THE FELONS OF
HARPERSFIELD

James Bosley

STRATTON
—PRESS—
Publishing Life

THE FELONS OF HARPERSFIELD
Copyright © 2021 **James Bosley**

Stratton Press Publishing
831 N Tatnall Street Suite M #188,
Wilmington, DE 19801
www.stratton-press.com
1-888-323-7009

ISBN (Paperback): 978-1-64895-602-7
ISBN (Ebook): 978-1-64895-603-4

Printed in the United States of America

Justice forever lost. Revenge needed found.

Generations of the family Porter have tormented the innocent lives involving local citizens of a small town in Southern Tennessee. Promised threats carried out, including brutal assaults and even murder. This is the story of the current generation.

One strong-willed sister and granddaughter, along with an undercover agent, labor to exact rightful payback.

This is the story of the current generation.

CHAPTER 1

THE FORD PICKUP truck's front bumper slammed into the rear bumper of the Honda Accord. The compact car's tires squealed while the driver nearly lost control of the vehicle.

"Hit the bitch again!" Murky shouted to Sterling.

"Yeah, knock her off the road!" Dalton added.

"That's Stacy Hughes drivin'. She's probably goin' into town to see her mama," Sterling assumed.

"Isn't she pregnant?" Dalton inquired.

"Yeah, she's got one in the oven," Sterling confirmed.

"Cool, we can take out two birds with one fuckin' stone. Hit her again, Sterling!" Dalton howled.

Sterling accelerated the pickup truck along rural route Martin's Way. The truck struck Stacy's Accord again. This time the Honda veered from the roadway and into a tailspin before sliding down to sudden stop into a shallow ditch. Two of the vehicle's tires blew as Stacy struck her forehead upon the steering wheel. She was dizzy but remained conscious. The impact caused her to bite down on her tongue, spilling seeping blood throughout her mouth.

Sterling, Dalton, and Murky continued along Martin's Way while trading high fives. As they passed the entrance into town,

Murky slung a nearly empty beer bottle through the truck's open passenger window, and it ricocheted off a green sign with white lettering that spelled out HARPERSFIELD.

*****

June 14
Harpersfield, Tennessee

WHEN ONE STARES into the direct line of light protruding from a bulb, the results are blinding random spots invading the eyesight. You would suppose that was the reasoning behind the invention of the lampshade.

Renee Stewart's lampshade was old and tattered, allowing the harmful light to pierce her tired eyes. Her digital clock at bedside displayed 3:00 a.m., a sleepless night. She pulled the blanket from her body and tossed the cover to the bedroom floor. She rolled off the mattress, draped on her robe, and headed outside for a breath of fresh air.

A summer's night. Hot and sticky. The humidity created small beads of perspiration that raced down her spine. The breeze had packed up and moved elsewhere in the world. Renee felt that if she were to stick out her tongue, she could taste the thick, moist air. She wished the stars in the sky above were ice crystals on a descent to cool her world a bit.

Renee gripped the railing of the porch as strands of her moistening dark hair begun to mat upon her forehead. She swayed slowly and softly with her eyes closed. Amid the heat and all the misery that came with it, she was still able to find a cool peace within her thoughts.

Childhood reminiscing of delightful times brought her present pleasure. The love of her grandfather kept her childhood as normal as circumstances permitted. He provided her security during her tender years as she matured to become a young lady. She recalled rushing up the driveway of the farmhouse while waving a paper from elementary school in her hand. A bright red letter *A* written in the teacher's penmanship sat atop the page. It was Renee's work that had earned

such a high mark. The assignment was to write an autobiography on merely one page, as best as a classroom of ten-year-olds could author. Renee wrote how her grandfather took care of her after the death of her parents. The closing line of her paper read, "My grandfather was sent to me by angels above, the winged saints didn't want me to be alone in this world." The teacher was astounded over Renee's writing abilities and detailed thought process at such an early stage of her young years.

Ike Stewart was proud of the essay. He probably glowed brighter than the author herself. He took the paper into town and showed it to anyone who would look and listen. His chest protruded outward when he would boast about his granddaughter receiving an A with him being the subject matter of such a fine piece of literature. Ike framed the paper and hung it on the wall in the hallway of the farmhouse.

As she scaled through her teenage years, Renee would spend many hours alone in her bedroom listening to music, mostly love songs as she would imagine a romantic adventure coming her way during her lifetime. She would visualize slow dancing with her strong man as she stepped around her bedroom with her arms extended out in the air. She would gently kiss him on the neck and then rest her head on his shoulder. Once, her brother, Nate, busted into her bedroom to announce that he was heading over to a friend's house when he caught Renee in the act of dancing with her invisible partner. Nate teased Renee for days over that display. It was after that when Renee installed a lock on her bedroom door. She was irritated at Nate for teasing her, but eventually, she saw the humor in it as well.

Nathan Stewart was not only Renee's younger brother; he was a great friend to her as well. Their relationship strengthened after the death of their parents. She would take time out of her busy teenage schedule to be sure to be in attendance for all of Nate's little league baseball games. She would sit next to Ike and root Nate on each time he came to bat. Nate would brag to his friends that his sister was a high school cheerleader, and his buddies would stare at beautiful Renee continuously when Nate had them over at the house. The siblings would often take the dogs for an evening walk and discuss what was going on in their lives at the time. They offered each other advice,

and at times the walks would end in a good heartfelt round of laughter. The talks that ended in tears always came with a hug of support.

Ike was lenient in allowing his grandchildren the company of their friends. They were permitted to have friends over at the house at any given time and needed not to ask permission to have pals spend the night. Many games of kickball took place in the backyard, and Nate became rather good at pitching horseshoes. Ike once competed for the county title in throwing horseshoes, and he passed on his skills onto his grandson. Badminton was popular as well. During the sporting events in the Stewarts' backyard, Ike would toss some hamburgers and hot dogs on the BBQ grill for all to indulge.

Her gentle thoughts were short-lived before her anguished feelings resurfaced. Even during times of peace-filled fun, an evil lurked over the town like a dark cloud. Although the young teens restrained from discussing the subject during their social gatherings, all were fully aware of the fear instilled in each of them. One unwanted visit, one turn of events, would destroy their laughter and smiles in an instant. There was simply no way of protecting each other; all you could hope for was that the evil remained away on any given day.

Using her forefingers, Renee gently rubbed her temples and took in a deep inhale of the summer-night air. She opened her eyes and viewed as far as the spotlight on the pole in the driveway illuminated. Now that she was twenty-one years old, the farm appeared a bit different to her somehow. As a child growing up on the land, it seemed larger, newer, and more vibrant. Now, through her young adult vision, she realized the farm was old and dying a slow death.

Renee Stewart was a beautiful young woman, and from photographs more than memories, she likened to the beauty of her mother, Beth. With her soft silky dark hair along with the rarity of soft blue eyes sparkling on a brunette, Renee radiated. Her hair parted on the right side, and her bangs flowed across the front of her upper forehead from right to left.

The brunette tresses fell just below her shoulder blades. The summer's sun lightened the dark hair just a bit. Not a dip of dye had ever touched her mane. Her blemish-free soft peachy skin tanned easily in the summer sun, and her figure was curvy and proportion-

ally correct. Her lips were full, and her cheeks slender. Renee stood at five feet eight inches and tipped the scales at one 108 pounds. She was an alluring, captivating young lady, and the male population responded well. Many people who exhibited the exceptional appearance as Renee displayed could become a bit conceited. However, Renee was virtually unaware of how beautiful she really was. She was three years out of high school, and besides a few dates, Renee had been single most of her life. She had a busy childhood helping her grandfather raise her younger brother Nathan.

Her grandfather, Ike, was a simple man who paved his way by farming corn and tomatoes throughout his life in rural Tennessee. Jack and Beth Stewart, Renee's parents, Ike's son and daughter-in-law, lost their lives in an automobile accident nearly fourteen years ago. Jack had been drinking but insisted on driving home from a barbecue gathering at a friend's house.

Jack lost control of the car that night in the Smoky Mountains of Tennessee, and by the time the mass of metal finally came to a rolling halt in the gully of a roadside valley, the entire vehicle was in flames.

Renee was eight years old at the time, and though she remembered her parents, the memories were becoming vague with time. Ike added to his life the responsibilities of raising the two children after the tragic accident. Ike's wife of forty-one years, Jodi, passed away as a result of breast cancer two years prior to the accident that took their only son. Jack took his mother's death hard, and his drinking increased.

Over the years since the death of his son, daughter-in-law, and wife, seventy-two-year-old Ike Stewart still worked the farm—on days his aging and aching bones would allow him to do so anyway.

Renee ran her right palm across the front of her neck as beads of moisture rivered down into her cleavage. Her polyester nightshirt, a number 27 Eddie George Tennessee Titans football jersey, was not soaking up her body's perspiration. She listened to the music of the singing crickets of the night. She then glanced at the decayed wooden steps of the porch and what remained of coats of paint applied throughout the decades. She was aware while stepping down from the porch in her bare feet, cautious of potential protruding splinters

in the wood. The cooling grass felt refreshing between her toes before she stooped to sit upon the lawn.

Renee rested her arms on her knees that were nearly up to her chest. She rocked slowly, slightly, back and forth, enjoying the serenity of the still night.

The quiet was soon disrupted by the squeaking sounds of the screen door being pushed open. She turned to observe her grandfather striding onto the porch, and Renee smiled at him.

Ike stepped up to a section of railing a few feet above Renee. "You couldn't sleep either, honey?" he assumed in his aging and raspy voice.

She shook her head as she turned back away from him. "No, Grandpa. I haven't slept a wink."

"I can't claim much better. Maybe a couple of hours at best."

Renee fidgeted a bit and then peered up to the starry sky above. "It's a year today." Her eyes clouded.

Ike sighed. "Yeah, I know. Believe me, I don't need remindin'. Could you use a hug?" he offered.

Without looking back at him, she nodded.

Ike paced down from the porch, moving a little less carelessly than she had done a few minutes prior. Ike's hair was silver but still nearly as thick as it was as a young man. He was five feet eleven inches in height and in good shape, despite his age. Being a hardworking farmer all his life had kept his body lean and muscular. His skin, as did his granddaughter's, tanned easily and deeply during the summer months to a burnt copper shade. He had the Stewarts' characteristic blue eyes, and even after more than seven decades of life, he was without need of eyeglasses. People claimed that Ike could see like a hawk. He had lost his decayed teeth through his thirties and had worn dentures ever since. His deceased wife, Jodi, would harp on him to drink milk and eat dairy products to encourage healthy teeth, but Ike resisted. He was strictly a meat-and-potatoes man.

The truth of the matter was that the male Stewarts of generations past had a history of teeth-related ailments. The females, though, experienced no such teeth-associated issues. Ike stated that God was eventually going to take either a man's hair or his teeth; you

simply couldn't have both. Ike wished it were his hair that left him; not much use in that other than to comb it. He would like to bite into an ear of corn without his teeth shifting. His skin was leathery from years of working the fields in the sunlight, and his arms contained age spots of brown islands, as he would put it. Ike was not much of a worrier when it came to life's struggles, but he had always cared deeply toward members of his family. When they were feeling blue, he was the first to try to lift their spirits. When things were so rough that he couldn't accomplish that task, his shoulder was always there to lean on.

He took a seat on the lawn next to Renee and placed a supporting arm around her shoulders. Within moments, she fell into a sob and rested her head onto his chest. He ran his hands and fingers through the back of her soft shoulder-length hair, "Hush now, honey. It's goin' to be okay. We must remember that Nathan is in a better place now. He's among the angels in God's kingdom."

She spoke through her weak, weeping voice, "I know, Grandpa, but it's still difficult to accept. What bothers me is when I think how horrible his last few minutes of life must have been like. I'm sure he was scared out of his wits."

Ike thought for a moment, but he could not summon up any comforting reply. He had pondered over the same issue more often than he'd like to admit. "We should try and not think about it in that way. Let's remember Nathan for how he lived. He did quite a bit for only bein' among us for eighteen years. Nate sure loved his baseball. Remember when I took him to the Reds game in Cincinnati?"

"Yeah."

"He was happy as a raccoon in a cornfield that day. When the Reds ran out onto the diamond, I swear I could hear Nate's heart poundin' from the seat next to me," Ike recalled.

Renee grinned. "Yeah, I'm sure Nate has put together a baseball game up there in heaven." After a few moments of silence, Renee sat up straight. "Do the police ever talk about it anymore, or is it a lost cause?"

Ike slowly rose to his feet as his back began to stiffen on him in a seated position. He brushed away a few blades of loose grass from

his pajama bottoms. "No, they really show no hope whatsoever. I saw Deputy Collins the other day, and there wasn't even a mention of Nate's case. I suppose they feel bad for botchin' it up. Has Murky given you any trouble lately?"

Renee frowned and exhaled. "Yeah, the usual creeps. I hate it when I am in town, and he spots me. He just stares at me like some sort of psycho stalker. I can just feel his eyes burn into me. It makes me want to throw up."

"Just ignore him, Renee."

"I try to, Grandpa, but he has a way of gettin' under my skin," she said with a groan.

He nodded. "Yeah, I know what you mean. Those Porters have been givin' people around here the creeps for generations. What about his brothers? Are Sterling and Dalton givin' you a hard time?"

Renee rolled her eyes. "Always."

"Well, I'd talk to their parents about it all, but you know that wouldn't do any good. Carter and Bessy are every bit as crazy as them boys are," her grandfather pointed out.

Renee's voice became nearly as soft as a whisper. "Grandpa, perhaps we should move away. So long as we live here in Harpersfield, the Porters are never goin' to leave us be."

His facial expression became a tad stern. "What, and leave the farm? Leave everyone and everythin' we have ever known? No, I'm not packin' up shop and runnin' like some scared rabbit because of some punks."

Renee slowly rose to feet. "Yeah, I know how you feel about that, Grandpa. If you're not movin', I'm certainly not leavin' you here alone. We'll tough it out and hopefully catch a break our way for once."

Ike embraced his granddaughter. "Listen, honey, it is looking like no sleep for us tonight. I'm goin' inside to put on some coffee and scramble up some eggs. Are you comin' in?"

She spoke into his shoulder, "In a little bit, Grandpa. I wanna listen to the crickets a little while longer."

"Good enough." He understood, slowly breaking from their embrace. He placed a gentle kiss upon her forehead. Ike then turned

and headed for the house. Within moments, he closed the screen door behind him.

Renee sauntered about twenty feet and then found a seat on an aged wooden lawn chair between the house and the barn. From there, the light on the pole just reached her with no room to spare. She inhaled a deep breath and raked her fingers through her hair. As she gazed at the large wooden sliding doors of the barn, she recalled a time shortly before her young brother's death.

*****

Renee was busy throwing hay onto the muddied dirt floor of the barn. An unusually wet spring had left the water table high and the surface soil soggy. The tractor's tires were sinking into the earth that was the barn floor, and the hay would help to solidify and strengthen the volatile soil.

"Need some help, Renee?" Nate offered. He was about to enter the summer before his senior year in high school, the same small school from which his grandparents, parents, and his sister graduated. Nate was eighteen and full of life. When the opportunity presented itself, Nate would talk baseball until somebody would shut him up. He didn't really date, though there were several girls in school whom he found attractive. However, Nate couldn't muster the courage to ask any of them out on a date. He was forward with everything else except the ladies. When it came to that, he was shy as they came.

He shared in his sister's blue eyes, but Nate's hair was a lighter ash blond. His build was lanky yet solid, consequently from working the farm. In addition, as his older sister had done, Nate bypassed the acne stage many teenagers suffered through. He inherited the clear Stewart skin.

"No, I think I'm okay here, Nate. Thanks for askin'. Did you finish feedin' the dogs?"

He removed his leather work gloves from his hands. "All fed."

Renee ceased pitching hay for a moment and wiped her brow free of sweat. "Why don't you take the rest of the day and do somethin' recreational? You've been poundin' away on the farm here for days on end. Go have some fun."

"Fun in Harpersfield?" He chuckled. "Where do you suppose I might find that?"

She thought about his comment for a moment before replying. "Good point."

"Well, there is a men's league softball game over in Waynesburg, I think I'll go and watch that."

"Just be sure to tell Grandpa before you leave," she reminded him.

"Yeah, I will," he responded. Nate then turned to walk away, but he hesitated. He spun back toward his sister. "Renee, can I ask you a favor?"

She grinned. "Sure."

He sighed. "What do you think of Murky Porter?"

"Why?"

"I'm just wonderin' is all."

Renee rolled her eyes. "Well, I think about Murky like I do the rest of the Porters. Like everyone in this town does. I think that those Porters are mean and nasty. Harpersfield would be a much better place without the Porters. You must know that I feel strongly about that because I rarely find somethin' bad to say about anyone."

He nodded in agreement. Nervousness developed in his voice. "So you wouldn't consider goin' out with Murky?"

She placed her hands on her hips. "Not in a million years. Why do you ask? Murky put you up to this, didn't he?"

Nate bowed his head.

"Well, you can tell him no deal. I can't believe he's now tryin' to use my brother to get to me. Why doesn't he just give up? I don't know how to make it more clear to him that I'm not interested. For cryin' out loud, this has been goin' on since grade school!"

"He's gonna to be pissed when I tell him," Nate indicated.

"Are you scared of the Porters?" she queried.

"Yeah," he admitted. "Who isn't?"

"I know they can be intimidatin', Nate, but I'm not goin' out with Murky for the sake of fear. The thought of goin' out with him makes me ill. Has he been botherin' you lately?"

"Yeah, him, Sterling, and Dalton have been roughin' me up. With words anyway. I have no doubt, though, that if provoked, they'll lash out beat the tar out of me."

Renee exhaled. "Damn, I despise those Porters. Okay…this is what you do, Nate. Whenever you're in town, whenever you're away from the farm, be sure to have a buddy along with you. Don't be caught alone."

He nodded. "Okay. I'll see if Johnny Mercer will go along to Waynesburg with me today. If he doesn't wanna go, maybe Grandpa will go."

"Do what ya need to do, Nate, but don't go alone. This'll probably blow over in a week or so. Until then, be careful."

"Okay, sis, I will. I'm goin' inside to call Johnny. I'll see ya later." He turned and headed for the house.

"Take the pickup truck, Nate! I'm goin' to need the car later!" she shouted to him.

He waved back to her in cooperation.

Renee took a deep breath before she returned to the task at hand.

*****

Renee slouched in the wooden chair and brought her hands up to cover her face.

She whispered into her palms, "I'm so sorry, Nate, I should have been more aware of the potential danger that lurked for you in the shadows."

"Coffee and eggs are up," Ike announced from the porch. "Come on in from the crickets, honey, and eat somethin'."

Renee rose from the chair. "Okay, Grandpa. I don't want ya to worry."

CHAPTER 2

Philadelphia, Pennsylvania

MARLA SIMMONS WAS seated in her living room during a late-afternoon hour on her favorite recliner. The television set was stationed a few feet in front of her, broadcasting CNN news. Marla was a retired agent of the Federal Bureau of Investigation, though she was only fifty-one years old. Marla spent twenty-seven years on the force and retired to conduct a career as a freelance private detective. While with the FBI, Marla specialized as a unique agent to communication crimes. When the Internet was introduced around the country and the world, her department became overwhelmed with cases. So much, in fact, she felt as though she was being swallowed up by the system. It was stressing her and keeping her up at night.

When Marla began to grow weary of nausea on a regular basis, that was enough for her. She resigned from the bureau and initiated the Simmons Private Detective Agency. Although she was now displaced from the FBI, she still maintained ties and connections within the bureau, activity for which the federal government was unaware of.

Marla was a looker through her young and midlife span. The years of stress had not physically caught up with her, and at fifty-one,

she appeared to be around forty years of age. She attributed this to only one evening each week of dining on meat, and the remainder of the week, she was a strict vegetarian. She dosed on four separate types of vitamins each day and had never smoked cigarettes. She drank alcohol in moderation and meditated for her spiritual well-being. Her gold-rimmed eyeglasses rested proudly on her lean nose against her brown skin. Her hair was dark with some gray sprinkled in.

She had considered of dyeing her mane in order to slow down the effects of aging, but then again, she deemed the gray served as a trophy of sorts, proving that she had lived a fast, hard life. A box of hair dye had sat untouched on a shelf in the bathroom cabinet for nearly a year. Her lips were smooth, and the natural texture of the light brown color required no lipstick. As a matter of fact, Marla's skin was unblemished, taut, and cosmetics would only suppress the glow of her warm facial features. She had kept her body in good shape, using exercise equipment she had installed in her basement.

Her shorthair yellow cat, Tulie, lay on the arm of the chair next to her while Marla worked on papers regarding recent cases within her agency.

Her business partner, Doolie Brookside, functioned mostly doing the footwork in Philadelphia and the surrounding areas while Marla handled most of the paperwork. Doolie insisted on going by Dule, stating that Doolie was a weak-sounding name for a man. At forty-nine, his desire for a woman's company had not subsided a bit. If anything, it had increased.

Dule Brookside had been a private detective for most of his adult life. He began his law career as a court reporter in Buffalo, New York. It didn't take him long to realize, even at a young age, that he wanted more to do with law than only report it. He wanted to investigate the dark side of the criminal world.

Dule was a tall pallid man, standing at six foot eight and was slender. He had lost a portion of his head of brown hair through his forties. His forehead shined where his skin was oily, which was most of the time, but Dule was one of those few fortunate men who appeared well with less hair. His throat was pronounced with a large Adam's apple. His nose was slender to match his body, and

his jawline was sleek. His voice was deep but lacked a degree authority. Dule's goals had always been set a little higher than his lack of courage would allow him to travel. Nineteen years prior, Dule was busted by local police for possession of cocaine. He served two years behind bars, and as part of his probation, he had gone through a lengthy rehabilitation program upon his release from prison. Dule had been clean of drugs since that day nineteen years ago. The agency he was working for at the time fired him. While putting his life back together as an ex-con, good cases just weren't coming his way. He spent over a decade in a run-down agency he operated on his own. Seeking a business partner to share the overload of cases, Marla came along and presented him with an offer, and their agency had since flourished. Dule was happier now than he had been in nearly twenty years.

Four months into their professional relationship, Dule and Marla became personal. They saw each other intimately on a consistent basis, but Marla was hesitant about making a full commitment. She had never married, no children, and enjoyed her time living solo. When Marla felt she knew Dule well enough to completely trust him, she informed him of a secretive group known as the Elite Four. She warned him that if he were ever to reveal the existence of the Elite Four, his body would be buried and never found.

Agent Marla Simmons was a copartner in the development of the Elite Four over eleven years prior. She and fellow agent Dennis Farrow covertly created the group to combat injustice around the country. It was exceedingly difficult to recruit as the members had to grasp the exact way that Marla and Dennis felt about the judicial system. Seeking this out without exposing their illegal concepts among FBI agents was not an easy task by any means. Dennis and Marla's methods were to casually speak of the judicial system in the presence of other agents and then to analyze their reaction before deciding to approach them with their notion. After a long-drawn-out process, five agents were eventually contacted privately, and of the five, four were recruited. The lone uncommitted agent pledged his secrecy in exchange for his life. To this day, FBI Agent Randy Delp had maintained the radical group and their identities to himself.

The Elite Four consisted of Agent Barry Stone, a seventeen-year veteran of the force. Barry was married with two children and resided in the suburban Phoenix, Arizona, area. Agent Anthony Becth was a twenty-four-year member of the FBI. Anthony was married with three kids. He resided in Gary, Indiana. Agent Janice Stark was an FBI agent with sixteen years of experience. Janice was divorced and lived in Concord, Massachusetts. Last but not least, Cole Walsh was an eight-year agent of the FBI. Cole was single and, at thirty-two years of age, had accomplished what some agents took an entire career to achieve. Cole had served in the US Army as a Green Beret specialist. He was sanctioned as one of the few marksmen on the force. It was said that Cole could shoot the Lincoln out of a penny at two hundred yards. Despite his younger age, Cole was assigned to cases that were usually reserved for more seasoned agents.

Agent Dennis Farrow, cofounder of the Elite Four, was shot and killed on duty six years prior. A drug smuggler that Dennis was investigating snubbed out the agent's life. It was an FBI case unrelated to the Elite Four activities. This left Marla as the sole coordinator of the Elite Four.

Marla broke away from her concentration with the paperwork at hand as a news story on CNN grabbed her attention. CNN anchorwoman Stephanie Kelimski reported the story with a photograph of one Nathan Stewart posted in the background. "Today marks the first-year anniversary of the murder of Tennessee resident, eighteen-year-old Nathan Stewart. The accused killer of Nathan Stewart, Murky Porter, remains a free man, though police are certain of his guilt. A botched typo on the search warrant led to the evidence obtained during the search of the Porter home to being thrown out of court. The evidence was overwhelming in pointing to Murky Porter as the killer. Murky himself had admitted to committing to the murder, but there is little police can do. The prosecution had to drop their case against Porter when the evidence was ruled insubmittable. Tom?" Stephanie threw the newscast back to anchorman Tom Browne.

"The Dow Jones saw an increase in stock trading today…"

Marla powered down the television using the remote control. She sat quietly in her living room for a few moments before nudging

Tulie from the arm of the chair. The feline landed softly on her paws and slowly moved for the kitchen. Marla reached for the telephone resting on the stand next to her chair.

Dule was positioned inside his car when his cell phone, new technology recently introduced to the world, rang. He grabbed the cell phone from the dashboard and raised the antenna. "Hello?"

"Dule, it's Marla. Where are you?"

He craned his neck to glance up at a sign. "I'm in the parking lot of Beanor's Restaurant on the west side."

"Why are you there?" she questioned.

"I'm watching Frank Meyers with a woman inside the restaurant. A woman that's not his wife."

"Get the photographs we need before heading back to the office."

He glanced at his 35mm camera lying in the seat next to him. "What's up?"

"I need you to go back to the office and get on the computer. First, find all the information you can on a murder case. The case is of victim Nathan Stewart of Tennessee. He was murdered a year ago today."

"Wait a minute, Marla. Let me jot this down," Dule requested. He reached into the pocket of his shirt and removed a small notepad and a pen. He opened the pad while scanning through the pages that had information already written on them. He stopped at the first blank page. "Okay, Marla. That's what name now?"

"Nathan Stewart of Tennessee. He was murdered a year ago today."

Dule scribbled quickly. "Okay, got it. Anything else?"

"Yeah, email the current available Elite Four agent and inform that agent to contact me within forty-eight hours. You remember the password to the program, right?"

"Yep, got it here in the ole' noggin'," he assured.

Marla rolled her eyes. "Call me when you complete both those tasks," she instructed.

"Will do, Marla. How about dinner tonight?"

She smiled. "Sure. About seven?"

"I'll be there."

"Okay, Dule. We'll talk about the information then. Bye now."

"Bye, my chocolate queen," he teased before kissing into the phone.

Marla moaned as she pressed the end call button.

Dule slid his cell phone back atop the dashboard and then reached for his camera. He shot several zoomed-in photographs through the restaurant's window of a Mr. Frank Meyers and his luncheon date, Ms. Angela Watkins. They kissed several times before opening their menus.

Dule whispered to himself, "Mrs. Meyers isn't going to like these photos. I gotcha, Frankie boy."

THE PORTER RESIDENCE sat on the outskirts of Harpersfield, which was a good thing, according to the locals. The house was an eyesore as it was generations in age with virtually no maintenance to speak of. Window shutters were either missing or barely hung onto the nearly paintless siding. Old long-ago-dead vehicles sat rusting away upon various sections of the property. Five doghouses surrounded the house, three behind the house and two in the front area. Two Rottweilers, a duo of pit bulls, and one Doberman pinscher completed the group of canines. A laundry line ran from the front porch to an oak tree some eighty feet in total distance. A screen door was missing, and the yellowing white front door was soiled from the porch surface up to the doorknob.

Off on the east the side of the property was a large area where the Porters burned their household trash, though it was illegal to do so in the county. The pile was two feet deep with ash as well as scorched aluminum cans and glass bottles. At times, it could be up to six weeks between incinerations, allowing the trash, maggots, flies, and other rubbish-seeking insects to accumulate. The foul odors of rotted meats and spoiled milk would surround the area on still days. Dog feces, some fresh, some whitened by the summer sun, spotted

the property like a minefield. The driveway was dirt and, during times of rain, was mud. Deep tire trenches caused a jamming, bumping ride along the driveway. The garage door had not been opened in over a decade, and inside was a rat pack of items and boxes with no room to walk about. An accumulation of worthless stash from generations of Porters occupied the garage floor and loft above. The lawn was spotty with crabgrass, rarely mowed, and the mailbox was completely rusted.

No house had ever stood within a half mile of the Porters' home. No one wanted to be their direct neighbor. Beyond the backyard and the three doghouses was a lame excuse for a farmed field. Carter Porter maintained somewhat of a cornfield in case the IRS came snooping around investigating how the Porters made a legitimate living. It seemed that for generations of Porters, they did not move away from home. For the most part, with exception of a few, this simply was a fact. At one time, the house was home to nineteen Porter family members aged three to eighty-eight.

Bessy Porter was a less-than-adequate housekeeper, and her husband, Carter, wasn't much of a worker outside the home. Carter could be frequently found inside the tavern in town, regardless of the time or day. The maiden, Elaine Marabess "Bessy" Lumas, was born and raised in nearby Webster, Tennessee. She was one of nine children. The large family resided in a double-wide trailer on the side of a hill on the outskirts of town. Behind the trailer was an outhouse to accommodate the overwhelming bathroom demands. Bessy's father, Don, performed little maintenance on the trailer or the property. The grass was overgrown as her brothers were lazy as well. Don ran with the boys as if he were their age. They drank frequently. It wasn't unusual for them to go through a case of beer each in a single day. Bessy's mother, Rhonda, constantly battled with manic depression and schizophrenia. Bessy could remember that it was as though being raised by two mothers, depending on which personality she was tuned into on any given day. The family was not close, and Bessy hadn't remained home much. She stayed over at different friends' houses most nights—that was until she met one Carter Porter. She was sixteen, and he was twenty. She met Carter at a party down along

the river's edge. Merely three days into their newly found relationship, and Bessy moved in with Carter in Harpersfield. She quit high school and devoted her life to Carter. One month later they were wed by the mayor of Webster after presenting a legal document signed by Bessy's mother giving her minor daughter permission to marry. Bessy would simply do anything for her husband. Illegal, immoral, or both didn't persuade her from performing her wifely duties. For instance, when she was seventeen, Carter created an encounter for her with his brother Steadman. Each time Steadman arrived home intoxicated (they lived together in the Porters' house), which was often, he would stare at Bessy with anxious eyes.

Before Bessy began drinking heavy, when she reached her twenties, she was an attractive young lady. Today, after years of consuming hard liquor daily, Bessy's beauty had all but deserted her. Steadman would pinch her on her backside and purposely rub against her. She did find Steadman to be alluring and handsome, and she enjoyed the attention, but she would never take it any further than that. She deeply loved Carter and would never do him wrong. Though she did find Steadman to be attractive, she didn't care for him much as a person. He was mean to her when he wasn't trying to seduce her. He wouldn't help around the house, and he was rude. Then one night, shortly after Carter and Bessy were married, something happened that she knew to this day changed things between her and Carter, though he refused to admit that it harmed their relationship.

Carter Porter, as with his male ancestors, was a large, solid-framed man. He stood at six foot four and weighed in at 240 pounds. His hands were large with long and thick fingers. His neck was broad while reaching up to his sharp jawline. His eyes were a dark green to the degree they nearly appeared gray in color. His nose pudgy, thin lips formed his mouth, while his chin narrowed and quickly tapered off. His full head of ashy hair was never groomed and rarely trimmed. A visit to a barber every four months was satisfactory for him. His ears were big but lay nearly flush to his head. At times he would sport a mustache and beard, but for the most part, he displayed jaws littered with unshaven face stubble in need of a fresh shave.

Though Porter men were not healthy eaters and consumed vast amounts of beer and whiskey, their ratio of body fat compared to lean and strong muscle was low. The Porter genes produced tall, stout, robust, vigorous, and powerful species of males. In all the past generations of Porter males, there existed not a single exemption to the rule. Simply put, if you were a male member of Porter evolution and descendants, you were sizeable, strong, mighty, ruthless, intimidating, and criminally inclined. Those who had regular contact with Porter family members—be they male, female, sister, brother, wife, husband, cousin, aunt, uncle, grandparent, or even their canines for that matter—would describe them as evil while some even cited the word *insane*.

Bessy was sitting in the living room at home wearing a nearly transparent nightshirt while speaking with her mother on the phone. She felt safe wearing such a revealing garment for now as it would be hours yet before Steadman would return home along with Carter after a night out drinking. The others in the home—Carter and Steadman's mother Edith, their sisters Francis, Yolanda, and Liddy—were all upstairs sleeping. Their uncle Raker and his wife Nora were also retired for the night. Their grandfather, Belmer Porter, had been sleeping since dusk. Carter and Steadman's father, Wridder Porter, passed years prior while skinny-dipping in Elder's Pond with his mistress. They were very intoxicated when Wridder drowned. His lover, Samantha Dyles, fifteen years his junior, drowned as well. Their nude bodies were discovered days later by a pair of fishermen.

Wridder, as with most of the Porters, was wild and out of control. He once shot a cop in Knoxville because the officer was putting a parking ticket on his Harley Davidson motorcycle. No one except Wridder was permitted to touch that motorbike. The police officer survived, although the bullet blew through his neck. Wridder spent six years in prison for the felonious assault. After serving out his sentence, Wridder Porter was more out of control than ever before. As with all the Porter women, Edith was frightened of her husband and let him do whatever he wanted to do without any static coming from her.

On this night, Bessy's haven was short-lived as the brothers came home earlier than their usual dawn arrival. It was just after

two in the early morning. The brothers had been involved in a fight inside the tavern and nearly beat a man from Waynesburg to death. The state police responded to the incident, so Carter and Steadman had to lie low for the rest of the night.

"You're on the fuckin' phone again?" Carter barked as he and Steadman entered the room. They were obviously intoxicated.

Using her arms, Bessy covered her body the best she could. Steadman glared at her and winked. She turned her eyes away from him. "I'm talkin' to my mother," Bessy reported.

"That mental case? She's goddamn nuts," Carter said with a smirk.

"Be that as it may, honey, she's still my mama. She's your mother-in-law now."

"Please don't remind me." Carter laughed. Steadman chuckled. "Hang up the phone. I have somethin' I wanna tell you."

After she bid her mother farewell, Bessy ended the call. "Before ya say anythin', Carter, I need to put on a robe to cover myself. I wasn't expectin' you all home just yet."

"Just hold your horses a moment. You'll be changin' clothes soon enough."

"What are ya talkin' about, Carter?"

Carter looked to Steadman. After exchanging mischievous grins and a nod of Steadman's head, Carter turned his attention back to his young wife. "Me and Steadman were talkin' on our way home. Steadman is goin' through a shitty dry spell."

"What does that mean?" she inquired.

"Well, if ya shut the hell up for a damn second, I'll tell ya!" he snipped.

"I'm sorry, Carter. Go ahead."

"As I was sayin', Steadman hasn't had much action lately. Not from a willin' woman anyway."

The brothers snickered.

Carter's facial expression then became more serious. "Bessy, I want ya to take care of Steadman. Show him a real good time tonight. I want ya to fuck his brains out. I've told him that you're a really good screw, so I'm gonna let him have a slice of my wife's sweet pussy pie."

"Carter, I don't understand. Are ya askin' me to have sex with your brother?" she wondered with a disgusted curl of her lip.

"Did I fuckin' stutter? That's what I said. Except I'm not askin' ya, I'm tellin' ya. I want you to go put on that sexy blue negligee thingie of yours."

"Carter, I bought that for our weddin' night. It's sentimental and all."

"I know, and you looked so damn good in it. So go put it on."

"It's very revealin', honey. I don't wanna wear that in front of Steadman."

"Oh, come on, Bessy. It shows off your pretty ass." Carter winked.

"That's because it's a thong," she explained.

"A thong, a song, or a ping-pong. Whatever it is, just put it on already," Carter demanded with a hard slap of his left palm upon the kitchen table.

Bessy knew the limit of where to take Carter's temper and pushed it no further. Carter had arrived at that "avoid at all costs" point regarding his lack of patience. Reluctantly, Bessy headed for the bedroom as the men settled into the living room.

After delaying for as long as possible, Bessy paraded into the living room wearing the very sheer and skimpy garment.

Steadman's eyes widened with satisfaction at the sight of her. Her skin chilled as she tried her best to maintain her eyesight on Carter and away from Steadman.

"Take a good look at that pretty ass, Steadman," Carter invited.

"Ya got a fine ass there, Bessy," Steadman growled. Steadman rose quickly behind Bessy and began to grope her. His large hands were roaming all over her nearly nude body. Bessy continued to look away from Steadman while maintaining looks at Carter.

"Are ya sure you want another man to have his way with me, honey?" she queried.

Carter jerked his head yes from his seated position on the couch. "Yeah, Bessy, but only family. If I hear of ya with another man other than my brother, I'll kill ya! Now, stop bein' so damn uptight and enjoy it. Steadman wants to screw ya bad."

Bessy didn't really want to go through with it, but to her aston-ishment, the more that Steadman fondled her, the more excited she became. As he rubbed her breasts, she rested her head back on his shoulder and moaned with unexpected pleasure. Steadman then pro-ceeded to help her step out from her negligee, though little assistance was needed. As if by some involuntary action, Bessy easily stepped out of her negligee. When she was completely nude and displayed before the men, Steadman laid her down on the living room carpet. Towering above her, Steadman lowered his pants. His penis stood rigid as the sight of her naked body excited him into an erection. Bessy was eager as well. The seven quick shots of bourbon she had consumed while putting on her negligee was now swimming around in her head, causing her to reveal her now keen willingness to have sex with Steadman.

Over the following hour, Steadman performed sexually with Bessy to her complete satisfaction. He was better than Carter when it came to sex. Much better. When he performed oral stimulation on her, it drove her wild with passion.

She was very enthused to return the favor to Steadman, some-thing that Carter must demand her to do with him. She stimulated Steadman orally for nearly ten minutes. During aggressive inter-course, Bessy watched as from sitting on the couch looking on, Carter masturbated. When Steadman ejaculated inside her vaginal walls, it was a welcomed occurrence by both him and Bessy. Not so for Carter. A moment after Steadman completed his ejaculation in harmony with Bessy's orgasm, Carter aggressively pulled Steadman from atop of Bessy. The men formed fists and nearly came to blows.

Bessy screamed at them that this was all their idea as she stood up from the floor. She made no attempt to cover her nude body. She asked them to halt their aggressive behavior and reassured Carter that she loved him.

A short time later while lying in their bed, Carter said nothing to Bessy. He simply turned his back on his wife and passed out into an alcohol-induced stupor.

In the months that followed, Carter shared his wife with Steadman on several other occasions. Though she enjoyed it and got

to the point of looking forward to engaging in sex with Steadman, she played it down in front of Carter's eyes. Only a single meeting did Steadman and Bessy go at it together without Carter's supervision of their act of lust. While initiating the sexual encounter, Carter passed out from an overindulgence of drinking. That night, Bessy and Steadman went at it like wild animals with raw lust and passion. She left fingernail scrapes upon Steadman's back.

Then one night, feeling unusually well, seventy-nine-year-old Belmer went out drinking with Carter and Steadman. Steadman hooked up with a gal from Waynesburg that evening and stayed the night at her house. Carter and Belmer arrived home intoxicated as Carter demanded that Bessy give the old man one last thrill while he still could perform. Belmer's health was deteriorating quickly, and he had very few days that he could simply rise from his bed.

Bessy had sex with Belmer that evening while Carter masturbated as an observer. She had recently reached nineteen years of age while Belmer was two weeks shy from turning eighty. She thought he was going to have a heart attack while he ejaculated inside her vagina, but he managed. Two weeks later and after several years of battling lung cancer from heavy smoking, Belmer passed away in his sleep. Carter claimed his Grandfather Belmer died a happy man because of the gift of Bessy's sex.

A year and a half following Belmer's death, Bessy had sex with both Carter and Steadman one night when Dalton was an infant. She conceived Sterling that night, leaving a cloud of doubt as to whether it was Carter or Steadman who fathered Sterling. It was just assumed that the baby was Carter's, and it was simply left at that. As for Dalton, he could have been Belmer or Carter's son. Bessy couldn't be certain of the old man's fertility, but she remembered hearing that a man in his eighties could still have potent sperm. She did recall that Belmer ejaculated a large amount of semen inside her vagina. More than she thought a man could serve. So the amount wasn't the question; the potency was. Again, it was left to assume that Carter was the father.

Steadman Porter was killed not long after Sterling's birth by a raging, revengeful husband from Webster. Carter was shot as well,

but he survived. With Belmer and Steadman out of the picture, Bessy again became pregnant, and this time there was no doubt that Carter was the father. Murky Porter was born nine months later.

Bessy passed her time in front of the television set with a bag of snacks at her disposal. Despite her habit of overeating and over-drinking, Bessy remained slim as a rail. Her green eyes were nearly always bloodshot and bagged below the sockets from years of con-suming rum and beer. She had needed eyeglasses for some time, but merely squinted rather than get a prescription. Her hair was light brown and at shoulder length. Her ears were rather small in diam-eter, a trait familiar with the Lumas bloodline. Her nose was long but not large. Her cheeks were round but not puffy. Her lips were a bit uneven, thin at the bottom while bloated along the top. She was fussy about maintaining her oral hygiene, however. Four times each day she would feverously brush her teeth, followed by a healthy swig and gargle of Listerine or Old Gran-Dad Whiskey. Though the rest of her physique was in desperate need of more suitable hygiene, her teeth were pearly white. Bessy could sport the same clothing daily until they nearly wore to rags. This wasn't unusual behavior among others within the Porter household as well.

Last year, Bessy had been attacked by one of the pit bulls when the dog reacted from the irritation of his fly-bitten ears. She had to fend the dog off with a mop handle in order to save her life. She required forty-two stitches on various areas of her tattered body.

Carter and the boys angered at her for striking the dog, Assassin, with the mop handle. She avoided Assassin at all costs now. She was not fond of the other dogs—Satin, Lucifer, Misery, and Undertaker—either.

After years of deaths within the family and a few moving on to places of their own, the large farmhouse was now home to only the immediate family members. Bessy was pleased to have three sons; she had always prayed she wouldn't conceive a daughter. She despised the thought of raising a daughter, expressing that girls were weak.

The boys—Dalton, aged twenty-four; Sterling, twenty-two; and Murky, twenty—all still resided at home. None of the three had a legitimate job, nor were they looking for gainful employment.

The trio did graduate from high school; however, they were not in attendance over half the school year and rarely did schoolwork assignments. Teachers simply issued the Porters passing grades based on their anxieties of the family retaliations. The Porter boys put money in their pockets by making marijuana and cocaine runs into Knoxville from time to time. They would pick up a bundle or two in the city, transport it back to the Harpersfield area, and supply the majority of the stock to local distributors while dealing and selling what remained of the drugs on their own in Harpersfield as well as several adjoining towns. When running low on funds, they simply robbed local businesses in Harpersfield. Wearing masks or displaying weapons wasn't necessary for out of fear, merchants simply handed over the money without hesitation and with no plans of reporting the theft to authorities. The vengeance over such actions would be horrendous and dreadful.

Some of the common traits the brothers all shared were foul manners, criminal records, body size, eye color, and decaying teeth. Besides Bessy's, there was not a toothbrush to be found in the Porter household. Like their father, uncles, and grandfathers before them, the three siblings were tall and possessed solid builds. Sterling and Dalton were both six foot five inches tall, while Murky stood at six foot four. All the boys' eye color was deep green and nearly a shade of gray. Both Dalton and Murky's hair color was a light shade of brown and Sterling's a shadow of rust. The boys would have been attractive to the opposite sex if their hygiene habits were improved. But then again, their violent personalities would be a turnoff for most females. Most is stressed, for there have been a few women over the years who found the Porters to be exciting bad boys.

Dalton's shoulders were broad and profound, his forearms thick with muscle, his biceps a pair of solid rocks. His midsection was tight and his thighs firm and thick. His dense hairline nearly swallowed his forehead whole. His brow line was piercing, as with all Porter males. The bridge of his nose was bumpy, results of many fistfights. He possessed a two-inch scar directly below his left eye, a result of a confrontation in a Knoxville bar. After initiating the fight, Dalton was sliced by a knife across the face, nearly severing his eye. The man dueling

with Dalton was large and mean, but not as evil as the Porters. Sterling and Murky were about ready to overtake the man in Dalton's aid, but Dalton waved them off, indicating he wanted to take the fight on his own. The battle raged on, and Dalton eventually overpowered the sizable man. Dalton ripped the knife from the man's hand, and what he did next shocked and disgusted the patrons inside the bar. Dalton pinned the man down on his stomach. Using the sharp knife, Dalton sliced the seat of the man's pants and underwear. He then cocked his arm back with knife in hand and plunged the blade into the man's rectum. The Porter boys laughed in celebration before fleeing the bar. The man nearly bled to death before he arrived at the hospital. The man refused to press charges in fear that the Porters would certainly kill him if he pursued the matter. The Knoxville police did charge Dalton with a misdemeanor weapons charge, but the case was low priority and became lost in the shuffle of the paperwork. It was not handled properly and simply not addressed.

Sterling could grow full facial hair, but he maintained a clean shave. Although his personal hygiene lacked his attention, he preferred his face smooth of hair. On some days, he shaved twice. He enjoyed the aroma that the aftershave lotion delivered to him, though it was a bargain off-brand that reeked of mint. He sustained his hair close to the scalp in military fashion. His front teeth were crooked and overlapped. Like Dalton, his Adam's apple was large and his dark green eyes close together. His shoulders were wide, with long powerful arms extending down to enormous hands. His legs were lean yet solid. Without mentioning, his brow line was piercing, as with all Porter males. His jawline was long and narrow and pointing at the chin's end. The outline of his mouth was rather tight in comparison with his other facial features. His nose size was proportional with his overall characteristics. He donned a tattoo of a naked woman on his left upper arm. Behind the nude woman was an ape with an erection and panting like a dog. Inked upon his right forearm was the US Marine Corps symbol, though he had never served. Below the symbol, the abbreviation of USMC was spelled out with Sterling's own definition of the representing letters. It read "United States Maniac Certified."

Murky's chin and upper lip area were always in a state of stubble. He didn't display a full beard, nor did he shave daily. The Porter men had deep alpha male voices, but Murky's was a lower note, even more profound. He shared the prominent Porter Adam's apple and tight eye formation and unique color. Murky displayed a chiseled jawline and overall facial structure that were characteristics and features of many professional male models. However, through the stubble, the rotting teeth, and collar-length messy hair, those attributes were difficult to discover. Like his father and brothers, Murky's build was solid, sturdy, unyielding, firm, and rugged. About 80 percent of Murky's back was covered in a colossal single tattoo. A full armor–bodied Viking was holding a spear in his right hand and a headless eagle in his left hand. Blood and feathers seeped from the Viking's mouth, suggesting that he had bitten off the head of the eagle.

*****

It was early evening when Sterling appeared in the living room where Murky and Dalton were watching television. Their parents were in Waynesburg attending a reverse raffle. Sterling stood while gazing at the television show airing. Murky and Dalton were seated on the worn sofa. A rerun of *Gilligan's Island* was playing.

"What the hell are you idiots watchin' this for?" Sterling taunted.

Murky and Dalton ignored him.

After a few moments, Sterling glanced around the living room area. "Where in the hell is the remote?"

"We're watchin' this, Sterling. You're not changin' the channel," Dalton asserted.

Sterling sneered. "I'll change the damn channel if I want to. Neither one of you worms are bad enough to stop me."

Murky squinted over at his standing brother. "Come on, Sterling. Don't be an asshole."

Sterling mocked Murky in a sissified voice. "Come on, Sterling. Don't be an asshole."

Murky extended his middle finger toward Sterling's direction.

Sterling snarled. "I'll break that finger off and ram it up your ass," he threatened.

Murky shook his right fist in the air. "Bring it on, motherfucker. I'll kill you like I killed Nate the masturbate last year."

Using the remote, Dalton turned off the television. "Why don't you two shut the hell up? You can't watch nuttin' around here."

The room fell quiet for a few moments before Sterling spoke up. "You know what, Murky? It's a year ago today that you wasted Nate. We should get some whiskey and celebrate."

Dalton's eyes widened. "I say we get drunk and go screw that whore over in Waynesburg."

Sterling nodded in agreement. "Sounds like a plan to me. Are you in, Murky?"

Murky sighed. "I wish I was gettin' drunk with Renee instead of you two rats."

"Man, would you shut up about her? I get sick of hearin' it," Dalton groaned.

Sterling slapped Murky on the back of his head. "Yeah, come on. Let's get drunk then drive over to Waynesburg and get one of Tammy's blowjobs. Man, that broad can suck a dick. A fuck and a suck for forty bucks. All three of us for a hundred. I sold some weed yesterday, got some cash on me."

"Okay...I'll go...The last time she blew me, I swear I came a quart," Murky said with a grin.

Sterling and Dalton laughed as the threesome headed out the front door.

CHAPTER 4

"I PRINTED THE documents and placed them inside this folder," Dule revealed, surrendering the folder across the restaurant's table to Marla.

"What's this?" she inquired, taking the folder from his hand.

"You know, the information you wanted on the Nathan Stewart case," he replied.

She nodded. "Good job, Dule. You're fast and with the program. But, of course, you're nice and slow when it counts." She winked seductively.

He playfully grinned at her. Dule surveyed the restaurant menu as Marla studied the contents of the folder, but not before placing her gold-rimmed eyeglasses upon her nose.

A waiter approached the table to top up their glasses of wine. "Are we ready to order?" the waiter queried.

Dule peered across the table. "Marla?"

Without glancing up from the folder, she instructed, "Order for the both of us, Dule."

"Okay then," he complied while looking back at the waiter. "We'll each have the Delmonico steaks, well done, and the lobster salad. Oh, and keep the wine coming. We're hailing a taxi home tonight."

"Very well," the waiter confirmed before retrieving the menu from Dule's hand. The waiter then traveled toward the kitchen area.

Dule drew a gulp of his wine while Marla was engulfed in the contents of the folder. Dule then spotted Frank Meyer and his wife seated at a nearby table. Dule imagined that when Mrs. Meyer's viewed the photos of her husband and his mistress the following day, there would be no further outings for Frank with his wife at his side.

"Listen to this, Dule," Marla whispered without glancing up from the folder. "The suspect, Murky Porter, is a free man. The police searched his parents' house and found the victim's blood on Murky's clothing that was hidden away in the basement. They also found the murder weapon, a knife. They found strands of the victim's hair on Murky's clothing as well. Nathan Stewart's DNA was all over the house. It's also believed that Murky's brothers, Sterling and Dalton, may have been involved in the murder as well."

"So why aren't these Porter boys behind bars?" he wondered.

Marla shook her head and rolled her eyes. "A technicality got them off. Our goddamn judicial system failed again. The search warrant was typed with the Porters' address as 2145 Dayton Road while the actual address is 2154. All the evidence was thrown out of court because that made the search illegal."

Dule lit a cigarette and then tossed the lighter onto the table. "That's the sort of bullshit that pisses me off. It gets under my skin. Sure, so I was caught with a little cocaine, but the bastards gave me two years in the pen. Then a dealer gets nabbed with pounds of the shit and only gets probation. I read in the paper the other day that some woman passed a bad check at a department store, and she got three years in prison. Then in the same paper, I read that some sicko raped his eight-year-old stepdaughter and only got six months for it. I'm telling you, the system is illogical."

Marla nodded her head in agreement. "It's reasons like those and this"—she held up the folder—"that the Elite Four was created. We're doing what we can to bring some righteousness to an imperfect system. I could give you examples of injustice all night long, Dule. It happens every day in this country. Rapists set free, abusers put into lame programs rather than jail time, murderers walk among us,

while drug dealers pay off judges and politicians. There are enough cracks in our system that if one could see it as an object, it would resemble a shattered windshield." Marla sipped from her wine and peered around the restaurant to be certain that none of the patrons were tuned into her and Dule's conversation before she continued.

"So when we are positive that an injustice has been committed"—again she raised the folder in her right hand—"such as this, we act. We take on a wrong and make it right. We bring needed closure. An eye for an eye. However, the key here is positive. We only take on about 5 percent of the cases we investigate. With the work we are doing, there cannot be a shred of doubt of a person's guilt."

"Are you going to assign this Stewart case to an Elite agent?"

Marla concurred, "However, it's not completely up to me. I present the case to the agent, then he or she determines if they agree with my outlook. If not, they just simply walk away. If they do concur, then we put our plan into action. By the way, did you look into the next available agent?"

He cleared his voice. "It's Cole Walsh. I emailed your request to him."

Marla beamed. "Good. Cole may be the youngest of the four, but he's the best."

CHAPTER 5

TAMMY PATRONI WAS sprawled naked on her bed with Sterling Porter atop of her. He had just finished his business with her and rolled away from her body. He slid to the edge of the bed and stood next to his pile of clothing. He began to dress as he looked over at Murky seated in a nearby chair. Murky was sharing a marijuana joint with Dalton. Dalton was wearing only his jeans as he had yet to fully dress after his turn with Tammy. She maintained her legs spread apart, revealing her exposed vagina as she waited for Murky.

"Come on, Murky. Get your clothes off and jump aboard," Sterling encouraged.

Murky hesitated, squinting through the bellowing smoke over at Sterling.

"What the hell are ya waitin' for?" Sterling grilled.

Murky groaned. "I don't know, Sterling. I think I'll pass. When I screw another broad, I feel like I'm cheatin' on Renee."

"What?" Sterling snorted. Dalton chuckled. Tammy rolled her eyes. "That bitch doesn't want anythin' to do with you. Why don't you get that through your thick skull already?"

"Don't call Renee a bitch, Sterling. I'll stab you!" Murky forewarned.

"Yeah, whatever, Murky. You don't scare me."

Murky pointed his right forefinger at Sterling. "You don't understand. I love Renee."

Sterling reached to the bed and cupped his right hand between Tammy's thighs. "This is what you should be lovin', little brother. This pussy is askin' to be fucked some more."

Tammy seductively winked.

"Now, get over here and get your dick wet," Sterling directed.

After another brief hesitation, while looking directly at Tammy's vagina, Murky stood up from the chair and began to eagerly disrobe.

*****

June 16
Cleveland, Ohio

FBI AGENT COLE Walsh turned from his computer inside his apartment and raised his cell phone to his left ear. In Philadelphia, Marla Simmons was lying on her sofa petting her cat that was perched upon her chest. Her telephone rang as she reached over to the nearby stand and picked up the receiver, careful not to dump Tulie on the floor.

"Hello, Marla Simmons speaking."

"Marla, it's Cole Walsh."

Marla sat up abruptly, spilling Tulie to the floor. The cat screeched and paced away aggressively. "Cole, how are you?"

"I'm fine, Marla, and you?"

"I'm doing good. How are things up in Cleveland these days?" she inquired.

"Oh, you know what life's like in a city. They call New York the city that never sleeps, but Cleveland isn't any different," he replied.

"Ditto here in Philly. Anyway, I assume that you received the email?"

"Yeah, I did. What's it all about this time?" he questioned.

Marla cleared her throat. "I think we have a definite go with this one. You know we can't discuss the details on the phone. So take a leave of absence from the bureau and cart your butt on down here

to my house in Philly. Of course, you know your pay will be covered by the general fund."

Cole rose from his chair and strode over to a large window in his apartment. He peered out to downtown Cleveland into the twilight of the evening. "How soon do you need me there?"

"Yesterday," Marla retorted.

Cole grinned. "Um…how about three days?"

"Two?" she dealt.

"Yeah, okay…I'll see you in two days, Marla." Cole pressed the end call on his cell phone and then tossed the phone onto the sofa. He remained standing at the window and whispered to himself, "I wonder what the case is this time around?"

Cole's reflection in the window was faint considering dusk was falling but was enough to reveal that he was equal in height to the Porter brothers. Cole weight-trained on a regular basis and was keen with his exercise ritual. He had coffee-colored hair trimmed at mid collar. His brown eyes fit well into his carved brow and slender cheeks. His jaws were clean shaven while his chin sported a goatee trimmed close to the skin. His neck was narrowed down but muscular. His chest and midsection were ridged with brawn development. His vast hands could collapse into mighty fists when need be. Though a man of Caucasian descent, Cole's skin appeared tanned year-round. His pace of saunter was confident but not cocky. Cole preferred dressing casual when not on duty with the FBI. It was T-shirts and Levi's at every opportunity.

Cole turned ladies' heads when he passed by, while a few went as far as openly flirting and offering their phone numbers to him. His voice was deep but easy, and his eyes were bold but kind, except when he was angry. When rage struck, Cole's eyes became piercing and cold. His facial expression was generally serious; however, it was not gravely looking. His toned skin was unblemished, and he bore just enough cologne to catch a hint of while standing next to him. His teeth were clean and aligned perfectly, thanks to his mother's insistence that Cole get fitted with braces when he was thirteen, though his teeth needed minimal alignment.

He had never married, nor did he have any children. At thirty-two, his life was busy, and he had little time for social calls. Cole Walsh realized at any early age, while in his teens, that he wanted to be either a soldier in the US Army or an FBI agent. He joined the army directly out of high school and served as a specialist in the Green Beret program. When enlistment was up, he decided to make a go at becoming an FBI agent. Two years after his service to the army was completed, Cole received his FBI badge.

This latest case, if he accepted it, would be his third as a member of the Elite Four. His initial situation was six years prior in New Orleans. An attractive but vulnerable woman, Myla Jansen, had spent two decades being physically abused by her husband, Raymond. Over the years, she had pressed charges against Raymond on four separate occasions. With each charge, Raymond spent little jail time. Some women were attracted to Raymond's good looks, though he was mean and disrespectful. The women whom Raymond dated and married were the type who had low self-esteem. However, Raymond was a handsome man and was picky about whom he paired up with. It was pretty ladies with less-than-confident attitudes for him. Myla thought many times to leave her abusive husband, but he threatened to kill her if she did. It turned out that she didn't have to leave him while still alive, as Raymond fulfilled his promise. During an argument, Raymond beat Myla's head against a heater pipe, crushing her skull. Myla lay deceased in the home for several weeks before a neighbor reported a foul odor coming from the Jansens' home. Police discovered Myla's decaying beaten body on the floor of the living room. They arrested Raymond on the spot, as he had remained living in the home despite his wife's dead body lying on the floor.

Raymond Jansen was charged with murder. In court, Jansen's lawyer claimed that his client had mental-related issues. That while growing up, Raymond's neglectful mother caused the adult Raymond to become violent. The lawyer's approach worked as the jury bought it. Raymond Jansen was sentenced to six months in a clinic and then set free. A year later, Raymond remarried, and within eight months, he was twice charged with spousal abuse.

Of the Elite Four members, Cole Walsh was assigned the case. Cole temporarily moved to New Orleans and landed a job at the same factory where Raymond was employed. He applied himself on developing a false friendship with Raymond. They would frequent taverns together, shooting pool and drinking whiskey. Raymond was under the impression that Cole was an ex-con, so he trusted Cole to be whom he appeared to be, a simple factory worker.

Over the next few months, Cole and Raymond's friendship strengthened, and eventually, Raymond invited Cole to his home. Cole then saw firsthand the despicable way in which Raymond treated his second wife.

****

"Hey, bitch, put some sandwiches and cold beers together. We got company," Raymond directed Cathy.

She bowed to his demand, and soon she was placing sandwiches and a cold six-pack of beer on the kitchen table in front of Cole and Raymond. Cathy squinted as Raymond grabbed a handful of her buttocks and squeezed tightly. Raymond chuckled, and Cathy nearly cried.

Cathy was nine years younger than the thirty-four-year-old Raymond Jansen. Her hair was naturally blonde and her eyes sky blue. Her figure was curvy and fit, her buttocks very shapely and alluring. Her breasts were natural, completely round and firm, given the look that they might be implants. She wore her blonde hair just beyond her shoulders, and her hygiene was very sufficient. Raymond was her first husband, and besides a few lame boyfriends growing up, she never was one to have enough confidence to date a decent man. Strong self-esteem should have come along with a young lady with such beauty, but was lost in her childhood, when her father would criticize her and her siblings.

She was raised in downtown New Orleans, one of seven children to Anita and Steve Tillman, in a poverty-stricken section of the city. Though her father drank and gambled away most of the family's income, he never blamed himself for his family's shortcomings. In the area where they resided, the crime rate was high, and it was a mix of

African American, Hispanic, and Caucasian population in the run-down neighborhood. Steve was prejudiced and despised blacks and Spanish-speaking people. Cathy and her sisters, Franny and Deloris, were few of the pretty white girls in the neighborhood. Whenever one of the girls would date a black or Spanish man, Steve would put a stop to it. One night, coming home from the bar earlier than usual, Steve arrived home intoxicated. The Tillman children, three girls and four boys, were staying at their grandmother's house for a few days in nearby Hollings, Louisiana. The county fair was in progress over the weekend, and the grandmother lived less than a mile from the fairgrounds. Steve did not want to wake his wife, Anita. She still retained a fair beauty even after six pregnancies. Two of the children, Deloris and James, were twins.

Anita, at forty-six, looked thirty-six and had passed on her family's trait of producing pretty women as daughters. Anita was obedient to her demanding and strict husband. However, Steve spent little time at home, and when he was there, for the most part, he was intoxicated and obnoxious.

What the children did not know was that Steve and Anita's sex life over the past few years was totally nonexistent. Steve was still very much attracted to his pretty wife, but he grew into a habit of sexual acts with prostitutes in New Orleans—more of the family money spent on his wayward ways. He salvaged his sexual urges for the wild, uninhibited sex he received by paying for it. Eventually, it took a toll on Anita, though she was unaware of Steve and the prostitutes. Steve had excused himself from sexual relations with Anita by stating his inability to gain an erection, a statement that was simply not true. She urged him to see a doctor, but he refused to do so.

As time passed, Anita felt neglected and her needs unfulfilled. For a spell of time, she was able to satisfy her urges through masturbation, but eventually, that just wasn't enough. Dwayne Harold, an African American man who lived next door to the Tillmans, was a handsome man. Though he was fifteen years younger than Anita, they began a friendship without Steve's knowledge.

Dwayne was divorced twice at his young age. He did have a live-in girlfriend who was unaware of Dwayne and Anita's relation-

ship. Dwayne had always fantasized about having sex with a white woman, so he set his sights upon Anita. What had started out as a friendship blossomed into sexual relations. In all the years of their marriage, Anita had never been unfaithful to Steve, but she succumbed to her needs and began engaging in sex with Dwayne on roughly a monthly basis. Dwayne's girlfriend was home nearly all the time; thus, Dwayne and Anita's sexual meetings took place at the Tillmans' house while Steve was away.

As Steve quietly moved up the stairs, Dwayne was in Steve and Anita's bed in the act of sexual intercourse with Anita. As Steve approached the closed door of the bedroom, he began to make out the excited moans generated from Anita. Steve pressed his ear to the door and heard Anita cry out during an orgasm. Steve's immediate thought was that Anita was masturbating, perhaps using a vibrator. That conclusion was dismissed when Steve heard Dwayne grunt as he ejaculated inside of Anita's vagina.

Steve, without hesitation, angrily kicked open the bedroom door. Steve Tillman reached for his gun in the dresser drawer, and despite Anita's cries for him to stop, Steve shot Dwayne Harold three times. He then turned the gun on his naked wife and placed two bullets into her chest. Dwayne and Anita both died from their gunshot wounds. Steve Tillman was sentenced to life in the Louisiana State Penitentiary.

The children lived with their grandmother until each of them turned eighteen. Cathy Tillman met Raymond Jansen while she worked the concession stand at a small stock car racetrack on the outskirts of New Orleans. Raymond frequented the track and came to know Cathy.

"Go sit in the corner, bitch," Raymond directed next.

Cathy's eyes widened. "What is that you say, Raymond?"

"The corner!" he barked.

"Why do you want me to do that?"

"Because a woman should be out of the way while inside the house while company visits. It rips her of any false dignity she might be falsely clinging to. A woman isn't smart enough to think that she's got dignity. Now take off to the corner for you, and keep your pie hole shut!"

It was obvious to Cole that Cathy feared her husband. Probably much like the late Myla had done before her.

"She doesn't have to sit in the corner. That's ridiculous, Raymond," Cole stated.

Raymond curled his lip at Cole. "Got something against a wife minding her husband?"

Cole rolled his eyes. "But she's your wife and not your slave."

"So what? Every now and then, you have to remind a woman of her place. Otherwise, she'll run you over like a stagecoach rushing from a band of thieves."

Cathy slowly and reluctantly moved toward a corner in the kitchen. She then stood with head bowed in shame before the men. Her eyes clouded with humiliation as her bottom lip quivered.

"Now, stay put until I say otherwise," Raymond instructed.

Cathy turned her eyesight away from the men in shame.

"Raymond, why are you chastening her like this?" Cole questioned.

He squinted at Cole. "What the hell is it to you? You like her or something?" Raymond then pointed at him. "I'll tell you what, Cole. You can look at her all you want, but if you so much as touch her, I'll mess you up. Don't even think about fucking my wife."

Cole now realized the opportunity he had been patiently waiting for since his arrival in New Orleans nearly three months prior. A situation where he could even the score for Myla and protect Cathy from the same fate as her predecessor.

"But I do have to say, if you fancied her, I'd understand, buddy. Mmmmmm, that's some mighty good pussy," Raymond mentioned. He then looked over at Cole.

Cole wanted to avoid any further mortification for Cathy, so he made a choice, and that was to surely anger Raymond. "Well, how about if I don't take your word for it and sample it for myself?" Cole grinned.

Raymond felt a rush of jealousy brewing within him, just as Cole hoped would happen.

Cole then accelerated the growing rage by winking at Cathy and commenting, "You are a fine-looking lady."

She began to find herself growing with excitement with Cole's interest.

"That's enough!" Raymond warned. "Stop looking at him, Cathy."

She hesitated.

"Now!" Raymond shouted.

She glanced away from Cole's direction.

"Stop flirting with my wife, you motherfucker," Raymond cautioned.

"Hey, take it easy. I can't help it, your wife has a nice figure," Cole complimented.

Cathy blushed and beamed. "Come on, Ray ole boy. Let me spend some time together with your wife. Whaddya say?" Cole suggested.

Cathy smiled.

"No way, man. She wouldn't want to you anyhow. Would you, bitch?" Raymond asserted.

Cathy cleared her throat halfheartedly. "Of course not. I love you, Ray."

Raymond curled his lip at Cole. "You see there, you're barking up the wrong tree, punk." Raymond then turned his attention back to his wife. "And I'll tell you what, bitch. If you ever touch another man, I'll twist your fucking neck like a pretzel," he promised. "Now, like I said before, keep your mouth shut."

Cole spoke up in order to maintain Raymond's looming agitation, "She can speak her mind. I'm enjoying her views, both orally and visually."

She grinned wide.

"Shut up, dude. Cathy, put your goddamn eyes back inside your head!"

She bit down her lip. "Now, Ray, don't get mad because I'm not doin' nothin. It's all in your head."

"Take your goddamn eyes off him. I won't say it again." Her husband lost his patience.

Cathy, with disappointment, turned to face the kitchen wall. Raymond shot up from his chair and rushed at her. He slapped her with a mighty force across the back of her head. Cathy's mouth banged into the kitchen wall, her lips bloodied while she grimaced in pain. The force of the blow caused her to drop to her knees.

Cole abruptly erupted from his chair. "Hey, what the hell are you doing with all this bullshit, Jansen? Knock it off, and don't hit her again."

"Stay out of this, dude," Raymond advised, "or I'll hit you next. Why don't you just leave? I'm sick of you making horny eyes at my wife."

Cole jerked his head no. "I want to stay. I want to talk to Cathy more." He realized that what he was doing was sure to enrage Raymond.

"Get out of my house!" Raymond demanded.

Cole turned to walk out the door and then glanced at Cathy's backside. "I'll call you sometime, pretty lady, when your idiot husband isn't around."

Raymond then rushed at Cole. He swung and connected with a punch to the side of Cole's head, near the temple. Cole's ears buzzed with a ringing sound as he took a stride backward—not to gather his senses, but rather to take aim with his right forearm. Cole's gun was holstered beneath his shirt, but at that moment, he didn't feel that he was in need of the firearm.

Cole lunged at Raymond, throwing his forearm with force up against Raymond's mouth. Raymond's head snapped back while his feet stumbled beneath him. He attempted to stabilize his falling body by grasping the kitchen counter's edge. He was unable to gain a firm hold and collapsed on the seat of his pants onto the kitchen floor. Cathy screamed before covering her bleeding mouth with her hands. Raymond reached up from a seated position and took hold of the handle on one of the kitchen drawers. He jerked the drawer open forcefully, spilling most of the drawer's contents onto the kitchen floor. Spoons, forks, butter knives, and steak knives crashed with a clanging sound to the tiles. Raymond grabbed the nearest of the steak knives in his right hand. He rose to his feet and beamed at the knife in his hand. He then glared at Cole. "I'm going to cut you up, man, you motherfucker."

Cole thought to pull his gun, but then hesitated, as he only wanted to go that route as a last resort.

Raymond made slow, calculated steps toward Cole. The member of the Elite Four stood his ground as Raymond and the knife approached.

"Put down the knife, Ray!" Cathy shouted.

He ignored her. Raymond then took a swinging stab at Cole. The blade missed Cole's stomach by inches as he shuffled his body quickly to the left. Raymond recoiled in preparation for his next attack. He lunged with the knife at Cole, who again moved out of harm's way. Raymond was unaware that he was dealing with a Green Beret as well as an FBI agent. His third, and last, attempt failed again. This time around, Cole was able to trap Raymond's hand beneath his right arm. He then launched a mighty blow with his head against Raymond's head. The head knock stifled Raymond, and he was barely able to hold on to the knife. Cole then intentionally set Raymond's hand free.

Raymond, now dazed, again confronted Cole with the knife in his right hand. Cole stepped aside and then grabbed Raymond's shoulder. He quickly twisted Raymond's body around so that Raymond's back was to him. Cole reached around Raymond's head with both his arms, gaining a firm hold. Cole then whispered into Raymond's ear, "Goodbye, Raymond Jansen, you murdering bastard. And this is for Myla." With a powerful jolting motion of his mighty arms, Cole broke Raymond's neck in two separate places. The snapping of the bones exploded like the crack of a baseball bat. Raymond's lifeless body relaxed and went limp. Cole released his grip, allowing Raymond's dead body to spill to the floor.

Cathy's face went pale before she ran to the living room. She halted abruptly and vomited onto the carpet.

Cole came to her aid. "It's okay, Cathy. It's over. He won't be bothering you ever again." Cole placed a supporting arm around her shoulder. "I had no choice. He was trying to kill me."

It wasn't that Cathy was saddened over her abusive husband's death; she was thankful to be finally free. She was in a state of mild shock and frazzled as it was the first time in her life that she had witnessed someone being killed.

The police arrived soon after, and it was eventually ruled that Cole Walsh acted in self-defense. Days later, as Cole prepared to

leave New Orleans, Cathy was gracious and appreciative of Cole, placing a thank-you kiss upon his cheek. Case closed, and Cole returned to Cleveland.

Justice served.

*****

Cole continued to gaze out his apartment window while recalling his second stint as a member of the Elite Four. It was two years ago when the assignment led him to the Baltimore area.

Paula Asner was accused of locking her seven-year-old daughter in a closet on and off over a three-year period. The child, Amber Asner, perished from starvation and malnutrition. During the trial, the lawyer representing Paula claimed that Amber was an unruly child who brought her mother grief. The jury didn't buy it. Paula was sentenced to twenty years in prison for voluntary manslaughter. After serving only six years of the sentence, Paula Asner walked away from incarceration as the result of a shock probation program. Within six months after her release, using a bogus identity and résumé, Paula landed a job with a nanny agency. While caring for a professional couple's child during the daytime hours, Paula was captured on hidden surveillance camera beating the child. The infant was hospitalized with multiple injuries, and sadly, another young life was lost.

In court proceedings, the tape evidence was thrown out as testimony for in the state of Maryland, a surveillance camera must be licensed. The professional couple did not realize this requirement, and the monitoring device was not officially listed. Again, Paula Asner walked away.

Cole Walsh, acting under an Elite Four assignment, rented a home in the Baltimore area under an assumed identity. With the knowledge that Paula Asner was in the area seeking employment, Cole ran an ad in the local paper. The ad read that a bachelor was looking for a live-in housekeeper. The pay was excellent. After interviewing six candidates, it finally paid off when Paula responded to the ad. Cole hired her immediately to start the following day. That evening, he reinforced the closet door with steel striping. He installed

a dead bolt lock that a mighty gorilla could not break. His plan was simple, and it was set.

The following day, Paula reported for first day of work. Before she arrived, Cole had placed three one-gallon jugs of water in the closet. No food. Shortly after her arrival, Cole paused until she neared the closet so he could easily force Paula inside the small closet. He locked the door behind her and was sure it was secure. He then left the house to never again return. Paula endured the following eight weeks screaming out for help to no avail. Cole left behind the water, as he wanted her to die a slow death. Starvation rather than a quick dehydration.

Just like Paula had done to Amy, it was a long, horrible nightmare of two months. She had to soil herself while captive inside the closet. When the water eventually ran dry, she drank her own urine to try to survive. She weakened to where she could no longer stand to her feet. The last few days, she was delusional. Paula Asner passed away in a slow, famished death. Her skeletal remains were not discovered until nearly a year later.

The local police could not gather enough evidence to pin the incident to any party. To this day, the mysterious case of Paula Asner remains unsolved. Justice bestowed.

Cole Walsh stepped away from his apartment window, ready to turn in for the night. Tomorrow he would deliver his temporary leave of absence notice to the bureau.

CHAPTER 6

June 18

COLE WALSH ARRIVED at the front doorstep of Marla Simmons's home in Philadelphia. He surveyed the immediate area before ringing the doorbell.

Within a minute, Marla pulled the door open. She smiled wide at him. "Cole Walsh, march your handsome butt right on in here."

Cole entered the house onto the river rock embedded into the floor of the entranceway. The house was simple yet with an elegant touch to it. Many of the awards and anniversary plaques that Marla received as an FBI agent were displayed on the walls of the entrance and kitchen area. Her retired badge was encased in glass and on the fireplace mantle in the living room. The house was very tidy as the tiled floor in the kitchen shined. The kitchen smelled inviting with cooking spices that were draped in a netted bag above the large wooden island counter.

Cole then noticed Dule Brookside seated at the kitchen table. Cole squinted toward Marla with a concerned expression.

"Don't worry, Cole. He's been informed and pledges full confidentiality," Marla assured.

Cole nodded, but with a doubt of confidence.

Dule rose from his chair and approached Cole with his right hand extended. "I'm Dule Brookside, Marla's assistant. I've been looking forward to meeting you, Cole Walsh. Marla tells me that you're one helluva agent."

Cole shook Dule's hand. "Yeah, well, Marla was a damn good agent in her prime as well," Cole complimented.

Marla grinned. "Why, thank you for the praise, Agent Walsh."

"Would you like something to drink?" Dule offered.

"Beer?" Cole sought.

"Coming right up," Dule confirmed.

"Come on in and have a seat," Marla invited, taking Cole by his right arm. She led him over to the kitchen table where Cole found a seat among five available chairs. Marla sat directly across the table from Cole just as Dule arrived with three cold bottles of beer. Dule then sat opposite Cole. Marla pulled a folder from her soft leather briefcase that was lying on the kitchen table. She then slid the folder across the table to Cole as he sipped his beer.

"There it is, Cole, the case we're looking at and considering. I'm committed to it. The guilt is doubtless. So take your time and read it over. Remember, the deciding vote is exclusively yours to make."

Cole opened the folder and began studying the contents.

The room was quiet for several minutes before Dule spoke to Marla. He whispered in an attempt not to disturb Cole's concentration. "I wrapped up the Meyers case today, Marla. When Barbara Meyers viewed the explicit photos of her husband's intimate meeting with his girlfriend, she about burst at the seams. She paid the retainer in full and declared she was heading for her lawyer's office."

Marla grinned. "Good job, Dule. What's the next case coming off the back burner?"

Dule swallowed a swig of his beer. "Taylor. Antonio Taylor. Antonio is a doctor. A heart surgeon at Philadelphia Memorial Hospital. Big bucks, you can betcha. He and his wife believe that their accountant could be embezzling money from them. The accountant claims the losses are from faltering stocks." Dule smirked. "But he's misplaced the documents to prove his claim of

financial misfortunes. The Taylors want us to try to find out if there is a deceiving paper trail."

Marla sipped from her beer before responding. "That could be a tough one for us, Dule. Those accountants are good at covering their tracks. What kind of deal did you set up with the client?"

"Three hundred dollars an hour plus expenses. Regardless of if we find anything on the accountant or not. If we do find something on the bookkeeper, then a ten-thousand-dollar bonus would be applied."

She bobbed her head. "Sounds reasonable. When do you need to get started?"

"I thought maybe in four to five weeks. I was thinking that you and I could get away for a couple of weeks. Maybe the Bahamas or Vegas?"

Cole glanced up from the folder for a moment to tease a grin Marla's way. He then returned his attention to the folder.

Marla smiled. "Yeah, Dule, we can do something like that."

"Great," Dule responded with obvious approval.

The kitchen then fell silent for a long minute.

Cole finally looked up from the folder then closed it.

"Well?" Marla nervously wondered. Dule hung on the edge of his chair in anticipation of Cole's riposte. This marked the first time that Dule had been involved this deeply with the decision-making process of the Elite Four.

Cole exhaled in a deep breath. "First off, I want to know why Dule Brookside here spent time in the pen."

Dule's eyes widened. Marla was not shaken by Cole's observation skills. She knew he was an excellent detective.

"How in the hell does he know that?" Dule quizzed.

Marla chuckled at Cole. "Enlighten us, agent."

Cole rubbed his jaw while observing Dule. "Prison-issued toothpaste has nyadine in it. Nyadine is in the chemical family of iodine and is used as a preservative. Now, what nyadine does over a period is it produces a tartar buildup along the gumline. What makes this plaque buildup unique is it has a very slight ivory tone to it. Just a touch dimmer than typical tooth enamel. You can only

get rid of the buildup with several intense teeth-cleaning visits to a dentist. You, Dule, have that buildup. Also, it takes at least a year of using prison-issued toothpaste to develop the required buildup. So you were in at least that long."

Dule brushed his gumline feverishly with his forefinger for a few moments. "Anything else, Sherlock?" Dule questioned sarcastically.

"Yeah, as a matter of fact, there is something else. I don't know if your cocaine use was a factor in your crime, but the faint broken blood vessels on the outside of your nose are a dead giveaway."

Dule cupped his left hand over his nose.

Marla covered her mouth to restrain from laughing.

"So I used to snort a little now and then. I don't anymore. I'm beginning not to like you very much, Cole," Dule claimed.

Cole scowled. "I'm not here to win you over, pal."

Dule stood abruptly from his chair and brushed by Cole on his way from storming from the kitchen.

Remaining seated, Cole reached up to Dule's neck with his right hand and pinched Dule's airway shut between his thumb and forefinger. Dule immediately struggled for air, but when he attempted to free his neck of Cole's hold, it triggered sharp pain to shoot up to his Dule's ears.

"Now, you listen to me, Dule, and you listen good. If you ever whisper a word about the Elite Four to anyone, they'll find pieces of your body no larger than a dime. Do you understand?" Cole threatened.

Dule quickly jerked his head yes as his face reddened from a lack of oxygen. Cole then slowly released his squeeze hold, and Dule gasped for air, followed by deep coughing. Dule nearly vomited while bending at the waist to gather in oxygen.

"Sit back down, Dule," Marla directed.

Cole then spun his attention back to Marla. "What the hell are you doing, Marla? I hope you trust that Dule will keep his mouth shut."

"Dule can be fully trusted, Cole. Just calm down, okay?" she promised.

Dule dropped back down in his chair. He rubbed his throat with his right hand while trying to soothe the ache. He now spoke with a rasp to his voice. "Damn it, Cole. You didn't have to do that."

"Just letting you know, Dule, that the Elite Four is not a game. This is serious business, and you'd better treat it as no less than that," Cole warned.

Marla waved her left hand. "Okay, okay…let's get to the subject at hand. Cole, what are your thoughts on the Nathan Stewart case?"

Cole delivered Dule one final warning glare before he looked back to Marla and replied, "No chance that the evidence was planted in the Porter home?"

"No. I looked over the police report several times. There is no indication of possible tainting of the evidence," she reported.

"This Murky Porter and his brothers. Do they have priors?"

She pulled another folder from her briefcase and opened it. "Murky Porter has five counts of breaking and entering, fourteen counts of disturbing the peace, three counts of assault and battering, and three counts of theft. Sterling and Dalton…ditto. These boys must do everything together. Strangely, all arrests were made by state, county, or adjoining town police—none from the hometown force. Each time, if the charges were not dropped altogether, the Porters were fined, sentences suspended, and/or assigned to community service. The fines have been paid sporadically, and not one hour of community service has ever been performed. You know that most courts don't follow up on these things. It's a sad situation."

Dule held his cold bottle of beer up against his stinging throat.

Cole peered at her. "Okay…I'll take on the case."

"Great!" Marla celebrated. "I'll visit the Stewarts down in Harpersfield the day after tomorrow to present our offer to them. You can take the next few weeks to prepare for the case. I'll call you and let you know if the Stewarts go for it or not. We'll communicate by cell phone rather than email, as Dule and I will be out of town for a little while. So I'll talk with you in a couple of days, Cole."

She rose from her seat simultaneously with Cole. They shook hands with an agreement.

"It was good seeing you again, Marla."

"Same here, Agent Walsh. I'll be expecting your reports throughout the process," she reminded him.

"You got it," he confirmed. Their handshake then gently broke away.

She then escorted Cole to the front door.

Cole eyed Dule and then winked. "See ya, Dule."

Dule did not vocally respond. He only waved his hand sharply.

Cole then stepped out of the house and to his black Dodge four-wheel-drive pickup truck parked at the curb of the street. The truck was Cole's personal vehicle and not part of the FBI-issued vehicles.

Soon, Cole Walsh was steering his vehicle away from Marla Simmons's house.

CHAPTER 7

June 20

MARLA IDLED HER sports car at the end of the long drive-way that led to the Stewarts' farmhouse in Harpersfield, Tennessee. She double-checked the address on the mailbox to the address in the case folder. Dule, who was riding beside her, confirmed that this was the correct residence. She pulled her dark blue Ford Mustang along the dirt driveway to cover the nearly six hundred feet of distance up to the house. She parked the car with a bit of dust rolling up behind the vehicle.

"You stay here in the car, Dule," she directed.

"Why? Oh, come on, honey. I want to see their faces when you tell them," he pleaded.

Marla gritted her teeth. "Don't give me a hard time with this. The only reason you're along is because we're driving to Las Vegas from here. These people are going to be overwhelmed with just me in there. They don't need the two of us making them even more uncomfortable. One of us is quite enough."

He growled in a low-toned, disappointed voice, "How long will you be?"

"No longer than I must, trust me. A small southern town like this Harpersfield is the last place a black woman wants to hang around too long."

Dule tapped at his holstered gun that was beneath his shirt. "Any shenanigans, and I got ya covered, my love."

"Thanks, babe." Marla then kissed Dule. "I'm going to pretend that you don't have a gun under your shirt. You're a convicted felon. It's illegal for you to carry a firearm."

"What you don't know won't hurt ya," he said with a wink.

Marla rolled her eyes as she popped open the driver's-side door. A low-toned alarm sounded, reminding her that she had left her keys in the ignition. She slid out of the driver's seat and closed the door, ending the sound of the alarm. Marla then moved around the front of the car and up to the porch of the aging farmhouse. She glanced around for any free-running dogs. Like her cat, Tulie, Marla didn't get along with dogs very well. After determining that the coast appeared clear, she stepped up the decaying, creaking steps of the porch. She reached the house where the screen door was all that was closed. She tapped on the aluminum frame of the door.

Inside, Ike was seated on the sofa enjoying an after-dinner coffee spiked with bourbon. Renee, in the kitchen, was putting away the now cleaned and dried dinner dishes. Ike rose to the sounds of the tapping upon the screen door while Renee hesitated her work in order to listen, as she could not see the door from her vantage point. She remained stationary for only a short moment before moving toward the door along with her grandfather.

Fearing that it could be the Porter brothers paying an unwanted visit, she accompanied Ike to the door. They peered through the screen door to view a stranger, a black woman, wearing gold-rimmed eyeglasses resting halfway down on her nose, standing on their porch. Ike looked at Renee in confusion before she shrugged her shoulders.

Ike slowly opened the screen door for the mysterious visitor.

Marla smiled and reached out her hand. "You must be Ike Stewart?"

"Yes, ma'am," Ike confirmed, not yet willing to shake her hand.

Marla maintained her extended hand. "My name is Marla Simmons. I realize that you do not know who I am, but trust me when I tell you that we need to talk."

Renee and Ike squinted at one another in perplexity.

Marla peered around and then whispered, "It's regarding Nathan's case."

Ike glared directly into Marla's deep brown eyes. "What about Nate?"

Marla slowly dropped her still-empty hand to her side. "I know this already sounds confusing, but we really need to discuss this inside. Do you mind?" Marla requested.

Ike looked to his granddaughter. After a hesitation, Renee nodded her approval.

"Come on in," Ike halfheartedly invited.

"Thank you," Marla replied before stepping inside the farmhouse.

Ike gestured with a nod for Marla to enter the living room. Marla immediately observed that the house was old, incredibly aged over the years. The furniture was well used, and the carpet was worn to its fibers. A small pendulum clock hung on the living room wall, ticking away with seconds. A sofa, recliner chair, a large dark-stained coffee table, and two wooden chairs (a flowery cloth cover on the arms) completed the furniture inside the living room. The house was old-fashioned, but it was maintained well. Things were orderly and clean. Marla attributed this to the presence of a woman residing in the household.

The east wall of the living room contained markings. Upon closer inspection, Marla deciphered that it was a series of growth charts. Three charts climbed the wall penned in red felt-tip marker. From left to right, the first chart had the name *Jack* above it. The next chart was titled *Renee*, and the last was headed by the name of *Nate*. Each notch on the charts was signified by feet and inches as well as the date, down to the age of the person in years and months. The television had a set of rabbit ears antenna atop of it, although cable and satellite television had come out decades ago. A large framed photograph that was taken what appeared to be in the 1980s was displayed on the wall above the fireplace. The man in the photograph,

which was obviously a younger Ike Stewart, had his arms around two women. Standing proudly next to Ike was a handsome young man.

Ike caught Marla eyeing the photo. "Those were two special ladies in my life. My lovin' wife Jodi and my wonderful daughter-in-law, Beth. They are no longer with us. Cancer took Jodi, and a car accident claimed Beth along with my son, Jack. A son any man would have been proud to claim as his own," Ike bragged with a shudder in his voice. "Fortunately, I still have a great gal in my life, my beautiful granddaughter Renee. She's every bit as pretty as her momma was."

Renee blushed. "Grandpa, you're just family is all. That's why you say that."

"No, it's true. You are a beautiful young lady," Marla complimented.

"Why, thank you so much for the kind words, ma'am," Renee responded, again slightly embarrassed.

Marla then spotted another photograph. This one was much more recent of a young boy donning a little league baseball uniform. The name of the team on the shirt was the sponsorship of one Tiny's Diner. He was wearing his baseball cap low on his forehead, causing the shade from the brim to obstruct the entire view of his face. Not utter obstruction though, as Marla realized by recalling the photograph inside her case folder that the young man was no other than Nathan Stewart.

"He liked baseball, huh?" Marla inquired.

"Oh, couldn't keep him away from the diamond," Ike confirmed.

"I tried to get him to pull up his cap for that picture, but he wouldn't listen. He thought he looked cool that way." Renee playfully rolled her eyes.

Marla then peeked out the bay window to see Dule eyeing her while pointing at his wristwatch. Marla took a seat on one of the two wooden chairs as Ike sat on the recliner chair.

"Can I offer you somethin' to drink?" Renee offered.

Marla raised her left palm. "Oh, no, thank you, I've had too much caffeine already today. But thanks just the same."

Renee located a seat on the sofa directly across from Marla.

Ike got down to the business at hand. "Now, what's this all about concerning Nate?"

Marla cleared her throat. "Mr. Stewart, what would you say if I offered to you justice for the murder of Nathan?"

Renee's eyes squinted. "What is this? A sick joke or somethin'?"

Marla shook her head no as her expression became critically serious. "I assure you that this is no joke."

"What are you, some kind of lawyer?" Ike inquired.

"Because if you are," Renee added, "the Porters have already been set free. It's over, there's nothin' you or we can do about it now. So please, don't be comin' here with your empty promises just to get some overpriced retainer."

"Believe me, I'm no lawyer."

"A reporter?" Renee drilled.

Marla jerked her head no. "Not a chance I'd be one of them sharks."

"Then I don't understand." Ike creased his forehead.

Marla pushed her eyeglasses a bit farther up on the bridge of her nose. "As I've told you, my name is Marla Simmons. I served over twenty years as an agent with the FBI. During those years, another agent and I formed a secretive group. Before I continue, I must warn the both of you that what you are about to hear must remain guarded. You are not to discuss it with anyone. If you do, we will just deny its existence, and you will need to be quieted. Do you understand?"

Ike and Renee looked at one another for a stifled moment before nodding their mutual understanding.

"Good," Marla confirmed. "Now first I must ask you, if I can practically guarantee justice for the murder of Nathan Stewart, would you accept my offer?"

"Of course." Renee was quick to respond.

Marla slid to the edge of her chair. "Okay…this is how it works…"

CHAPTER 8

THE PORTER BOYS saw Sterling's rusty pickup truck swing into the dusty parking lot of Harpersfield's lone tavern. Joe's Place was known for its cheap draft beer. It was also a tavern where the Porters' father frequently visited. Upon catching sight of their father's pickup truck in the parking lot, Sterling, Dalton, and Murky decided to go inside the roadhouse for a beer with their dad.

Sitting at the bar were three patrons. In the barstool next to Carter Porter was Tammy Patroni, a prostitute from Waynesburg. Earlier, she was stroking Carter's erect penis beneath the bar. Several stools down from her sat the gentle town drunk, Mason Turner. Mason was nearly fifty-nine years old but appeared to be seventy, and his liver had taken on decades of hard drinking. His hair was nearly completely gray now, and his eyes drooped with heavy bags of skin below the sockets. His ears were large, making his face appear thin and narrow. His long nose curled down at the end, giving him the presence of a wizard from a children's storybook. He limped for about twenty feet each time he rose from a seated position until his tight back loosened up a bit, likely results of sitting on nonsupportive barstools for years. He lived alone these days after going through four marriages. Mason was an undersized man at five feet eight inches tall

and weighed a mere 140 pounds. Mason would rather drink than eat. He was a quiet man for the most part and easygoing. He was never one to cause any trouble.

Joe's Place was mostly bar area. There were two small tables with three chairs at each of them, but rarely did anyone take a seat at the tables. There was a time when the tavern served food; an aged, outdated menu sign still hung on the wall and would testify to that. The menu was so antiquated that owner Joe Skidmore decided to keep it in place as a historical display. A hamburger with fries on the menu was only sixty-five cents. The menu in place was well before Joe's time of managing the tavern.

A bit down farther the street, Tiny's Diner had become more popular with meals over the years and virtually shut down the tavern's business of dining. Joe Skidmore was thirty-four and the third generation of Skidmores to own and operate the tavern. His parents, Malcolm and Janey Skidmore, gave up the ship to Joe five years prior after Joe sobered up. They weren't going to hand over the ownership and let Joe run the business when he couldn't control his own drinking. His marriage to Judy Martin changed Joe's ways, and he cleaned up his act. Malcolm and Janey appreciatively handed over the family business with Judy being in the picture. They had since moved to retire in Florida.

They realized now how peaceful life was in Southern Florida while not needing to deal with the Porters. They wouldn't even consider coming home for a visit. Joe and Judy traveled to visit them twice a year in the Panhandle State. Joe's hair was worn short in military style, though he had never served. He hated dealing with hair, so he just shaved it close to his scalp. From what hair was visible, like the Skidmores before him, Joe was graying early in life. It was okay though; it bothered him none. The stubble on his face, which he sported even though Judy wished for him to shave, poked through with wired hair from beneath the surface of his face. Joe had the type of skin that looked like it had been gone over with sandpaper. No blemishes, just a leathery look about it. His eyes were blue, and his ash-blond eyebrows lay light on his tanned skin. He enjoyed gardening, and during the morning hours before the tavern opened for the

day on afternoons, he and Judy could often be found working their garden at home, soon following sunrise on most days.

Three years prior, just as the garden was nearing harvest, the Porter boys took it upon themselves to destroy the crop. Trailing down the road drunk and disorderly, they drove Sterling's truck up onto the Skidmores' land and purposely threw the truck into spins throughout the garden. Over 90 percent of the crop was lost. The Skidmores' preparations for canning were all for naught. Judy and Joe witnessed the cruel criminal act and reported it to Sheriff Bob Harvey. All that was done about the incident was the Porters were issued a warning citation, which they ripped up in Bob's face.

Since the Skidmores reported the Porters to the police, the retaliation would be forthcoming. This time the Porters set fire to the Skidmores' home. Joe and Judy barely escaped with their very lives. They moved into the back room of the tavern for nearly a year as their home was rebuilt. That time, Joe and Judy simply let matters be. Being that Harpersfield was a small town, only two state alcohol licenses were issued each year in the area. Joe's Place and Darton's Gas Station held the only permits.

Emma's General Store did sell alcohol, but without a permit. Sheriff Bob Harvey acknowledged this, but portrayed as though he was unaware. The tavern did host an annual pig roast in the yard behind the establishment each July. It was a popular event that usually sold tickets to nearly everyone in Harpersfield as well as to those residing in the adjoining towns of Webster and Waynesburg. It profited well, and Joe kept the Porters away from the event by dividing the profits with them, 70 percent to 30 percent. Of course, it was Joe who only received 30 percent. However, he realized that if the Porters showed up even once at a pig roast, all future festivities would be lost. Their crazy antics would surely chase away the attendees of the annual gathering.

The Porters made a good profit from the roasts, so they stuck to their agreement of not attending the festivities.

The Porters relied on dirty money as none of them had a legitimate job. It was difficult for Joe to hand over such a large sum of money each year to the Porters. He could have used the money to fix

up his house, put some of it back into maintenance for the tavern, and take his wife on a nice vacation. However, he was fully aware the money purchased peace, and how could you put a price on that? He had thought about squeezing back a bit on the Porter's cut, but he feared the risk. It could mean a beating or, even worse, his life at the hands of the Porters if it were ever disclosed. Over the years of the roast's profits, Joe had paid the Porters their share in full.

The tavern was practically home to Mason Turner. He had been around long enough to see the tavern age over the decades. He could recall when the barstools were wooden and patrons tossed peanut shells on the floor. This was planned as it made walking on the floor cushioned with shells a unique experience. Today, Joe proudly displayed new shining black-and-white tile on the floor. No longer were shells tossed about, except by the Porters, but Joe did not scold them for doing so. He recognized what the price would be to do so. He would certainly have taken some hard knocks.

The three Porter brothers entered the tavern through the beat-up screened door. They spotted their father immediately and made their way toward him. Sterling grinned at Tammy after she winked at him.

Dalton placed his arm around his father. "Hey, Pop, buy us a beer."

Carter nodded to the bartender to fulfill the request. "What the hell are you boys up to this evenin'?" Carter good-humoredly interrogated.

Dalton and Murky plopped down on barstools next to their father. Sterling rubbed Tammy's breasts on the outside of her blouse.

"Nuttin' much," Murky reported. "Kinda bored."

"Why don't you boys go over to the stock car races tonight over in Webster?"

Dalton nodded. "Hey…that's a good idea. There's always some nice Webster pussy walkin' around there."

"Wanna go to the races?" Sterling asked Tammy.

She nodded her acceptance.

"For Christ sakes, Sterling," Carter groaned while rolling his eyes. "You're supposed to screw a whore. You don't date her."

Sterling angered but did not backtalk his father.

"She's ridin' in the back of the truck if she goes," Murky asserted.

"That'll be fine," Tammy acknowledged.

Dalton shook his head.

Three draft beers were then delivered by Joe Skidmore before Carter tossed two one-dollar bills on the bar. The bartender swiped up the bills in his hand and then slid them into the cash register.

Murky smirked at Dalton. "Let's have some fun. Watch this."

Mason was looking straight ahead while minding his own business.

"Hey, Turner," Murky threw his voice the length of the bar. "What the fuck are you lookin' at us for?"

Mason turned his insecure attention to Murky. "Huh? I wasn't lookin' at nothin'."

"Leave him alone, Murky. He's not doin' anyone harm," Tammy pointed out.

Murky ignored Tammy's plea and continued to badger Mason. "You stink, Mason. Why don't you take a bath?"

The truth of the matter was that Murky could have practiced some personal hygiene of his own.

Mason was becoming visibly anxious. "Okay, Murky, I will. I'll clean up when I get home. Whatever you say. I don't want any trouble, young man."

Murky gulped a long drink from his beer and then stood from his barstool before moving toward Mason.

"Go get 'em, Murky," Sterling coached as Murky passed him on his way to the other end of the bar where Mason was stationed.

Dalton pushed himself up from the barstool to shadow Murky. Carter beamed as he observed his sons in action. Murky and Dalton came to a stand next to Mason.

"Are you gettin' smart with me, Turner, the slow learner?" Murky grilled.

"No, I'm not, Murky. Please leave me alone," Mason pleaded. "I'll go home, just please leave me be."

Dalton chuckled at Mason's vulnerability.

"Nope, I can't do that, Mason. I must set an example. Nobody, and I mean fuckin' nobody, stares down the Porters."

Joe interluded. "Don't do it, Murky, or I'll call the cops. Mason hasn't done anythin' but sit there quietly while mindin' his own."

Carter leaned forward in his barstool. "If you touch that god-damn phone, Joe, I'll break your damn hand."

Joe swallowed hard and raised his hands in a surrendering fashion. "Okay…, Carter…no cops."

Carter eased back into his barstool.

Murky reached up and slapped Mason on the back of his head. The blow caused Mason's baseball cap to flip off his head and onto the bar. "Stand up, Turner!" Murky demanded.

"Please let up, Murky."

"Stand up, Mason. Don't make me pull you up, or I'll get more pissed off," Murky warned.

Reluctantly, with ringing in his ears, Mason rose to his feet. "Murky, I'm beggin' you not to hurt me. My bones are gettin' old, and they ache all the time."

Murky chuckled, and in one quick fluent motion, using his left fist, he punched Mason in his throat, shocking the airway.

Mason grabbed at his throat, trying to regain his breathing. As the man struggled, Dalton reared back and kicked Mason in his groin area. Mason doubled over in excruciating pain and then collapsed to the tavern floor.

Before Dalton and Murky moved away from the fallen gentleman, Murky kicked Mason upon the left side of his face. Mason groaned out in pain as his body trembled. He coughed deeply, gagged several times, and spit while attempting to clear his airway.

Dalton and Murky broke into laughter as they returned to their individual barstools. Sterling delivered to each of his brothers a high five.

"You boys have some wound-up energy." Carter chuckled.

Murky glared at Sterling. "Next time, tell your whore to shut the hell up."

Sterling peered to Tammy. "Yeah, keep your damn mouth shut, except when you're blowin' me."

The Porters laughed in harmony.

Tammy, taking the threat seriously, succumbed to Sterling. "I'm sorry. I'll keep my place next time."

"Let's go to the races!" Dalton proclaimed.

Soon, the three brothers were loaded up in the cab of Sterling's pickup truck with Tammy sitting on the wheel housing in the bed of the truck. They pointed the rig toward Webster and accelerated down the road.

Mason was still coughing for air from time to time.

"Get to your worthless feet, Mason. You disgust me, you spineless twerp," Carter growled.

Mason struggled to his feet.

"Now get the hell out of here!" Carter commanded.

Mason nearly fell as he staggered out the tavern's door.

As the tavern's television behind the bar aired the local news and echoed into Carter's ears, he recalled an event along with his now-deceased brother, Steadman, from years prior. After the siblings had read an article in a nationally published hunt-and-game magazine that the county of Gaines in the state of Tennessee had produced some of the finest stag deer bagged over the previous five years, the duo decided to take a hunting trip to that county when deer-hunting season opened in less than a week's time.

*****

"We'll park my truck right here," Steadman confirmed as he brought his vehicle to a halt in an open field of tall grass.

"Looks as good as place as any to me." Carter nodded from the passenger's seat.

The Porter brothers—Steadman, twenty-six years old, and Carter twenty-three—arrived at a previously uncharted territory for the duo as this marked the first for either one to be within the borders of Gaines County, some ninety-five miles northeast of their hometown of Harpersfield. Unbeknownst to them, they had parked Steadman's vehicle in the boundary of Hartsgrove, Tennessee, a small town; however, their exact landing spot mattered none to them.

Within ten minutes, the had their loaded hunting rifles strapped to their backs while heading out to the nearby timberline at sunrise in hopes of bagging a trophy buck on the opening day of deer-hunting season in the state.

After some four morning hours of slowly stalking the forest floor without success of shooting a single deer, let alone even spotting their intended prey of a large buck, the young brothers began to grow bored and restless.

"I wonder whose property we're trespassin' on?" Carter chortled.

"I don't really give a shit," Steadman retorted.

"Fuck, matters to me none either," Carter confirmed. "Just thinkin' out loud is all."

Steadman then pointed ahead of their position. "There's an incline up just a bit there. Let's get the hell up there as it's probably overlookin' an open field. Should give us a good vantage point of any deer meanderin' around the area. Remember, we traveled all the way up here to drop a buck. Never mind any doe bitches. We can put down plenty of sissy venison back home. This hunt is all about antlers. The bigger, the better."

"Gotcha, bro," Carter verified.

At the top of the crest, the Porters did indeed gain a decent view of a valley's field below their roost. However, the basin was currently unpopulated of any quarry they were seeking. Some three hundred yards below their perch were two houses that dotted along the flatland where the tall grasses gave way to groomed lawns. The households were about five acres separated in distance without any another structures within sight.

Peering through the scope of his high-powered rifle, Steadman sighted in on a young man working on a van in the driveway of his residence. The vehicle's hood was raised with the novice mechanic wrenching away at the engine and its components.

Steadman nudged his brother's shoulder. "Raise you scope, Carter. We might have somethin' to tell us if we have our damn firing sticks on target."

After peering through his rifle's scope, Carter, without sympathy, encouraged, "Looks like damn good target practice to me."

"Okay, keep your scope on him while I fire my rifle to tell me exactly where my bullet strikes."

"Covered," Carter affirmed.

Taking steady aim, Steadman focused the crosshairs of his rifle's scope to rest upon the head of the unsuspecting young man. Steadman inhaled and then squeezed the trigger. The echo of the rifle's blast was engulfed by the van's noise of acceleration by the makeshift mechanic. The

young man was struck by Steadman's projectile directly behind his right ear. The lead traveled through the target's head and exited above his left brow. The unaware victim was killed instantly as his upper body leaned into the engine of the van.

"Perfect fuckin' shot, Steadman," Carter celebrated.

"Where did I hit him?"

"Right behind his ear. That moron didn't stand a chance." Carter snickered.

Steadman lowered his rifle to scan over the firearm. "Yes sir, little brother, we got these sticks dialed right in, alright."

Just as the wayward brothers were about to turn around to head back down the incline, a young lady suddenly appeared from out the front door of the house while holding a tall glass of iced tea in her left hand. She was oblivious to what had just transpired in the driveway of their home.

Spotting her presence, Steadman motivated his sibling. "Ah, Carter, my brother. Your target practice has just arrived."

Carter wickedly grinned. "That she has. That she has." He then gained a solid stance, crouching on one knee before raising his rifle's scope to his right eye. After scanning for a few moments, the target eventually came into view through the magnified sights. "I don't know if I'd rather screw her or shoot her, but today I'll just blow her ass away. Steadman, scope on it for me and let me know where my shot lands."

Steadman raised his scope to his right eye. "Covered," he grunted.

As the young lady made her way to the van, Carter steadied his scope's aim upon her. As the attractive young lady attempted to deliver the cold refreshment to husband, she noticed that something wasn't quite right.

"Duane?" she inquired. "How about a cold drink, honey?" Upon further inspection, Elaine soon came to realize that her husband was not responding. With her left hand, she gripped her husband's left shoulder. "Babe?" It was then that she discovered the bullet hole behind his right ear.

Abruptly turning toward the desolate road, Elaine began shouting, "Help!" repeatedly.

With the rifle's scope crosshairs aimed directly upon her facial area, Carter squeezed the trigger of his firearm.

The blast from the shot rang out moments after the flying bullet entered Elaine's opened and bellowing mouth before exiting the rear of her head. Her body collapsed upon the driveway a few feet in front of the idling van.

"The mouth, Carter. You shut that bitch up," Steadman approved.

Carter made mocking actions of buffing the barrel of his rifle using the sleeve of his shirt.

As if what had just tragically transpired was completely normal, the Porter brothers were matter-of-fact. "Well, with all that ruckus, no Bambi's gonna be around now," Steadman noted. "Let's hike our way back to my truck and go find the nearest bar in this town."

Less than an hour later, the deceased bodies of young newly-weds Duane and Elaine Bowman were discovered by neighbor Kenne Williamson on his way home from a day's work. The couple's demise was immediately ruled as homicides by the Gaines County medical examiner. However, local authorities were left with little evidence at the scene.

Being it was deer-hunting season, one accidental shooting was within a realm of possibilities, but not two down by separate bullets at the same location.

At dusk that evening, Steadman and Carter were drinking their share of alcohol inside Dottie's Hartsgrove Pub. The television set perched on a shelf behind the bar was airing the local six o'clock newscast. Anchorman Myles Darwin reported as a recent wedding photograph of the young married couple appeared over Darwin's left shoulder. "The bodies of Hartsgrove residents Duane Bowman and his wife, Elaine, were discovered by a neighbor earlier today in the driveway of their home. Both victims of gunshot wounds to the head. Police report that their deaths are being investigated as homicides, but officials are left with little evidence at the scene. The Gaines County Sherriff's Department is requesting that anyone with information on this case to call the office at 555-1222. This is not being considered as a deer-hunting accident."

"What the hell is goin' on with people anymore?" bar patron Cletus Gurley questioned out loud.

"You got me, Gurly." Fellow tavern attendee Albert Noles shrugged his shoulders.

"I mean the guy was merely wrenchin' on his rig, and pow, some asshole shoots the dude. And as if that weren't enough, he takes out the wife too."

With Steadman and Carter having bellies full of beer and aching for a physical confrontation, Steadman raised the forefinger of his left hand while addressing Cletus, "Hey, what the hell did he just call you?"

Cletus pointed at himself.

"Yeah, you dumbass. Did that fat shit just call you a girlie? I'd kick a motherfucker's ass if he called me a sissy." Carter chuckled.

Cletus peered at Steadman. "The name is Gurly, G-u-r-l-y, you idiot."

Steadman winked. "Don't make me get up from my stoop here, G-i-r-l-i-e."

"Is that right, a-s-s-h-o-l-e," Cletus countered.

Albert placed his right palm upon his friend Cletus's chest. "Take it easy, Clet. Those are some big dudes."

Cletus pushed Albert's hand away. "The hell with that, Noles. These out-of-town deer hunters waddle here into our town durin' the season and think they're all that and stuff. I'm tired of the bullshit."

"Um, I wouldn't push the envelope on this one, Gurly. Somethin' telling me those boys are not all there, if you get my drift." Albert issued a final caution.

Cletus, consumed with an ample quantity of liquid courage, did test the waters. "Hey, you all get one evening a year away from your wives, and you get all wild and shit, is that it? You henpecked and whipped lassies."

Several patrons chuckled over Cletus's comeback. But not Albert. "Clet, you need to let this one go. Those guys…well… they look like ones not to mix with."

Cletus winked at his friend. "No worries, Noles. Just sit back and watch me take care of these sorry excuses for bullies."

It was well known around the local municipality that Cletus Gurly was not one to mess with. Although a fair man and not one to start a conflict, he was the individual to stop most wayward men in their tracks. However, as with the other locals in the tavern, he couldn't imagine the magnitude of the hard knocks territory he was to embark on.

Cletus Gurly was a large man by standard measures. He stood at six feet four inches in height and weighed in at 240 pounds. He

was considered the gentle giant in the small town of Hartsgrove, and as barroom tallies went, he had never been on the losing end of any physical confrontation.

Steadman raised his mug of beer. "Hey, girlie, don't get your pink panties all in a bunch now."

Cletus huffed, "I'm coming over to teach ya a thing or two about Hartsgrove bein' a take-no-bullshit kinda town."

Steadman shook his head. "Nope. You're coming over here to get your faggot ass kicked."

Cletus sat his mug of draught beer on the bar. He then rolled his neck, generating cracking sounds of his muscles loosening. The Hartsgrove patrons inside Dottie's tavern then began chanting, "Clet...Clet...Clet!"

Inspired by the bystanders' encouragement, Cletus moved toward Steadman while the Porter brother calmly rose from his barstool. As Cletus stepped by Carter, the younger Porter commented, "You're a dead man walkin', dumbass."

That sentence was articulated in such an eerie and serious tone that it cast a bit of uneasiness inside Cletus. But undaunted, Cletus Gurley arrived face-to-face with Steadman Porter.

Using his right index finger, Steadman pointed to his own right-side jawline. "Take your best shot. A freebie before I trash you. Let's see what ya got there, girlie boy."

Cletus reared back his right arm and delivered a full and powerful fist to Steadman's right cheek area. The powerful blow firmly snapped Steadman's head to the left; however, the Porter brother's legs and feet remained stable in a solid stance.

Cletus, as well as the observers in the tavern, were set back over Steadman's strength to resist such a commanding blow. Steadman merely rubbed his jaw for a moment before declaring," My turn, girlie." Using both hands simultaneously, Steadman grasped each of his challenger's ears, and in one fluent motion, he delivered a forehead-to-forehead butt that instantly broke Cletus's nose and displaced his left-side eyetooth. Blood spewed from Gurley's now-flimsy muzzle. Cletus buckled at the knees as he leaned into the bar. Steadman then took to landing unremitting punches to Cletus's head and facial areas. With each powerful punch, Cletus was slowly descending to the tavern floor below. His hair

and face were becoming matted in his own blood. He was even dripping blood from his left ear.

After Cletus's complete collapse to the floor, Steadman continued to attack the fallen man. It was then that a frightened and upset Albert Noles took flight for the tavern's door to escape the mayhem. As he darted forward, Carter came to believe the man was coming on an attempt to rescue his friend from Steadman's brutal beating. Carter abruptly rose from his barstool and landed a mighty right-handed fist to Albert's chin. The strike knocked Albert unconscious as his body tumbled to the floor near his fallen friend. Carter, not yet satisfied, commenced to stomping on Albert's head with his large right boot. Noles's body was jarred with each kick, and blood began to seep from his nostrils.

"Enough!" proprietor Dottie Hadley screamed from behind the bar. "Get your asses out of my place, now! I'm callin' the cops."

Seeing the woman quickly punch in numbers on the phone behind the bar, Carter ceased his attack upon Albert to turn his attention to Steadman, who was still assaulting the unconscious and broken Cletus Gurly. Carter grabbed Steadman by the collar of his shirt. "We gotta go now, Steadman. This place gonna be swarming with cops soon."

Steadman jerked away from his brother to continue his beating upon what was now a nearly lifeless victim of his aggressiveness.

"Steadman, right here and now! We gotta make tracks, dude!"

After landing a final mighty blow to the bloodstained face of Cletus Gurley, Steadman joined Carter with scurrying out from the tavern.

They piled in together inside Steadman's pickup truck in the parking lot of Dottie's Hartsgrove Pub. After speeding away into the darkness of night on a side road, the brothers calmly and in a matter-of-fact approach recalled their day. "Well, no deer, but we did get in some practice on moving targets." Steadman winked from the driver's seat.

Carter nodded. "Yep, and got to kick some ass too."

They chuckled in harmony.

*****

Although witnesses provided the responding police officers to the Hartsgrove Pub with detailed descriptions of the assailants,

authorities were never able to pinpoint who the men were or where they hailed from, for that matter.

Cletus Gurley spent four days in the ICU unit of a local hospital and eleven days hospitalized altogether before finally being discharged.

Albert suffered permanent hearing loss to his left ear as well as a discolored right eye.

The mysterious shootings of Duane and Elaine Bowman were never resolved.

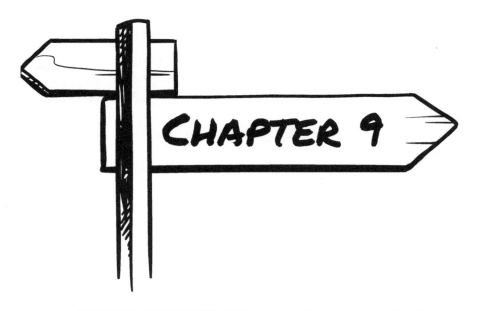

CHAPTER 9

"THERE ARE FOUR FBI agents who work outside the general structure of the law's guidelines who bring justice when our system fails. I'm a cofounder and coordinator of the Elite Four," Marla explained. She then showed her credentials to the Stewarts, including her current driver's license, retired FBI badge, and her present-day detective agency's business card.

"The government allows them to function?" Renee inquired while looking over Marla's documents.

Marla removed her eyeglasses from her nose and folded the frame in her right hand. She then swayed her head no. "Of course not. The government is completely unaware of the Elite Four's existence. If those in power ever come to know of our presence, we'll be shut down promptly and most likely sentenced to prison time."

"What exactly is it that this group does?" Ike questioned.

"Well, Mr. Stewart, the laws of this country were originally written to protect the innocent public and to properly punish criminals. Unfortunately, over the years, those principles have become lost within the smokescreens that lawyers have thrown at our courts. The results are that criminals now have more rights than their victims. I could go on with many examples, but it has progressed so badly that

it's become general public knowledge. Lighter sentencing, lower set bails, if any bail costs at all, and as with most anything else, at times, bribes play a part as well. The obstruction of our judicial system is evident each day. However, again as with most anything else, people tend not to react to things until it hits home—as it has in your case." Marla opened her eyeglasses in order to perch them back upon her nose. She then tapped the folder that was resting on her lap. "It's completely obvious, without a shadow of a doubt, that Murky Porter, with help from his brothers Sterling and Dalton, murdered Nathan. An address typo set these killers free. Those three boys that killed a grandson and a brother are free to live on with their lives and walk among us."

Renee's eyes clouded.

"So how can this Elite Four help?" Ike inquired.

"Well, actually, the members of the Elite Four work solo. It's one agent per case. Though they know who each other are, they rarely see one another. If an agent accepts a case, I then contact the family of the victim if that case requires it. That is why I am here today. We have an acceptance by an Elite Four agent to take on Nathan's case if you and Renee give us the go-ahead. Upon your acceptance, if achieved today, the assigned agent will arrive here at your farm in about three weeks. The agent will explain his plan to you at that time. Again, I cannot express the importance of confidentiality."

Renee fidgeted on the sofa for a moment. "What's the agent's goal?"

Marla glanced around the room and then whispered, "An eye for an eye. The agent will come here to exterminate Murky Porter. He will execute Murky within the means of the law. He will create a situation over time to try to draw Murky out to attack the agent. This way the agent can legally take life in self-defense."

Renee swallowed hard and looked to her grandfather. The room fell quiet with only the ticking sound of the pendulum clock.

"How much would this cost us?" Ike wondered.

"Not a cent. The agents are paid through a general fund that the five of us contribute to as well as private donations. Very off-the-record donators who wish to seek justice as deeply as we do, only from behind the scenes."

Long moments passed before Ike peered to Renee and inquired, "What do you think?"

Without hesitation, Renee slid to the front edge of the sofa and eagerly nodded.

Ike looked back at Marla. "Okay, let's do this."

Marla beamed. "Bless you. You won't be sorry. Nathan will now rest in peace. Your assigned agent is one Cole Walsh, and believe me when I say that you hit the jackpot with him. Cole is an excellent agent. Like I said, he'll arrive in about three weeks. The agent will keep me updated as this case unfolds, but the two of you won't ever see me again." Marla then closed the folder before rising from her chair.

Ike fought his way out of the sinking recliner while Renee stood up from the sofa. The trio moved toward the front door of the farmhouse.

Marla stopped at the door and turned to glance at them. "Don't question the actions of the agent at any time. The agents always have the option of shutting down the case if they feel they're not getting cooperation. Remember that these agents are unique individuals. They are highly trained, Cole foremost, and they can get moody at times. Just sit back and watch this man at work, and you'll be amazed. I'm not certain on how he will approach this case, but be rest assured that by the time he arrives here, he'll have it all planned out."

"We'll be sure not to step on his toes," Ike confirmed.

Marla then extended her right hand. "Okay then, it was very nice meeting the two of you."

This time around, Ike eagerly shook her hand. Marla then turned her attention to Renee, still extending her hand. Renee strode by Marla's hand and embraced the woman. Marla was stunned for a moment before she accepted the gesture of kindness.

Renee whispered into Marla's ear, "Thank you so much for bringin' justice to Nate's murder. It means everything to us."

"You're certainly welcome, young lady."

Their embrace broke with Renee wiping her cheeks free of tears. Marla quickly opened the screen door before breaking into tears of her own. Before striding out onto the porch, she inquired, "Do you folks own any dogs?"

"Yeah, we have five. Why?" Ike asked.

Marla's eyes widened. "Where are they right now?"

"They're locked in the barn," Renee replied. "If we let them run free without watchin', them Porter brothers might get a hold of them to torture them."

Marla shook her head as she moved onto the porch. Without turning to look at them, Marla remarked, "Those Porter boys will soon meet up with a mighty foe. When it all comes down in the end, the last person I would want to be is a Porter."

Ike and Renee beamed at each other.

Marla Simmons then stepped down from the Stewarts' porch and marched in the direction of her car idling in the driveway.

CHAPTER 10

"WHERE THE FUCK is dinner?" Carter growled out while standing next to an empty kitchen table.

Bessy hurried into the kitchen. "I'm sorry, Carter. I'm runnin' behind today."

"Sorry doesn't feed me, Bessy. Talkin' about behind, I'm gonna play with yours a bit." Carter then rubbed her backside.

She slapped down a frying pan upon the electric coil of the stove and quickly turned the dial setting to high. She then reached for the refrigerator door as Carter took a seat at the table. She pulled out a jug of milk from the refrigerator and poured about three cups of the white liquid into the pan. She then returned the milk to the refrigerator and then fetched a plate of about a dozen pig hocks. She plunked the hocks one by one into the heating milk.

"Carter, you reek of beer," she commented.

"Shut the hell up, Bessy."

"You've been at the tavern again, huh?"

Carter raised his middle finger at her. "Don't be cookin' up all those hocks. Our boys won't be here for dinner this evenin'."

Bessy planted her hands on her hips. "I swear them boys are never home. Where are they now?"

"Over in Webster, at the stock car races."

Bessy sighed. "I hope no one gets them in any trouble over there. The cops there can be brutes."

He boasted, "My boys can take care of themselves. Don't mess with the Porter boys if ya know what's good for ya."

*****

MARLA ACELERATED HER Ford Mustang out of Harpersfield as quickly as she could without chancing a speeding ticket.

"These small southern towns make me uneasy. For the most part, the people are wonderful. But the bad apples are rotten to the very core," she asserted.

Dule, seated next to her, lit a cigarette. "We're on the road now. You'll be fine. Did the Stewarts take the deal?" he inquired.

Marla nodded. "With enthusiasm. Of course, they were set back at first, like everyone else before them. Eventually they warmed to the idea and accepted it wholly."

"So what happens next?"

"I phone Cole and tell him it's a go."

"He's a bastard," Dule indicated.

Marla cracked a slight grin. "Oh, he just bruised your ego a bit, Dule. He could have really hurt you if he wanted to."

"Jesus, Marla, you make it sound like this guy is some sort of a superhero."

"Maybe he is," she suggested.

"You wanna sack this guy or something?" Dule curled his lip.

Marla purred. "Hmmm…saddle up with Cole Walsh? That'd be a nice ride for any gal," she playfully teased.

Dule glared at her.

"Oh, take it easy, Dule. I'd never stray on you, honey."

Dule reached over and gently took her hand that was free of the steering wheel. While she steered the sports car from the back roads and onto the interstate, she asked Dule, "Honey, will you be a saint and get my cell phone out from the glove box?"

He opened the glove box and delivered the cell phone to her. Marla traded watching the road before her and placed a call to Cole's cell phone.

Cole was lying back on his sofa listening to a CD when his cell phone began to ring. Using a remote, he lowered the stereo's volume. He then reached for his phone on the nightstand. "Hello?" he greeted into the phone.

"Cole?" Marla's voice inquired.

"Yeah."

"It's Marla. I left the Stewarts' farm in Harpersfield about an hour ago. They accepted the arrangement. I told them you'd be there in about three weeks."

Cole grinned into the phone. "It's a date," he confirmed before depressing the end call button. He gripped the remote and jacked up the volume of the stereo and then gulped from his glass of bourbon on ice.

CHAPTER 11

June 29

RENEE DROVE THE Chevrolet Cavalier down along the long dirt driveway on her way to go grocery shopping with her grandfather. Ike steadied himself in the passenger's seat during the bumpy ride on the uneven surface.

"I gotta put the blade on the tractor and level this driveway," he reported.

When they arrived at the end of the drive where the dirt met pavement, the three Porter brothers were grouped outside Sterling's parked pickup near the Stewarts' private drive. Murky stood with his arms folded while staring directly at Renee inside the car as she steered the vehicle past the trio of hoodlums. Murky blew her a kiss. Ike sneered at the brothers while Dalton shook his fist at the old man. Renee accelerated the car a tad more than customary to escape the tense situation. Her hands trembled and her eyes watered with both fear and anger.

"I hate those boys so much. They give me the creeps!" she acknowledged.

Ike patted his granddaughter on the back of her hand upon the steering wheel. "Help will be here soon, honey. Just remember not to tell anyone. And try to keep from sayin' *hate*. It's such a harsh word."

She grinned at the thought of Ike continuing to teach, though she was now into her twenties. The thought of the agent's eventual arrival helped to ease some of Renee's apprehensions. "I won't tell a soul, Grandpa."

CHAPTER 12

July 8

WHY THE HELL are you boys just lyin' around the house on such a sunny afternoon?" Bessy wondered out loud. She was seated on the sofa while clutching a can of beer. Carter was leaned back in a recliner chair glancing at his sons lounged throughout the living room area.

"We're bored out of our damn minds," Dalton complained.

"Yeah, ain't nobody around to mess with," Murky reported.

Sterling shrugged his shoulders. "Where the hell is everyone?"

Carter leveled his recliner chair before taking a large gulp of whiskey from his glass. "I'll tell ya where everyone's at. Today is the day of Skidmore's goddamn pig roast."

"Oh, that's right. I forgot," Dalton groaned.

"How come we are never invited, Pop?" Murky knew the answer, but asked just the same.

"Joe pays us good money to stay away," Carter predictably replied. "It's because all those lame fucks there don't know how to really raise hell and party it up. I tell ya, if we Porters were there, it'd be a different scene than what them assholes are used to."

The boys chuckled.

"So why don't you just go? The hell with the money. Have your-selves a good time," Bessy suggested.

Carter snapped his fingers. "Yep, let's go, boys, and I'll still take Joe's money. The last one in my truck is a fuckin' sissy."

Hooting and hollering, the four Porters piled into Carter's truck and were soon off for town.

At the pig roast festivity at Joe's tavern, a crowd of nearly sixty people were gathered, with more expected to arrive during the eve-ning hours. An outside bar beneath a pavilion was stocked with bot-tles of liquor and wine. Two kegs of beer were tapped with more barrels waiting in the cooler inside the tavern. Long tables were sit-uated on the floor of the pavilion where ample supplies of dishes of food and snacks were lined up. Placed around the open lawn area were plenty of picnic tables to accommodate the crowd. Although the purchase of a ticket included all you could eat, it did not cover the purchase of beverages. Most side dishes were prepared by locals happy to donate their time and efforts to the annual event. Joe hap-pily took over the duties of roasting the full pig.

A country and western bar band from Webster was beginning to set up their sound equipment onto a makeshift stage near the pavilion. The pig roast event ran noon to midnight on each second Saturday of July annually.

"Lookin' like this year is goin' to be another great turnout, Joe," Jim Tinelberg commented. He and Joe were near the roasting pit as Joe stoked the fire beneath the rotating swine.

Joe nodded. "That it does, Tiny. Sold quite a few tickets. You can already see that some folks from Webster and Waynesburg are here as well as our regular locals. I just hope we have enough roasted pork to go around." He chuckled.

Jim assured, "Porky there is one big piggy. I'm sure there will be more than enough."

"Oh, I wanted to thank you for donatin' the huge tub of potato salad from the diner as you do every year."

"Are you kiddin' me? Pam wouldn't have it any other way. It gives her a year's worth of braggin' rights, ya know." Jim chortled.

With the end of Jim's comment falling faint and weak, Joe noticed Jim peering over his left shoulder while his jaw dropped. Joe quickly turned his head to take in the dreaded sight of the four Porter men making their way toward the gathering.

"Oh no, not them," Jim wheezed.

Joe was quick to toss his stoking pole aside before engaging in a stiff pace to try and cut off the unwelcomed guests before they reached the masses. Before Joe could head off the foursome, they were among the guests.

Joe than came face-to-face with Carter. "What the hell are you doin' here? This isn't part of the arrangement we made together, Carter."

"Oh, fuck that deal, Skidmore. Not only are my boys and me here to party, but you're also still gonna pay me my cut."

Joe, after working so hard to proudly put this day's events together, lost his cool with Carter. "I want you and your sons to leave now. Right now, Porter!"

Without blinking an eye, Carter quickly grasped his right hand around Joe's throat. "I'm gonna give you one and one only, Joe, to blow off a little steam. But you mouth me one more fuckin' time, and I'll slap you up on that spit along with the goddamn pig. Now, get the hell outta my face." Carter then released his grip along with a hard shove, which nearly sent Joe tumbling to the ground.

As much as it pained Joe in doing so, he quickly realized what line he was crossing and not to push it any further.

"Ladies and gentlemen, you'll be pleased to know that the party cavalry has just arrived to deliver to you all a pig roast like you've never seen before!" Carter shouted. The Porter brothers howled.

Some of the locals, completely aware of the acts of cruelty they were about to face, hurried toward the exit.

Again raising his voice Carter announced, "And any of you losers who leave shall be hunted down tomorrow and dealt with in the harshest manner. So you best go sit your asses back down."

Reluctantly, all complied.

Those in attendance from the Webster and Waynesburg areas were astounded over how this man and his sons controlled the local citizens. Most had certainly heard terrifying stories and rumors

regarding the Porter family of Harpersfield, but very few had ever witnessed it firsthand, and that was about to change.

Among the invitees of the pig roast were two married couples from Waynesburg who were close friends. Grant and Brenda Delaney as well as Russ and Carla Clarke were first-time attendees of Joe's annual pig roast. None of the four were often in Harpersfield before today. They were flabbergasted over what was transpiring before them. It was if someone had just taken the wind out of the festivity's sails.

"This is completely uncalled for," Grant relayed to their small group. Grant Delany, thirty-seven, was an over-the-road truck driver for a living and was a rather large and thick man. He sported a long beard that nearly extended to his collar. He was an easygoing man but accepted no flak from anyone.

"I agree, babe, but let's stay out of it just the same and give it a bit of time to blow over," his wife Brenda advised. Brenda Delany, thirty-five, was lean and slender. Her long ash blonde hair she often wore in a ponytail. She worked at Walmart in Waynesburg.

"I agree with Brenda," Carla spoke up. "I see no positives in us getting mixed up in this town's mess." Carla Clarke, thirty-four, was husky for a woman, with a rounded face and bleached blonde hair. She was a stay-at-home mom for two children.

Russ Clarke was a thirty-four-year-old man of average build, but his job as a city roadworker included occasional heavy lifting in contributing to strong arm muscles. Russ was a fair-minded man, but was short in patience and at times could be a hothead.

He shook his head in disagreement over the wives' concerns. "No, what sort of men would Grant and I be if we just let shit like this go down right in front of our eyes? I say we go over there and shut this thing down in its tracks."

Grant was quick to concur. "I'm with you, buddy. Let's do this."

"Guys, I wouldn't do that." Brenda let out one last cautious worry.

Already making their decisions, Grant and Russ began making their way toward the Porters. Like most any other out-of-towner, they had heard their share of Porter tales, but felt they were most likely overfueled and exaggerated. They were simply bullies who needed to be confronted before they would back down.

Grant Delany and Russ Clarke couldn't have been more wrong with their assumptions.

"Look, two guys over there are on their way toward the Porters." Henry was quick to point them out to Emma. The store owners were huddled together near a table of food. "Boy, if they know what's good for them, they better head the other way."

"Oh no, those poor men." Emma shook her head.

Spotting the direction that the same duo was taking, Renee, seated at one of the picnic tables along with Ike, whispered, "Grandpa, those men are gonna get themselves hurt or maybe even worse."

"I see, young lady. I reckon this isn't gonna turn out well at all," Ike predicted.

Grant and Russ arrived to stand before the Porter men who had yet noticed the men as they approached.

Grant was the first of the two to speak up. "Hey, guys."

This gained the Porters' attention upon the confronting pair.

"It's obvious that no one wants you fellas around here, so how about you all take your circus side show on the road and away from here, huh?"

"Yeah, we'll be more than happy to escort you all from the property," Russ added while protruding his chest.

"Hey, look, it's Batman and Robin," Dalton taunted.

Murky chuckled. "Ah, the caped crusaders have come lookin' to get their asses kicked. Where did you park the Batmobile anyway? I wanna take it for a spin."

The Porters snickered in harmony.

With his temper beginning to flare, Russ persisted. "Very funny, assholes. Now, about that escort, how about we walk you all on out of here? I won't ask again."

None in the group of Porters were set back by any sort of measure.

Carter rubbed his chin with the fingers of his right hand and countered with, "Ah, thanks for the offering, Robin, but I think we'll pass on that escort. How about instead we just knock the hell out of both of you?"

Grant asserted, "Yep, you four against us two. That's typical bully behavior in a nutshell."

"You're a whiner, ain't ya, Batman." Carter winked. "Nope, not anyone here gonna say we didn't battle fair and square and all. So I'll tell you superheroes what. It'll take only take but one of us Porters to clean up this sissy mess before us. Just a one is all. So go on ahead now and pick one of us, and let's get it on."

The trio of brothers were quick to raise their right arms and in unison chanted, "Pick me. Pick me. Pick me!"

Carter chuckled sarcastically. "Okay, sorry about that. The boys are a little anxious to be the one who gets to pound the dog snot out of you fuckheads. Alright, boys, alright. Simmer down for a minute. We'll do paper, rock, or scissors. The winner gets to tango with Batman and Robin here."

"Grant and Russ will trash only one of them," Brenda was quick to claim to Carla, who nodded in agreement.

After several rounds of the childhood antic, Sterling emerged as the victor.

"Yes!" Sterling celebrated with cracking his knuckles in preparation for his soon-to-be duel with the confronting men.

Dalton and Murky booed the outcome of the contest.

Russ then proclaimed, "Look, we're not going to gang up on your one son and kick his ass right here in front of everyone. That would make us as much a bully as you all are."

Carter nodded. "You're right, Robin. You're not gonna kick Sterling's ass at all. He's gonna kick both your asses."

"When we do trash your son, you all are gonna jump in to rescue him. That's how this works, right?" Grant surmised.

Carter raised both of his hands. "Nope, not at all. Straight up, I swear. If Sterling can't hold his own, which, trust me, he will and then some, then he'll deserve takin' an ass whoopin'." Carter then looked to Sterling. "I'm damn tired of all the talkin', son. Go get 'em, boy."

As if Carter had just released a vicious dog, Sterling rushed the two men. Sterling's initial attack landed a solid right-hand punch to Grant's beard and striking the man's chin below. The mighty power of the blow sent shockwaves rolling around inside Grant's skull. The man stumbled back and tumbled to the ground on his buttocks

while his world was in a spin. He had been on the wrong end of a fist before, but never with so much strength and control.

As Grant shook his head while trying to gather his senses, Russ landed a strong punch of his own, directly making impact with Sterling's forehead just above the eyes. The contact was clean and flush and with enough energy behind it to sting Russ's knuckles. Russ every bit expected his solid strike to send his opponent plummeting to the lawn, but instead, Sterling's head barely jerked, let alone any movement of his solid footing.

"Is that all you got there, Robin the boy wonder?" Sterling winked.

Before Russ could make a move to shield himself from Sterling's certain retaliation, the Porter brother struck his foe directly in the throat with a well-calculated left fist. The hit struck with such a force that it lifted Russ from his feet. Upon landing, Russ lost his footing while tumbling to the ground near his fallen comrade. Russ was left gasping for any intake of air that he could generate.

It was then that Grant was able to struggle to his feet, though his foundation was wobbly at best. He threw an errant punch at Sterling with minimal strength behind it. The wayward and off-target swing left Grant exposed to Sterling's ensuing assault, in which Sterling kicked his right leg while burying his heavy boot deep into the pit of Grant's stomach. The defeated man dropped to his knees, only to have his merciless adversary strike once more with a hard right fist to the left temple area. Grant was knocked unconscious before folding up to the grass below and upon his chest.

Sterling then turned his attention to Russ, who was still fighting for a breath of air. Sterling strode with three wide steps before taking a leap and landing his entire body upon Russ's head and neck area. Upon lifting himself from his landing, Sterling delivered a powerful left elbow strike to Russ's right jaw, breaking bone in the process. Like his friend before him, Russ was rendered unconscious.

Confrontation was over with Sterling practically unscathed. As Sterling was being delivered high fives of congratulations from his father and brothers, Brenda Delany rushed out from the crowd to attack Sterling. Storming upon the eldest Porter brother, Brenda began striking Sterling's back with hard-driven slaps delivered by

both hands. The strikes did nothing to affect the tall bold young man. He simply took a solid grip on her right wrist before headbutting her into oblivion as Brenda, bleeding nose and all, crumbled to the ground near her husband.

Carter cleared his throat before elevating his voice yet again. "Any other foolish takers before we finally get this party off the ground?" After a short spell of eerie silence, Carter declared, "Well, my sons, party your asses away."

The brothers began to run amuck throughout the grounds of the gathering. As Carter stepped by the unconscious Grant Delany, he purposely delivered a strong right-boot kick to the fallen man's head. "Oops, didn't see ya there. Sorry...not."

A rush of 911 calls rained down upon the Harpersfield Police Headquarters from the pig roast gathering. The calls were being received at such a fierce rate that dispatcher Delores Sampson was nearly pulling her hair out. She was forced to turn away from the phones to grab hold of the station's radio microphone. "Sheriff Harvey, you there? Please pick up."

After a few seconds, but what felt like an eternity for Delores, the radio cracked open from the other end. "Right here, Delores. What's goin' on?"

"Hey, Chief, I'm gettin' more emergency calls from Joe's pig roast than you can count on two hands. You need to get on over there, pronto!"

"Might be a fire out of control from the roastin'. Frank and I are ten minutes away out on Martin's Way. Let callers know we are en route."

"Will do."

At the pit where the pig was being roasted, Dalton unzipped his pants to pull out his penis and urinate on the swine. Sterling forced a nearly full glass of whiskey down Mason's throat. Murky, as he sprinted by the picnic table where Renee was seated, quickly grasped his right palm on her T-shirt over her left breast before continuing for his planned destination.

"He's the real pig here and not that thing spinning on the spit," Renee mentioned to her grandfather.

Murky easily jumped a low-standing chain-linked fence separating the tavern's property and a neighbor's land. Rushing toward a small storage shed, he easily pried open the shed's door, snapping a lock in the process. Inside the shed, he fumbled through the contents until he came across a tool he thought to be useful—a pickax. Throwing the tool's long handle on his left shoulder, Murky exited the small storage building to again scale the fence. Upon his return to the tavern's grounds and using the pickax, he punctured both kegs of beer at the base of the barrels, allowing the contents to spill onto the floor of the pavilion.

Behind the outdoor bar, Dalton grabbed hold of a full bottle of Jack Daniel's Whiskey and twisted off the bottle cap. After consuming two lengthy gulps of the whiskey, he extended his right arm before heading into a trot to sweep away a long line of liquor bottles to crash and shatter to the floor below.

Using the same pickax, Murky pounded away the spit rod's latching mechanism until it broke free, allowing the entire carcass of the pig at roast to plummet onto the fire, embers, and ashes below.

Carter was busy kicking over the country band's amplifiers, monitors, and speakers. Only when the Porters' rampage and rummaging finally tapered off did they notice that most all the festival attendees had vacated the grounds. Carla Clarke had managed to get her husband and friends alert enough to make their way to her SUV to drive them to the hospital in Waynesburg. The only souls remaining were Joe Skidmore sitting with his back against the tavern's rear outside wall while his head was lying on his knees, and his wife, Judy, was seated next to him doing her best to comfort his devastating disappointment.

As the yard grew with an eerie quiet, Carter broke the silence. "Well, this all just went from loads of fun to downright borin'. Let's head home, boys, and get drunk as skunks."

As the Porters stepped past Joe and Judy, Carter growled, "I'll be by tomorrow for my cut, Skidmore. We'll have a beer and shoot the shit. If there's a pig roast next summer, we'll be sure to stop on by."

The Porters chuckled on their way to Carter's truck.

About five minutes after the Porters' departure, the Harpersfield police cruiser pulled into the deserted parking lot of Joe's Tavern with

overhead lights flashing in the dusky conditions of late evening. After emerging from the patrol car, Sheriff Harvey and Deputy Frank Collins scampered their way to the yard behind the tavern. Before them was a sorrowful sight to behold. The roasting pig was in flames atop the firewood and charcoal within the pit. Broken glass, liquor, and gallons of beer saturated the floor beneath the pavilion. Prepared food was strewn about the area, and the makeshift stage for the band was in disarray.

Looking upon the desponded couple of Joe and Judy Skidmore, Sheriff Harvey asked, "What the hell happened here, Joe?"

Raising his head from his bended knees for a brief moment, Joe replied, "In one word, Bob. Porters."

The sheriff cleared his throat. "Oh, I see. Well, we'll take a drive up to their place to have a word with them."

Judy rolled her eyes. "Yeah, you do that, officers."

Twenty minutes later, Sheriff Harvey gingerly steered the patrol car along the Porters' driveway. As he placed the cruiser into parking gear, he looked over to his sidekick. "Ready for this, Frank?"

From the passenger's seat, the deputy exhaled. "Not really, but let's get it over with."

As the only Harpersfield police officers were preparing to exit the cruiser, the vehicle was suddenly surrounded by the Porters' savage canines. Carter and his sons were seated on the front porch sharing a bottle of bourbon, watching the event unfold in the driveway.

Sheriff Harvey, while keeping close tabs on the snarling dogs, carefully rolled down the driver's-side window. It was nearly nightfall now. Shouting out through the partially opened window, Bob called out, "Hey, Carter, how 'bout callin' off the greeting party? We need to talk."

Carter stood from his lawn chair to shout back, "All is good, Harvey! They'll only bite if ya look at 'em."

The brothers chuckled.

"Seriously, call them off, Carter," Bob nearly begged.

Carter nodded at his sons. "Go ahead and round them up to the barn. Let's hear what the good sheriff needs to ramble on about."

After nearly five minutes of the Porter brothers corralling the vicious canines into the barn and returning to the porch at their

father's side, only then did Bob and Frank finally emerge from the patrol car. As the pair of officers stepped up onto the porch, Bob nodded. "Carter, boys."

"So, what's got you all up in knots tonight, Harvey?" Carter grumbled.

Bob slightly bounced as he replied, "Well, Frank and I just came from Joe's place. You know, the tavern."

Murky rolled his eyes. "We know the place, dumbass."

Again, Bob cleared his throat. "Yes, right, of course. Anyway, today was the annual pig roast held there at the back of the tavern. Well…"

"I'd like to get twenty bucks for each time you say the word *well*," Dalton said with a snicker.

The other Porters chuckled.

"Um, yes, well…" Bob stuttered along. "Anyway, when Frank and I arrived, the place was in complete shambles. I've only spoken with Joe and Judy thus far, but I plan to speak with others who were there. Um…were you all there at the pig roast by chance?"

Carter exhaled a long trail of cigar smoke. "Yeah, we stopped by for a cold beer and a taste of roasted pork. Good stuff, ya know. We were just mindin' our own beeswax when some sorta ruckus broke out. Probably some out-of-towners with a bit too much to drink. So not wantin' to get all involved and shit, we just got the hell out of there."

Bob nervously scratched his neck. "Is that how it all went down, boys?"

Carter sneered at the sheriff. "Are you askin' my sons if their father is fuckin' lyin'?"

Harvey was quick to back off. "No, no, not at all, Carter. Just need collaborating accounts to officially complete my report is all."

In harmony, the brothers nodded their endorsements of their father's narrative, with Sterling adding, "And I got sucker-punched from some idiot I didn't even know. See that little bump on my damn forehead?"

Inspecting Sterling's forehead, Bob scribbled into his notepad.

Frank then spoke up. "Um, Sterling, if you could describe your assailant, perhaps we could identify him and bring him in for questioning."

Sterling creased his eyebrows at Frank. "Like I said, deputy, I didn't see the asshole."

Scribbling in his own notepad, Frank pressed, "And after this unknown man who sucker-punched you, you didn't retaliate?"

"Who said it was a man? I mean if it was a he, then he punched like a girl." Sterling mischievously grinned.

The Porters sniggered.

"So, man or woman, did you strike back?" Frank questioned.

Sterling shook his head. "No, sir. I was a good boy."

"Are we about done here?" Carter sought with growing impatience. "It's dark now, and my boys wanna see if we can spotlight a deer or two."

Bob was quick to mention, "Now, Carter. It isn't deer season, and even if it was, spotlightin' is illegal. It's called poachin'."

After spitting a concoction of tobacco juice from his mouth, Carter claimed, "It's only poachin' only if you shoot the varmint. Nope, not our plans at all. Only to hit them with the light to watch them in their natural grace is all."

The brothers chortled.

With his notepad still open, Bob inquired, "Anything further you all want to add to your accounts of what transpired at the pig roast earlier today?"

Murky raised his right forefinger. "Yeah, tell Joe the brain is slow, that next year he should roast the pig above the fire and not in it."

The Porters roared into laughter.

Bob nodded to Frank that it was time to depart the premises.

As the Harpersfield lawmen stepped down from the porch, Carter firmly suggested, "Close the case, Andy and Barney. Remember, we know where you live."

Back inside the patrol car, Frank looked to Bob. "Not guilty again, right?"

Bob hastily tossed his notebook aside. "Right."

CHAPTER 13

July 17

RENEE APPROACHED THE farmhouse after a long and hot morning of tending to the cornfield. When she was about two hundred yards from the farmhouse, a black pickup truck came into her view. The truck was parked in the driveway next to the house. Atop the hood of the truck, a stranger was seated. Her heart raced as did her pace while closing the distance between them. She removed her leather work gloves as she strode up near the front of the pickup truck.

"Are you, I hope, the company we've been expectin'?"

He nodded. "Cole Walsh," he announced, extending his hand as he slid down from the hood of the truck. He landed on his feet, standing near her.

Renee admired his masculine build, his strong arms and protruding chest lining his T-shirt, and she noticed that Cole certainly appeared intimidating. She figured that he'd have no difficulties handling himself if physically confronted. He was immediately attracted to her soft tanned skin and her southern sway, as well as her full lips and blue eyes, deep blue eyes that set off her silky brunette hair. He

welcomed the way her firm, full breasts filled her T-shirt beneath the straps of her overalls.

He quickly took his line of vision from her breasts to Renee's blue eyes when she cleared her throat. "I'm…" she began.

"Renee," he concluded.

"Um…yeah, that would be me. You're late. We've been waitin' for days now. You were supposed to be here like six days ago," she was quick to point out.

He lowered his arm after realizing she was not intending to shake hands. "No definite date was confirmed. I'm not late, it's just that your anticipation is early."

The screen door of the house swung open before Ike, holding on to a couple cans of beer, paced out onto the porch. He made his way over to Renee and Cole. "I see that you've met Cole," Ike confirmed, looking over to his granddaughter.

Renee glared at Cole. "Yeah…we just met," she verified. Renee then took an abrupt turn to head inside the farmhouse, treading along quickly.

Ike looked at Cole and shrugged his shoulders. Ike then handed one of the cans of beer over to Cole.

"I think Renee and I got off to a sluggish start," Cole reported. He then pulled back the tab on top of his can of beer.

Ike glanced back toward the farmhouse. "Oh…she'll come around. She's upset about the delayed arrival of Nathan's justice, is all. I explained to her that we were not promised an exact date, but she gets edgy when she becomes anxious."

Cole squinted. "Well, talk to her about adjusting her attitude, Ike. I have no tolerance for playing games or to deal with negativity."

Ike cleared his throat, feeling a bit awkward and embarrassed. "Will do. I'll see to it."

"You say that the guesthouse next to the barn is my quarters?"

Ike nodded. "You'll find all that you need in there. Furniture, TV, bathroom, and a bed are all inside. The mattress is in good shape."

"Does the shower work?"

"Sure does. Hot water never runs out. Will you be eatin' with us each day or goin' out?"

Cole surveyed the property as far as he could view from his current vantage point. "I'll eat here. That'll be fine."

"Renee's a good cook," Ike added. "The only thing to get in town is a greasy burger at Tiny's Cafe. Well, truth be told, Tiny's food is pretty decent. You need to travel to Webster or Waynesburg to find somethin' more like a good stew or steak dinner. I grill up my own steaks. I'll treat ya to a thick slab of beef sometime, Cole."

Cole bent to pick up his duffel bag from next to the truck. "I think I'll go take a shower and then grab a nap. It was a long drive. This evening, the three of us will get together and discuss the plan. Okay, Ike?"

"Sounds good. Dinner's at six."

Cole nodded before moving toward the guesthouse. He was not particularly fond of being short with Ike and Renee, but he realized that personal feelings simply could not shape between an agent and clients. It was counterproductive. So he wanted to establish those boundaries from the get-go.

DEPUTY FRANK COLLINS was stationed outside an old abandoned bowling alley on the western outskirts of Harpersfield along Martin's Way. He reached inside his patrol car to unclip his radio mic from the dashboard.

"Boss?" he muttered into the radio.

"What is it, Frank?" Sheriff Harvey responded.

"Ah…Bob…I'm out here at the Memory Lanes Bowlin' Alley checkin' the old structure as we do from time to time. Well…you're not goin' to believe what I found inside, beneath the old bowlin' shoes shelves."

Bob growled, "Just spit it out, Frank. What is it?"

"I found marijuana. Lots of the stuff. A bundle the size of a bale of hay. And white powdery material, about ten bricks in plastic bags. I'm willin' to bet it's cocaine."

Bob's eyes widened. "Are ya certain?"

Frank crowed proudly from behind the radio. "I'm sure. What do you want me to do with it?"

Bob thought it over for a moment. Bob and Frank weren't exactly two seasoned officers as far as experience dealing with drug trafficking. It was, for the most part, speeding citations, driving under

the influence, bar fights, and occasional domestic violence calls. The sheriff was nearly certain that this find had something to do with the Porters, but pinning it on them was another thing.

"Um...load it up in the patrol car and bring it on in. We'll weigh it and then report it to the state police before we pour an accelerant over it to torch it."

"Will do, Bob."

"And, Frank, how many times do I have to tell you that when we're on duty, you call me sheriff? Especially over the radio."

"Oops...sorry, sheriff," Frank corrected himself. He then tossed the radio mic through the open patrol car's window, landing it on the passenger's seat. Officer Collins then traveled back inside the vacant building to retrieve his discovery.

*****

COLE WALSH STOOD upon the small porch of the guesthouse smoking a cigarette.

"You don't seem like the type that would smoke," Renee commented. She seemed to have appeared out of nowhere.

"Where did you come from?" he inquired.

"I was lookin' around the guesthouse makin' sure there are no snakes hangin' around. They take a likin' to callin' the guesthouse home sometimes. Are you frightened of snakes?"

Cole shrugged his shoulders. "Snakes do bother me somewhat. Spiders, on the other hand, I have no issues with."

"Spiders and snakes don't affect me too much. I hate bats. Flyin' rats is what that they are."

"I know what a bat is," he snipped.

She folded her arms. "Are you in a rotten mood today or something? I would hate to think that you are like this all the time."

He ignored her inquiry. "Can you point me toward the crime site? I want to look around."

"It's in the woods, behind the cornfield. I can run you back there on the tractor, or we could walk."

"Walking will be fine. Lead the way," he directed.

Renee turned from him and began striding toward the rear of the property. Cole snuffed out his cigarette on the wooden porch and then leaped from the deck. He moved quickly to match her progress.

"What do you mean that I don't seem like the type who would smoke?" he questioned.

Renee maintained a rigid pace as they approached the cornfield. "Well…you're fit and all. You definitely exercise, work out, to keep in shape. So I thought that you probably wouldn't smoke."

"I only smoke about five cigarettes a day. Do you smoke?"

"Only when I'm drinkin' alcohol, which isn't very often."

They marched along the eastern border of the large cornfield as the evening crickets began to sing. It was less than two hours to dusk.

"Do you have any brothers or sisters?" Renee inquired.

"You can save the 'You don't know what it's like to lose a sibling' speech. I lost a sister when I was fifteen. She drowned in Lake Erie after going for a swim while she was intoxicated. She was at a friend's party along the lakeshore and wandered off. Her body washed ashore two days later. She was eighteen and my only sibling."

Renee sighed. "My father did somethin' similar. He was drinkin' and drivin' when the car crashed, killin' him and my mother."

"That is why you live with your grandfather?" he assumed.

Renee concurred, "Yeah…He raised Nate and I after the accident."

The duo then arrived at the rear of the cornfield along the edge of the woods. With her still leading the way, they entered the wooded area.

"Does your grandfather hunt deer?" he asked. He then avoided a small hanging branch that whipped toward him after she swiped through it.

"He used to. Nate hunted deer every year."

"I bet there are some nice stags on this property," he mentioned.

"Nate shot a twelve-point buck about four years ago. He had the head mounted. It hangs in the barn."

Cole asked, "Have you ever deer hunted?"

Renee choked up. "Me? I myself couldn't kill any livin' thing." She then hesitated for a moment. "That's why I'll never understand how anyone can take another's life."

Nothing more was revealed as they covered the following four hundred yards before arriving at the site of the crime.

Renee's eyes clouded as the pair came to a temporary halt. "Here's where it happened," she informed him.

Cole placed his hands on his hips and peered around the immediate area.

"Nate was inspectin' corn in the field that afternoon. Officer Collins and Sheriff Harvey believe that the Porter brothers approached Nate in the cornfield and then lured him out here in the woods before stabbin' him."

Cole exhaled loudly. "Small-town cops. Nate wasn't lured out here."

"How can you be sure?" she questioned.

"If the Porter brothers would have lured Nate out here into the woods to kill him, they wouldn't have come so deep into the thickets to find adequate cover. Less than a hundred feet into the timberline would have been sufficient. No, the Porters chased Nate out to this richer part of the woods."

Renee placed her hands over her mouth.

"Does that make it harder for you to accept?" he asked.

Renee nodded before removing her hands away from her mouth. "I found some ease in thinkin' that it was an ambush and over quickly for Nate."

Cole bit his lip and shook his head no.

*****

Nate Stewart was busy on that hot day in June. He was gathering sporadic ears of corn inside a bucket to take back to the farmhouse for his grandfather's inspection. Ike examined the randomly selected ears for invasive microbes and general kernel health. Nate then heard rustling in the corn on that still and quiet afternoon. He stopped collecting corn momentarily to peek around. His line of sight was limited by the tall stalks of corn that surrounded him. After a few moments of not detecting any further noise, Nate returned to the task at hand. Within several minutes, Nate overheard the rustling sound again and ceased picking ears of corn from the stalks. His heart began to race before he figured it must be

Max making the clatter. Max was one of their five dogs, but the only one that tended to roam about the cornfield at times.

"Here, Max. Come here, boy," Nate called out.

Nate was expecting to hear Max's panting any moment. Stillness. With some apprehension, Nate gingerly returned to gathering corn. After another few moments had elapsed, Nate, with bucket in hand, turned to head back to the farmhouse. He then came face-to-face with Murky Porter. Sterling and Dalton were flanked behind Murky.

Nate felt an instant surge of fear sting through his body. His mouth turned dry as his hands trembled. He dropped the bucket that contained the selected ears of corn. Nate's voice slowly dragged with nervousness. "Hi...Murky... What are you...guys... doin'...out here?"

Murky's face grew with an unpleasant grin. "Nate...Nate...Nate the masturbate. You didn't come through for me."

Nate bit his lip. "I tried, Murky. She just doesn't want to go...out with you."

Murky raised his arms out to his side. "Why wouldn't she want to go out with a fine male specimen such as me?"

Dalton and Sterling chuckled.

Murky looked back at his brothers and barked, "Shut the hell up." Murky then turned his attention back to Nate. "So, what do you think I should do about your failure, masturbate?"

Now, Nate wished Max were about. The dog would protect Nate long enough so that he could make a run for the house.

"Fuck em' up," Sterling egged on.

"Kick his ass into the next county," Dalton furthered.

Murky raised his left hand while extending the forefinger above his shoulder without turning around. This was his signal for his brothers to stifle.

"Now, masturbate, maybe we can work somethin' out here. How about I spare you a beatin' if you get me some naked pictures of Renee?"

Dalton smirked.

"I'd like to see those pictures," Sterling remarked.

"Only I see them!" Murky warned.

Nate cleared his throat. "Murky, I couldn't get anything like that. Even if I could, I wouldn't do it...She's my sister...I wouldn't...give you photos of her like that."

Murky's expression became one of irritation. "Then you tell me, masturbate! What the hell am I supposed to do with you?"

"Rip his balls off," Sterling growled.

Murky now allowed his bothers' participation with the ordeal.

Dalton and Sterling took a step nearer from behind Murky.

Murky drew in his nasal passages to spit a phlegm concoction into Nate's face.

Nate sickened at the feeling of Murky's phlegm sprayed upon his face. Sterling and Dalton snorted. Nate quickly pulled the bandana from his back pocket to wipe his face free of the foul mess.

"You don't want to mess with me, masturbate. I'll hurt you, and I'll hurt you bad," Murky warned with an eerie calm. Murky's eyes squinted to where they were nearly closed. "I'm mad. Real fuckin' mad. When I get mad, masturbate, I do crazy shit."

Nate's legs began to tremble.

Dalton rubbed the outside of his pants to be sure his hunting knife was inside his pocket. "Let's cut one of his fingers off."

Murky glared at Dalton. "Can't you see that I'm tryin' to negotiate with masturbate here?" Murky then turned his attention back to Nate as he stepped up next to him. He placed his arm around Nate. Nate closed his eyes in fear. "Okay, masturbate, you can get me those pictures, can't you? Sneak inside Renee's closet, and when she's changin' clothes, snap a couple of pictures. It's that easy, and then I'll spare you an ass kickin'."

"I won't do that to Renee." Nate stood by his principles.

Murky slapped Nate on the back of his head. "That's not the answer I need to hear, masturbate."

Nate opened his eyes. "Please leave me alone, Murky. I'll talk with Renee again to see if she'll go out with you, but I'm not takin' any revealin' snapshots of my sister for your twisted enjoyment."

Murky took his arm from around Nate's shoulder. He then crouched down next to Nate's legs. "You've failed me, masturbate. So why should I give you another chance?"

Nate grew a little angry and frustrated. "Murky, she doesn't want to go out with you. There's nothin' I can do about that."

Murky smirked before announcing, "Get 'em, boys!"

An instant surge of tremendous fear commanded Nate's body, causing his legs to engage into a full run. He abruptly spun away from the Porters to take to a terrified getaway through the stalks of corn.

Dalton and Sterling began a sprint after Nate as Murky stood upright. He was soon joining the chase.

Nate navigated the stalks with a fast pace, maintaining his hands and arms in front of him. He parted the stalk's sharp-edged shoots as best as he could. Some leaves made it through his guard, however, causing small shallow cuts about his face and arms.

Dalton, Sterling, and Murky were all battling with the same type of slashing to their skin. Nate then realized that if he stood any chance of getting away from his pursuers, he had to leave the cornfield. They detected his location by the movement of the stalks' tall tassels above, and he could be easily heard storming through the noisy stalks. He turned his direction toward the rear of the cornfield. Nate didn't want to run the Porters toward the farmhouse where they could harass and perhaps hurt his grandfather and sister.

A few hundred yards were covered when Nate cleared the cornfield. There were some three hundred feet between the end of the corn and the beginning of the woodland. This jaunt would leave him exposed in the open. Nate sprinted as fast as his feet would carry him, but just before entering the woods, Dalton emerged from the corn. He spotted Nate racing into the woods.

"Over here!" Dalton shouted and whistled out to his brothers, who were still in the corn maze. Murky and Sterling heard Dalton's shout of direction, so they turned their run toward that path. In less than a minute, Murky and Sterling sprung out from the corn to join Dalton near the entrance of the woods.

"Nate ran in there," Dalton reported, pointing toward the woodland.

Nate stood behind a tree, trying to gather his breath. He did not hear Dalton's shout, so he felt that he was safely hidden in the woods.

The Porters, being excellent game hunters, decided to enter the woods quietly. They were careful with each step not to rustle any fallen dried leaves or to break any twigs beneath their boots.

Within five minutes, Nate's breathing had calmed, and he figured to stay put behind the tree, hoping the Porter boys grew frustrated with not placing Nate in the corn and that they departed.

Just as Nate became comfortable, Sterling spotted him standing behind the tree. He motioned with his head to his brothers, and soon Dalton and Murky spotted Nate as well. "Let's rush him," Dalton whispered. With that, the brothers engaged in a full run toward the tree.

Nate's eyes widened as he heard the Porters' aggressive approach. He peered around the tree to see the brothers closing on him quickly. Nate's heart raced as he turned away from the tree to begin to run through the woods.

"We gotcha now, Nate!" Sterling yelled.

Nate knew that if he could make it to the creek side, there was an old abandoned fruit cellar near the bank of the creek where he could hide. The entrance to the cellar was overgrown with vines, and only if you knew exactly where the cellar was located could you discover it. Nate knew of the exact location of the cellar.

Nate was about fifty yards in front of the pursuing Porter brothers and about two hundred yards from reaching the creek side when he made a critical mistake. As he attempted to leap a fallen tree, Nate's foot hooked onto one of the log's branches. Nate's body slammed to the ground with force, knocking the air from of his lungs.

Before Nate could recover and get back to his feet, the Porter brothers had him surrounded and towered above him.

*****

"Are you sure he was chased out here?" Renee quizzed.

Cole nodded. "Let me ask you something. Is there a haven near here?"

She gave him a confused look. "What do you mean?"

"A house, a barn…a hidden back road…an old cabin maybe?"

She thought it over for a moment. "No, nothin' like that. It's all wilderness for miles. The only thing I can think of is that there is an old fruit cellar down by the creek. Nathan and I would play in it like it was a secret fort when we were kids."

"How far is the cellar from here?" he inquired.

She pointed. "Just over that next ridge. Why?"

"Would the Porter brothers have knowledge of the cellar?"

She shook her head. "I wouldn't think so. No, I wouldn't see how they would know about it. Nate and I pretty much kept it a secret. Of course, my grandfather knows about it, he's the one that built it decades ago." Renee hesitated as her face reddened slightly. "I found out, when I was a teenager, that my grandfather actually used it years ago to store moonshine."

Cole smirked. His focus then became more acute. "That is probably where Nate was headed before the thugs ran him down."

She glanced to the ridge and then back at Cole. "Yeah, you're probably right. But I don't like to think about that afternoon and what poor Nate must have been put through. You know that day, I thought about takin' Max's, that's our largest dog, chain off and lettin' him run around the property. Max enjoys doin' that now and then. If I had set him free, Max would have tracked down Nate to accompany him. Max really liked Nate. That dog would have protected Nate even it would have cost that dog his own life. I was literally approachin' Max before I changed my mind." Her eyes began to cloud. "But I didn't do it. I didn't set Max free. If only I had, this entire tragedy may have had a different outcome."

"Perhaps. But you can't go around second-guessing yourself. You had no way of knowing that your brother was in any immediate danger. It's not healthy to badger yourself."

"I know, but we all do it from time to time," she countered.

"Not me," he responded.

"You don't?" she asked with a skeptical tone.

"I don't live that way. Things happen in life for a reason. You know, they call it fate. We may not always know why things happen the way they do, but that doesn't matter because they happen anyway. So I just focus on the things that I can change or control and leave it up to fate to take care of everything else."

"I don't believe you can do that. Most of us would like to think that we can pull that off, but we can't. Worry and wishin' you could change somethin' about the past exists in each of us. So when you say you can bypass all that, well, you're full of hot air, Cole." She squinted at him.

"Is that right?" He glared. Then his facial expression lightened a bit. "Well, maybe I do…just a little."

"Uh-huh," she rebutted.

He shook his head. "Anyway…we're straying from the subject. Let's head back to the house before the old man begins to worry."

CHAPTER 15

DALTON STEPPED THE full weight of his right boot on Nate's left hand. Nate grimaced in pain. Dalton smirked at Nate. "You'll run no more, boy."

Sterling grabbed a fistful of Nate's hair to pull him up to his feet. Sterling glared at Nate with eyes that were as cold as ice before he slammed his forehead against Nate's nose. The force of the blow shattered Nate's nose. Blood spewed out from Nate's nostrils. Nate weakened and wanted to fall to the ground, but Sterling maintained his grip on his hair, keeping him upright.

Dalton pulled the hunting knife from his pocket and then whistled over to Murky to gain his attention. Dalton then tossed the closed knife about thirty feet over to his younger brother.

Murky caught the knife in his right palm. He slid the blade open from the knife's casing to admire the metal shining in the afternoon sun. He then stepped directly in front of Nate, who was being held captive by Sterling.

"Masturbate, do you remember the farmer over on Meyer's Pass? You know, the one that always gave people shit about ridin' their ATVs and dirt bikes even when we weren't on his property? That guy was an asshole. His name was Parker. Do you remember now? You

should, Pop tells us your grandpap use to supply Parker with moon-shine. That shit made that motherfuckin' Parker even nosier."

Nate nodded about remembering Parker, though he knew nothing about the moonshine. He did recall though that Dan Parker was a farmer over near the Meyer's Electric Company's property. Dan simply disappeared about four years prior and had not been heard from since. The police found his farmhouse in order, and they fig-ured that perhaps Dan died out in the wilderness somewhere while deer hunting. A heart attack or stroke, perhaps. Eventually, as the police insisted, someone would stumble across Dan Parker's skeletal remains out in the timberland. There had been no such discovery of Dan's remains over the years.

Nate now spotted the knife in Murky's hand. His eyes widened, and he began to scream out. Dalton stepped forward to place his hand firmly over Nate's mouth.

Murky continued, "Well, that goddamn Parker went too far one day. We were ridin' our ATVs mindin' our own beeswax when that bastard called the cops. It would have been no big deal, but it wasn't Frank or Sheriff Harvey that showed up. We could have han-dled them. No, that goddamn Parker called the state police. They took our ATVs and put us in jail for the night just because Sterling got a little mouthy with 'em."

"The bastard cop kept callin' us hoodlums. The son of a bitch," Sterling remarked.

Murky nodded and then continued, "It cost us five hundred bucks to get our machines back."

"All because of that asshole Parker," Dalton chimed in.

"Well"—Murky picked the story up again—"Parker had to be taught that you don't mess with the Porters. We dragged that moth-erfucker off his tractor and out to the woods. We took turns and beat the hell out of that bastard. We then kicked Parker's head like a soccer ball for a spell before we buried him alive. We used two shovels and a pick that we brought with us. We dug the hole so freakin' deep that nobody is ever goin' to find Parker." Murky chuckled.

Murky then stepped up to Nate. Nate trembled and bit down on Dalton's hand. Dalton only grinned at the pain and did not pull

his hand an inch back from Nate's mouth. Nate looked into Murky's cold gray eyes. Nate begged for mercy with a fearful expression on his face. Murky showed no sympathy. The youngest Porter boy then reared his right arm back and plunged the long sharp blade of the knife into Nate's stomach.

The blade's entry caused a painful burning sensation throughout Nate's midsection. Murky then pulled the blade from Nate's body. He then carved another plunge, this time into of Nate's chest, slicing his aorta. Nate's internal bleeding poured to fill his chest cavity within seconds. His esophagus packed with the red liquid as he could no longer breathe. Blood seeped from his mouth and oozed between Dalton's fingers. Nate was now losing consciousness as Murky completed a third plunge of the sharp blade into Nate's ribs, puncturing the left lung.

Sterling released his grip on Nate's hair, allowing Nate to pile up on the ground. Nate coughed up blood before he eventually lost his life. Murky stabbed Nate's fallen body an additional four strikes for assurance that Nate was indeed deceased. Murky then stood upright with the victim's blood sprayed upon his clothing and face. Dalton had red stains on the sleeve of his shirt. Blood from Nate's shattered nose was painted on Sterling's forehead and splattered on and in his ears.

After nearly a full minute of hush after the stabbing was completed, Dalton spoke up. "We don't have any shovels with us."

Sterling inhaled a deep breath and sighed. "So whatta we goin' to do with the body?"

Murky bit down on his lip as he folded the bloody knife shut. "We just leave it here. Nobody will find it by tomorrow night. We'll come back then to bury it."

"Why not tonight?" Dalton questioned.

Sterling spoke up, "Because if you remember, you dickhead, we're goin' to Knoxville tonight to pick up a bundle. If we don't show, we'll lose the whole package. Then how do you suppose we get money?"

Dalton nodded. "Oh yeah, that's right, I forgot."

"It'll be fine until tomorrow night. We'll come back in the darkness to bury masturbate," Murky planned.

The following day, in the early evening, after spending the entire day searching for Nate, Ike ambled into the woods headed for the fruit cellar where he had a jug of moonshine hidden below the wooden floor. He needed a gulp of the firewater as his nerves were shot. Renee was driving to each of Nate's friend's homes after a day of searching for her missing brother. Ike then stumbled upon the most horrid sight in all his years. Lying in a dried pool of blood was his fallen grandson. Ike quickly dropped to his knees to check Nate for a pulse. Nate's skin was cold and turning gray. There was no pulse. Ike lifted Nate's stiffening upper body into his trembling arms. Ike cried out a cry that was so deep with hurt that it was eerie sounding and bone chilling.

CHAPTER 16

COLE WAS ENJOYING each tender bite of the beef roast that Renee prepared in an all-day sauté inside a Crock-Pot. It had been quite some time since he last eaten a home-cooked meal. The dinner was complete with a baked potato, steamed green beans, and blackberry pie for dessert.

"Bein' a single man, you probably live on fast food?" Ike assumed about Cole from across the dining room table.

Cole swallowed his mouthful of potato before replying, "Pretty much. I've made the Wendy's location across the street from my apartment independently wealthy."

Renee chortled from her seat at the table.

"Where is home?" Ike inquired.

Cole cleared his throat. "It's not necessary that you know that."

Renee spoke up. "Cuyahoga County, Ohio."

Cole smirked sarcastically. "My license plates?"

She nodded.

"Cleveland, to be exact."

"Oh, I've been there," Renee suddenly revealed. "Two summers ago, my friend, Stacy, and I drove up to Cleveland to visit the Rock and Roll Hall of Fame."

"My apartment is less than two miles from there," Cole disclosed.

"Are ya home much?" Ike asked.

"Not really. Well, when I'm working on a Cleveland-based case, I'm home more often," Cole explained while lifting his fork filled with green beans.

"What about your family?" Renee queried. "Do you see your parents often?"

Cole sighed. "What is this? My life is not the issue here. Besides, it's none of your business."

Renee raised the palm of her left hand. "Well…excuse me for asking."

Cole chewed his food while glaring at Renee.

After dinner, Cole, Renee, and Ike were perched about on the front porch of the farmhouse. Cole and Ike were sipping on glasses of bourbon. Renee was tasting a glass of red wine.

Cole lit a cigarette. "What I'm about to say demands your complete and full attention," Cole clarified, calmly and precisely.

Renee and Ike looked to Cole with complete concentration.

"As you already know, I'm an agent with the FBI. But while I'm here in Harpersfield, I'm merely a basic John Doe. There will be no discussion of my FBI status within or outside of the home. I'm not going with an alias, so use of my real name will be fine. What the outside world needs to believe is that I'm a hired farmhand. From what I've read about the case and what you have told me, Murky Porter is obsessed with Renee, right?"

Ike and Renee nodded simultaneously.

"Okay, we'll go with that and use it against him," Cole strategized.

Ike and his granddaughter appeared befuddled.

"What do you mean?" Ike questioned.

"Renee and I have to eventually portray that we are becoming emotionally and intimately involved with each other."

She rolled her eyes.

"Believe me, I don't like the idea any more than you do, gal. However, we can bring Murky out to the forefront, and he'll make a mistake out of jealousy. That's when I can make my move, legally."

Again, Ike and Renee looked confused.

"Okay, here it is in a nutshell. I need to have reason to be here to satisfy the FBI as well as other local and state law-enforcement agencies' investigations. When I take down Murky Porter, I must have justifiable reason as to why I did it and why I'm here. I planned this all out over the past weeks. We portray that Renee and I met two years ago when she was visiting Cleveland."

She interrupted, "How would you have known that I was in Cleveland two years ago when I just told you that durin' dinner tonight?"

Cole rubbed his jaw, running the tips of his right hand's fingers over the stubble of a beard. "I had a background check done on everyone involved with this case before I made the trip down here. Credit card transactions tell a lot about a person, Renee. You used your credit card to pay for your hotel room at the Motel 6 in Willoughby, a town just east of Cleveland. You were there from July 6 through July 9."

"Oh…wow," Ike spoke with amazement.

"That's kind of creepy." Renee added, "That you could know that so easily."

Cole continued, "So we met in Cleveland and then remained in touch through email and telephone calls after you returned home. This spring you informed me that your grandfather needed a farm-hand for a few months and if I knew of anyone that could fit the bill. I volunteered my services as I had been laid off from a factory where I was employed as a welder. Our intentions, however, are more about us becoming romantically involved than me helping around the farm."

She shook her head no. "I don't think I can do this. I'm not so sure if I even like you."

Cole squinted. "The same here, but it's the only way this will work."

Ike interluded, "You can do it, honey. You were a good actress in high school."

"Oh, Grandpa. Those were dinky little high school plays. With written scripts at that."

"Well, you were good at it," Ike confirmed.

Renee felt proud over her skills as an actress. "Yeah, I guess I can look at this as an actin' challenge."

"This has to come across natural," Cole pointed out. "We don't need an overplayed performance from you as if you're vying for an Oscar."

She curled her lip at him.

He ignored her gesture and continued, "So over the next couple of weeks, I pose as a farmhand. Then we slowly begin to show, Renee and I, that we are becoming an item. We'll be seen around town holding hands and, just because we have to, kissing from time to time."

Renee extended her tongue from her mouth and made a motion as if she were sticking her left forefinger down her throat.

Again Cole disregarded her negative gesture. "Word then gets around that this new man in town is wooing the Stewart girl. We all know how news travels fast in a small town."

Ike firmly nodded his head in agreement.

"Then Murky becomes enraged with jealousy and plots to attack me to get me out of the picture. When he does, I take care of him in self-defense. End of the Murky story, Nate's murder justified."

"Sounds like a solid plan to me," Ike remarked.

"Yeah...well, you're not the one who has to kiss him, Grandpa," Renee complained.

"It's all for Nate, Renee," Ike reminded her. Ike then offered them a good night and made his way inside the farmhouse to retire for the night. This left Cole and Renee alone on the porch.

Several moments of tongue-tied silence prevailed between them. Renee then cleared her throat to finally break the dead air. "So what is it like to live in Cleveland?"

He shrugged his shoulders. "It's like living in any other city, I guess. Sirens blaring most of the time, traffic jams, the homeless sleeping in the streets."

"That doesn't sound very appealin'," she noted.

"Oh, there are beautiful parts of Cleveland as well. We have a renowned zoo, ports on the lakefront, The Rock and Roll Hall of Fame, as you are aware, professional sports teams, good fishing...and if you want to get out of the hustle and bustle of the city, the countryside is not too far of a drive. Amish farm communities are within

an hour's trip. It's like anything else, Renee. You need to look beyond the surface to discover the beauty within."

She sighed. "Now you're soundin' like Grandpa."

"I believe that there is some good in everyone, if you look hard enough."

"I don't completely agree with that," she indicated.

"Why is that?"

She rose from her chair and slowly paced along the boards of the porch. "My grandfather says that you should never wonder what your life would be like if things were different, that you have to live with the cards you're dealt, and to make the most of what you have. I understand what he is tryin' to say, that you shouldn't dwell on things that you cannot change or control. But I have to admit that I am guilty of wonderin' from time to time." Renee ceased her stride to lean against a porch railing before continuing. "I can't help but to think about what life would be like if my parents were still alive. What they would look like today, if I would be any different with my ways under their direction? And Nate, he would have been a young adult now, what would his plans be? We are taught to love God but not necessarily understand him. That's difficult to do at times. I accept him as my lord and my savior, but I most certainly do not always agree with him. Why is it that some of the best people in the world die while evil criminals are left to live on? So to say that there is good in everyone is a blanket statement that should be carefully considered and defined a bit further. As we in Harpersfield already know, and you will soon learn, there are no—I repeat, *no*—good traits within the Porter family. Not even a slightest hint. Not one single fiber of righteousness flows through their cold veins. I have seen them so cruel at times with absolutely no signs of mercy or remorse. You can look as hard as you want past the surface of the Porters, but you'll find no splendor within those monsters."

Cole nodded and then exhaled. "I guess I should take back my statement then."

"No, it's a good philosophy that you should always carry with you. Just because there are a few exceptions to the rule, that shouldn't spoil your positive outlook on humanity as a whole."

Cole sipped from his bourbon. "What I do for a living pairs off good against evil. That is if you consider"—he lowered his voice to a whisper—"the FBI as good. Not everyone would agree. Take the Waco, Texas, incident for an example. Regardless, we agents, for the most part, are upright individuals, I honestly believe that, or I wouldn't be a member of the agency. Like any other operation, we have our flaws, our few bad apples here and there. But our goal is to do decent work for the people of this country. In most of the head-to-head combats that I have witnessed between good and evil, good prevails virtually every time. Though there are the rare occasions when evil prevails, but it is only a matter of time before they are caught. A temporary setback for the righteousness, I suppose you could say. In the end, karma is a powerful entity. I've seen it at work too many times not to be a believer." He leaned nearer to Renee. "Tell me this, as a team, do you feel that we could overcome and conquer the Porters?"

She hesitated and then fidgeted. "I want to be a cheerleader for the good team, of course, I really do, but I have never seen the Porters lose in any confrontation. It's a tall order, so we'll just have to cross our fingers and see how it all pans out. The way I see it, we have nothin' to lose—well, our lives perhaps, but what is life here with the Porters and their torment nonetheless? I guess what I am sayin' is that the odds are certainly against us, but I'm ready to go for it just the same. So I am pledgin' to you that I am in this for the long haul."

He readily grinned. "That is all that I can ask for."

She teased, "So we finally agree on somethin'?"

He taunted, "Um…don't play too much into it, we are still poles apart."

The playful expression washed away from her face. "There are just no breaks from you at all, is there?"

"You give an inch, and they will take a mile," he countered.

She rushed the screen door of the farmhouse and slung it open. "Then I shall bid the jerk a good night," she snipped.

"Don't let the bedbugs bite!" he shouted through the screen door. He waited until he heard her bedroom door slam shut. He shook his head as made his way to the guesthouse.

CHAPTER 17

OVER THE FOLLOWING ten days, Cole worked as a farm-hand and made his appearance known around town. He completed runs for dog food, seeds, garden tools, and for whatever else for which he could find an excuse. He befriended townsfolk as word of his presence was fired around Harpersfield like a slingshot. He came to discover the peace, other than the Porters' shenanigans, that a small town had to offer. His hectic life in the city had its way of playing on his nerves, which at times translated into restless sleep. But here in Harpersfield, Cole had been getting some of the best rest of his life, and it felt refreshing. He was also becoming aware of the love and warmth that was shared within the Stewart home between Renee and her grandfather—a comforting, secure feeling that was never felt in the Walsh household.

Beyond the farm, on the horizon, was one of many peaks that sprouted up from the Smoky Mountain Range. The mountains were a beautiful, peaceful sight that Cole seized during the morning and evening hours. A light foggy mist developed at the top third of the mountain during the evening hours and into the morning light. Cole imagined that it must be like paradise up there for the wildlife that resided in the wilderness. Somehow the grasses of Tennessee seemed

greener than the lawns up in Ohio. Such a rich green, in fact, that the grass nearly appeared blue. He supposed that the bluegrasses of Kentucky extended down through the Tennessee valley, but he was too embarrassed to ask. And the sky…the sky was a deeper shade of blue in this part of the country, he was nearly certain of that. The air was crisp and clean, and a hint of freshly plowed and growing fields pleasantly tickled at the sense of smell. Yeah, these were the splendid surroundings that Cole found that he needed to recharge his outlook on life, his strength, and his overall health. It just made everything fall into prospective; it made a man think more clearly. He could see reasoning as to why the townspeople were proud to call this place home.

*****

July 29

COLE SWUNG OPEN the large door of aged wood as he stepped inside Arnold's Feedstore of Harpersfield. Inside for a primary visit, Cole was a bit set back over the expanse of the store's plentiful square footage. For a feedstore in such a small community, it was rather spacious in size. Although portions of available shelving space were unoccupied, the inventory of merchandise inside the store was rather abundant.

He glanced around as he approached the counter where a boxer dog was peacefully lying on the wooden floor next to a display of animal-themed postcards. The canine looked to Cole with gentle eyes. Cole stooped to pet the boxer, who welcomed the attention. Suddenly, shuffling out from the backroom to behind the counter, a man appeared and grinned. "Well, howdy there, stranger. That there is Eugene, Gino for short. He really seems to like ya, but then again, he likes everyone. Not much of a watchdog." The man chuckled. "But my buddy in both busy and not-so-busy times. So, what I can do ya for today, sir?"

Cole patted Eugene one last round before rising to the counter. "Dog food." He then reached into the right pocket of his jeans to

remove a crumpled note that Renee had sent along with him. "Um…
three forty-pound bags of Purina multibeef mix."

The man nodded with recognition. "Ah, that would be for the
Stewart clan. Yep, they are about due." After a moment of thought,
the proprietor then snapped his fingers. "Oh, you must be Ike's newly
hired hand I've been hearing about."

Cole shook his head. "Doesn't take much to spread around
here, yes?"

"Oh, it would blow your mind how quickly it all goes 'round."
Extending his right hand over the counter, the man greeted him.
"Nice to meet ya. Chuck Arnold here, owner and operator of this
here feed and seed shop. Most outsiders think Arnold is the first
name, but no, it's my last. Sorta strange to have first names as first
and last." He chortled. "But just the same, it's me."

Charles Arnold was sixty-eight years old and had been running the feedstore for nearly five decades and was employed at the
same establishment for fifty-four years and counting. The only son
of original owners, Norman and Edith Arnold, Chuck began his
lengthy career at the store at the tender age of fourteen. He and his
wife of forty-nine years, Meredith, had four adult children and nine
grandchildren. However, none of the Arnold family members were
interested in inheriting the feedstore as wishing not to deal with the
antics of the Porter family. But for Chuck Arnold, operating the feedstore was all he had ever done and all he had ever known. Over the
years and through several generations of the Porters, he had been
openly robbed countless times over and was once beaten severely by
Steadman for falsely being accused of shorting the Porters of cash
during one of their up-and-front robberies of the store.

Chuck was short and broad. At five feet and seven inches tall
and 178 pounds heavy, he was as round as he was erect. His gray
hair, once abundant, was now thinning and scarce. He sported rather
thick-lensed eyeglasses and wore a collared shirt with the Arnold's
Feedstore emblem sewed on the right chest area. Meredith, his shy
and withdrawn wife who rarely left the confines of their home in
Webster, had been on him for nearly a decade to sell to the store and
finally retire, but Chuck wasn't quite ready to hang up his hat just yet.

Shaking hands, Cole returned the greeting. "Cole Walsh here."

"Well, Cole, the Stewarts' biweekly order of dog food is as sure as the rain, so I always have it pushed aside and ready for pickup. I'll just put it on Ike's tab. He's always good for it. So follow me, and we'll get ya all loaded up now."

"Um, this feedstore is rather big for supplying such a small town."

Chuck nodded. "Yep, that it is for these days. But there was a time when this store was the only one of its kind for miles around. That was before Webster and Waynesburg got all built up and stuff. For many years, this place supplied farmers from all around. But even with today's competition, we still do alright."

As they passed a row of shelving leading to the dock area, Chuck had a flashback from years ago when Carter and his brother Steadman paid an unexpected and unwelcomed visit to the feedstore just past closing time as Chuck was locking up shop for the night.

*****

After Chuck kicked away the wooden block that wedged open the entrance door to the feedstore, something he had done religiously over the spring and summer months, the large door was slowly swaying closed only to have a large opened palm grab the door's frame to halt its progress.

Chuck swallowed hard when he came face-to-face with Carter Porter.

"Howdy, Chuck." Carter sarcastically winked. "It's been a spell since we last spoke. How the hell are things, Arnold?" Without invitation, Carter stepped inside the feedstore with his brother Steadman directly behind him.

In a shaky and nervous voice, Chuck uttered, "Carter. Steadman. How are you fine gentlemen doin'?"

Carter glanced around the store for a moment before inquiring, "How's business been lately? I've noticed while passin' over the last month or so a good number of vehicles in the parkin' lot."

Steadman raised a box of birdseed from off a nearby shelf before examining the label and then tossing it over his left shoulder, allowing the package to plummet to the wooden floor below.

"Um…guys…I was just closin' up for the night. Is there somethin' I can do for you all?"

Carter spit a collection of tobacco juice onto the floor of the store. "Well, yep, actually, there's somethin' you can do for us. Empty that safe of yours and hand it on over to us. It's been a while since you've met your dues, Chuckie."

Chuck cleared his throat. "Um, yes, sure thing, Carter and Steadman."

The brothers then followed the edgy proprietor to the back room of the business. Under a desk and beneath an area mat was a small floor safe. With trembling hands, Chuck was eventually able to maneuver the combination dial to unlock the safe.

"All that's in there, Arnold," Steadman growled.

From his knees, Chuck nodded as he reached inside the safe. After collecting the full contents from the box, he rose to his feet to timidly face the Porters to hand over a small stack of bills.

Carter snatched the bundle from Chuck and readily counted the cash. With the tally complete, Carter glared at Chuck. "What the heck is this, Arnold? There's less than two hundred bucks here. You holdin' out on us, you motherfucker?"

Chuck abruptly shook his head. "No, Carter, I wouldn't do that. I had no idea you guys were even goin' to show up this evenin'. That's the one and only safe, I swear. That's all the cash sales for today, the rest was credit cards." There was no hidden stash.

"Then where in the hell is the rest?" Steadman snarled.

"There is no rest, Steadman. Yes, business has been pretty good recently, but today bein' a Monday, it was a bit slow. All last-week sales I've already banked and paid bills this mornin'. I've got two kids with braces on their teeth, and I had to have new lines dug for my septic system at home. Expensive things, guys. Sorry, but that's all I can spare right now…and I really can't spare that, but it's all yours. Please just let me be now. Please."

Steadman reached out with his left hand to grab the collar of Chuck's emblemed shirt. "Come on, Arnold, you connivin' son of a bitch. You're gonna lead us to your hidden stash."

As Steadman pulled him across the floor of the store, Chuck pleaded, "Guys, please, I assure you there is no stash. I swear it now. I've given you all that I have. Everythin'."

Unconvinced, Steadman maintained forcing Chuck through the store. "Where, Arnold? Where the hell is it?"

"Guys, I'm tellin' you the truth. There's nothin' more. God as my witness."

Carter, in close pursuit, scorned, "Ain't no God gonna help your sorry ass now."

Steadman then pinned Chuck along a series of shelves. Coming face-to-face, Steadman pointed his left forefinger less than inch away from Chuck's left eye. "I'm gonna only ask you one more time, you feed-store asshole. Leads us to the stash."

Sobbing, a terrified Chuck Arnold begged, "Please, please, there is no secret stash. If there were, I'd take you right to it."

"Wrong answer," Steadman confirmed. He then began to land solid punches with his right fist upon Chuck's head and facial areas. Soon, blood began to ooze and spray from Steadman's beatings. Carter then joined his brother in the thrashing of the feedstore's vendor.

By the time the Porter brothers were through with their assault, Chuck Arnold was unconscious and clinging to life. To add insult to injury, and before departing the premises, the brothers went on a rampage throughout the store using their pocketknives to slice open bags of feed and seed, allowing the contents to spill out onto the floor. They broke several windows and heaved items about in devotion to complete disarray.

Chuck was eventually discovered hours later, just before daybreak inside the feedstore, by then-acting Sheriff Nelson Hughes after a concerning call placed by Meredith Arnold regarding the whereabouts of her missing husband. Chuck was rushed to the hospital in Waynesburg, which was the beginning of a lengthy recovering period for the battered man. It was general, but unspoken knowledge, that this all was the doing of the Porter men. But fearing repercussions, the victim, as well as local law enforcement, chose to look the other way. The official report given by Chuck Arnold and encouraged by Sheriff Hughes was that the assailants attacked from behind without the victim getting a good look at them. Also, in the statement, the sheriff's department's ensuing investigation at the scene was unsuccessful in collecting sufficient evidence linking any individuals to the crime.

Years later, Chuck Arnold still dealt with scars from the unprovoked attack upon him, both physically as well as mentally.

*****

"Right over here." Chuck pointed to three large bags of dog food stacked near the swinging doors leading out to the loading dock. "That's the Stewart order there. Did you back up to the dock?"

Cole nodded.

"Alrighty then, let me open these doors, and I'll help you get all loaded up." After positioning the doors in a locked open position, the men slid the bags of feed onto a flatbed dolly.

Once on the dock, Chuck then noticed Murky, Sterling, and Dalton approaching and quickly excused himself from the immediate area. "Sorry, my friend, but I think I just heard the front door open. A customer to tend to."

"No problem," Cole mentioned. "I can handle the loading."

"Good. Just leave the dolly here on the dock. That will be fine." With that said, Chuck quickly disappeared back inside the store.

Cole tossed the last large bag of dog food into the bed of his truck that was backed up against the wooden dock extending out from Arnold's Feedstore. It was here, for the initial time, that he witnessed the Porter brothers other than in photographs. Sterling and Dalton were leaning against the dock's support poles about ten feet from Cole's truck after seemingly appearing from out of nowhere, though Cole did hear their quiet approach. Murky was seated on the dock's edge with a pinch of chewing tobacco in his jaw.

Cole nodded his head as a greeting, as if he had no prior knowledge of who they were. None of the three boys returned the friendly gesture. They only eyed Cole. The bulky size of the Porter brothers initially startled Cole. He was aware by their descriptions on paper that they were tall and of unwieldy build, but you had to view them in person to place it into proper perspective. Cole was nearly equal in size, but his muscular structure was more defined and toned than any of the three brothers. However, one could tell immediately that

the Porters were extraordinarily strong. They were constructed thick and solid with virtually no body fat of mention.

"Who the hell are you?" Sterling grilled.

"Oh, hi there. I'm Cole," he replied while extending out his right hand. "I'm working up at the Stewart farm."

Sterling committed no movement to shake Cole's hand.

Cole cleared his throat and dropped his arm back to his side.

"How long you gonna to be workin' up there?" Dalton inquired.

Cole squinted. "About another two or three months, I suppose. Old man Stewart doesn't get around so well anymore, so I'll stay through the harvest, I would guess."

"You're from Ohio. How did you get this job down here?" Sterling summoned, looking at the truck's rear license plate through the openings of the dock's wooden floor.

"Oh," Cole explained, "it's a long story."

The three brothers then glared at Cole as that was insufficient information.

"Um...I was visiting the Rock and Roll Hall of Fame up in Ohio. Renee Stewart and her friend Stacy came up there to visit the hall where she and I met. We became friends and emailed each other over the past two years or so. Well, I've been laid off from my job the past year, and when she told me her grandfather was hiring, I jumped at the chance."

"Well...you'd better not be jumpin' somethin' else up on that farm," Murky warned.

Cole played, as planned, that he misinterpreted Murky's admonition. "Oh, I'm clean. I didn't jump bail and run from the cops or anything like that."

Murky shook his head, and his brothers chuckled. Murky figured that Cole was too foolish to try to explain further. He also imagined that Cole was excessively dumb and would not attract Renee.

"Just get on back up the hill, hired farm boy," Murky directed. "You may see me come around from time to time. I'm courtin' Renee."

Cole stepped down from the deck. "Okay, see ya later, Murky."

At that second, Cole realized that he just made a vital mistake.

Murky glanced over his shoulder at his brothers than back to Cole with a squint. "How the hell do you know my name?"

Cole, needing to think quickly and lightning fast, uttered, "He said your name a little bit ago." He pointed at Sterling.

The brothers couldn't exactly recall if Sterling had spoken Murky's name. It left just enough uncertainty that Cole was able to get away with the mishap.

Murky retorted, "Are you sure that Renee hasn't been talkin' about me?"

Dalton slapped Murky on the back of the head. "You're fuckin' dreamin'. That girl doesn't want anything to do with you. Get that through your thick skull already, you idiot."

Sterling and Dalton sniggered.

"Dalton, if you hit me in the head again, I'll chop your filthy hand off. I'll hurt you, and I'll hurt you bad," Murky rebuked in all seriousness.

Dalton, out of tediousness rather than fear or intimidation, calmed his taunting. "I'm just messin' with ya, Murky."

"Does the Stewart gal talk about me?" Murky echoed to Cole.

"Um…I wouldn't know. I don't really talk with Renee. I just talk with Ike," Cole replied.

Sterling spoke up. "You know that old man is an ole shiner? He used to run firewater. Some people say that he still brews a little of it time to time."

Cole shrugged his shoulders. "That's no business of mine."

Murky slid from the edge of the dock to step toward Cole. As he moved past Cole, Murky nodded in a gesture for Cole to follow him. The two stepped aside together about twenty feet from the dock.

Murky spit out a spew of tobacco juice. "What's you name again?"

"Cole."

"Well, Cole the mole. I need you to do somethin' for me. I want you to talk to Renee while you're up there on that farm. Tell her that she should go out with Murky Porter. Can you remember that? Murky Porter."

"I don't talk to her much."

"Well, see that you talk to her about this," Murky demanded, forcefully patting Cole on his chest.

Cole nodded.

"Good boy, mole." Murky winked. "I think we'll get along fine." He then placed his arm around Cole's shoulder. "Just don't do me wrong. You don't want to mess with me. I'll hurt you, and I'll hurt you bad."

Cole desired to break Murky's neck right then and there, but he must remain patient. Instead, he nodded in understanding.

Murky took his arm from around Cole and grinned mischievously, "Get your ass back up to the farm and get to work on my mission. Don't fail me, Cole the mole."

"Come on, Murky!" Dalton shouted. "We're goin' to Waynesburg for some pussy!"

For a flash, a very brief moment, Murky could view past Cole's facade to see the calculated rage inside the man's eyes. He was left wondering, but eventually dismissed it.

"Gotta go, Cole the mole. Can't really say I enjoyed the company though." Murky bid a sarcastic farewell before stepping away.

When Murky moved out from earshot, Cole mumbled to himself, "Same here, punk."

During the drive back to the farm, Cole commended himself on another display of controlled patience. He realized it was a vital component in order to succeed in his business. It hadn't always been that way, however. He was a hothead in his younger days.

Cole glanced at the rearview mirror and ran the tip of his finger along the path of a quiet scar upon his forehead. The scar was about two inches in length and had faded some over the passing years. He viewed it as a reminder of what happened when you lose your cool.

Cole's father, Ted Walsh, was a Cleveland police officer nearing retirement. He had taught Cole much about patience of being a lawman. Ted had no knowledge of the existence of the Elite Four. Cole's father was quick to tell of his profound proudness that his son was an FBI agent.

Cole's mother, Kathy Walsh, was not an attentive mother as Cole and his sister, Becky, grew up. Kathy spent nights dosing on

pain pills and days sleeping them off. When she was out of medication, she replaced the pills with whiskey. About the time Becky and Cole were heading for their beds for the night, Kathy was just getting up. His father worked days, so Cole often wondered when his parents communicated. Becky did most of the housecleaning, laundry, and prepared the meals. Shortly after her eighteenth birthday, Becky attended a party at a friend's house who lived on the shores of Lake Erie. Since turning sixteen, Becky began to drink hard liquor, obtaining it from her mother's stash that Becky had discovered. Kathy noticed the drop in her whiskey inventory, but she merely deducted that she had been drinking more.

Over the next two years, Becky's alcohol consumption became nearly as heavy as Kathy's. Cole attempted talking with Becky about her excessive drinking on several occasions, but Becky honestly believed that she had it under control.

That night at the party, Becky was extremely intoxicated when she decided to go for a swim. She wandered off alone and stepped onto the beach. It was a warm night, but it was windy. The waves on the lake had picked up with intensity to over six feet in height—not favorable conditions in which to swim. Becky stripped off her clothes and then stumbled toward the rough water. She wandered into Lake Erie until she was waist-deep in water. She then dove into a passing wave. She did not surface until after she had drowned. Cole was fifteen years old at the time, and suddenly he was an only child. The Walsh household was always gloomy after Becky's death.

Ted Walsh worked in the heart of the city and realized that he didn't want his family to reside within the striking distance of the excessive crime that big cities fester. When Cole was five years old, Ted moved his family to a suburb thirty miles east of Cleveland in the moderate-sized town of Mentor, Ohio. It was here that the Walshes could reside in a peaceful community, and Ted's commute to work was thirty minutes or so. Cole had numerous friends as he grew up in Mentor, but not exactly one he could call his best friend. He had different hobbies than most of the other boys his age. Cole found an interest in weight training when he was twelve while most of the other boys in the neighborhood rode their BMX bicycles or jumped

onto their skateboards. At fourteen, Cole landed an after-school and weekend job bussing tables at a Perkin's Restaurant that was within walking distance of his home. His objective for the income was to join a fitness club a few miles from his house.

Heisley Road Racquet and Fitness Club membership was expensive, but to Cole, it was well worth it. They had all the state-of-the-art weight-training equipment. He purchased a ten-speed bike as well to ride back and forth from his residence to the club. At sixteen, Cole had his first real intimate experience with a member of the opposite sex. It began when Cole met her father. Karl Palmer was a member of the Heisley Club. Karl worked afternoons as a security guard at the nearby Perry Nuclear Power Plant facility. Being that Karl worked afternoons, his workouts at the club took place during the morning hours, as did Cole's. Although the Heisley Club was an exceedingly popular establishment, the crowds were minimal between ten in the morning and noon. Sometimes, it was downright slow. Cole liked it best when many of the members were not around. It gave him free rein of the equipment. It was during these times that Cole came to know Karl and eventually Karl's daughter. Cole didn't have any problem attracting girls, but he was shy toward the opposite sex.

Karl invited Cole to his home in the town of Perry, fifteen miles east of Mentor. Karl sought for Cole to see his home gym, and he wanted to take Cole fishing on Lake Erie in his boat. Karl picked up Cole in Mentor one Saturday morning and brought him back to the Palmers household. Karl's wife, Annie, was a very gracious hostess and made Cole feel immediately welcomed. Karl and Cole toyed with the home gym for a bit and then began to prepare the boat for an afternoon of fishing.

As they prepped the boat, a red Dodge Neon pulled up in the driveway. An alluring young lady stepped out of the car, and she immediately made eye contact with Cole. Her hair was long and soft. Her light brown mane curled naturally around the frame of her alluring neckline. Her skin glowed peachy, and her green eyes ran deep with color. She smiled with perfectly aligned pearly white teeth at Cole. She was a hint overweight with a round attractive face. Her perfume was perfect, an aroma that drew men's attention like a magnet.

She was Karl and Annie's sixteen-year-old daughter, Marie Palmer. Marie was a junior at Perry High School and a popular girl with her classmates. She was involved with school activities, and despite her nominal weight problem, she was a particularly good cheerleader for the football team and a member of several academic clubs. She was registered with the National Honor Society with a 3.8 GPA.

On this day, Marie was wearing a pair of black silky shorts and a red T-shirt with the words Perry Cheer Squad printed across her large breasts. By the color of her shirt and her car, Cole was sure that red was her favorite color. Her legs were tanned and smooth, and her toenails protruded out the front of her sandals painted in a quiet ivory shade. What Cole found enticing was that her fingers were slender for a large-framed girl, and her natural fingernails were long and manicured well. Cole knew at this young age that one of his favorite assets on a woman was her soft, feminine fingers and fingernails. His other enjoyment on a woman was…well, her backside. Though Marie wasn't obese by any stretch of the imagination, her body framed more weight than what would be ideal for her. Even with the extra pounds, Alicia's backside was shapely pronounced. She was what most women envied—one who could carry the additional weight without sacrificing her alluring figure. However, to Cole, attraction was only a mere formality. It was what was on the inside that mattered most to him.

Marie did date now and then, but she hadn't landed a young man with quite the handsome exterior such as Cole Walsh. She already had visions of showing off her new and very handsome boyfriend to her friends. Her smile to his direction was something Cole could not immediately decipher as either friendly or flirtatious. He decided to ride it out for a spell to see if she was indeed attracted to him. His initial feelings were that he found her to be a young lady he would like to ask out on a date. But he had to test the waters with her first.

She remembered her father mentioning something regarding having a young man from Mentor over to the house, but Marie never imagined that he would be so handsome. Or as the girls her age liked to refer to as "hot." Their meeting each other was a bit awkward due

to Cole's bashfulness toward the opposite sex. He cleared his throat after releasing a weak-sounding voice as his face reddened slightly.

That evening, upon Karl and Cole's return from fishing, Karl insisted that Cole stay for dinner. After dinner, Cole, Marie, Karl, and Annie chatted together on the back patio. When the time arrived, Marie volunteered to drive Cole home. Karl saw no problem with it, but Annie was a bit apprehensive. She had just met Cole that day. After reassurance from Karl that Cole was an upstanding young man, Annie agreed to allow Marie to provide Cole a ride home.

Cole began to feel a bit more comfortable around Marie. But somehow, she shifted her persona when she escaped from the company of her parents. Her innocence transformed into a bit of wildness. She forwardly questioned Cole if he was a virgin. He was indeed, but he thought that was none of her business. She then queried Cole if he knew anyone who would buy them some wine or whiskey. He didn't. She drove them down to the lakeshore to Mentor Headlands Park, although those were not the verbal directions Cole relayed to her of the location of his home.

Less than a minute after Marie parked her Neon, she was all over Cole in the passenger's seat. Cole didn't exactly reject Marie that evening in the park as it marked the very day that he lost his virginity in the front seat of a Dodge. Cole enjoyed the experience; however, he came to realize that he preferred a woman who would have been less aggressive. A bit more challenging.

Marie wanted to continue to see Cole on an intimate basis after that day in the park, but Cole politely shut it down before it could get off the ground. Cole remained friends with Karl, but he turned down future invitations to the Palmer household.

As with everything else that he did, Cole pursued weight training completely through to his goal. His body became sculpted with strong and defined muscles. When he achieved the point of where he wanted his physique to be, he modified his workouts to maintain that ideal build. He was marked with protruding muscles, but not so much so that he resembled a contestant for the Mr. Universe title. Rather, his bodily frame was enough to intimidate men and yet remained alluring to women.

When Cole was seventeen, he attended the police academy in Akron on a high school student program. He graduated from the program with honors. Shortly after he progressed from the academy and during his senior year in high school, Cole entered a nightclub with a few buddies, all using bogus ID cards. Cole was the designated driver since he rarely drank alcohol. Because of his mother's slavery to the bottle, he was frightened to consume. A female in the club took a liking to Cole's good looks. Unfortunately, she was there with her boyfriend. That didn't stop her from continuously eyeing Cole's direction. The boyfriend soon became wise to her interest, and he approached Cole. The man was older than Cole, but he wasn't any larger. Cole was intimated as the man's irritation was apparent. He accused Cole of flirting with his girlfriend. Cole knew now that he should have just walked away, but instead, his hot head came to surface. He said something to the man along the lines that it's a free country.

Before Cole could react, the man landed a hard punch to Cole's forehead. The man was wearing a large US Marine's ring, and the sharp-edged stone cut a path along Cole's forehead. Blood spilled out from the gash and dribbled down into Cole's eyes. Cole reached behind himself to grab hold of one of the barstools. Before the marine could act in response, Cole brought the stool down onto the man's head. The girlfriend screamed out, and the disc jockey in the club immediately halted the music.

Nearly everyone's attention turned to Cole and the marine. The man, nearly unconscious, fell to the carpeted floor near the bar. Within minutes, two uniformed Cleveland police officers rushed inside the club. Cole and the marine were both arrested. Cole's father was able to persuade the police force to drop the charges on his son. They agreed, being that Ted was a veteran of the force. However, a stipulation was added. Cole must join the military service or face full-assault charges. Cole was happy to comply. He was already engrossed with joining the army.

The following month, Cole turned eighteen, and he quickly enlisted in the US Army. Two months later, merely days after graduating from high school, Cole was off to boot camp. He served the

following forty-eight months in the army and emerged as a Green Beret Specialist. He remained in the reserves over the next four years to perfect his position. Directly after his initial four years of military service, Cole joined the FBI as a student of the academy.

His father, the army, and the FBI all contributed to teaching Cole patience. He has nearly mastered patience over the years since that night in the club. Cole's fuse has grown in length since he was a hotheaded young man.

CHAPTER 18

July 31

"IT'S TIME WE are seen together in town," Cole instructed Renee. She was feeding the dogs inside the barn. The canines were rustling around her ankles and legs in anticipation for their upcoming meal.

She poured about three pounds of dry dog food onto the dirt floor of the barn, and the dogs, in unison, took part in the feast. Renee glanced up at Cole and giggled at the dog's eager actions.

Cole shook his head and chuckled at the pets' enthusiasm. "So, I thought the three of us can take a drive into town," Cole conveyed.

Renee sighed and rolled her eyes.

Cole squinted. "Don't concern yourself, Renee. We're not at the romantic stage yet."

"Good," she responded in relief.

"Good," he echoed. "Let's say in an hour. Meet Ike and me at his pickup truck." He began to step away. He then halted his progress and turned back to address Renee. "Shower and change into something nice in case we run into Murky."

She believed that he was being tongue-in-cheek with her in some sort of twisted manner. "Shut up and stop teasing me."

She then could tell by his dry expression that he was not taunting. "I'm serious. I want you looking nice in case we run into Murky. It's all part of the plan. Without committing, I want you to give Murky the idea that there could be a chance you'd go out with him."

"Why?"

"Because when we take the plan to the next stage, it will make his jealous rage that much more intense."

"I don't know if I can pull this off. I despise Murky and his brothers."

"I can certainly understand that. But we need to do this. I thought you were a good actress?"

"I can be when I need to," she confirmed.

"Well then, need to. Remember, this is for Nate," he reminded her.

She hesitated before nodding her willingness.

"See you in an hour," Cole reinforced as he stepped away.

Renee knelt to pet the canines. A few minutes had elapsed since Cole exited the barn when she heard a noise from behind her. Her heart raced with anxiety, and a nervous lump developed in her throat. Suddenly, a hand touched her shoulder. She leapt upright and screamed.

"Honey, it's me," Ike quickly blurted out.

She pivoted to view her grandfather inside the barn. "Grandpa, you scared the daylights outta me! What are ya doin' sneakin' up on me like that?"

Ike squinted. "You're a bit jumpy aren't ya?"

She pushed her hair behind her ears. Renee then brought out a rubber band from her pocket to secure her hair into a ponytail. "Yeah, well, perhaps I'm a bit on edge. This Murky thing has me all jittery."

"That's why I came out here. I waited until Cole left so we could chat alone. I'm thinkin' that maybe we should call all this off. Whattya think?"

"Why are you considerin' that, Grandpa? Don't you want to see justice brought to Nate's murder?"

"Of course I do, but at what price?" His eyes clouded. "I've lost a wife, a son, a daughter-in-law, and a grandson. You're all I have left, Renee. If I lose you, they might as well bury me."

She took his left hand into her right hand. "Grandpa, there are no certainties in life. None of us know what tomorrow has in store for us. We merely take each day as it comes. People, loved ones, friends pass through our lives, and then one day they are suddenly gone. That's just the way it is. However, one should never make themselves so emotionally dependent on another to a point where they couldn't function without that person. We humans owe it to ourselves and our loved ones to be self-sufficient when need be. When we place such a burden of our own existence upon another's, that's a lot of unfair pressure on the one that we love."

Ike nodded his head in understanding.

"Now, as for the justice thing. I'm frightened over how this is unfoldin', but you questioned at what price. How can we put anything above rightin' Nate's murder? That is the way I see it anyway. If it were the other way around, if it were Nate here today and I was in my grave, he'd be doin' all he could to bring justice to my death. So I can surely do the same for him. I'm completely aware of the high risk involved with doin' this. I understand it could have tragic results, but I'm willin' to take that chance. I'm makin' the decision right here and right now to approach this thing at full throttle. If we continue with this at anything less than a full commitment, that's when a mistake could take place. So I'm not hesitatin' or second-guessin' any longer. I'm dedicated to see this thing through."

Ike pulled Renee into an embrace. He then placed a gentle kiss upon her forehead.

*****

DALTON, STERLING, AND Murky were hanging out at the only gas station in town. The Arco Station was owned by the Darton family and had been for decades. Fred Darton was managing the station for the current generation. His twenty-three-year-old son, Merle, worked at the station, awaiting his turn to take over

the reins someday. Conditions hadn't changed much over modern times in Harpersfield, and that rang true for the Dartons' station. The four beverage coolers were aged some thirty-five years and had been repaired numerous times. Duct tape held together some of the cracks in the glass doors. A bronze tray with the Coca-Cola insignia hung on one of the walls, stating that a bottle of Coke was merely ten cents—a price that had long since expired. The lettering on the tray was barely legible from the effects of aging. A scaled-down plastic Firestone Tires sign swung from the ceiling on a rusted chain, though the station hadn't dealt in new tires for over a decade.

The fuel pumps were still the rotary type, displaying price and gallons in plastic rolling figures. Nearly every pump in the country was now digital, but not for Fred Darton's locale. The solo public restroom was unisex, and a display of oil cans sat on a rack near the bathroom. The packaged appearance of the oil, mostly Quaker State brand, revealed its time. It had been seventeen years since oil had last been packaged in cardboard containers. Plastic bottles were now the norm, so the Quaker State oil on the rack was nearly two decades old. Fred did stock updated oil on a rack next to the counter; he just hadn't gotten around to moving out the old rack over the years.

His wife, Beverly, came to the station monthly to clean up after Fred and Merle. She mopped the worn tiled floor and washed the windows. Fred placed only a bit of his profit back into the station, and it showed.

The Porter brothers each had a can of beer in their hands, drinking the cold liquid in the hot afternoon sun. Fred and Merle were seated behind the station's counter. The Porters stood at the open doorway.

"Why the hell don't ya get some air-conditionin' in here, Fred?" Sterling moaned.

"Cost too much, Sterling. A man doesn't make much of a livin' in gasoline these days," Fred reported.

"Get that lazy shit Merle to do some repair work on cars and trucks," Dalton suggested, with no regard that Merle was there in attendance. Merle glanced at Dalton. Dalton flipped his middle finger at Merle.

Fred looked to his overweight son. "Yeah, why don't ya? You know mechanics."

"I hate gettin' greasy, Pop," Merle responded.

Fred peered at the Porters. "There ya have it. He's worthless help 'round here," Fred teased.

"We could kick him around for ya a bit," Sterling offered.

Fred swallowed hard as Merle's eyes widened in fear. "No... no, boys. Please don't do that. Merle, he doesn't mean any harm. Do ya, boy?"

Merle anxiously shook his head no.

Murky slugged a long drink from his beer before he demanded, "Give us a twelve-pack and a carton of smokes."

Fred quickly rose to his feet. He reached inside the cooler behind the counter and removed a twelve-pack of cold beer. He then reached above his head and fetched a carton of cigarettes. He placed both items on the counter and rang them up on the cash register. "That'll be sixty-four dollars and seventeen cents," he announced.

Sterling and Dalton chuckled. Murky spoke up, "There'll be no charge today, Fred the unmade bed. You give us the brew and smokes, and we won't kick the shit out of your fat, lazy son."

Fred was swift in agreeing with the deal. "It's all yours, Murky. Please just don't hurt Merle."

Sterling grabbed hold of the twelve-pack as Dalton snapped up the carton of cigarettes. The duo walked out of the station to toss the items inside Sterling's truck. Murky initially made the motion as if he were going to follow his brothers out from the station. Instead, he reached forward and gained a grip on the open door. He then pulled the door closed, trapping him inside the station with Fred and Merle.

Fred began to tremble and sweat a bit more.

"Come here, Merle the girl," Murky insisted, waving his hand toward himself.

"Murky, please," Fred pled.

"Get the hell over here, Merle. Don't even make me come around that counter to fetch you."

Merle reluctantly rose to his feet. He looked to his father. "Pop?"

Fred began to sob.

"Get over here, fat ass," Murky bellowed one last word of warning.

Sterling and Dalton overheard Murky's roar as they stood next to Sterling's pickup truck. They snickered.

"You'd better do as he says, son," Fred voiced in a shaken tone.

Merle hesitated as long as possible before Murky's eyes turned cold and gray. Merle then moved gingerly around the counter to stand before Murky.

"Why don't you lose weight, ya fat ass?" Murky drilled. Merle could only shrug his shoulders. "Punch me, Merle the girl," Murky directed.

"What?" Merle inquired with confusion.

"Punch me. Let's see if ya can strike any harder than a girl can."

Merle's hands quivered in fear. "I don't wanna punch you, Murky. I've never hit anyone before."

"Punch me, Merle the girl, and I'll give you a Twinkie," Murky offered before he scoffed.

"I'm not gonna hit you."

Murky nodded. "Just as I thought, Merle the girl. You're a wimp. Get out of my face. You disgust me."

Merle was delighted to oblige, but as he turned to saunter back behind the counter, Murky kneed him solid in the lower back. Merle hollered out in pain as he collapsed to the floor on his knees.

"Murky, please leave him alone," Fred begged for mercy.

Merle reached his left hand behind his back to protect the area that Murky had just attacked.

Sterling and Dalton came rushing inside the station. They sneered at the sight of the fallen Merle. Sterling then stomped on the back of Merle's right hand flat onto the tiled floor. Sterling's large black boot rattled the knuckles of Merle's hand. Again, Merle buckled in pain. Fred then glanced over to Dalton, who was making a mighty fist with his right hand. Fred cried out, "Protect your head, son!"

Merle's hands were unable to reach up to his head in time before Dalton landed a hard fist to the back of Merle's head. The world went into a spin for Merle as he gasped for air. Fred now rushed from behind the counter to help protect his son. He placed himself

between Merle and the Porters. Fred raised his hands before himself. "Please, boys...please, I'm beggin'. Merle has had enough. You know that I know your father well. Carter and I used to run together all the time. I'm the one that introduced your father to your mother. Please show mercy on your father's longtime friend." Fred formed his hands in a praying fashion. "For the love of God, please leave my boy alone."

Dalton, Sterling, and Murky grinned at each other. Dalton then stomped on Fred's left foot. Fred grimaced in pain as he plunged into the counter. Sterling then rushed Fred and delivered a mighty punch to Fred's mouth. The blunt of the blow shattered the top-front portion of Fred's dentures. A cut opened on the inner top lip of Fred's mouth. Blood seeped over his bottom lip like a dripping faucet.

Murky then gripped his right hand firmly around Fred's throat, cutting off his airway. "We're takin' what's in the register. Do you have a problem with that, Fred the unmade bed?" Murky growled.

Fred feverishly shook his head no.

Dalton cautioned, "You'd better not plan on callin' Harvey or Collins."

Fred again shook his head.

Sterling jumped over the counter to press the No Sale button on the older-style cash register. The drawer opened with a ring of a small bell. Sterling removed the cash from the register and then stuffed it inside his pants pocket. He then leaped back over the counter.

Murky released his grip from around Fred's throat. Fred wheezed for air and coughed. "We'll be back tomorrow. Darton's fartin'," Murky claimed.

"Yeah, we'll be back to drink a beer and shoot the shit. We won't rob ya again for a few months." Dalton sneered.

"Remember, no damn cops," Sterling counseled.

After a few moments of silence, Dalton directed, "Come on, let's go. This is borin'. Let's go smoke a joint on the deck of the feedstore."

Soon, but not soon enough for Fred and Merle, the three Porter boys strode out from the station.

Fred made his way over to his fallen son. He knelt, and before he spoke to Merle, Fred wiped some of the blood away from his

mouth with a handkerchief. He then rubbed Merle's back with the palm of his right hand. "Are you okay, son?"

"It hurts, Pop," Merle reported.

"I know. Does it feel like anything is broken?"

Merle shook his head.

"Okay, try to stand up."

Merle, slowly and aware of each movement, rose to his feet. Fred came to a stand alongside his son. Merle grimaced and gripped his lower back with his left hand. He then peered at his father. "Pop, your teeth."

"It'll be okay, Merle. I have another set. Let's get you home so your momma can take care of your bruises. She's gonna be so upset about her boy gettin' hurt."

"We have to close the station first, Pop," Merle pointed out.

"There's nothin' much left worth takin'. They cleaned us out. But we'll lock the door just the same."

"You can't call the cops," Merle indicated.

"I know, son, I know better than to do that. The Porters would hurt us worse than they just did. Besides, Harvey wouldn't do much of anything at that. As always, we'll take our lumps and bruised pride and move on now."

CHAPTER 19

"WHY ARE YOU ridin' in the back of the truck?" Renee quizzed Cole. Ike was in the driver's seat of the pickup truck while Renee was about to lower her head to sway onto the passenger's side. Cole had leaped into the bed of the truck.

"I'm just a simple farmhand riding into town with the folks that hired me," Cole explained.

"You can sit up here with us. With you back there, it's like takin' one of the dogs for a ride," she compared.

"The plan is not ready for that just yet. Quite frankly, neither are you," Cole observed.

Renee sneered at him. "Suit yourself." She then, with aggression, slid into the truck's cab. Ike and Cole snickered. "Just drive, Grandpa," she insisted. Ike placed the truck in gear and trekked toward the road.

During the ride, Ike reached his right hand behind his head to slide open the divided rear window of the truck. He communicated with ample volume for Cole to hear him over the noise of travel, "Where in town are we headed exactly?"

"Let's see if we can spot the Porters' truck," Cole replied, speaking into the wind.

"Okay then," Ike confirmed.

"What if Murky comes on to me too aggressively?" Renee queried.

Cole teased, "We'll give you two space to be alone."

Renee squinted. "Haha…very funny." She then glanced down at her chosen attire and hoped that the short low-cut blue sundress was not too inviting. "Seriously, what happens if Murky gets out of hand?"

Ike and Renee's expressions grew with looks of concern.

"Don't worry," Cole reassured, "I'll have you covered the entire time. I have a feeling I won't need to interlude. Something tells me that you'll be able to control Murky like a trained puppy."

She swayed her head in disagreement. "Nobody has ever been able to control those boys. They're ruthless."

"Trust me," Cole encouraged.

"You'd better protect her," Ike advised.

"It'll be fine, old man, I promise. I wouldn't place Renee in a situation that I believe I couldn't handle."

"Just remember, Cole, we're not dealin' with some run-of-the-mill punks here. These boys are calculated slaughterers. I'm not only talkin' about Nate. I think the Porters had somethin' to do with Dan Parker's disappearance as well," she noted.

Cole nodded. "I looked into that case as well. You could be right. I know what we are dealing with. Just follow my plan, and everything will be fine."

Renee gazed toward the Smoky Mountain Range through the truck's open passenger window. The summer breeze wafted back the bangs of her dark hair a bit. Her soft blue eyes watered as a reaction to the wind. Her delicate tanned skin glowed in the sunlight that was radiating down from the sky above. Renee had a very slight overbite, which bit at her bottom lip ever so vaguely. Her teeth were pearly white. This trifling overbite added to Renee's radiant sensual appearance. It individualized her, although the blue eyes with the dark hair did a good job of that on its own. She tended to pull the sides of her hair behind her ears. Renee was raised in an atmosphere that could have easily allowed for a tomboyish development, but her feminine qualities ran too deeply and triumphed. Renee was a hardworking farmer, but she was every bit a delicate young lady as well. Her body

was toned and slim at the waistline. She took after her mother, who always maintained her petite figure regardless of her diet.

Renee thought about her past intimate relationships, though there was not much to recall. Murky Porter's obsession with her extended back to grade school, and all the area boys were terrified of him. Murky's intimation of any male that showed an interest in her had them running for the hills before Renee and her suitor had time to get a potential relationship off the ground.

Only one outlasted Murky's actions…for a brief interval anyway.

*****

Dillon Niles began chatting with Renee at the county fair during the summer of her seventeenth birthday. Dillon was from the neighboring town of Webster, so he was oblivious of the potential danger for communicating with Renee Stewart. He did not know who Murky Porter and his brothers were, and Renee was not about to tell him. Renee and Dillon shared the next four afternoons and evenings together attending the fair before the festive event closed for another year. Dillon was eighteen and a senior at Webster High School. Renee was a junior at Waynesburg High. Harpersfield was too small a community to support their own high school.

They went their own ways after the fair closed, but Renee couldn't stop thinking about him. They had kissed several times—her first real kiss from a member of the opposite sex. Renee was a virgin, as pure as they came. Dillon hadn't stopped ruminating about Renee either. For some reason, which Renee still couldn't reason, she and Dillon had not exchanged telephone numbers. In September, when school resumed, Renee went on about Dillon with her classmate and friend, Stacy Hughes. After weeks of hearing about Dillon, Stacy encouraged Renee to track him down. They came up with a plan: go to a Webster High School football game and hope to bump into Dillon there.

One Friday night in early October, Renee and Stacy attended the Webster Lions versus the Montville Pirates football game. The plan couldn't have fallen together any better for Renee. Before the end of the first quarter, she met up with Dillon Niles next to the home team bleachers. By the second quarter, they were kissing behind the bleachers, leaving

Stacy alone in the crowd to fend for herself. She didn't mind though. Stacy realized that if things were the other way around, Renee would sacrifice for her.

By the fourth quarter, Dillon and Renee finally emerged from behind the bleachers. Renee's lips were chapped from all the kissing. This time, they were sure to exchange telephone numbers.

Renee playfully screamed with excitement into Stacy's ear during the drive back to Harpersfield. Renee was certain that she was falling in love with Dillon. The following weekend, Dillon paid a visit to Renee at the farm in Harpersfield. They enjoyed a good part of the day strolling around the land hand in hand, stopping occasionally for a kiss. It was a humid early October day in Tennessee, warm enough to swim. They approached the clear-watered pond situated on the far south section of the property. The pond was nestled in a small secluded field and surrounded by woodlands. It could only be seen from a proximity. Ike had the pond dug decades ago for emergency irrigation purposes. As far as water holes went, this specific one was unusually crystal clear as it was fed by an underground natural spring. The bottom of the pond could be viewed at a depth of over four feet.

Dillon held Renee in his arms at the pond's edge. Dillon wasn't tall; he had the average height for an eighteen-year-old young man. His hair was light brown with eyes that matched. He was of a slight chunky build, but he held the weight well on his solid frame. To Renee, he was a great kisser. But now, Dillon was ready for a little more than merely smooching.

So was Renee, though she herself wasn't prepared to admit it. Dillon kissed her; he kissed her deeply and passionately. For the first time in her life, Renee could feel a man begin to caress her breasts. Using both his palms and fingers, Dillon caressed her breasts from outside her shirt. Renee began to feel all warm and fuzzy inside. She could sense his erect penis filling his Levi's as it pressed against her right hip.

Dillon broke the kiss from their lips and began pecking her neck area, including her earlobes. Renee responded by leaning back her head and softly purring. He then pulled at her T-shirt from inside her Levi's. Dillon, in one fluent motion, pulled Renee's shirt up and over her head. The warm air was now tickling her exposed skin. He tossed her shirt to the ground and then anxiously went to work with unhooking her bra.

She tittered at his frustration over finding it difficult in releasing the bra from around her breasts. His fingers were trembling with excitement and were not working well for him.

Finally, she took over the task and unfastened her bra. Slowly, as she watched his eager eyes, she pulled the bra away from her breasts. Her full breasts stayed firm in the unsupported air, and her nipples were erect with excitement. His eyes widened at the sight before him. Dillon now caressed Renee's breasts flesh to flesh. She responded by placing the palms of her hands on the back of his hands to guide his movements.

"Let's skinny-dip," she whispered.

"Yes!" he eagerly agreed.

She observed as Dillon quickly removed his clothing. When he was down to just his underwear, she anxiously waited to see her first completely nude male. Dillon pulled his boxer shorts over his hips as his erect penis sprung out. Renee was slightly embarrassed at her first sight of an erect penis other than in pictures inside a Playgirl magazine that Stacy had stashed in her barn. But then again, those magazine shots didn't contain erections; the penises were limp. She thought that Dillon's rigid manhood was average in size, but then again, she had nothing from her past to compare it with. She wasn't sure if Dillon was a virgin as she was, but with his easiness of disrobing in front of her, Renee figured he had done something along these lines in the past.

Dillon beamed at her before running to the water's edge and then diving into the pond. He soon surfaced with the water level at midchest, facing Renee, who was still holding on the bank, bare from the waist up.

"Come on in, the water's fine," Dillon invited.

She snickered and looked around the immediate area to be sure that Dillon would be the only soul to witness her entirely disrobed. Once Renee was satisfied with their solitude, the young lady reached for to the button at the front of her Levi's. She dislodged the button and then quickly pulled down on the zipper. She then kicked the tennis shoes from off her feet. She swayed her hips as she pulled her jeans down over her hips and then off her legs. She tossed the bundled pants onto the ground next to her T-shirt and bra. She was now down to only her panties, and without hesitation, she slid the undergarment past her ankles. The panties merged with her pile of clothing on the ground. She was quickly preparing to jolt for the water.

"Wait!" Dillon shouted while extending his arms into her direction. Renee halted her motion and then looked to him in confusion. She was excited to be naked along with the young man, but she was also bashful over it being first time. She was anxious to conceal her nudity within the depths of the pond.

"Why do you want me to stop?" she inquired.

"I want a long look at your body," he replied with a roguish grin.

She playfully wheezed. "Geeze, Dillon." Renee did not attempt to cover herself, allowing Dillon to take in the full view of her nudity.

Dillon thought, and rightfully so, that Renee was beautiful. Her breasts were full and firm. Her pubic hair was dark, silky, and shaped in a perfect triangle.

"Okay, Dillon," she said, feeling a bit awkward, "can I jump into the water already?"

He extended his right index finger. "Wait, just one more minute," he requested, making a circular motion with his finger. "First, slowly turn around."

"What?" She again blushed.

"Spin, Renee. I want to see that pretty butt of yours," he bid.

"Why?" she queried with a slight giggle.

He shrugged his shoulders. "I don't know why. It's a guy thing."

"Alright, if you say so." She rolled her eyes. Renee then began to slowly rotate her body. With her back to him, Dillon enjoyed the sight of her fit, firm, and shapely backside. When she completed her turn, she rushed to jump into the pond, feet first.

After some playful splashing, sexual foreplay commenced. Within the next ten minutes, Renee Stewart was a virgin no more. After their mutually satisfying session of making love, the couple dressed and cuddled together, lying upon the pond's shore. It was then that Renee felt a need and a responsibility to inform Dillon of the Porters and their evil capabilities.

"Dillon, um, I need to explain somethin' to you, but I'm not certain of where to begin to properly articulate it to you."

Slightly puzzled, Dillon propped his head up on a bent elbow. "Well, it's probably best to just come right out with it instead of thinkin' about it too much."

"Yeah, I know." She sighed. "It's just…I'm just afraid it might run you off, and I've become so fond of you and all."

Dillon squinted. "Is it a boyfriend? Do you have another boyfriend you haven't told me about?" he inquired with a worried tone to his voice.

Renee gently squeezed his right hand. "No, no, it's nothin' like that. I wouldn't do that to you."

He gasped. "Whew. You had me scared there for a minute. Well, that's the worst possible thing I could come up with. So whatever it is you need to tell me, it can't be all that bad. So just spill it and get it over with, gal." He winked at her.

Renee came to a seated position and nervously wiggled her feet. After clearing her throat, she exhaled. "Okay, let's start with this. How many times, prior to today, have you been to Harpersfield?"

After he thought it over, Dillon replied, "Oh, about a dozen times over the years, I would say. I mean, there are many more conveniences in Webster being that it's a larger town than Harpersfield, so there's not much need for people in Webster to come here for anything. But my dad prefers a certain brand of crabgrass killer that the Webster feedstore doesn't carry, but the Harper Feedstore stocks it. When he'd get a spell over bein' fussy about our lawn, we'd pile up in his pickup truck to make the trip here. As far as I can recall, each time it was in and out. I don't know why he was so focused on gettin' out of town so quickly. There was one trip though when we did stop at a diner for lunch and—"

"That would be Tiny's Diner. It's the only one in town," Renee interrupted.

Dillon snapped his fingers. "Yep, that's the place! Damn, I could never remember that name, and it drove me crazy. Anyway, I remember I had a cheeseburger and fries, and Dad ate a hot dog and chips. The food was actually tasty. The root beer, I recollect, came right from the barrel on the counter. Boy, the best root beer I've ever tasted."

Renee nodded. "For a small-town diner, Tiny's would have to rank somewhere up near the top."

"Well, Dad wolfed down his lunch like I never seen him eat before or since," Dillon continued. "I mean, I only had two bites of my burger down, a single fry, and a sip of drink in me when Dad suddenly announced it was time to pay up and leave. I told him that I had only

began to eat, and he told me to gather it all and bring it with me, and I could finish eatin' durin' the drive back to Webster. I remember bein' a bit stunned 'cause I never seen him act like that way. So during the trip home, I asked him why we always leave Harpersfield so fast whenever we go there, and he told me it was none of my business, and I was always to keep it that way. Wherever that meant." Dillon shrugged his shoulders.

Again, Renee cleared her throat. "I understand what your dad meant."

Dillon's eyes widened. "You do? How would you know that? Do you know my dad?"

Renee shook her head. "Of course not."

"Then how do you know what he meant by it wasn't any of my business, and I'm always to keep it that way?"

The twitching of feet intensified as she gazed upward at the clear sky above. "Because it all ties in together with what I'm about to tell you."

Now feeling restless, Dillon stood and raised his arms parallel to his hips. "The more this progresses along, the more confused I'm becomin'. Please just come out with it."

She rose to her feet as well and then brushed a bit of debris from her clothing. She gently took hold of Dillon's left hand. "Come on, let's go for a walk, and I'll fill you in on everything."

As the couple strolled together upon the fallen leaves of autumn, Renee sought, "Dillon, tell me your view, um, outlook regardin' Harpersfield?"

"What do you mean exactly?"

Renee strived to define her inquisition a bit sharper. "Um, in your eyes, your assessment of Harpersfield?"

After a few more steps, Dillon shrugged his shoulders. "I don't know. I suppose I would say it's a small quaint town nestled among the Smoky Mountains. People of modest incomes who are easygoing and friendly. Where everyone knows everyone. A one-traffic-light town, as a metaphoric."

"We actually have two traffic lights," Renee playfully pointed out. "Well, that's if you count the flashin' yellow caution light at the intersection of Harpersfield Road and Lexington Lane."

They shared a chortle.

The mood once more returned to a more serious ambience.

"So how's my assessment of your town?"

Renee nodded. "Nearly dead-on. Yes, humble people here in Harpersfield, both financially and with modesty."

"Why do I feel a 'however' is coming down the alley?"

"Well, because that's exactly what is about to be delivered," she disclosed. "However, for generations now, a certain family here in Harpersfield has reigned their terror on this town in ways you could never imagine. Oh boy, get me started on this, and you won't believe your ears."

He cleared his throat. "You mean like a menace to the town?"

"Menace is putting it very mildly and grossly miscalculated. You see…it's…well…without a better use of words…pure evil. Vile and diabolical in a lot of ways."

"Are we talking about some sort of twisted cult here?"

Renee shook her head. "No, not exactly. It's not a large worshipping group, per se. As a matter of fact, there are very few members. But those limited participants who do fit in accomplish as much as a sizable band could ever achieve."

"So how many members are we talking here?"

"Well, the numbers have fluctuated over the years with both births and those who passed away, but the current club, if you want to put it in that context, consists of four participants. A father and his trio of sons."

Dillon was a tad confused over the report. "Are we talking that a mere four individuals are wreaking havoc over the entire town of Harpersfield? I mean, what is the total population of Harpersfield anyway?"

"The welcome sign in town states the head count at 342, but that updated sign was erected some five years ago. Although I suppose with the natural cycles of life and death, the number remains fairly in that ballpark."

Dillon computed. "So what you're telling me, what you're expecting me to believe and accept, is a group, club, or whatever they are and with simply four members are wreaking havoc and controlling an entire community of over three hundred strong? That's like 98 percent versus 2 percent. That…that just doesn't add up, Renee. Not to mention that a fraction of the 98 percent is law enforcement."

Renee ceased their pace for a moment. She slid her hand from Dillon's hand in order to rub her throbbing temples. "I know…I'm fully aware this all seems to make no sense on paper, but paper doesn't always reflect genuine life. And real life here in Harpersfield is that this town is

most certainly ruled by the vast minority, period. It isn't numbers against numbers, but rather by intimidation and carryin' out threats to the very letter. Controllin' through fear, insecurity, coercion, force, bullyin', and disregard toward human dignity and life. Extortion, blackmail, pressure, cruelty, and brutality. You mix that formula together and top it off with a heaping spoonful of nonexistent remorse of any kind, and you discover a very toxic force to be reckoned with. You see, Dillon, it's not about figures, but rather the characterization of protecting your loved ones and the self-desire to survive is what it all boils down to. Once manipulation has been created and established on a large scale, it becomes a mighty force to defeat.

"There exists a family in this town who have this all down to a science. I suppose one must reside here to utterly understand it all. Yes, exceedingly small towns have their tranquilities, but they are also exposed to possible monopolies. To control and dictate a diminutive community is a much simpler task to accomplish than regulating a greater population, especially when said party confines and restricts law enforcement as well. So this is not a paper thing, but rather, it's reality."

Dillon took hold of Renee's right hand to continue their stroll. "I stand corrected, hon. Supply me with details, gal."

Renee warmed to the sound of Dillon's reference to her as "hon." However, her temperament again turned somber. "The family's surname is Porter. Throughout generations here in town, they have run unruly and virtually control most aspects of Harpersfield. To resist the clan certainly means retaliation by the Porter family members, and the outcome is not a pretty thing for the activist or their loved ones."

"And the police force plays no role in shutting down these Porters?"

Renee shook her head. "Remember, law enforcement affiliates have family and loved ones as well. It's that threat from where the Porters generate their bullyin' and control. It's important that you recognize that the Porters' threats are real...very real. Their barkin' isn't futile. It most certainly includes a mighty, mighty bite."

Dillon interjected, "Wait. Now that we are discussin' this, it brings to mind of some 'stories'"—Dillon used his fingers to create quotation marks—"drifting around Webster about several wrongdoings going on in here in Harpersfield, but most write them off as exaggeration or even fables."

Renee raised her left palm. "You can bet they are facts. Probably most of them anyway. However, most accounts don't extend outside the borders of Harpersfield as the source or sources would fear being exposed and therefore subjected to the Porters' retaliation."

"I'm getting a clearer picture of it all now," Dillon pointed out.

Renee grinned with reservation. "I'm sure you believe that you are, but really, you have no clue of the magnitude of the situation."

"Such as?"

Renee again ceased their walk. "You're really not comprehending that these Porters are capable of committing acts that are difficult to put into context or general understanding. One must think outside the box to utterly understand their fiendish behaviors. Some beyond the borders of this town without exposure to the Porters may be quick to dismiss it all as myths or fabrications. But unless you witness it all firsthand, it's difficult to believe, and this I recognize."

"You make it sound as though they are monsters," Dillon interjected.

"Oh, was I being that easy on them?" Renee made her point with all seriousness to her voice.

Dillon gulped. "That bad?"

"Crueler."

"Holy crap," he muttered.

Renee opened her mouth, but not a word escaped from her lips. She closed and then opened her mouth again before beginning to structure her words. "But it gets even worse, Dillon. The Porters consist of three brothers and their father, Carter. The sons are Sterling, Dalton, and Murky. They range in ages from twenty to twenty-four. One in particular, Murky, the twenty-year-old, has held a torch for me for years. Of course, I want nothin' to do with him, but to say he is persistent would be an understatement. Any young man who has ever shown interest in me, even the slightest, Murky shuts him down in fashion as only a Porter can do."

Dillon slid his hand from her hold. His facial expression was one of deep concern. "What is it exactly that you're tryin' to say? Am I in any sort of danger? Should I even be here in town?"

Renee spoke softly in order to maintain somewhat of a calmness. "It's okay, Dillon. No one is goin' to see us out here in the woodlands. But

we really do need to be careful. Havin' you comin' to Harpersfield, now that I really think about it, is probably not a good idea. From now on, we'll meet in Webster exclusively."

With a bit of a frustrated tone, Dillon grumbled, "I don't know why you would place me in such a vulnerable position? I mean…I don't get it. I really thought you liked me."

Renee grabbed his forearm. "But I do like you, a lot, as a matter of fact. And that is why I…well, I acted a bit selfish over this…us. I was worried if I told you about the Porters that you wouldn't come visit me."

"That decision should have been mine to make and mine only."

Renee bowed her head. "I know, I know, and for that, I'm so sorry."

Dillon paced back and forth for a few moments before speaking up. "So what do we do now? What's the plan? Sneak me out of Harpersfield as if I'm some sort of fugitive or somethin'?"

Renee reluctantly nodded.

"Oh, this is simply great. What if this Murky or his brothers spot me durin' my getaway? Huh? What then?"

"They won't. We'll get you outta here safe and sound," she claimed with a slight uncertainty to her voice.

"No, no, let's just say I don't make it without bein' detected. That the Porters make me out durin' my escape. What then, Renee?"

She attempted to touch his shoulder, only to have him step back away from her. Renee tried to reassure Dillon, "Look, we are goin' to get you outta here in one piece. I know these woods like the back of my hand, and there is a tract we can take that will hide us in the woodland nearly the entire way to the farmhouse."

Dillon snapped his fingers. "Oh, now I get it. It's now makin' sense to me as to why you directed me to park my truck behind the barn."

"Look, this will be the one only time you will come here to Harpersfield to see me. Goin' forward, I'll come to Webster to see you."

"That is if I'm still alive!"

She adjusted her direction in the woods. "Come on, we need to go in this direction."

While Dillon began to follow her, he nervously glanced around the forest. "How far is it to my truck?"

"About fifteen minutes, if we maintain a steady pace."

When the couple arrived where the woodlands emptied into an open field, about six hundred feet of distance stood between them and Dillon's truck parked behind the barn.

"Should we make a sprint for it?" he questioned.

Renee shook her head. "No, that would make us stick out like a sore thumb. It's quite a distance from here to the road, but just the same, we could be observed by passersby. I suggest we casually walk without any briskness to it."

Dillon nodded in agreement.

"Are you ready?" she prepped.

Again, he bobbed his head. Dillon could sense that Renee was riddled with feelings of guilt. As they began to step out into the open field, he gently took her left hand into his right hand. She smiled warmly at him.

As the pair carefully made their way across the field, the Porter brothers were traveling along in Sterling's truck on a drug run to deliver the goods they had picked up in Waynesburg. The receiver and tri-county distributor of the drugs, one Doug Fentworth, was awaiting the Porters while idling in the decaying parking lot of the abandoned bowling alley.

Just as Renee and Dillon were making progress across the field hand in hand, Sterling's truck, with the Porters inside, passed the Stewart farm, and the timing couldn't have been worse. Sterling was driving while Dalton was to his right on the cab's bench seat. Murky was pinned to the passenger's door as the trio were shoulder to shoulder.

Murky drew in a gander through the passenger's window and to the Stewart property as he had often done. It was then that he witnessed Renee crossing the field with a young man he hadn't seen before. The distance was a bit too far for Murky to make out detailed facial features, but he was certain it was Renee, and the hand she held was positively a male's and not a female's. A fact that Murky was able to deduct was that the male in question was shorter in height and heavier in weight than that of Nate Stewart, Renee's brother. So if it wasn't Nate, Murky was left with but one conclusion: this mysterious fellow must be Renee's latest suitor.

"What the hell?" Murky mumbled at the truck's closed passenger window. He then shouted, "Sterling, stop the damn truck!"

Sterling looked to Murky, perplexed. "What?"

"The truck, you asshole. Halt and turn around. Now!"

"What the hell has gotten into you suddenly, Murky?! I'm not turning around. We're already running behind schedule."

"Turn around now, you motherfucker!" Murky demanded.

Sterling applied the truck's brakes, bringing the vehicle to a screeching halt upon the pavement of the road.

"Sterling, what the hell do you think you're doing? We can't be late, or Doug vacates the deal, and we are screwed out of our money!" Dalton complained. "You know how it goes. On time or lose your dime. Now, stomp on it, and let's get to the old bowling alley already. And, Murky, you shut up."

Murky, ignoring Dalton's warnings, persisted, "Turn this rig around, Sterling, or so help me, I'll slice you from ear to ear!"

Sterling began the process of pointing the truck in the opposite direction when he growled, "Stick your threat in your ass, Murky. I'm only doin' it because I'm curious about whatever it is that has your panties all in a bunch."

Dalton snickered.

"If you got somethin' to deal with, you have exactly two minutes to get it done, and we are headed back the other way. Got it?" Sterling asserted.

Dalton groaned. "If we lose this deal because of you, Murky, I'll be taking it out on your hide."

As the truck was nearing another pass by the Stewart farm, Murky instructed Sterling, "Now slow it down. Down to a crawl."

Sterling let up on the accelerator pedal and applied a bit of braking.

"Where the hell did they go?" Murky grumbled.

"Where did who go?" Dalton probed.

After determining the field was now deserted, Murky extended his left arm before Dalton and pointed toward the now-isolated ground. "There in that field a minute or two ago was Renee walking with some guy and holding his hand. I'm gonna kill that bastard."

Sterling brought the truck to a complete stop in order to closely examine the area in question. "There's not a soul out there, Murky."

"Yeah, you're just seein' shit, dude," Dalton pointed out. "You're so obsessed with that Stewart girl that your sorry excuse for a mind is messin' with you." He chuckled.

"I'm fuckin' tellin' you guys, they were there when we passed the first time," Murky insisted.

Dalton looked sternly upon Sterling. "Come, bro, and get us turned back in the right direction before Doug bails on us."

"Yep, let's go get our funds," Sterling agreed.

Behind the Stewart barn, Dillon was relieved to be crawling inside his pickup truck. "Whew, looks like we made it," he said while winking at Renee through the open driver's window. He then turned over the truck's engine.

"You be careful drivin' home," Renee bid. With that, she placed a tender kiss upon Dillon's lips. "I'll drive up to Webster to see you in a few days."

"Sounds perfect," he replied. After one last short kiss between the couple, Dillon began to make his way along the farm's lengthy driveway.

Meanwhile, some three hundred feet up the road from the Stewart farm, Sterling swung his truck off the roadway, careful to avoid a nearby ditch. After pointing the truck into their original direction, the brothers returned to their previous path with no time to spare. The instant they were in the process of gliding past the end of the Stewart driveway, Dillon, driving his pickup truck, appeared at the driveway's end where the dirt met pavement. Dillon was preparing to make a left turn onto the road, which would establish a travel in the opposite direction of the Porters' route. Dillon was completely unaware of the Porters' close proximity to him; the left turn was simply the proper course toward Webster.

Murky was quick to spot Dillon and his vehicle preparing to depart the Stewarts' driveway. By this time, Sterling had his truck up to speed when Murky barked, "There's that cocksucker leavin' Renee's place. That motherfucker is a dead man walkin'. Turn it around and follow that son of a bitch, Sterling."

Dalton swayed his head side to side. "No…no…no, and hell no. We ain't goin' through that bullshit again. Not happenin'."

"Murky, quick, get his license plate number, and we'll deal with it later," Sterling suggested.

Peering into the sideview mirror and viewing the rear of Dillon's pickup truck after Dillon pulled onto the road, Murky began to recite the plate number. "KNB 4696…KNB 4696…KNB 4696." Murky then went through the clutter inside the truck's glove compartment. "KNB 4696…KNB 4696."

In a sissified voice, Dalton mocked and teased Murky, "Mr. KNB 4696 had his dipstick inside my Renee's oil pan."

Dalton and Sterling roared with laughter.

Refusing to be agitated, Murky continued his chant. "KNB 4696… KNB 4696…KNB 4696." At last, Murky was able to get his fingers on a stub of a lead pencil with just enough of a point exposed to make it possible to write. However, the next obstacle was then discovered—something to scribble on. Murky frantically searched for scrap paper, cardboard, or any substance that could be utilized within the contents of the messy glove compartment, without success. The compartment's inventory was a pair of greasy work gloves, small tools, and a variety of insignificant screws, nuts, and bolts.

"KNB 4696…KNB 4696…KNB 4696." As a last resort, Murky turned his left hand upward to expose the palm. As he continued the chant, using the stub of the pencil, he carved the letters and numbers upon the skin of his palm. "KNB 4696…KNB 4696… KNB 4696." As Murky pressed the pencil's point into his skin, spots of blood appeared. One he was satisfied he had completed the task, Murky laid his head back against the seat's headrest.

Out of some twisted form of respect, Dalton handed a nearly empty bottle of Jack Daniel's Whiskey over to Murky. Dalton said, "Wow, bro, that was some manly shit right there. Take a gulp or two. Well-earned now. That was some Porter bravery right there, dude. Stuff like that is what separates us from the weak motherfuckers."

"Porters!" the brothers barked in unison.

With that said, Murky accepted Dalton's offer and emptied the bottle's remaining liquid with two sizeable gulps.

When all was said and done, the brothers were able to complete their rendezvous with Doug Fentworth, and a sizable profit obtained was the result.

The next day, Murky Porter made his way inside the Harpersfield Police Station. Sterling and Dalton waited outside in the parking lot. At the reception desk was fifty-eight-year-old Delores Sampson. A familiar sight, Delores had been employed at the Harpersfield Police Department since she was twenty, some thirty-eight years ago. She was a jack of all trades—secretary, dispatcher, file clerk, as well as a registered CPA who

prepared the vast majority of Harpersfield's residents' annual federal and state tax returns. Delores was married to Hank Sampson and had been for nearly thirty-four years. They had two boys, Harlen and Karl. Both sons were now adults and helped work and manage Hank's automotive repair shop, Sampson's Wrenching and Painting Automotive Garage, known by the locals as simply Sampson's, at the corner of Pine and Oak Streets on the west end of Harpersfield. Hank and Karl managed auto repair duties while Harlen was one of the most renowned auto body men in the tri-county area.

Like most families in the small town of Harpersfield over the years, the Sampson group had experienced the madness firsthand of the Porters in some form or another. To date, the Porters had robbed the Sampson shop nearly a dozen times. As with other business owners in the area, they declined to press charges in order to avoid retaliation from the evil family unit.

The Harpersfield site was their secondary shop as their main service store was now located in Waynesburg, where they now resided. Around a decade prior, Hank, Delores, and their sons moved away from Harpersfield area to Waynesburg when they had their newly built main store erected there in town in order to avoid the Porters as much as possible. Not wishing to abandon their original location altogether, the Sampsons ran the shop in Harpersfield on Tuesdays and Saturdays of each week. On those days, Hank's brother, George, handled things at the Waynesburg location. Since the drastically reduced hours of their operations in Harpersfield was established, it did help to increase auto repair business for Fred Darton's service station.

Thus, upon the appearance of a Porter at the station, Delores became immediately uneasy.

"Where's Bob?" Murky growled. "I wanna talk to Harvey now."

Delores cleared her throat. "You mean the sheriff?"

Murky sneered. "No, I mean Harvey. There's nothin' sheriff about that fat-ass coward. Now, are you goin' to go after him, or do I go fetch him?"

Delores immediately stood from her chair. "Take it easy, Murky. I'll go gather him up right away."

Murky sarcastically waved her on her way. Within a few moments, Sheriff Harvey apprehensively appeared in the lobby. He timidly nod-

ded at the unexpected visitor. "Good afternoon, Murky. What can I do for you?"

Murky moved toward the station's entrance door while waving the sheriff over to his location. By habit and instinct, Delores began to follow the sheriff. Murky then barked, "Just Harvey. For cryin' out loud, mind your own beeswax, Sampson."

Delores immediately succumbed. "Of course, Murky. I don't know what I was thinkin' after all. I have some files to attend to anyway." Delores abruptly returned to the seat at her desk.

Sheriff Harvey cautiously approached Murky. "Is something wrong, son?"

Murky glared at Bob. "Don't ever call me son. I'd fuckin' puke if you were my father."

Bob was quick to wave his right hand. "No, Murky, I wasn't implying anything at all. A figure of speech is all. No harm, no foul."

Murky then revealed his left palm to Bob. The sheriff was a bit taken aback at the sight before him. "Jesus Christ, Murky, did you carve that into your hand?"

"Two things, Bob the slob. One, never mention my name and Jesus in the same sentence. And two, who the hell do you think carved it other than me? I swear you're one stupid son of a bitch. Now, run this plate for me," Murky directed, pointing at the letters and numbers etched upon his palm.

"What's that you say?"

Murky was losing any patience he was attempting to retain. "Fuck, are you both ignorant and deaf? Run this plate number, Bobby."

Bob raised his hands before himself. "Now, wait just a minute, I can't do that. I can't run a plate for just anyone. Not for Joe Public, anyway. It's a law enforcement rule. Sorry, but that's the way the cookie crumbles."

Murky audibly exhaled. "I'm only gonna say it one more time, Harvey. Run the fuckin' plate."

Delores rose from her chair and cleared her throat. "Is everything okay over there, sheriff?"

Murky peered over Bob's left shoulder to lock eyes with Delores. "Sit your ass back down and shut the hell up," Murky directed.

A chill pumped through Delores's bloodstream as she quickly plopped down in her chair.

"As a matter of fact," Murky pursued, "just get outta here."

Needing no further encouragement, Delores shuffled off to the ladies' restroom, forcing the door closed behind her.

Murky then turned his attention back on the sheriff. "Run the goddamn plate, Harvey. Do yourself a favor and don't make the mistake of thinkin' this is a request."

Bob waved his hands in a surrendering fashion. "Of course, Murky, of course, will do. No need to get riled up. Since you chased Delores away, I don't know how to work the office system myself, so let's make our way to the radio into my office and have Frank make the plate on the patrol car's computer."

In Bob's office, with Murky leaning against the doorframe, the sheriff took hold of the CB radio's microphone. After pressing the talk button, Bob called out, "Frank, over."

"What's up, boss?" Deputy Collins responded.

"Where are you?"

"Just left Tiny's Diner. Had a late lunch. Ain't much hungry today for some reason."

Bob nodded. "That's fine. Listen, I need you to run a plate number for me."

"Well, I had plate number 3 at the diner," Frank teased. After a brief moment of radio silence, Frank attempted to recover from his feeble joke. "Oh, never mind. Go ahead, chief."

Bob then silently waved Murky to approach him. Reading from Murky's engraved palm, Bob sounded off into the microphone, "Plate number KNB 4696. That's KNB 4696."

"Tennessee?" Frank cracked back.

Bob glanced to Murky, who then nodded. "Yes, Tennessee, Frank."

"Why do you need the plate run?" Frank asked.

Bob rubbed his forehead. "It's a long story, deputy. I'll fill you in later."

Frank's typing sounds upon the computer's keyboard cracked over the radio's transmission. After inputting a bit more information in the patrol car's computer, the deputy responded, "Alrighty then, you got something handy to write with?"

The sheriff quickly swiped a pen and notepad from atop his desk. "Go ahead, Frank."

"The vehicle is registered to one William Niles, 3846 Cold Springs Road over in Webster," Frank reported.

"Let me read that back to you. William Niles, 3846 Cold Springs Road, Webster. Right?"

"You got it," the deputy confirmed.

Before Bob could muttered another word, Murky snatched the note from the sheriff's hand before marching for the station's exit.

While watching Murky push open the door, Bob mumbled to himself, "Oh boy, whatta you and your brothers up to now? Lord only knows."

*****

The Porter brothers drove to Webster that afternoon to pay Dillon a visit.

Dillon spent the following twenty-four days in the Webster hospital, the initial six days in the ICU, over the assault and beating he undertook at the hands of the Porter brothers. The severe trouncing left Dillon with several permanent scars, three missing teeth (which he eventually had replaced with partials), a busted eardrum (for which he only recovered 30 percent of hearing capabilities in his left ear), a fractured jawbone, a laceration an inch in length at the back of his neck (a result of the large ring Sterling was wearing as part of his right fist), a splintered socket of his right eye, four broken toes on his left foot (the outcome of Dalton's heavy boot stomp), a broken left forearm, bruising of the liver and kidneys, and three cracked ribs that pierced and collapsed Dillon's right lung. The doctors described it as nothing short of a miracle that patient Dillon Niles survived his serious and brutal injuries.

William and Karen Niles had discovered their son savagely beaten and unconscious in their driveway and quickly called 911. They also came across the horrific sight of their family pet, a miniature collie named Buddy, lifeless and hanging by twine from the elm tree near their garage.

In the end, the Niles family refused to press charges as they feared that any backlash from the Porters would simply be unbear-

able. Although Dillon was fully aware of whom his assailants were, he simply reported to the police that the attack was an ambush, and he didn't get a look at the aggressors.

Bob Harvey read of the attack in the local paper and chose to look the other way.

Dillon Niles ceased all future contact with Renee Stewart. She was hurt at first, believing that perhaps she had given in with sexual intercourse too soon in their developing relationship. That he had lost respect for her. The last Renee had heard about Dillon Niles was that he was now married with a baby on the way. He moved away from the immediate area shortly after the brutal beating—a ruthless attack at the hands of the Porter brothers that Renee was unaware of.

Renee wasn't certain if Dillon was even in the state of Tennessee any longer.

There was a brief period when Nate's friend, Johnnie Mercer, showed an interest in Renee. They kissed several times inside the barn, but she was not comfortable with the situation. She found Johnnie handsome and attractive, but she was eighteen, and he was only fifteen. She stopped the activity before it amounted to anything further. Johnnie stopped coming around after Nate's death. He took his best friend's demise extremely hard. She heard that Johnnie was now racing cars down in Charlotte, North Carolina. He was trying to break into the NASCAR circuit as a driver.

When Renee self-reflected, she acknowledged that she was a very sexual person. However, with Murky Porter lurking around every corner, she hadn't had many opportunities to satisfy her desires. With Dillon, it was exciting, but she wanted so much more.

*****

"Earth to my granddaughter. A penny for your thoughts," Ike teased.

Renee looked quickly from out of the truck's window over to her grandfather. "Oh, I'm sorry, Grandpa. I drifted away there for a few minutes."

He nodded. "Yeah, so I noticed. Is somethin' troublin' you, honey? If you're frightened to face Murky, we can back out of this right here and now."

She cracked a half smile. "I never like facin' the Porters, but we need to do this." She then glanced back through the now-closed rear window of the truck to view Cole looking out at the mountains. "I don't care for Cole much. He's arrogant. But I know that he's here to help, and for that, I trust him. So long as he is overlookin' the situation, I feel okay with it."

"He has to be," Ike commented.

"Huh?" she questioned.

"Cole. He must be arrogant. Have you tried thinkin' about what his life must be like?"

She bit down on her lip and shook her head no.

"Renee, I've raised you better than that. Never judge without wearin' the accused boots. This man, Cole, faces the country's worst hardened criminals year after year. He probably sees more death and cruelty in one year than we will see in a lifetime."

She hadn't considered his demanding lifestyle before. "Well, he chose to live that way," she pointed out.

Ike nodded. "That's true, but remember, he serves us. Cole, and agents like him, do their best to rid America of its offenders."

She rolled her eyes. "God, Grandpa. You make it sound as though he's a superhero or somethin'."

"In a sense, he is," Ike retorted.

"Well, it doesn't mean that I have to like him."

Ike took his eyes off the road for a momentarily to glance at her. "Try lookin' at the world in a softer light."

She stared at him for a second before turning her eyes back out the window.

Ike shifted his eyes back on the road ahead of them. "Lucy Nichols," Ike grunted.

"What are you talkin' about now, Grandpa? Who is she?"

"Lucy was a gal I went to school with."

Renee delivered a lopsided expression in Ike's direction. "You only went to school until the eighth grade."

"That might be so, but I went to school with Lucy just the same."

"Well, okay…but what does that have to do with anythin'?"

Ike pushed a pinch of tobacco into his cheek. "Lucy was a pretty girl. She had dark hair, about the color of yours, and it was naturally curly. All the boys teased her, but it was because deep down, they really fancied her. We all would have traded our favorite baseball cards in exchange for a kiss from Lucy, but of course, we buddies weren't about to admit that to each other. There was a boy in our class. His name was Homer Miller—"

She interrupted, "Homer? That poor kid with a name as such."

"That was sort of a popular name back then. Anyway, Homer always had a thing for Lucy, more than the rest of us did, and he wasn't ashamed to show it. He'd carry her books for her, give her his puddin' at lunchtime, and hold her shoes for her while she twirled around on the monkey bars during recess. Of course, I'd try to get a look up her skirt while she was suspended from the bars." He chuckled.

"Grandpa!" Renee scolded and shook her head.

He cleared his throat. "But as much as he tried, Homer couldn't gain Lucy's interest whatsoever, not in the way he hoped for anyway. She liked another boy named Wesley Burns. Wesley was a recluse. He always sat in the back of the class by himself, but for some reason, Lucy took a hankerin' for him."

"Is this going somewhere, Grandpa?" she inquired with a sigh.

He nodded before spitting a ball of tobacco juice out the truck's window. "As much as Lucy tried, she couldn't gain Wesley's interest, not in the way she hoped for anyway. So do you see now?"

Renee looked at him completely baffled and shook her head.

"If it's there between a man and a woman, if it's meant to be, it doesn't need to be forced. It will just come naturally. Homer didn't end up with Lucy, and Lucy didn't end up with Wesley. It was a crazy, mixed-up situation. They would have to wait until later in life before they would have a chance to find the one that was truly meant for each of them."

"I suppose that you are now goin' to tell me that Homer, Lucy, and Wesley found their soul mates one day and lived happily ever after?" she forecasted with a bit of sarcasm.

He shrugged his shoulders. "I wouldn't know, I never saw them again after the eighth grade."

Renee rubbed her temples. "Sometimes, you're a silly man, Grandpa."

They both chuckled.

CHAPTER 20

THE PORTER BOYS jumped from atop the feedstore's dock to begin a walk across the street in unison.

"Damn, I'm stoned," Dalton announced. "Where did this shit come from, Sterling?"

Sterling glowed proudly. "I have my connections."

Dalton chortled and then began to outright laugh while trying to control his outburst with little success.

"Dalton, act right, dignified. Not like a stupid monkey," Murky warned. He possessed low tolerance for silly antics.

"Lighten up, Murky," Sterling stated.

Murky extended his middle finger up at Sterling. They then stepped up onto the sidewalk.

"Let's get a burger at Tiny's," Sterling suggested.

Outside the entranceway of the diner stood two plexiglass-enclosed pay-for newspaper boxes standing side by side, complete with coin slots. The left-side booth contained the daily edition of the local paper, the *Waynesburg Gazette*. The front-page article was titled "Local Farmers Hoping for More Rainfall." The stand to the right displayed the weekly version of the *USA Today* newspaper headlined with "Missing Hikers—14 Months of More Questions Than

Answers" and "Senator's Daughter Remains AWOL." Positioned above the headline was a photograph of a couple holding hands. It was a white woman and a Hispanic Mexican male, both appearing to be in their later twenties. The small print below the photograph read, "Hikers Heidi Solare and Manning Gomez."

The adventurous couple had gone missing two months prior to the murder of Nathan Stewart.

The Porter bothers scanned the *USA Today* headline through the plexiglass.

Murky scratched his head in a mocking state of confusion. "I wonder what happened to them?"

The brothers chuckled in unison.

"No mixed-race bullshit in these parts—not in our town. No can do," Sterling casually commented before pulling open the diner's entrance door.

*****

It was a mild warm April day in the lower Tennessee Valley. Twenty-six-year-old Heidi Solare and Manning Gomez had just emerged from heavy woodland just north of Webster, Tennessee, on a leg of their planned four-month-long hiking adventure across the southern United States. They were still in the early stages of their venture after completing southern Kentucky and northern Tennessee. Their efforts initiated in Wheeling, West Virginia, with their final destination being that of Saint George, Georgia, the southernmost tip of the peach state before the Florida border. The entire trek was estimated to be a span ranging from March 30 through July 22.

The couple had just wrapped up a three-day hike and camp within the tall timber of the Tennessee Southern Valley. Their next move was to hitch a ride to the nearest town for a single night's stay in a motel before continuing on the following morning with the next phase of their journey, which would find them entering the northern regions of North Carolina.

As they stationed themselves upon the loose gravel of the road's shoulder, Heidi gave Manning a kiss of good fortune before they extended their right thumbs in hopes of obtaining a ride. Both hikers were weighed down with heavy backpacks and in need of a restful night's sleep.

Heidi was an attractive young woman with natural blond hair she wore at shoulder length. Her blue eyes sank into her puffy cheekbones, and her lips were slim. Her build was solid but not stocky.

Manning was average in height and kept his full head of hair in a short buzz cut. His body was lean, but muscular. His root beer—brown eyes sat on either side of his nose, which tapered at the top. Typically, his face was clean-shaven, but not wanting to be hassled with the daily razoring upon his jaws during the couple's hiking adventure, he allowed the growth of a mustache and beard. Together, they made a fine-looking couple who was planning to get married in less than six months in the near future.

Less than four miles north of the couple's location, Sterling Porter steered his pickup truck into a Speedway Service Station some seventy miles southwest of Knoxville and headed in the direction of Webster. The brothers were trekking their way home after rounding up a supply of drugs from supplier Jed Weaver.

The truck pulled up to one of the available fuel pumps. After placing the vehicle in the parking gear and shutting down the engine, Sterling looked to his brothers in the cab of the vehicle. "We need to get gas in a can to ignite the trash pile at home. Pop has been on our backs to get it done."

From the middle position of the truck's bench seat, Dalton peered back through the truck's rear window to the bed of the truck. After scanning the truck's bed, he snarled, "Well, where is the gas can, bro?"

Sterling then gazed back at the truck's bed before snarling back, "Fuck, motherfucker! I forgot to bring the can!"

"You moron," Dalton groaned.

Murky, from the right passenger's seat, rolled his eyes and then waved his right hand toward the station's store. "Just go inside and buy a gas can, and then we'll fill it up, you stupid degenerates."

Sterling raised his left forefinger. "Oh yeah, we can do that."

Murky rolled his eyes. "At times it's a downright shame to claim you two as blood."

In unison, Sterling and Dalton glared up at Murky with disdain. Murky, realizing he might have pushed the envelope a bit too far, retracted. "Oh sure, get all pissed off at me now. The one who has your back no matter what. I was just soundin' off was all."

Sterling and Dalton eased, but merely a bit.

Murky squinted his eyes. "Now, don't make me go about hurtin' you and hurtin' you bad."

In harmony, the brothers traded high fives before Sterling made his way to the station's store to purchase a gas can.

Soon, Sterling returned with an acquired ten-gallon-capacity container and promptly filled it with fuel before sliding the vessel along the bed of the truck. The brothers then continued the travel on their return to Harpersfield.

"We'll grab a ride soon, babe," Heidi reassured Manning as very few vehicles continued to pass by their roadside perch.

Manning nodded with little confidence. "I hope so, honey. I'm all about out of stamina. I need a soft bed rather than the hard forest floor of our tent."

Heidi extended her right thumb to a passing vehicle as she retorted, "The comfy mattress is coming up soon, my love. Merely a compassionate commuter away is all. Hang in there."

After over a half dozen or so passing motorists failed to offer the couple a ride, an incoming pickup truck loaded with the Porter brothers was on its approach.

"Look, a fuckin' Mexican and his white bitch up ahead tryin' to hitch a ride," Murky pointed out. "I say run over the spic and his bitch."

Sterling nodded but then offered, "I got even a better idea. Let's give them a ride."

Dalton's eyes widened. "I like Murky's idea better. Don't give that wetback and his sorry excuse of a white cunt a lift."

"Ah, but we give them a ride to where we want to take them and not where they want to go." Sterling winked.

Murky growled his approval. "Let's do this."

Sterling eased the truck's accelerator as the rig approached the hitchhiking pair.

Noticing the approaching vehicle dropping in speed, Heidi celebrated, "Here it comes, Manning. Our transportation to a soft bed."

"Hallelujah!" Manning was pleased.

Sterling edged past the couple before braking the truck to a complete stop on the shoulder of Route 86 South.

Heidi and Manning jogged some twenty yards to meet up with the idling vehicle and its kind occupants offering them a lift. Heidi approached the open passenger's window where Murky was stationed. She explained, "We're heading to the next town, Webster. I think a sign a little way back displayed the town as six miles from here."

Without looking directly at her, Murky nodded. "That's on our way. Hop in the bed of the truck."

"Thank you so much," Heidi extended her right hand to Murky. He made no movement to exchange in a handshake with her. She then lowered her extended hand and shrugged her shoulders.

Peering over Heidi's left shoulder from behind her, Manning bid, "Thanks, gentlemen. Greatly appreciated indeed."

Manning Gomez was born and raised in Lansing, Michigan, three years after his parents legally migrated from Mexico. Although he spoke Spanish as well as English, the latter was his fluent language. Manning was as much American as any of the brothers inside the cab of the truck.

Wanting to entice the couple to board his pickup truck, Sterling indicated, "No problem at all. We're headed that way anyway. So it's not like we're goin' out of our way. Hop on in the bed, and we'll be in Webster in about ten minutes or so."

Eager to seek some of the comforts associated with proper bedding and a warm meal, Heidi and Manning tossed their heavy backpacks into the bed of Sterling's truck, followed by climbing on board themselves.

Widening his eyes slightly, Manning commented to Heidi, "Man, those are some awfully big dudes."

She nodded in agreement. "That they are."

Sterling accelerated his vehicle back on the rural route. Once up to speed, he looked to his brothers in the cab of the truck. With the rear window slid closed, their passengers could not hear them.

Sterling suggested, "I say we take the spic and his white bitch out to Elder's Pond."

Dalton nodded. "I know what you're thinkin', bro. The middle of nowhere."

"Yep," Sterling confirmed.

Within another passing mile upon the roadway of Route 86 South, Sterling veered his truck from the main thoroughfare to continue south upon the rustic Martin's Way.

Noticing the sudden change in direction and scenery, Manning consulted with Heidi. "Hey, honey, this doesn't seem to be the direction to that town of Webster. Why did they make that turn?"

"Um, good question, babe. Let me see what's up," Heidi conveyed. She lightly rapped on the truck's rear window.

Without turning his head in her direction, Dalton reached his right hand over his left shoulder to slide the rear window open.

Heidi spoke into the slot of the now-open window. "Hey, guys, what's up? Why are we going in this direction?"

Again, without bothering to turn his head while staring straight ahead, Dalton reassured, "Yep, this is another way to Webster, a faster direction, a shortcut. We'll be there in no time." With that simply said, Dalton slid the window closed.

"I'm not liking this at all, Heidi." Manning sounded a bit worried. "Something's just not right."

After a long moment of quietly assessing the situation, she assumed, "Oh, I think we are overly exhausted and being a bit paranoid. Look, these locals know the back roads like no one else ever could imagine. I'm sure, as with the vast majority of southern people and their generous hospitality, these gentlemen are merely getting us to our destination as quickly as possible."

Not completely convinced, Manning suggested, "Hey, we're close enough to town now that we could foot it from here. Let them know we're ready to be dropped off. Even offer them a twenty for gas and their trouble."

Sensing Manning's increasing uneasiness, Heidi agreed. "Okay, will do, babe. We can make it on our own from here." Again, Heidi knocked on the rear window.

On this occasion, Murky reached over Dalton's right shoulder, and while turning his head to make eye contact with Heidi, the youngest Porter brother slid the rear window open. "What?" he snarled.

"Uh, look, guys. My fiancé and I are fine at this point. Another hour or so of daylight left, so we can make our way to Webster from

here, no problem. We appreciate the lift and plan on giving you some gas money. So if you'd be so kind to pull on over, we'll head on our way."

Murky grinned. "Sure, no problem at all. Thanks for the gas money, but not needed. A stop sign is just up ahead, and we'll let you off there. You all have a great evening now." He nodded before sliding the window closed.

Heidi then relaxed as she looked to Manning. "Yep, we are both exhausted beyond reasoning. I'm thinking we need to stay in the motel for two nights to fully rest up and get our senses right."

"Yep, I agree," Manning agreed and peacefully surrendered.

As Sterling's vehicle approached an upcoming stop sign, Heidi and Manning refitted their packs to their backs, but not before Manning needed to slightly move about a filled gasoline can snagging a strap of his gear. Heidi brushed off a bit of rusted dust her pants had collected while she rested against a coiled old chain. The couple prepared to depart the pickup truck's bed as the stop sign neared.

"Shouldn't he be slowing down?" Manning assessed.

As the stop sign distance closed, Sterling accelerated the vehicle, speeding through the desolate intersection.

"What the hell is he doing?" Heidi fretted.

Manning swallowed hard. "Um, this isn't good, honey. Use your cell phone to call 911."

She fumbled through her backpack before finally locating her cell phone. She powered up the phone, only to discover they were currently out of range to gain any reception.

"What is it?" Manning tensely inquired.

"No signal," she regrettably reported.

Manning, in a panic, suggested, "Then we make a jump for it."

Her eyes widened. "Think about it, Manning. We're traveling over seventy miles per hour. It'd be suicide."

"Well, then what?"

Heidi, after several moments in thought, said grimly, "We'll just wait it out to wherever they are taking us. Upon arrival, we'll try to negotiate or even escape. Nothing much else we can do at this point."

Manning tapped the outside of his left thigh with his palm. "What the hell is it they could want from us?"

"Money, I would suppose."

Manning recommended, "Perhaps we could flag down any passing motorists.

"Look around you, babe. Not another vehicle in sight. We're on a side road out in the sticks."

Just then, Sterling's truck abruptly left the paved roadway and into an open field. The ride became extremely bumpy and jarring. The hitchhikers were bounced around the bed of the truck as they attempted to grab hold of the bed's side to support their uncontrolled movements. One large jolt slammed Manning's forehead into the truck's wheel well, nearly rendering him unconscious.

After a lengthy and turbulent journey, Sterling finally brought the vehicle to a sudden stop.

The hitchhikers were attempting to gather their senses as the Porter brothers climbed from the cab of the truck. Dalton reached behind the bench seat of the cab to retrieve a 30.06 loaded hunting rifle complete with a high-powered scope. Sterling reached for his .357 magnum handgun from the rear side of his belt. Murky joined his brothers to the tail end of the truck.

Waving his firearm and then lowering the bed's tailgate, Sterling ordered the frightened couple out from the truck.

Reluctantly, Heidi and Manning complied while sliding off the now-open tailgate. Standing in confusion, Heidi questioned, "What is it you want from us? We have a bit of cash on us, but not much. Perhaps sixty or seventy bucks, but it's all yours if you'll just let us on our way."

Murky squinted. "Don't need your spare change. That's merely morsels to us. No, what we seek money can't buy."

"What then?" she inquired apprehensively.

Murky folded his strong arms. "So, you two, you a couple?"

Through a shaken voice of fear, Heidi jerked her head in confirmation. "A little over three years now."

Murky spat upon the ground near her hiking boots. "So tell me why, bitch? Why ya fuckin' a spic?"

"Please desist from using that ugly word," she requested.

Murky glared at her. "No? Well then, how about wetback?"

She quickly became aware that they were in extreme danger. "Look…um…my dad is an especially important man in a high posi-

tion. If something were to happen to me...us...he'll utilize every resource available to him to track down those responsible."

Heidi's father was US Senator Hal Solare from the state of Michigan. The Porter brothers took no concern over her enlightening warning.

Dalton then nodded at Heidi. "You always do the talkin'? Your Mexican boy there, henpecked and pussy whipped, is he now?"

Sterling and Murky chuckled.

She squinted. "Manning is free to speak if he wishes to do so."

Obviously anxious and uneasy, Manning didn't utter a single word.

Murky then began to pace in a circular motion around the standing couple. "Typically, bitch, me and my brothers would be havin' a rodeo while riding your pretty ass. But we ain't gonna be rammin' our cocks into that spic dick–polluted pussy of yours."

Although intimidated and uneasy, Heidi, believing she was simply dealing with criminal wannabes for which she couldn't be more mistaken, blurted out, "Okay, what's it gonna be, guys? This is getting old. Just take our cash and let us move on already."

Murky ceased his pacing and glared at her. "Not that simple, white trash. You brought this wetback onto our turf. So now, as natives of this area, we need to wash the germ away from our hands. You see, any white gal who screws a wetback is a spic herself."

It was now apparent to Heidi that she had extremely underestimated the brutality of the men standing before her, and any recovery was all but impossible at this juncture.

"Um...let's...talk this over." She stumbled over her words. "Look, you...just let us go, and not a word shall ever be spoken about this incident. Right, Manning?" She desperately looked to her fiancé.

He eagerly nodded in agreement.

Murky crouched down and mischievously grinned. "Not all simply that brown and white, with pun intended. Nope, we let you go on your way, and who knows how many more spics will want a free hall pass here in our town?"

Sensing that situation was escalating out of control, Manning reached into his pants' right-side compartment and pulled out a small pocketknife. He quickly slid the three-inch blade open and began to wave it about.

Not set back by any means, the brothers chuckled in unison.

"What the hell ya gonna do with that?" Sterling insulted.

Murky nodded. "Go fetch a real blade, Sterling."

The older brother paced to the truck's cab and stretched his left arm beneath the driver's seat to obtain an encased dagger. He gripped the weapon in his right hand as he pinned the handgun under his right armpit. He then handed the holstered blade over to Murky.

Slowly and meticulously, Murky slid the ultra-sharp double-edged ten-inch blade from its leather casing. "Now, this a stiletto, brown boy. A blade so sharp it reflects sunlight. But…I'll tell ya what I'll do. We'll trade knives, with me taking your pathetic excuse of a pocketknife and arm you with this fine specimen right here. If you win the match, you both can walk free. It's not up for negotiation. All or nothing. So hand me your sorry-ass pocketknife, and here's the blade of wet dreams for you."

Sensing no choice in the matter, Manning nervously exchanged weapons with Murky.

"This is absurd," Heidi complained with a renewed spell of boldness. "This bullshit needs to stop right here and now. Come on, Manning, we're getting the hell out of this foul situation. Appreciate the ride, guys, but daylight is waning, and we need to hike to town to get a room for the night. Go play your twisted games elsewhere and with other unfortunate participants. Our tenure of being your puppets has come to its conclusion. If you have a problem with that, too damn bad."

Sterling sarcastically grinned. "Nice try, bitch. But not good enough."

Heidi placed her hands on her hips. "Is that right now? You don't have the balls, punks. I've got your badge of fake courage in my back pocket. What the hell do you think you're going to do, kill us?" She scoffed.

Sterling meticulously raised his handgun with careful aim between Heidi's eyes. He then squeezed the trigger.

The bullet struck Heidi's forehead with a violent jerk of her neck with blood and brain matter splattering throughout the immediate area, killing her instantly. Heidi's lifeless body folded to the ground below.

Sterling's coldly responded with just one word. "Yes."

"Good shot, Sterling," Dalton approved. "That spic-fuckin' bitch was gettin' on my nerves."

Manning was wide-eyed with shock as he had just witnessed the sudden slaying of his fiancée.

Murky, calmly and callously, nodded toward Heidi's collapsed body. "See that there, brown boy? Huh, wetback? That's what happens when you don't do as the Porters say."

Manning was completely beside himself, as if this were all some horrendous nightmare, and he wanted so badly to wake up.

"So, upfront and true to a Porter's word," Murky projected, "you and me, we have us a knife fight, Mannin', slicin' you up is what I'm plannin'. And if by some damn miracle you champion over me, well, my brothers here will let you walk free."

Manning swallowed hard. "And if I refuse to spar with you?"

Again, Murky nodded at Heidi's lifeless body.

Manning, still numb with trying to absorb Heidi's demise, looked to Dalton and Sterling. "Do I have your word on it?"

Dalton shrugged his shoulders. "Well, you don't have much goin' for you right now. But yeah, our word is solid. You win, you walk. But in that pea brain of yours if you think for a moment if you have a prayer against a Porter, well...let's just say I wouldn't want to be ya."

Glancing upon his fallen fiancée once again, anger began to over-take his fear. Here he was, now armed with the sharpest, longest, and most fierce-looking stainless-steel edge he had ever held in his hands. And his foe only possessed a three-inch blade of a Boy Scout–issued pocketknife.

With newly found confidence, along with a burning desire for revenge, Manning positioned the large dagger before himself while point-ing the blade in Murky's direction. "Let's do this, you cracker hillbilly. This Mexican American is going to slice your white punk ass up!"

Murky smirked while looking to his siblings. "A spic thinkin' a taco is the prize."

Sterling and Dalton chuckled.

Murky then bid to Manning, "I'll give the first three stabs before I even raise this sorry excuse for a knife. Ready now, are ya, wetback?"

Without hesitation, Manning rushed toward Murky. Raising his right hand brandished with the sharp dagger, he took a sweeping slash at Murky's facial area. Murky quickly stepped aside while sliding the toe of his left boot before Manning's left hiking boot. Murky's opponent tripped and stumbled before tumbling to the ground, nearly administering a self-inflicted stab wound to his stomach in the process.

Sterling and Dalton chortled.

Murky mockingly shook his head. "Just like any stupid spic. Gotta mind your own weapon, shithead. That's one free stab. Now, get your lazy ass up."

Manning slowly rose to his feet. He turned to face Murky. "I got you this time, you Tennessee hillbilly."

Murky extended his arms at his hips. "Bring it on, brown boy."

Manning, more determined than ever, again rushed his adversary. During this attack, Manning used the tactic of trading the dagger between his left and right hands, attempting to confuse Murky.

The Porter man displayed not even an ounce of concern as his rival closed the distance between them. Manning seized the opportunity to take a straight-lined plunge with the dagger aimed at his challenger's upper torso. With the point of the sharp blade inches away from penetrating Murky's chest cavity, Murky raised his left forearm while maintaining the open blade of the pocketknife pointed downward his right palm. Manning's forehead came crashing into Murky's thick and mighty arm before the blade could reach his foe's physique. Manning's head snapped back before he careened to the left of Murky's stance and crashed into a small mound of brush.

"That was free stab number two, shithead. One to go," Murky tallied. "Better make it your best shot. After it, I'm footloose and fancy-free, motherfucker. You'll be pushing up daises with your white bitch."

As Manning struggled to his feet with blood seeping from his lower lip, Murky added, "You Mexicans screwin' white pussy irks the hell out of me. But in some ways, I get it. I mean, if even I was a brown dude, I wouldn't want to screw any spic cunt. Not only are they fat, ugly, and stinky, they nag, nag, and nag. Who would want to stick their dick in that?"

Dalton and Sterling snickered.

Finally arriving at a full stand with shaky knees and a bleeding lip, Manning pledged, "I'm going to kill you, mountain boy."

Murky mischievously grinned. "Not today, brown boy. Not only am I going to cut your heart out, I'm also gonna track down your mama for a blow job and cum in her bucktoothed mouth."

Enraged, Manning roared a growl and charged at Murky at a full dive. His third attempt with the sharp blade did make contact, but

merely a shallow cut upon Murky's left outer thigh, hardly deep enough to cause spotting of blood.

Murky shoved Manning's body to the right. Manning again lost his footing while crumbling to the earth.

Simultaneously, Dalton and Sterling each raised three fingers of their right hands.

Murky lifted his right hand grasping the opened pocketknife. "That's three and out, Mannin', with piss-poor plannin'. It's now a free-for-all. Get your black ass up off the ground, and let's rumble, motherfucker."

Manning—exhausted, enraged, vengeful, and believing he maintained the advantage with his superior weapon—rose to his feet with poise. He brushed away a few loose brush endings from his shirt before glaring at Murky. Waving the dagger in his right hand and through tears of anger, Manning growled, "Heidi and I were going to get married in September. I love her, man. I love her. But no…no…you all just stole that away from us. We were going to settle down after this long hike and have a couple of kids. Buy a house, a new vehicle or two, and Heidi planned to be a member of the local PTA. All gone in a moment at the hands of punks like you!"

Murky shook his head. "You spics never stop complainin'. Screw your own race, Mexican, and leave ours be."

Manning roared as he attacked Murky. "I'm so going to kill you!" He took a swinging whack with the large dagger aimed at Murky.

The Porter brother ducked away from the swipe and then trapped Manning's right forearm beneath his right upper arm. The long-bladed dagger dangled in Manning's hand for several moments before tumbling to the ground below. Murky then forcefully headbutted Manning, forehead to forehead. The mighty blow and nearly knocked Manning unconscious.

Murky then released his captor's arm, allowing Manning to drop to his knees. Murky then strode over to the fallen dagger and grasped it in his right hand. Maneuvering to face his opponent who was still on his knees, Murky stood before Manning. "You had me the entire fight, you stupid ass. You see, I gave you three free stabs. I made certain to say stab, and that locked you in on that. But all you merely had to do was…" Murky traded the dagger's grip in his right palm with the blade itself. He then reared back his right hand to his shoulder. "Throw it."

Murky then released the coiled tension of his right arm, slinging the dagger into a perfect tumble into Manning's direction. The sharp double-edged blade embedded deep inside of the Manning's chest.

Manning swayed, coughed up a spew of blood, and then collapsed face-first upon the field's grass. After one final twitch, Manning's life withdrew from his battered body.

Without regret, remorse, or shame, Murky approached Manning's corpse to dislodge the dagger from his chest.

"Cool shit," Dalton praised.

As Murky wiped clean the fresh blood on the knife's blade onto Manning's shirt, he inquired, "What do we do with the bodies, bros?"

"Let's just toss them into Elder's Pond," Dalton suggested.

Sterling shook his head. "Nope, they would surface after a few days."

Dalton understood and then offered, "We'll bury them."

Murky rolled his eyes. "Dalton, do you ever listen to yourself? You see any shovels or a backhoe? Fuck no, you don't."

"Don't push it any further, Murky," Dalton snarled.

In the fading light of the forthcoming sunset, Sterling glanced at the filled five-gallon gas can in the bed of his truck. He nodded. "We burn them."

Murky agreed. "Fuckin' A."

Dalton then added, "And dump their charred asses in Elder's old house well."

"Now you're thinking, Dalton." Murky winked.

Dalton beamed.

Sterling further planned, "Okay, we pile up their bodies near the pond's edge on the bare clay so we don't start a brush fire. After they're charred, we'll throw them in the back of the truck and then over to the old well. Ain't nobody had any business with that old hole in the ground for years now. We push back the lid, dump the bitch and spic deep into the well, before sliding the lid back over and then getting the hell out of here."

"Let's do it," Murky and Dalton sounded off in unison.

After working together to move the deceased bodies of Heidi Solare and Manning Gomez to the pond's edge, Sterling unscrewed the cap of the five-gallon gas can before pouring and saturating the bodies with the flammable liquid. After the final drops of the fuel fell upon the victims,

Sterling directed, "Okay, boys, step on back. This is going to get wicked, and wicked fast."

Dalton and Murky stepped away from the pond's shore. Sterling searched about for anything ignitable. He then spotted a dried-up pine-cone. Taking the fir tree's long-ago dropping into his left hand, Sterling touched the open flame of his cigarette lighter to a single fin of the pine-cone. After a flame to the ignitor commenced, Sterling heaved the blazing cone upon the saturated figures. After a massive initial swoosh of flames, the targeted sources settled into a steady burn.

Well into the darkness of night, the brothers slid the charred remains of Heidi and Manning into the bed of Sterling's truck. At the sight of the well, the trio encountered an ordeal. Some twenty years prior, county engineers had positioned a thick concrete lid on the old well to prevent access to the pit deep in the earth from any accidental mishap from children visiting the now state park area. This was temporary as the final plan was to collapse the old well and fill it with soil to eliminate any remaining depth. However, over the decades of exchanged elected officials and budget issues, a conclusion to the issue was never achieved.

As strong as the Porter brothers were, even in unison, they could not budge the four-foot-thick concrete lid on the old well. After a thought process, the siblings executed a plan to uncoil the heavy linked chain in the bed of Sterling's truck to attach to the well's covering to the trailer hitch of the vehicle. After some maneuvering, they succeeded in moving the thick slab of cement a sufficient distance in order to dump the scorched remains of Heidi and Manning into the abyss of the deep well. In the same manner, they replaced the lid to its former position.

CHAPTER 21

THE PORTER TRIO strode inside Tiny's Diner. The owner of the diner, fifty-four-year-old Jim "Tiny" Tinelberg, was sorry to see the brothers enter. They rarely paid for their meals, and other patrons would usually depart quickly after the Porters' entrance into the eatery. It was obvious to Tiny that the boys were under the influence of drugs, which made things even worse. Jim figured he was at least a bit fortunate on this day. The boys' visit was between lunch and dinnertime rather than during a peak period. The only other customer at the moment was seated at the counter, sipping on a cup of coffee (which was secretly spiked with rum).

Mason Turner quickly lowered his cup of coffee down on the countertop and headed for the door of the diner. Before he could make his way to the door, Sterling grabbed hold of the collar of Mason's shirt. "Hey there, Turner. What's your hurry?"

Mason nervously fidgeted.

"It seems someone robbed your friend, Fred Darton. You know, Harpersfield used to be a quiet town. Now there are maniacs runnin' about." Sterling sarcastically winked.

Dalton chuckled. Murky grinned.

"Who do you suppose robbed Darton and his worthless boy?" Dalton asked.

Mason trembled as he shrugged his shoulders. Whether it be Tiny's Diner, Darton's Station, or Joe's Tavern, poor Mason Turner could not catch a break from the wrath of the Porter family.

Tiny placed his hands on his hips from behind the counter. "You boys let Mason be. He's not doin' anything to you."

"Shut the hell up, Tiny," Murky cautioned.

Jim Tinelberg's wife, Pam, sauntered from the kitchen to behind the counter and stood next to her husband. She glanced nervously at Jim. If there were such a thing as a saint in Harpersfield, this would be Pam Tinelberg. Pam, even at fifty-one, was still an active woman in the small community. Her once solid brown hair was now sprayed with sections of gray, making her appear a bit older than she was. She wore a gold cross around her neck, and she could be seen around town at times toting a Bible. She taught Sunday school services at the local church and had done so for nearly thirty years. If the Porter brothers did possess a soft spot, and it most certainly was not overly tender, they would give Pam a tad of respect, at times, with a little more regard than how they treated any of the other folks in town.

Pam was the one who fed them when food was scarce at their home. When the Porter brothers were growing up, there were times when their father would go on drinking binges and their mother just stayed in bed. The cupboards and refrigerator eventually ran themselves dry. A young Murky, Dalton, and Sterling would ride their bikes into town and stumble into Tiny's Diner. Pam, against her husband's wishes, would feed the boys, sometimes for days at a time.

Pam cleared her throat, and in a soothing voice, she requested, "Murky, Dalton, and Sterling. Please let Mason be. He's not doin' well. The doctor says that his blood pressure is really high."

"Cool," Dalton responded to the information. "Let's see if we can get Mason's heart to explode."

"Yeah," Sterling eagerly agreed.

Murky glanced over to Pam. She formed and moved her lips with a silent, "Please." He firmly shook his head no. Pam, disap-

pointed, moved back to the kitchen so that she wouldn't have to witness what was about to take place.

Dalton then landed a hard punch into Mason's chest. Mason buckled over in pain.

"Is it still beatin'?" Murky asked sarcastically, inquiring about Mason's heart.

"I think so," Dalton reported.

"Here, let me give it a shot," Murky offered.

Dalton stepped aside.

Murky grabbed Mason's hair and stood the old man upright. He then delivered a heavy left fist near the area that Dalton had just struck. The blow sent Mason back a few steps.

"Enough!" Tiny shouted.

"Shut up, Tiny, or you're next," Sterling warned, pointing at Jim.

"Bessy, this is Pam Tinelberg," Pam announced into the telephone's receiver. "Your boys are here at the diner, and they're out of control. They are harmin' Mason Turner badly."

Bessy sipped on her can of beer while standing next to the kitchen table inside the Porter's home. "Well, what the hell do you want me to do about it, Pam?"

"If I put one of them on the phone, will you tell them to stop?"

"They ain't gonna to listen to me," Bessy assured.

"For the love of God, Bessy, at least try," Pam pleaded.

"Fine…put one of em' on," Bessy growled.

Pam marched the cordless receiver out to the counter. The first of the boys that she spotted was Sterling. "Sterling, you're wanted on the phone," Pam proclaimed.

Sterling turned his attention from Mason's beating and glared with confusion at Pam. "For me?" He pointed to himself. She nodded while holding out the receiver into his direction. Sterling approached the counter and snatched the receiver from Pam's hand. He lifted the handset to his ear. "What?"

"Sterling?" Bessy inquired.

He rolled his eyes. "What do you want, Ma?"

"Whatever it is that you boys are doin', stop it," she half-heartedly directed.

"No can do, Ma. We're havin' some fun with Mason Turner."

"Now, you boys be nice," Bessy requested.

"Yeah, sure, Ma," Sterling snickered before setting the receiver down on the countertop. He then returned to the mischievous cruel actions along with his siblings.

Pam picked up the receiver. "Bessy?"

"I did what I could do. Now leave me alone. And don't call the cops on them boys. They'll get ya back if you do, and it'll get ugly," Bessy cautioned before ending the call.

"Oh, look…Mason's spittin' up some blood. Cool!" Dalton pointed out.

Sterling clapped his hands together and then shouted, "Fuckin' A!"

"Come on, Mason. One more should give ya that heart attack." Murky smirked as he moved toward Mason.

Pam's eyes widened as she caught a glimpse of Tiny eyeing a wooden box on a shelf behind the counter. Inside the box was a loaded handgun he kept in case of a robbery attempt on the diner. He had never needed to resort to using the handgun, but this could be a situation that called for extreme action.

"No, Jim!" Pam snapped. She came to realize that this incident was about to escalate out of hand, and someone may become seriously injured—or worse. She felt she must put a stop to it now.

She moved quickly from behind the counter and positioned herself in between Mason and the Porter brothers. She extended the palm of her right hand out to the brothers. "Stop! That's enough! You're gonna kill him, for Christ sakes!" Pam trembled in fear, as it was a known fact that the Porter boys showed no mercy to anyone.

An awkward silence filled the diner as the trio glared at Pam. Tiny made a quiet step nearer to the small wooden box. Mason collapsed into a chair at a nearby table.

Pam attempted to reach the threesome any way that she could muster at that moment. "Remember when I used to feed you boys when no one else would?" The Porters then looked to one another. She continued her effort to tap into any compassion that may still be

within the brothers. "Dalton, you used to always ask for crackers and grape jelly. Ritz Crackers, never saltines," she recalled.

Dalton grinned as he recollected.

"And you, Sterling. You enjoyed salami sandwiches, fried on the stove, crispy and greasy, but not burned," she pleaded. Sterling favored the way the fat from the fried salami saturated the bread.

She then turned her attention to Murky. "And for you, Murky, it was peanut butter and sliced banana sandwiches. More peanut butter than banana." Pam nodded. "Then I'd blend each one of you a tall milkshake."

Tiny began to believe that his wife could be making some headway and thought that he could help things along. "Sometimes I bought you boys cigarettes before you weren't of age yet," Tiny reminded them.

Pam glared at her husband as she was unaware that Tiny once supplied cigarettes to minors. She would most certainly talk to him about that later. As for now, the task at hand needed immediate attention. She took advantage of the brief stalemate to wave her hand behind her back. It was her signal for Mason to move safely out from the diner.

Mason made his move and stumbled out the door.

Dalton stepped toward the door before Pam slid in front of him. "Did you boys come in for a burger?" Pam questioned. After another tense moment of silence, the three boys finally headed for the counter. Pam let out a long sigh of relief.

*****

Ike steered the pickup truck along Harper Street. They passed by Mason Turner, who was stumbling along on the sidewalk.

"What's with Mason? He looks as though he's seen a ghost," Ike wondered.

"He's probably had a snootfull again, Grandpa," Renee assumed.

Ike then glanced ahead and spotted Sterling's pickup truck parked curbside. "There's the Porters' truck," Ike pointed out.

Renee's heart raced, and her mouth ran dry as she spotted the vehicle as well. She quickly parted the rear window of her grandfather's vehicle. "They're here, in town," she tensely informed Cole.

"Good," he responded. "Exactly where?"

"I just seen them through the diner's window," Ike reported. He then brought his pickup to park a few spaces down from Sterling's rig.

Renee's hands began to tremble.

Cole realized that he needed for her to remain calm. She had to be convincing. He attempted to ease her worries. "Hey, it's going to be fine. I'm always carrying my gun, and I'll be watching your every move. The two of you go on inside, and I'll stay out here in the bed of the truck. I can see inside the diner from here."

Renee's eyes widened. "What do you mean you're stayin' out here? If you're not goin' in with us, then I'm not doin' this."

"Listen to me, Renee. It must be this way. At this point, we want Murky to believe that there is nothing between you and me," Cole planned.

"There isn't, nor will there ever be," she snipped.

"Oh, believe me, I agree," Cole retorted.

Ike chuckled to himself.

"Now, let's get back to the strategy at hand. The two of you go inside to get a bite to eat. I'll watch carefully from out here. Renee, you give Murky a little interest. Just enough to raise his hopes. If something begins to go wrong, just run your right hand through your hair, and I'll be in there faster than you can say help."

"But why do you have to stay out here?" she pressed.

"It's all part of the scheme. I met Murky and his brothers the other day, and I played the dumb farmhand. I'm sure he thinks I'm too dumb for you to have any interest in me. That's good at this point. We must keep it that way for now. I'll stay in the back of the truck like a simple hired hand would do," Cole explained.

"What do I say to Murky?" she wondered.

"What does he typically say to you?" Cole sought.

"He'll ask me out on a date. He always asks me out, and I always tell him no."

"Well, today, don't say no, but don't exactly say yes. Are you following what I'm saying?"

She nodded her understanding.

"You can pull this off, Renee. Just recall your actin' skills. They're good," Ike claimed.

The compliment delivered to her a boost of confidence. "Okay...let's do this. Cole, you'd better not take your eyes off us for even one second. These guys are mean and nasty."

"I promise," he pledged.

Renee inhaled in a deep breath before she popped open the passenger door.

Dalton lit a cigarette just as the diner's door swung open with the familiar sounds of cow bells attached to a leather strap at the entrance to the restaurant. He turned to view Ike and Renee entering the diner. He nudged Murky with his elbow.

Murky turned his head to observe Renee Stewart, the love of his life, arriving at the diner.

Ike's stomach churned as he despised being in the same room with the murderers of his grandson. Renee deeply hoped that they would eventually pay dearly for taking her innocent brother's life.

Sterling swung in his stool to stare at Ike. "Hey there, shiner. Got any firewater you want to part with?"

"I don't make or run that stuff anymore," Ike returned.

"Oh, bullshit," Dalton snipped.

Ike and Renee quickly located seats at one of the small tables.

From outside, Cole observed intently.

Jim strolled out from the kitchen to behind the counter. "Hello, Ike and Renee. How are the two of you today?"

"Hello, Tiny," Ike greeted back. "We're fine. How 'bout yourself?"

Renee was becoming uneasy as Murky endlessly ogled in her direction.

"Oh, I'm doin' alright, can't complain. Even if I did, who would listen?" Jim teased.

"How's Pam?" Ike inquired.

"She's doin' good. She's in the kitchen grillin' up some patties. Can I get you folks a menu today?"

Ike glanced to Renee, and she shook her head no.

"I think that we know what we'll have, Tiny," Ike answered.

"Very good." Tiny understood as he grabbed his order pad and approached the table.

"Go take their high-cholesterol order, Tiny." Sterling smirked.

Dalton chortled. Murky continued to gaze at Renee.

Tiny ignored the remark as he clicked open his ink pen. "What'll it be, folks?"

"A couple of sodas, and I'll have the bacon cheeseburger," Ike ordered.

"Fries with that?" Tiny questioned.

Ike nodded.

Renee looked up at Tiny and smiled. Tiny and Pam had always been kind to her and Nate. Pam would talk to her for hours at times about boys, school, and other topics. She came closer than anyone else in replacing the things that Renee's mother would have furnished during her upbringing.

Tiny used to take Nate and some of the other boys in town fishing along the Shannon River north of Webster.

"I'll have the grilled chicken salad," she kindly ordered.

Tiny scribbled down their order on his pad, though he could memorize such an order. He enjoyed using the pad; it gave the diner a bit of an old-fashioned charm. "Dressin'?" he queried.

"Ranch," she confirmed.

"Comin' right up, folks," Tiny indicated. He then turned and headed back to the kitchen area, dressed in his spotless white apron.

Murky rose from his stool at the counter, and Renee could view his approach from the corner of her eye. Her heart raced with anxiety. She recalled her acting skills, and now was the time to deliver. She took a quick glance out the diner's window to be certain that Cole was indeed viewing the action inside the eatery.

"Hi there, beautiful," Murky leered, standing next to the table.

Renee did not look up at him.

Murky then glared at Ike. "Lose the seat, old man. Find another table."

Ike reluctantly stood to find a seat at a nearby table.

This angered Renee. "Please don't speak to my grandfather like that."

The diner fell eerily quiet. No one ever spoke to Murky or his brothers with such frankness. Not if they preferred the manner for which their teeth were currently aligned.

Ike promptly gazed out the window to Cole and was about to signal to him when Murky shocked everyone. "I'm sorry, babe, you're right. I should have been nicer to the old man."

Renee had never fully realized that she contained this sort of power over the ruthless Murky. She had never tested the waters so deeply before.

Dalton and Sterling looked at one another in a chuckle.

"You're a cream puff wimp, Murky," Dalton taunted.

"Shut your damn mouth, Dalton," Murky cautioned.

"Hey, if you ever eat some of that fine pussy that's sittin' over there, Murky, you have to let us smell your breath," Sterling suggested.

Dalton snickered.

"If you assholes don't shut up right now, I'll hurt ya, and I'll hurt ya bad," Murky warned.

Both Dalton and Sterling extended their middle fingers at Murky after he turned away from them.

Murky took the seat that Ike had vacated. "You haven't been goin' out with anybody, have ya?" Murky questioned her.

Renee shook her head no. She was doing her best in not telling Murky to go to hell.

"Well, that's good, cuz I'd have to break the guy's bones. Whaddya say we go down to the river next weekend together? There's gonna be a bonfire party there." Murky was waiting to hear her decline for the hundredth time.

"What do people do at a bonfire party?" she inquired.

Murky was pleasantly astounded over her delayed reaction in turning down his invitation, "Party like animals. Drink, smoke, and some go swimmin'."

"Well, I don't really drink very often," she commented.

"That's okay, babe. Sterling scored some great weed."

"I don't smoke pot," she revealed.

He glared at her. "Well, you can fuckin' start!"

She now realized that she had only a limited amount of control over Murky and not to push the envelope any further. He was like a time bomb set to detonate at any second. She sighed and carried out the best of her acting skills. "I don't know, Murky. I'll have to think about the river thing."

"Are you serious?" He nearly stuttered with apparent excitement in his voice.

"Give me time to think about it. I'll let you know by next weekend," she reported.

"This is so cool," Murky declared. "I can't believe that you're finally goin' out with me!"

"*Might*." She was certain to clarify.

"Might…okay…I'll take might for now. How 'bout we celebrate by goin' in the back room right now and screwin'?" he requested.

The idea of him touching her, of her engaging in sex with Murky Porter, appalled her. "Geez, Murky, slow down," she retorted.

"Oh, you're right, babe. It's just that I love you so much that I want to do the nasty with ya so bad."

Dalton and Sterling puckered their lips at each other in a silly gesture. "I love you so much," Sterling ribbed.

"Do you wanna go in the back room and screw?" Dalton mocked and then chortled.

"Last warnin'!" Murky advised, glaring over at his mocking brothers. He calmed immediately when he glanced back to Renee. "Well, if we do go to the party together, we'll ride in Sterling's truck. Dalton can jump in the back."

"I'm not ridin' in the back of the truck like that monkey outside is doin'," Dalton claimed, referring to Cole.

"Fine then, Dalton. You don't have to go," Murky surmised.

"Oh, I'm goin'. It's guaranteed pussy at those bonfires. I'll just take Dad's truck," he responded.

"Whatever, Dalton." Murky sighed. He then transformed his attention back to Renee and winked. "What time should we pick you up?"

Jim then appeared with the two glasses of soft drinks. "What are you doin' over there, Ike?"

Murky groaned and folded his arms to his chest. "Shut the hell up, Tiny. Can't you see that I'm tryin' to talk to my gal here?"

Jim sat the drinks on the table and then moved away, slightly angered.

"I didn't say that I'd go," Renee was quick to confirm.

"But you didn't say no," Murky pointed out.

"I didn't say yes," she followed.

"You'll let me know soon," he insisted.

Renee, reluctantly but showing otherwise, nodded.

Murky clapped his hands together. "Yes!"

"Fetch our burgers, Tiny," Dalton demanded.

"They're comin' right up!" Pam shouted from the kitchen. Soon, Pam emerged from the kitchen holding on to a large tray. She sat the tray down on the counter near Dalton and Sterling. She shuffled two burgers from the tray and slid the plate onto the counter in front of Dalton and Sterling. She then picked the tray up and strode around the counter. She moved to the table where Ike was seated and served up his bacon cheeseburger with a friendly smile. "I swear, Ike Stewart, each time I see you, you get even more handsome."

Renee grinned at Ike.

"Why, thank you, Pam." Ike slightly blushed.

"Oh, that's stupid. You can see all the moonshine wrinkles on his face. His liver probably looks like a pickle." Murky chuckled.

Sterling and Dalton sniggered.

Ike was noticeably bruised by the comment. His appearance had indeed aged with definitive markings from years of heavy drinking.

"That wasn't very nice to say, Murky," Pam commented.

"I wasn't tryin' to be nice," Murky retorted.

Pam then placed Murky's hamburger in front of him, followed by Renee's salad. Pam marched away in haste, not wishing to be near Murky any longer than she had to be.

"You know, if you want to have any chance with me at all, you have to begin by bein' more respectful of my grandfather," Renee asserted.

Murky observed as Ike gingerly brought the cheeseburger to his mouth. Ike's dentures had long needed replaced, but he liked the way they fit. A new set would be uncomfortable through the break-in

period. His hands were frail as they slightly trembled with weakness. His gray hair was protruding over the rim of his upper ears and, by his own standards, needed a trim. He just hadn't gotten around to driving over to the barbershop in Waynesburg.

Ike was not completely alone in life, but he seemed lonely. He had not pursued an intimate mate over the years while raising Nate and Renee. Now that he was open to the possibility of a partner, his health was failing him.

When eyeing Ike, most people would show some heartfelt sympathy, but not Murky Porter. In fact, Murky found the need to further humiliate the elderly man. "Hey, Ike high as a kite, Pop tells us that you once screwed a married woman and that the husband took after you with a knife. How the hell did that all go down?" Murky drilled.

Renee was stunned over Murky's accusation. Certainly, this couldn't be true. That would mean that her grandfather was unfaithful to her now-deceased grandmother.

Murky brought up the sensitive subject to try to stain Ike's high standing in Renee's eyes.

Ike reddened slightly. Ike most certainly realized that it was not wise to lie to the Porters, so he looked to Renee for understanding. "That was back in my drinkin' days."

"It's true then?" she questioned.

Ike reluctantly nodded.

"Grandpa, how could you?"

Murky slyly smirked.

"It's not what you're thinkin', Renee. I was makin' a run one day over in Webster. It was many years ago. There was still a market for shine in those days. It was a bit cheaper than store-bought booze, and underage drinkers could get their hands on it. One of the stops that day was at Wally's Hardware Store. Wally Reynolds and his wife, Emily, owned and ran the store. The Reynolds were young, in their twenties, and weren't runnin' the store very well. Profits were down, and they were strugglin' to keep afloat. There's an auto parts store at that location these days, where the hardware store used to sit. Anyway, Wally wasn't a drinker. He was a businessman. He'd sell the moonshine from behind the store. We'd deliver over fifty gallons a

month to Wally. What I mean by we, Max Chamber and I. Max was a fairly major distributor of moonshine, and I was his runner. Max had many connections, includin' ties with organized crime. Well, on this particular day, we were at the hardware store for two reasons. The first bein' to deliver the monthly gallons of firewater, and second was to collect on Wally's delinquent account. That's why Max was along with me that day."

Ike paused telling the story for a moment to take a bite from his cheeseburger. The attention of the diner occupants was entirely focused on him as he continued.

"Wally had promised me the prior month that he would have payment in full this month. Max was there to ensure Wally kept his promise. Unfortunately for Wally, he couldn't pay his bill—in full, anyway. Max was prepared to beat Wally severely or possibly even kill him. Emily could sense the danger, and she stepped around from behind the store's counter. She pleaded with Max to show her husband mercy, but to no avail. Max didn't have any compassion. He could throw a harmless baby to a pack of wolves and think a-nothin' of it. Her beggin' was gettin' her nowhere until she done somethin' that caught us all off guard. At the time, Max, Wally, Emily, and I were the only people inside the store. Emily then offered her body to Max for his sexual pleasure in exchange for sparin' her husband a brutal beatin'."

"I like this Max guy." Dalton grinned.

Sterling nodded his head in agreement. "Yeah, a take-no-shit motherfucker, just like we Porters."

Ike sipped his beverage, had another bite of his sandwich, and then resumed. "Wally begged of her not to do it, but she was determined to save her husband's neck. Max's eyes widened as he was instantly interested. Emily was a beautiful young lady, a looker for sure, and Max was an overweight man in his fifties. He warmed to her offer, and then he presented a deal. Ten minutes in the back room with Emily Reynolds would buy Wally another month to come up with the money owed. Wally immediately declined the offer, not wanting to put his wife through such an ordeal, but Emily reluctantly accepted. Then Max added one more stipulation that I wasn't

expectin'. I was to be sexually fulfilled by Emily as well. She hesitated before eventually agreein'. She really had no choice, as there was no negotiatin' with Max Chamber. I had no say-so in the matter either. The boss had spoken, and you just didn't cross Chamber, period. His thinkin' was that the wife had to give it up to him and the delivery-man to really teach Wally a hard lesson.

"Before I could think about somethin' to try to curb Max's enthusiasm, Max was tearin' at Emily's clothin' as she shuffled toward the back room of the store. Soon, the noises of sex came echoin' from the back room, causin' Wally to plug his fingers into his ears. When Max was finished with Emily, he emerged from the back room tuckin' his shirt inside his pants. He then announced that it was my turn with Emily. My plan was to go in the back room and act as though I had sex with her when actually I was not intendin' to go through with it at all. I loved my wife and wasn't about to be unfaithful her. But what I hadn't figured on was that Max followed me back there to Emily. He wanted to watch."

Renee grimaced in disgust.

"Now, I was male, normal in every way, and seein' Emily with no clothes on and willin', well…started my fire. After an initial resistance, I ended up havin' sex with Emily. The followin' month, I returned to Wally's Hardware Store to collect and deliver. This time around, Max wasn't with me. Well, Wally Reynolds was havin' a difficult time acceptin' the fact that Max and I had our way with his wife. He came at with me with a large knife. I escaped from the store just as he was about to stab me. I ran out to the street, and he continued to pursue me. He chased me down the street, wavin' that knife at me. Of course, many people in town saw this. I was able to safely make my way back to my truck, and I got the hell out of there.

"Word traveled around Webster about the incident, and eventually, the tale made its way back here to Harpersfield. When my dear Jodi confronted me about it, I confessed it all. She and I nearly divorced, but I gave it every effort to repair things between us, and we were able to salvage our marriage."

"Did ya ever screw Emily again?" Dalton asked the awkward question.

Ike gave Dalton a look of disgust and shook his head no.

"Well, I would have did her again. She sounds hot," Sterling remarked.

"Whatever happened to Wally, Grandpa?" Renee wondered.

"Well, I refused to deliver there any longer. Max took over the account. I heard that Wally couldn't pay his bill and that Max grew tired of sex from Emily to put off payment. He wanted to be paid in cold hard cash. Wally tried, but he couldn't produce all the money. Wally's car was found at the bottom of the Sulfur River, and unfortunately, Wally was inside the vehicle."

Renee bowed her head. "That's so sad."

"No, it's not," Dalton spoke up. "That fuckin' idiot Wally had it comin' to him. He didn't pay up. If one of our distributors didn't pay up, they'd suffer the same fate."

It's common knowledge in Harpersfield that the Porters dealt in drugs. Local law enforcement confiscated any drugs that they could locate, but did little else to solve the problem.

Renee then noticed Murky was staring at her from across the table. He was looking at her with excited eyes. She felt extremely uncomfortable. "You about ready to go, Grandpa?" she queried.

Ike sensed her uneasiness. "Sure, we need to head back to the farm."

Murky rapidly broke from his trance when he realized that Renee was planning to depart. "Wait, you can't leave just yet," Murky insisted.

Renee anticipated a problem and nearly ran her right hand through her hair to signal Cole into action.

Murky stood from his chair and plunged his left hand into his Levi's pocket. He then pulled out his large hand, which was formed into a fist. He lowered his sizable fist down in front of Renee and slowly opened his fingers. Lying in the palm of his hand was a diamond ring with a white gold band. The ring appeared awfully expensive.

Renee was surprised, and though she was taken back by the ring's beauty, there was no possible way that she would accept the gift.

"Here, Renee, it's all yours. I got it a long time ago, and I carry it with me every day, waitin' for the right chance to give it to you," Murky revealed.

Sterling craned his neck to gain a glance at the ring. "Damn, Murky, that's some rock. Now, stop actin' like a blubberin' pussy-whipped wimp. Shameful to the Porter name!"

Dalton snickered.

Murky got angry. "Shut your mouth, Sterling. You have no room to talk. You run around town datin' that whore Tammy."

"Yeah, well, I didn't give Tammy a goddamn ring. You're a moron. You can get some of that pussy without the butterin' up and bribin' the bitch. I bet I could get some of that if I wanted it," Sterling claimed. He then winked at Renee.

She quickly looked away from his direction.

Murky abruptly turned to glare at Sterling. "One more word out of you about my love for Renee, and I'll hurt you, and I'll hurt you bad," Murky advised.

Sterling held the palm of his right hand up at Murky. "I'm not gettin' into this with you, bro. I'd have to rip your balls off and stuff them into your mouth."

Again, Dalton snorted.

"Dalton, shut your mouth," Murky and Sterling said simultaneously.

Dalton flipped up his middle finger at both of his brothers.

Although the Porter brothers often threatened each other with violent attacks, they rarely squared off toe to toe physically. Each, in their own belief, was the alpha male of the trio, but the group also respected the extreme size, power, and strength of their siblings. Individually, they were fully aware that any bodily confrontation between them, regardless of who may triumph in the end, would be a bloody mess and would probably be a fight to near death. The rare physical confrontations did indeed end in a virtual tie without any true champion. Both participants would be simply left licking their own wounds. An unspoken reverence and apprehension for one another was in existence.

They all were well above average in height, strength, bulk, fighting skills, and downright callousness. If the Porter brothers adopted any respect and/or regard for any individual, it was exclusively between one another.

Murky then spun his attention back on Renee. The picturesque ring was still resting in his palm. "Go on, babe, take it. It's yours, and I want to see ya wearin' it every day."

"Murky, I can't accept such a splendid gift. Though I appreciate the offer, it's way too expensive and improper seeing that we are not...not...well, not even a couple." She utilized the excuse. If the ring were coming from someone whom truly she cared about, she would certainly be prepared to receive it. The piece of jewelry was absolutely stunning. Moreover, Renee was certain that Murky hadn't purchased such a posh item under honest terms. It was either stolen or purchased using drug money.

"I know it's worth lots of money, but still, I want you to have it." Murky continued to make his case.

Dalton mocked Murky by means of a girlie tone to his voice. "Why, Murky Porter, I do declare. For little ole' me? Such a beautiful ring. Must I give you a blow job for such a generous offer?"

Sterling roared with laughter.

Murky quickly slammed the ring onto the tabletop and turned to Dalton in a full run. He covered the distance between him and Dalton in a flash. He vaulted in the air and tackled Dalton from off his stool. The brothers slammed to the floor in a bear hug.

Outside, Cole stood up in the bed of the truck to get a better assessment of what was transpiring inside the diner.

A thing about the Porter brothers, the three of them were extremely skilled at fighting. Their father enrolled them in the Golden Gloves Boxing program as they were growing up. Dalton took first place in the county finals. Sterling finished second in state, and Murky won two major tournaments. When pinned up against each other, there was usually no winner. They ended up beaten, bloodied, and bruised.

"Get the hell off of me, Murky!" Dalton demanded.

Murky rolled off Dalton before both men rose from the floor to a strong stance, facing each other. They formed fists with each of their hands, and they snarled. Dalton lunged forward and landed a punch to Murky's jaw, sending Murky treading back a few steps.

Murky retaliated with a strike of his own to Dalton's forehead, sending Dalton's ears abuzz.

Sterling looked on with a grin painted upon his face.

Outside, Cole leaped off the bed of the truck and quickly headed for the diner's door.

Pam raced from out of the kitchen and shouted, "Dalton, Murky! Please don't fight in here!"

It was then that the mutual unspoken respect the Porter brothers held for one another came to surface with Dalton and Murky lowering their defenses simultaneously.

But the timing was insufficient and too late. Jim had seen enough. He reached for the small wooden box and quickly popped open the lid. He took hold of the handgun to raise the barrel toward Murky and Dalton. Jim had no intentions of firing the loaded pistol; he just wanted to intimidate the boys out from the diner.

Sterling observed the gun in Jim's hand, and he quickly reached for his own handgun tucked inside the waist of his pants. Only the Porter boys knew that Sterling had the weapon as he sported his long shirt over the beltline.

Sterling aimed the barrel of his handgun less than an inch from Jim's temple. "Drop the fuckin' piece, Tiny," he warned.

Jim then saw Sterling's pistol on him at point-blank range. Murky and Dalton broke away from their dueling actions to peer over at the counter. Pam placed her hands over her mouth and released a muffled scream. Ike plugged his ears with his fingers, and Renee's eyes widened.

Cole reached beneath his shirt to take a grip on his own handgun, but left it holstered for now. He waited just outside the door of the diner until the last possible moment. He must keep his FBI identity secret if at all possible. If he came rushing through the diner's door with gun in hand, the entire scheme, the whole plan, would simply be over in bringing justice to the murder of Nathan Stewart. It would all be vaporized the very second Cole would be forced to flash his badge. Murky would remain a free man. The Porters would then know that he was much more than a mere farmhand.

Sterling slowly stood up from his stool, careful not to take the pointed gun off Jim. Sterling then glared at Jim. "I'm only goin' to say this one more time, Tiny. Drop the gun."

The tension inside the diner was thick and tense.

"Drop the gun, diner man," Cole whispered to himself. He then placed his grip upon the door's handle.

"Oh, Jim!" Pam cried. "Drop the gun, honey, or he'll shoot you."

Jim squinted, looked to the three brothers, angered, and then slowly and reluctantly lowered his weapon.

"Now, drop it, Tiny!" Sterling demanded.

Jim reluctantly released his grip on his gun, allowing it to drop to the diner's floor with a thud. He ground his teeth together as Sterling made his way around the counter while still pointing his gun at Jim. Sterling kept his eyesight on Jim as he bent to pick Jim's handgun up from the floor. He then tossed Jim's gun over to Murky, who made the catch. Sterling then punched Jim in the face with the same right hand that was holding the gun. The hard blow dazed Jim as the butt of the gun slashed him across the cheek.

Pam shouted, "Please stop, Sterling!"

Sterling then shook his finger at Jim. "Tiny, don't you ever point a gun at a Porter again. Fuckin' never ever! If you do, I swear I'll unload my gun into your head." Sterling then kicked Jim in the groin area, causing Jim to wince in pain and collapse to his knees.

Pam raced to her husband's side. Sterling jumped back over the counter.

Murky examined Jim's handgun. "I'm keepin' the pistol, Tiny." He then tucked the firearm into the waist of his pants.

"Come on, let's go. We gotta make a run to Waynesburg. We got some deliveries to make," Dalton reminded his brothers.

Cole quickly stepped back to the pickup truck to leap into the bed of the truck.

Murky strode to the table where Renee was seated. "Don't forget your ring, beautiful."

"Murky, I'm sorry, but I can't accept the ring," she declared. She then plucked the ring from the table in an attempt to hand it over to him.

"No, you keep it," he insisted.

She shook her head no.

Reluctantly, Murky grabbed the ring from her palm. He then stuffed the ring back inside his pants pocket. He mumbled, "Someday you'll wear my ring forever. Are you goin' to the bonfire with me or not?"

Renee would have rather ate a pound of raw liver than go out with Murky Porter. However, she realized she must do what she had to do in order for the plan to avenge her brother's murder to succeed. She forced herself to reply, "Give me a little time to think about it."

His eyes widened, and he beamed. "Is that a maybe?"

With a forced motion, she nodded.

"Fuckin' A!" Murky celebrated. "I'll ask you again in a few days. We'll have a blast. Bring your bikini because we'll swim. Wait, don't bring your bikini. Most everyone skinny-dips. Wow, I can't wait to skinny-dip with you!"

"I can't wait to see the fine pussy that must be between that Stewart girl's legs," Sterling commented while licking his lips.

Renee was becoming nauseated over the entire episode in the diner. Pam tried to help Jim to his feet, but he was too dazed, and the full brunt of his weight was too much for her to manage. She wanted to get Jim to the back room where the first aid kit hung on the wall.

"Shut the hell up, Sterling!" Murky screeched.

"Murky, you have to slow down. I didn't say that I would go. I said maybe," she confirmed.

"Okay, I'll take a maybe. It's lots better than a no," he figured.

"Come on, Murky. Let's hit the road," Dalton pressed as he and Sterling were now positioned at the diner's door.

"Alright...alright. I'm comin' already," Murky snipped. He smiled at Renee before finally stepping away from her.

When she was certain he could no longer see her face, she rolled her eyes as part of a gesture of an expression as if she were about to vomit. Dalton, Sterling, and Murky then departed the diner. Ike quickly stood to move behind the counter to assist Pam with getting Jim to his feet. Renee moved swiftly to the kitchen and dampened a small hand towel with cold water. She carried the compress to Pam,

who now had Jim seated upon one of the stools. Pam used the cold compress to help stop Jim's cut from bleeding any further.

"Those boys are of the cruelest form," Pam indicated.

Outside the diner, the three brothers strode past Ike's pickup truck on their way to Sterling's vehicle.

Dalton pointed at Cole sitting in the bed of the Ike's truck. "Hey look, it's the trained monkey."

Sterling grabbed hold of his own groin area. "Does the monkey want a banana?"

The Porters laughed in unison.

Cole ignored their taunting of him and maintained his composure. Cole performed his dumb farmhand role as he waved. "Hi, Murky, how are you today?"

Murky then winked at Cole. "Hey, I've almost got Renee. You keep tellin' her what a great guy I am. You can throw in there that I'm a stud too. Remember, Cole the mole, don't fail me. If you do, I'll hurt you, and I'll hurt you bad."

Cole forced a nod of his understanding, appearing as though he was intimated by Murky.

The brothers lightheartedly slapped each other around while making their way to Sterling's truck.

CHAPTER 22

"**WHAT'S UP WITH** you tonight, Marla? You were staring off into space at the blackjack table," Dule inquired. He and Marla were seated on barstools inside a casino lounge in Las Vegas.

She swirled the Scotch and water inside her drinking glass. "After being an FBI agent for as long as I was, you develop an intuition. Mine is telling me that this case in Tennessee is trouble. Something's not right. I know Cole is the best at what he does, but something's going to backfire miserably. I can't quite put my finger on it, but it's there."

"Cole seems like he can take care of himself plenty."

"Yeah, well, sometimes in this line of work, even Superman might inadvertently uncover some kryptonite," she pointed out. Marla then reached inside her purse and pulled out her cell phone.

"What are you doing?" he queried.

"I'm thinking about calling it off and getting Cole out of those mountains in Tennessee," she responded.

"You can do that?"

Marla glanced at Dule over the top of her eyeglasses. "Of course I have that option. You don't think I would have created a group that I had no power over, do you? I have the last say on everything

regarding the cases. If I want an agent to withdraw at any point, they withdraw. It's that simple, no questions asked. I've only had to use my trump card on two occasions, but it's happened."

Dule placed his left palm on the back of her right hand. "Just remember, Marla. If you make that call, then the murderer in Harpersfield continues to walk around a free man."

She sighed profoundly. "Yeah...I know. Maybe I'll wait until tomorrow. Cole is due to call in with his first report on the case. I'll see where things are then." She then slid her cell phone back inside her large purse. The couple then sipped from their drinks simultaneously.

"Dancing around with one's morals can play hell sometimes, huh, Marla?"

"What are you talking about now, Dule?"

He leaned closer to her. "You know, like with this current case. You want to do what is right, but at what cost? Is it really up to us as individuals to decide the fate of others? Isn't that what our judicial system is for, even when it fails at times? Believe me, I am no cheer-leader for our government's feeble system, but at what point do we take it into our own hands to see that justice prevails? I don't know, perhaps it's not up to us or any system to judge and punish. Maybe that's God's job exclusively. What if, for argument's sake, the Elite Four was wrong once? What if they terminated a party that was later found to be innocent?"

She shook her head. "That can't happen, it's impossible. We do not take on a case unless guilt is as plain as the nose on your face."

Dule touched his large nose.

"Um...sorry, Dule, I was only trying to make a point. Um... an association."

He cracked a half smile.

"Anyway, if there an ounce of doubt, we do not take on the case."

He exhaled, "Boy...there is just no room for wiggle there."

"We don't allow for any."

A man then walked by and realized he was holding a lit cigarette in his hand. He glanced around nervously and quickly sat the ciga-rette on the edge of the bar near Marla and Dule.

Marla fidgeted. "What is that guy doing? This is a nonsmoking establishment."

Dule laid his pack of cigarettes on the bar in front of him.

"Dule, put out the cigarette the man left behind," Marla directed.

"No, wait, I'm making my point here."

Within a few moments, the aroma of the burning tobacco invaded the nostrils of the bartender. The bartender snapped his head in the direction of the billowing smoke. He spotted the burning cigarette on the bar, and then he set his sight on the pack of cigarettes placed in front of Dule. The bartender aggressively approached Dule. "Sir, there is no smoking in here. Now please put your cigarette out, or I'll have to ask you to leave."

"That's not my cigarette," Dule informed him.

The bartender creased his forehead. "Yeah right, buddy, and I'm Mickey Mouse. Now, put your damn cigarette out or leave."

Dule raised his palms. "Okay...okay...I'll put it out." Dule picked up the cigarette and dunked it into his nearly empty glass. He then looked smugly over to Marla.

She nodded. "Okay, Dule, point well taken."

"Well, I've played enough blackjack this evening," Dule stated. "Now, how about we go up to our room, and I'll play with black Marla?" He winked.

Marla giggled deeply as she playfully slapped him on the arm. "Oh, Dule, you're so feisty. Okay, let's go."

*****

COLE SAT ON the small porch of the guesthouse listening to the serenity of a warm summer's night in the Smoky Mountains. As Renee had done at times, he listened to the welcoming music composed by the crickets. He sipped from his glass filled about a quarter of the way with Jack Daniel's whiskey. He then inhaled a long drag from his cigarette. He exhaled, and through the billowing smoke, in the still air, he noticed Renee making her way toward the guesthouse. Her dark hair shone from the light of the pole next to the driveway. She was wearing a pair of cut-off denim shorts and a simple white

blouse. The shorts revealed her long, slender, and smooth legs. The blouse was buttoned up, covering her cleavage, but the forms of her full breasts could not be concealed from view.

Cole enjoyed the sight as she made her way across the lawn. He only had on a pair of Levi's jeans. Recently he had completed his daily regimen of sit-ups and push-ups. He brought a chin-up bar with him and installed it in the doorway between the bedroom and the kitchen of the guesthouse. Fifty chin-ups had satisfied him earlier as well. After the demanding workout, he went through the cool-down period and then had a shower. He put on his Levi's and nothing else, as he was not expecting company on this night.

He thought about stepping inside for his T-shirt before Renee arrived at the porch, but there was not enough time to do so before she shuffled up the four wooden steps that led to the porch.

During the first few moments, Cole and Renee enjoyed the view of one another's appealing physiques. She had noticed before that Cole was fit, but now she could view just how firm he was. His body was chiseled with sculpted muscle. Along with his full head of hair and deep eyes, she did find him to be extremely attractive. Physically anyway. She didn't care so much for his attitude.

It had been a spell since Cole had been in bed with a woman, especially one of Renee's beauty. He couldn't help but to let his eyes roam, a little more obvious than what she was doing with her line of sight upon him.

She cleared her throat to bring his attention and his eyes up to her line of sight. "Murky Porter has called here three times tonight. God, I sure hope you know what you're doin', FBI man."

Cole abruptly stood from his chair and pointed his forefinger in her direction. "Do not speak those initials. We've talked about this. You never know who could be lurking in the shadows."

Her face reddened with embarrassment over breaching one modest rule. Renee completely understood the risks of such a security violation. "I'm sorry," she mumbled.

He peered out into the darkness. "No worries, I think it'll be okay this time. Not ever again though."

"I said I was sorry," she let out.

He squinted. "I heard you the first time."

She curled her lip at him and then whispered, "Anyway, Murky is takin' this façade hook, line, and sinker. I'm not goin' to be able to hold him at bay much longer. When the telephone rings, my skin just crawls. Can you imagine what that must be like? Your brother's killer callin' you."

"No one claimed this was going to be easy. You just have to trust me on this."

"That's askin' a lot. I don't know if I can go through with this. My nerves are about shot."

"Well, find the strength. You're doing this for your fallen brother."

She bit down on her lip. "Can I have one of those cigarettes?" she requested, glancing at the pack of Marlboros lying on the deck of the porch.

"I thought you said you only smoke when you drink hard liquor, which is rarely?" he taunted.

"I am goin' to have a cigarette tonight, okay? Fine, I'll have a slug of bourbon as well. Now, can I have a ciggy, please?"

He nodded his head toward the pack. "Help yourself."

Renee bent to pick up the pack of cigarettes, and as she did, her blouse fell slightly away from her chest. This allowed Cole a view of the top portion of her bare breasts, to his satisfaction. Her skin was silky but firm, and the portion of her cleavage that he could view was perfectly sculpted.

She then stood upright with the pack of Marlboros in her hand. She plucked one of the cigarettes from the pack and placed the butted end between her lips. "Light?" she requested through the cigarette planted between her lips, causing it to bounce.

He reached inside the front pocket of his Levi's to take hold of his lighter. In doing so, his pants lowered about an inch, which exposed the top edge of his pubic hairline. The sight of this caused Renee's heart to skip a beat. It excited her. She was barely able to control her excitement from reaching an expression upon her face before she quickly looked back to his facial area.

Cole had not detected her enthusiastic reaction. He then handed the lighter to her. Renee lit the cigarette and puffed. She kept the

smoke inside her mouth and without inhaling. The smoke escaped from her mouth in one forced release of air pumping from her lungs. She then returned the lighter to Cole. She watched as he plunged the lighter back inside his pants pocket, and she again gained the view as before.

"So what's next?" she questioned, flipping back her hair.

He sipped from his glass. "I'm thinking that I might try to reach one of the three Porter brothers," he replied.

"What do you mean by reach?" she inquired. Renee then drew in another drag from her stick of tobacco. Her left eye closed from the irritation of the smoke billowing up from the burning end of the cigarette. She exhaled again without inhaling and then pulled the cigarette from between her lips, holding it in an awkward fashion between the fingers of her right hand.

"The odds are that one of the three must have somewhat of a conscience," he anticipated.

She chuckled sarcastically. "Believe me, not in this case. You try findin' one of those boys, and you might discover yourself reachin' for a branch while hangin' from a tree."

"Are you trying to tell me that all three are evil to the very core?"

She nodded. "That's exactly what I'm tellin' you. It's pure wickedness with all three of them. There is not a compassionate side to any of the brothers. Their father is the same way. I guess you could say that it's genetics." She then tossed the pack of Marlboros back down onto the porch floor.

"So I have no chance of getting one to turn on the others?"

She shook her head. "Absolutely not. Those Porters are sewn together."

"Okay, you grew up with them, so you'd know better than I. I'll drop that notion."

"Good choice," she agreed. "So what's next?"

He raked his fingers through his hair. "Well, we give Murky a few more days to run on high hopes before we shatter his false dreams. You're just going to have to put up with the phone calls for now."

She rolled her eyes.

"We're going to have to spend more time together," he instructed.

"This is gettin' worse as we go along," she declared.

He angered marginally. "I don't like the idea any more than you do."

She raised the palm of her left hand. "Okay, okay. We'll do what we need to do."

After a few moments of awkward silence, Cole articulated in a calmer voice, "We need to convince Murky that it was going to be you and him before you unexpectedly fell for me."

"He'll try to kill you," she assured him.

"Exactly." Cole nodded.

She motioned her head with understanding, but then asked, "What if he gets to you before you get him?"

Cole shrugged his shoulders. "That's a risk that comes with the territory. I need for him to threaten my life with a weapon before I can make my ultimate move."

"Are you goin' to try to deal with all three brothers?" she pondered.

He rubbed his sharp jawline. "If necessary, yes. I hope it works out along those lines. That way I can completely rid Harpersfield of its cancer."

"I don't know. Those Porter boys are tough customers. They set out to win with no regard to fairness or compassion for human life." She then elicited another drag from her cigarette, only to allow the smoke to seep slowly from her mouth. Again, she failed to inhale. Cole took the next drink from his bourbon.

After an inelegant moment of fidgeting, Renee cleared her throat and queried, "So, for how many years have you been workin' out?"

He smirked. "What makes you believe I work out?"

She rolled her eyes. "Oh, come on, you have some muscle mass goin' on there."

"Why do you want to know?"

"Just curious is all."

"Curious or attracted?" he teased.

"Curious," she bit out. "You sure are conceited!"

"No...no, I'm not really. I'm just taunting you is all. I started weight training when I was in my teens. How about you?"

She pointed to herself. "Who, me? I don't work out."

He looked her over. "It sure looks like to me that you do."

She blushed. "Really?"

He nodded.

"I suppose it's because of all the hard work on the farm."

"Whatever the reason, it sure is working," he complimented.

Again, she flushed. "Okay, would you please stop goin' on, already?"

Upon discovering that she didn't take well to compliments, he decided to let her off the hook by shifting the subject. "Tell me, Renee. What are the local cops like around here? Why don't they take these Porters off the streets?"

Renee then grabbed a seat on one of the two wicker chairs on the porch. She crossed her long smooth legs as Cole's eyesight ran along the length of her exposed skin. Again she cleared her throat to remove his attention away from her body. He quickly glanced up to her eyes, slightly embarrassed. She was relishing his attention, but she wasn't about to allow him that knowledge.

"Sheriff Harvey and Deputy Collins are good people, they really are. They do their best to a certain extent. But then again, like all citizens in this town, they fear the Porters. Rumor has it that Carter Porter once beat Sheriff Harvey to near death over a game of pool. Deputy Collins has a wife and two children, one's just a baby. I don't think, to him, that the Porters are worth leavin' his kids fatherless. So the two of them virtually look the other way and permit the Porters do their evil things. You see, if they arrested the Porters and charged them, the Porters would easily make bail, and the time before any trial could commence, the police and their family would be in grave danger. If they are called to a disturbance involvin' the Porters, they don't always respond, and when they do react, they don't do much about it. They would never lock the Porters up, as that would be a big mistake. It was one of their secretaries, Mattie Freeman, who inadvertently typed the Porters address incorrectly on the search warrant over Nathan's murder."

"You don't hold that against her, do you? I mean, it was a critical error, but I'm she didn't do it intentionally. Besides, it's the sheriff's job to make sure it all is correct before executing the warrant."

"Of course I don't hold it against her, but it wouldn't matter much if I did. Mattie is dead."

His eyes widened. "Dead? How did that happen?"

Renee sighed. "Suicide. She shot herself in the head with her husband's handgun after her blunder set Murky free. I suppose she simply couldn't forgive herself. It's a shame. She was such a nice lady."

Silence, other than the cricket's chirping, overtook the porch for a few moments. Cole sipped from his glass, and Renee drew in another mouthful of cigarette smoke. The exhaled cloud seeped from her mouth. She had yet to inhale a single draw.

"Are you going to smoke that or waste it?" he wondered out loud.

She squinted. "What the heck are you talkin' about? I'm smokin' it."

"No, you're not smoking it. You're simply puffing on it."

She rose from her chair. "Okay then. Watch this." She then took a significant drag from her cigarette. With her mouth filled with smoke, Renee hesitated for a moment while realizing that if she went through with this action, she would likely be sorry. Nonetheless, she wanted to prove to Cole that she was tough for a woman, although that image did not fit her well. Renee was too gentle, soft, and all around womanly to pull off the hard act. She was a lady through and through.

Renee closed her eyes and then inhaled the smoke from her mouth into her lungs. Immediately, she felt her airway slam shut and her throat spasm. Her lungs burned, and her eyes watered. She tossed the cigarette from the porch and then bent at the waist. She coughed a deep cough repeatedly.

Cole chuckled as she held the palm of her left hand up at him. He continued to snicker until he came to realize she was having a difficult time catching a breath of air. He moved over to her. "Okay, Renee, take a slow breath in through your nose."

She attempted to follow his directions, but her airway was not cooperating. Instinctively, he tried to soothe her by rubbing his hand on her back. After another spell of coughing, Renee was ultimately able to take in some air. Soon, her coughing was replaced with rough breathing as her dizziness began to subside.

"Are you going to be okay?" he inquired with a slight tease-filled grin on his face.

She nodded while remaining in a stooped position.

Cole could view the contours of her shapely backside as her shorts had risen to her upper thigh. The lower portion of her butt cheeks had seeped below the hem of her shorts. He took in the sensual sight longer than he anticipated that he should, until he heard the familiar sound of her clearing her throat. Again, his face reddened a bit with embarrassment at being caught gazing at her body as she was eyeing at him over her shoulder. His eyes glanced quickly away as she stood upright to turn toward him.

"Enjoyin' the sights this evenin', are ya?" she asked with a bit of harshness. She appeared as though his gazing was offensive to her, but in reality, she found his obvious sexual interest in her tantalizing and exciting.

He nearly stuttered. "Sorry…um…sorry."

"Well, try keepin' your eyes inside your head, okay?"

He nodded. Renee then rubbed her stomach for a moment. The inhale of the cigarette's smoke had her feeling nauseated.

"So I can't really expect any solid support from the local police?" Cole questioned.

She shook her head no, and in a voice still gravelly from her failed attempt at smoking, she replied, "Not at all."

"You need to weather the Murky storm for a few more days then. We need to get his hopes to their highest point. Then we'll trip him up. A stroll through town together holding hands should be sufficient. When Murky calls you after that, you tell him that you suddenly realized that you have strong feelings for me, so you won't be going out with him after all."

"Okay," she responded, "but he's going to be super crazed. I hope you know what kind of monster you're about to unleash."

He squinted. "Let me worry about that."

Again, a brief hush consumed the porch. Then in a calm, serene voice, Renee curiously probed, "What are your parents like, Cole?" Renee believed that people are like a garden in many ways. She could recall her grandmother and her mother's vegetable garden each year

and how they showed pride with working at it. A garden grew to become what it was according to how it was nurtured along the way. If one took care of a garden, then the harvest would be healthy, plentiful, and hardy. If one neglected a garden, the weeds would invade the plants and choke them off at the stem. It was not a mystery to mankind that you get out of something what you put into it.

It was a shame to Renee that not every garden in life could grow beautifully and productively. No, there would always be gardens where the gardeners were not attentive, and the plants rotted away. They were some vegetables that do survive neglect to become vigorous plants, but that yield was far and few between. For the most part, a shoddy gardener produced poor reaps. A prosperous, rewarding garden required a gentle touch, but a stern hand when needed. A delightful garden demanded plenty of sunshine and had to be watered at strategic times. It was a balance that must be met for a garden to have positive results by the efforts put forth by the gardener. Of course, sadly enough, there were those few plants that refused to grow healthy regardless of the amount of tender loving care the gardener provided it. However, good gardeners had the odds in their favor that the garden they sowed shall grow magnificently and make them proud one day.

Carter and Bessy Porter's gardening hadn't been much to be desired, and their rotten plants showed it. Ike Stewart was a caring, hardworking gardener, and Renee hoped that she had made him proud of his harvest.

Cole was startled by her inquiry. "Why do you ask?"

She shrugged her shoulders. "I dunno. Just wonderin' is all."

Cole sipped from his bourbon before revealing, "Well, because of my mother"—he raised his glass in front of himself—"I'm really careful with this stuff. She drank a bit too much. Well, she drank a whole lot. She was a good mother. I mean, she never beat us or anything like that. She just missed out on a lot of mine and Becky's childhood because she was either medicated, intoxicated, or sleeping off a hangover."

Renee pressed her lips together as she believed that must have been difficult to grow up with.

Cole continued, "Dad's a cop in Cleveland. He's going to retire soon. He's a good guy. He really made up where Mom lost ground. He was deeply hurt when Becky passed away."

"Does your father know you do this…this sort of thing outside your…" She was poised not to break the "Don't mention the FBI" rule. "Um, regular job?"

He shook his head no. "Of course not. I mean, he certainly knows what I do for a career, but he's unaware of the additional undertaking."

She leaned against a support pole on the porch. A slight breeze had picked up to gently lift her soft dark hair. "Does that bother you? Does it bother you that your father doesn't know?"

"Yeah, sometimes. I know that he would agree with the concept, but not the execution of it. He's a by-the-book kind of guy all the way. So it's just best he doesn't know." Cole then hesitated before he decided to elaborate. "My childhood was okay. I'm not disturbed by it or anything like that. I don't believe that my parents were exactly in love, but I never doubted that they loved their children. My father was a strict disciplinarian, so I knew not to tread certain waters. He ruled with a strong hand, and in some ways, I'm glad that he did. It made Becky and me walk a straight line, which I believe makes one a responsible adult. I never really heard my parents argue. My father refused to have turmoil inside the home. Though I could sense when they weren't on speaking terms at times. All in all, the Walsh household wasn't a terrible place by any means."

Her eyes saddened for a moment. "I barely knew my parents. They were killed—"

"Thirteen years ago, in an automobile accident on Route 46 in Bainbridge Township. That's about thirty-five miles north of here. Your father had been drinking and lost control of the car, a blue Ford Focus license plate number JLK-4938. Jack and Beth Stewart were killed instantly."

Renee shook her head at Cole. "Sometimes you're just plain spooky."

"It's my job, Renee. I gathered all I could before I made the trip down here."

She was fascinated and intrigued. "What else do you know about me?" She then moseyed over to a wicker chair to reclaim her seat.

"Okay then." He held up his right forefinger. "But with no interruptions."

She nodded in agreement and playfully grinned.

He took a quick sip of the bourbon before enlightening her. "You grew up here in Harpersfield, the first eight years with your parents, and then from there, with your grandfather. You're the older of two siblings. You attended Waynesburg High School and graduated three years ago with a grade point average of 3.6. You were a cheerleader both your freshman and sophomore years. You withdrew from that when you were a junior because you picked up extra classes. College prep courses. You haven't gone off to college because since Nate's death, you don't want to leave your grandfather alone. You once dated a guy named Dillon Niles. The Porters took care of that. The brothers beat Dillon to within inches of his life and then trashed and robbed the Niles home. Dillon and his parents did not press charges because they feared retaliation from the Porters. That's exactly how those animals get away with the antics they bestow upon the population."

Renee did not know exactly what had become of Dillon until now. She was speechless.

"Your best friend is Stacy Hughes, but you don't see much of her these days. She's pregnant and married, living in a trailer park in Waynesburg. You didn't get your driver's license until you were seventeen. You failed the test three times when you were sixteen. Finally, your grandfather signed you up for a driver's education course. You passed your first try after completing the program."

Cole drew another sip of bourbon and then resumed.

"You have no criminal record, though once when you were eleven, a stolen skateboard was found in your possession. You bought it from a fellow student at school not knowing that it was stolen. Your favorite of the dogs on the farm is Merlin. You were a Girl Scout Brownie from the age of six until ten. After that, you lost interest in the program. You didn't play any sports in high school. Your studies were more important to you. You like to cook, especially a good

chuck roast. You drink occasionally, but not often. You obviously don't smoke"—they both chuckled—"and at times, you can be a bit stern with your opinions."

Renee sat with her eyes widened and her jaw opened. "It's like you've read my diary. Except I don't have one."

"Oh, but you do. We all do." He then whispered, "It's called government files."

She was astounded. "You gathered all that from files?"

"Mostly. The rest came from your grandfather," Cole revealed.

She giggled. "Boy, Grandpa has a big mouth."

Cole stooped down to pick up his pack of Marlboros. Soon, he was lighting one of the cigarettes placed between his lips.

Renee yawned. "The greatest enemy of good morals is fear. People will do things outta anxiety that they would normally not do. Fear is the drivin' force that leads to the demise of people's fine standards. They are forced to sacrifice their decent principles in order to adapt to fear. I've witnessed it here in Harpersfield all my life, thanks to the Porters. It's not an easy thing to do to surrender what you hold so dear to yourself. It's not a good transaction at all. Your dignity is tested, and sometimes it's lost. The Porters have stolen away the moral fiber from most of the people in this small town, and it's a downright shame. I'm not sure why Murky hasn't tried the fear factor on me, but his brothers sure have. Murky shuts them down though. He won't allow them to intimidate me. But I'm no different than anyone else. If the Porters made me choose between my life or the life of ones that I love, or doin' whatever it is they wanted me to do, I'd have to go along with their demands. That's where terror overtakes good morals. Thank god the Porters haven't done that to me...not yet anyway."

Cole appreciated conversing with Renee. She was not only beautiful but intelligent as well. "Yeah, you're right there. Our first line of defense as humans is our instinct to survive. So when someone succumbs to the Porters' threats and drops their proud values in order to get by, we certainly can't judge them for that."

"What is the most disgraceful thing that you have done out fear?" she questioned.

He hesitated.

"Oh, come on. You can tell me," she persisted.

Cole exhaled big. "When I was eleven, before I started weight training, I was a small guy. One day I spotted a go-kart resting curbside in front of our house. My dad was at work, Becky was at a friend's, and my mom was, well, sleeping of course. I walked out to the roadside to investigate as to why someone would just abandon their go-kart."

"That was strange," she added.

"I looked around the immediate area, but I didn't see anyone, so I decided to take a seat on the go-kart to see how it felt. I started to imagine that I was a driver in the Indianapolis 500."

She giggled. He chuckled.

"Suddenly, a brutal-sounding voice yelled out to me, 'Hey, Walsh, get the hell off my ride!' I looked up to see Baron Johnson and his sidekick Ray Carnes approaching. Now, Baron was a few years older than me, and he was the bully of the neighborhood. I had no idea that the go-kart belonged to him, and it later turned out that it was actually stolen. Anyway, Baron and Ray had been riding the go-kart around the neighborhood before it eventually ran out of gas." Cole tasted his drink before picking back up on the story. "I was stymied with fear because I knew that anything associated with Baron Johnson was bad news. The kids in the neighborhood called him BJ behind his back, but never to his face."

"Why would they be frightened to call him by his initials?"

"Well, they were his initials alright, but to us kids, the letters stood for something else."

"What?" she inquired.

"You know." He gestured by waving his hand near his crotch area. She gazed, baffled. "No...what?"

He cleared his throat. "You know, BJ, um...initials used to indicate, um, oral sex...blow job...BJ for short."

She chortled before clearing her throat. "Oh, now I see why Baron would take offense to that. Please continue."

"I stood up from the go-kart and backed away as they approached. Baron warned me to stay put, so I fearfully complied.

He set the filled gas can he was carrying down on the ground and told me to kneel in front of the red container. I hesitated before he slapped me hard on the back of my head. I knelt before the can, and then he shoved my face in front of the flexible hose. He made me inhale those gas fumes for nearly two minutes. By the time I was allowed to stand up, I couldn't balance from the dizziness. They laughed as I stumbled around the yard until finally, I threw up. I was so humiliated. I had a blasting headache for three hours after that."

"That Baron was an idiot," Renee snarled. "Did you tell your parents what happened?"

Cole shook his head no. "My dad, the cop, would have had Baron arrested, and that would have made things unbearable when that hoodlum got out of jail with his sure-to-be vengeance upon me. You know, just like the Porter syndrome asserts itself. So I kept it all to myself."

She nearly reached for his hand, but lacked the assertiveness to do so. "That must have been terrible."

He bowed his head in shame. "Yeah, it was, and I didn't do a damn thing to try to stop him. I was scared. Another example of what fear can do to a person."

"Did you retaliate on this Baron guy when you got older and bigger?"

He exhaled smoke from his cigarette. "I didn't have to. Shortly after he turned twenty-one, he got involved in a bar fight inside a tavern in Cleveland, and he was stabbed to death."

Renee slid her hair back behind her ears. "Well, I don't wish death upon anyone, but that guy certainly had it comin' to him."

After a few moments of collecting himself, Cole inquired, "How about you, Renee? When has fear ever controlled you?"

She squirmed in her chair, producing the familiar squeaking sounds of wicker. "Promise not to tell?" She impishly glanced at him with puppy-dog eyes.

He shot his right palm up into the air. "You have my word."

"Alright then…There are old abandoned mines around the area, productive coal mines from long ago. This expanse used to be a real central core for coal, but not so much anymore. The mines

were deserted decades ago and have since either been filled in or have collapsed on their own with time. But a few of them still exist. One summer day, when I was about ten, my best friend Stacy and I were bored out of our minds. I mean, there is only so much a kid out of school for the summer can find to do in Harpersfield.

"So not being able to come up with much else to do, we decided to go mine exploring. All the parents in the area repeatedly warned their children to stay away from the old mines, and ours were no different. But we'd play it cool and only go inside the mines a small distance. The mine shaft we decided to explore that day was behind the Gerts' store. Stacy and I slid back the plywood that covered the shaft's entrance and gingerly, while daring each other, stepped inside.

"Just ten feet down the shaft where the daylight still shined inside, I came face-to-face with a bat that was hangin' from the wall of the mine. A big bat—I mean a big bat! I must have startled it as it peered at me through its beady eyes and snarled with its pointy teeth. Though they are blind, I know, but that bat sure seemed to have its eyesight fixated on me."

Her eyes widened, and Cole's eyebrows raised.

"I screamed out, and not even knowin' what I was screaming about, Stacy screamed as well. We crawled up and out of that shaft in a flash with that bat flutterin' around behind us.

"Once we made it out of the mine, the bat stayed inside the shaft, thank god. We jumped up and down and quickly ran our hands through our hair. It was then that Stacy began to laugh. She laughed hard as she pointed at...at...at, well, my crotch area. I looked down to see that I had urinated in my shorts. I was so embarrassed."

Cole tried his best, but he was unable to control himself before he busted out in a hardy laugh.

"Hush now, Cole, it's not all that funny." She angered a bit.

He attempted to tighten his lips, but like a dam with a hole in it, he couldn't hold back. He hooted until tears slowly rolled down from his eyes. "You pissed in your pants!"

She folded her arms. "Well, I prefer to call it urinated in my shorts, but go ahead, have your fun."

He spoke as he continued to howl, "Oh, come on…Renee… you have to admit…that…it's humorous."

She remained slighted until her lips slowly begin to quiver. She then grinned and joined Cole in his laughter. "Well, that bat…it scared the hell out of me! Well, my pee as well."

They both continued with laughter for a spell before slowly subsiding. They wiped tears from their eyes.

"Oh, that was too good," Cole expressed, nearly out of breath.

"Yeah, fear sure is a strange and powerful emotional reaction," she agreed. Renee then stood from her chair and yawned. "I think I'm gonna call it a night. It's been a long day, and I'm exhausted."

She hesitated for a moment while anticipating a good night wish or something along those lines coming from Cole. He made no such gesture, merely taking a drag from his cigarette. Renee shrugged her shoulders and then strode down from the porch.

As she made her way across the lawn toward the farmhouse, Cole called out to her, "Hey, Renee!"

She halted her walk to turn to look at him. "Yes?"

"One more thing about you…you're wearing light blue undies." He winked.

Renee shook her right fist at Cole in a playful manner. She then turned away from him and continued to walk toward the farmhouse.

Just before she stepped inside the house and through the screen door, Cole raised his voice so that she could hear him. "Good night, sweet dreams."

She smiled while remaining turned away from him as she glided inside the farmhouse.

August 1

IT WAS JUST after daybreak when Sheriff Bob Harvey steered the only Harpersfield patrol car ever so slowly through the heart of town along Harper Street. Sitting next to him in the passenger's seat was Deputy Frank Collins. The building roofs, as well as the lawns around town, were still damp from the morning dew. The sunlight was trekking above the horizon and piercing through the windshield of the patrol car. It was twenty-eight minutes past six o'clock.

Both officers, the entire police force of Harpersfield, already had their sunglasses perched on their noses while shielding their eyes from the bright morning spears of sunlight.

Sheriff Harvey was overweight. He had been chunky throughout his life. From a pudgy kid growing up in Harpersfield to a man now nearing fifty-two years of age, he had been plump. He was a victim of male pattern baldness at a young age. Only the sides and lower back of his head of hair remained before he was twenty-five years old. About ten years ago, he began to shave what little remained of his head of hair from his scalp. Bob's maintained the slick appearance

ever since that first day's bout with the razor. The folks of Harpersfield called him cue ball—at least they did so behind his back.

What personally annoyed Bob regarding the loss of hair on his head was his inability to grow a robust mustache or beard. He felt that a definitive mustache and beard would offset the absence of hair upon his head. He grew what facial hair he could muster and never placed a razor anywhere near the sporadic growth, although the crop was barely beyond the stage of peach fuzz. The sheriff had been married twice and divorced twice. He had been a single man over the past eleven years, and he had become accustomed to flying solo. Bob had two daughters from his first marriage who were now grown and resided in different parts of the United States. He sent the girls to a private school in Knoxville as they grew up, nearly breaking him financially. This minimized his daughters' exposure to the Porter family.

Deputy Collins had a hair problem as well, except his predicament was too much hair. He could grow a full beard from smooth skin in less than six days. He did shave each day, sometimes twice. Rarely did he sport a beard, and then that didn't last for long before he broke out his razor. His wife, Elizabeth, was not partial to facial hair on a man. His light brown hair was thick and difficult to comb, especially first thing in the morning. Hair sprouting out from his chest protruded up and over the collar of his uniform's shirt. Frank was born thirty-four years ago with nearly a full head of hair. He had just as pertinent of a hairline now as he did then. His mane hadn't receded an inch. He would complain about his thick hair at times, but not while in the company of his boss. It was a touchy subject to discuss around Sheriff Harvey.

Frank was thin, and the visible veins in his arms formed a map upon his forearms. His perceptible Adam's apple bounced when he spoke with his deep-toned voice. His left front tooth was chipped in half, a result of his temper about ten years ago. Frank was driving nails into the new siding on his house. Unwittingly to him, he was using the wrong type of nails for the job. The nails were stubborn to sink into the siding. Some bent, some snapped. Out of frustration, Frank reared back aggressively with the hammer and caught himself in the mouth. The hammer's blow cracked the tooth in half. It was

then that Elizabeth insisted that Frank enter an anger management course over in Webster. The program had helped Frank to relax and not to react with such a short fuse, although Frank's aggressive temperament had done little to boost his courage.

"Collins, we have to start crackin' down on the Porters a little harder before the state comes down on our asses hard," Sheriff Harvey asserted.

Frank fidgeted in his seat. "If you don't mind, sheriff, I'd like to be around to see my baby grow up."

"I wasn't bein' completely serious. Just sayin' it is all. It just feels good to say it sometimes."

Collins sighed with relief.

"No," Bob continued, "I've been around these parts for too long to know better than to lock horns with the Porters. Carter was an absolute bastard when we were growin' up."

"He still is," Frank added.

Bob nodded in agreement while keeping his eyes on the road. "Yes, that he is. Did I ever tell you about the time when Carter and his brother Steadman tortured that woman up at Fowler's Mill?"

Frank reluctantly shook his head no. He was not comfortable hearing war stories about the Porters. It reminded him of the potential danger of his job.

"Well, Carter and Steadman trapped this woman up by the mill. I think Carter was about fifteen and Steadman seventeen. The woman, Mary Wellford, was a wife and mother livin' over in Webster. She was about thirty-four at the time. She was leavin' work after her shift at the mill and was walkin' toward her car. Carter and Steadman were all drunken up and sittin' inside Steadman's truck near the entrance of the mill. Well, at least Steadman was sittin' in the parked truck. Carter was off in the brush pissin'. Steadman spotted Mary walkin' toward her car, and he took a likin' to her. Mary was an attractive woman from what I understand. Anyway, he watched as she swayed toward her car, unaware that she was in the vicinity of a couple of hoodlums. Steadman yelled through the open window of the truck for Carter to hurry up with his business. Carter made his way quickly back to the truck, nearly pissin' on his pants in the process."

"How do you know all the details?" Frank wondered.

Bob turned the patrol car along its slow course onto Vine Street. "Are you kiddin'? Steadman was a braggart. He couldn't keep his mouth shut. If Steadman was involved in somethin', which was often, the whole town knew about it."

Frank nodded.

"So," Bob continued, "Carter hops back inside the truck just about the time Mary was duckin' inside her car. Carter and Steadman followed Mary until they came up on a remote section of Martin's Way about eight miles outside of Webster. You know where that is, it was remote back then, but that new truck wash place is there now. It was there that they ran her off the road where her car slid into a ditch. Steadman leaped out from his truck to pull Mary out from her car. She screamed at the top of her lungs, but there was no one other than Carter around to hear her cries of distress. Steadman and Carter took turns rapin' that poor lady. When they were done with her sexually, they couldn't just leave her be—no, not the damn Porters. They had to beat her, and beat her they did. They completely caved in the side of Mary's face with their bare fists. Steadman bit off part of her left ear, and Carter pulled out six of her teeth with a pair of pliers."

Frank grimaced. "Jesus Christ, Bob."

"Well, it's fact. I mean, you just can't make up shit like that, Collins. Anyway, they left her for dead lyin' along Martin's Way. A few minutes after the Porters sped away, a passin' dairy truck found Mary battered next to her wrecked vehicle. He rushed Mary to the hospital. She spent five long weeks in the hospital. She did finally regain consciousness, but she was a vegetable, unable to speak, walk, or remember who she was.

"Well, Steadman bragged about the incident to nearly anyone who would listen. Carter tried his best to keep Steadman's mouth shut. The police had no physical evidence linking the Porters to Mary's attack, but it was common knowledge that they did it. Today's forensic technology wasn't available back in those days. Mary's husband, Rick Wellford, eventually caught wind of the rumors comin' out of Harpersfield. He took to his gun one day to avenge the ruthless attack on his wife. He drove here to Harpersfield and found Carter

along with Steadman inside the tavern. He opened that gun up and let it bark. He fired four shots altogether, hittin' Steadman twice and Carter once. A bullet that went astray lodged in the wall behind the pool table. That bullet is still in that wall today. Steadman passed away a few hours later. Carter spent a week in the hospital after they removed a bullet from his stomach. Rick Wellford got life in prison for killin' Steadman.

Carter was furious that his brother was shot and killed. About a year later, Rick and Mary's son, Ronnie, who was twelve and now livin' with his grandmother in Webster, disappeared on his walk to school one day. He was never seen again, and the body of the boy has never been found. Carter was not one to run his mouth like Steadman did, but somehow, everyone knew that it was Carter who nabbed that boy. His sick way of avengin' his brother's death."

Frank ground his teeth, "Man, those Porters are goddamn animals."

Bob parked the patrol car curbside on Vine Street. The officers remained inside the vehicle.

"I was always frightened that the Porters would get a hold of one of my girls. Now, I'll admit that I don't exactly take care of the Porters like I should, but God as my witness, if they had ever touched a hair on one of my daughters' heads, I would've killed them," Bob claimed.

"What is it do you suppose makes them so evil?" Frank quizzed.

Bob let go of a long sigh. "Who's to say, Frank? I dunno. Maybe it's a chemical imbalance in their brains or somethin'. There are some people that just can't be helped, that can't be reached."

Frank rubbed his eyes. "Feels like the pollens are gonna be up today."

"Did ya remember to bring your inhaler thingy?"

"Yeah…I got it here in my pocket," Frank replied.

CHAPTER 24

COLE STIRRED IN his morning sleep as he perspired. He was dreaming about something that took place in his past. Something that disturbed him deeply.

*****

As part of a drug sting, the FBI raided a house in Columbus, Ohio, that was distributing crack cocaine. Usually this would be a local police operation, but this distributor had loose international ties with drug lords and kingpins. Cole was a member of the raid that afternoon. Tony Gerney was the distributor, and he had three prior drug-related arrests. Tony had money, dirty money, enough to buy big fancy lawyers and reduced sentences for his crimes. This time though, the FBI caught him with enough cocaine to put him away for life. Six people occupied the house that day—Tony, his girlfriend Tina, his partner Aaron Kessler, and two of Tony's and Aaron's thugs. Also inside the house, was Hadie Thompson, a young lady strung out on heroin.

The FBI had timed their raid perfectly. Tony and his thugs were caught off-guard, and the arrests went off without a hitch. Cole discovered Hadie as the last occupant inside the house. She was in an upstairs

bedroom sprawled out on the bed. Her clothes were soiled and looked as though they had been on her body for weeks. Her arms revealed multiple tracks where she had been injecting heroin into her veins. Through her inadequate hygiene, Cole could see a beautiful young lady. Hadie was so out of it that she didn't even realize that Cole was removing her from the house. Cole could have arrested her as part of the sting, but he chose to admit her in a rehabilitation center instead.

Hadie stayed in the center for nearly a year while Cole visited her on a monthly basis. When she came out of rehabilitation, she was clean, sober, and healthy. Her beauty now shined through, and twenty-four-year-old Hadie Thompson was ready to start her new life.

She credited Cole for saving her life. She had no family to turn to and nowhere to go. She could have stayed at the city mission for a spell, but Cole feared that if left alone, she might fall back into using drugs. He decided to move her up north a bit to his apartment in Cleveland. There he could watch over her until she could get on her feet.

Weeks turned into months as Hadie and Cole grew closer to one another. She landed a job as a waitress at a local Denny's Restaurant and was beginning to do well for herself. At some point, Cole and Hadie fell in love with each other. They began sharing the same bed as well as the same dreams.

Cole was called out of town on a case for weeks. He called daily to check in on Hadie. The first week she was there to answer each call. Then her availability became sporadic. After several weeks of instability from her, Cole withdrew from the case and caught the next flight back to Cleveland. He rushed to the apartment fearing something was wrong. He crashed through the door to see that the apartment was a mess with clothes and dirty dishes lying in each room. He rushed through the bedroom door to find Hadie lying on the bed, nude and nearly unconscious. A hypodermic needle was on the stand next to the bed.

Cole's eyes watered. "Oh no, Hadie, please no."

Hadie stirred and moaned at the sound of his voice. Her voice was weak and distorted. "Cole, honey, what are you doing here? You…um… weren't supposed to be home yet…yet."

Cole sat on the edge of the bed and ran his hand through her long blonde hair. "Why, Hadie?"

She sighed. "I lost my job. I didn't know how to tell you. They said they were cutting back...back. Yeah, right...they just found about my past...my past."

He took her gently into his arms. "It's okay, Hadie, people lose jobs every day. You'll find another job, it'll be okay. This junk you're using isn't going to make things better, it just makes it worse." Cole then kissed her on the forehead and gently laid her body back down on the bed. He whispered to her, "Is there any more in the apartment?"

She raised her hand and, with a frail finger, pointed to the dresser. He stood up from the bed and approached the dresser. He opened the top drawer to see three full vials of liquid heroin, with one that was nearly empty. He sighed as he took the vials into his hand. He stepped into the bathroom and flushed the contents of the vials down the toilet. He then returned to Hadie's side. "Promise me, babe, that tomorrow you'll let me put you back into rehab. Okay?"

She nodded in agreement.

He then smiled at her. She delivered a weakened grin.

The following morning, moments before Cole opened his eyes, he could feel her cold skin against his body. Her body temperature had dropped over the nighttime hours, and without looking, Cole knew that Hadie had passed away sometime during the night. She died of cardiac arrest due to the heroin abuse for nearly eight years. All he could do was hold her lifeless body and weep before calling the coroner.

Two days later, he found her diary tucked between the mattress and the boxed springs. The only entry for each day were the same eleven words: "God, please help me, I can't do this on my own."

*****

Cole abruptly woke on the bed inside the guesthouse. His breathing was heavy, and his heart raced. He sat up on the bed and rubbed his eyes.

Renee, inside her bedroom in the farmhouse, woke almost simultaneously as Cole. She had a rough night of dreaming about her parents and Nate. Suddenly, her telephone on the nightstand rang.

She wondered who it could be at such an early hour. She picked up the receiver. "Hello?"

"Hello, beautiful," Murky's voice greeted her from the other end of the call.

She couldn't stomach Murky, especially so early in the morning. "What do ya want?"

"Hey, whoa. You're grouchy in the mornin'. I'll have to remember that when we get married," he commented.

In a bad way, Renee wanted to tell him to go straight to hell. However, she realized what the plan entailed. This was one of the unpleasant sides of the strategy. "What are you doin' up so early anyway?" she inquired.

"I haven't slept. I've been thinkin' about you all night. I jerked off while thinkin' about you," Murky admitted.

She squinted and stuck her tongue out. "That is so disgustin'."

"No, not at all, darlin'. It's a compliment to you."

She shook her head. "Well, do me a favor and don't compliment me again."

After a brief silence, he asked, "What are ya doin' today, sweet thing?"

"Why?"

"I was just thinkin' we could meet this evenin'. Say, at around seven at Full Moon Drive-In over in Webster?"

She looked confused. "They haven't shown a movie at that drive-in for years. It's closed."

"Exactly." He laughed into the receiver. "We'll make our own movie, a dirty movie."

Now she began to feel nauseated. "Murky, it's too early in the mornin' for my mind to work. You'll have to call me later."

"Okay then, beautiful. Later it is. I'm goin' to get some shut-eye and dream about you. If you're naked in my dream, I'll wake up with a hard-on."

She rolled her eyes. "That's more information than I need to know. I have to go now," she declared before abruptly ending the call. She then screamed at the telephone, "I hate you!"

Ike, who was brewing a pot of coffee in the kitchen, overhead Renee's anguish. He scampered to the end of the hallway and raised his voice, "Are you okay back there?"

She shouted back through her bedroom door, "Yeah, Grandpa, I'm okay. I'll be out in a minute." She then sat up in bed and then stood on the floor, leaving her blanket on the bed. She was only dressed in a pair of panties, attired like she wore most every night. Sometimes, during the cold of the winter, she would wear a T-shirt to bed. But it was summer, a hot summer at that, so no T-shirt or bra was needed. Her fully bared breasts perked in the morning sunlight streaming through her bedroom window. The same window that suddenly crashed into her bedroom with shattering glass.

Cole's body lunged through the ground-floor window, and then he rolled onto the carpet. Renee was stunned at the sudden intrusion, and her eyes widened as she again screamed. Cole quickly ascended to his feet in a fighting stance and looked frantically around the room.

Ike stepped quickly down the hallway toward Renee's room.

"What the hell are you doin'?" Renee shouted.

"I heard you scream," Cole reported. "Are you okay? Is Murky in here?"

"I'm fine. He was on the phone. I screamed at the phone after we hung up. Jesus Christ, you scared the hell out of me!"

Ike attempted to turn the doorknob, but it was locked.

"I'm sorry," Cole apologized. "I thought you were being assaulted."

She felt a safe and secure comfort knowing that Cole reacted and responded so quickly and decisively. Renee was about to approach him to reassure Cole that she was okay, but it was then that she realized that she was standing before him clad in only her panties. Her breasts were completely exposed to him. She promptly crossed her arms in front of breasts. "Get out of my room, Cole!"

"What is goin' on in there?" Ike inquired with deep concern to his voice.

"It's okay, Grandpa," she answered, again through the locked bedroom door. "It's only Cole comin' to what he thought was my rescue. He'll be comin' out now."

While keeping one arm covering her breasts, Renee reached with her other hand to gain a grip on the blanket lying on the bed. She whisked the blanket up to her body and wrapped it around herself. "Will you please get out of my room?" she again requested.

Cole relaxed his fists and opened the palms of his hands. "Yeah, okay…sure. I'm sorry."

"It's okay…just get out of here, please."

He moved toward the door and unlocked the knob before pulling open the door. Ike, leaning on the door, spilled into Cole's chest before gaining his balance.

"Whoa there, old man," Cole said as he grabbed hold of Ike to stabilize him.

Ike looked to his granddaughter wrapped up in her blanket. "Are you okay, honey?"

"Yeah, Grandpa, I'm fine. It's just that Murky was on the phone, and he upset me. When I screamed, Cole thought I was in danger, and he came crashin' through my window."

Ike grinned. "It's nice havin' a bodyguard, huh?"

"Well, yeah. But the bodyguard doesn't need to see the actual body he's protectin'." She blushed.

Ike chuckled.

"I'm sorry, Renee. I'll clean up the broken glass mess," Cole offered.

Without looking in his direction, Renee nodded.

Ike then patted Cole on the shoulder. "I'll get the broken glass later. Come on, Cole, let's go out to the kitchen. I gotta fresh pot of coffee on."

"Okay, Ike, sounds good," Cole accepted. Cole then sauntered from Renee's bedroom first, and then Ike closed the door behind them.

When she was certain that they had departed, Renee allowed the blanket covering her body to drop to the floor. The nipples of her breasts were standing erect. She was sexually excited that Cole had viewed her in such a vulnerable fashion. However, she was not about to let him know that.

Renee then stepped out of her panties and tossed the silky undergarment into a nearby laundry basket before heading for the bathroom directly off her bedroom to shower. As the warm water

spilled over her body, Renee resisted to touch herself with masturbation, but rather to think of something that would cool her existing sexual surge, her exhilaration.

Thoughts of Murky Porter would certainly do the trick of destroying her current sexual awareness. But the memory that rushed into her mind, one that she wished she could forget, returned in a fury. She shivered as she recalled the events of that autumn day when she was seventeen.

*****

Renee strolled down the long driveway of the farm to retrieve the daily mail. It was early afternoon, and usually Ike was quick to get the mail a bit after its arrival in the morning hours. However, Ike had been down with the flu the past twelve hours, so Renee took on the task. She hummed the latest song that was hot on the charts that she heard on the radio a few minutes prior as she continued along the driveway. The autumn breeze was warm that day as it tickled at the fire red and bold yellow leaves on the trees that were nearing their time to descend to the ground below. She wore shorts that day, figuring there wouldn't be many days remaining that she could do so. The winter winds would be setting in soon, and the shorts would be put away until springtime. Her top was a loose-fitting T-shirt, and as she was about to discover, it would prove to be a good choice on her part.

As she neared the mailbox along the side of the road, she began to feel a bit uneasy. A sense of insecurity invaded her body, as if she had swallowed a hot drink and could feel it seep down inside of her chest and finally ooze into her stomach. She opened the door of the mailbox and reached inside. She pulled from the box a teen magazine she had a subscription to, a few bills, and a birthday card from Myra Cooper addressed to Nate Stewart, although his birthday was nearly a month away.

Renee grinned at the thought of the pretty girl from over in Steven's Pass who was sending her brother a birthday card. Nate was in Memphis competing in a four-day softball tournament with his fall league team. He had been gone for two days, and it would be two more until he returned home. Renee would put the card on his dresser to be sure that he received it.

She shut the door to the mailbox, tucked the mail under her arm, and was about to head up the driveway when she was startled.

"Hello, Renee, the love of my life," Murky claimed.

The sudden intrusion of his voice over the breeze and the rustling leaves on the trees caused her to jerk her body and lose her grip on the mail. The documents plummeted to the driveway.

Murky had been hiding out in the deep ditch across the street. He was now standing twenty feet behind her.

"Damn it, Murky, you scared the tar out of me!" she snipped.

He snickered.

"Very funny!" she continued to scold. "Where did you come from anyway?"

He nodded toward the road. "I was in the ditch."

She bent to pick up the mail. "I don't even want to know why you were in the ditch," she groaned. She then realized that in this position, her shorts were elevating up her legs toward her buttocks. She quickly snatched up the mail and stood upright to discover that Murky had been indeed ogling at her backside. "Is there somethin' I can do for you, Murky Porter?" she asked hastily.

He winked. "Yeah, marry me."

"Not in a million years," she responded.

He curled his lip at her.

"Where are your brothers anyway? The three of you are always together."

Sterling and Dalton then stepped out from behind a large pine tree near the road.

Renee nodded and muttered, "I should've known." She was nervous enough with Murky near her, but now with the three Porters within striking distance, she became stifled with fear. The vastness of distance to the farmhouse seemed to grow in her mind.

Sterling and Dalton joined Murky at the end of the driveway.

"What are ya doin' for the rest of the day, sweet thang?" Murky queried.

She shrugged her shoulders and then looked up the driveway. From here, it was a bit too far for the farmhouse to be within her sights. The farmhouse nestled behind a row of tall brush off to the right of the driveway. She could see the brush, but it seemed to be marching off farther into

the distance. She cleared her throat. "I...um...I have to take care of my grandfather. He hasn't been feelin' well."

"That old man probably drank too much moonshine last night," Dalton sneered.

"If ya can't hold it, don't drink it," Sterling added.

Renee shook her head no. "That's not it at all. He has the flu."

"Call a hangover whatever ya want to, Stewart," Dalton spat out.

Murky turned his head to look at his brothers. "You two morons show Renee some respect."

In a sissified voice, Dalton yelped, "You two morons show Renee some respect. I am Murky Porter, and I am sooooooo pussy whipped."

Sterling snickered.

"Sterling, Dalton, shut your sewer holes, or I'll hurt you, and I'll hurt you bad," Murky warned.

Sterling and Dalton mocked as if they were trembling with fear.

Murky then focused his attention back on Renee. "So, baby, why don't we say that you come by the house this evenin'?"

Renee wanted to put him off, but she realized that she needed to be tactful if she wanted to make it back to the farmhouse intact. "I already told ya, Murky. I have to take care of my grandfather."

Murky shoved his hands into his pants pockets and then rocked on the soles of his boots. "So you're sayin' that if your grandfather wasn't sick that you'd come over to my house?"

She twitched nervously. "Well, no...not exactly."

He brightened. "Oh, I see, you want me to come by here instead."

She exhaled as she attempted to be diplomatic. "Murky...why don't you find a gal who wants to be with you? That girl just isn't me. Sometimes it's there for two people, and sometimes it's not. I'm sorry, Murky, but I don't now nor will I ever feel that way about you."

He squinted and growled, "I feel that way about you. You'll just have to learn to want me. Whatever it takes to do that, you'd better get on with it."

The sounds of an approaching car had the four of them gazing out to the road. Passing by slowly after spotting the foursome were Deputy Frank Collins and Sheriff Bob Harvey inside the Harpersfield patrol car.

Renee sighed relief, but it was short-lived. Bob stopped the car as Frank rolled down the window. "Is everythin' alright here?" Frank called out.

Renee shook her head no and waved for them to come to her rescue.

"Get the hell out of here, Bob and Frank, before we break your necks," Sterling warned.

Slowly and reluctantly, Frank rolled his window up, and Bob steered the patrol car away from the immediate area.

Renee's heart began to race with trepidation.

Murky turned to peer at her with a fiery, angered gaze. His eyes appeared to turn gray. "I love you, Renee, but that is only goin' to carry you so far. I'm gettin' tired of tryin' to court you with no results."

She was at a loss of how to respond without offending him. She gave it a go. "Murky, I'm sorry, I don't know what to tell you. You can't force someone to want to be with you. You should stop tryin' to court me. It is never goin' to happen like you wish it to be."

Dalton growled, "Face it, Murky, the only way you're gettin' any of that pussy is to take it by force. I say that we all screw her, right here and right now."

"I second that," Sterling agreed.

"No!" Murky bit out. "Only I do it with Renee! But you two goons could hold her down for me while I take her. Maybe after I have my way with her, she'll fall in love with me. Take her down, brothers!"

Dalton and Sterling shuffled toward Renee.

She had to take flight; she needed to find the strength in her trembling, fear-jellied legs to make a run for the farmhouse. But she realized deep down inside that she simply couldn't outrun the Porters. They were tall, strong, and fast afoot. She was in a foul situation that was turning uglier by the second.

Run! she fired off inside of her mind.

Just as the tingling sensation of adrenaline flowed down her legs, a pickup truck went speeding by the driveway. The driver of the truck did not detect the foursome on the Stewarts' driveway.

"Oh, fuck no!" Dalton wailed. "That was Pop. He'll kill us if he makes it home before we do. We haven't done lick around the property today."

It was immediately apparent that Murky, Dalton and Sterling were panicked and intimidated—something that was rarely seen from the trio.

"Let's go!" Sterling demanded. "We'll shortcut it through Wiles' field."

As rapidly as they had appeared some ten minutes prior, the Porters were gone in a flash.

Renee shuddered all over as tears of liberation streamed down her cheeks. She began a walk up the driveway, but it soon turned into a hardy jog.

*****

Renee slowed the flow of hot water to allow the cold water to dominate the shower's fall. She quivered to wash away the dreadful memory of that day from her thoughts.

CHAPTER 25

IT WAS JUST past ten in the morning, Las Vegas time, when Marla Simmons's cell phone began to ring. The phone was sitting on the nightstand next to the bed.

Marla and Dule were sleeping away an extremely long night behind them into the late morning hours in each other's arms. It was nearly daybreak before they finally drifted off to sleep. Their clothes were scattered about the hotel room as a result of what was a sex-filled evening for them.

She forced her eyes open and reached for the ringing phone. Dule stirred but did not wake. She pressed the call button. "Hello?" her raspy, groggy voice greeted the caller.

"Hello, Marla, it's Cole."

She immediately sat up in bed. "Cole, I've been thinking about you quite a bit. How's it going in the hills of Tennessee?"

"So far everything is on schedule. These Porters…they are certainly ruthless."

"Is it something you can maintain a handle on?"

"Well, I haven't turned up the heat just yet, but the rising of the thermostat is commencing come this evening. I'll then know better on how to access the situation," he pointed out.

She grasped the phone with both hands. "Listen, Cole, I'm seriously considering backing out of this one. I have a bad feeling about it that simply won't go away. What do you think?"

Cole squinted as he paced the guesthouse floor. "Please don't pull the plug on this, Marla. We need to get these killers off the street."

It became her turn to squint. "These? What do you mean by these? You're only to take care of Murky, not the other two brothers."

"Marla, if I leave two behind, I might as well leave all three. This trio of brothers are pure evil and inseparable. They work as a team. If I put Murky down and leave it at that, Sterling and Dalton will make this town their own revengeful playground with their rage. It's already bad enough that the town is virtually within their control. I have to take out all three brothers for this to be entirely effective," he explained.

She bit down on her lip. "Boy, I don't know about this, Cole. You need to let me think it over. In the meantime, it's Murky only. Am I making myself perfectly clear? Remember, it's my decision, not yours."

He reluctantly ceded, "Yeah, I know, Marla. I won't expand the mission without your go-ahead."

She smiled with a bit more ease. "Good. Now, call me tomorrow and update me on the impact of the raised thermostat. Got it?"

"Will do. Can I ask where you're at?"

Marla glanced over at a sleeping Dule as she replied sheepishly, "I'm in Vegas. Gambling a little and exercising with Dule, if you know what I mean." She giggled.

He chuckled. "Yeah, I gotcha. Just don't wear Dule out. He seems a little soft to me."

"Oh, anyone less than Iron Man is soft to you, Cole," she indicated.

"Yeah...well...perhaps. Anyway, I'll speak with you tomorrow."

"Okay. Be careful, and good luck."

"Thanks," he said before ending the call.

Marla stared at her phone for a moment as she whispered, "I hope for your sake, Cole, that my intuition on this one is wrong."

*****

"WHAT THE HELL are you lookin' at?" Sterling badgered Beverly Darton. Sterling was standing guard outside the laundromat on Harper Street guzzling a beer while Dalton and Murky were inside robbing the change machine.

Beverly was about to enter with a bag of soiled clothing in her hand. Beverly was forty-seven but appeared sixty. Diabetes had taken its toll on her, especially over the past six years. Her skin was leathery and her hair very thin, unusually thin for a woman. She sported bifocal eyeglasses as the disease had eaten away at her retinas. She was unable to maintain a steady weight, so as a result, she was extremely slim. Her kidneys were failing her as well as she needed to resort to wearing Depends Adult Diapers rather than standard underwear beneath her clothing.

Beverly did love her son, Merle, very much and was doing her best to remain in his life as long as possible. She continued to glare at Sterling.

"What the fuck is your problem, woman? Stop lookin' at me like that, or I'll rip your eyes out!" Sterling warned.

Beverly, in fear but resilient, spoke softly yet sternly at Sterling. "Yesterday, you and your savage brothers hurt my Merle."

"Yeah...so?" he snarled.

"His father and I were up with Merle most of the night. He was in pain, a lot of pain. Merle has never done anything wrong to you boys. You just do things like that for no reason. You and your brothers are sure to burn in hell."

Sterling smirked, and then his eyes narrowed. Before she had an opportunity to make any sort of move, Sterling had her by the arm in a tight grasp. "Listen here, bitch. You never speak to a Porter like that. Ever! You need to learn some manners and know your place." He then raised his right hand and backhanded her with a hard slap to her facial area.

Beverly's frail neck snapped to the right with force. Her ears rung, and her legs weakened. She dropped the bag of laundry to the sidewalk. Sterling then punched her in the stomach. Beverly keeled over and collapsed to the concrete below. Her left cheekbone caught the corner of the laundromat door, which laid open a cut on her face. Blood streamed from the incision that ran along her face down to her neck. She was nearly unconscious.

Dalton and Murky stepped outside to see Beverly folded up on the sidewalk.

Dalton chuckled. "What the hell did you do, Sterling?"

"I just kicked her ass. Comin' at me about her worthless boy, Merle. Dumb bitch." Sterling then drew in his nasal passages and spit a concoction of phlegm onto the sweater that Beverly was wearing. It was her favorite sweater that she donned even during the heat of the summer. She chilled easily as another condition of her disease.

Murky smirked and then reached for the zipper of his Levi's. He pulled out his penis and then urinated on Beverly's legs, her exposed, scraped legs protruding out from her hiked-up sundress resulting from the sudden fall.

Sterling and Dalton cheered. Before striding away, Dalton sent a hard kick into Beverly's ribs. She grunted out in pain and gasped for air. The three boys snickered in unison as they moved around the corner toward Sterling's truck. Soon, they were speeding away.

Parked across the street from the laundromat during the entire assault on Beverly Darton was the Harpersfield police cruiser. Inside the vehicle sat Sheriff Harvey and Deputy Collins.

"Is she alive?" Frank wondered.

"I dunno," Bob replied. He then turned the ignition key. "Let's just get out of here. We didn't see nothin'."

"Jesus Christ, Beverly is such a nice lady, and she's sick. Those ruthless bastards!" Frank barked.

"Yeah, well, what the hell do you want to do about it, Frank? Huh? There's nothin' we can do. We get involved in this, and we'll be the next ones sprawled out on the sidewalk." Bob then placed the patrol car into gear. He drove the car slowly past the fallen Beverly Darton and continued a track away from the area.

"Use your cell phone, not the radio, and make an anonymous call to 911. Get an ambulance out here from Waynesburg," Bob directed Frank.

Deputy Collins pulled the cell phone from his belt to place the emergency call.

Beverly Darton—beaten, tattered, soiled, and unconscious—was barely able to breathe on her own. Her body trembled slightly, and her heartbeat was erratic. Fortunate for her that she had administered a shot of insulin less than an hour before, and the blood from her cut had clotted. Her bag of laundry lay on the sidewalk with some of the clothing spilled from the opening of the plastic bag. Beverly Darton would get no laundry done on this day.

CHAPTER 26

COLE SAT ATOP the barn's roof smoking a cigarette.

"What the hell are you doin' up there?" Ike questioned. His hands were cupped around his mouth as he stood on the ground looking up at Cole.

"Just enjoying a smoke, Ike."

"Up there?"

"It's all part of the preparation."

Ike shook his head in misunderstanding. "Are you comin' down?"

Cole rose to his feet. "I'll be right there." To Ike's amazement, Cole stepped off the roof's edge and grabbed hold of the large gutter pipe running down the wall of the barn some thirty feet in length. Cole, maintaining the bulk of his weight leaning toward the barn, slid down the galvanized piping. By keeping his weight toward the pipe, he was sure not to pull the pipe's anchors out from the wall. Those results would be a painful outcome for Cole. Within seconds, Cole was standing on the ground next to Ike.

Ike pointed up to the barn's roof. "How'd you get up there?"

"That same pipe," Cole replied.

"There's a ladder inside the barn," Ike pointed out.

"Maybe next time." Cole grinned.

Ike then echoed his earlier question. "What were you doin' up there?"

"Like I said, preparation. Before I go to the next level with this case, I need to self-reflect. Make sure that I'm on the right page. I separate myself from the world and then ask myself if I'm doing the right thing."

"And are you doin' the right thing?"

Cole nodded. "I believe so, yes."

"So you gonna get those Porter boys?" Ike probed.

"You can bet the farm on it," Cole promised.

Ike smiled wide and then suddenly turned somber.

"What is it, Ike?" Cole was curious.

"Oh, what you just said about preparation, it just got me to thinkin' about a bad memory is all."

"Are you going to tell me?"

"I want to. It just feels strange to talk about breakin' the law in front of a lawman."

Cole glanced around the immediate area. "It's okay, you can speak about it freely, Ike, just be careful with any references to my occupation."

Ike reddened. "Oh, right, sorry, Cole."

"So go ahead, I want to hear about this experience you had."

Ike exhaled. "Back in my shine-runnin' days, we had two cars and two trunks full of firewater to deliver over in Waynesburg. What I mean by we were me and three of Max Chamber's cronies. Max was the boss man of the operation. No matter how much you prepared for a run, it was always unnervin'. We were to take as many back roads and secret trails as we could to stay off major highways and paved roads. One leg of the journey took us through a wooded area on a path just wide enough to accommodate the vehicles. It was dark, really dark, that night as the heavy cloud above blocked out any moonlight.

"I remember feelin' scared that night. I was always frightened to run the shine, fearin' gettin' caught and goin' to jail. But the fear I felt that night was different somehow. The farther we journeyed into the woods, the faster my heart raced. I was sweatin' like a whore in church, and though it was humid that summer night, my sweat was cold. Somewhere in the darkness of the night, somewhere along that

trail, the leading car struck something. I was drivin' the car behind the front runner with one of the cronies ridin' shotgun. It all happened in an instant, but I knew...I knew it was no deer that we hit. It was as big as a deer...but it was no deer. What that front car hit...was...well...human. Now, why there was someone out in those woods in the middle of the night was beyond me, but we hit someone just the same.

"It was by the headlights, though they were bouncing about over the rough terrain, that I caught a glimpse of that person lungin' off the trail after the car struck him." Ike's eyes clouded as he continued. "I wanted to go back, to turn around and help whoever it was that we just hit. I slowed the car to try to find a place to turn around when the thug next to me placed the barrel of his gun to my temple. He ordered me to drive on, or he'd blow my brains out. I was certain that if I didn't comply with his demands, he would have shot and killed me. I had to punch the gas pedal and continue our way to Waynesburg.

"At our drop-off point, the subject of the struck man wasn't even discussed. I checked the newspaper carefully over the next two weeks about maybe the police discoverin' a body out in the woods, but never heard a thing about it. I mean, whoever it was in those woods that night was hit hard. But I never did find out what became of that man. I still think about it from time to time. It used to drive me crazy...so much in fact that I went out to those woods years later posin' as if I were deer huntin' and frantically searched the area. I thought maybe I'd come across some human bones or somethin' like that, but I found nothin'." Ike rubbed his eyes. "I suppose it will always remain one of life's mysteries."

"Mason Turner," Cole confirmed.

"Huh?" Ike questioned, baffled.

"It was Mason Turner that was hit that night," Cole informed him.

Ike's eyes widened. "Mason? Our Mason Turner? Harpersfield's town drunk?"

"That's him."

"How could you know that?"

"Like I said before, I checked out everything about this place before I came here. Mason sought medical attention that night over

at the hospital in Webster after being found stumbling along Martin's Way by a passing trucker. His right leg, right hip, and several ribs were broken. He had to have surgery to place pins and screws into his bones."

Ike nodded. "Now that you mention it, I remember Mason bein' gone for a while after that night."

Cole snuffed out his cigarette. "Of course, we both know that it was never discovered who was responsible for hitting Mason with their vehicle or why Mason was out in those woods that night for that matter. Mason wouldn't talk to the authorities. It was feared by both Mason and the police that it was the Porters who were responsible. With Mason refusing to press charges, the police gave up on searching for the culprits."

Ike sighed. "God, what a relief it is to know that who we hit that night didn't die. But I think I know why Mason was in the woods that night."

"Why is that?"

"Well, Mason's nickname used to be Mason Jar. You know, moonshine is kept in mason jars. Well, he was most likely tryin' to learn our route. He was probably hopin' that we'd turn our back for a moment, and he could run off with some of the shine. Sometimes Mason just doesn't think with his head. Um...you're not going to arrest me, are you?"

Cole chuckled and placed his hand on Ike's shoulder. "No, Ike, I'm not going to arrest you. I think we can let it slide. But you, me, and Renee have to stop talking outright about references to my profession."

Ike covered his mouth with his fingers. "Oops, again, sorry."

*****

SHERIFF HARVEY AND Deputy Collins were taking their dinner break at Tiny's Diner. It had been a little over three hours since the Porters' assault on Beverly Darton. She was now in a hospital in Knoxville after being life-flighted from Waynesburg's medical center. Her vitals had finally stabilized, and it appeared that she would pull through the terrible ordeal. Fred and Merle had rushed to Knoxville

to be at her side. News of the attack had already spread around Harpersfield, but nobody spoke of it out in the open, only in whispers.

The sheriff bit into his hamburger before a drop of grease dribbled from out of from the bun. A bit of mayonnaise pushed its way into Bob's peach-fuzzed hair above his upper lip. Frank sat next to him at the counter, eating from his plate one French fry at a time. He had passed on a burger today; his stomach was still weak and nauseated at the thought of leaving Beverly Darton bleeding in the street.

"Who's the stranger in town?" Pam Tinelberg asked. She was behind the counter drying some drinking glasses with a small hand towel.

Bob glanced up at her with his mouthful of hamburger and bun. He shrugged his shoulders.

Pam teasingly placed her hands on her hips. "You mean to tell me that we have a handsome stranger here in Harpersfield, and the local police have no idea who he is?"

"We haven't seen him yet, but believe me, we've been told. People in this town run their mouths plenty," Frank commented.

Pam leaned onto the counter nearer to the officers. "He's stayin' up at the Stewart farm. I saw him in the back of their pickup truck yesterday."

"Ike must need an extra hand up there on the farm. He's not gettin' any younger," Bob pointed out.

"Well, that good-lookin' stranger can give me a hand anytime," Pam teased and giggled.

"You're a married woman, Pam," Frank lectured her.

"Oh, cool your afterburners, deputy, I'm just kiddin'. A gal can look, ya know."

"I'm plannin' on takin' a drive up to Ike's place tomorrow and look into who this guy is. I heard that he has Ohio plates on his truck, which strikes me as odd. Why is he all the way down here for a lame farm job?" Bob pondered.

Frank squinted. "I dunno. Perhaps he simply likes it down here."

"Maybe...or perhaps he's a wanted man by the police up in Ohio. Did you ever think of that?"

Frank shook his head no.

"See, that's why I'm the sheriff, and you're the deputy."

CHAPTER 27

RENEE HEARD MUSIC originating from the guesthouse as she made her way onto the porch. She peered through the screen door to view Cole, clad only a pair of Levi's, stretching his muscles and having a completely determined and serious look upon his face. He hadn't noticed Renee spying on him. She continued to secretly watch from the left edge of the screen door and out from his direct line of sight. He jumped up and grabbed hold of the chin-up bar. He performed several quick pull-ups, causing the muscles in his chest to protrude and define themselves. The muscles in his arms and shoulders pumped full of adrenaline. Cole's physique was sturdy, strong, and bold. Renee found the sight extremely appealing and alluring.

Cole released the bar to land on his feet. He then reached for his handgun and holster on the bed. He picked up the holster first and strapped it around his back and chest. He checked the fit and adjusted the strap snug. He then attained his handgun, a black .357 Magnum, and seated the gun inside the holster. He then moved for a second gun, a silver .44 Magnum, and placed that gun in the back waistline of his Levi's.

Cole slipped on his T-shirt just as the music was winding down. Renee slipped quietly away to head back to the farmhouse. Cole was unaware of her presence as he prepared mentally for the upcoming trip into town.

Renee continued to stroll until she was behind the barn. She stooped to pluck a daisy from the ground and then slid the stem of the flower behind her ear. The soft petals of the daisy rested next to her glowing cheek. She stepped slowly and directionless as her thoughts of finding real love someday came rushing into her thoughts. She observed as a pair of squirrels ran together up the side of a tree. She covered another sixty feet before leaning against a tree. Just as she felt she was all alone in her world of thought, she discovered that was not the case at all as Ike startled her from behind.

"A penny for your thoughts," he bid.

Renee gasped and quickly snapped her head toward him. "Grandpa, you scared the daylights out of me!"

"Sorry, honey, I didn't mean to alarm ya," he apologized.

"What are you doin' out here anyway?"

He slid a pinch of tobacco inside his jaw. "Oh, I was checkin' on the corn. I was goin' to take a dozen ears or so to Tiny when we go into town in a bit, but it's not quite ready. We haven't had enough rain this summer."

She nodded. "Yeah, it has been a bit dry, though it did pour the other night."

"It's not a downpour that we need. An all-day steady rain is what would do the trick. The soil could use a good saturation."

"After all these years, have you ever found yourself growin' tired of farmin', Grandpa?"

"Well, I don't know if I have grown tired of it, but it can be frustratin' at times, for sure. A farmer depends so much on Mother Nature, and that gal can be unpredictable."

"So what's kept you goin' at it all these years?"

He spit a bit of tobacco juice onto the grass. "Oh, that's easy It was your grandmother, God rest her soul. She had a way of keepin' me in line, makin' sure I stayed on the right track. She was wonderful woman, and I was lucky to have had her."

"You and Grandma were so much in love. You could see it whenever you two were in a room together. Did you love Grandma the instant you first saw her?"

Ike shook his head no. "I don't put much into that 'love at first sight' stuff."

"Why not?"

"It's impossible to love someone without knowin' who they are first. You learn a person, get to know them first. Then if you fall in love, you love their heart and not their shell. Loving someone for the way that he or she looks is superficial."

"Yeah, but I think it's important that you be attracted to the person."

"Attracted and picky are two different things, Renee. Attraction isn't just physical, it's rational as well. Perhaps when you first set eyes on someone, it doesn't quite tingle inside your shorts..."

"Grandpa!" she lightly scolded.

He reddened a bit. "Well, you know what I mean. But with time and gettin' to know that person, suddenly you're tinglin' like a wild animal."

She blushed. "Your way of puttin' things could use a little work. But...what if...you find the one that excites you physically...as well as warms your heart as you come to know them?"

"Well then, you have found a love that is grand. But it's usually one or the other. Rarely do we find the perfect match. I was blessed that I found that in Jodi Maxwell." An awkward moment of silence took over before Ike teased her, "Does a buck have your shorts a-tinglin'?"

She playfully landed a slapping strike upon his left arm. "No... and I wouldn't tell ya if that were true."

Ike chuckled.

Renee became a bit somber.

"What's on your mind, honey?"

She sighed. "I'm not exactly sure, to tell you the truth. I'm just lookin' for answers, I suppose."

He nodded. "Yeah...I don't think we ever stop doin' that, seekin' answers to some of life's questions. Which riddle are you tryin' to solve this time?"

Not being certain that she wanted to discuss it, she hesitated.

"It's me, honey, good ole Grandpa. You know you can tell me whatever it is that's on your mind."

She smiled warmly. "Yeah, Nate and I could always talk to you."

He hugged her. "You bet you can. Now what is it?"

Ike stepped back as Renee cleared her throat. "Sometimes I feel like I'm puttin' myself into some sort of a fantasy dream world, you know, imaginin' things that will probably never come to be. I worry that I am settin' myself up for a huge letdown."

Ike grinned and shook his head. "You're a true hopeless romantic, aren't you?"

"You make it sound like a jail sentence, Grandpa."

"Well, honey, in a sense, it is. You can't believe that a relationship between a man and a woman could be flawless. It can't be. You must separate fairy tales and romantic novels from real life, or you are headed for disappointment. I'm not sayin' that you can't find real happiness, but you need to keep it in perspective. Your future husband, whoever that may end up bein', is going to have flaws as well you have flaws. No human bein' is perfect, honey, and neither is any relationship. But when two people really love each other, the imperfections become part of what you love about each other."

She nodded with understanding. "Thank you, Grandpa." She kissed him on the right cheek.

"Oh, you're welcome, child, but there's more you're not tellin' me."

She fidgeted a bit. "You know me well, don't you?"

He winked.

Renee exhaled loudly. "Well, I know I haven't had any real experience at love yet...but it just seems to me, so I thought, that when you meet that special someone that you'd feel somethin' right away. Like your heart beatin' rather strangely, or your throat goin' dry... or your breathin' becomes erratic whenever you are around that person. I've met some guys that I thought were good-lookin' or nice or both, but nothing felt out of the ordinary. Separatin' fairy tales and romantic novels and puttin' them aside, shouldn't one feel somethin' differently when the right one does come along?"

He rubbed his chin. "You do feel somethin' different when the right one comes along. You just don't realize it until later on. Love is so much more important, critical, and meaningful than infatuation or lust could ever be. You can feel attracted to a person but not necessarily like them as an individual, or you might not be attracted to a person but like who they are. Love, with real love, all the right things come together at the same time. But it takes time, not goin' to happen overnight."

"So you could sense that unique feelin' for that special someone, and you don't realize that you are feelin' that way at the moment?"

"Exactly," he claimed. "Sometimes it comes out in strange ways."

"What do you mean?"

"I call it the denial stage. It will almost seem like you despise this individual, when actually, you have fond feelings growin' inside for this person."

She narrowed her eyes. "Grandpa, if you're insinuatin' that this is what I'm feelin' regardin' Cole, you can just forget it. I think he is arrogant, and he's not my type."

Ike threw his palms up in the air in surrendering fashion. "Hey, put your guard down. I'm not talkin' about anyone in particular. Just talkin' is all."

She began to pick at the bark on the tree. "Besides, I don't think that Cole knows what love is."

"Oh, and you do?" he jeered.

"I spent my entire teenage years readin' all about it, watchin' movies about it," she retorted.

"That makes you an expert on the subject, huh?"

She chuckled. "That's a silly hypothesis, isn't it?"

He gently took hold of her left hand, lowering her fingernails away from the bark of the tree. "Listen, honey, you're playin' too much into all this. Love isn't somethin' that you make happen, it's not somethin' you can force. It needs to occur naturally, and as with most cases, it happens when you least expect it. So relax, live your life, and love will take care of itself in the meantime."

She huffed. "I may not know everything there is to know about love, but I am certain of one thing."

"What's that?" Ike sought.

"That I sure do love my grandpa," she replied.

They embraced.

*****

IKE STEERED THE truck into town with Renee seated next to him. Again, Cole was riding in the bed of the truck. Ike pulled the vehicle against the curb in front of Tiny's Diner and parked there. Cole jumped from the bed of the truck and quickly opened the passenger's side door for Renee, part of the manners that his mother had taught him.

Renee rolled her eyes. "Oh geez, this is goin' to get corny, is it now?"

"All part of the act. Believe me, I emphasize the word *act*," Cole countered.

Renee curled her lip at him as she slid from the passenger's seat.

Ike leaned his head back and sniggered. He then popped open the driver's door to gingerly lower his feet to the pavement below. "I don't spot Sterling's truck about," Ike reported.

"They'll be around soon enough." Renee was certain. "They always are, they're parasites."

Cole, with some apprehension, extended out his right hand and offered it to Renee.

She inhaled a deep breath and squinted. "Do we really need to that?"

"Just hold my damn hand, Renee. It's not going to kill you," Cole growled.

Renee flung out her left hand aggressively. "Okay…please don't raise your voice at me," she requested.

He took hold of her hand, and they shared an awkward moment over their show of affection. Her smooth skin felt soft and delicate to him. Warm and comfortable. She was pleasantly surprised that this action hadn't seemed so dreadful to her after all. But she was too headstrong to give him the satisfaction of knowing that. Rather, she kept it all business.

"Let me know the very second we can break from this hold. Hopefully, it will be before I throw up." Renee then made a mockery of a motion of sticking the right forefinger of her free hand down her throat.

"Come on, you two. Let's get steppin' along," Ike directed with a playful smirk. Ike was warming to the idea of liking Cole, and he enjoyed seeing a good guy holding on to his granddaughter's hand, even if it was just an act.

The trio made their way to the sidewalk with Ike leading the way by less than a full step. He reached inside his pants pocket and pulled out a pair of thin leather gloves.

Renee appeared confused at her grandfather as he began to slip the gloves onto his hands. "Where did those gloves come from, Grandpa? I've never seen them before," she asked.

"I keep them in the chest in my bedroom. These here are my fightin' gloves, honey. I put 'em on if I know I'm a-goin' to be fightin'," he explained.

Cole immediately ceased walking, causing Renee to halt as well. "Whoa, hold on just a minute here. Ike, you will not be fighting. I'll take care of Murky Porter and perhaps his brothers and only I. Do you understand?"

Ike, who had stopped his stride as well, lowered his head and mumbled, "Yeah...sure, Cole. I understand good enough. I just thought maybe you'd want a little help."

"Negative, old chap. What the hell can you do at your age? Those boys would chew you up and spit you out."

Ike sighed. "Yeah...I suppose you're right." He then pushed his empty gloves back inside his pants pocket. He then continued his stroll with a little less zip to his step.

Renee nudged Cole at his side as she glared at him.

He now realized that he was a bit too stern and insensitive with Ike. "Hey, listen, Ike, I didn't mean anything by that. It's just that I need to do this within the guidelines of legal self-defense. That will entail me having to eat some crow from those boys before I can fully react. Only I will know when the time is right, okay?"

Ike nodded and then beamed. "Yeah...I understand good enough, like I said before. But I'll tell ya what, in my prime, I could

hold my own. I used to knock 'em down durin' a ruckus inside the tavern. Now, don't get me wrong, I took a lickin' from time to time, but I also dished out some punishment of my own." Ike made the gestures of throwing a few punches into the air before him.

Renee and Cole grinned.

"I betcha did, Grandpa."

They arrived at the corner of Harper and Vine Streets. They observed as far as they could view along Vine Street, but did not spot Sterling's pickup truck.

Suddenly a voice greeted Renee from behind.

"Hey there, girl."

Renee startled. She jarred her body, jerking her hand out of Cole's relaxed grip. Cole turned his head to see a young lady with strawberry blonde hair with sprinkled freckles upon her cheeks. She was seven months pregnant with a young man standing directly behind her. He was clad in a black T-shirt with the Harley-Davidson emblem across his chest. His face was splattered with a sporadic growth of a beard and mustache. His head of ash blonde hair was clean and combed. He appeared to be in his young twenties.

"Jesus, you sure did spook, Renee. What's up, gal?" the pregnant girl inquired.

Cole put it together who the stranger was just as Renee spoke her name.

"Well, Stacy, you snuck up on me like some sort of predator."

"Sorry, I just turned the corner, and here you stood. How ya been?"

Renee then moved toward her friend and hugged her. As their embrace parted, Renee glanced down at Stacy's midsection. "I should be askin' you that. How's things comin' along with the baby?"

Stacy rubbed her stomach. It was seven and a half months ago when she and Donnie went out on a date. Their first date together. It was a party over at the Jennings Farm. Alcohol beverages were abundant, and Stacy consumed her share. Donnie took part in the drinking festivities as well. In their shared state of intoxication, one thing led to another. The following month, Stacy missed her period. Her mother made her firm stance known of her opposition to abortion. Though she was of legal age to make her own decision, she abided by her mother's wishes.

Donnie, figuring it was the proper action to take, asked Stacy to marry him. Reckoning it was the right thing to do for the upcoming baby, she accepted his proposal of matrimony. However, these circumstances were manufactured. Donnie and Stacy were completely aware that the baby was not Donnie's. They were married by the mayor of Waynesburg in a private ceremony with only the two sets of parents attending. Renee was hurt that Stacy did not invite her to the ceremony, but she understood the reasoning behind it.

Donnie worked at Fowler's Mill for minimum wage. The couple resided in a trailer park in Waynesburg. Renee was nearly certain that Stacy wasn't in love with Donnie, but she was afraid to ask. One thing that stood out with Renee's assumption was that Stacy did not take on Donnie's surname. She had remained a Hughes.

Donnie continued to stand on the sidewalk behind his pregnant wife. He made no effort to show any affection toward her. He nodded at Cole, and the gesture was returned.

"I'm doin' good. The baby is due in seven weeks. It's a boy. We're goin' to name him Thomas."

Renee lifted her right forefinger. "That's a good name, I like it. Especially if he goes by Thomas and not just Tom or Tommy."

Stacy leaned toward Renee and whispered, "Who's the good-lookin' guy? God, he's a hunk."

Stacy's words could be heard by all, so Renee supposed that whispering was useless. "Oh, it's not what you think, Stacy."

"Oh, sure it isn't." Stacy giggled.

"Okay, think what you want."

Stacy glanced for a long moment at Cole, and then she smiled.

Donnie showed no reaction of possessiveness or jealousy. "I'm Donnie Turmac," he announced, extending his right hand out to Cole.

Cole shook his hand. "Cole Walsh."

Donnie appeared nearly dwarfed compared to Cole's large frame. Donnie stood at five foot eight inches tall and weighed a mere 145 pounds in comparison to Cole's six-foot-four-inch stature and a firm, fit 230-pound frame.

"So you're going to be a father soon?" Cole noted.

Donnie chuckled nervously. "Yeah."

"Well, congratulations."

"Thanks."

To Cole, Donnie seemed less than ready for the upcoming baby. It could be nerves and anxiety over starting a family at such a young age.

Stacy sighed. "So, Renee, is Murky Porter still botherin' you these days?"

Renee placed her hands on her hips. "Yep…he is so relentless."

"He's still botherin' you even though you have a beau now?"

"I told you, Stacy. This isn't what it appears to be."

Stacy swayed her head with a look of disbelief on her face.

Renee sighed. "Forget it."

Stacy looked to Cole. "Well, whoever you are, you'd better watch your back. Murky will be pissed when he sees Renee with another. The Porters are not ones to rile up. God, I hate those fuckers."

"Stacy!" Renee scolded her friend's foul language. Renee had nothing against the F-word, so long as it occasionally came from a male's mouth. She believed that the striking word was too strong for a lady to apply under any circumstances.

"Well, Renee, I do hate them. They bring that word out of me. I'm sorry."

Donnie then spoke up. "We just saw them Porters about an hour ago over in Waynesburg before we drove over here. They were cruisin' around in Sterling's truck. Probably lookin' for more trouble. We headed the other way and decided to get out of Waynesburg for a spell. When them brothers come to town, it nearly becomes like a ghost town. People either get the hell out of Dodge for a while or lock themselves up in their houses. Heck, some of the businesses even put out their Closed signs. So we took a ride here to visit Stacy's mama. With some luck, the Porters will be gone when we get back to Waynesburg."

Ike shook his head. "They're such a menace."

All quietly agreed.

"Donnie signed up for the police academy over in Knoxville. It's the crash course they offer so he can become a cop in half the time it typically takes. He wants to be an officer in Waynesburg. He just can't carry a gun for the first year."

"Well, that's a good trade to get into, huh, Cole?" The moment Renee completed the sentence, she realized that she had made a huge mistake.

Cole glared at Renee.

"Oh, you're a cop, Cole?" Donnie inquired.

Thinking fast on his feet, Cole replied, "Um no, Donnie, I'm not. What Renee meant is that my father is an officer up in Cleveland."

"That's cool," Donnie responded.

"Anyway, we have to get goin'. We called ahead, and Mama's got dinner on, so we have to head up to the house," Stacy informed.

"Okay, Stacy. It was so good to see you," Renee bid before embracing her friend once again. "When the baby's born, give me a call, and I'll come by to see little Thomas."

"Will do, Stewart girl."

Stacy and Donnie waved as they headed out of sight.

"I'm so sorry, Cole. Sometimes I speak before thinkin'." Renee was quick to apologize.

"It's okay, I think I repaired it. Well, we're not going to accomplish much today with the Porters out of town," Cole pointed out.

"Let's head over to Tiny's for a bite," Ike suggested.

"We might as well. I didn't have any time today to prepare dinner at home," Renee conveyed.

Cole extended his hand out to Renee. She gasped. "We don't need to hold hands anymore today. The Porters aren't here."

He nodded. "We can fuel the rumors that are certain to shoot around town. From what I've seen so far, word travels fast around Harpersfield."

She chuckled. "You sure got that right."

Visibly appearing reluctant, but welcoming from deep inside her, she accepted Cole's strong hand once again.

The trio headed inside Tiny's Diner with the sound of the ringing bell perched atop of the door. Jim was behind the counter and Pam inside the kitchen. Young lovers sixteen-year-old Macy Donalds and seventeen-year-old Paul Hartman were seated at one of the diner's small tables. They were holding hands across the table and whispering their conversation with each other. Three tables to the left sat Yen Wiles and his wife Patti. Yen was a farmer around the same age

as Ike. Yen and Ike had been friends for many years, and they used to frequent the taverns together from Waynesburg to Webster. Patti never cared much for Ike. She was one to blame her husband's wayward antics on bad influences from others. Ike, in her opinion, got Yen into more trouble than he bargained for. The truth be told, when Yen was away from Patti, he could get rowdy.

Yen wasn't oriental, though his namesake might have suggested so. Yen was the nickname his father coined him with as a young lad. He used to call to his son Yen-me-your-ear. Over time, the name shortened to Yen, and it stuck. Yen's real name was Charles, and Yen, like Ike, still worked his farm, but he made minimal progress as compared to his younger years. He typically hired a farmhand for the summer months, but not this season. This year he had promised to spend more time with Patti and let the farm go for the summer.

Yen and Patti were an odd couple, physically anyway. He was slender, and she curvy and chunky. Patti was a homebody and introverted. She had little, if any, claims to a social life. Yen was more outgoing, but at times he could be found cooped up at home with his wife for weeks on end. He felt caged, and when he broke out for a spell, he took it all in aggressively.

Seated at the counter were Sheriff Harvey and Deputy Collins. Bob was dipping his plastic spoon into the ice cream sundae in front of him. Frank was sipping on a cup of coffee.

Macy and Paul glanced up to the door at the sound of the bell. They quickly then returned to their private conversation.

Macy Donalds had a secret, a troubling problem. She held inside a tragic account that happened to her about two years prior. She had just turned fifteen a few days ago. She was riding her bicycle along a path in the woods between her house and her young friend Tina Matthews' residence. The ride was about three miles in length, which was a bit over a mile through the woods.

*****

Macy pedaled swiftly as fast as she could. She despised being in the gloomy woods, but to travel around the shortcut would add an hour to

her ride. She wanted to get to Tina's place before dusk. She and her friend were planning an overnighter at Tina's house. They had microwave pop-corn, several teen movies, and two liters of Mountain Dew at their disposal. Her ride took her past Elder's Pond.

It was so named after a farmer, Nelson Elder, before he was killed in a tornado. The powerful storm destroyed his farm about forty-five years ago, and all that remained was the farm's irrigation pond. Nelson had no living relatives to claim the farm, so the state of Tennessee took over the land. They permitted public fishing in the pond, and they stocked it annually.

Macy's luck was about to run out for on this day, Carter Porter and his sons were fishing in Elder's Pond. Sterling first detected the sounds of Macy's bike racing through the woods, and then he spotted the young girl riding along the ridge above the pond. Macy did not notice the Porters at the pond below.

Soon, all four of the men witnessed her ride along the ridge.

"That's Macy Donalds," Sterling pointed out.

"Yeah…she's a cutie. She's gettin' to have a nice ass on her," Murky declared.

"Big tits too. I think her boobs might be bigger than her sister Julie's, and Julie is two years older," Dalton added. "Damn firm looking too."

"Boy, I'd like a piece of that pussy," Sterling bid.

"Well, what the fuck are ya boys standin' around here for? Go fetch her pretty ass," Carter directed.

The boys dropped their fishing poles simultaneously and took off on a sprint toward the ridge to about fifty feet in front of Macy's prog-ress. They hunkered down next to the path where Murky picked up a thick fallen branch from the ground. They hid behind the brush as Macy approached. When her bike reached their point, Murky leaped out from the brush and jammed the branch into the spokes of the bike's front wheel. The wheel abruptly stopped rotating, and Macy flipped over the handle-bars. She crashed to the ground twelve feet in front of her bike facedown, forcing the air out from her lungs.

Carter Porter was making his way up the ridge about the time Macy was gasping for breath. Dalton immediately pounced on her back, and when Macy discovered it was the Porters, her heart froze with fear. She tried to scream, but ample air hadn't yet returned to her lungs. Dalton

area on his knees at her side and ejaculated onto her breasts her facial areas. She could feel the warm semen splatter on her at several locations about her chest, jawline, forehead, and nose.

Carter, Dalton, and Murky guffawed as Sterling squeezed out the remainder of his semen onto her face. Macy, unable to focus any longer, passed out. When she came to about thirty minutes later, the Porters were thankfully gone. She was scared, battered, bruised, and had dried blood in her mouth. Her vagina was sore, blistered, and throbbing in pain while her facial area was crusted with dried semen. However, she was pleased to be alive. She stood up and gingerly put her clothing on.

Today, she was still not certain as to why the Porters left her to live, but she knew that she would never tell anyone of the horrible events of that day. She didn't show up at Tina's for the overnighter. Instead, she rode her hobbled bike back home and reported to her parents that she had a terrible bike crash in the woods. That's all she told them. Macy thought about reporting the gang rape to Sheriff Harvey, but she knew that he wouldn't do anything about it other than run his mouth, and then the entire town would know about her humiliating day in the woods. To this day, whenever she saw any of the Porters, Carter more so, she'd like to kill them all. She had tried to move on emotionally from that awful day near Elder's Pond, and though there were no physical scars that remained, the same could not be said regarding her mental well-being.

What Macy did not know is that after the gang rape, while she was unconscious, the Porters were planning to kill her and bury her body out in those woods. A pair of Tennessee Park Rangers saved her life while on a routine patrol of the state pond and surrounding area. The Porters spotted the armed rangers, and the assaulters moved quietly out of the vicinity. The rangers were unaware of what had transpired on the ridge just above them. The rangers had completed their routine patrol before Macy became conscious again.

*****

Yen craned his neck up at the sound of the bell to spot his long-time friend Ike Stewart entering the diner. His face grew with a wide grin as he waved. "Hi ya there, Ike."

Patti kicked Yen's shin beneath the table. She then squinted ghastly at Ike.

"Hey there, Yen. How ya been, old boy?"

"Oh, can't complain, but my shin hurts now."

"Darn right it does," Patti snipped.

Ike shook his head before he moved toward the counter. He grabbed a stool at the bench with Renee finding a seat next to her grandfather. Cole plopped down on a counter stool between Renee and Sheriff Harvey.

"Hello, Ike, Renee," Jim Tinelberg greeted. He nodded at Cole. Cole waved.

"Hello, Tiny," Renee responded. Jim sat a glass of water in front of each of them.

"Whatcha got goin' on for today's special?" Ike queried.

"Reuben sandwich and chips for $3.75."

"Does that include the soda?"

Jim rolled his eyes. "No, it does not. At that price, I'm already givin' away the chips."

"Lean corned beef on that Reuben?"

"Always, Ike."

Ike thought it over for a moment and then ordered, "I'll have a cheeseburger and fries."

Jim shook his head. "Then why did ya ask about the corned beef?"

Ike grinned. "I know ya like to brag about it."

Jim's stern expression softened, and he smiled. "Yeah…you're right there."

Sheriff Harvey took a few moments to look Cole over.

"How about you, Renee?" Jim pondered.

"Did Pam fry up some chicken today?"

"She sure did. Want mashed potatoes with that?"

Renee nodded.

Jim then looked to Cole. "And you, sir?"

"A cheeseburger and fries will be fine."

"Good enough, folks. I'll put your order in right away with Pam." Jim then headed for the kitchen area.

Bob Harvey rose from his stool to stand next to Cole. "Hello there, stranger," he greeted, extending his right hand out to Cole. "I'm Sheriff Bob Harvey."

Cole looked at Bob. Although Cole remained seated while Bob was standing, they were nearly the same height. He returned the handshake. "Cole Walsh."

"What brings you to these parts, Cole Walsh?"

"Work."

"All the way down here from Ohio, are you now? I know that, you see, because I'm a lawman."

Renee thought to herself that Cole knew more about the law than Bob could ever comprehend.

"Oh, I thought perhaps it was from the plates on my pickup truck." Cole smirked.

Yen laughed aloud. Again, Patti kicked him.

"No work up there in Ohio, no?" Bob probed.

Cole exhaled. "I'm not a threat to your town, Sheriff Harvey. I'm just a hardworking man earning an honest dollar."

Bob rubbed at the dried ice cream that was pasted in his facial peach fuzz. "Well...it's my job to serve and protect."

"Yeah...right!" Yen barked.

Patti kicked him.

"Damn it, Patti, you keep hittin' the same tender spot."

Bob squinted at Cole. "Ohio. That's the buckeye state, right?"

Cole lit a cigarette. "Yep, that it is."

"Ever go to any of the Ohio State football games?"

Cole shook his head no as he exhaled smoke from his cigarette. "Can't say that I have. I'm from northern Ohio. The Bucks play farther south, down in the Columbus area."

Bob pointed his finger at Cole. "Ha! See how I got you to tell me which region of Ohio that you're from? It's called good detective work," Bob boasted proudly.

Cole raised his eyebrows and chortled. "Yeah...you're a helluva detective, sheriff."

Renee snickered quietly to herself.

Bob adjusted his belt and holster to a looser fit around his pot-belly. "Well, Frank and I put up with no shenanigans around here in Harpersfield. If you break the law, you'll answer to us."

Deputy Collins spoke up, "Leave him be, sheriff. He's doin' nothin'."

"Bob, why don't you do somethin' about those animals the Porters?" Yen growled.

Patti kicked again.

"Quit it, Patti! It's really startin' to hurt tons."

She glared coldly at him.

Bob turned to look at Yen. "Hush up now, Yen, you don't know the half of it. I have those Porters right where I want them. It's just a matter of time before I haul them all in."

Frank bowed his head in shame. He knew that he and Bob would never confront the Porters. They were simply the Porters' puppets.

Yen waved the back his left hand at Bob in disgust.

Bob then turned his attention back to Cole. "Anyway, keep your nose clean, and you'll have a pleasant stay here in Harpersfield. But if you cross the line, I'll be on you like fleas on a mangy mutt."

Cole did well to control speaking what was actually on his mind. Instead, he maintained the calm atmosphere. "Okay, sheriff, you don't have to worry about me. I'm a law-abiding citizen."

Bob nodded his head at Cole before he sat back down at the counter.

Macy and Paul then stood up and headed for the front door. As they passed where Cole was seated, an unexplained feeling deep within overtook Macy. A good, secure, and comfortable feeling. She was drawn to Cole, but not in an affectionate manner, though she thought that Cole was very handsome, but in a protective sort of fashion. She couldn't piece it all together, but it was there just the same.

Macy looked at Cole, and he glanced at her simultaneously. It was as if, in that exact moment, it was merely the two of them in attendance inside the diner. She smiled warmly at him while Cole delivered a reassuring grin. Somehow, Macy realized that Cole was a savior, some sort of hero. She kept her eyes on Cole until she was completely out the door.

"What was that all about?" Paul inquired Macy outside the diner. He and Macy began to walk toward his car.

"I don't know, I felt somethin' that I can't describe."

Paul did not possess a jealous bone in his body. "You seemed at peace when you looked at that guy."

"I guess that's one way to describe it. That man, he's, well, he's special in some way. I just can't put my finger on it as to why. Different is what I'm tryin' to say, I suppose. A cut above the rest. Why he is here in Harpersfield is beyond me. Do you believe in ESP?"

"I dunno know about all that supernatural stuff, but I do know that a woman's intuition is a strong force that must be respected. I learned about that from both my mama and grandma as I grew up."

Back in the diner, Bob and Frank were getting ready to leave. "How about the check, Tiny?" Bob requested. Jim had returned from the kitchen area to behind the counter.

Ike stood to head for the bathroom. As he strode behind Cole, he stumbled on a loose tile and nearly tumbled to the floor below. To help retain his balance, he impulsively grabbed hold of the back of Cole's T-shirt. The tension created on the backside of Cole's garment caused the front of his shirt to tighten around his chest. The outline of his gun and holster became apparent at that juncture.

Both Bob and Frank spotted the telling bulge beneath Cole's shirt. They could immediately observe and confirm that it was a holstered handgun. Bob became nervous, and Frank swallowed hard. Their shared immediate thoughts were that Cole must certainly be an armed criminal of some sort.

"Grandpa!" Renee blurted out as she moved quickly to help stabilize Ike.

"I'm okay, honey."

Cole was unaware of Bob and Frank's discovery. Cole spun in his stool to help with Ike.

Ike waved off Renee's and Cole's offers of assistance. "Stop your fussin', you all, I'm fine. I just need to go to the men's room." Ike then made his way to the restroom.

Renee sat back down as Cole spun to face the counter again.

"Here's your check, Bob," Jim announced.

Bob was still staring at Cole.

"Sheriff?" Jim bid.

Bob then broke away from his thoughts of Cole's concealed weapon and looked at Jim. "What's that, Tiny?"

"Your check, here it is," Jim replied, attempting to hand the slip of paper over to Bob.

"Um… just put it on my tab, Tiny."

Jim was confused over Bob's lack of attention. "Okay, sheriff, will do."

Bob then signaled to Frank for them to step outside the diner together. They quickly rose to their feet and headed for the door. The bell sounded with the aggressive opening of the door.

Bob nervously paced on the sidewalk outside about ten feet to the left of the diner's entrance.

"What are we goin' to do?" Frank inquired. The deputy was noticeably tense as he tapped his right boot on the concrete.

Bob ran his left palm over the smooth surface of his scalp. "I dunno, Frank. We gotta think this through…and fast."

"Maybe we can call the state police and have them run a background check on this Cole Walsh?" Frank suggested.

Bob nodded in agreement. "That's a good idea, Frank. But criminals don't use their real names. I bet the name Cole Walsh is an alias."

"Yeah…you're right. So what do we do?"

"Well, this Cole, which isn't his real name, I'm sure, is probably wanted up north. Maybe he robbed a bank or somethin'. Whatever sort of criminal he is, he has a gun. I think we're gonna need to take care of this one ourselves. We wait out here, and when he comes out, we'll arrest him."

"Okay, but we'll have to draw our guns. If you say we can't draw our guns, I won't be part of arrestin' him, Bob."

"Okay, Frank, we can pull our firearms. But make sure Pam doesn't see us, or she'll throw a fit. You know how she dislikes guns and violence."

Back inside the diner, Ike took bites from his cheeseburger while he talked with Yen, who had made his way to the counter,

to Patti's dismay. She remained at the table, pouting. Cole removed the pickles from his cheeseburger, and Renee sprinkled salt on her mashed potatoes.

"What do you want out of life, Cole?" she explored.

"What do you mean?" he wondered.

"I mean, do you want a wife and kids someday?"

He bit into his cheeseburger. He waited to swallow the food before replying. "I'm not completely closed to the idea, but I never give it much thought either."

She stated, "Well, if you're goin' to do somethin' like that, you'd better get on with it soon. I mean, how old are you now? About twenty-seven or eight?"

"Thirty-two," he revealed, just before his next bite of his burger.

She swung her head. "The clock is tickin', Cole."

He hadn't really thought about it in that manner. He was still young but getting a little older to be starting a family. He was not certain if that was what he desired after all. He believed that he would be simply fine with being single for the rest of his days.

Ike was correct; Renee was a hopeless romantic. When she was thirteen, she used a bath towel and fashioned the towel the best she could to resemble a veil wrapped on her head. She would sketch flowers on small poster boards using pastels. She would don one of her mother's long dresses. Though Beth was deceased, some of her clothing Ike passed down to Renee. Using the long hallway of the farmhouse as a church's aisle, Renee glided across the floor to approach her imaginary groom as she hummed the wedding march. Her face reddened when she was caught in the act by her grandfather. But rather than tease and embarrass her, Ike took hold of her hand and asked if he could have the honor of giving away the bride at her wedding. She locked arms with Ike, and together they slowly stepped along the hallway.

Renee realized even back then that she was a romantic. That sat fine with her. Now that she was older, Renee comprehended, more so after her chat with Ike several hours prior, that life wasn't a storybook fairy tale, but she still had the burning desire to be swept off her feet at her eventual wedding someday.

She fidgeted in her seat. "Is there a special lady waitin' for your eventual return to Ohio?"

He shook his head to indicate no.

She nibbled at a spoonful of mashed potatoes.

"How about you?" he questioned. "When are you planning to take the plunge and then have some kiddies?"

Renee sighed. "Well, I was hopin' to go to college first, but that's not workin' out. I dunno. I want to have all my babies before I'm thirty."

"Well, you and Murky best get busy then," he playfully taunted.

She impishly slapped his right arm. "Shush up now, Cole. I wouldn't touch Murky for a million dollars."

"When I was growing up, our neighbor was an old guy that had no wife. His name was Andy Tate. Why I remember him so vividly is that I used to cut his lawn in the summer and shovel his driveway during the winter months. He'd pay me very little, but I did it just the same. He was a tall man, and even in his older years, he looked healthy and strong. One evening when I was sixteen, I brought this girl home that I had been dating to meet my parents. Andy was sitting on his porch when I pulled my car into the driveway with her in the passenger's seat. The following day, I went next door to mow Mr. Tate's lawn. He stepped out into the garage as I was filling the mower with gasoline. He remarked that the girl he had seen with me the previous evening was pretty, but he warned me to beware."

"Beware of what?" Renee was curious.

"He told me that all women are gold diggers, that they are only interested in how much money a man can put forth for them."

She raised her eyebrows. "You don't believe that, do you?"

He sipped his ice water before answering. "Of course not, but old Mr. Tate sure seemed convinced. He told me that was why he had never married, why he had been a single man all his life. He went on to say that he was happy that way. No wife to nag him, nobody to answer to. He could come and go as he pleased, and his earned money was his money and his only."

"Did he seem happy to you?"

"Not really. He seemed to be man without direction. Mostly grumpy and bitter when I did converse with him. He spent most of

his time alone. I can't recall a single time that he had company. His house was never decorated during the holiday season, and sometimes weeks would go by without seeing him come out from the confines of his house. When I was about twenty and home on a thirty-day furlough from the army, old man Tate passed away, and for some reason I felt compelled to attend his funeral. Besides the funeral home director and the pastor, I was the only one at the cemetery to pay respects to Mr. Tate."

"No family at all?" she inquired.

"If he did have any family, they didn't attend the memorial service."

She hung her head. "That's so sad."

"Yeah, I guess it was sad. It was rumored around the neighborhood that Mr. Tate left behind a very hefty bank account. My mother's friend, Linda Maze, worked at the branch of the bank where Mr. Tate done business, and she told my mom that he had willed all his money to the Prevention of Child Abuse Organization located in Chicago, Illinois. I'm sure there is a story behind that."

Renee plunged her straw into her glass several times. "Maybe if Andy would have taken on a wife, his life would have been better for him."

"Perhaps."

She then stirred her water using the straw. "You're not going to end up bein' like Mr. Tate, are you?"

Cole lit a cigarette and shrugged his shoulders. "I would hope not, but you just don't know for certain."

"Well, I would expect that at least you'd pay your teenage lawn worker a bit more of a reasonable wage," she taunted.

He chuckled as he exhaled smoke. After a quiet pause, he offered, "I admire your strength."

She blushed, as she always had done when encountering a compliment. "That was a genuinely nice thing to say, Cole. Thank you very much."

"Well, it's the truth. You're willing to face the killer of your brother to gain perspective and to keep the faith. You can even find a moment or two for humor in all the madness. This is profoundly serious, and you completely comprehend that. But you also realize

that a laugh from time to time is healthy and required in order to keep your head on straight. Nate must have loved you very much, Renee."

Her eyes brimmed with tears. "I sure miss him."

"I know what you mean. Sometimes I expect Becky to come walking through the door, though I know she never will."

Suddenly, neither were very hungry anymore. They pushed their plates away in unison.

"Do we need to hold hands when we walk out of here?" she queried, secretly hoping that the answer would be yes.

He grinned. "No, I'll let you off the hook this time. I think we established enough today to get the rumor mill fired up."

She did her best to act relieved. "Good, I was gettin' sick of holding your hand."

Cole ground his teeth. "Well, you don't have to worry about it again today."

"Good!" she retorted.

Ike, Renee, and Cole walked out from the diner and headed toward Ike's pickup truck. They then witnessed Bob Harvey and Frank Collins aggressively approaching them with their handguns at full draw.

"What the hell are you doin', Bob?" Ike drilled.

"You have a criminal stayin' with you, Ike," Bob informed. "Now step back out of the way, Ike, and let us do our job."

"Put your hands up!" Frank barked at Cole.

"What the hell for? I haven't done anything," Cole challenged.

"Get your hands up now!" Bob bellowed.

Cole reluctantly raised his hands.

Bob marched toward him and frisked Cole's chest area to locate the holstered handgun. "Whaddya got here, my friend?"

Cole, though he did not want to reveal his status to the good sheriff and his sidekick, found no other option. In one quick, fluent motion, Cole dropped his right hand to gain a strong grip on Bob's throat, pinning the airway between the thumb and the forefinger. Immediately, Bob was unable to breathe. Cole glared at the sheriff with a glare that seemed as though they could burn through steel. Every ounce of compassion drained from Cole's blue eyes. "Drop the gun, sheriff."

Bob did not immediately comply. Cole tightened his pinch. Bob's ears and face transformed into a dark shade of red due to lack of oxygen and blood flow.

The sheriff, out of options, then dropped his weapon to the sidewalk below with a single clanking sound.

Cole maintained his grip on Bob's throat.

"Hold it right there!" Frank screeched, his gun still pointed at Cole. He was trembling. "Let go of the sheriff, or I'll shoot!"

Cole responded in a calm, easy, yet stern voice, "Take that gun off me, deputy. You're not shooting anyone."

"Let go of the sheriff. He can't breathe. You're under arrest," Frank commanded, still waving his gun at Cole.

With his free left hand, Cole reached up and pressed his hand against his own chest. The calculated pressure released a latch that held his holster together. From under his shirt, the holster sprung open, and his handgun descended from its perch and traveled along Cole's stomach. The gun then spilled from the bottom of Cole's shirt, where he clutched the gun perfectly. He quickly raised the model .357 Magnum, his favorite of his four handguns, and aimed the barrel directly at the deputy. He cocked back the hammer with a definitive, threatening clicking sound.

"I'm only going to say this one more time, deputy. Drop the damn gun, or I'll sweep your head from off your body."

With what little sound that Bob could muster, he demanded, "Drop the gun, Frank, you idiot."

Frank released his grip on his gun, and it tumbled to the pavement, bouncing in double sequence before it settled.

"Kick the firearm over to Ike," Cole directed.

Ike beamed as he was delighted to be part of the excitement.

Cole glanced around quickly to be sure no one was witnessing the events as they unfolded. The streets were empty of people.

Frank kicked with his right foot, sending his gun skidding across the concrete. The gun traveled the few feet to the waiting Ike Stewart. Ike stooped and eagerly picked up the firearm from the sidewalk.

"Now, Renee, scoop up the sheriff's gun," Cole instructed.

She bent picked up the loaded weapon.

Cole then moved in direction of an alley between Tiny's Diner and Emma's General Store. He led Bob into the alley. Ike, Renee, and Frank followed as well.

Cole pinned Bob against the brick wall of Tiny's Diner exterior. "Now, you listen good," Cole articulated, his face less than an inch away from Bob's face. "I'm going to release your throat, and then I have something to show you. So you move nice and easy, got it?"

Bob nodded in understanding.

"Before I let go of the sheriff, deputy, get over here where I can see you."

Frank moved against the wall next to Bob. Cole then released his mighty pinch, to Bob's relief. Bob gasped for his full breath of air. He coughed and bent at the waist.

Suddenly, Frank rushed at Cole. Quick to react, Cole sprung aside, and Frank's momentum caused him to stumble and crash to the ground.

Renee attempted to hold back, but she chuckled. Ike sniggered.

"Get up!" Cole barked. "Get back over against the wall."

Frank stumbled back to his feet and brushed the dust and dirt from his uniform. Embarrassed, he plopped back up against the wall. Bob's face was slowly returning to a healthier shade of pale.

Cole reached in his back pocket to pull out his wallet. He snapped open the wallet before Bob and Frank, revealing his shiny FBI badge.

Frank's eyes nearly bulged out from his head. "Holy shit, Bob, he's FBI!"

The sheriff and his deputy then looked up at Cole as if he were a god.

Bob swallowed nervously. "What's the FBI doin' here?"

Cole plunged the wallet back inside his pocket. "That's exactly none of your business, Sheriff Harvey. I will tell you boys this. If I hear one word around town about the FBI being here, losing your badges will be the very least of your worries. Is that crystal clear?"

During a customary FBI procedure dealing with this type of undercover operation, Cole would have Bob and Frank detained until the case was completed. This would assure secrecy, but this

was not a run-of-the-mill FBI event. In this instance, he couldn't confine them.

Frank readily nodded in agreement. "You don't have to worry about me, Agent Walsh. My lips are sealed."

Cole glared at Bob while speaking to Frank. "I'm not worried about you, deputy. From what I've gathered, it's the sheriff here who has loose lips."

Bob held his right hand out in front of himself. "I promise, Agent Walsh, not a word."

"This is not a game. Do you understand?" Cole continued to stare at Bob.

Again, Bob swallowed and snapped his head yes. Cole delivered the sheriff one last scowl before he moved out from the alley.

Bob was left rubbing his aching throat. "Give me my gun, Renee," he requested in his now graveled voice.

Renee, striving to maintain her snickering, handed the firearm over to Bob. Frank reached out to Ike to gain the return of his weapon.

"I think it's best that you boys heed Cole's warnin'." Ike winked.

CHAPTER 28

"WE'RE GONNA NEED even more weed and snort next week, Weaver," Sterling informed Jed Weaver.

Jed was one of the largest distributors of marijuana and cocaine in nearly all of Southern Tennessee. Jed was forty-two but looked fifty-two, and he coughed on a consistent basis. He was tall and thin and sported numerous tattoos sporadically spread out all over his body. His skin was pale and flushed. His stringy brown hair was disheveled, and he had a constant cigarette hanging from his mouth.

Sterling, Dalton, and Murky were inside Jed's house in Knoxville to pick up their monthly supply of the drugs. The ongoing arrangement was that Jed received 85 percent of all sales, but he was fully aware that he was fortunate to see 70 percent from the Porters. He gave no friction though; he knew the Porters would break him in half if he did so.

Jed's wife, Marissa, sat on the arm of the sofa next to Jed as he weighed up the sets of drugs. Marissa was twenty-nine and had been a heavy marijuana and cocaine user for nearly fifteen years. She married Jed for the free continuous supply of the drugs and all the dirty money he had accumulated over time. She was pretty, but she did not take good care of her appearance. Her long ash blonde hair stopped at

midback and was a tangled mess. Her eyes, which Dalton adored, were a turquoise blue. On one occasion or another, Marissa had sex with each of the Porter brothers with Jed having full knowledge of the acts. Again, he would not create waves with the Porters. He had seen them turn downright evil in a wink of an eye, something that Marissa had been spared of witnessing—that was until on that particular afternoon.

Hank "Tank" Sanchez then trudged into Jed's living room. Tank was twenty-eight-years old, six feet seven inches tall, and tipped the scales at a solid 380 pounds. He was built robust and had a continuous cold expression painted on his face. His bottom lip was pierced with a silver stud about the size of a jellybean. His neck was as thick as his jawline, giving him the appearance that he had no neck. His head was shaved bald of hair with a lengthy scar streaming across his forehead. He was of a mixed race with his mother being Jamaican and father a full-blooded Mexican. Hank was raised in a hardened childhood in the city streets on the shady side of Buffalo, New York. His father, Juan Sanchez, also an oversized man, was a lifetime criminal now serving a thirty-year sentence in the New York State Penitentiary after his third conviction for armed robbery. His mother, Lila Harris Sanchez, was a prostitute on the streets of Buffalo who passed away some five years prior after contracting HIV from one of her Johns.

Hank was the only offspring of the married couple and was left to fend for himself throughout his dismal childhood. Hank grew into a tough, bitter, shallow, and mean-spirited adult. He was as strong as an ox and had dropped many men to their backs during physical confrontations. Hank made his living as a bodyguard to wealthy criminal bosses. His reputation of being a ruthless and unbeatable brute of a thug allowed him to charge top dollar for his bodyguarding services. Crime bosses across the country would outbid each other in order to gain employing Hank Sanchez for their very own purposes.

Over the prior month, Jed Weaver had been the highest bidder while securing Hank's services for a minimum of eighteen months. Hank was always armed with a handgun, but unless his boss's life was under attack, he preferred hand-to-hand combat with any foe. He took pride and joy in beating a man into oblivion, and to him, the larger his opponent may be, the better.

"Who the fuck is the gorilla?" Dalton questioned.

Tank glared at him.

"Gentlemen, this is Hank 'Tank' Sanchez. I recently brought Tank on board as my bodyguard to protect my well-being as well as interests," Jed announced.

"Yeah? Whattya payin' Big Foot?" Murky probed.

"Plenty," Jed retorted.

"So, Tank," Dalton smirked. "If I were to, say, punch Jed in the jaw, you'd come at me?"

Tank firmly nodded.

"Well, you wouldn't be much of a bodyguard after I sprawled your big ass out on the floor now, would ya?" Dalton winked.

"Yeah, Tank the mind's blank. You need to be even bigger than your ugly ass is to fuck with us," Murky asserted.

Hank took an aggressive step toward the Porters.

Jed threw his right arm out in front of Hank. "Um, you don't wanna do that, my man. Trust me. You can virtually kick the ass of the entire free world, but ya don't wanna tangle with these boys. They'll chew you up and spit ya out."

"Lightweights," Hank mumbled.

"Did someone toss you a banana? I don't remember tellin' ya to speak!" Sterling barked.

Marissa whispered to Jed, "Tank is an extraordinarily strong man. I think he could take those three."

"He couldn't handle just one of them. Believe me, wifey, the Porters would win by whatever means it took. I have simply never met any man stronger than each one of them individually, let alone collectively. I can guarantee none of the three have ever lost a fight... ever. There are merely but a handful of men in the world who are truly a cut above the rest with might, skill, and unyielding determination, and you are presently looking at three of them as we speak."

Marissa swallowed hard.

"So tell me, Tank, have ya had a piece of Jed's wife too?" Dalton chortled.

"Shut up," Marissa bit at Dalton. Actually, the answer was yes. Though Tank had only been around the Weavers for a little over

three weeks, he had sex with Marissa on two separate occasions. Jed had no notion that this had taken place.

"I'll say it once, Jed, shut your bitch up," Dalton cautioned.

Jed gripped her leg with strong pressure. "Stifle it, Marissa."

She looked to the Porters, and their eyes appeared to be spinning into a cold shade of gray. She felt a chill crawl along the surface her skin.

"I wanna take ya on, ape man. Call it practice. I've dropped guys as big as you before," Dalton confirmed.

"You guys aren't exactly small," Marissa added.

"You would know," Sterling winked.

Marissa blushed.

"You really wanna tangle with me, motherfucker?" Hank grunted. "I'll twist you like a pretzel and then piss all over your ugly fucking face."

"Hank, um, don't do this..." Jed tried to interrupt in order to save his own bodyguard.

Hanks raised his right palm at Jed seated on the sofa. "No worries, boss. I got this fucking pussy punk's ass. He'll be kissing my boots while blubbering out his sorriest pleads to me. Then I'll chase off his sissy brothers."

"Hey, gorilla," Dalton taunted. "After I kick the ape shit out of you, I'm gonna look up your mama and slide my huge meat stick inside her ugly pussy. Past the stench of course."

Hanks glared coldly at Dalton. "My mother is dead, dickhead."

Dalton merely shrugged his shoulders. "It'll just make it easier to rape the cunt is all."

Jed nervously raked his fingers through his messy hair.

Marissa began to tensely chew on her fingernails.

Hank cracked his knuckles one at a time and then declared, "Time to beat some respect into you, Porter, you motherfucking pussy."

Murky leaned back in his chair. "Your mistake, Big Foot about to get the boot. Trash him, Dalton."

"Come on, guys, not inside my house," Jed pleaded.

Hank and Dalton ignored his appeal.

Dalton stepped over to Hank and offered up his jaw. "Take your best shot, King Kong," Dalton taunted.

Hank looked to Jed for approval.

"I wouldn't do it, Tank." Jed gave a final warning.

Hank moved a step back from Dalton.

"You damn wimp," Dalton chortled. "Just as I figured."

"Some bodyguard ya got there, Jed," Sterling said with a chuckle.

Dalton raised his right forefinger and then stipulated, "But no backing out of this, you cocksucker. You said stupid shit that can't be taken back. Nobody"—Dalton then raised his voice—"and I mean nobody speaks to a Porter that way and walks away! You're mine now, you overgrown pussy and sorry excuse of a bodyguard." Dalton was still offering Hank a free shot at him.

Now on the sudden defensive, Hank took a hefty swing at Dalton. The hard punch landed squarely upon Dalton's jaw. The force of the massive blow caused Dalton's head to jerk violently to the left, but his feet stood their ground. Hank beheld Dalton in amazement. He just struck Dalton with all his strength, and it didn't budge Dalton an inch from where he was stationed.

Dalton rubbed his jaw and then snickered wickedly.

Hank, shocked by Dalton's stamina, stumbled back a few steps.

"The rumble is on now," Dalton announced. "Here comes you worst fuckin' nightmare, Tank!" Dalton then rushed at Hank as Hank did his best to fend off the attack. It soon became apparent to Hank that Dalton was too much to handle. He was simply too strong, and his fighting skills were well polished. He moved with the precision of a trained boxer, which the Porters happened to be.

Before Hank could fully react, Dalton landed four solid punches to Hank's head and facial areas. Blood spewed from Hank's nose, and his eyetooth propelled out from his mouth. His ears rung, his jaw burned, and the room began to spin around him. Dalton gripped the pierced stud injected into Hank's lower lip and ripped it from Hank with a forceful yank. Hank's lower lip split open, and blood oozed out from the open wound. Dalton examined the steel stud for a moment and then jammed it deep inside Hank's left nostril. The large man grunted out in excruciating pain as Dalton applied pressure on Hank's now-broken nose. Dalton then kicked Hank in the groin. Hank doubled over and tumbled to the living room floor.

Although Dalton reined in Hank on his own, Sterling and Murky felt compelled to join in on the action. Murky kicked Hank several rounds in the ribs. Dalton leaped and brought his full weight down on Hank's right leg, breaking the bone at the shin with the sounds of a cracking baseball bat. Hank shrieked in agony. Sterling then kicked Hank in the head, knocking Hank unconscious. The three brothers then traded turns kicking the fallen man in the head. His jaw broke, and his body jerked with convulsions.

"Please stop!" Marissa cried out. "You're killin' him!"

The Porters continued to assault Hank Sanchez. Marissa rushed to them and grabbed Sterling by the shoulders. "That's enough already!"

Sterling turned to face her, and after an evil grin, he landed a solid punch to her forehead. Marissa's head snapped back as she crashed to the floor. She was stunned and out cold. Jed did nothing to help his wife, fearing the Porters would certainly attack him as well.

The boys assaulted Hank for several more rounds before they finally eased up.

Sterling then snatched a large bag of marijuana and three bricks of cocaine from the coffee table before the threesome headed for the door.

"See ya next week, Jed the living dead," Murky calmly bid.

Jed quickly dialed 911 in order to try and save Hank's life, but only after hiding his large supply of drugs.

On their travel from Knoxville back to Harpersfield, Sterling glanced out the driver's-side window in Webster to catch a view of some teens playing a thrown-together soccer match on a high school field when the scene stirred a memory for him.

*****

Harpersfield farmer Dan Parker was a busy man, not only with the daily tasks demanded of a grower and cattle raiser, but also with his persistence of nibbing into the business of others. Dan's forty-three acres of property butted up with the Meyers' power company's land equipped with gridded towers transferring electrical power to local communities.

Although Dan Parker had no say-so of what transpired on the Meyers' property, he made any activity on the land an event of his interest anyway.

Dan was fifty-eight years old, and after two divorces, he was currently single while casually dating a woman from Webster. He was of average height, standing at five feet ten inches tall. His arms were short and stout, as were his legs. Dan was overweight with a rounded face and protruding eyes. He bore an untrimmed rust-colored mustache that obscured both his upper and lower lips. His head of hair was thinning and lacked proper grooming. Overalls were his choice of attire, and he was rarely seen dressed in any other fashion.

His first wife, Darla Jean, passed away at the tender age of twenty as a result of an erupting brain aneurysm. Darla and Dan were planning on starting a family, but it was never to be. Three years after her unexpected passing, Dan married his second wife, the former Norma Reynolds. Over fourteen years of marriage, the Parker couple produced two children. Hannah was their firstborn, followed by a boy two years later they named Grant. At the age of seven, Hannah was diagnosed with childhood leukemia and unfortunately failed to celebrate her ninth birthday. Her death destroyed Dan as well as the Parkers' marriage. After the divorce, Grant resided with his mother with Dan having visitation rights every other weekend. Eventually, Norma remarried, but Dan chose to remain single.

Grant Parker was now thirty-four and husband to Clara. Together they brought a daughter, Mandy Mae, into the world who was now ten years old and Dan's only grandchild. Grant, having little interest in following his father into the farming business, was a shift manager at Walmart in Webster and Clara a cashier at a local Marathon Service Station. They resided in a modest home on the north end of Webster. Dan would visit Mandy Mae at every opportunity, and the two had grown close.

However, Dan was a bitter man regarding the sudden death of his first wife and the youthful passing of his only daughter. Dan wasn't one to consistently drink alcohol, nor did he indulge in recreational drugs, so his outlet was at being a nosy and prying man upon the affairs of others. He figured if he couldn't be happy and content with his own life, others should suffer in misery as well. Dan Parker wasn't a bad person, merely misguided in animosity.

Now and then, the Porter brothers would ride their ATV and dirt bikes on the Meyers' acreage. Overextending his authority over the area, Dan at times would call the sheriff's office to complain when the Porter brothers were riding their machines over his property line.

Sheriff Harvey and Deputy Collins would respond only to determine that the Porters were not exactly crossing the border between the farm and the power company's property. Although there were a few breaches along the border here and there, rather than confronting the Porters, the Harpersfield police force chose to look the other way.

After years of frustration, Dan Parker decided to bypass the local sheriff's office and placed a call to the Tennessee State Police as the Porter brothers ran rampart on their off-road vehicles near his property. Tennessee state police officers Martin Cline and Jasper Walker soon arrived at Dan's door. After explaining that the riders of the off-road vehicles had ignored the provincial authorities to restrain and desist their activities, he felt he had no other choice but to go over the heads of local law enforcement.

Officers Cline and Walker then approached the recreational riders in a calm and friendly manner. They had no prior dealings with the Porter brothers, so neither had any inclination of what they were about to face. After hand signaling the Porter brothers to halt and shut down the engines of their all-terrain vehicles, Jasper Walker took charge. "Look, guys, you are trespassin' on private property, and it needs to stop here and now. I'm as much a fan of off-roadin' as the next guy, but respectin' private property comes along with the activity. So load up your off roadies in your pickup truck over there and move on out. We don't want another call regardin' this again. Alright then?"

Murky hopped off his motocross bike to approach the officers. Noticing Officer Cline's nametag on the officer's uniform, he was quick to try and make his case. "Well, Marty spoilin' the party, you see, we're not on any private property. This land is owned by Meyer's Electric Company and not part of Parker's acreage."

Martin placed his hand on his hips. "It's Officer Cline to you, and this property is as private as the farmer's land. So unless you have written permission from the electric company to ride upon their land, then I repeat for the last time. Load your off roaders and move on out."

"And if we don't?" Sterling chimed in from his seated position on the solo ATV.

"Well, we'll be happy to arrest the three of you and haul you on in," Officer Walker reacted.

Dalton grunted from his perch on the other dirt bike. *"All because that Parker has a bug up his ass? We ain't botherin' that nosy fucker."*

Taking a deep breath while trying to reassess the situation, Martin attempted to reach a compromise. *"Oh, come on, gentleman. Aren't there other places you can take your ridin' to? It's all open country in this neck of the woods. Let's just wrap this up and call it a day. How about it?"*

"Load 'em up, guys. Let's go," Jasper added.

In defiance, Sterling informed the uniformed officers, *"Yep, you bet no problem at all. We'll load up when we're done ridin', but we ain't done just yet."*

"Oh, but that you are," Jasper confirmed.

"Did my brother stutter?" Dalton sassed. *"We're done when we say we're done."*

Simultaneously, the Tennessee state police officers drew their handguns while pointing at the Porter trio.

Murky chuckled, *"Wow, firearms pulled for simply riding our machines. You guys are pathetic."*

"Hands up and hands up now!" Martin demanded. *"You're under arrest for trespassin' and failure to comply with the orders from respondin' officers. Now, carefully put your arms behind your back. This minute!"*

Left with no other options on the table, each Porter brother placed their hands behind their back. With only two sets of handcuffs between them, Martin completely cuffed Murky while Jasper cuffed Sterling's and Dalton's right wrists together.

After spending overnight incarcerated at the eighth precinct's state police station in Knoxville, the brothers were released the following morning with a court date pending in the near future. Their off-road vehicles had been confiscated, and after satisfying a fine of five hundred dollars, the machines were released from the compound and loaded onto Carter's pickup truck. Carter had driven to Knoxville to bring his sons home.

On their travel back to Harpersfield, Carter inspired his sons to enact revenge on Dan Parker. Murky, Dalton, and Sterling weren't in

need of any further encouragement regarding the issue, but Carter's cheerleading added fuel to the already burning fire.

Six days later, Dan Parker was busy plowing a field on the southeast section of his land when he noticed the Porter brothers on foot and approaching his position. In the distance, he spotted Sterling's pickup truck parked at the edge of the timberline. As the trio neared, Dan grew increasingly anxious.

Murky stepped directly in front of the tractor's path and raised his right palm. Reluctantly, Dan brought his tractor to a halt. Sterling raised his left hand, signaling the farmer to shut down the tractor's engine. Dan felt he had no other option but to comply.

After the dying engine's last muffle, Dalton spoke up. "Farmer Dan, get your sorry ass on down here now."

Dan, noticeably shaken, attempted to stall for time. "Howdy, guys. As you can see, I'm tryin' to get this field plowed before sunset. What can I do for you all?"

Impatiently, Dalton waved Dan off the tractor. Unenthusiastically, Dan submitted to the demand. Now at ground level along with the Porters, Dan tried small talk. "Nice day today, huh? They're callin' for rain overnight is why I'm tryin' to get this area of the field turned up. Hey, I haven't crossed paths with your dad for a spell now. Tell him I said hey, okay?"

Murky then stepped face-to-face with the farmer. "We're all goin' to take a stroll together into the woods, Parker the barker. Let's go."

Dan cleared his throat. "Oh, hey, guys, I'd sure like spend some time with y'all, but like I said, I really need to get my work done here. Another time perhaps?"

Sterling uttered a single word. "Woods."

Dan timidly slid his hands inside the pockets of his overalls. "Um, yeah, sure…we can hang out together for a bit. Plenty of daylight left to get my plowin' done."

Once the foursome was hidden away among the tall trees and undergrowth, Murky extended his right arm across Dan's shoulders. "Well, Parker the barker, all your barkin' has your ass in a sling now, dumbass. You should have kept it a low growl, but hell no, you had to go yelping to the state boys."

"Yep, asshole," Dalton furthered.

Murky lowered his arm from the farmer's shoulders before beginning to pace a circle around the worried man. "So, Parker the barker, we're gonna do what is done to any unruly mutt. We're gonna put that yapping bastard down."

"You should have been a good boy, Odie," Sterling remarked.

Murky looked to Sterling with confusion.

"You know, Odie. The dog in the Garfield comics."

Murky squinted at his older brother. "Go stand in the corner and put your dunce cap on."

Dalton chuckled.

"Fuck you, Murky," Sterling grunted.

Murky then focused his attention back on Dan as the farmer pleaded, "Please, guys, I'm beggin' you for mercy. I have a precious ten-year-old granddaughter who thinks all the world in her grandpa."

Not a single eye was batted.

"You should have thought about that before pickin' up the phone, Danny boy." Dalton winked.

In desperation, Dan began with erratic offerings. "Look, I make but a modest livin', but I could probably scrape up about five or six thousand dollars for you all. That's like two thousand bucks each, fellas. Whaddya say, and we'll call it even."

Sterling snickered. "We can add, you fuckin' moron."

"Actually, it's division," Dan felt obligated to point out.

Sterling abruptly slapped Dan across the face with the back of his large left hand. "If I say it's addition, then that's what the hell it is."

"Right. You're right, Sterling, it is addition. My mistake. I'm sorry."

Murky then ceased his pacing to crouch down before Dan. "Don't need your money, Dan the man no one can stand. Any other stupid ideas?"

Doing his best to think on his feet, the frightened man offered, "Um...well...look, I've been seein' a gal from over in Webster for about two years now. Her name is Hilda. Well, anyway...let me speak with her, and maybe...perhaps I can talk her into doin' a favor for you all."

Dalton crossed his arms across his chest. "What sorta of favor?"

"You know, favors." Dan detailed the word favors using his forefingers in a gesture of quotation marks.

"She'll suck and fuck us." Murky chuckled.

Sterling snickered. "Parker, we've seen you with her in town at times. Don't go buyin' her no ring. Get a lease instead. That bitch is one ugly mutt."

"Ruff!" Dalton chortled.

Murky then rose to a standing position. "Besides, if we wanted to hump her, we'd just do it. We don't need her damn permission first. Looks like you're outta options there, Parker the barker."

With widened eyes, Dan implored, "Please...please don't do this, guys. I'm so sorry I called the state police. My little Mandy Mae would be heartbroken to see her grandpap all beaten up and busted."

Dalton then made their intentions clear. "Who said anythin' about the rug rat ever seein' you again?"

Dan's expression grew solemn as he swallowed hard. Before the farmer could utter another word, Dalton landed a mighty left-handed punch to Dan's right-side temple. Dan's ears buzzed, and his legs buckled. He dropped to his knees before Murky. Rearing back his right leg, Murky sent a powerful kick with his heavy boot to Dan's upper nose and forehead area. The strike rendered Dan unconscious as his limp body collapsed upon his back and to the forest floor below.

"In the mood for a round of soccer?" Sterling asked his brothers. "See those two tree trunks side by side over there?" He pointed them out. "That's the soccer field's goal, and Parker's head is the ball. We kick until the soccer ball crosses the goal, and we score."

Mocking as if he were announcing play-by-play action over a stadium's speaker system, Dalton broadcasted, "Now up are members of the Porter team with a number of free kicks in their pockets. Ladies and gentlemen, and ladies, remove your panties please, we give you Murky, Sterling, and Dalton, the hardest-kickin' soccer players of all time."

The trio then simultaneously took a taunting bow.

Over the following ten minutes or more, the Porter brothers exchanged turns at kicking Dan Parker upon his head and facial area. With each massive blow, Dan's body inched nearer toward the trunks of long-ago fallen oak trees. Eventually, the beaten, bloodied, and battered head of one Dan Parker finally crossed the imaginary goal line between the two tree trunks. The fallen and beaten man from the neck up was now unrecognizable.

Using three shovels the brothers had tossed into the bed of Sterling's truck before making their way to Parker's farm, the strong brothers, working in unison, excavated a deep hole of nearly seven feet in depth in the deep woods before preparing to dump Dan's body into the makeshift grave. After dragging Dan's beaten body to the lip of the chasm and ready to tumble him into the hollow distance below, Parker suddenly coughed up a spew of blood before wheezing in an inhale of air.

"Can you believe that fat ass is still alive?" Sterling tittered.

Murky then settled the sole of his left boot upon Dan's right hip. "Not for much longer," he nonchalantly commented before unlocking his knee and sending Parker plummeting down into the tomb.

Without hesitation, each brother took hold of their individual shovels and began tossing soil upon the still-breathing body of Dan Parker. After completing the filling of the morbid gravesite, the brothers brushed dropped leaves and nearby fallen branches upon the freshly dug earth to help conceal the location, though it was very unlikely that anyone would ever stumble across the spot in such an isolated and remote area.

After burying the frantic man alive, the Porters simply returned home to sip on cold beers.

No ruing, no remorse, no regrets.

CHAPTER 29

RENEE STOOD GAZING out the bay window of the farmhouse with a mug of steaming tea in her right hand while observing a driving rainstorm. An occasional flash of distant lightning illuminated the night's sky. Like she did at times, she thought about how wonderful Harpersfield would be if the generations of the Porters had not made this town their own.

While she was attending high school, she investigated the founding of the town using reference books at the Webster Library. What she discovered was revealing and interesting. John Emmett Harper settled in the town in the year 1805 along with his wife, Margaret "Maggie" Harper. They had three children, James, Robert, and Patricia. Their farm was situated where the police station now stood. Eventually, additional families settled into town as the Harper children grew up. Patricia Harper, at the tender age of sixteen, met and fell in love with one of the recent settlers, a seventeen-year-old by the name of Eldie Porter. Eldie and his farming family had migrated from England to find opportunity in the then-young United States. Eldie's parents, Horace and Charlotte Porter, were soon in trouble with the law. The reference books didn't state exactly what the charge was, but Horace and Charlotte both were sentenced to jail time.

The Harpers opened their home to Eldie Porter, who was suddenly parentless, and he moved into the Harpers' farmhouse. Soon after, Patricia and Eldie were wed. They saved enough money and settled into a farm of their own near what was now a strip along Martin's Way. They had three offspring named Ward, Vincent, and Henrietta. While the children were still young, Eldie had become an enemy of most of the townspeople. At one time or another, he had done most of them wrong. In one terrible occasion, as a result of an ongoing feud with George Stewart, Renee's great-great-grandfather, Eldie shot and killed every head of cattle on the Stewart farm, the same land that Renee and Ike presently called home. Eldie was sentenced to four years in jail. While he was away serving his sentence, Patricia found another man and filed for divorce. When Eldie returned to Harpersfield after serving his time in Memphis, he shot and killed both Patricia and her new husband. Eldie then turned the gun on himself.

Ward and Vincent carried on the Porter tradition of wildness and criminal activity. As a wayward team, it was believed that they raped over sixty women in the lower Tennessee Valley. Each time, out of fear, all pending charges were dropped. Vincent was eventually shot and killed by a vengeful young lady that the Porters had previously raped.

Ward married one Gloria Forester. Together they parented five children. The oldest son, Belmer, would eventually become Carter Porter's father and Murky, Dalton, and Sterling's grandfather. Belmer was a hell raiser in his own right and taught Carter the felonious tactics of the Porter family. Throughout the generations, the Porters' torment on the small town of Harpersfield and immediate surroundings had not deteriorated a bit.

The lights inside the farmhouse flickered, as they had been doing the past thirty minutes. Ike was fast asleep, undaunted by the thunderstorm raging outside. He and Renee had witnessed the power of these Tennessee storms many times before, and they had grown accustomed to the effects. The bulk of this storm had passed, leaving behind a steady rain and faded thunderclaps.

A quick flash of lightning helped Renee spot a figure in the driveway. She anticipated the next flash, concentrating on the area

where she saw the figure. The following strike was rapid, but she was able to put the image in perspective. It was Cole seated upon the hood of his truck in the pouring rain.

She shook her head in disbelief and mumbled to herself, "What are you doin' now, you fool?" She set her cup of tea on the windowsill and grabbed an umbrella from the doorway closet. She pushed out the door while extending the umbrella into its fully opened position.

"What the heck are you doin' out here in this foul weather?" she pressed while approaching Cole.

"Charging my battery," he responded.

She glared in confusion at the truck.

"My personal battery, not the truck's."

"What exactly are you talkin' about now?"

Cole was wearing a Cleveland Browns hat with rainwater spilling over the brim. "There's nothing like a good rain to cleanse one's soul. To help clear your mind."

"Well, can't you do that, whatever it is you're goin' on about, inside the house and out from the lightnin'?"

"Lose the umbrella and join me," he invited.

She shook her head no. "I think one nut on the farm is plenty."

"Are you always this uncomplicated?" he inquired.

She was immediately offended. "Would you like to clarify that?"

He leaned toward her. "It's not that so difficult, Renee. You're so damn predictable, it isn't funny."

"Why? Because I don't do idiotic things such as you do?"

"You don't do anything. Not out of your typical patterns anyway. Sometimes it's healthy to throw caution to the wind. I'd be willing to bet if you were invited on a spontaneous luxurious trip to… let's say…Hawaii, with all expenses paid, you wouldn't go because who would feed the dogs?"

"I'd go," she snipped.

"No…no, you wouldn't."

Stillness fell between them with only the sound of the falling rain pelting on the hood of his truck.

Deep down inside, Renee was fully aware that Cole was accurate with his assumptions. She had never been one to take chances,

to travel off the beaten path. She always stuck with safe odds and the game plan. She didn't consider that her outlook was dull; she felt that it was merely being a responsible individual. Some dubbed it conservative; Renee preferred to describe to it as maturity. There were times though when she would have enjoyed making herself cut loose a bit, to be a little free-spirited, but she hadn't been capable stepping over that imaginary line. Her grandfather most certainly was one who was spontaneous, and Renee felt that he would encourage her to do as well, but Ike simply lived and let live. Renee understood that with the right amount of persuasion, a solid formula of conditions, she could stray from her rut...somewhat anyway. She just required someone to prove to her that it was fine to roam from predictability from time to time.

"Go back inside, Renee. You're cramping my style," Cole criticized.

"You're such a jerk!" she barked, before marching back toward the house.

Cole, on the other hand, had been accused more than once of living a lifestyle quite the opposite of Renee's path. He went about his life without structure and could live out of a duffel bag for weeks at a time and think nothing of it. He didn't care for planning or ordained schedules. He dealt with matters on a whim and didn't give much thought about tomorrow so much. Though there were times when he wished that his life contained a tad more stability and direction. A right lady, a proper mate, who could give his wayward path a little more course and meaning. However, although he did appreciate his freedom as a bachelor, he also recognized that being put into check now and then wouldn't necessarily be a bad thing.

Renee turned around to storm back outside of the farmhouse, this time without the umbrella protecting her from the descending rain from above. Her hair and clothes were wet as she reached Cole and his truck. "So you tell me, big shot, what is so rational about this?" she inquired while raising her arms.

"It's not insane, if that's what you're implying."

She placed her hands onto her hips. "I'm standin' here in the rain gettin' wet from head to toe. I could be catchin' a cold and be sick for days. My clothes will be wet and difficult to take off. The

water is uncomfortable and rollin' down my back. And you are tryin' to tell me that this is alright, that it is normal? I think it is unwise, miserable, and just downright twisted. You get caught in the rain, as we all do from time to time, but you voluntarily don't consciously rush right out into it."

"That's an old wives' tale," he retorted.

"What the heck are you goin' on about now?" She raised her voice through the pounding rain.

"Rain causes illness. That just isn't true. Viruses cause sickness, not water falling from the sky. That's ridiculous."

She brushed her matted hair away from her forehead. "Explain William Henry Taft then."

"Who?" He squinted at her.

"Are you kiddin'? You work for the federal government, and you don't know that William Taft was one of our presidents?"

"Oh, that William Henry Taft," he taunted.

She growled, "Yeah, well, anyway, he gave his inaugural speech in the pouring rain and died of pneumonia less than a week later."

"He was unknowingly carrying the virus before he even gave that speech." Cole pushed her claim aside.

"Oh, so now you're a doctor, huh?"

"No…I'm not a doctor, I'm just practical. If exposure to rain causes pneumonia, everyone would have caught it."

"That's not completely accurate, Cole. Not everyone is a knucklehead like you are to purposely stand out in it."

"Ouch," he continued to taunt. "For the record, I'm sitting and standing in the rain. So tell me, who do you take after, your mom or your dad? Which one was the conservative one? As deep as you've dug your boots into the unyielding soil, I'd say they both were probably unadventurous."

Her eyes teared, mixing in with the rainwater streaming along her cheeks. "I wouldn't know the answer to that. I barely remember them. Let's change the subject. I don't want to talk about my parents."

He leaned forward. "Why, because they are deceased? You don't discuss your parents because they are no longer with us?"

"Yes!" she exclaimed.

"That's pretty lame."

She got angry. "What the heck do you expect me to do? Keep bringin' up the hurt again and again?"

"No, but you could stop whimpering about it," he advised.

"You're a careless bastard!" Renee howled before turning back toward the farmhouse.

Cole slid from rain-soaked hood of his truck and quickly closed the distance between them. He grabbed her right arm to spin her to face him. "Listen to me, Renee, you're going about this all wrong. You should be remembering your parents before the accident and not after. You're so channeled in on their deaths, that is all you think about. Recall your mother's smile, your dad's grin. Your mom's gentle voice, the pleasant way she kept the house smelling. Your dad's snoring, his grilling burgers over charcoal briquettes on a Sunday afternoon. Anything about them living and not dying. You're allowing them to slowly fade from you memory."

Renee smiled a bit through her tears.

Cole's voice came to be more soothing. "When the subject comes up, when you talk about your parents, it should be with delight and not in despair or turmoil. Don't feel cheated because they were taken from you, but rather feel fortunate and blessed that you had parents at all. Some children grow up who can never make such a claim. So when you think of them, rejoice knowing that although they no longer roam the earth, they still live inside your heart. The same goes for when you recollect memories of Nate as well."

After a passing moment, Renee acknowledged, "Now that I really think about it, I suppose I've been throwing my own pity party."

"Don't fret. We are all guilty of that from time to time. It's easy to get involved in our own sorrow, but it's not that difficult to move on with life with a degree of acceptance if you truly apply yourself."

"Thank you, Cole," she whispered.

"Ah…you'd better get in out of the rain." He remained modest. "After all, you don't want to catch a cold." He playfully winked.

She grinned and giggled. "It's all not so bad after all." She then glanced momentarily deep into his eyes before spinning and jogging back to the farmhouse.

After peeling off her wet clothes and showering, Renee crawled into her bed. She recalled fond memories of her parents and Nate during happy times while a smile slowly developed upon her face before she peacefully drifted off into a restful sleep.

CHAPTER 30

August 2

RENEE THUMPED THE breakfast dishes and silverware onto the table. Ike, seated at the table enjoying a cup of coffee, cleared his throat. "Somethin' wrong this mornin'?"

"Last night, Cole was outside in the storm sittin' in the rain. Then he told me that I'm not spontaneous. In other words, I'm borin'. I think he is ridiculous," she snipped.

Ike grinned. "I think it bothers you because ya like him."

Renee became wide-eyed. "That's insane! I'm not eatin' with you guys. I'll be in my room."

NEARLY AN HOUR later, the telephone in Renee's bedroom rang.

"Hello?" she answered.

"Hi, honey, baby doll, beautiful. It's your man, Murky here. I'm sorry I didn't get back to ya yesterday. Me and my brothers ran into somethin' unexpected," he explained.

In truth, Dalton, Murky, and Sterling, after having their way with Tammy, engaged in a bar fight with a few local Webster men. To the Porters it was good fun, but to their opponents, it was an

extremely painful experience. Two of the four men ended up with broken bones. All four required stitches to close wounds. The Porters were practically unscathed.

Renee bit her tongue to keep from telling Murky to back off. "Well, you don't need to call me every day."

"Sure I do. You're my true love."

"No...no, I'm not, Murky. I have not agreed to go out with you at all."

"But you're thinkin' about it."

"That isn't exactly a yes. If you want any chance with me, you're gonna need to give me a few days to think things over. Until then, you're gonna to have to leave me be, no more phone calls," she clarified.

"Whatever it fuckin' takes. I just wanna lick ya all over," he moaned. He then delivered a kiss through the phone's receiver.

Renee felt sick. "I gotta go, bye."

"Okay, honey. I'll call ya in a few days."

She quickly ended the call before Murky could utter another word.

*****

THAT AFTERNOON, RENEE was inside the barn tending to the canines. She had fed each of them and was now grooming Max after tending to Merlin's coat. Cole entered the barn and hopped up on the tractor. He was slowly developing into a genuine farmhand as he was assisting Ike out in the cornfield.

"You hurt me with your words last night," she asserted without glancing his way.

"I'm not here to make friends, Renee," he countered as he turned the ignition key to the tractor. The tractor's engine came to life, producing more noise than they could speak across. Cole then steered the tractor out from the barn.

*****

THAT EVENING, RENEE noticed Cole stepping across the lawn. She observed as he leaned something against the light pole out-

side her bedroom window. When he moved away from the immediate area, he left behind a section of cardboard inscribed with a red marker spelling out the handwritten words, "I'm sorry, Renee." Under the illumination of the pole's bulb, she could make out his declaration.

Renee beamed as she retired to her bed for the night.

Hours later, Renee had lengthy and vivid dream.

Renee Stewart and Stacy Hughes were seated at a table near the bar inside a tavern. The time period was during the days of the Wild West, cowboys, horses, and guns. The bartender was Jim Tinelberg, and above his head behind the bar was a wooden sign carved with the words Tiny's Tavern. His wife, Pam, was busy polishing the bar after a patron had spilled a shot of whiskey.

Deputy Frank Collins, donning a flannel shirt and a cowboy hat that was too small for him, nailed a wanted poster to the wall of the tavern using the butt of his gun. The poster was of the Porter brothers, wanted dead or alive. The poster was complete with black and white photographs of each brother and offering a five-hundred-dollar reward for their capture.

The music being played by the piano player, Macy Donalds, was a quick beat that Yen and Patti Wiles found easy to step to upon the tavern's wooden dance floor. Renee's grandfather, Ike, waddled inside through the swinging tavern doors. He was sporting a pair of rawhide pants over his full-bodied thermal underwear, allowing the top of the undergarment to act as his shirt. He made his way to the table where Renee and Stacy were perched while enjoying glasses of red wine.

Stacy was wearing a rather revealing dress, cut exceptionally low at the breast area. Her hair was tight in a bun, and her eyelashes were painted in black mascara. Her perfume was aromatic and heavily applied. Renee was clad in a full-covering light blue dress with a matching hat. A blue bow was tied at her collar.

"Grandpa, you march right back on home and put some clothes on!" Renee scolded while grasping a Chinese-made handheld fan in front of her face, waving it aggressively for some fresh air. The tavern's atmosphere was filled with cigarette smoke and the foul aroma of whiskey.

Ike checked over his attire. "Why, I am dressed, granddaughter."

"I would hardly call that dressed. You look as though you just rolled out of bed." Renee rolled her eyes.

"I hope I'm underdressed as well…Ya know, a pregnant gal without a proper suitor has to find an admirer before she grows too large. This skimpy dress should do the trick." Stacy winked.

"You call that a dress?" Ike teased. "That's barely a handkerchief." He snorted.

Stacy, embarrassed, stood from her chair hastily. "I'll talk with you later, Renee," Stacy bid. "Ike." She nodded before scurrying out from the tavern.

After Stacy departed, Renee reprimanded Ike. "Grandpa, that wasn't a very nice thing to say to Stacy."

Ike grabbed the seat vacated by Stacy. "Perhaps it wasn't, but Stacy is too much of a lady to be dressed like a prostitute. She isn't goin' to find the right man among the savages who frequent this downtrodden establishment."

Renee glanced around the tavern. At the bar, nearly passed out, was no other than Mason Turner. Emma Gert slapped Henry Gert's hand as her husband reached for the large jar of pickles on the counter of the bar. Sheriff Bob Harvey, wearing a cowboy hat that was too large for him, which caused Renee to suppose that he and Frank should swap caps, was trying to talk his way into being Tammy Patroni's company for the night. Tammy, dressed even more revealing than Stacy, was openly flirting with the sheriff. It was obvious that she was the town's prostitute.

Renee exhaled. "Yeah, I suppose you are right, Grandpa. All the good men in this town are either married or dead at the hands of the ruthless Porters." Renee moaned. She then curled a lock of her hair around her forefinger. "But…US Marshall Cole Walsh isn't a married man.

Ike grinned mischievously. "No, that he isn't. Are ya takin' a likin' to him, young lady?" Ike ribbed.

Renee's eyes widened as she increased the pace of fanning herself. "Why, no, I most certainly am not. He's too arrogant for my likin'."

Ike was not convinced and displayed so with a doubting smile.

Renee realized that he could see right through her.

"Be that as it may, I wonder why the US Marshall is here in town anyway?" Ike pondered.

Renee pointed to the wanted poster behind Ike.

He turned to look at the placard briefly before spinning back toward Renee. "Well, we have a sheriff, ya know," Ike verified.

Renee then directed Ike's attention to Bob Harvey, who was giggling along with Tammy as he tried to slide his hand beneath her dress.

"Oh, I see now why the marshal is here," Ike conceded.

Renee nodded.

Suddenly the swinging doors of the tavern's entrance swooshed open with the Porter brothers striding inside.

Macy hit a couple of off-key notes on the piano before she quickly rose from her seat and scurried away to a far corner of the tavern. Bob Harvey retreated from next to Tammy and cleared his throat before he cowardly nodded a welcome gesture to the Porters. Frank Collins quickly dipped beneath the bar.

The Porter brothers were all clad in cowboy attire, but each had a bandana covering their mouth and nose. The three outlaws were heavily armed with two side pistols each in their belt holsters.

Dalton pulled his bandana down to his neck to reveal his identity as he announced, "If you all have money in the bank, well, ya don't any longer."

The Porters hooted in sarcastic harmony as Murky and Sterling disclosed their identities as well, though all the townsfolk already knew who they were.

"Yeah," Murky contributed, "next time ya all deposit a bit more, or I'll hurt ya, and I'll hurt ya bad."

Sterling snorted. "Tammy, come on over here to me, my pussycat."

Tammy sauntered over to Sterling to plant a long kiss upon his lips. Dalton squeezed her backside while she kissed his brother.

Renee's heart raced, and she swallowed a dry knot of fear as she witnessed Murky lusting at her with wishful eyes. His spurs jingled as he moved across the wooden floor toward the direction of Renee and Ike.

He arrived at a stand next to the seated Renee. "Well," Murky growled, "if it isn't my fair lady in waitin'. I'm here now, darlin', so how about a big wet kiss for your man?"

"Leave Renee be, Murky Porter," Ike grumbled.

"Shut your trap, you old shiner, before I fill ya full of lead," Murky warned.

"Don't harm my grandpa." Renee was frightened.

Murky grinned slyly at her. "Well, my sweet darlin', Porters don't bring harm to family. So all ya need to do is marry me, and then Ike here becomes family. That way, ya never would need to worry about Ike gettin' hurt."

Renee fanned herself ever so briskly. "I wouldn't marry you, Murky Porter, if my life depended on it."

Murky creased his nose and snarled, "Well, that might just end up bein' the case if ya remain so stubborn about it."

Renee trembled as she stood and reached her hand out to Ike. "Come on, Grandpa, let's head on home."

Ike rose to accept her hand, and together they attempted to step around Murky.

The Porter brother then grabbed hold of Renee's arm and squeezed tightly. "Not so fast, Renee. We haven't finished our business here yet."

"Ouch! Murky, you're hurtin' me," Renee sniveled.

"You'll be in a lot more pain than this if ya don't start cooperatin' with me."

Ike reached his point of tolerance and took a punching swing at Murky. Dodging out of the way, Murky chuckled, and he kicked Ike's feet out from beneath him. Ike plummeted to the floor, forcing the breath from his lungs.

"Grandpa!" Renee gasped as she tried to kneel to his aid, but Murky's hold on her was too strong for her to move about.

"Tell me that you'll marry me, Renee, or I'll beat the hell out your grandfather, right here and right now."

"Kick his ass, Murky!" Dalton cheered from behind.

"Kill the shiner," Sterling added.

Murky then kicked Ike in the stomach with such force that Ike's body lifted from the floor. Ike grimaced in pain.

"Okay…okay…Murky," Renee pleaded. "Please leave my grandfather alone."

"You know the magic words, Renee. Say them," Murky barked out.

Renee hesitated.

Murky reared back his leg to again strike Ike.

Before he could inflict further injury, Renee interluded, "Stop, Murky! Stop and I'll say it!"

He pulled her closer to him. "Okay, then say it, Renee, I'm waitin'."

She exhaled. "Murky…I…I…will…I…" As much as she wanted to protect her grandfather from further assault, she just couldn't bring herself to declaring to Murky that she would marry him.

Murky angered but arrived at a compromise. "Okay, let's just consummate it with a kiss." He then puckered his lips and closed his eyes as he anxiously awaited the soft feel of Renee's lips upon his.

In a sissified tone, Dalton mocked Murky, "Since you won't say that you'll marry me, how about a big wet kiss to seal it? I'm Murky Porter, and I'm such a wimp when I'm around Renee Stewart."

Sterling and Dalton laughed in unison.

Murky opened his eyes and glared at Dalton. "Shut your sewer hole, Dalton, or I'll hurt you, and I'll hurt you bad." Murky then returned his attention to Renee before he whispered to her, "Kiss me now, Renee, or I'll harm your grandfather."

She understood that Porter threats were genuine, that they did what they stated. She must kiss his foul mouth. But how could she possibly go through with such a disgusting act without falling ill?

She suddenly realized that this was the key to her quandary. "Um, Murky, I don't think that you want to kiss me right this moment."

He squinted. "And why the hell not?"

"Because I think I'm comin' down with a bit of the flu."

He shrugged his shoulders. "I don't mind. It's worth it to me just to finally get a kiss from your sweet lips."

Her heart dropped as her plan failed. There was no further delaying tactics that she could conjure up. It was either kiss Murky now, or her grandfather would be severely battered.

"Come on, Renee, I'm growin' impatient here," he pressed.

Reluctantly, she slowly puckered her lips. He grinned wide before creasing his lips and closing his eyes. She stepped forward and leaned toward him.

When their lips were less than an inch from meeting, the tavern's doors suddenly swung open. This time US Marshall Cole Walsh strutted inside the demoralized establishment.

Renee beamed at the sight of the intimidating lawman, as did the other townsfolk.

Cole could see and sense immediately that the Porters were up to no good. He played it off while taunting, "What's the special today, Tiny?"

Jim nervously cleared his throat as the Porters glared at Cole. "Um…fish. The fish is really good today at a fair price."

"Sounds good, Tiny. Serve me up some of that delicious fish and a draught beer." Cole then grabbed a seat on one of the barstools.

Murky motioned to Dalton to handle things.

Dalton shuffled to stand behind Cole. "Why don't ya get your fish to go and head on outta here?" Dalton sternly suggested.

Cole spun in his stool to face him. "You know, it is a nice day outside. It sure would be nice to eat beneath a shade tree, but then I'd have the flies and ants to deal with. Naw, I think I'll eat in here, but thanks for the thought just the same."

Dalton sneered. "You mock me. Nobody ridicules the Porters."

Cole looked over the three bothers. "Oh, well, that's a shame there. You're such easy targets."

The patrons collectively needed to hold their breath in order to restrain from laughing out loud. But then a sudden fear overtook the crowd as they knew that Cole would need to deal with serious backlash that was certain to follow.

Dalton quickly reached for his holster to grasp his handgun, but he was not as quick as Cole in drawing his firearm. Before Dalton could take aim, Cole fired his weapon purposely, blowing off Dalton's cowboy hat. Sterling was the next to reach for his gun. Cole took precise aim at the next Porter at the end of the bar and fired. The bullet struck Sterling in the hand, knocking the gun from

his grip. Murky reached for his gun, and as he acquired aim at Cole, Renee stomped on Murky's boot with her high-heeled shoe. Murky dropped his gun before he hopped around in agony. Cole fired his gun with accuracy, where he hit Murky's belt buckle with the blast. The buckle collapsed, causing Murky's pants to fall to his ankles, revealing his thermal underwear. The patrons roared into a round of laughter. Using both his guns, Cole then fired at the floor next to each of the brothers' collective feet, causing them to dance right out the door of the tavern.

A burst of applause by the townspeople erupted as Renee rushed to Cole. She leaped into his arms, and he swung her around the room. "You're my hero. Forgive me for my forwardness, Marshall Walsh," she said before kissing him.

As the kiss ended, she realized that amid all that had transpired, her emotions got the better of her, and she had gone too far by smooching Cole. She immediately stepped from him and cleared her throat. "Sorry about that, Marshall."

He teased, "No, you're not. You've wanted to do that for a while now."

She turned red. "God, I can't believe how arrogant you are!" She then marched out of the tavern.

"Come on back, Renee! I was only having a bit of fun," Cole called out.

Ike winked at Cole before he went in pursuit of his granddaughter. Outside the tavern, Ike was hurrying to try to catch Renee and her brisk pace.

"Slow down, child!" Ike called up ahead.

She stopped so that Ike could close the distance between them.

"What is your problem, honey?" he inquired.

She pointed to herself. "My problem? I don't have a problem. That stuck-up Cole is the one with a problem."

He smirked. "You sure do like him, don't ya?"

She rolled her eyes. "Let's just go home, Grandpa."

Outside the farmhouse near her bedroom window, a rooster crowed, waking Renee for another day in her life.

CHAPTER 31

August 3

COLE AWAKENED TO a pounding upon the guesthouse door, which interrupted the chirping sounds of the early morning birds. Ike's elevated voice from outside then invaded the confines the guesthouse. "Come on, Cole, up and at 'em, boy. I want to take ya somewhere to show ya somethin' this mornin'."

Cole sat up on the edge of the bed and rubbed his eyes. With a groggy moan, he said sleepily, "What is it, Ike?"

"Just come on. Get ready and you'll see," Ike replied as his voice faded off into the distance.

Cole stood, yawned, stretched, and then cleared his throat. He needed a breath of fresh air to help wake him. While still only clad in his underwear, he whisked open the door, and to his surprise—as well as hers—Renee was just outside the door. Cole quickly shifted to stand partially behind the door.

Renee turned her head away from him. "Um…sorry." She blushed.

"What are you doing standing on the porch anyway?" he rebuked.

"I was just waitin' on you to get ready. Grandpa can get restless when he's headstrong about goin' somewhere."

Cole squinted. "Where are we going anyway?"

"I can't tell you. Grandpa would have my skin if I ruined his surprise. Now, come on and hurry on up. We'll be in the truck waitin'," Renee explained before scurrying from off the porch.

After over an hour's drive over some tight, rough back roads, they finally reached their destination.

Ike pointed out the truck's window. "There it is, Cole, in all its glory," he proclaimed with pride.

Cole peered up at the tall wooden wheel that was resting in a narrow river. "Yeah, it's a mill. So?"

Ike winked his right eye and then snapped his fingers. "Yeah, but it's not just your everyday run of the mill." Ike made a pun. "No sir, this is a very special mill."

"Looks like any ole' mill to me," Cole specified, "though I haven't seen many mills in my life."

"She's a beauty," Ike asserted. "Come on, I'll show ya."

Cole leaned from the confines of the truck, and Renee slid out following her grandfather's exit from the driver's side. The trio approached the mill that had an abandoned operation shack near the giant wheel.

"You see, Cole, these smart engineers from up Knoxville way had this ingenious idea that they could supply electricity to several towns around here by just buildin' and usin' this here mill." Ike spit out a bit of tobacco juice and then continued. "Well, the concept was good, though sometimes things don't work out like they do on the drawin' board. I was one of forty-two men that erected this mill decades ago. It took us nearly three years to complete the job, and this here mill has never served one flicker of electricity to anyone."

The threesome arrived at the operations shack.

"Why not?" Cole inquired, suddenly interested.

Ike rubbed the stubble on his chin. "Well, some folks say that it is the work of ghosts, the spirits of the Indians. They say that along this here riverbed is an old Indian burial ground, and the souls of those Indians buried here are payin' back the white man for stealin' their land. That these souls casted an evil spell upon the mill."

Cole's eyes widened.

Ike chuckled. "But I say that the wheel is just too damn heavy for the shallow river to turn it over."

Cole grinned tentatively.

"You don't believe in ghosts and goblins, do you, Cole?" Renee teased.

Cole cleared his throat. "Do you?"

She giggled. "Of course not, that's silly."

"Just 'cause ya can't see somethin' doesn't mean it doesn't exist," Ike stated.

She rolled he eyes. "Grandpa, you may have scared me when I was a little girl with your spooky stories, but I'm a grown woman now. It will no longer work."

Ike smiled warmly. "Yes, that you are."

She moved a step closer to Cole to continue to taunt. "So you didn't answer my question. Do you believe that spirits inhabit the earth?"

He squinted. "Why is it so important for you to know?"

She shrugged her shoulders. "It tells somethin' about a person's character."

"You mean it lets you know if they are crazy or not."

Renee creased her forehead in a playful manner. "Perhaps. Now, are you goin' to answer the question or step around it?"

Cole lit a cigarette as Ike peered inside the window of the shack. Cole exhaled smoke before he replied, "Are you asking me if I believe in life after death?"

"I believe in life after death," she pointed out. "I believe in God and heaven above. What I'm askin' you is if you believe that the dearly departed roam around here on earth in the form of spirits?"

Cole inhaled a long drag from his cigarette and then replied, "I read once where a man had lost his wife of twenty-three years to heart disease. He was so lost without her that he had just about given up on life, and he wasn't even fifty years old yet. He became a loner, a recluse. Except for his job, he never left his house. This went on for over two years until one day he heard a knock at his door. When he answered the door, no one was there. Before he closed the door, he glanced down to spot a box lying on the doorstep.

"He brought the box inside the house with him. The box was a heart-shaped container of candies. You know, the type that loved ones give on Valentine's Day, except it wasn't that time of the year. He slid open the box. Inside, the candies had been removed and replaced with a single bar of candy. It was a Snickers bar, which was the type of bar that his wife packed in his lunch each day. It was his favorite. Also, inside the box was a Cuban cigar. He smoked a Cuban cigar each Friday evening after work. But he had not smoked a cigar in the two years since his wife's death.

"Also inside the box was a handwritten note, but it was written so neatly it nearly looked typed. It read, 'Darling Dyno, my heart may have failed me, but it shall never stop loving you. Now, you need to get out a little more, you're looking pale. Don't worry about me, I'm fine. We'll be together again someday. Until then, enjoy the rest of your life. Love, Daisy.' Now, their nicknames for each other were Dyno and Daisy, and this man never told a soul about those endearments. So he takes this note to have it analyzed by writing experts, and it turns out that it is not of ink or gel or lead or of any origin of writing utensil they had ever seen before. The florist that delivered the box said that he dropped off the box, full of candies and no note, the day before this guy found it on his doorstep. Anyway, he is going on with his life now a happier man knowing that he'll join his wife again someday."

Renee was mesmerized for a moment, and then she became skeptical. "That is a bunch of garbage."

"Why don't you believe something like that could happen?" Cole questioned.

Her eyes clouded a bit. "Because Nate and I were very close. If there were a way, he would contact me to let me know he is okay. He would do it."

"Well, I'm telling you that I read that story."

"In which magazine?"

He broke into laughter. "I read it in the *National Enquirer*."

Ike turned and chuckled.

"Cole Walsh!" she snipped before playfully slapping him on his left shoulder. "I should heave a rock at you!"

"Easy now, Renee," Cole kidded. "I really don't have an opinion on ghosts."

"Between you and Grandpa, I never know what to believe," she chortled.

"Hey, you two, come on over here and help me break inside this shack."

"Grandpa, that's illegal," Renee warned him.

"No, no...honey, it's nothin' like that. Hangin' on the wall inside is a framed photograph of us men who built this here mill. Nobody comes out here anymore, so I want that picture to hang in my room at home."

"Oh, I see. Why didn't you just say so in the first place?" Renee now approved.

Renee and Cole made their way to join Ike at the shack. The door was boarded up, and a rusted lock was in place.

"Think we can get inside, Cole?" Ike inquired.

Before he had an opportunity to reply, Renee said, "With some precision leverage between us three, we can probably pry open the door, right?" Renee looked to Cole.

"Well, I had an easier way in mind. You see, I could—"

"What, my way isn't good enough?" she goaded.

He snubbed out his cigarette on the ground. "Fine, we'll do it your way," Cole ceded.

Ike took hold of one end of the board crossing the door, Cole the other end. Renee found a grip near the center of the board.

"Okay then," she directed. "On the count of three, we all pull together. Ready? One...two...three!"

The trio worked in harmony pulling back on the board. The board creaked for a moment but did not budge.

"Again!" Renee barked. "One...two...three!"

Again, they heaved. The barrier didn't dislodge, but Renee did. She lost her grip on the board, and the force of her leaning backward carried her into a stumble and to an eventual tumble to the ground.

Ike and Cole chuckled as she landed on her backside.

"Very funny," she snipped before Cole helped her to her feet.

"I knew that wasn't going to work," Cole indicated.

She huffed. "Then give your way a try, smartie."

"Okay then," Cole agreed. "You'll want to stand back, Ike."

Ike moved away from near the doorway. Cole reached beneath his shirt and hauled out his handgun. He took quick aim at the lock and fired. The shot echoed out throughout the river valley. The lock snapped in half and twirled around the metal ring before it plummeted to the ground below. Cole then stuffed his weapon back inside its holster.

"Show-off," Renee grunted.

Cole threw his hands out to his sides. "What? You wanted the door open, right?"

"Are you always so dramatic?" she growled.

He bit back, "If you were a man, I'd take you out behind the woodshed and teach you a lesson."

She gestured with a wink. "Yeah, you'd like to get me behind the woodshed, but it's a pipe dream that's never gonna happen, cowboy."

Ike intervened. "Are we gonna stand around yappin' our gums all day? Let's get inside the shack and check things out."

After pushing open the creaking wooden door, Ike strode inside the aged shack with Renee and Cole in close pursuit. The walls were bare except for the photograph that Ike was after, along with a mess of cobwebs.

Ike plucked the framed picture from the wall and held the photograph while he studied it. "This room, this shack used to be full of controls. Of course, once the project was declared a failure, they took all the equipment with them," Ike informed the two. "It's a shame as two good men lost their lives buildin' that wheel. I remember the first one to go, it was Eugene Spratz. Eugene was the sculptor, as we called him. He formed the wooden spokes to fit precisely within the wheel. He'd measure then cut, measure then cut until he got it exactly right."

As Cole and Renee listened to Ike, their hands inadvertently brushed together on their backsides. Cole thought to move his hand away, but then decided that he would leave it in place so long as Renee allowed him to do so. Her skin against his skin felt soft and warm.

Ike explained further, "One day, Eugene was workin' on a stubborn angle, and he was determined to get it done by nightfall. He

stayed up top of that wheel a bit too long past dusk. As he eased his way down, he miscalculated his footin' in the fadin' evening light, and he stepped off the railin'. He fell nearly eighty feet to his death.

"The other man, Hank Loomis, was a father of three. He lived up near Webster. He was in the gearbox makin' adjustments one mornin' when the big boss showed up. The boss wanted to see the wheel turn, so he came in here to the shack and hit the controls. When the gears engaged, they chewed up Hank like a mulcher. These were all good men"—he pointed at the photo—"and we gave it our all to build this damn mill."

Cole felt self-confident that he could now reach for Renee's hand as she had maintained her hand near his. Perhaps it was time they held hands with meaning rather than play-acting as part of the plan to lure Murky Porter into Cole's trap.

His hooked his forefinger around her pinky finger. To his disappointment, she abruptly pulled her hand away from him, and she did not look directly at him.

Cole fidgeted as he was a bit ashamed. "Um…Ike, are you still in touch with any of those men?"

Ike shook his head. "Many of them have since passed away or moved on to other parts." Ike then stepped toward Renee as he pointed to a zone in the photograph. "See that man there, honey?"

"Yes, Grandpa."

"That is Everett Turner. He's Mason's daddy."

"Really? That's interestin'," Renee stated.

"Yeah, and he drank nearly as much as Mason drinks," Ike said with a snicker.

"Are there any Porters in that photo?" Cole questioned.

Ike blurted out, "Heavens no, no generations of the Porters ever made an honest livin'."

Cole glanced up at the ceiling above Renee's head. Then in one fluent motion, he grabbed Renee around her waist and brought her body to his body with her back to his chest. He then placed his wide palm tightly over her eyes.

"What do ya think you're doin'?" she snipped.

He didn't respond as he lifted her up into his arms and moved them quickly out the door of the shack. She began to kick. "Cole, let me down! Have ya gone crazy or somethin'? Let me go!"

Once safely outside the shack, Cole sat her down and uncovered her eyes as Ike stepped out from the shack. Renee kicked at Cole several times before landing a strike upon his shin. Cole hopped around and winced as he reached for his pain-stricken shin.

"Why the hell did you do that for?" Cole barked as he limped about.

"You were tryin' to grope me!" she bit.

"Oh, don't flatter yourself, Renee. I was doing nothing of the sort."

"Then what do you call it?" she snarled.

Cole's temper flared. "Renee, you need to learn to allow people to explain before you jump to conclusions."

She folded her arms in haste. "Okay…explain away, I'm waitin'."

"I glanced up above your head inside the shack and saw something you wouldn't want to see. There are bats inside that shack, about a dozen of them hanging from the ceiling."

She swallowed hard. "Bats…you mean bats as in bats?"

He nodded. "Bats…as in bats."

She brushed her clothing as if to mop away anything clinging to her. "Oh my god! I hate bats!"

"Exactly. That is why I got you out of there," Cole clarified.

After settling down a bit, Renee hung her head. "I'm sorry…I didn't know."

Cole, still feeling somewhat down after Renee pulled her hand away from him a bit earlier, remained a tad harsh. "Well, I hope you have learned to not be so quick with judgment of others."

"I said I was sorry," she huffed.

"Well, tell my aching shin that!"

"I thought that you were tryin' to feel me up," she retorted.

"Oh, give me a break. You're too young for me, you're still a puppy."

"Maybe it's just that you're gettin' too old," she shot back.

They glared at each other as Ike whistled loudly and then said, "Okay, you two, that's enough. Time to call a truce, already." He then

stepped by Cole and Renee on his way back to the truck. "I swear, I can dress you two up, but I can't take you anywhere."

Cole and Renee lightened up and then broke into a chuckle.

During the ride home, Cole had his left arm, by force of habit, stretched across the top of the truck's bench seat. Ike continued to tell of how the mill was erected while he steered as they traveled along some of the most beautiful landscape that Cole had ever witnessed. The warm breeze coming through the truck's open windows gently caressed Renee's dark silky hair. Cole was transfixed at viewing her through the sideview mirror on his side of the truck.

Renee, seated between Ike and Cole, was unaware of Cole's ability to gaze at her by using the mirror.

As he watched both the magnificent landscape and Renee's beauty, Cole became captivated. Ike's voice merely converted to nothing more than background noise to him. Slowly, Renee's tired blue eyes closed, and her head leaned back against Cole's forearm. He wondered if perhaps that was a calculated move on her part? Or was it that she was merely drained? Or maybe she believed that his arm was a section of the truck's seat? Or perhaps...could it be that she was sending him a silent signal, a message that she was growing fond of him?

Trying to decipher her move had Cole frustrated. He decided to leave things where they were until he had further proof of her true intentions over the upcoming days.

CHAPTER 32

RENEE AND COLE strolled along Harper Street hand in hand, this time with a bit less reluctance by both parties involved. Ike was in tow, filling his jaw with chewing tobacco. They had yet to discover that they had missed the Porter brothers in town once again. Dalton, Sterling, and Murky were in one of their visits out of town to Tammy Patroni.

Cole peered inside each business that they passed while looking for the Porter boys. The laundromat was empty of customers at the moment. Tiny's Diner had seven patrons, none being whom Cole was seeking to find. The feedstore results were no better, and next was Darton's Gas Station.

"Let's go in for a soda," Ike suggested. "I haven't seen Fred or his boy for a spell."

"Where in the hell are those Porters?" Cole anguished.

Renee shrugged her shoulders. "I dunno. They're usually hangin' around town. It figures, when ya want 'em around, they can't be found."

They followed Ike inside the station. Fred was standing behind the counter, and Merle was seated in his favorite chair eating from a bag of potato chips while watching a game show on a small television set.

"Hi there, Ike," Fred greeted with a smile.

"Hiya, Fred. How are ya and the boy?"

Merle waved without glancing up from the television.

"We're doin' better now that his mother is home," Fred replied.

"Did Beverly go on a trip?" Ike asked.

Renee removed three cans of soda from the cooler and passed them around.

"Oh, you didn't hear?" Fred pondered with a bit of irritation to his voice.

"Hear what?"

"Those goddamn Porter boys beat Beverly. She spent days in the hospital up in Knoxville."

"Jesus Christ. What the hell did they beat her for?"

Fred shrugged his shoulders. "Ya know when it comes to those ruthless brothers, a reason isn't always needed."

"Is Beverly goin' to be alright?" Renee expressed worriedly.

"Yeah, but she's in for some healin' time."

"Did you tell the sheriff?" Ike wondered.

Fred exhaled quickly. "Yeah, but that's not gonna matter much. You know that."

Ike nodded.

Fred then reached his hand across the counter. "Hi there, I'm Fred Darton."

Cole stepped to the counter to shake Fred's hand. "Cole Walsh."

"Welcome to these parts. Say hello to Cole, Merle."

Again Merle waved without glancing up from the game show.

Fred rolled his eyes. "Anyway, Cole, workin' up at Ike's, are ya?"

Cole nodded. "I'm sorry to hear of your wife's misfortune."

"Yeah, well, I hope those Porters get theirs someday."

"Sometimes these things have a way of equaling out," Cole commented.

Renee secretly grinned.

"We can sure pray for that," Fred consented. "Of course, Beverly's beatin' was bad enough, but not nearly as terrible as what they did to poor Nate."

"What do we owe ya for the sodas?" Ike quickly changed the subject.

Renee's eyes clouded.

"Three bucks," Fred reported.

"They'll kill us all someday," Merle mumbled.

"What is that you say, Merle?" Fred questioned.

Merle lowered the television's volume using the remote clasped in his right hand. "They, the Porters, they'll kill us all one day. What's to stop them?"

"God," Ike retorted.

"With all due respect, Mr. Stewart, God is good, but the evil that runs in the blood of them Porters is demonic. I've grown up in this town like everyone else, and if we are completely honest with each other, we'd admit that there is not a single drop of kindness in those hoodlums. But we are all so headstrong to keep callin' Harpersfield our home that we're willin' to take the chance of bein' killed at the hands of the Porters."

"You're bein' a bit paranoid, Merle," Fred weakly suggested.

"Am I really, Pop? I don't think so. It's like we all know it exists, that it's out there each and every day in our lives. But does anyone really do anything about it? No, they don't. So we just sit back and let the bomb tick away."

"What would ya suggest we do, Merle?" Renee kindly sought.

Merle shrugged his shoulders. "I don't have any answers, Renee. Ya know, I read a lot, mostly news events and such. I read in *Time Magazine* a while back that our judicial system is the most forgiving system in the world."

Cole found a need to speak up. "It's all about deterrent. Something our system desperately lacks."

"Exactly," Merle quickly agreed. "There are criminals in this country that walk away with a mere slap on the wrists where in other countries they would be serving a long time in prison. Hard time, not this near country club conditions that inmates in this country experience."

"Jesus, Merle, you sit over there staring at the TV day in and day out, and then all of a sudden you come out with all of this. You're somethin' else, you are, my boy," Fred claimed.

"Well, Pop, one can learn much more by listenin' rather than talkin'," Merle pointed out.

"That's very true," Renee concurred.

"What would you know about not talking?" Cole teased her.

She playfully slapped his right arm.

"You make it sound so gloomy, son. We all know what the Porters do, and yes, we do look the other way a bit too far, but we must. No matter how bad things get, we need to have some peace in our minds. If that's lookin' the other way, then so be it."

"But it'll only get worse, Pop. Ignorin' it isn't gonna make it go away. I'm scared. I'm scared all the time. I'm so down over bein' scared."

A brief silence overtook the station.

Ike cleared his throat before speaking up. "I'm scared too, Merle. We all are. I learned long ago that ya need to try your best to stay out of the path of the Porters. It's your only line of defense. I know it sounds cowardly, but it's about survival."

Renee nodded her head toward Cole, gesturing for him to reveal his mission to the Dartons in order to ease their weary minds.

Cole shook his head no.

After another reflecting silence, Merle raised the volume on the television set. He returned to watching the game show as if he hadn't spoken a word.

Thirty minutes later, after the strolling trio passed by Sampson's Wrenching and Painting Automotive Garage, Cole noticed a vacant lot containing only a set of concrete steps that simply led nowhere. A total of six steps completed the solid block of cement. Cole inquired, "What's with the stairway to only empty air?"

"Oh, that's where the Harpersfield Catholic Church once stood for many years," Renee reported.

"What happened to it?"

"It burned to the ground about fifteen years ago. It was arson, and you can bet who lit the match. But like everything else, the Porter family walked away uncharged and unscathed."

Cole squinted. "Why burn down a church?"

Renee shrugged her shoulders. "I was only about six at the time. I remember when it happened, with the Waynesburg and Webster

fire trucks here in town. I don't really know many details. Grandpa could tell you more about it than I ever could."

Now curious, Cole looked to Ike. "What about it?"

After placing a pinch of chewing tobacco in his jaw, Ike began his recollection. "Yep, the ole Harpersfield church. Growin' up and well into my older years, I spent a many of Sunday mornin's sittin' on a pew in that house of worship. It wasn't a large buildin', but no need for it to be for such a small town. Anyway, I remember a plaque hangin' next the front door readin' that the church was one of the first buildin's erected after the very foundin' of Harpersfield so many years ago. And right there is where it stood for nearly two centuries until it was torched from existence about fifteen years ago.

"Throughout the functionin' years of the establishment, tryin' to retain a father to head the church was a struggle. The Porters simply ran them out of town, one after another. Some would hightail it directly after an initial threat comin' from Carter and his brother Steadman. There were few of the holy men who tried to stick around a bit longer, but none really made it more than a year or two before packin' up and headin' out. In hindsight, I think the church was out of business more than it was in session. The Porters would damage the vehicles and homes of the preachers, and if that weren't good enough, they would physically attack them. The one I recall best was Father Samuel Beck. A good man and nice fella. He preferred for people to call him Father Sammy."

Halting their progress in front of the now-vacant lot, Renee asked, "What became of Father Sammy?"

Ike scratched his head. "Oh boy, honey, this was all back some years ago, but I'll do my best to remember all I can. Father Sammy's wife was Rachel. A very shy and quiet lady, and like her husband, she was truly kind. They hadn't produced any kiddies together yet but were plannin' on startin' a family soon. Well, Sammy was one the few preachers over the years who wouldn't allow the Porters' intimidation to force him down from his post. You see, the Porters didn't want a man around town teachin' and preachin' the gospel. Every Porter I've ever known are atheists.

"The first thing Carter and Steadman did to Sammy was damage the man's car. A Chevy Nova, if I remember correctly. Anyhow, I suppose the make and model isn't important. But damage the vehicle they certainly did. Sammy's car was parked behind the church late one evenin' while the clergyman was alone inside the facility. The Porter brothers busted every window and flattened all four tires on the Nova. They also ripped out the entire fuse box and drove a large screwdriver through the radiator.

"Even after the vandalism, Sammy was determined to stay on as the town's only clergyman. A few weeks later, it was Sammy's house that the malicious brothers targeted. You know the house, Renee. It's the Radcliffs' place these days out on Tarbell Road."

She nodded. "Oh yeah, the brick house."

"That's probably the only reason it still stands today. If it were a wooden home, I'm sure the Porters would have torched it. Atheists and arsonists is what they are. But on a day when Sammy and Rachel where out of town runnin' errands, what the brothers did do was pour five gallons of motor oil into the well that supplied fresh water to the home. It had been rainin' that day, so the ground was saturated when they drove Steadman's truck over the lawn and tore up the yard until it was like a mud pie complete with ruts, grooves, and ridges. They broke each and every window in the house and burned down the storage shed with all the equipment inside. On the asphalt driveway while usin' a can of spray paint, they left a message behind, which read, 'Leave town and take your damn God with you.'"

Cole shook his head. "Where were the police through all this?"

Ike rolled his eyes.

Cole surrendered. "Oh boy. Forget that I even asked."

"Anyway, even after all that, Father Sammy still refused to pack up and move on. By golly, that followin' Sunday, there he was preachin' away in front of the congregation. I'm not sure if he was brave or foolish or a bit of both. Frustrated over the situation, the Porter brothers waited for a few weeks until they could catch Sammy and Rachel home alone. Sammy was busy grillin' burgers out on their patio while Rachel was preparin' the table inside the house for dinner with the radio playing gospel music. The brothers parked Steadman's

pickup along the side of Tarbell Road near the Becks' driveway before slippin' onto the property on foot. Soon, they were on Sammy before he had a chance to know they were on his land.

"Steadman attacked Sammy from behind by placin' his large palm to the back of the clergyman's head and forcin' him face-first down on the hot gratin' of the charcoal grill."

"Ouch." Cole grimaced.

Renee's eyes widened. "That poor man. But, Grandpa, how do you know so many details?"

"Oh, Steadman was the biggest braggart in the entire county. If he was involved in somethin', eventually all became aware of it. But of course, the Porters still remained untouchable for local law enforcement."

Renee nodded in disgust. "Then what happened?"

"Well, while Steadman was busy assaultin' Sammy, Carter slid inside the home and set his sights on an unaware Rachel Beck. She could not hear her husband's attack out on the patio over the gospel music playin' on the radio. So Carter snuck up behind her and wrapped his forearm around her throat. He powered her body down upon the dining room table and...well...forcefully had his way with her. By the time the Porters finally left the premises that day, Sammy was scarred for life physically and Rachel emotionally. Needless to say, the Becks' exit from Harpersfield soon followed.

"Over the followin' twenty years or so, other clergymen would come and go, but only for short stints. The church would sit idle for long periods in between. Even after Steadman was shot and killed, Carter still ensured the church would remain a lost cause. So about fifteen years ago, I suppose after Carter grew tired of dealin' with incomin' preachers, he simply set fire to the church. Rumor has it that his sons, who were just little guys back then, helped their dad with his arson activity."

"That's twisted," Cole groaned.

"Yet another horror story from that despicable family." Renee sighed.

CHAPTER 33

MARLA'S CELL PHONE sounded as she and Dule were on their long drive back to Philadelphia after spending time in Las Vegas. She pulled the phone from out her purse. "Hello?"

"Marla, it's Cole."

"Where have you been? You were supposed to call me yesterday," she scolded.

"I know, sorry. Nothing much happened yesterday, so I thought I'd wait to call you today. There's not much to report today as well. I haven't crossed paths with the Porters over the past few days."

"I'm still having bad feelings about this case, Cole. If you want to stay down there, you'd better start convincing me now."

Cole spoke in a low seductive voice as he teased, "I'll give you a passionate kiss when this is over."

"Why, Cole Walsh, you have my heart a-fluttering." She giggled.

From the passenger's seat, Dule glared at her.

"Come on, Marla. Let's go through with this case. These boys are terrorizing this small town."

"There you go, speaking in plural again. It's boy, Cole, not boys. Murky only. I'm not authorizing the other two if I indeed keep this case in operation."

"Okay, I'll take the deal. Murky only."

She hesitated and then groaned, "Oh, I just don't know about this one."

"I'll do this for you. Give me two weeks, and if I haven't completed the mission within that time span, I'll crawl home with my tail between my legs."

"You'll have to come to Philly and be my toy for a day," she kidded.

Dule forcefully cleared his throat.

"You run a delightful bargain, lady," Cole said with a chuckle.

"Seriously, you have one week from today."

"A week?" he complained.

"Take it or leave it."

"Okay...okay. I'll take it."

"Call me tomorrow, Cole."

Cole tossed his cell phone onto the bed before heading outside the guesthouse and toward the barn. Just before placing his call to Marla, Renee had stopped by the guesthouse to inform Cole that Ike would like to speak with him in the barn. Renee then headed back to the farmhouse, so Cole believed to be the case.

"Here he comes, Grandpa," Renee gasped excitedly as she peeked out the door of the barn while peering out to the lawn. Ike and Renee had previously devised a plan to play a practical joke on Cole.

"Okay, honey." Ike was as hyped up as she was. "Take your stick and hide behind the tractor. Hurry now."

Renee scurried across the barn floor, and then she slid behind the tractor with a fallen tree branch about an inch in diameter in her hands. She chuckled with anticipation.

"Be quiet now, child, or you'll give us away," Ike directed.

"Okay, sorry, Grandpa," she replied.

Cole approached the barn and then stepped inside. He nodded at Ike. "You wanted to see me?"

Ike played as if he was unaware of what Cole was inquiring about. He squinted. "How's that?"

"Renee said that you wanted to see me about something. I'm sorry it took so long, but I was on the phone. So what is it?"

Renee pressed her left palm over her mouth to keep from being heard from her hiding spot.

Ike then suddenly acted as if he recalled. He snapped his fingers. "Oh, that's right, yeah. I wanted to ask you a favor."

"Sure, what is it?"

Ike's expression grew shameful. "Well, I'm not foolin' anyone about me gettin' older, you know, enterin' my twilight years. Okay... so I'm already in my twilight years. Anyway, I was wonderin' if you'd give an old man one last chance at redeeming his pride."

Cole appeared confused. "Um...what are you talking about?"

Ike's chest protruded outward as he pulled up on his pants a bit. "I'll have you know that in my heyday, I was a darn good arm wrestler, one of the best in the county as a matter of fact." Ike then bent his arm at the elbow and pointed at his bicep. "I still have some left in me, you'd better bet I do."

Cole threw his right palm in the air. "Hold on right there, old-timer. If you are asking me to arm wrestle with you, you can just forget it."

Ike's appearance became one of disappointment. "Why not?"

"Because, Ike, you have gotten up there in years, as you said. You just admitted that yourself."

"Yeah...so?"

"You might get injured if we arm wrestle." Cole expressed his concerns.

Ike then landed a fairly firm punch on Cole's upper left arm. "Oh, hogwash. You're just 'fraid is all."

Renee pressed her palm tighter over her mouth.

"That's ridiculous, Ike. Why would I think that you could possibly be a challenge to me? Why would I be afraid to arm wrestle an old man?"

"Maybe because you might lose? Don't worry, Cole, I won't tell anyone," Ike jeered.

Cole chuckled. "Okay, Ike, bring it on."

Ike buttressed his elbow on the workbench. "Now, don't hold back anythin', Cole. Give me all ya got 'cause I plan on doin' my best to put a whoopin' on ya."

"Yeah, okay, old man, if you say so," Cole taunted as he brought his elbow to the bench. The men then grasped hands.

"Okay, Cole, on the count of three. Are you ready?"

Cole nodded.

"One…two…three!" Ike barked. Ike immediately carried power to the leverage contest, but Cole had little difficulty holding him steady. Ike then leaned in with his body weight, but still, Cole did not budge. Ike could see that Cole was strong, but he didn't expect this much resistance. The man was very strapping indeed. To Ike, it seemed as though he was trying to move a truck.

Renee peered out with her line of sight shooting between the seat and the engine of the tractor. She steadied the stick in her hands, waiting for the exact moment to arrive.

Ike dug into the barn's dirt floor with his boots as he grunted with strength. His face reddened as he gasped for air. Cole was burning no energy at all.

"Listen, Ike, you want to quit this nonsense now?"

Ike shook his head as he inhaled a deep breath and found a resurgence of strength. He moved Cole's arm, but just a smidgen of a distance. Ike appeared as though he was about to pull a muscle or, worse, have a heart attack, so Cole decided it was best to end this match. He sprung the mighty muscles in his arm into action. In one demanding swoop, Cole slammed Ike's arm to the bench top.

With flawless timing, Renee snapped the stick in half over her knee. The crack of the branch sounded similar to a human bone breaking.

Ike shrieked out in phony pain and crumbled to the floor. "Oh my god!" Ike shouted. "Oh my god, my arm is broken!"

Cole's eyes widened as Ike gave the impression of going into a convulsion of pain. "Holy crap, Ike! I am so sorry! I am so sorry, man…I didn't mean to hurt you!" Cole gasped as he dropped down to Ike's side on the barn floor. "See, this is exactly why I didn't want to do this, old man. Let me see your arm, hold on, just wait here, I'll go for my phone and call for an ambulance…Better yet, I'll get my truck and drive you to the hospital."

Ike's expression then turned from grave to a grin and then to a hardy laugh. "Can we stop along the way to have a beer?" Ike scoffed.

Renee then moved out from behind the tractor with the snapped stick in her hands. She roared with laughter. Ike and Renee's laughter grew with intensity. Ike had to wipe tears from his eyes as Renee bent at the waist.

Cole glared at them.

"You should've seen your face, Cole," Ike playfully taunted. "It looked as though you'd seen a ghost."

Ike sprung to his feet, but Cole remained on his knees. Ike patted the back of Cole's left shoulder. "That was one of the funniest things I've ever seen, Cole," Ike continued to jeer.

Cole rubbed his eyes with his thumb and forefinger.

"You went for it, Cole, hook, line, and sinker," Renee added through her laughter. "Or should I be saying hook, line, and stick?" She playfully taunted.

Ike howled with laughter.

Cole rose to his feet. His expression was not one of lightheartedness, but rather of complete seriousness and disgust. He continued a defiant stare at Ike and Renee until their laughter slowly faded and then subsided altogether.

After a long moment of awkward silence, Ike cleared his throat and nervously grinned. "Say somethin', Cole."

Cole narrowed his eyes.

"It was just a practical joke, no harm, no foul," Renee informed insecurely. It was obvious that Cole was annoyed. Renee and Ike fidgeted and swallowed hard.

Cole's eyes clouded. "I was on assignment in the military when our brigade came upon the enemy unexpectedly. Intelligence told us that we couldn't expect to reach enemy lines until the following day, but here we were, finding ourselves surrounded by enemy soldiers before we could react. We were beaten, tortured, and some of us left for dead. The rest of us were dragged into their camp and locked up in bamboo cages. They took turns assaulting us. One of the bastards then started to stab my best friend repeatedly. All I could do was watch as my friend bled profusely.

"Then one night, we attempted an escape, but as we crawled beneath the fence, one of us got his wrist caught in the fencing. The

enemy was closing in on us quickly, so I was left with no choice but to break my fellow soldier's arm to get him out of that fence. I'll never forget his screams of pain when I was forced to snap his bone."

Ike and Renee's mood turned very somber. Renee felt ashamed. "We're so sorry, Cole. We didn't know. Will you please forgive us?" she pleaded.

Cole shook his head no. "I'm sorry, but I can't do that."

Ike and Renee hung their heads.

Cole cleared his throat. "I can't offer acceptance of your apologies simply because there is no truth to that story." Cole then burst into hearty laughter of his own.

Renee and Ike realized that Cole had turned the tables on them and that they had been had.

Ike clapped his hands. "Oh, you are good, Cole. You are damn good." Ike joined Cole in the laughter.

Renee playfully shook her left forefinger at him. "Cole Walsh, you are terrible. I should put you over my knee for a good spankin'," she joked.

Cole grinned and winked.

"Wait," she teasingly growled, "I take that back."

The trio shared a robust round of amusement.

Renee enjoyed what she had just witnessed. She believed one of the most important attributes that a man could possess was a strong sense of humor. Cole's humor appeared to be fine and healthy.

CHAPTER 34

IKE WAS PROUD of his open-fire grilled steaks. He purchased the fresh beef, never frozen, cuts from Jack Miller's cattle farm on the outskirts of Webster. Over the years he had developed his own special marinade sauce and soaked the steaks in the concoction at least twelve hours before cooking.

Renee and Cole sat on wicker lawn chairs observing Ike prepare the open fire for cooking the steaks. He meticulously stoked the hot ambers before placing the grill rack atop two old tractor rims above the low flames to tickle the meat. "Now, the secret to a good steak is to cook it slow, the more unhurried the better. I'd say the best steaks take a good two hours to grill. That's true with sex too. The slower the better." Ike winked.

"Grandpa!" Renee chided.

"Well, it is," he defended.

Cole chuckled. Renee blushed. She quickly changed the subject. "Anyway, what's the next move regardin' the Porters?"

Cole sipped a swallow of his beer. The crickets were beginning to sing with the surrounding dusk conditions. Cole then lit a cigarette.

"I asked you a question, Cole."

"You're not going to like the answer."

"Well, I'll do what I gotta do to avenge Nate. So what is it?"

Cole, frustrated, said with a sigh, "I called in today and was only given one additional week of time with this case."

"I thought it was on for as long it takes?" she speculated with widened eyes. "What happened?"

"The deciding power has spoken. An uneasy feeling about this is brewing at the top. I had to practically beg to get another week. She wanted to pull the plug today."

"Well, what can be accomplished in a week?" Ike questioned.

Cole exhaled smoke. "We need to speed things up."

"How?" Renee conjectured.

Cole took another swallow of beer. "You need to go to that party at the river with Murky."

Renee, without hesitation, shook her head. "Oh, no way. I'm not doin' it."

"It's the only way, Renee."

"Why?"

Cole leaned forward with a creak to his wicker chair. "We need to get Murky's hopes soaring high and then pull the rug out from beneath him. We can accomplish that by you going to the party with him, and then the following day he sees you and I together."

"There is no way that I am goin' anywhere with Murky Porter alone. Forget it."

"I'll be right there," Cole confirmed.

"What?"

"Yeah, I'll be there watching over you. You tell Murky that your grandfather demanded that you bring along the jerk that's working for him on the farm."

"I won't have any problem with the jerk part," she snipped.

He curled his lip at her. "Anyway, Murky spends time with you at the party, his hopes inflate, and then the next day we burst his bubble. That's sure to cause him to attack me, and that's what I need to happen in order to execute."

"I don't know, Cole. It sounds dangerous for her to go to that party with Murky," Ike cautioned.

Cole leaned back in his chair. "It's the only way to get this done as quickly as required. I'll keep a constant eye on Renee."

Only the sound of crackling firewood could be heard for long moments before she spoke up. "Okay, I'll do it," Renee proclaimed. "Only because of my enduring love for Nate. But, if even for a second, you fail to protect me, Cole, I swear I'll kick you square in the... well...where the sun doesn't shine!"

"Renee!" Ike returned a scold.

They all joined in on the mirth.

Several hours and a trio of consumed steaks later, Ike headed to the farmhouse to retire for the night.

Cole placed more wood on the fire, bringing the ambers back to flames. "Your grandfather sure can cook a mean steak. He should bottle and sell that secret marinade he goes on about," Cole complimented.

Renee stared into her glass of wine while he could sense her somber mood by the light of the fire.

"What's on your mind?"

"Everyone in town is gonna hear about me goin' out with Murky. They're sure to think I'm a terrible witch for betrayin' my dead brother."

"You put too much emphasis on what people think. My father always told me that what people think about me is none of my business. I don't give a damn what people contemplate about me."

"Evidently."

He glared at her. "What's that supposed to mean?"

"Oh, nothin'," she retorted before consuming another a sip of her wine.

He lit a cigarette. "You won't get any pampering from me, Renee. I'm sure being raised by your grandfather was a powder puff experience, but I'll lay down no layer of foam for you to fall on."

She squinted at him. "You think that losin' your parents as a child is easy? Growin' up here on the farm wasn't pampered by any means. It's hard work. Where do you get off on judgin' others?"

"I wasn't passing judgment on anyone. Just stating facts is all."

"God, I feel like comin' over there to slap you across the face, Cole Walsh."

"What would that prove?"

"Nothin', it would just make me feel better."

Silence prevailed for several moments before Cole sounded off, "Do you know what your problem is?"

"No, but I'm sure you're goin' to tell me."

"You're so uptight because you're horny."

Her eyes widened, and then she glared at him. "That is so ludicrous!" she retorted angrily.

"I don't see any guys hanging around."

"I just haven't found the right one yet," she defended.

He chuckled as he continued to taunt, "Yep, that's your problem. Your lawn isn't being mowed."

She stood abruptly from her chair. "I hate you!"

He sighed. "Ah, come on, Renee, sit back down. I'll stop badgering you a bit."

She folded her arms.

He ceased laughing. "I promise. Have a seat, please."

Renee hesitated before sitting back down. "What about you, Cole? I don't see a ring on your finger, and I haven't heard you talk about any girlfriends. Perhaps you're not gettin much action yourself?"

"Perhaps."

After another moment of hush, she inquired in a softer tone, "Have you ever been in love?"

"Ah...yeah...once."

"What was her name?"

"Hadie."

"That's a pretty name. What happened? Did she grow tired of your foul attitude?"

Cole's eyes clouded momentarily. "Hadie is no longer with us."

Renee swallowed hard. "Oh, I'm sorry...I didn't know."

He displayed to her the palm of his right hand and shook his head.

"Can I ask how it happened?"

"Drugs. An overdose."

Renee became baffled. "You dated a drug addict?"

"It's a long story."

"You don't have to tell me about it if you don't want to."

"I'd rather not talk about it."

"That's fine…I'll tell you about the only time I was in love, okay?"

He nodded.

"Well, you already know that his name is Dillon Niles. I met him at the fair. I wasn't sure for a while if I loved him, but when I look back on it now, I realize that I did in some sort of way. Ya know, young love can be confusin'. It's difficult to decipher between infatuation and love at a young age. Well, now that I think about it, it probably was just a case of infatuation. But it sure seemed like real love to me back then. What is it that Donnie Osmond calls it? Oh yeah, puppy love. Not that I'm an avid listener of Donnie Osmond's songs. Sadly and eventually, Murky caught word of Dillon. After the brothers paid Dillon a visit, he avoided me like the plague after that."

"How do you put up with it? Most people would have lost control by now."

"You mean Murky and his brothers?"

He nodded.

Renee closed her eyes. "It sure isn't easy. I'd be long gone from this town if it weren't for my grandpa. He refuses to move away, and I'm not leavin' him here alone."

The fire crackled and Renee yawned.

"You'd better head on in and get some rest," he suggested.

"No, I want to talk with you more, if that's okay with you," Renee said.

He grinned.

"Only because you're the only one out here to speak with," she quickly recovered. "Let's take a wander down the driveway so I can stay alert."

They strolled together along the edge of the long driveway guided by the light of the moon silhouetted against the sky above. She considered to take hold of his arm to support her walk, but then she deemed that he might take such an action in another manner. She maintained her hands at her side. "How will I know at the party if it becomes necessary for me to signal for your help?"

"You'll know. You might be a little tedious, Renee, but you're intelligent."

She frowned. "Is that supposed to be some sort of twisted compliment? I'm not amused. Why do you think I'm dull?"

"Well, I guess it's not completely your fault. I mean, how can you socially develop with any meaning in a small and secluded town such as this?"

"Have you always been so insecure?"

"What the hell are you talking about?"

"When people continuously run down others, it's usually because they are not confident in themselves."

He ceased walking. "I don't know if that's exactly it, but you may be on to something. I live frightened most of the time."

She was surprised at his confession.

"I've never told anyone that before."

"Really?"

He shook his head no.

"Then why did you tell me?"

He shrugged his shoulders. "I feel comfortable around you, I guess."

"Why is that?"

They continued strolling.

"I can't completely explain it, but believe me when I say there haven't been a handful of people that I can declare I feel comfortable with. I see so many wayward individuals in my line of work. It's refreshing to be with someone who is completely honest and up front."

"You can be decent when you want to be." She cracked a smile.

"Yeah, well, don't tell anyone."

She giggled. "Fear is a complicated matter," Renee examined. "It's the very force that the Porters use against people. Without fear, they would be powerless. I try not to live with fear, but it's so difficult to keep it from overtakin' you at times. I suppose God instilled fear in us as a warnin' mechanism. Like if ya touch a hot stove or somethin'. When I was in my young teens, I had reached a point where I grew tired. I know I was young, but I was tired of the problems that life brought with it. My parents were dead, Murky never let me alone, and I felt trapped inside the boundaries of this town. I thought to end it all, but I emphasize the word *thought*. I would have never

actually gone through with it. But it got me to thinkin' about things. About life in general. I realized that I was tryin' to carry the world upon my shoulders. I decided to restructure my thinkin' the way I looked at things. I promised myself that I would only worry about things that warranted worryin' about.

"I guess the most important thing I learned is that one cannot control the actions of others. People are gonna do what they're gonna do regardless of what you say about it. We are accountable for our own actions, and I wasn't going to feel guilt or shame any longer over what someone else might have done. I'm a true believer in fate. What I don't mean is that life is one big blueprint. What I'm tryin' to say is that events happen for a reason. Reasons that we are not supposed to know about. Everything has meanin', every action has an outcome. It's up to us to put the pieces of the puzzle together and understand it. That's not so straightforward at times. It's all about balance, I suppose. For every certain number of good people, there is a bad one. For several good deeds with merit to them, there is a dastardly act. A world filled with righteous people would be great, I suppose. However, it'd be a bit borin', wouldn't ya think? I guess with any degree of excitement comes frustration. I'm not sayin' what the Porters do to people is excitin'. It's disgustin', but it sure isn't borin'.

"You're right when you say that I live in a rut, but I like it that way. At least I know each day where I'll land with my good morals and my kindness toward others. I suppose I could use a little more spontaneous action in my life, but that usually leads to worry and thoughts that are unsettled. I enjoy peace of mind, and livin' in a controlled environment delivers that to me. Sure, there are times when I lay in bed at night and sigh over the thoughts of bein' humdrum, but at the same time, I can close my eyes with a clear conscience. So if that's bein' a tedious person, so be it. I'll take dull over inner turmoil any day of the week."

Cole froze his stride and, to her surprise, ran his left hand through her dark, silky hair. "When I say that you are dull, I guess it's because I'm a bit envious. I wish I could be more like you, but quick actions run in my blood. You're right when you say that an unsettled life leads to a mind that's not completely at peace. But then

again, I can't just sit back and watch life pass me by. I need to jump in there and grab it by the horns. I suppose the both of us should seek a middle ground between our extremes. Perhaps that will come with age, perhaps not. But you're not completely correct when you say we can't control the actions of others. I know we can't point everyone in the direction we'd like them to travel, but we can have some influence if we keep speaking up. We just can't keep sticking our heads in the sand and hope that all bad things just simply go away. It's safe to remember, what we may think is right, the other person may believe is wrong, and vice versa. It's all about opinions. Who really knows what is right and what is wrong? That's where laws and morals come in, to set some guidelines anyway.

"I believe I have learned why some people take good or bad to extremes. It's about attention. Somewhere along the line in their life, they have felt left out. They want to draw attention to themselves in order to feed their need to be accepted or at least noticed. Unfortunately, some of the attention seekers are those that set out to gain that notice through bad deeds. Bad will get you attention quicker than good ever could. You're right in saying that people are held accountable for their own actions. We are simply humans sharing this world. We are surely not all trained physiologists to deal with every kink in each other's minds. For the most part, we are all within a normal range, whatever that may be. We can't take it on to ourselves to feel responsible for those that stray wayward. It's not our fault, and it's not in our control. It's not really labeling you dull, Renee. It's called being mature."

She smiled as they continued with their walk. They strolled and talked for another forty minutes before making their way back to the farmhouse. After an exchange of good nights, Cole headed back to the guesthouse. Renee's heart felt warm as she shut the screen door to the main house.

Nearly an hour later, Cole sat on a chair he had moved near the front window of the guesthouse. He rested his chin on the windowsill as he gazed out into the warm summer Tennessee night. After nearly ten minutes of quiet thought, his eyelids began to grow heavy. It had been a long day, and drowsiness was catching up with him.

Just as he was about to rise from the chair and head to bed, he spotted Renee's bedroom illuminate from across the lawn. He watched as she took a seat in front of her dresser with a large mirror attached to the rear of the piece of furniture. She was wearing a pair of soft blue thin pajamas as she stroked her silky dark hair with a hairbrush. Her back was to Cole, so he felt safe with spying on her. Suddenly, his eyes were no longer closing.

The air was still and quiet while the sky above was clear with the glowing stars of the night. This gave Cole a good line of vision and the ability to hear the radio station she was playing. As he maintained his attention on Renee and her beauty, he couldn't help but to wish that it were his fingers and not the brush that was stroking her hair.

When satisfied with her now tangle-free hair, Renee pulled the back of her hair up from her neck and used a rubber band to secure it into a ponytail. With the back of her neck exposed, Cole imagined kissing her skin gently.

Renee then reached up onto the dresser to switch off her lamp before heading to bed when she noticed the guesthouse window's reflection in her mirror. Instead of reaching for the lamp, she shut off the radio. She carefully studied the reflection for a moment before she made out that Cole was watching her through the window. She grinned to herself and mumbled, "Cole, you are so silly at times." She then decided to rib at him a bit. She rose from her chair to abruptly attack her open window.

Cole sprang to attention, but he was too late to move out from her sight.

She raised her voice at him across the lawn. "You know, Cole, in most states, it is illegal to be a peepin' tom," she taunted.

He stuttered, "I…I…I…was looking…at the…stars above."

She playfully snickered and slyly grinned. "Uh-huh, sure you were. Since when are the stars inside my bedroom?"

"Your bedroom? I…wasn't…you don't think…I was looking in your…bedroom, do you?" he queried with a reddened face.

She squinted. "What are you still doin' up anyway? You have to be exhausted. I know that I am."

Cole shrugged his shoulders. "I'm tired but not sleepy, if that makes any sense."

Renee smiled warmly. "How about a nightcap?"

"Sure," he eagerly replied.

"Well then, pour yourself one," she taunted and then closed her bedroom window.

He mumbled to himself, "That was good. I have to admit, that was really good." Cole then closed his window and crawled into bed.

CHAPTER 35

MASON TURNER WAS perched upon his usual barstool inside Joe's Tavern. He was the only remaining patron on this night since the others had gone home nearly an hour prior. The news was broadcasting on the television set positioned on a shelf above the bar. Newscaster Mindy Hilton was anchoring the news from the WJYT studio in Webster. Mason wasn't really listening to the broadcast; he was admiring Mindy's full breasts that were pouring out from her low-cut dress.

"She sure has a set of lungs on her, huh, Mason?" Joe pointed out as he brought Mason a fresh beer.

Mason's face reddened. "Oh, I was just listenin' is all."

Joe chuckled. "Is that right now? Nobody actually listens to Mindy, not men anyway. So you won't mind if I flip the channel then?" Joe teased.

"No…don't go to the trouble, Joe. You can leave it where it's at."

"I thought so," Joe chortled. Joe went about his business of washing glassware and then filling the beer coolers.

When the newscast ended, Mason stared blankly at Joe.

"What is it, Mason?" Joe probed.

"I was married four times," Mason began. His voice was clear and without stumble, slurring, or a stutter. Over all the years of drinking,

Mason had mastered controlling his voice regardless of how intoxicated he was. "Four times"—he held up four extended fingers of his left hand—"and each time I couldn't hold on to her. I dunno, I think I'm meant to be a loner, and I was merely forcin' the issue of marriage. I'm not such a bad guy, ya know. Yeah, I drink a little—okay, a lot... but I never beat my wives or anything like that. Hell, they were all bigger than me. They could have kicked my butt if they wanted to."

Joe grinned. "No, Mason, you're not a bad guy."

"Then what's the problem? Why is it that some of us find the right one while others spend a lifetime lookin' for it, only to come up empty?"

"If I knew the answer to that, Mason, I'd be a wealthy man."

"How are you and Judy doin' these days?"

"We're fine. I have a great marriage."

"So Judy is the right one for you?"

"Oh, definitely. I got really lucky when I landed her."

"How did ya two meet? I know that she's originally from Waynesburg."

"Believe it or not, I was passed out when we met." Joe chuckled.

"Huh?" Mason appeared confused.

Joe placed his hands on the bar to support his body as he leaned over the sink. "I was goin' through a rough time. I was drinkin' quite a bit back then. I'm not sure why, I suppose I just didn't want to face most days sober. My mind worked too much, and the alcohol shut it down."

"I know whatcha mean," Mason agreed as he raised his bottle and then gulped a swig of beer.

"Well, I was at this pig roast over in Waynesburg—that's where I got my idea of the annual pig roasts I hold here—but anyway, while the pig was roastin', I had myself some pre-dinner drinks. Quite a few, as a matter of fact. By the time I realized that I'd had too many drinks in me, it was too late. My world was spinnin', and I couldn't keep my balance. I remember people's faces were cloudy and blurry, but I could sure hear them laughin' at me. I eventually hit the ground, and from what I am told, I landed rather hard.

"Of the people that were there, only one came to my aid. I woke up beneath one of the tent roofs with my forehead bein' wiped down

with an ice cube. I focused in on quite a beauty. Her hair was light brown and her eyes as green as a deep runnin' river. I immediately fell into those eyes. She smiled at me and asked if I was gonna be okay. I think I was able to mumble yes. Her beauty had me stymied, though my head was throbbin' with pain from the fall.

"I asked her how long I'd been out, and she told me about two hours. She had stayed with me that entire time. When I questioned her as to why she came to my rescue, she said she wasn't sure why. That she was just drawn to me. I asked her out on a date right then and there. She promised to go out with me if I vowed to cut down on my drinkin'. I did her one better. I promised to quit drinkin' altogether. I haven't had a drink since that day. Judy does more for my spirit than alcohol could ever do. It's kind of peculiar that I serve the stuff, but I don't consume it. I'm not even tempted. No offense, Mason, but if it weren't for Judy, I was headin' down a road that would have had me sittin' behind a drink like you do each every day of the week. A year later, Judy and I were married, and it's been a gem ever since."

"But why no kiddies?" Mason wondered.

Joe smiled with pride. "We just found out last week that Judy is pregnant."

Mason raised his drink. "Well, congratulations are in order, barkeep."

"Thank you, Mason. But don't say anything just yet. Judy wants to announce on her own soon."

"Not a word, Joe. Maybe I can pass out at a pig roast one day and find the love of my life," Mason joked.

"I wouldn't count on it, Mason. That was truly a lucky incident for me."

"Well, I plan on passin' out just the same."

Both men hooted.

*****

Bessy Porter mumbled in her sleep. She mumbled again, and then she snorted, which woke her up. She was in a slumped position

on a lawn chair in the front porch of the Porter home. She had been drinking heavily and was passed out for the past several hours.

It was well past midnight when she pried herself up from the chair to begin a stumbling sequence on her path inside the house. Before she reached the door, she heard sounds in the still of the night coming from the barn. It wasn't a night owl or crickets. She listened intently as she swayed and heard more commotion coming from the barn. She made her way across the lawn, nearly tripping in the process, until she reached the barn. Bessy pressed her right ear against the wooden door and listened closely. She then heard a muffled woman's shout before it was quickly quieted. She then listened to Sterling growl, "Shut the fuck up, or I'll bash your face in!"

Bessy pushed open the door of the barn. It was dimly lit inside the outbuilding, and she could only make out two figures on the floor of the barn. She reached for the light switch next to the door and flipped it upward. A large light in the center of the barn illuminated the building inside. A buck naked Sterling turned to look at his mother.

"What are you doin' out here in the middle of the night, Sterling?" Bessy quizzed.

"Just havin' some fun, Mom. What are you doin' up?"

Bessy then noticed a pile of woman's clothing scattered about on the barn's floor along with Sterling's clothing. Then she glanced to observe that Sterling had four feet and four legs before she completely focused to realize that a pair of a female's feet was mixed in with her son's. Bessy moved closer to discover that Sterling had the nude woman trapped below him with his left hand covering her mouth. The hostage opened her eyes wide as she realized who she was.

"Sharon?" Bessy inquired.

The woman nodded a frightened yes.

"Remove your hand for a minute, Sterling, I want to talk to her."

An impatient Sterling rolled his eyes. "Well, hurry up, Mom." Sterling then eased his grip over the woman's mouth.

She gasped for air and sobbed.

"Sharon Greene, I haven't seen you in a while. How is the family?" Bessy conversed as if they were sitting at the kitchen table having coffee.

"Oh, thank god you're here, Bessy. Please help me. I'm bein' raped!"

"Come now, Sharon, you're bein' a little dramatic, aren't ya now? My boys are good boys. Sterling's just toyin' with ya a bit."

"Yeah," Sterling grunted.

"No…no…Bessy, I was dragged here against my will," Sharon anxiously reported.

"That can't be true, right, Sterling?" Bessy looked at her son to confirm.

"No way, Mom. Her car was broken down up on Martin's Way. I offered to help her, and she said she'd repay me with sex."

"Well, see there, Sharon, you must pay your bills. It's not nice to offer somethin' and then back out at the last minute."

"This is insane, Bessy. You couldn't possibly believe that I want to share intimacy with this…this animal. I'm a happily married woman and a mom!"

Bessy scolded, "Don't you call my son an animal. I'll whoop you like a redheaded stepchild if you don't mind your manners, Sharon!"

Sterling again covered Sharon's mouth as she screamed into his palm, but it was barely audible through Sterling's large palm.

"Where are your brothers, honey?" Bessy calmly asked Sterling.

"They went on to bed. They were tired. They said they'll have a slice of this broad in the mornin' if she is still here"—he then glared into Sharon's eyes—"and still alive."

"Well, make sure she pays up, son, but there is no reason to harm her unless she gets too scrappy. I'm headin' inside for a beer and then to get some shut-eye. Turn off the light when you're done."

"Okay, Mom, good night now."

Bessy turned to leave the barn. "It was nice seein' you, Sharon. Tell John that Carter and I said hello."

"Bessy, help me for cryin' out loud!" Sharon shouted into Sterling's hand.

Bessy shook her finger at Sharon. "Do yourself a favor, Sharon, and just settle down and go with it. You don't want to get Sterling all riled up now. Hard tellin' what he might do." Bessy then exited the barn.

Sharon Greene was a thirty-four-year-old housewife and mother of two from Webster. Sharon was a light brown–haired beauty. Her

shoulder-length hair was naturally highlighted with soft browns, and her eyes were coffee toned. Her olive skin easily tanned during the summer months. Her nose was pudgy yet quaint, and her firm jawline was supple enough to be feminine. Sharon kept herself in great shape knowing that a healthy body led to good bone structure and muscle tone. She was well versed on human anatomy as Sharon was a licensed physical therapist who traveled on business throughout the county to the homes of her patients. Although she was raised in Webster, she knew of the Porters, first by reputation, and secondly, about six years ago, she treated Bessy Porter in the office for a fractured vertebra she suffered in what she claimed to be a farming accident. But Sharon knew better. She had seen the likes of this type of injury before with women who were victims of spousal abuse. But Bessy refused to come clean and stuck to her story of a farming accident.

Sharon tried taking Bessy under her wing to get her to tell the truth so that she could arrange to have the woman protected by the proper authorities. She invited Bessy to her home on several occasions, trying to befriend her. However, it all went for naught as Bessy wasn't about to squeal on Carter. Bessy quit showing up for therapy for her back, though she wasn't through with her planned sessions of treatment.

On this night, Sharon had been on her way home to Webster from Waynesburg, taking a shortcut through Harpersfield. Usually, she avoided Harpersfield and took the longer way, but the session with her patient, Mr. Haines, lasted longer than expected. He was experiencing a rough time with his ailing knee, and Sharon stayed longer. It was late, and she wanted to get home.

Along Martin's Way, Sterling's truck seemed to have come out of nowhere and ran her off the road and into a ditch. She begged and pleaded for the three brothers to let her go, and though she had never met the boys personally, she soon realized that they must be the dreaded Porter brothers. Her pleas failed as the trio pulled her from her car. While Dalton held her captive in the truck, feeling her up as he did so, Murky and Sterling guided her car over the ridge and sent the vehicle plunging into the depths of the Sulfur River. They then kidnapped her back to their house.

Murky and Dalton were nearly sleeping on their feet when they stumbled inside the house, stepping by their mother on the front porch, who was passed out on a lawn chair. Sterling forced Sharon out to the barn where he was now violating her.

"Bessy, please come back here and save me!" Sharon cried out. "For the love of God, help me!"

"You mention God around me again, and I'll use my fuckin' dagger to lay open your neck earlobe to earlobe, bitch." Sterling then tightened his mighty grip around Sharon's throat, which completely cut off her airway. "Listen to me, lady. We can do this easy, or we can do this rough. It's up to you, but either way, we're gonna screw. So what's it gonna be?" He loosened his grip so that she could speak.

She coughed for several moments as the oxygen rushed back inside her lungs. She was wheezy, weary, and nauseated. Her voice was shaky and scratchy. "Please, young man, show some mercy and let me go. Don't worry, I won't tell a soul about any of this."

He squinted his eyes as they turned into a deep cold abyss. For a second, Sharon could have sworn that Sterling's eyes turned lifeless and gray. He gripped her throat again, collapsing her windpipe, as he rammed his large erect penis inside her vagina. Sterling's strength was so powerful that Sharon could not struggle to move from beneath him. He introduced intercourse at such a force that it tore at her vaginal walls. She shuddered out in pain as she tried her best to gain a breath of air. It became alarmingly apparent to Sharon that Sterling was not going to allow her to breathe again until he had completed his cruel act upon her.

Sharon desperately wanted to survive; her babies and husband were waiting for her at home. She wished to see the sun in the morning and many mornings thereafter; she so desired to see her kids through high school and then onto college. She wanted to grow old with John. Sharon Greene needed to survive this ordeal; she was not prepared to die, not tonight, not this way. She must do her part to help bring this ordeal to its conclusion as quickly as possible. If Sterling took too long to reach his goal, if he lingered on too far, she would die of asphyxiation.

Sharon began to sway her hips to match his rhythm. She tightened her vaginal muscles to massage his penis.

Sterling moaned with pleasure. "That's it, bitch, you're likin' it now, aren't ya? Oh yeah, baby, women love the Porters' big cocks. Mmmmmm...fuck good, baby, like a wild animal."

Sharon stepped up her motions to a higher level. She imagined a deeply hidden sexual fantasy that she had held inside for years to help lubricate her vagina. Also, though she despised what Sterling was doing to her, his organ was much larger than John's, giving her a sense that she hadn't felt before. In the right situation, it would be an exciting sensation. But not like this.

"Oh, you're gettin' wet now, lady...I knew once I got inside ya that you'd like it. Fuck like no tomorrow, bitch."

That statement held true for Sharon as she must bring him to an ejaculation before she lost her life. She raised her hips to meet his thrusts. Finally, she could sense he was nearing climax. His penis throbbed with excitement inside her as he ground his teeth. She bucked and squeezed her vaginal walls around his penis.

Sterling grunted out as his semen shot and sprayed inside of Sharon's vagina. His body trembled; she was nearing unconsciousness from lack of oxygen. At the last possible moment, Sterling collapsed on top of her, releasing his grip from around her throat. The first deep inhale of oxygen taken in by Sharon was like breathing in razor blades. Her lungs filled as her world spun around her.

Sterling trundled off her nude body as his breathing was rapid while he slowly descended from his height of sexual excitement. Sharon rolled onto her left side and brought her knees to her stomach to help ease her severe cramping. She could feel Sterling's semen ooze out from between her legs and seep down along her inner thighs. She grew ill over that awareness. She coughed. She coughed hard and deep, nearly vomiting on the floor of the barn.

It took Sharon nearly five full minutes to gather her wit and senses about her. She was hampered by a tremendous headache as she shamefully crawled to the pile of her clothing on the floor. She took hold of her panties and was about to pull them on when Sterling stopped her. "What the hell do you think you're doin'?"

She sobbed out, "I'm dressing, and then I'm goin' home!"

"Oh no, you're not, not yet."

Her eyes watered as she looked at him. "Please…you've had your perverted, twisted fun. I just want to go home…to take a bath to scrub away the events of tonight and forget that this ever took place."

"How do you plan on gettin' home? Your car is at the bottom of the Sulfur River." He chuckled.

"I'll walk…I'll hitchhike," she mumbled. She then slid her panties over her ankles.

"Keep them off!" Sterling forcefully demanded.

She wept. "Please…please let me go home to my children. They are just little kids wonderin' where their mommy is."

"Not until my brothers have a piece of your pussy. I promised them, and we keep our promises to each other. They will have their way with you in the mornin', and then we might let you go on your way. We'll see if ya hump them as good as you fucked me."

"I beg of you, let me go home."

He shook his head. "No can do. Besides, you ain't gonna hitch no ride at this time of the night, and I sure ain't takin' your sorry ass home. Nope, you're here until mornin', so you might as well sleep on the floor with me, all naked and stuff." He snorted perversely.

Sharon could take no more. She certainly could not go through a series of two more rapes at the hands of the Porters. So it was then that she lost control, that she snapped. She had to get out of there. She simply had to gain her freedom, even if that entailed going on the run without her clothing, then so be it. She thought to lie next to Sterling, play like she was sleeping until he drifted off to sleep, and then she would sneak away.

Just as she settled in on that plan, he ruined it by rumbling, "Yeah, you sleep here with me, but not before we do it again."

No, Sharon Greene would not spend another second beneath the sweating man with a foul odor. No, she would rather take her chances and flee. She then came up with plan B.

"Can I at least step outside to relieve myself?"

Sterling made an expression of confusion.

"To urinate?" She attempted to clarify.

"Oh, you need to bust a piss." He then understood.

"Well, I prefer to more subtle about it, but yes, I do, if you don't mind."

He shrugged his shoulders. "No, I don't give a shit if you do."

It worked; she was going to escape!

"But you don't have to go outside. You can piss in here, on the floor. It's only dirt. Me and my brothers piss in here sometimes."

Plan B was wrecked. She was left with no choice but to flee for the door.

Sharon abruptly stood to her feet and raced for the door of the barn. Sterling was quick to react as he sprung to his feet. While she wrestled with the door's latch, Sterling was on her in an instant. She cried, turned, and began to swat at him. She kicked, slapped, bit, and shouted, "Let me go, you bastard! I have a family. I have children who need me. Now let me go, damn it!"

"Shut your pie hole!" Sterling barked.

Sharon landed a solid kick to his upper thigh, though she was aiming for his groin area. The strike jammed her toe, but it was effective as pain was delivered up Sterling's thigh and into his left hip. He winced and released Sharon. She turned to grab hold of the door's latch. After fumbling a bit with trembling hands, she fought the door open. Just as she was about to run from the barn to taste freedom, Sterling grabbed a handful of her hair. He pulled her back to him with such vigor that it lifted her from her feet and stunned her neck. He then lifted up Sharon from beneath her armpits. "Settle the fuck down, bitch!" he snarled. She spit in his face and then kneed him in the stomach. Sterling nearly dropped her to the floor below but was able to maintain his hold on her. His eyes unmistakably turned a shade of gray as he roared like an angry lion. He became unglued with rage.

Sterling peered around Sharon's shoulder and spotted a pitchfork hanging from a pole on a sturdy wooden peg. While holding Sharon up off her feet, he growled as he walked her across the floor of the barn toward the prongs of the sharp tool.

At two feet from the pole, Sterling planted his feet to heave and release Sharon onto the pitchfork. The prongs shot through her back

and exploded out from her chest. Her blood sprayed and splattered to the floor below. She was able to look down at the sharp iron points that had plunged through her chest cavity. Her eyes widened as her mouth filled with blood. She gagged, and then she choked.

Sterling was intolerant and shoved her body deeper onto the jagged prongs. Sharon's body shook violently before it suddenly went limp. Sharon Greene lost her life with her body suspended three feet from the floor.

Sterling, with an unnatural calmness, dressed and then exited the barn, shutting off the light before he closed the door. He strolled across the lawn toward the farmhouse, knowing that in the morning, his father and brothers would help him dispose of Sharon Greene's body.

Sterling Porter crawled into his bed and soothingly drifted into a sleep, as if he had just spent the last few hours reading a peaceful book. No conscience, no nightmares, and no regrets.

CHAPTER 36

August 4

USING A ROD and reel lent to him by Ike, Cole was taking in the hot afternoon sun fishing in the pond on the remote area of the farm. Ike had gone into town to run errands.

Cole heard someone making their way through the woods near the pond, so he ducked away out of sight behind some brush. He thought it a possibility that the Porter brothers were roaming around the property. He wanted to observe what they may be up to.

Within a few moments, Renee appeared from the woods, making her way down the bank of the pond. Cole was about to step out from the brush when he hesitated. Renee looked around the area carefully, and after not spotting anyone, she began to disrobe. Cole dipped down deeper into the brush, keeping his eyes on her.

Renee assumed that Cole went to town with her grandfather. She then pulled her shorts off her legs and tossed the garment to the ground.

Cole figured she was going for a dip in the pond in her bra and panties. To his pleasant surprise, Renee removed her undergarments, standing fully nude at the water's edge. Cole became incredibly

excited at the sight of her beautiful body. Her legs were smooth, her breasts were perfectly round, and her nipples were deep pink. Her skin was tanned, and her brunette hair tickled her shoulders in the summer breeze. The triangle of her dark pubic hair was pronounced against the light skin where the sun didn't reach.

She gingerly stepped into the water waist deep and then submerged beneath the water. She surfaced after several seconds and then swam in a circular direction.

Cole waited for several minutes before he moved away from the brush, acting as though he had just arrived at the pond. She screamed when she spotted him, being certain that her naked body remained beneath the water's surface.

"What are doin' here?" she asked, nearly out of breath.

"I came to fish," he replied.

"I thought you went with Grandpa."

"Uh-uh."

"Um…"

"Going for a swim? I bet the water is warm."

"Ah…yeah, it is."

"I brought my trunks in this tackle box here, perhaps I'll join you?" He actually had no swimming trunks with him.

"There's seaweed in here. You probably don't want seaweed on you."

"What are you talking about? That water is crystal clear."

This reminded her that the water was transparent. She aggressively treaded the water to cause ripples around her. "Why don't you fish rather than swim?"

"Fish now? With you splashing about, no fish will bite. I think I'll just swim," he teased.

"Cole, um…um…I don't have any clothes on. You're not comin' in here!"

"Oh, I see." He sheepishly grinned.

"Will you please grab my clothes over there and toss them into the pond for me?"

"I'll just turn my back while you get out of the pond and put on your clothes."

"I'm not fallin' for that, buster, I know you'll peek. Please, just fetch me my clothes."

The combination of the warm water waving between her legs and her attraction toward Cole had her sexually excited and stimulated. She would very much like for Cole to jump into the pond and join her, but she was not going to give him the privilege of knowing that.

Cole made his way down the bank and pointed. "These clothes?"

Renee growled impatiently over his playfulness. "Yes, those items."

"If I toss them in, they'll get wet. How about you just come out and get them?"

"Throw them in here already, Cole!" she demanded.

"Okay, okay. I'd say not to get your panties all in a bunch, but of course, you're not wearing any at the moment." He continued to taunt.

She curled her lip at him. He then tossed her shirt and shorts into the pond. She quickly swam the short distance and gained hold of the clothing before they could sink to the bottom of the pond. Her face reddened. "Okay, now the rest of it."

He raised up her pink and white flowered cotton panties in his hand. "This?"

She rolled her eyes. "Yes, that. The other thing too."

He held up her bra with his other hand. "This?"

"Damn it, Cole, throw them in here!"

"I don't know, Renee. It seems to me you should at least keep some of your attire dry."

"Forget it, I have my shirt and shorts on now." Renee then swam to shore. She emerged from the pond with her soaked shirt and shorts clinging to her body. With her wet clothes snuggly fitting to her naked body beneath, it left little to the imagination as to how beautiful and tight Renee's body was.

Cole nearly licked his chops as he gazed upon her breasts, wishing and imagining that his hands were cuddling the robust roundness of her sopping, heaving mounds as he caressed her nipples between his fingers. Her silky waterlogged shorts were tucked inside her vagina, creating the form of a groove as well as the outline of her vaginal lips visible to him. Again, Cole could not help but to gawk.

She aggressively plucked her undergarments from his hands before stepping into her shoes to storm up the bank of the pond.

"Ah, come on back, Renee. I was only having some fun with you."

"Go to hell, Cole!" she shouted from the woods on her march back to the farmhouse.

Cole tittered to himself.

*****

IKE WAS SEATED outside on a bench in front of Emma's General Store enjoying a pinch of his favorite chewing tobacco that he just purchased inside when Mason Turner came stumbling by. Mason did not notice Ike on the bench as he approached.

"Mason, where are you headed? What happened to you? You don't look so well. Was it the Porters again?" Ike interrogated.

Mason grabbed at his sore ribs and winced as he nodded.

Ike shook his head. "Those ruthless hoodlums. Will they ever stop?"

"I don't think they'll ever cease and desist, Ike. They seem to enjoy hurtin' folks." Mason stated the obvious.

Ike nodded and then spit out a concoction of chewing tobacco juice. "Yeah, I suppose you're right, Mason."

"Well, unfortunately, I'm one of their favorite targets."

"Have ya ever tried talkin' about it with Sheriff Harvey?" Ike wondered.

Mason released a sarcastic snicker.

Ike chuckled. "Yeah, right, lame idea."

Mason gingerly let his body down to take a seat next to Ike on the bench.

After a brief hesitation, Ike asked, "Mason, have you ever thought about movin' away from Harpersfield in order to rid your life of the Porters?"

Mason nodded. "I sure have. I think we all probably have at one point or another. But this is home, and it's hard to imagine livin' anywhere else but here." Mason then pulled a tin flask out from his shirt pocket. He unscrewed the lid and sipped a swig from the whis-

key inside. He then handed the flask to Ike, who then had his own taste of the liquor.

"I know what ya mean, Mason, about this bein' home and all, but sometimes I question myself if the decision to stay here is selfish of me and not the best thing for my granddaughter." Ike sighed.

"Renee is a strong person, Ike, and you should be proud. She'll be simply fine. Everyone knows that the youngest Porter has his sights set on her, but we also know she wants nothin' to do with the likes of him. But bein' that he has a hankerin' for her probably keeps her safe from the Porters and their soulless wrath."

"Yeah, it probably saves my skin as well. I know them Porter boys would like nothin' more than to knock me around a bit. But Murky keeps them at bay 'cause of his feelins' for Renee," Ike reckoned.

Mason took in another swig of whiskey before he placed a hand on Ike's left shoulder. "I haven't gotten the chance to say how sorry I am about Nate. He was a good boy."

Ike's eyes clouded. "Yes, that he was. I hope them bastards rot in hell for takin' my grandson away from me."

Mason nodded. "Somehow I think they will eventually, somehow they will. We can all pray." Mason then sensed that it was time to change the dark subject. "Have I ever told you about the time when Renee saved my dog?"

Ike brightened a bit. "No, she hasn't told me either. What happened with your dog?"

"Well, you know Rex?"

Ike nodded.

"Well, that old German shepherd doesn't get around much these days. The vet says he has chronic arthritis. Anyway, it was about seven years ago when Rex was still spunky that it happened. I was throwing a stick into Elder's Pond, and Rex would leap in and retrieve it. I was kind of daydreamin' and not payin' attention."

Ike looked doubtful.

"Okay, okay, I was drunk. Anyway, I lost track of how many times I sent that dog into the water. He'd go after that stick no matter how many times I heaved it in the water. Rex was gettin' very tired, but I kept sendin' that stick out in the pond. It got to

the point when his exhaustion wouldn't allow him to swim any longer. He went under, came up yelpin', and then went under again. When it finally dawned on me that my dog was drownin', I started yellin' out for someone to help. Lady Luck was shinin' down on Rex and me that day as it just so happened that Renee was ridin' her bike across the ridge above the pond when she heard my cries for help. That young lady, with no regard for her own safety, raced her bike down that ridge. About halfway down, the bike was movin' too fast, and she lost control. She tumbled down the remainder of the ridge.

"At the bottom of the drop, she sprang to her feet, though both her knees and her elbows were bleedin'. It was obvious that she was in pain, but she wasn't goin' to allow that to stop her. She dove into that pond and saved Rex. I couldn't thank her enough. I offered her some money as a reward, but she refused it. You raised an exceptionally fine young lady there."

Ike, proud as a peacock, boasted, "Renee is a true gem. But why didn't you jump in and save Rex?"

Mason's eyes widened. "Are you kiddin'? I can't swim. Never learned how."

"Really?" Ike seemed surprised.

"My parents rarely let me out of the house as I grew up. They kept me caged up and away from the Porters. About the time a youngin' learns how to swim, I was cooped up at home instead."

Ike exhaled. "Yeah, those Porters have altered the course of all of our lives throughout generations. Perhaps one day it will all even out."

Mason took a long swig from his flask before handing it over to Ike. "Well, we can always hope, we can always hope. Anyway, I'm gonna git before the Porters might come around. I'm goin' home to doctor up my wounds. I'll see ya around, Ike."

Ike handed the flask over before Mason rose to his feet and began to stumble away.

"Stop by the house for a visit sometime, Mason," Ike called out in invitation.

Mason waved a friendly gesture back at Ike out before moving out of sight.

*****

THAT NIGHT, COLE sat on the porch of the guesthouse with a glass of Jack Daniel's in one hand and a lit cigarette in the other. He was still basking at the sight of Renee's beautiful nude body from earlier in the day. His mood turned somber, however, when he recalled a time in the army when a naked girl didn't work out so well.

*****

Platoon Sergeant Henry Rikes was big, strong, and demanding—a military man his entire life and one helluva Green Beret in the Special Forces. Some three thousand men enlist each year in the Green Beret program, and only a few dozen make it past Officer Rikes's rigid rituals to become a Green Beret. Most cadets don't survive the first two weeks of the six-week program.

Cole Walsh was one of the few who did make it, but because of a twist of events, he nearly flunked out. Henry's daughter, Tara Rikes, was young and beautiful. She would visit her father on base at times, and during those visits, she would always find a moment or two to flirt with Cole. She had seen cadets come and go, but Cole's handsome looks drew her to him like a magnet. Henry was very protective of his daughter. Cole was very attracted to Tara, and over weeks of flirtatious behavior, against his better judgment, he began arranging secret trysts with her.

Tara turned out to be sexually kinky, which Cole didn't mind at all. She was wild with sexual ambitions, but in her past, she had few sexual partners. For the most part, she acted out her fantasies while masturbating alone in her bedroom. But with Cole, it was different for her. She felt that with him, she could let it all out in the open.

One of the things they did together was have Cole take photos of her, Polaroid photos of her nude and in vulnerable positions. Cole kept the photographs locked away in his army-issued footlocker. One evening while Cole was on security patrol, one of the platoon cadets discovered

that the lock on Cole's trunk was not completely engaged. Earlier, Cole had opened the locker looking for cigarettes, and inadvertently, he did not get the lock completely closed. When the platoon cadet discovered the photos of the naked Tara, his eyes widened at the sight of the eight photographs as he shuffled through them. Soon, he was sharing the photos with the rest of the men in the squad. Cole stepped inside the bunkhouse to see the men passing around the photos. He angered as he rounded up the revealing pictures.

Just as he was heading toward his bunk to stow away the personal photographs, Sergeant Rikes burst into the bunkhouse to throw a surprise inspection. The platoon came to attention at the sight of Henry and froze in their tracks. Cole's heart pounded as the sergeant glared at him.

"What do you have there, Walsh?" Henry barked.

Cole didn't answer.

"Answer me, goddamn it!"

"These are personal, sir," Cole weakly sounded off.

"There's nothing personal in the army, son. Walk them over here to me."

"This cadet would rather not, sir."

"Walsh, you step over here right now, or I'll break your fucking legs! Do I make myself clear?"

Cole realized that he had no choice in the matter. He reluctantly moved to face Henry. The sergeant extended his hand, and Cole, with apprehension, handed the photos over to him.

Henry glanced at the top photograph of the stack, which revealed Tara lying naked on a bed and licking her lips. Henry looked no further. His hand trembled as he lowered the photos to his side. His eyes were so occupied with anger that they nearly ruptured out from his face. "Fall out!" he shouted. "Everyone get the hell out except Walsh here."

The cadets rushed the door and were soon outside.

Henry stepped in front of Cole. He did not look at Cole directly in the eyes, but rather stood at Cole's side and stared straight ahead.

"If I ever see you within ten feet of my daughter again, I'll kill you," the sergeant whispered with a serious tone.

"Yes, sir."

"I want you out of my platoon."

"No, sir. This cadet, with all due respect, is very sorry, sir. But he wants to stay in the platoon and become a Green Beret, sir."

"I want you out of my army, Walsh."

"No, sir."

"Out!"

"Please no, sir. I will not quit."

"Fine, have it you way, asshole. But I'm telling you right now, Walsh, I'm going to make your life a living hell."

Cole stood in silent fear as Henry turned abruptly away. The sergeant tossed the photos into the flames of a burning barrel outside the bunkhouse door.

Henry made Cole's life extremely difficult over the following months, but Cole endured. Cole never went near Tara again. Upon graduation, Cole received the declaration of becoming a Green Beret. There was a silent mutual respect between him and Henry on graduation day, though it was not spoken in words.

*****

Cole observed as Ike made his way across the lawn to the guesthouse in the dark of the night.

"I just wanted to tell you that Murky just called, and Renee is upset. Would you come up to the house and talk with her?"

"Yeah, sure. I'll be there in a couple of minutes, Ike."

Ike made a gesture to walk back toward the farmhouse, and then he hesitated. He turned back to face Cole. "Ya know, young man, I've been around for quite a few years. Over seven decades, as a matter of fact. I've seen people come, and I've seen people go. I've lived through wars and some awful hard times. But through it all, I had my beautiful Jodi to help guide me along. God, I miss her dearly. People need people, Cole, that's a fact of life. Keep goin' through life like a lone wolf, and that's what you will be, alone.

"I had a wonderful and loving mother. Of course, that was many moons ago. The one most important thing my mother taught me about was understandin' that God didn't intend for us to go through life on our own. That is why He the Lord created other people and

opposite sexes. She told me to reach out to others and to accept them into my life." Ike stopped to place a pinch of tobacco into his jaw. He then continued. "I don't know if it's a macho thing with you, and with all due respect, but it's not wise to isolate yourself from people that care or could care about you. Life is tough enough without goin' and placin' ourselves out on an emotional remote island just because of our stubborn pride."

Cole squinted. "I came here, Ike, to do a job and not to get lectured on the ways of life."

"Who's lecturin'?" Ike asked, pointing to himself. "You won't catch me lecturin'. The good Lord knows I've strayed a bit wayward in my life from time to time, so I have no room to talk. I'm just sta-tin' facts is all. I've never seen a lonely, happy man before."

"Are you trying to play matchmaker for your granddaughter? Is this what this is all about?" Cole wondered as he snuffed out his cigarette.

Ike chuckled aloud. "Heavens no, I wouldn't do that. Renee will be simply fine. She doesn't need you, per se. She'll find herself a nice gentleman one day, I'm sure of it. Whoever he is, he'll be one lucky man. Renee was raised to take care of her man."

"Well, don't tell her I said so, but she sure is pretty."

"That she is." Ike smiled and glowed with pride. "Well, I best head back up to the house."

"I'll be up that way in a few."

Renee was sitting on her bed looking out into the night's dark-ness when Cole entered her room through the open door.

"I heard that Murky called," he revealed before quietly closing the door behind him.

Renee's eyes clouded. "You know, Nate trusted me. It's not like he looked upon me like a replacement for his mother, but after our parents died, it strengthened our bond. He would hand over to me his money that he earned doin' odd jobs to save it for him, and he would share his tales with me. He knew that I would never tell another soul of our secret talks. Nate confided in me, and he trusted me. Now, just a few minutes ago, I agreed to go out on a date with the scumbag that killed my little brother. Somehow, I feel like a dirty person for betrayin' Nate."

"Nobody is betraying anyone. You're doing this to avenge Nate's death. If it were the other way around, he'd do the same for you."

"That doesn't make me feel any better, but thanks for tryin'. I could almost smell Murky's foul breath over the phone when he chirped with excitement that I agreed to go to the river with him tomorrow night. I wanted to tell him to rot in hell."

Cole found a spot to sit next to her on the bed. "He will rot in hell, this I can promise."

A tear slid down her cheek. She needed reassurance, and Cole realized that. He awkwardly placed his right arm around her shoulders. Renee responded with her head falling into his chest. She sobbed.

"Crying is healthy." He attempted to ease her mind.

"Then why does it feel so rotten?" she quizzed.

He cleared his throat. "Well, it's the aftereffects that are rewarding, not during...um...you know...You feel better after a good cry..."

"Okay, Cole, you're nearly stutterin'." She cracked a tiny grin. "You can slow down, I know what you are tryin' to say, and thank you."

He warmly tightened his hold on her. "Good, because sometimes I have a problem when trying to express my feelings."

"Only sometimes?" she taunted and chuckled.

"Okay, okay...Hammer away at Cole if it makes you feel any better. I can take it."

She was about to snuggle up against his shoulder when it dawned on her that they were showing signs affection. She quickly rose from her bed and broke his hold on her. "I'm goin' to be alright now, so you can leave my room now, thank you."

Cole stood from the bed and raised his arms from his side. "What are you so afraid of?"

She rubbed her forehead. "Nothin'...I don't know...I don't want to get into this right now."

"Get into what? The conversation or us?" he pondered.

She raised her eyebrows as she looked at him. "Us? There is no us."

He lowered his arms and turned abruptly to leave the room. On his way out, he grunted, "Sorry to have bothered you."

She exhaled loudly and then lightly slapped herself on her forehead before she collapsed onto her bed.

CHAPTER 37

"YOU'RE LATE THIS week. Ya know I don't like late," Carter conveyed.

"I'm sorry, Mr. Porter, but my Honda wouldn't start. I had to use Donnie's truck," Stacy Hughes explained. She had just walked in through the storage shed's door of Emma's General Store. This was where she and Carter had been meeting weekly for the past two years. Even before she became pregnant, Carter insisted that they meet weekly, even during times she was on her menstrual cycle. That mattered none to Carter. Stacy reluctantly agreed to these meetings after Carter had threatened to rape her mother. Stacy grew up in Harpersfield, so she was fully aware of the authenticity of threats coming from the Porters. They carried them out, plain and simple.

Only three people knew of Carter and Stacy's trysts. Besides the two participants, her young husband was aware of the meetings. Donnie also knew that the baby Stacy was carrying was not his, though they led everyone to believe so. Without a shadow of doubt, the upcoming baby was Carter's as he was her solo sexual partner. Donnie and Stacy had never engaged in sexual intercourse. Donnie and Stacy were merely friends helping each other through a rough time in their lives. Stacy was in need of a father for the baby, and

Donnie was anxious to move out of the house away from his strict, abusive father.

Carter wanted Stacy to abort the baby, but she was completely against that option. Carter lied to Stacy before the pregnancy, claiming that he had a vasectomy, but he simply didn't want to wear a condom.

Carter nodded his head in a downward motion, and Stacy knelt before of him. She hesitated before unzipping his trousers. She reached inside the open zipper and pulled out his semi-erect penis. As she did with each meeting, she stroked his penis until it was rigid. She then took the large organ into her mouth.

"Damn, Stacy, you sure can suck a mean cock." Carter moaned in pleasure. "If I didn't already have a wife, I'd take ya home with me."

Over the following ten minutes, Stacy continued to orally satisfy Carter before she rose to her feet. She then began to disrobe. "I haven't told anyone about us, Mr. Porter," she reaffirmed.

"I wouldn't give a fuck if ya did." He snorted.

"I know, but I'd rather keep it a secret, please."

"As long as you keep suckin' and fuckin', I won't say a word."

She now stood before him completely nude.

"You're still a hot piece of young ass, even with the big pregnant belly." Carter flattered her in his own demented way.

"I guess I'll take that as a compliment." She rolled her eyes.

Carter lay down on the wooden floor. He pulled up a small sack of potatoes to use as a makeshift pillow. "Come on over here, you naked redhead, and sit on my face."

"Mr. Porter, can we just do it and get on out of here? I'm havin' a rough evenin' with the baby. He's been kickin', and I have cramps."

"Ya should have gotten rid of the fuckin' rug rat," he protested.

"How can you say that about your own baby?" she asked, nearly coming to tears.

"It's a boy, right?" he sought out.

"Yeah, the ultrasound revealed it's a boy. I'm namin' him Thomas."

"As long as it's a boy, I guess it'll be alright. But you're not namin' him Thomas. That's sissy soundin'. I like Brutus. Name him Brutus. There was a Brutus Porter a few generations ago. He was a crazy motherfucker. Yeah, Brutus."

"But I wanna name him Thomas."

"Brutus!" Carter insisted. "If ya don't name him that, I'll kill the little fucker."

"Okay, okay, Mr. Porter, Brutus it is." She reluctantly conceded.

"Now, come on over here, and straddle your pussy down on my dick," he directed.

Like she did each week, Stacy placed her mind and thoughts elsewhere while she and Carter engaged in sexual relations. She thought of a pretty place, a place other than the small towns in this area. A place where the sun always shined and there were coconuts growing in the trees. Where the sky danced with fluffy white clouds. A place where everything was ideal and exactly right.

She quickly dressed after Carter ejaculated.

"Why are ya always in such a hurry, red?" he inquired, still breathing heavy from the sexual act.

"I have to get back to Waynesburg."

"Why?"

"Donnie will start to worry."

"The hell with that punk." Carter rose to his feet and then tucked his penis back inside his pants. "Let's go get a beer at Joe's."

"I'm not drinkin' while I'm pregnant, Mr. Porter."

"Why not? That boy is gonna be a Porter. He'll drink plenty, you can be sure of that." Carter chortled.

"Be that as it may, I'm not startin' Thom—um, Brutus off early."

"Bessy drank when she was pregnant. Anyway, just go on your pathetic way. You're a bore."

After dressing, Stacy hesitated before walking out of the shed. "Can I ask you a favor, Mr. Porter?"

"You can ask all ya want, red. Doesn't mean I'll do it," he growled.

"Will you force Murky to back off Renee Stewart? You're the only one he will listen to."

"Why should I do that? That boy has a hot spot for the girl. He wants her so bad, he can taste it."

"Yeah, well, Mr. Porter, with all due respect, Renee doesn't want Murky," Stacy revealed.

"Why should you give a shit?"

"She's my best friend. I know that this Murky thing really upsets her."

"Really?" Carter questioned, rubbing his jaw.

"Yeah, it gets to her, and it scares her. If you could get Murky to back off, it would be great for Renee. He'll listen to you, Mr. Porter. Please take care of it, okay?"

"Well, everything comes with a price, ya know. I'll tell ya what, red. You bring that pretty Stewart girl along with you next week. She gives me a suck and fuck, and I'll cool Murky's jets for her," Carter proposed. "That Stewart girl is young and gorgeous. I'd like to get my face buried between those milky thighs."

"She won't do it, Mr. Porter."

"How do you know she won't?"

"I know Renee well. She won't go for that. Please, just talk to Murky."

"No suck and fuck, no talk to Murky. That's my final offer."

"Mr. Porter, that has two chances of happenin'. Slim and none." Stacy then committed a mistake, although she was not speaking in a serious manner. "Maybe I'll take care of it myself and just run Murky over with my car."

Suddenly, Carter grabbed Stacy in a choke hold with his large right hand. He lifted her up against the wall of the shed until her feet were nearly three feet above the floor. His eyes appeared to turn gray. "Don't you ever fuckin' threaten a Porter! If ya ever say somethin' like that again, I'll rip that baby out of your stomach and feed ya both to the Sulfur River! Do I make myself clear?" he roared.

Through her closed throat, Stacy choked out the words, "Yeah…Mr. Porter. I'll never say…anything like that again. I promise…I'm sorry."

He released her throat without easing her downward. He simply allowed her to crash to the wooden floor below. She scraped her left elbow and jammed her jaw.

"Now get the hell out of here, I'm tired of lookin' at ya. And don't be late next week."

Stacy struggled to her feet and stumbled out the shed as she wept.

CHAPTER 38

August 5

THE MINSTER RIVER runs along the border of Harpersfield and Waynesburg. The river was once polluted as a factory upstream in Bontman County was releasing chemical waste illegally into the river. Eventually, the EPA discovered the source and shut down the factory. Nearly three decades later, the river now ran clear and clean. The fish had long since returned while many avid fishermen could be spotted along the banks of the Minster on any given day of the week. A particular section of the river's bank, on the Harpersfield side, lay level for about nine hundred feet in length. This was a popular spot for teenagers and young adults alike. Party Central is how it was commonly referred to. It had been a lover's lane even back in the days of the polluted waters. High school pregnancies had been conceived at Party Central. There had also been three alcohol-related drownings in this section of the river over the prior decades.

This night was muggy, stale, and without a hint of a breeze. The bonfire was ablaze, and the kegs of beer had been tapped. Partygoers from Harpersfield, Waynesburg, and Webster frequented the weekend activities on a regular basis, and this Friday night was no differ-

ent. Some eighty-five partygoers were at this neck of river to bash the night away.

Back at the Stewart farmhouse, Renee slipped into her Levi's, trying to talk herself out of going to the river with Murky Porter. He was due to pick her up any minute now, certainly along with his brothers.

"Are you about ready?" Cole inquired, startling her as he poked his head inside her bedroom.

"Can I dress without your supervision? Do you mind?"

Cole cleared his throat. "Why didn't you close your door completely?"

"Because we respect somethin' around here called privacy. Of course, that was until you arrived."

Cole made a face.

"That animal isn't here yet, is he?" she wondered while zipping up her pants.

"No, haven't seen him."

"You mean them. His brothers will be along too."

"Are you serious? He'll bring his brothers along on a date he's finally landed after years of trying?"

"The Porters are always together, period."

"I wonder how he'll react when you tell him that I'm coming along?"

She shrugged her shoulders. "I dunno. It could get interestin'."

A vehicle's horn then sounded from the driveway.

"Well, we're about to find out," Cole said in a steely voice.

Renee's hands began to tremble. "You'd better protect me."

Cole winked. "I've got you covered. No worries."

"Well, let's do this then...for Nate." She exhaled.

"You gotta tell us what prime pussy tastes like, Murky," Dalton requested. He was seated between Sterling and Murky inside Sterling's truck.

"Shut the hell up, Dalton. I'm not tellin' you shit about the woman I love. It's time you jumped your ass back to the truck's bed so Renee can ride up here with me."

Dalton turned his attention to Sterling, who moaned. "Don't fuckin' look at me, Dalton, I'm drivin'. Get your ass on back there."

Reluctantly, Dalton climbed over Murky and out the passenger's door of the truck. He jumped into the bed of the truck.

"You're a lucky bastard, Murky. Renee is a fox. I'd like to be gettin' some of that," Sterling declared.

Murky flipped up his middle finger at Sterling.

"You're a touchy fucker when it comes to her," Sterling said with a snort.

The farmhouse front door swung open, and Murky's heart skipped a beat as he viewed Renee step out onto the porch. She was clad in a tight pair of denim jeans. The pants formed to her shapely backside, of which Cole had already taken in the enticing scene. A soft blue T-shirt fit snuggly around her full breasts. Her glowing makeup was applied to perfection, touched off with a lightly applied dark shade of pink lipstick. Her deep blue eyes blazed in the fading light of the day.

From behind her, Cole could see her silky dark hair shine in the sunset as she strode along with the graceful flow of a lady. It was all natural for her. The look, the walk, the charisma that followed her every movement. What made Renee stand out from other beautiful women was that she simply didn't have a lone conceited trait within her earnest personality.

She was fully aware of Murky's attendance. She could see him from the corner of her right eye, but she wouldn't look directly upon him. He was wearing a black sleeveless T-shirt that revealed the tattoos inked on his upper arms. On his right upper arm was a dark blue dragon with yellow eyes and breathing in bloodred fire. On his left arm was a full-bodied black panther. Captured in the panther's sharp claws was a rooster. The panther was licking the fowl. Below the tattoo were the words "Pussy Loves Cock."

Murky quickly slid out from the truck and stood next to the open passenger's door. "Hello, beautiful. Cart your pretty ass on over here and give me a kiss."

Murky's grinned turned sour when Cole appeared from behind Renee.

"What the hell are you doin'?" Murky rebuked Cole.

"Um…oh…the old man wants me to tag along for whatever reason. I'd rather stay here and watch reruns of *Gilligan's Island* on TV, but it's the only way he'll allow Renee to go tonight."

"You've got to be kiddin' me," Murky grumbled.

Dalton and Sterling snickered in harmony.

Renee forced herself to look at Murky. "Do you want to go out with me or not, Murky? Because if you do, he needs to come along as sort of a chaperone. You've brought your brothers, so my grandpa said I need to bring Cole."

"This is bullshit!" Murky snapped. "You're twenty-one years old. The bastard shiner can't tell you what to do any longer."

"He's not demandin' me to abide, merely requestin' I respect his wishes, which I fully intend on seein' through. So does that mean our date is off?" she inquired.

After a long hesitation, Murky pointed at Cole. "You ride in the back with Dalton, Cole the mole."

"That's fine," Cole replied.

"And stay out of my fuckin' way tonight too," Murky cautioned.

Cole winked. "No problem at all. I got my can of Pepsi in my bag here and a comic book. You ever read the *Trotter the Otter* series? I know the title sounds a bit lame, but that mammal gets himself in some binds at times. He's like a superhero of the stream where he lives."

Murky looked blankly at Cole. "You are one stupid motherfucker, mole."

"Trotter the ass kicker?" Dalton joked. He and Sterling shared a hearty round of laughter.

Murky then softened as he turned his attention back to Renee. "Your carriage is waitin', my darlin'."

She gritted her teeth before stepping down from the porch.

Along the way to the gathering at the river and in the bed of the truck, Cole falsely appeared to be fascinated as he read from his comic book. Dalton, sitting behind the cab of the pickup truck to ward off any winds generated by the travel, lit a marijuana joint. After exhaling a deep inhale, Dalton then presented the smoldering joint over to Cole. Raising his left palm in a polite manner, Cole turned down the offering, "No, thank you. I don't smoke the stuff."

Dalton then attempted to pass along his opened whiskey bottle to Cole, who shook his head. "That either."

After swigging from the bottle, Dalton commented, "You're one borin' motherfucker, you are. Dumb as a rock too."

Cole nodded and, in complete seriousness, mentioned, "My mother says that as well."

Dalton nearly choked as he exhaled more smoke. "Wow, that's really fucked up."

Cole continued to appear as if he were actually reading the contents of the comic book.

Dalton leaned forward a bit before asking, "So tell me something, asshole. Have you been screwin' the Stewart girl?"

Cole looked up from his comic book and squinted. "What do you mean, Mr. Porter?"

Dalton rolled his eyes. "It's Dalton and none of that mister crap."

Cole nodded.

"So are you screwin' her or not?"

Cole shook his head no. "Renee is a good girl. We're friends is all."

Dalton settled back against the rear of the truck's cab. "Well, that a good thing for you. You go and play hide the sausage with that gal, and my brother will cut your dick off and feed it to you." Dalton chuckled.

"Yes, sir." Cole cleared his throat.

"Dalton, you moron. No mister or sir bullshit."

Cole answered, "Okay, Dalton."

After a few moments of awkward silence, the Porter brother inquired, "How old are you anyway?"

"Thirty-two."

"Ever been laid?"

Cole glanced up from his comic book. "Once. I meant more than one time. Just with one girl. She was my girlfriend about ten years ago."

"Shit, man, you haven't had any pussy in ten years. We gotta get you some tail tonight. Tammy will be there, and she'll give it up to ya. Wanna get your dick wet?"

Cole shook his head. "I'd be too nervous."

After another exhale of smoke, Dalton shrugged his shoulders. "Whatever, dude. You know, and not in a fag way or anything like that, but you're a strappin', good-lookin' dude. If you could get some balls about yourself, you could be dippin' into some of the prime pussy out there in the world. You know, the top-shelf stuff that me and my brothers can only get by forcefully takin' it. But what the hell, it's all good in the end, yeah. Anyway, you bein' all shriveled up in a shell, you're missin' out on some fine snatch." Dalton then glanced at the opened comic book's cover featuring the illustration of a river otter sporting an outfit complete with a cape. Inscribed on the chest of the costume was the name Trotter.

After another swig from his bottle, Dalton raised his left forefinger. "Let me give ya some advice that you better heed, Trotter the Otter fanboy. If you try to be some sorta fucked-up superhero for that Stewart gal, Murky will break your neck. So you best keep that otter right there inside in the comics."

"I will, Dalton. Thanks."

Dalton chuckled. "Don't thank me. Personally, I'd enjoy watchin' my brother trash your stupid ass. Just sayin' is all."

Cole then spotted an aged chain coiled up on the floor of the truck bed. It took all the patience he could muster up from not taking the chain and wrapping it around Dalton's neck. But with all that was at stake, Cole resisted the temptation.

After inhaling the joint to it's very end, Dalton snickered. "Oh, you can bet your dumb ass that Murky gets a sweet slice of that Stewart pussy tonight, whether she wants to part with it or not. Matters none to him." Dalton then nodded. "Yessiree, Trotter wannabe, that girl's pussy will be dripping with Porter cum by night's end."

Cole was fuming inside. Trying his best to remain in character, Cole asked, "Even if Renee doesn't want to?"

Dalton squinted. "Did I just stutter or somethin'? She has no say-so in the matter."

The group soon arrived at the river where the party was in full swing. Renee was fighting off Murky's advances, as she had done the entire ride inside the pickup truck on their way to the party.

Cole stationed himself back among the crowd, but maintained a constant eye on Renee.

"Murky, for cryin' out loud, give me some room to breathe. You have me backed up against this tree. You need to cool your jets and give me a bit of space, or this date is over!"

"Okay, okay…I'm backin' off. For now, anyway."

"Let's talk about somethin' other than sex or marriage or us havin' kids. Let's talk about…I dunno…my dogs. I have some great dogs. Max is a—"

"Borin', fuckin' borin'," he indicated.

"Hello there. You certainly can't be from around here," Brenda Farlow invaded Cole's space.

"What makes you say that?" Cole queried after looking over the attractive young lady.

Brenda was twenty-four and resided in Webster. She was a lifeguard at the local YMCA and remained in great shape. Her blonde hair was wavy and fell to the middle of her back, and her eyes were a deep blue and teal mix.

"You're too damn good-lookin' for me to not to remember you. What's your name?"

"Cole."

"Well, hello, Cole. I'm Brenda." She smiled warmly.

Cole was instantly attracted to her, as were most men. "What brings you down here tonight, Brenda?"

"Drink a little, and if I meet the right guy, smooch a little more."

"I can smooch with the best of them," he boasted.

Brenda giggled. "I bet you can. How about you show me?"

"Believe me, Brenda, I'd love to, but I'm too busy tonight."

She squinted. "Busy? At a party?"

Renee glanced over to witness Cole chatting with the pretty young lady. To her astonishment, Renee sensed a sudden surge of jealousy.

"Yeah, well, I can't explain it, Brenda. If you need some smooching, you'll have to find it elsewhere. I can't give you the attention that such an attractive girl such as you deserves. Not tonight anyway."

"Are you sure?" She winked flirtatiously.

"You are certainly making this difficult. But I'm going to have to politely decline. Perhaps another time."

"Okay, Cole, suit yourself. I'll be around if you change your mind." Brenda ran her tongue across her pearly white teeth before she faded back into the crowd.

Cole closed his eyes for a moment to help curb his excitement.

Dalton and Sterling sat on a large log that had rough seats carved out of the trunk. Each had a beer in their hand, watching the crowd by the light of the bonfire.

Every partygoer was fully aware of the Porters' attendance and their strong hold on both towns of Harpersfield and Webster alike. Each attendee was sure to nod at the brothers in a sign of regard, respect that was generated out of fear, but revered just the same. The last place anyone wished to be was on the wrong side of the felonious trio of brothers.

"Which broad is goin' to be the one that we fuck tonight?" Sterling mulled over.

Dalton swallowed a gulp from his beer and then pointed. "There's a redhead over there."

"She's a little too fat."

"Well, don't be too damn choosy. I'm gettin' a hard-on already."

"If we're goin' through the hassle of rapin' the bitch, at least she's gotta be hot," Sterling dictated.

Dalton nodded in agreement.

CHAPTER 39

SHERIFF BOB HARVEY sat at the counter inside Tiny's Diner nursing a cup of stale coffee. Deputy Frank Collins had parted for home, leaving Bob in the diner with Jim and Pam. The large Friday evening crowd enjoyed their share of the weekly fish fry and were now home or on their way there. It was the only day of the week that Tiny's Diner attracted many patrons from surrounding towns. Jim took pride in his secret recipe of the breading mix with which he coated the fish fillets. It was spicy, crunchy, and was every bit promised as advertised.

Jim was now putting away menus behind the counter while Pam was in the kitchen washing up pots and pans. Jim and Bob watched the newscast on the television behind the counter that Jim only switched on when the evening was winding down. WJYT Newscaster Mindy Hilton was anchoring the news. "Webster resident Bruce Greene has reported his wife, Sharon, as a missing person. Sharon was last seen a few nights ago while leaving the residence of Mr. Steven Haines in Waynesburg after a physical therapy appointment at his house. Mrs. Greene is a physical therapist." A photograph of Sharon was displayed in the background over Mindy's right shoulder. "Mr. Haines has been officially cleared of any involvement regarding Mrs. Greene's disappearance. Police are asking anyone who

has any information about the whereabouts of Mrs. Greene to call the Webster Police Department at 404-555-1919."

As the newscast broke to commercials, Bob commented, "I bet the husband killed that missin' woman."

"What makes you think so?" Jim asked with a toothpick rolling around on his lips.

"Call it police gut instinct. Yeah, they will probably find her remains beneath their concrete driveway years from now." What Bob didn't know was that the body of Sharon Greene was buried over ten feet deep beneath an old abandoned pickup truck on the Porters' property. Using an aged backhoe that Crater had stolen some years prior, the father and his sons excavated the makeshift grave before tossing Sharon's deceased body into the depths below. They then poured a twenty-pound bag of lime over the corpse to help reduce any odors associated with human decomposition. After burying Mrs. Greene, the foursome pushed the junked pickup truck overtop the fresh grave site.

"But the Webster Police need to wait to get enough on this guy to arrest him, and that's hard to do without a body. If her body were here in Harpersfield, I'd know it, and I'd find her. Nothing gets by me here. I'd turn over every stone in town," Bob boasted.

Changing the subject, Joe mentioned, "I'm sure there's another party goin' on at the Minster River tonight, Bob, bein' that it's Friday and all. Don't you ever go down there and patrol it? I'm sure there are many shenanigans that go on up there. Hell, there was some wild parties back when we were teens. I can only imagine what it must be like now."

Bob cleared his throat before producing a weak excuse. "Of course I would patrol that riverbank, but it's out of my jurisdiction."

"Oh, it is not, Harvey. The southern bank is in Harpersfield, and you know it. You just don't go up there 'cause you know the Porters hang out there at times."

Bob quickly sought to alter the topic. "Have you seen that stranger that's been workin' up there at Ike's place?"

"Cole? Yeah, I met him. Remember, he was in here the other day when you were here too. He seems like a nice enough guy. Why do you ask?"

Bob tapped on his coffee cup. "Well, there's more to him, but I can't say what." Bob knew that Jim would try to drill out the details.

"What are you talkin' about?"

"Let's just say that things aren't what they always appear to be."

"Is that right? What part of Cole isn't a farmhand?"

"I didn't say anything of the sorts."

"Sure ya did. Now, are you gonna to tell me, or sit there until you burst at the seams?"

Bob snuggled up to the counter. "Okay, but you can't tell a soul."

"Wait a minute, Bob. Pam, come on out here for a sec. The gossip is about to hit the fan."

She quickly stepped behind the counter, wiping her hands dry of dishwater with a cloth towel. "Oh yeah? Whatcha got for us, Bob?"

"You two can't say a word that Cole Walsh...is an FBI agent. He showed Frank and me his badge. Now, I dunno know why he's here, but I have a couple of theories. I think that..."

*****

MURKY GREW TIRED of listening to Renee ramble on, so he grabbed her around the throat. Cole made a quick step toward the duo. Renee kicked Murky in the left ankle with force. He released her throat when he reached for his throbbing ankle.

"You bitch. That hurt!"

"Well, you were chokin' me!"

"You ever kick me like that again, I'll send your teeth down your throat!" Murky threatened.

She glanced nervously over to Cole and then back at Murky. "I'm sorry, Murky."

"Kiss me and make me feel better," he requested.

Renee could not bring herself to do so. "Murky, if you let me take this date at my own pace, you'll get a better response from me. I'm kinda shy on a first date, and I'm just not ready yet, okay?"

"Damn it, Renee, you're teasin' the fuck out of me."

"Go get us a beer, Murky, and we'll start over again."

He grunted. "I'll be right back."

"There she is, the fuck of our night." Sterling pointed at Brenda Farlow. "Damn, she's blonde as blonde can be. Ya know, she probably has blonde hair on her pussy. That drives me wild."

Dalton and Sterling rose simultaneously from the log. "Let's go drag her into the fuckin' woods," Dalton suggested.

"Sterling? Dalton?" Tammy Patroni spoke up as she approached them. "I didn't know you fellas were here tonight. How's it goin'? Are ya horny? I'll give ya some on the house tonight." Tammy was unaware that she has just saved Brenda Farlow from certain rape.

"Hiya, honey." Sterling beamed. "Take me and Dalton out in the woods for a romp?"

"Well, Sterling, ya know I'll do anything for you, baby."

Dalton and Sterling eagerly followed Tammy away from the riverbank.

While Murky made his way to the keg of beer, Renee quickly stepped over to Cole. "I'm not goin' to be able to hold off that beast much longer. Don't even suggest that I kiss him. I'd throw up on the spot," Renee proclaimed.

"Why did he choke you?" Cole asked.

"Because he wanted me to stop talkin'."

Cole chortled.

"Stifle it, Walsh."

He cleared his throat to gain a more serious tone. "What do you want to do? We can call it off."

"What do you think? I want to avenge Nate's murder, but I can't stand Murky's hands all over me."

"Play it by ear, Renee. If it becomes too much for you, just wave me over."

"Yeah, but then that foils the plan."

Cole then spotted Murky making his way back from the keg. "You'd better move back on over there. He's on his way back."

She bit her lip before quickly turning away.

Cole wanted to avenge justice nearly as much as she did, but it was a fine line when it came to her overall safety. He increased his focus on Renee and Murky.

"I fetched us a beer," Murky reported to Renee.

She had made her way back to their spot merely seconds before him.

"Thanks," she said before taking the beer from his hand.

"I want ya to spit in my beer," Murky requested.

Renee nearly choked on her sip of beer. "You want me to do what?"

He placed his cup of beer near her mouth. "Spit."

"Why in the world do ya want me to do that?"

"Well, you won't kiss me yet, so I'll taste ya that way."

"That's twisted, Murky."

"Spit in the fuckin' beer."

"No."

"You're tryin' my patience, Renee. Spit!"

Reluctantly, she spit into his cup.

He mischievously grinned before slurping down his beer.

Renee felt her stomach churn.

"You see, darlin', that's love."

"No, Murky, that's gross."

He rapidly reached to grab a handful of her hair from the back of her head. He leaned her head back and kissed her hard on the lips.

Cole took several quick steps toward them, but Renee displayed the palm of her left hand to Cole as Murky continued to force the kiss between them. Cole halted his progress, and then he sensed an unexpected surge of envy overtake him. He sputtered to shake off the sudden unexpected feeling.

Finally, Renee was able to break away from Murky. "Damn it, Murky. Don't ever do that again!"

Cole realized that he needed to be the one who decided if this was becoming too dangerous. Renee's love for her brother would certainly cloud her better judgment. Enough had been completed tonight to set up the next stage of the plan for the following day. As for now, Cole had to get Renee away from Murky without revealing who he really was.

Suddenly, he developed a plan. He dashed quickly behind a tree to call 911 on his cell phone. He reported to the dispatcher that someone was in the act of drowning and gave the location as Party Central along the Minster River.

*****

THE EMERGENCY DISPATCH barked over the radios of local and state law enforcement and rescue workers. Sheriff Bob Harvey missed the call as his radio was turned off while he spread rumors with Jim and Pam inside the diner.

*****

IKE WAS PERCHED upon the porch of the farmhouse nervously rocking in a wicker chair. He was worried sick about his granddaughter in the company of one Murky Porter. He commenced to question himself as to why he had been so stubborn to remain residing in Harpersfield. It was home, not just by land, but by heart and soul. Generations of Stewarts had resided here and endured the hardships of the Porters for many years passed, so why shouldn't Ike stick it out? It made sense to stand by your convictions, to live where you wanted to reside. It's the USA, the land of freedom, so you can hang your hat wherever you want to perch it. But was it just stubbornness or loyalty for him to remain in the only area he has ever called home? Was sacrificing the safety of his granddaughter worth it all? Maybe they should move, but to where? He was entering his elderly years now and would certainly find it difficult to adjust to anywhere other than Harpersfield. If he relocated, Ike would go from knowing everyone to being surrounded by strangers. Who would purchase the farm? Who would move onto the Stewarts' precious land? No, he'd stay for now, play it by ear. Cole was here now. Everything will be fine...right?

*****

MARLA LEANED BACK in her living room recliner, enjoying a nightcap of rum. Tulie snuggled up at her feet. Dule wanted to share the night with her, but Marla needed her occasional time alone. The grandfather clock ticked away as the only sound in the chamber. She was still struggling with her uneasiness over the case taking place

in Tennessee. Cole was a top-notch agent, she acknowledged this, but it was doing little to comfort her.

Marla fidgeted in her chair, causing Tulie to spring to her feet in a huff. The feline jaunted out from the room. The apprehensions that Marla was feeling over this current case caused her to recall a circumstance years ago that nearly had a very tragic ending.

*****

A suspect in the Philadelphia area had been making threats over a citizen's band radio airwaves for several weeks. Reginald Grissom was anti-government, and he was letting his feelings known in a series of threats. He claimed that he planned to attack the Capitol building in Washington, DC, and then he was going to punch out a senator. Any threat to the government and their officials were immediately turned over to the FBI by local law enforcement.

It took about eight days for the FBI to pinpoint Reginald's position by tracing his radio transmissions. Reginald was sly and intelligent and knew that his time was limited while on air before he could be traced. Ultimately, he stayed on the air a bit too long, and the feds nailed down his position. With the address confirmed, agents Marla Simmons and Dwayne Mayweather were assigned to apprehend Grissom.

"This should be an easy one. The guy is an airbag. All talk, no action," Dwayne conveyed to Marla as they stalked up to the front door of Reginald's residence.

"Well, just the same, stay on your toes. You never know," Marla countered.

"I'm sure Reggie is a cream puff." Dwayne chuckled. He then knocked firmly on the front door. "FBI, open up."

A little elderly frail woman opened the door. She was wearing a colorful sundress and was well groomed. She invited the agents inside the house without apprehension. The house was quaint and tidy. The carpet was plush and looked nearly new. The house smelled warmly of a cooking roast and fresh bread. The aged woman led the agents into the living room, showing off her healthy house plants.

"This fern nearly died a few weeks ago, but I've managed to nurse it back to shape. And over here, that baby's breath flower will grow an inch a day if I don't promptly trim it."

"Ma'am, I'm agent Dwayne Mayweather, and this is Agent Marla Simmons. May we ask who you are?"

"Certainly. I'm Liddy Grissom."

"Well, Liddy, you're related to one Reginald Grissom, I assume?" Marla interrogated.

"Why, yes, I'm his grandmother, ninety-four years young and still cooking." She grinned.

Marla and Dwayne were puzzled.

"I allow Reginald to live here with me because he doesn't have a job or a place of his own. Can I ask what this is all about?"

"Can you tell us where we might find Reginald, Liddy?" Marla promptly inquired.

"Oh, he's probably in the bunkhouse above the garage. I swear that man spends most of his waking hours up there talking on some sort of radio."

"Could you direct me to that room?" Dwayne requested.

"I sure can. Follow me."

Liddy walked slowly, so Dwayne had plenty of time to catch up with her.

"You stay here in the house, Marla, in case he makes a run for it through here. I'll follow the old gal and apprehend ole' Reggie."

"Okay then, Dwayne. I'll cover in here, just in case."

After Dwayne and Liddy had moved on, Marla thought to pull her gun and ready herself, but she recalled Dwayne commenting that Reginald Grissom was probably a cream puff that's been hiding behind his radio. She decided to retain her gun in its holster.

What Liddy had not known was that about an hour earlier, Reginald had come inside the house and went upstairs to a spare bedroom in order to nap. The knocking of the agents at the door had awakened him. He was inside the house, and Marla was unaware that he was now moving quietly down the stairs.

Marla roamed around the living room, looking at Liddy's plants and photographs on the wall. Again she thought to ready her gun but did

not do so. Suddenly, the familiar click of a revolver pistol being engaged sounded from behind her. She turned abruptly to see Reginald pointing a .357 Magnum directly at her head. He was a mere three feet from her.

"Lose your gun, FBI agent," Reginald directed.

Marla raised the palms of her hands. "Now, wait a minute, Reginald, you're already in plenty of trouble. You don't want to go this route. Put the gun down."

"Drop your weapon on the floor now!" he demanded.

Marla could tell by the look in his eyes that he'd use his gun if needed. She slowly reached inside her jacket and dropped her gun to the floor.

"Kick it over here."

Reluctantly, she kicked the gun, and it tumbled across the carpet to Reginald. He placed his foot on top of her gun. "What are you doing here in my grandmother's house, nigger?"

Marla got angry at his racial comment, but realized she must keep things from overheating. "We have a warrant for your arrest. You've been threatening the government."

"You're goddamn right I have. This democracy sucks. You have your towel heads, nips, spics, spades…and the list goes on and on. They come here and on taxpayers' expense, and everything is handed to them. Jobs, houses, college, and their own businesses. Where is America for the Americans? You Africans make things even worse. Living on welfare and having babies to get more food stamps. You're breaking the working man's wallet."

Regardless of the potential danger, Marla felt a need to speak up in retaliation. "Grandma tells me that you don't work, Reggie. So what gives with that?"

"Where is my grandmother?"

"I had an officer take her to the station where she'll be safe," Marla fibbed. She didn't want Reginald to be aware that another agent besides herself was on the premises.

He awkwardly grinned. "You're not a bad-looking woman. Not bad at all. Take off your clothes."

Marla's eyes widened. "Excuse me?"

"You heard me, drop your laundry."

She made no movement.

He leaned the pointed gun nearer to her. "Now!"

Over the next few minutes, Marla reluctantly removed her clothing, leaving her standing completely nude in front of Reginald.

"My my my…you sure are pretty for a black lady. I'd screw ya, but I don't do races other than my own. Instead, I think I'll shoot you."

She could see by the look in his cold eyes that he was completely serious. Marla could also perceive his hand tighten around the gun that was pointed at her head. She closed her eyes, and at the sound of the gun firing, she shook, expecting to feel the impact of the bullet. Instead, there was only the crack of a firearm, but no pain that followed. No burning sensation. No jolt.

She snapped her eyes open to see Reginald Grissom lying on the carpet in a pool of his own blood. She looked quickly behind her to see Dwayne with a smoking gun in his hand. He had sent Liddy next door considering the pending danger. Dwayne's shot was precise, striking Reginald between the eyes. Reginald was dead before he hit the floor.

Marla felt a tremendous spell of relief and rushed into Dwayne's arms.

Dwayne awkwardly squeezed her arm and offered her a grim smile. "You should put your clothes on, Marla."

She quickly realized she was still naked and rushed to put on her clothes.

*****

During the investigation that soon followed, items were seized from Reginald's radio room atop the garage for evidence to wrap up the case. Three citizens band radios were confiscated. A diary that threatened the life of five US senators was discovered. In addition, two rubber blow-up dolls used for sexual pleasure and nearly forty ounces of marijuana were confiscated from the room. The FBI helped to relocate Liddy with new living quarters after she decided she no longer wanted to stay in that house.

Dwayne and Marla remained partners for another three years after the Grissom case unfolded until Dwayne was promoted. In those three years, he never allowed Marla to forget that he once saw her when she was naked, and she never forgot that Dwayne saved her life.

CHAPTER 40

BACK IN PARTY Central, sirens blared in the distance and grew nearer by the minute. Soon, it became apparent to the partygoers that the emergency vehicles were headed their way. The underage minors scattered while Sterling, Dalton, and Tammy came rushing out from the woods. Tammy was barely dressed.

"Murky, it's the state boys. I can tell by the sound of the sirens. Let's get the hell out of here now!" Dalton shouted.

Murky left Renee standing in her tracks as he joined his brothers on a run for Sterling's truck. Within moments, Sterling had the truck spitting gravel from beneath the rear wheels.

Cole rapidly moved over to Renee. "Come on, I got to get out of here too. I can't show my ID to the state police."

"I can't believe that punk just left me here stranded and alone," she stated.

"I knew he would. In fact, I planned on it. I'm the one who called 911. Now let's get the hell out of here."

The first of the two police cruisers slid onto the river's bank with an ambulance close behind. Cole and Renee disappeared into the woods with Cole leading the way. The partygoers who had chosen

to stay wondered what all the excitement was all about as the police officers made their way quickly down the bank.

"Hey, what's up, officers?" partygoer Vince Bucky asked.

"Where's the drownin' victim? Is he or she still in the water?" State Police Officer Mark Daniels inquired as he removed his shoes, ready to leap into the river.

"What are you talkin' about?" asked Vince's girlfriend Sherry Spence.

"We got a call that someone here was drownin'."

"Oh, bummer call, officer. No drownin' goin' on here," Vince reported.

"Who placed the call?" Officer Daniels asked in anger as the other officers and two paramedics joined him on the riverbank.

The eleven remaining partygoers shrugged their shoulders.

"Okay, let's clear it out, everybody!" Mark demanded.

A few mumbles were heard as the partygoers disassembled.

"Where are we goin'?" Renee pondered as a low-hanging branch scraped her on the neck. "Ouch! Darn it, Cole, please slow down. It's hard to see, it's so dark."

He halted his fast-paced gait about ten feet in front of her. "Well, come on, Renee, and keep up."

She slapped Cole on the arm. "A gentleman would guide a lady through the dark woods, not leave her hung out to dry."

"Okay. Grab my arm and step quickly. Keep your head behind my back so branches don't swipe at you."

"It's a little too late for that." She pointed to the scratch on her neck.

"Sorry. I had to get you separated from Murky. It was about to get out of control."

"How'd you know he'd just leave me like that?"

"I've seen the type. I've dealt with them for years. They're selfish people, only looking out for themselves and their cohorts in crime."

They eventually made their way into a clearing and up to a shoulder of a back road. The road was dark and quiet. The summer breeze tickled at her silky hair that Cole could view in the moonlight. Her skin glowed with a bronze tan. Cole felt that in this moment

of time, he was gazing upon the most beautiful woman he had ever laid eyes on. He sank deeper into her blue eyes, and the vibes he sensed radiating from her warm heart were robust. For a moment, he thought of taking her into his arms and kissing her gently and passionately. Then picking her up off her feet and walking her along the road and kissing her again. He dreamed of laying her down in the tall grass and making sweet love to her.

Renee snapped her fingers. "Hello? Cole, are you in there?" she probed.

He did not immediately respond.

"Cole, are you feelin' okay? Do you wanna sit for a spell?"

"Huh?"

"You sure are actin' awfully peculiar. Are ya back from wherever it was that you drifted off to?" She giggled.

Cole finally broke from his trance over Renee's beauty and his undeniable attraction toward her. "Do you know where we are exactly?" he queried.

Renee glanced around the immediate area for a moment. "Yeah, we're on a stretch of Martin's Way that runs between Harpersfield and Waynesburg."

"How far to the farm?"

"I'd say about eight, maybe nine miles."

"Which way?"

She pointed to her left.

They began hiking along the shoulder of the road. "You can let go of my arm now, Renee. We're out of the woods." He attempted to play off the powerful attraction that he held for her. He had to keep their relationship professional. The Elite Four rules called for it.

She hadn't realized that she was still holding on to his arm. She quickly jerked her hand away. "Well, excuse me. I didn't know it bothered you so much. Am I that unappealin' to you?"

"Why, is it that you want me to find you pretty?" he grilled.

"No. I was only wonderin' is all."

"Don't let it go to your head, Renee, but you are an extremely beautiful young lady," he complimented.

"Well, you're not so bad lookin' yourself, Cole. However, that doesn't mean that I like you other than a friend. And that's scant at best."

"You've made that crystal clear more than once."

She quickened her pace to move in front of him. She then turned to pace in a backward fashion in order to face him. "Who in the heck do you think you are anyway? God or somethin'?"

"No, don't be ridiculous. That was a stupid question."

"Oh, so now I'm dumb, is that it?"

"No. A bit insecure perhaps."

"Why would you say that?"

"You were just fishing for a compliment."

"I was not! It was just conversation, but of course, there's no talkin' to you. You're so stuck on yourself, you don't even hear what others are sayin'."

"I'm not stuck on myself."

"Yeah, right." She chuckled. "If you could kiss yourself, you would."

He raised his arms. "I don't know where you get all that from, but I am not conceited by any means. I think you get that confused with my sense of humor."

She pointed a finger at him and creased her forehead. "You have a sense of humor? Hmmm…somehow that has slipped by me."

He attempted to step around her, but she wouldn't allow him to do so. "What's the matter, Cole, does the truth hurt?"

"No, but misjudgment is frustrating."

"So I got you all wrong, is that it?" she asked.

"Mostly…yes."

Renee huffed. "Well, maybe I don't want to bother gettin' to know who you are."

"You know, you just won't admit it."

"And why would that be?" she snapped.

"Because you like me, and that scares the hell out of you," he said with a wink.

She clapped her hands. "There goes your arrogance again."

"There is nothing wrong with a bit of confidence and respecting who you are. As long as you have some modesty mixed in as well."

She quietly agreed with him; she was aware this was how he really was. He was good-looking, charming when he wanted to be, well-mannered, caring, and unselfish. She was scared; she was frightened of having her heart broken. But Renee was stubborn and determined to get one up on him over this conflict. "There's an exceptionally fine line there. Confidence is sometimes conceived by others as cockiness."

"And so is speaking your mind."

"Are you tryin' to say that I'm too forward?"

"I think you could be more selective over your words at times before you speak. A bit more diplomatic and sensitive to other's feelings."

"I am. I care about a person's feelins' more than most people do."

"I realize that, but does the rest of the world realize that?"

She was humbled and bowed her head a bit. "I really come across like that?"

He shook his head. "Not at all. I was just showing you how it feels to be misjudged."

"Cole!" she said, exasperated. Renee then stumbled on the edge of the pavement and tumbled onto the dirt on the shoulder of the road. Cole recognized that her spill didn't injure her physically, but rather her pride.

He continued on, stepping around her. He was upset over her comments.

"Well, thanks a lot for helpin' me get up." She raised her voice at him. She rose to her feet and wiped the dirt from her clothes. She then jogged to catch up with him. Suddenly, a set of headlights came over the horizon.

"Oh no, I hope that's not the Porters," Renee said fearfully.

"Move off the road and over to the bushes in case it is them. I'll tell them we became separated at the party, and I haven't seen you."

She scurried down the roadside embankment and a few feet into the wooded area. The lights brightened as the vehicle approached, temporarily blinding Cole. He couldn't make out the vehicle until it came to a stop on the road next to him.

"Need a lift?" Jim Tinelberg asked. Jim and Pam had closed the diner for the night and were headed home in their Ford Explorer.

"Sure, that would be great, thank you." Cole then looked back into the wooded area. "It's okay, Renee. It's Jim and Pam from the diner."

Cole waited until Renee made her way to the vehicle before he opened the rear door. Renee slid into the SUV without so much as glancing Cole's way.

"You're welcome," Cole slyly remarked.

"Hello, Jim, Pam," Renee greeted, ignoring Cole.

He found a seat in the rig while Renee slid across the back seat against the opposite side door, putting as much distance as she could between them. Cole shook his head.

"Thank you for the lift. How was business at the diner tonight?" Cole asked after shutting his door.

Jim and Pam wondered why Cole and Renee were out this way at this hour of night without a vehicle but decided not to probe.

"Business was steady. The fish fry always does well. Do you want dropped off at the farm?" Jim asked.

"Yes, please," Renee responded.

A mile down the road, Cole noticed Jim watching in the rear-view mirror between glances at the road as he steered the SUV. Pam stared straight ahead, not moving a hair. Immediately, Cole could sense that the sheriff had let the cat out of the bag.

"So you have family in these parts, Cole?" Jim inquired.

Jim and Pam were part of an easygoing southern town; an FBI agent in their back seat might as well be a celebrity.

"No, Jim, I don't."

"What brings you to these parts then?" Jim inquired.

Pam snuck a light smack onto her husband's lap, signaling him to cease asking the agent questions.

"Is something wrong?" Cole asked, leaning forward in his seat.

Jim cleared his throat. Pam spoke up, without looking back over her shoulder, "The sheriff tells us that you're FBI."

Renee's eyes widened as she looked down at the floor.

Cole chuckled aloud. "Oh yeah, right. What will I be tomorrow, an astronaut? Then maybe the next day I'll be a professional baseball player?"

After a few moments of silence, Pam and Jim broke into laughter. "I can't believe we fell for Bob's crap. We've been 'round him long enough to know better," Jim admitted.

"We're sorry, Cole," Pam added.

"Think nothing off it, no damage done. I'm just a simple man making his way through life."

"You might want to add that you're egotistical, Cole," Renee snipped.

Jim and Pam grinned.

He ignored her.

"I thought you two were becomin' an item. I saw you holdin' hands the other day," Pam remarked.

"Well, you should have taken a picture, Pam. You won't ever see that again," Renee confirmed.

Again, Pam and Jim smirked.

"Why don't you relax?" Cole requested.

"You're right. I'm sorry, Jim and Pam."

"It's quite alright, Renee. We understand occasional squabbles," Pam acknowledged.

MURKY, DALTON, AND Sterling each grabbed a barstool inside Joe's Tavern.

"Damn, that was close. Why the hell was the state boys doin' at the river anyway?" Dalton pondered.

"It pisses me off, man. I had Renee eatin' out of my hands." Murky pouted.

"Did ya hump her?" Sterling explored.

"No, but I would have. It was just a matter of opportunity, which the state boys fucked up."

Dalton swatted Murky on the back. "Why did ya leave her there, you bonehead?"

"Dalton, if you hit me again, I'll hurt you, and I'll hurt you bad."

Dalton played as if he was shaking in fear.

"Why did ya leave her, Murky?" Sterling persisted.

"I dunno, I wasn't thinkin' right. Everything happened so fast. She'll get home somehow. Mole can walk her home, but he best not touch her!"

"What will you boys have?" Joe asked from behind the bar.

"A pitcher of beer," Dalton ordered.

"I'm gonna get drunk, and you guys can drop me off at Renee's place. I'm goin' to climb in her bedroom and lick her all over," Murky planned.

"Oh man, Murky, you gotta bring her panties home so we can smell 'em," Sterling insisted.

"I might, if you morons don't tell her."

"We won't," Dalton pledged.

"Get us a pair each," Sterling demanded.

"Don't push it, Sterling," Murky ground out.

Murky, as with the rest of the Porters, had problems accepting things that didn't go their way. He shouldn't have had to fight so hard over all these years to get Renee to come to him. She should have bowed at his feet at first calling. He had considered on several occasions to exterminate her, to slay her away. If he couldn't claim her as his very own, no one else ever would. Renee, though she was unaware of the situation rolling around inside Murky's mind, was basically down to her last strike. If she would have turned him down on this date of accompanying Murky to the river, he was planning on ending her life by means of his own hands.

Now that she went out on a date with him, he believed that Renee was growing closer to becoming his wife. However, she must first comply with the rules that go along with being a Porter woman. Only speak when spoken to. Never ask where the man has been. Drink and get intoxicated with your husband. Have dinner ready each evening, even if you're not certain he'll be coming home. Engage in each and every sexual act to his desire, and if she ever mentioned the word *divorce*, she was a dead woman walking.

Murky's heart ran cold to the world, and he wouldn't have it any other way. He, like his brothers and relatives before his time, had never felt a morsel of remorse for the wrongdoings they had committed. One event he was particularly proud of happened one summer's day in Knoxville. He and his brothers were in the city and stopped at a grocery store to buy beer.

*****

"What kinda beer do ya rats want to get?" Murky asked his brothers. They were standing in front of the beer cooler in aisle 5.

"Stroh's," Dalton replied.

"Piss water," Murky stated.

"Bud Light," Sterling suggested.

"Not enough zip to it. I'll pick it. You dickheads don't know your beer," Murky claimed as he reached for a twelve pack of Miller Genuine Draft. The brothers began walking up the aisle when they spotted an adult male accompanied by an older woman. It was obvious that the man had a mental disability. His walk leaned to the right, and he limped. His right hand was frozen into a claw. His lower lip was large, and it drooped away from his bottom teeth. He wore thick-lensed eyeglasses and heavy clothing, even though it was a hot summer day.

Donald Curnell was shopping with his elderly mother as he had always done. Donald was born thirty-six years ago with a brain tumor. By the time he was fourteen years old, the tumor had grown to the size of a grapefruit. Despite the doctor's attempts to control the tumor, it spun out of control. Donald was normal in every way, but it came time when the tumor had to be removed in order to save his life. The decision to go through with the operation took place when Donald was sixteen. The surgeons entered Donald's skull when he was merely seventeen.

It was completely explained to the Curnell family that Donald would suffer a degree of brain damage as a result. There was no conceivable way to remove the entire tumor without taking some of Donald's brain along with it. If any of the tumor was to be left behind, it would just continue to breed. The doctors removed the entire tumor and nearly a third of Donald's brain in the process. The operation was a success as Donald was tumor-free. However, Donald went from being a normal young man to mentally handicap overnight. His memory, physical movements, and bodily functions were all affected. His speech became extremely slurred, and his twenty-twenty eyesight was lost forever. Donald was left near legally blind. He resided with his parents; he simply couldn't function on his own. The Curnells loved their son and planned on taking care of him for however long they lived. Elizabeth Curnell took her son

Donald with her nearly everywhere she went. Keeping Donald's mind occupied warded off his spells of depression. Her husband, Stan, took care of Donald on the weekends, giving Elizabeth a well-deserved break. It was Tuesday in the supermarket when Elizabeth and Donald had the misfortune of crossing paths with the Porters.

"Hey, look, it's a tard." Sterling chuckled.

After nineteen years of dealing with her boy in his state of derailed mind, Elizabeth had grown accustomed to rude people pointing out her son. However, on that day, she hadn't realized the magnitude of the dire situation. She didn't know the Porters and what they were capable of.

"Check out his pants. He looks like an idiot." Dalton laughed.

The boys then surrounded Donald.

"You drool like a freak," Murky snorted.

"Okay, gentlemen, you've had your fun. Time to move on now," Elizabeth politely suggested.

"We'll move when we want to, you bitch!" Sterling snapped.

Elizabeth immediately realized that she wasn't dealing with something out of the norm. She became nervous and took hold of her son's arm. "Come on, Donald, honey, we're done in here for the day. Let's pay for our items and head out for the van."

"Hey, we're not done with him yet!" Dalton barked.

"Oh, yes, you are," Elizabeth stood her ground.

Big mistake.

In unison, the boys' eyes seemed to turn gray as they stared her down. Elizabeth's throat became dry as she tried to swallow.

"Hey, Don the tard-on, do you wanna beer?" Murky offered.

Donald shook his head no.

"He can't consume alcohol while on his medication," Elizabeth reported.

"Man, that would suck not to be able to drink," Dalton stated. "Have ya ever been laid, Donnie? We know a gal that'll give ya some pussy, you tard."

Donald appeared confused and began to tremble.

Elizabeth's eyes clouded. "Enough! Now you leave us be, or I'll call the police," she warned.

The Porters despised the word police. Using the twelve pack of beer as a weapon, Murky swung the packed beer and hit Elizabeth on the right side of her head with a violent blow. Her knees buckled, and she collapsed to the floor in the aisle. Donald began to sob as he observed his mother struggle in pain. Murky then stepped up to her and kicked Elizabeth in the stomach. Donald reached down for his mother. Sterling grabbed hold of Donald's fingers and twisted them in a fashion that brought instant pain to Donald's hand. Donald winced in pain.

"Come on, let's take the tard for a ride," Sterling growled.

Donald had no choice but to follow Sterling wherever he led him. His fingers were throbbing with pain and on the brink of breaking as Sterling tightened his grip. Dalton looked out around the corner of the aisle and waited until the coast was clear. The Porters then led the frightened Donald out of the store and into Sterling's truck, shoplifting the beer along the way. Dalton jumped into the bed of the truck. Murky and Sterling secured Donald between them on the bench seat. They drove Donald into Waynesburg fifty minutes away, forcing him to drink beer along the way.

Sterling whipped his truck into Tammy Patroni's driveway while sounding his horn.

Tammy looked out her window and giggled at the boys' antics. "What are ya boys doin' here today? It's not your regular day," Tammy inquired. "And who is this?" She questioned the identity of Donald.

Sterling led Donald into Tammy's house in the same fashion in which he escorted him out of the grocery store. "We picked this tard up at the grocery store. He's never been laid, so you're gonna fuck him," Sterling insisted.

"Don't I have a say-so in this?" Tammy teased.

"Nope," Dalton snarled.

Murky slid Tammy a hundred dollar bill.

"Well, okay then. I gotta Franklin handed to me, let's get it on," Tammy bellowed.

The group made their way inside Tammy's bedroom. The bedroom intimidated Donald. The waterbed was covered with bright red satin sheets. A large mirror was attached to the ceiling above the bed with figures along the wooden border of the mirror. The shapes were of people

engaging in sex in a variety of positions. The room was well lit, too lit for any sort of intimacy. But Tammy's clients didn't visit her for a romantic evening. They wanted to see the flesh they were paying for. The bedroom reeked heavy of perfume and melted candle wax.

Tammy stepped out of her clothing as she approached the bed. Within five paces, she was completely nude. She stood before the boys and teased with a sly grin at Donald. Before the operation, Donald did have a girlfriend in high school. But shortly after the procedure, she couldn't accept the new Donald, and she broke off their relationship. Donald had intercourse with his girlfriend several dozen times, so Tammy was not the first woman that he had perceived nude. However, his memory did not serve him well, so Donald might as well have been a virgin.

Donald enjoyed gazing at Tammy and her nakedness, but at the same time he was embarrassed, so he glanced away.

"No no no, Don the tard-on, you gotta take a good look at that pussy. Tammy has a fine bush and a nice-lookin' set of lips between them legs of hers," Murky described.

"Why, thank you, Murky Porter." Tammy licked her teeth.

"Lie down and spread your legs, Tammy. That'll get the tard's engine started," Sterling directed.

Tammy lowered herself onto the red sheet and did as Sterling instructed.

"There now, take a look at that, tard," Sterling declared. Using his large hands, Sterling forced Donald to turn his head and to view Tammy in her most vulnerable position.

"It's all for you, Donald," she whispered seductively. Tammy thought that the boys were doing something nice for Donald, a gift of sorts. But Tammy had been around the Porters long enough and should have known better than to believe that. No, this was not a kind gesture. This was no party for the breaking of Donald's virginity. What this was for the Porters was to humiliate a mentally challenged person. It was yet another case of their misguided sense of humor and cruelty to others. Tammy was about to discover how low and nasty the Porters could be.

As the situation deteriorated, Tammy was enjoying the situation less and less.

"Take your clothes off, Don the tard-on, and stick your dick inside Tammy," Murky instructed.

Donald shook his head nervously.

"Take your clothes off and fuck that broad!" Murky demanded.

Donald hesitated. Murky stepped abruptly to Donald and slapped him with a powerful force using his open right hand across the face. The blow sent Donald's thick eyeglasses flying across the room. Tammy was rudely awakened to the seriousness of the situation.

"Murky!" she bellowed. "That wasn't necessary."

"Shut your mouth, Tammy," Dalton warned.

"Now do ya take off your clothes, tard-on? Or do I hit ya again?" Murky questioned.

With his face still stinging, Donald reluctantly removed his clothing down to his underwear.

Tammy compassionately switched from the seductive mode to the motherly style. She sat up in the bed and draped the sheet across her body. "It's okay, Donald. I won't hurt you. Just come on over here and sit next to me. All we really have to do is just talk, if you'd like."

Murky growled, "Bullshit, bitch. I paid ya a hundred bucks, so you're screwin' the tard-on."

"You can have your cash back, Murky. I don't want the money at the expense of this poor man's dignity."

Sterling rushed at Tammy and backhanded her across the mouth. Tammy's head jerked, and she plunged back on the bed. She rolled on the bed, in too much pain to speak.

"No whore of mine is gonna talk back to the Porters," Sterling declared.

In complete fear, Donald took a chance to run. He moved as quickly as his nearly crippled body could carry him. The Porters merely had to jog to catch him. They did so as Donald was making his way through the front door of the house. Dalton pushed Donald from behind, sending Donald tumbling down the seven concrete steps. The boys laughed. Murky rummaged through Tammy's purse on the kitchen table and retrieved the hundred dollar bill. He stuck the bill in his pocket. He also came across a red felt marker pen inside the purse. He slid the marker in his pocket as well. The Porters then forced Donald back into Sterling's truck and sped away from Tammy's house.

Inside the house, Tammy nursed her swollen and bleeding lip.

The Porters punched, slapped, and kicked Donald as they drove around portions of the county. As they made their way along a seldom-used dirt road near the Waynesburg and Harpersfield border, they approached a small bridge constructed of railroad ties.

"Let's dump the retard. This is getting borin'," Sterling groaned.

"Yeah, I wanna sit up front," Dalton said through the open rear window of the truck.

"Okay, stop at the bridge, Sterling." Murky pointed to the crossing ahead.

Twelve feet below the bridge was a ravine that ran with overflow from the Sulfur River during periods of heavy rains. Most of the year, as it was then, the ravine was a dry creek bed. Ridged rocks lined the bottom of the gully.

As they stood on the bridge, Murky used the felt-tip pen to write a message upon Donald's forehead. Dalton and Sterling guffawed when they read what Murky had written. The Porters then lifted Donald from his feet despite Donald's reaction to fight free. The Porters were simply too strong for him. The Porters then took a reluctant Donald by force and spilled him over the bridge railing. Donald screamed out during his fall from the bridge. A bit of luck was with Donald that day as his physique missed a series of sharp rocks by inches. His body slammed down on a bare area of the ravine. He was instantly knocked unconscious. The Porters sped away in a round of warped laughter.

*****

When Donald regained consciousness, he roamed for hours clad only his underwear. Without his eyeglasses, the world was all but a blur. His body was beaten and torn; his mind was numb. Finally, a passing motorist discovered him and rushed Donald to the hospital in Webster.

Elizabeth and Stan Curnell learned of the news regarding their son's rescue, and they rushed to the hospital. Donald spent four days recovering in the clinic, and his forehead had to be scrubbed free of red marker spelling out the words "I screw my Mommy."

Sterling, Dalton, and Murky were picked up a week later and arrested by the state police. Hours after their arrests, Carter produced bail money, and the brothers were released from custody. While they awaited trial, Carter paid the Curnells a visit. He simply explained that if his sons were sent to prison, he would kill their handicap son.

The Curnells promptly dropped all charges pending against the Porters.

CHAPTER 42

IKE STOOD FROM the porch swing as he heard Renee and Cole approaching up the darkened driveway. Soon, they were within his line of sight aided by the light on the pole.

"Well, you just don't know how to treat people. You just assume that everyone is a bad guy," Renee snapped.

"That's not true. I don't think that way." Cole defended himself.

"Sure you do. I watch the way you look at people. Everyone is a suspect in some way, right, Cole?" Renee catechized.

"You've got me all wrong."

"Do I really? I don't think so."

Ike grinned and then whistled. "Hey, you two, put your claws down for cryin' out loud. You sound like a couple of cranky coonhounds."

Renee softened her tone as she approached the porch. Cole continued toward the guesthouse after nodding at Ike.

"Hello, Grandpa, what are you still doin' up?"

"Well, child, I couldn't sleep with you out there dealin' with the Porters. How did it go?"

"It was disgustin', Grandpa. Murky made me spit in his beer, and then he forced me to kiss him."

"How'd ya get away from him?"

"Cole called the state police and told them that someone was drownin' just to get them to come rushin' to the scene. When the state police arrived, the Porters hauled tail."

"Sounds like Cole did some good thinkin' on his feet."

"Well, don't tell him that. His head is already big enough."

Ike bit his lip to keep from chuckling. "How did ya get home?"

"Jim and Pam picked us up."

Ike stretched and yawned. "Callin' it a night, gal? I know I am."

"You go on ahead, Grandpa. I'm goin' to stay out here in the night air and simmer down a bit."

"See ya in the mornin'," Ike bid as he headed inside the house.

She paced on the grass while making occasional grunting sounds. Renee then glared at the guesthouse for a few moments before she stormed into that direction. She rapped firmly upon the door.

Cole whipped the door open. "What do you want now?"

"I'm not done with you yet. Will you please come out here?"

"Why? So I can put up with more verbal abuse? I've had enough for one day, thank you."

"I'm just tryin' to show you that you can be hardheaded sometimes."

"So why does it matter? A little while longer, and I'll be out of your life forever. Why should you care?"

She lightened up. "I have to go out to the barn to feed and check on the dogs. Will you do me a favor and go with me? I don't want to be lurkin' around in the dark not knowin' where Murky might be."

He hesitated before stepping outside the door. "Let's go and get it over with."

Renee slid the large door of the barn open and was greeted by the canines happy to see her. She weaved her way through the active dogs and over to the feeding tub. She poured from a large bag of dog food, and the feasting was on. She maintained her attention on the dogs, not looking directly at Cole, and explained, "I'm under a lot of stress over this whole thing, so please don't pay too much attention to my attitude."

"Well, your attitude could use some adjusting."

She planted her hands on her hips. "Jesus, Cole, I'm tryin' to apologize. Alright?"

"Then just come out and say it! I'm sorry. Is it that difficult? Watch. I'm sorry…Renee."

Renee sighed and mumbled, "I'm also sorry, Cole."

Within a few minutes, the dogs were fed and petted. Cole slid the large door shut before he and Renee made their way back toward the houses. When they reached the guesthouse, Renee did not hesitate to continue her path to the farmhouse.

"You're welcome," Cole grunted.

"Thank you." She half grinned.

"Good night," Cole bid.

She waved her right hand without turning around or slowing her pace. Cole jogged to catch up with her brisk walk. He grabbed her arm and whisked her around to face him. The pair looked deeply in each other's eyes. Their hearts pounded with excitement and feelings of sincere passion. Neither one could hold back any longer. They craved, wanted, and needed to be together intimately.

They fell together in a passionate, aggressive kiss. Their lips met with force, and their teeth grinded together. The kiss intensified as he picked her up into his arms. He carried her into the guesthouse without breaking their kiss and shut the front door behind them with a kick of his boot.

*****

"SEEN MASON TONIGHT, Joe?" Sterling questioned.

"No, I haven't, why?" Joe reported. The bartender was trying to pry a cork out from a bottle of red wine. A bar towel hung over his shoulder, and a toothpick poked out from the corner of his mouth. The bar's countertop, as usual, shined in the overhead lights.

"I wanted someone to pick on. That fuckin' Mason is a joke."

"Mason's done nothin' to you boys. Why don't ya leave him be?"

"Mind your own business, Joe." Dalton pointed a finger at him. Joe cleared his throat. "Sorry, Dalton."

"Come on, you shitheads, give me a ride to Renee's," Murky slurred.

"Let's get him there before he cries," Dalton said with a smirk.

As the tavern's door swung shut behind the brothers, the cork plunged up and out of the neck of the wine bottle.

*****

RENEE'S BREATHING WAS rapid as Cole peeled away his thin T-shirt.

"Damn, you have a nice chest," she complimented breathlessly.

He leaned his head back and moaned with delight as she kissed and nibbled at his chest. He pulled her body up to his, and they swallowed each other in a lust-filled kiss. His hands ran down her back and stopped at her buttocks. He gently rubbed and squeezed her shapely backside as she grinded her hips into him. She then reached between their waists and tugged at the button of his Levi's until she had it dislodged. Her left hand slid inside his pants where she rubbed his erect penis through his underwear to his pleasure. He pulled her blouse off her shoulders, popping the buttons in the process. He then slid the blouse over her arms and tossed the garment to the floor. Before Cole's next move, Renee reached around and unhooked her bra, allowing it to slide from her breasts to the floor. Her erect nipples glided back and forth against his bare chest as she swayed her body. With his right hand, he gained a firm grip upon her left breast, pleased with the full size and firmness of it. He rolled her swollen nipple between his thumb and forefinger, causing Renee to throw her head back and gasp out a pleasurable moan. She maintained a strong grip on his penis through his underwear.

"God, I want you, Cole," she whispered, trying to catch her breath.

"You are a very sexy woman, Renee. You have me on fire."

"I want to taste you," she purred. Renee then knelt and dragged his Levi's down to his ankles. She gained a grip on his underwear and yanked the undergarment down to his bundled-up Levi's. His penis stood at attention and throbbed before her face. She took his penis into her right palm and slowly stroked his erection.

Cole's legs trembled as he grinded toward her. She leaned her head toward him and teased him by placing her lips less than an inch from the tip of his long penis. "Are you ready for this?" she asked seductively.

He nodded anxiously.

Renee licked her lips before she took his pulsating sexual organ inside her mouth. His buttock tightened as she worked and caressed her tongue over the surface of his hardness. She cupped his testicles into her left hand and cuddled them gently while her mouth worked feverishly on his penis. Renee was exceptionally wet between her soft, slender legs. Her breasts rubbed his thighs as she consumed as much of his penis into her mouth as she possibly could, but to her pleasant surprise, Cole was larger than the average male. She accepted him to the very rear of her throat, still leaving nearly half the length of his manhood exposed. She pressed her full lips against his skin and dragged with a slow rhythm in a back-and-forth motion. Renee could feel him throbbing against her teeth.

He grabbed handfuls of her hair and pushed her into him, nearly choking her in the process. Renee allowed his penis to spring from her mouth before she slid her tongue up and down his stiff shaft. After several more minutes of her orally pleasuring him, Cole needed more of her. He took hold of her upper arms and hauled her up to him. He picked her up into his arms and gently spilled her onto the bed. He kicked off his Levi's and underwear before joining her on the mattress. She welcomed him with an inviting smile. He placed kisses upon her neck as Renee tossed her head back. He licked a trail down her neck until her reached her breasts. He alternated her nipples between his lips, nibbling each with his teeth. She grabbed at his short hair as her thighs pulsed. She could feel his hardness press into her outer thigh, and she rubbed him with her leg. "Mmmmmm, Cole," she whispered.

Cole moved his mouth to her left earlobe and nibbled as his hands work feverishly on her breasts. "I want you, Renee," he growled.

"You've gotten me so hot, Cole. Take me!"

He kissed down along her neck, across her breasts, along her tight stomach, to the top of her slacks. He opened the button of her pants with his teeth and then lowered the zipper in the same fashion. She was nearly out of breath as her hips bucked. He rose to his knees and gripped at her pants. He pulled the jeans down her legs and past her feet. He then flung the slacks to the floor. Like a lion on the

prowl, Cole swooped his face between her legs. He placed kisses on the crotch of her light blue lace panties. She grinded her hips into his face. He licked her panties, pressing his tongue so that she felt the inviting probe. "Oh, gawd, Cole. Take my panties off already!"

Cole could now detect the alluring scent of her excitement through the material, and it was captivating and inviting to his nostrils. He clutched each side of her panties, and with a sudden jerk of his strength, Renee's panties tore away from her hips. He hurled the torn panties across the room, landing them on one of the chairs. Renee's excitement escalated as she lay completely naked in front of him.

He gazed at the beautiful sight between her legs, the dark triangle of her pubic hair. Her region was of soft silky pubic hair rather than coarse and kinky. This was to Cole's liking. The folds of her vaginal lips lay cuddled and were visible beneath strands of the silken pubic hair. Again, Cole lunged his face between her legs. He placed several kisses upon her mound while working his way toward her wetness. He placed a lengthy kiss upon the lips of her vagina. She grinded her crotch into his face. His tongue began to work by parting her vaginal lips while he licked up to her clitoris. Renee dug her fingernails into the bedsheet, and she blurted out a lengthy purr. His jaw was soaked with her wetness as he seized her sweet offerings.

"You taste so good, Renee," he gasped between his strokes of licking.

Renee's voice was cracking. "It's all yours to enjoy."

He continued to stimulate her orally as she aroused her own breasts. She arched her back as she orgasmed into his welcoming mouth. Her body shook while she grinded harder into his face. Her heart raced as she climaxed for a second time. She became more vocal with the release of her pleasurable moans.

He slid his hands beneath the cheeks of her firm buttocks and lifted her hips nearly a foot off the bed. She swayed her midsection side to side to meet the rhythm of his tongue. Renee orgasmed for the third time, trembling and gasping for air. Cole then gently lowered her to the mattress.

"Cole, take me! Take me, Cole!" she pleaded.

He positioned himself on his knees between her spread legs. She reached to him, taking his hard penis into her soft hands to guide him inside her vagina. But before Renee committed them to intercourse, she caressed her clitoris using the swollen tip of his penis, moving it a circular motion and purring as she did so. She stroked his rigid shaft as she continued to stimulate herself with the head of his member. She continued to purr as he leaned back his head while he received pleasure from her actions.

After a spell, Cole became anxious to enter her, and she could sense this by his body language. Renee grinned playfully at him while she welcomed his penis into her vaginal lips. He filled her as he leaned his hips toward her. Her eyes rolled back in her head at the feel of his throbbing penis inside her. He hesitated as he enjoyed the sensations of her inner vaginal walls tightening around his stiff penis. Cole then plunged back and forth as Renee countered by bucking her hips. Her wetness saturated his erection as they melted together in a firm embrace.

She rose into his arms, and he held her as Renee bobbed up and down upon his manhood. She quickened the pace and then slowly rocked on his erection. Her breathing intensified, and she placed a series of kisses on his neck. Her hard nipples rubbed against the tight muscles of his chest as his throbbing penis massaged her inner vagina. She pinned her fingernails into the skin of his back. Again, Renee picked up the pace of her rocking motion, sliding her vagina lips up and down upon his shaft.

Cole moaned into her ear, further exciting her. She arrived at another orgasm as her vagina constricted around his large penis. She ran her fingers through his hair as they gazed deeply into each other's eyes. She held his stubbled jaw in her hands, and they kissed deeply as she maintained her motion with her hips. Cole gripped her soft, smooth, tight buttocks with his large hands and guided her motion to meet the rhythm of his grinding hips. His testicles met the cheeks of her buttocks as he buried himself completely inside her. She hurled back her head, and her hair flowed through the air. She gasped as she again climaxed, this time upon his throbbing stiffness. She was experiencing multiple orgasms for the first time in her life,

to her pleasurable liking. Their hips became synchronized, creating a sexual intercourse in perfect harmony. The stimulation was intense for both. His heavy breathing was now matching her intensity level. She then swayed her hips side to side as well as up and down. By the expression of satisfaction on his face, Renee knew that this action from her felt especially good to him—and to her as well. She sensed another orgasm nearing, and Renee wanted them to peak together this time. She was now moving her hips in a circular motion.

"Fill me up, Cole. I want to feel you go off inside me. Fill me up, Cole," she gasped. She quickened her motion, intensifying the throbbing of his penis. "Go for it. I want to feel it."

Cole's thighs tightened, and she knew he was approaching climax. He took her right nipple into his mouth, and she moaned out with delight. "You feel sooooooo damn good, Renee," he rumbled.

"You too. Set off inside of me. I need to feel it. Explode, baby. Explode inside me!"

Cole grunted deeply as he ejaculated with force. Renee felt the warm liquid firing off inside her vagina as she peaked as well. Their sex-created bodily fluids blended as they trembled and quivered with stimulation.

"That's it. Let it shoot, baby. It feels so damn good!" She purred her approval. He continued to ejaculate as his semen began to ooze out of her filled vagina. She could feel the warm fluid flow from her vagina and down along her buttocks. Renee bucked her hips wildly. "Empty inside of me."

Cole completely drained inside her as his body shook. She caressed his penis with her vaginal walls a few additional moments after he completed ejaculating. She then came to rest on his lap with his now-relaxing penis still inside her. They each took a few moments to gather their breaths.

"That was fantastic, Renee," he murmured, still trembling.

She whispered, "You liked?"

"Oh yeah."

"Me too."

They kissed while collapsing onto the bed together.

*****

THIRTY MINUTES LATER, Cole and Renee were sleeping in each other's arms. At the end of the farm's long driveway, Sterling's pickup truck pulled up carrying the three intoxicated Porter brothers.

"How the hell are ya gonna get home, Murky?" Sterling questioned.

"I'll walk."

"It's over six miles," Dalton reminded him.

"I know where we live, asshole," Murky slurred.

"We'll just wait out here for ya," Sterling suggested.

"It's gonna take me about an hour," Murky declared.

Dalton chortled. "Shit. You fuck like a rabbit. You'll cum in less than a minute. You ain't foolin' us a bit."

Murky punched Dalton in the upper arm. "You two just best not peek in the window and see my beautiful Renee naked. I'll kill you if you do," Murky warned.

Dalton and Sterling could sense that Murky would react violently to such an act.

"We'll stay put in the damn truck," Sterling confirmed.

Murky then leaped down from the vehicle.

"Go get her, stud boy," Dalton cheered.

"Yeah, and bring us back her panties," Sterling added.

Murky then jogged up the Stewarts' driveway.

CHAPTER 43

"WHAT ARE YOU doin' up so late?" Joe quizzed Bob as the sheriff made his way to one of the barstools. Joe poured Bob his usual cup of coffee.

"Oh, I can't sleep. Somethin' heavy is goin' on here in Harpersfield, and I'm not in on it. That really ticks me off," Bob claimed before sipping the hot liquid.

Bob gained Joe's undivided attention. "Why? What's goin' on?"

The sheriff glanced around the tavern to see only Mason Turner, who stumbled inside the tavern minutes before Bob's arrival, bowing his head in a drunken stupor at the other end of the bar.

"You can't tell a soul, Joe, but we have an FBI agent here stayin' in Harpersfield. He's undercover posin' as a farmhand up at Ike Stewart's place."

Joe's eyes widened. "Why do you suppose the FBI is here?"

Bob whispered as Joe leaned on the bar, "Frank and I have come across some hidden dope lately. The FBI could be onto a major drug ring, and Harpersfield could be a main vein of that ring."

Joe chuckled. "Harpersfield a drug-traffickin' central station? Give me a break, sheriff."

"Then what else could it be?"

"Maybe it's about Nate Stewart's murder."

"Naw, it can't be that. That's all done and settled. The FBI can't do anything about that. Murky and his brothers walked away from that, and there's nothin' that can be done about it now. It has to be somethin' else."

"Well, I know that Ike doesn't run moonshine like he used to, so that couldn't be it. Maybe this agent is just on vacation."

Bob squinted. "In Harpersfield?"

Joe snickered. "Yeah, you're right. Who in their right mind would vacation in this run-down town?"

"Well, for whatever the reason he is here, you can't say a word, Joe. He'll have my badge if this gets out."

Joe motioned as if he were zipping his lips closed.

"Not even your wife," Bob added.

"Judy wouldn't say anything."

"Okay, you can tell her, but nobody else." Bob then looked over at Mason.

"Oh, don't worry about him none. A parade could march by right now, and Mason wouldn't have a clue," Joe chortled.

Bob nodded. "Help me get him into the patrol car, and I'll take him home."

Joe stepped around the bar and headed toward Mason. "Come on, Mason, stand up. The sheriff is goin' to give ya a ride home."

Joe stood quietly behind the bar after Mason and the sheriff had departed the tavern. Only the soft grinding noise coming from an overhead ceiling fan could be heard. The television was on mute, and the juke box was silent. Joe continued to wipe down a now-clean drinking glass as his thoughts deepened.

He recalled running around the streets of Harpersfield as a young lad. Those were the days before Dalton, Sterling, and Murky were born, but the town still had to deal with Carter and Steadman. One of Joe's goals early in life was to become a professional moto-cross racer. He saved his hard-earned allowance and other money by doing odd jobs to purchase a yellow Yamaha YZ125. Joe loved that motorcycle, which he proudly displayed the number 18 on the side plate. After taking care of his daily chores and after school hours,

Joe would ride that motorbike at every opportunity. With time, Joe became exceptionally skilled on that motorcycle. He then entered an amateur invitational in Knoxville. Out of 214 competitors in the 125 class, Joe took fourth place overall. He was presented a ribbon, and he displayed it on his bedroom wall. He felt that with a little more practice, he would be a cut above the rest in the motocross world. Just as it all was coming together for him, Carter and Steadman tore it apart.

Joe was sharpening his riding skills on a bumpy trail along the ridge of the Sulfur River one afternoon. Carter and Steadman were in the area poaching deer when they heard Joe's motorcycle approaching. The Porter duo stood on the path and held up their hands for Joe to stop. Joe knew that if he did not comply, Carter and Steadman would track him down later and beat him severely. Reluctantly, Joe brought his beloved motorcycle to a halt in front of the Porters.

Steadman pushed Joe off the seat and took over the motorbike. He and Carter then took turns riding and dumping the motorcycle to the ground. Neither could ride very well. Joe could only hope that he would get his motorcycle back in one piece.

After about thirty minutes, Carter and Steadman had their fill of riding Joe's motorcycle. However, instead of simply handing the bike back over to the owner, Carter and Steadman had other cruel plans in mind. Together, and at the sounds of Joe pleading for them not to do it, Carter and Steadman guided and then pushed the motorcycle down the ridge while watching the machine plunge into the depths of the Sulfur River.

The young Joe could only watch teary eyed as his number 18 faded into the deep clouded water of the river, never to be seen again. Carter and Steadman had a good laugh, but Joe's heart was heavy. Before they left the weary Joe alone, they found a need to punch and kick him several times.

It was days later, after breathing difficulties, that Joe's mother took him to the doctor to discover that he had three broken ribs.

Joe's motorcycle sank that day, as did his dream.

Joe Skidmore finally left the clean glass on the bar. One by one, he shut off the tavern's lights for the night.

Chapter 44

DULE SAT AT the bar in the lounge of a hotel a mere block from his apartment. He peered around nervously, primarily at the lounge's entrance. Soon, the company he expected stepped through the door. Dule raised his right hand to signal the man and woman of his location.

FBI agents and Elite Four members Barry Stone and Janice Stark made their way to Dule. Barry was a well-defined black man with muscles that protruded beneath his suit. He shaved his scalp bald and sported a goatee. He was six foot four and had large hands. He was thirty-eight years old and divorced twice. His sixteen-year-old son, Daniel, was talking about entering the police academy, which made Barry proud. Barry was an exceptionally intelligent man who could have gone on to be a scientist or perhaps a mathematician. However, law enforcement and detective work was his passion.

Janice appeared to be anything other than a tough FBI Agent. She stood at five foot eight and was fit. Her natural blonde hair was wavy and swayed down to her shoulders. Her eyes were green, and her peachy skin was flawless. She was an attractive woman at thirty-four, and she once completed an undercover stint as a stripper in a

nightclub, and soon she had a following of numerous male fans. She was divorced, about three years now, and no children.

Barry and Janice were two of the top agents in the FBI as well as superb Elite Four agents.

Barry shook Dule's hand. "Why did you call, Dule? And where's Marla?"

"Marla won't be joining us tonight," Dule revealed as he invited them to have a seat.

Barry and Janice settled in at the bar.

"What's this about?" Janice probed.

Dule took a moment to absorb the sound of her sweet voice. He melted at her soft tone. "Let me buy you two a drink first before we get down to business."

CHAPTER 45

MURKY YANKED THE screen out from outside Renee's opened bedroom window and then climbed inside.

Cole's eyes opened as he lay with Renee in his arms on the bed inside the nearby guesthouse. He heard Murky's cunning entrance into the farmhouse. Cole slid out from the bed, careful not to disturb Renee. She rustled and mumbled a bit, but remained asleep. He pulled on his Levi's and quietly stepped out onto the porch. He spotted the window screen leaned up against the house and knew that it must be Murky creeping inside of Renee's bedroom.

Inside the bedroom, Murky squinted in the darkness to make out Renee's bed. He slid onto the bed and whispered, "I'm here, beautiful. I'm sorry I left ya at the river. I've come to give you the cock that you yearn for." He reached for her, only to come up empty-handed. "Renee?" he blurted out, only to receive no answer. "Where the hell is she?"

Murky then scaled back out the window with Cole observing his every move. He leaped to the ground and shuffled down the driveway, disappointed and disappearing into the darkness of the night.

When Murky reached the truck at the end of the driveway, Dalton jeered and taunted, "See, I told ya it'd take stud boy just a few minutes. A fuckin' bunny rabbit."

"Where the hell are her panties, Murky?" Sterling pressed.

Murky jumped inside the pickup truck, crushing Dalton against Sterling. "Dalton, I swear I've had about enough of you. One more word, and I'll kick your ass up between your shoulder blades," Murky threatened.

Dalton swiftly and without warning gripped his hand around Murky's throat, blocking his younger brother's airway. Murky attempted to pull Dalton's hand away but without success.

"Let's try to remember who's the big brother here, Murky. Because if ya piss me off enough, I'll trash you."

"Let go off him, Dalton. I don't want to listen to the both of you fight. I'm too damn tired, and I just want to get home and sleep," Sterling groaned.

Dalton released his mighty grip from around Murky's throat. Murky gasped for air and coughed.

Sterling pulled the truck onto the road.

Murky caught his breath and mumbled, "When you least expect it, Dalton, it's comin' back at ya, I swear."

Once he was convinced that Murky had left the premises, Cole returned inside of the guesthouse and snuggled up to Renee.

*****

"I WANTED TO discuss Marla with you two. I wanted Anthony Becth here as well, but he's too involved with a current case to just pick up and leave," Dule explained.

"So what about Marla? Is she okay? Is she ill or something?" Janice inquired with concern in her voice.

Again, Dule took a moment to absorb her delicate sound. "No, Marla's not ailing, but still, I'm worried about her."

"Why?" Barry asked in his deep voice.

Dule sipped a drink from his glass of scotch and then sighed. "You know Cole Walsh?"

The agents nodded.

"Well, he's on a case now that has Marla spinning. She's uncomfortable with it, and I can see it in her eyes that it's disturbing her deeply."

Barry shrugged his shoulders. "It comes with the territory. Marla knows that better than anybody."

"It's different this time around. Marla is really letting this one get to her. She wants to pull Cole off the case, but he keeps bargaining with her."

"Marla can fold the case at any time, that's the rules," Janice affirmed. "Cole is not one to break the rules. If she hasn't pulled him off the case, she must feel it's still worthwhile."

"I think she turns to putty in Cole's hands," Dule shared.

"Marla? No way. She's one of the strongest-willed persons I know," Barry stated.

"So why did you have us jump on a plane?" Janice pressed.

"I want you two to help me convince Marla to close up shop with this case."

"We can't do that. That's not how it works. She calls the shots, period. We're not even to contact her unless she contacts us first," Barry made clear.

Janice added, "You're asking us to break code, to bend the rules, and we won't do it."

Dule exhaled long and deep. "That's it? You won't help me out with this at all?"

"No," Barry was quick to respond. "Don't tell Marla that we were here in Philadelphia. Now, I'm going to grab a room and get some shut-eye. I'll fly out in the morning. Take care, Dule."

Dule reluctantly waved to Barry as the agent shuffled away from the bar.

"Wait up, Barry," Janice bid before she gulped down the remainder of her daiquiri. "Bye, Dule." Janice moved quickly across the tiled floor in her high heels to join Barry at the door of the lounge. "I'm going to get a room as well. I don't want to fly out tonight."

Barry grinned and winked. "Wanna split the cost of a single room?"

"Why, Barry, I see you once in a blue moon, and you're flirting with me?"

"Yeah, that I am. Now, let's get that room, you gorgeous blonde."

"Can I trust you to be a good boy?" She chuckled.

"No...no, you can't."

"A room together will be fine then." She took hold of his arm. They stepped out of the lounge together.

Dule swirled ice cubes in his drink before lighting a cigarette. He rubbed his tired eyes.

"Something the matter?" the bartender asked.

Dule groaned. "I think my gal could be falling for another."

"Wow, that's tough, my man. The next drink is on me."

Dule waved an appreciative left hand.

Chapter 46

August 6

JUDY SKIDMORE, JOE'S wife, was trying to keep her hands busy and her mouth shut. She was folding clothes at the laundromat in the early morning, listening to small talk coming from Emma Gert, who owned and ran the town's general store. Emma was sixty-one and seemed to be tired nearly all the time. She worked long hours at the store, and being a miser, she refused to hire help. Her husband, Henry, worked the few hours that Emma did not, though Henry was reaching seventy and had arthritis. As with Tiny's Diner, Emma's General Store was a hot spot for gossip. Judy was bursting at the seams to tell Emma about the FBI agent in town, though she promised Joe she would remain hush about it.

"Then I heard that Beverly Darton spent a few days in the hospital after the beatin' the Porters gave her. Of course, Bob Harvey won't do anything about it. I heard while Beverly was away, Fred and Merle messed up the house plenty. They can't fend for themselves without Beverly around. I swear that if my Henry put my house in such disarray while I went away for a few days, he'd feel my wrath

when I got home. Anyway, I guess Pam Tinelberg is takin' care of cleanin' the house until Beverly heals up."

The room fell quiet of conversation, with only the sounds of washers and dryers humming along. Judy worked feverishly at folding clothes until she couldn't hold it in any longer.

"Um, Emma, did ya know that Ike Stewart hired a farmhand for the summer?"

"Of course, Judy. You know nothin' gets by me."

"Have you met him?"

"No, I haven't met him yet. I saw him walkin' along Harper Street with Ike and Renee the other day. He's a good-lookin' man."

"Is that all you know about him?"

Emma immediately tossed her magazine on top of a clothes washer. "Is there more?"

Judy hesitated. "I'm not really supposed to say."

Emma nearly licked her chops. "Come now, Judy, do tell. You know your secret is safe with me."

Again, Judy paused, knowing that Emma's statement of secrecy simply wasn't true. "His name is Cole, and he's...well...he's an FBI agent."

Emma brought her hand to her chin. "Is that right? My goodness, what is the FBI doin' here in Harpersfield of all places?"

"I don't know, but I guess the sheriff thinks it might have somethin' to do with a drug ring."

Emma chirped, "In Harpersfield? That Bob Harvey is a loon."

"Just the same, it's just plain weird that the FBI is here."

"I bet it has to do with Florence Brickhammer," Emma predicted with a snap of her fingers.

"Why would it have to do with the mayor of Waynesburg?" Judy questioned.

"Well, she's up for reelection in the fall."

"So?"

"The FBI is probably here to make certain that no shenanigans go on durin' the political contest. I hear she's up against some well-to-do gentleman originally from Webster who recently relocated to Waynesburg. There's a rat in the woodpile there, I tell ya."

Judy rolled her eyes. "I'm sure that the FBI is not concerned about some small-town mayoral race, Emma."

Emma shrugged her shoulders. "Well, it was just a thought. Ya never know with the FBI."

"Be that as it may, don't tell anyone about this, Emma. Mum's the word now."

*****

MARLA CEASED EATING her toast as a baffled expression formed on her face. "What's with you this morning, Dule? You look as though you swallowed a canary."

She and Dule were eating breakfast at a quaint eatery in downtown Philadelphia.

Dule waved his fork. "Oh, it's nothing, Marla. I was up late last night is all."

"Late? Why?"

He reached across the small table and took her hand. "I'm worried about you, baby."

"About me? Why are you concerned about me?"

"Come on, Marla, you're not fooling me a bit. I can see this current case with Cole Walsh is taking its toll on you."

She sipped from her hot coffee. "They all do, Dule, you know that. Every case has a way of driving nails into me. I've dealt with it for decades, so it's nothing new to me. Stop worrying."

"This one is different. You're becoming distant."

She grinned as she sprinkled sugar on her grapefruit.

"What?" he inquired.

"I think you're jealous."

"Jealous of what?"

"Cole Walsh."

"That's absurd," Dule argued.

"Yeah, I believe you're jealous," she teased. "Don't fret. I think it's cute."

"I'm not jealous. I'm worried."

"Call it what you want. You don't have to concern yourself where Cole is involved. He and I have a business relationship only. We only tease each other. Come on and get with it, my darling. You know that I'd never play around on you." She puckered her lips, and Dule leaned in to kiss her.

Dule had grown extremely close to Marla—something that hadn't happened often in his life.

Dule was never close to his father as Jerry Brookside was basically a loner who should have never married Francis Lyles. But he did marry her, and together they bore two children. Dule's sister Kelly was three years his senior. It was Francis who took care of all the children's wants and needs. Jerry worked long hours at his automotive repair shop, and when he was home, he was withdrawn. He only spoke when necessary, and Dule could recall that his father would spend countless hours working on jigsaw puzzles. Dule didn't remember ever seeing his father drink alcohol, but he was sure that his father was on some sort of medication. The reason Dule assumed this was the case was because his father would hide away for days at a time, and his mother would mumble about Dad not taking what the doctor ordered. Francis would force Jerry to take his medicine during those times. Whatever the medication was, it didn't exactly turn Jerry into a social bug, but at least it brought him out from the confines of his bedroom.

Francis was the very glue that held the family together. After the children were grown and on their own, Francis filed for divorce from Jerry. After weeks of living apart, Francis returned to the home. Dule was happy to see his parents reconcile, but he was confused. Dule loved his mother very much, and she was one of the few people he had been really close with. He worried about her returning to the dreary home that Jerry built. Dule questioned his mother's actions, and she explained to him that she feared that Jerry would become desperate and do something drastic to himself if she would have not returned to him. The request for divorce was withdrawn from the courts.

Kelly Brookside married early. She was eighteen, and John Hewitt was twenty. Eight months after the wedding, Kelly gave birth to Dule's nephew Joshua. That timetable explained the rush

to get married. John studied to become a psychologist, and at Kelly's request, he tried to reach the inner mind of Jerry Brookside. Jerry regretted this plan of action and stopped speaking to John altogether. Eventually, Kelly became estranged from the family, despite attempts by Francis to keep it all in harmony. Kelly turned her back on Dule as well, though he had done nothing offensive toward her.

Francis returned from grocery shopping one day to discover Jerry's dead body hanging from the rafters inside the garage. Twine was wrapped several times around his neck and around the rafters. In a note Jerry left behind, he stated that the medicine had never set him free of his anguish. He ended it all that day in the garage.

Dule was saddened deeper than he thought he would be over his father's death. He knew his father was troubled and that each day of his life was a struggle to get through. At the very least, he was at peace now.

Francis moved in with Dule for about a year before she met Robert Raines. Francis changed under the influence of Robert. She began to dress wild and act immature. Robert was one of those men who was in his late forties going on his teens. Dule didn't care for the way that Robert was demanding of Francis. Dule was certain that behind closed doors, Robert was striking his mother. The day that Francis announced that she was moving out and moving in with Robert, Dule and Robert had a confrontation that ended in a fist-fight. Francis sided with Robert, causing her and Dule to drift apart.

It was a bittersweet time for Doolie Wayne Brookside. The mother he was close with was soon married to a man that Dule couldn't stand to be in the same room with. His sister Kelly was all but gone from his life as well. However, Dule's career as a private detective was flourishing. He then met Debra Novotony while in a cocktail lounge one night. Debra was an attractive woman, and though she was ten years older than Dule, she looked his age. Over the following months, Dule spent more and more time with Debra. Their relationship grew, and Dule fell in love with her. However, there was something about Debra though that didn't spell out on the surface. She would seem desperate at times. She would borrow money from Dule and would

come up short in paying him back. Dule didn't mind though, since at the time he had money streaming in.

Eventually, Debra moved in with Dule, and they began to share everything, including a bank account. It was nearly a year before Dule discovered that they were virtually broke. At one time, there was over eighty thousand dollars in the mutual bank account. It was currently down to less than two thousand. He confronted Debra about the lack of funds, and she finally confessed her secret. Debra Novotony was a cocaine addict.

Dule was floored over the news and wondered how a detective such as himself could overlook such a significant habit. But Dule then made another mistake. Instead of arranging for Debra to seek help with her addiction, he joined her.

Together over the next few years, Debra and Dule snorted their stable financial world up their noses. When the money ran dry, Debra, behind Dule's back, began to prostitute. She ran amuck with the wrong type of guys, did them wrong, and the body of Debra Novotony was found in a roadside ditch nearly decapitated. The murderer or murderers were never apprehended.

The brutal killing of Debra caused Dule to self-reflect. He put his detective agency on hold and entered a rehabilitation center for six months. He came out clean and began to rebuild his life. When his agency eventually floundered, he turned back to cocaine. Then came the dreadful day when he was busted by the police for possession and spent two years in prison. Dule had not touched cocaine since that day.

Dule had grown very close to Marla and he wanted to protect that.

"Cole is supposed to call me today to give me an update. He has five days remaining down there in Tennessee, and the clock is ticking," Marla confirmed.

CHAPTER 47

RENEE STEWART OPENED her eyes and found herself face-to-face with the sleeping Cole Walsh. She smiled as she ran her fingertips across his lips.

He stirred and awoke as she gently kissed him.

"Good mornin', Cole," she whispered.

"Good morning, you beautiful southern belle."

She purred softly and snuggled up to him. "What's on the agenda for today?"

"How about we spend the day together?" he warmly suggested.

"I like the way you think."

"Okay then, let's get on up, grab some breakfast, and then decide what we'll do next."

"You know"—she kissed his neck—"we could stay in bed a little while longer."

"And I like the way you think."

They kissed passionately and then again indulged in each other.

*****

"GET THE FUCK up, Murky!" Carter barked. "And wake your brothers. You shitheads haven't done a damn thing around here lately. I need some help with the chores. Now, get the hell up."

Murky sprang up in his bed. "Okay, Pop. We'll be right out."

"Well, see that you are. Don't wake your mother. She went to bed last night skunk drunk."

"Yes, Pop."

*****

"HE'S FBI, AND we don't know why he's here," Emma informed her husband Henry. They were busy opening their store for the day.

"That's strange, and it's gonna drive you wild, Emma. God forbid somethin' goin' down in this town, and you don't have a handle on it," he chortled.

"You just give me a bit of time, and I'll find out."

"Oh, I don't doubt that for a moment."

"You have any hunches about it?" Emma sought.

He rubbed his jaw with his arthritis-stricken right hand. "Nope, none that I can say for sure. I will tell you though, I think that Stewart girl is fallin' for our agent."

"What makes you say that?"

"Are you kiddin'? It was written all over her face the other day when they were walkin' hand in hand along Harper Street. Yessiree, bobcat tail, that girl's got the bug bad."

"You still got the bug for me, Henry?"

"Always will, my love."

*****

A FEW HOURS later, the bell above the door of the general store rang out as Cole and Renee entered the establishment. Henry and Emma were stationed behind the counter. Emma handed Mason

Turner his bag with a purchased bottle of wine inside. Mason nodded at Cole and Renee as he sounded the same bell upon his exit. Emma nudged Henry to bring his attention to the couple that just arrived.

"Hello, Emma, Henry," Renee greeted.

Henry nodded.

"Hi, Renee. How are ya today?" Emma welcomed.

"I'm fine."

"And your grandpa?"

"Fine. Emma, can we get a half pound of sliced of turkey lunch meat and a small container of potato salad please?"

"You bet, Renee. Goin' on a picnic, are y'all?"

Renee beamed. "Yeah, we thought we'd go up to Memsey's Ridge."

"Oh, it's nice up there this time of year. The waterfall is probably dried up though," Henry mentioned. "Haven't had much rain this summer, nothin' to speak of really."

"It rained heavy the other night, Henry," Emma reminded him. "Came down in buckets nearly the entire night."

"Oh, that's right, so the waterfall is probably workin'," Henry predicted.

Emma glanced quickly at Cole.

"Emma, Henry, this is Cole Walsh. He's workin' up at the farm," Renee introduced.

Henry waved.

"Hello, Cole. Gonna be in these parts long?" Emma probed.

Cole retorted without directly answering her question, "Is the potato salad made with mayonnaise or Miracle Whip?"

"I make it both ways, which do you prefer?"

"Miracle Whip."

"You got it."

Cole and Renee then made their way down one of the aisles to locate the varieties of bread.

"They know," he whispered.

"Know what?"

"That I'm FBI."

"How can you tell?"

"Believe me, after doing this for years, you just know. That sheriff won't shut his mouth."

"Smooth it over like you did with Jim and Pam."

"That's a one-shot thing, Renee. It's getting out of hand now."

"What do ya want to do?"

"Well, if they come right out and ask, of course, we'll deny it. Let's just hope I get to Murky before the stories do."

"Anything else from behind the counter, Renee?" Emma called out.

"No, I think we can get the other items out here on the floor."

"Where are you from, Cole?" Emma again called out.

"Cleveland, Ohio."

"Oh, I've been there once. My sister's boy played ball for the Cleveland Indians team at one time, and we went up there to see him play. Of course, that was many moons ago."

"Ever go to any Indians games, Cole?" Henry asked.

"Yeah, every so often."

"What's a man from Cleveland doin' down here?" Emma sought.

Cole again muttered to Renee, "Trust me on this. Just go along." Cole called back, "I work for the Farmer's Bean Institute. We're sent out to different parts of the country to check on bean crop."

Renee snickered quietly and lightly slapped Cole on his right arm. He firmed his lips to keep from chuckling.

Henry raised his arms at Emma. "That explains it then."

Emma was not yet completely convinced. "I didn't realize that Ike had a bean crop. He's always planted corn."

Renee and Cole approached the counter with their selected items in hand.

"Yeah, that's right, Emma, Ike is a corn farmer. But he's thinking about switching over to beans beginning next year. There's a little more money in beans these days than corn. I'm here to survey the land and check soil minerals for potential bean crop. At the same time, Ike expressed he could us a hand around the farm for a bit, so here I am."

Emma rang up their items on an old cash register that was long outdated.

"Well, that sure clears up a lot, Cole," Henry pointed out.

From behind the counter, Emma indiscreetly kicked her husband's ankle, signaling him to hush.

"How's that?"

"Well, let's just say that the rumor wheel in this town could use a bit of grease in its axle," Emma indicated.

Outside the store, as they were walking toward the truck, Renee laughed aloud.

*****

MURKY MOVED QUIETLY along the floor of the living room, heading for the telephone.

Carter stepped out from the kitchen. "What the hell are you doin', Murky?" Carter growled.

Murky halted in his tracks, his heart racing. "I need to use the phone, Pop."

"Is that right? You figure you can stop workin' when ya want? I don't remember givin' the okay to stop. Don't try my patience, boy, I'll rip your head off your shoulders. Now get back out in the field with your brothers and do some goddamn work."

"Just one quick call, Pop. Please?"

"Get out to the field, Murky!" Carter shouted.

Murky quickly scampered out of the house.

*****

"WHY IS THIS place called Memsey's Ridge?" Cole inquired. He and Renee were resting on a blanket next to a pool of water. Before them, a waterfall spilled over from a tall and rocky crest above.

"It's sort of a sad, twisted story," she answered.

"Tell me."

"Well, it hasn't always been known as Memsey's Ridge. As my grandfather explains, it was once called Miner's Point. I guess the coal miners use to come here and wash the coal dust from their bodies after a long shift underground. Anyway, that all changed one sum-

mer years ago. One of the generations of the Porters, Raker Porter, had a twelve-year-old daughter named Memsey. Raker was one of the few Porters who wasn't a violent person, but he sure was strange. They say that he had tar paper pasted over the windows of his house, never lettin' in the light. His wife, Nora, died when Memsey was a baby. Some people claim that Raker killed Nora, but it was never proven. Raker was into witchcraft and sorcerers. He used to go into Webster to check out books from the library about devil worshippin' and rubbish like that.

"Well, one day, he forced his daughter, Memsey, up to the pinnacle of Miner's Point, right up there." Renee pointed upward. "And then forcefully dumped her over the top of the falls. By the time her body hit the water below, the impact was like hittin' a slab of concrete. Memsey was killed instantly. Raker claimed he was saving the town by sacrificin' a young virgin to Satan. That if he hadn't done it, Lucifer had plans to burn down the town and all the people in it.

"Raker was arrested for manslaughter but somehow made bail. The tale goes that Raker was a quiet but significant distributor of marijuana and black-market pain pills throughout the state of Tennessee and had tens of thousands of dollars stashed away. Dirty money, ya know. He wasn't a producer or runner of the illegal substances, but coordinated drop-off points as well as a variety delivery points. He covered his tracks well and was never suspected nor arrested. He may have been an oddball, but he was super sly. While he was out waitin' for his trail, Nora's mother, Memsey's grandmother, seventy-eight-year-old Cora Reid, shot Raker dead with a high-powered hunting rifle. Property of her late husband, Albert. She then turned the gun on herself. So in lieu of Memsey Porter's tragic and untimely death, the town council officially changed the name of this place to Memsey's Ridge."

Cole swallowed a bite of his sandwich. "You're right, that is twisted."

"Most things are when it comes to the Porters."

Renee snuggled up to Cole. He swigged a long drink from his bottle of sweet tea.

"When I was in the army, something happened once that I'll always remember. As part of the Green Beret program, we had a grueling obstacle course that we had only two weeks to perfect. The Green Beret program is the only curriculum in the armed services that train you to be individuals. To be selfish and to look out for yourself and not your fellow soldiers. You were trained to penetrate enemy lines and kill, period. No one, not even your fellow soldiers, were to hinder your assignment in any way. If they lagged behind, fell and broke their ankle during the heat of a mission, you were to leave them or even shoot them.

"This one guy in my platoon, Dale Hinks, was determined to become a Green Beret like his father before him. However, Dale just barely made the minimum size requirements, but his heart was plenty big enough. He completed all the stages of training, all except the obstacle course.

"During our final week, Dale had yet to pass the obstacle course, and that was one of the requirements to becoming a Green Beret. It came down to his last chance, and though I had already passed the course days prior, we were still required to run the course. Unless the ones of us that had previously passed committed a major infraction on the course, we were in. The part of the course Dale found to be difficult was scaling a twenty-five-foot wall with ropes anchored and dangling down from the top. The catch was that you had to scale the wall using only one arm. It demanded precise timing, or you'd crash to the ground every time. That day, I scaled the wall directly in front of Dale. Once at the top of the wall, my next move was to slide down the other side of the wall and continue to the next obstacle. I hesitated, watching over my shoulder at Dale struggling with that wall, knowing it was his last opportunity to conquer. The drill sergeant was screaming at me to move on, but I wanted to help Dale to scale that wall. I wanted so desperately to help him, but I knew that if I did that, it would count as a major infraction. I would fail out of the program one day before I graduated, but Dale would have become a Green Beret. I struggled with my decision, and with a final warning from the drill sergeant, I left Dale behind and slid down the other side of the wall.

"The following morning, those of us who passed the program, fourteen of us out of 168 that had started six weeks prior, received our diplomas and became official Green Berets. That afternoon, Dale Hinks was found in the latrine. He was hanging from the rafters by his rifle strap bound around his neck. He took his own life rather than face his father as a failure. To this day, I regret not turning around on that wall, and if I had to do it all over again, I would have reached for Dale."

Renee softly rubbed Cole's left forearm. "You did what you thought was right at the time. Don't badger yourself over it. It sounds to me like Dale had more issues than just climbin' a wall. Not everyone in this world can be saved, Cole. Sometimes things just have to run their course…no pun intended."

"Yeah, my father gave me the same speech once. Can I ask you something?"

"You can ask me anything, honey," she whispered. She then kissed him on the neck.

He cleared his throat. "What do you believe love is?"

Renee grinned and then teased, forcing him to clarify his inquiry. "Well, that depends. What kind of love we are we talkin' about? There's the love for God, parents, siblings, friends, and even pets. Which one do you wanna know about?"

"The love shared by mates. Between a man and a woman."

"Oh," she continued to tease, "that type of love."

"Oh, just forget it." Cole became frustrated.

"No no no…I'll answer the question," she conceded with seriousness and sincerity. Renee's heart began to pound feverishly. Her throat ran dry as she anticipated that he could be leading up to saying that he had fallen in love with her, which was something she wanted to hear badly. She was certain that her heart was sinking into his soul.

Renee Stewart was sure that she had completely fallen for Cole Walsh. Renee had never felt so close to any man before, causing her to acknowledge that the relationship she once shared with Dillon Niles was no more than an adolescent crush. These feelings that she held for Cole were much deeper and profound. If he were to tell her that he loved her, she was prepared to reveal the exact words back to him.

"It's difficult to put it into words, and I haven't had much experience with it. I can remember the way that my parents looked at each other. That was unquestionably love. I know my grandfather loved my grandmother. You could just tell by the way he took care of her."

Cole added, "I've seen it before too, but sometimes you observe couples together that you just sense who simply are not in love. It just becomes routine for them, a habit, so they simply remain together. Then there are those who are with a mate for the sake of just having a mate. They can't take being single. But single isn't so bad."

The latter part was not what Renee was hoping to hear. "Single can be lonely sometimes, Cole."

"Perhaps, but it's better than spending your life with someone you don't genuinely love. I believe love is overrated. I think people become more accustomed to being together more than they actually love each other." Cole spoke from experience. He realized that his parents had merely remained together out of force of tradition more than love itself.

"That's a grim way of lookin' at it."

"It's the truth."

"So you don't think that true love between a man and a woman exists? That it all merely becomes a habit of bein' together?"

"For the most part, yeah, I do. I mean, people still care for each other, but with the passing of time, other things become stronger than their weakening feelings for each other. It's about being comfortable, like the way an old broken-in pair of boots feel. Then there are those that are together for many years, decades, a couple of generations even, and the love they share is as strong as the day they met. Those are the exceptions to the rule, and it's rare."

"Boy, some gal must have really broken your heart at one time."

"I think that women put more value into love than men do."

Renee concurred, "Oh, I agree with that statement. Men can be cold sometimes, but then they can also be very lovin'."

"Sometimes I just think we'd be better off as humans without all this love business."

"I respectfully disagree with that statement. Fallin' in love and bein' in love is part of who we are. Sharin' your life with another is an important component in the human makeup. I know it can be scary to fall in love. Your first reaction is to protect your heart from bein' potentially broken. But like everything else in life, love doesn't come with any guarantees. You just need to go with the flow, and if things don't work out, you just have to move on with your life. You'll eventually rebound and find yourself a better person for the experience. Sometimes, Cole, a person just has to take a chance and roll the dice."

After a long hesitation, Cole, in a low voice, returned with, "Yeah, maybe you're on to something there. I'm not so sure that I want to love. I don't know if that's selfish or merely a protective device. I wonder if anyone can be truly happy in a relationship? I've seen people stray from their mate and do them wrong. Women are difficult to keep content."

"That was a sexist remark if I ever heard one, Cole Walsh. Men can be just as confusin', ya know. I think that if two people are justly in love, that alone satisfies their every need."

"Love is not a cure-all, Renee."

"I realize that. I'm realistic."

"There is so much that has to fall into place for a relationship to work well. The way I see it is that if a mate tries to change you, then they don' really love you for who you are. If two people can be completely who they truly are and are happy with that, then that's real love."

"I don't believe in tryin' to change people. That's like puttin' them inside a cage."

"I know one thing I wouldn't try to change about you," Cole said.

"What's that?"

"Your southern accent and drawl with that soft voice. It is so damn sexy."

"Why, Cole Walsh." She giggled. "You can be a real charmer when ya wanna be."

As they cuddled together, Cole mentioned, "I don't know if it's just me, but I find it sort of strange to name a memorial after a young girl who was murdered at the very site."

Renee creased her eyebrows. "You know, I never thought about it quite that fashion. But now that I do, it is kinda gloomy in a way."

"Well, at the very least, the loss of an innocent life hasn't been forgotten."

Carved into the lower stones of the ridge near the memorial's entrance was a statue of a young girl bowing her head while clutching a stuffed teddy bear in in her right hand. Inscribed below the effigy where the words "The Memsey Porter Ridge Memorial. You may not have been with us for many years, but you shall be remembered for many years to come. Your neighbors of Harpersfield."

Renee held Cole a little closer. After checking the area and comfortable that they were completely alone, they made love upon the blanket.

*****

"WHAT ARE YOU doin', Bob?" Deputy Frank Collins questioned the sheriff as they were on patrol about Harpersfield.

"What are you talkin' about, Frank?"

"You're runnin' your mouth just like Cole warned us not to do. I stopped for a cup of coffee a little while ago, and the diner was buzzin' about the FBI agent that's in town."

"I didn't say anything."

"Give me a break, sheriff. I certainly didn't say a word, so it had to come from you."

"It just pisses me off, Frank, that the FBI has somethin' cookin' here in town, and they haven't involved us. We're the law here, for cryin' out loud."

Frank hesitated and then sighed. "Yeah, it kinda has me annoyed too."

"Well, I say that we try and find out what this Cole's assignment is all about. If we can close the case before he does, we'll look great."

"Bob, we're talkin' about a highly trained FBI agent here. I hardly doubt we could match wits with him."

"Who said we have to match wits? We just have to be sneaky as alley cats."

CHAPTER 48

"**CAN WE GO** now, Pop? It's nearly dark, and we've been in the field all day," Sterling complained. He was standing in the musky and dingy living room of the Porter residence, dirt-stained and tired. Bessy was intoxicated and seated on the couch with a bottle of beer in her right palm. She paid no attention to Sterling. Carter was smoking a stout cigar while leaning back in a recliner chair.

"Did ya rats dig that irrigation ditch?"

"It's done, Pop."

"Get the hell out of here then. I'm sick and tired of hearin' the damn whinin'. Feed the goddamn dogs before you leave."

*****

"**HE HASN'T CALLED**, has he?" Dule asked. He had just stepped out of the shower and was towel drying. He grabbed a pack of Marlboro cigarettes from the nightstand next to the bed and lit one of the tobacco sticks.

Marla was at the mirror brushing her hair, her cell phone on the dresser in front of her. She and Dule were at her house preparing to go out for dinner.

"Dule, you need to concentrate more on our cases at the agency rather than what's going on with the Elite Four. Besides, Cole will call. He said he would."

Dule glanced at his watch before sliding it on his wrist. "It's after eight. If he's going to call, he'd better make it soon."

Marla bit her lip. "Have you ever had a bad feeling about something that won't go away?"

"Yeah, baby. Just before I was busted, I thought about flushing the cocaine down the toilet. Something was just telling me it was about to backfire in my face, but I didn't react to my inner thoughts, and I paid a hefty price for it."

"Do you think I should call this case off?"

Dule shuffled over to her, and from behind, he placed his hands on her shoulders, looking at her reflection in the mirror. "Marla, you know about these things better than I do. I'd like to see justice brought to this case as much as anyone else, but at what cost? Is it worth the risk? These are things you must answer for yourself and arrive at a decision. This straddling the fence is going to drive you crazy."

Marla sat her hairbrush down and sighed. "Well, after tonight, Cole only has four days left on this case. He's good, really good at what he does, but he will have to pull off a miracle to wrap this up that quickly."

"So why go through with it? Why not just terminate the case when he does call tonight?"

"I'll sense what his demeanor is when he calls." Marla turned and kissed Dule. "Get dressed and let's go to dinner. I'm famished."

*****

COLE AND RENEE sauntered inside the tavern to pick up their phoned-in order of chicken wings and potato wedges for dinner.

"Hello, Renee," Joe greeted.

"Howdy there, Joe. We're here for some takeout. Also, along with our dinner order, a twelve pack of Miller Genuine Draft, a bottle of Jesper's Blush red wine, and a fifth of Jack Daniel's please."

"Comin' right up, young lady."

Mason Turner lifted his head up from his stupor and weakly waved at Renee. She smiled at him. Cole and Renee exchanged several kisses as they waited on their order.

She glanced back at Mason and then looked to Cole. "Mason is such a gentle soul. He wouldn't harm a fly, yet the Porters torment him on a regular basis."

"The Porter types have no compassion, hon. Maybe we can bring some much-needed peace into Mason's life soon."

"I hope so. But what do you mean by us? Are we partners on this case now?" She eagerly grinned.

"We have been since the start," he replied with a wink.

"Do I get a badge?" She pouted her lips.

"Don't push the envelope," he teased.

"Here ya go, Renee. That'll be sixty dollars and seventy-one cents," Joe proclaimed while placing the items on the bar.

"You rob the people in this town, Joe," she playfully teased. Renee then reached inside her pants pocket.

"I got it," Cole offered while pulling out his wallet from his Levi's pocket. As he opened the wallet, he was sure to keep his badge away from Joe's sight, but Mason got a good look at it, and his eyes widened.

Cole handed the bills over to Joe.

"Thank ya, much, stranger. Renee, are you gonna introduce me to your boyfriend?"

Renee blushed, both at her neglecting to introduce Cole and the word *boyfriend*, though she liked the sound of it. "Sure, I'm sorry. Cole Walsh, this is Joe Skidmore."

Cole and Joe shook hands. "Nice to meet you, Cole. Workin' up at Ike's, are ya?"

Joe was a bit suave than the others in town were, so Cole hadn't noticed that Joe was aware of his FBI status.

"Yeah, I'm helping him with the season's crop."

"Well, it seems that more than just harvestin' produce is goin' on up there this time of year. You two make a fine-lookin' couple," Joe complimented.

Renee took hold of Cole's left hand. "Thank you." She beamed.

"Tell your grandpa that I said howdy now."

*****

THIRTY MINUTES LATER, Sterling, Dalton, and Murky were making their way into town. Dalton and Murky were arguing, as usual, while Sterling's thoughts drifted back to when he was fifteen.

*****

Bessy had been drunk for days on end, staying in her bedroom. Carter was in Knoxville over the past week and was due home that day. Sterling and Dalton had abducted Mary Cumberson, a pretty housewife who worked as a successful real estate agent in Webster. She and her husband Karl made their home in Waynesburg, near the border with Harpersfield. Karl was a plumber for a top-notch outfit in the Knoxville area. As far as Harpersfield's standards went, the Cumbersons were well-to-do. They resided in the priciest house in town and had expensive vehicles. They had a daughter and a son, neither older than six.

Mary was a looker, turning men's heads as she passed by, but she was a lady throughout. Many of the men in town would comment on her beauty while noting that Karl was a lucky man. Mary was five foot five, thirty-two-years old, chestnut hair, and deep green eyes. She was fit and liked to wear sundresses on the weekends, which revealed her curvy shape well. She loved her husband and never toyed back with all the flirtations she received while in downtown Waynesburg. It was all innocent gestures, until the Porters decided they had heard enough talk about Mary's beauty, and they wanted to have some fun with her.

That afternoon, Mary was running an errand in Harpersfield, a new listing of a log cabin home on the banks of the Minster River where she merely needed to place a For Sale sign on the property, though she avoided the small town whenever possible. She was planning to bring her children along with her, but at the last minute, Karl decided to take the children up to Memsey's Ridge for the afternoon so they could have some fun swimming. Mary planned to meet up with her family for a picnic lunch at Memsey's Ridge after completing her task at the cabin home.

Dalton, Sterling, and Murky were hanging out in front of Darton's Gas Station when Mary pulled her red Lexus up to the pumps. She was

wearing denim shorts that day as it was hot and humid, nearly one hundred degrees. The brothers watched as she stepped out of the car to pump her gas. Her legs were slender, smooth, and well tanned. The breeze tickled at her shoulder-length brown hair, and her casual top smoothed to her full breasts, though she was wearing a bra. Her back was to the Porters as she fueled the car while the brothers gazed at her backside. Dalton was nearing seventeen at the time and Murky about to turn fifteen.

"I say we get us some of that," Dalton indicated.

"That would be so cool," Sterling affirmed.

"I can't think of a better way to breaking in Murky. I mean, to lose your virginity to a hot piece like that would be great. Whaddya say, Murky? Want to lose your virginity to that hot bitch?" Dalton inquired.

Murky eagerly nodded.

"Well, let's do this then," Dalton confirmed.

They waited until Mary finished fueling her vehicle and then walked inside the station to pay. As she passed the boys, she nervously smiled at them. Like everyone else in the area, Mary feared the Porters.

Sterling moved like a cat to Mary's car and leaped into the back seat. He rolled off the seat and down to the floor. Dalton and Murky jumped into Dalton's old Chevy Nova. They prepared to follow Mary out of the station. Less than a mile down the road, Sterling startled Mary from the back seat of her car and put the blade of his large knife to her throat. He ordered Mary to drive up to the Porters' house.

Inside the house, they tied and duct-taped Mary's hands and feet to the bedposts and then tore off her clothing. They each took turns forcing sex with Mary, and she sobbed during the entire ordeal. After Murky, the last of the three, rolled off her, Dalton went in his parents' room to get the Polaroid camera. Bessy stirred in her drunken state and asked Dalton what he and his brothers were doing. Dalton simply told her the truth without apprehension. Bessy only stated for them to return the camera when they were done using it.

They snapped photographs of Mary, bound and naked. It was at that time that Carter came home. He was invited inside Dalton's bedroom to have his turn with Mary, which Carter took full advantage of. While Carter was on top of Mary, Bessy sauntered into the bedroom to see her husband engaging in sexual intercourse with another woman. Bessy

simply stated that she needed more beer and whiskey from the store when everyone was done with what they were doing. She then stumbled back to her own bedroom. When Carter completed having his way with Mary, they warned her that if she told anyone about the afternoon's events, that they would harm her children. They then set Mary free. She spoke of the incident to no one in order to protect her children, though it damaged her deeply.

A couple of weeks later, Karl Cumberson was mowing his front lawn when Dalton, Sterling, and Murky came driving by. Dalton parked his car on the road in front of the house and walked up to Karl. He handed Karl the explicit photos of his naked and bound wife. Dalton laughed as he shuffled back toward his car.

Karl's anger at the Porters soared as he shuffled through the photographs of Mary. He rushed at Dalton, with Sterling and Murky quickly spilling out of the car. Karl took a swing at Dalton, but missed. The brothers than roughed up Karl on his front lawn, leaving him behind in pain, bleeding from his lip and nose. Karl struggled to his feet. He ran the lawnmower over the photographs, mincing them into pieces. He then rushed inside to hold and comfort his wife.

The following day, the Cumbersons vacated their home abruptly and moved to Knoxville without telling anyone where they were headed. They put their house on the market, but it stood empty over the past nine years as no one in the immediate area could afford such an estate. Recently, Karl and Mary had reduced the price of the house, but still no interest had been forthcoming.

Mary Cumberson had come to terms with the horrible events that unfolded that afternoon in Harpersfield with the help of a professional therapist as well as her supportive husband. Since the day they abandoned their home in Harpersfield, the Cumbersons have not returned to the small town.

*****

"The day you can kick my ass, Murky, is the day that hell will freeze over," Dalton declared.

"I could if I got mad enough, Dalton. You'd better believe I could put a whoopin' on you," Murky claimed.

"Would the two of you stifle it? Man, that shit gets old. Either beat the snot out of each other, or shut the hell up!" Sterling barked.

*****

IKE, RENEE, AND Cole enjoyed their drinks as they sat on the porch of the farmhouse while the fading sun gave way to dusk.

"Where do we stand on the plan, Cole?" Ike inquired.

"I haven't given it much thought today, Ike. I'm going to think about it in the morning, and then we'll put it into action some-time tomorrow. I only have four days remaining to get this done." Suddenly, Cole's eyes widened. "Oh, damn it. I forgot to call in to Marla. If you two will excuse me, I'll be back in a bit."

Cole quickly made his way to the guesthouse where he had left his cell phone.

"I'm likin' what I'm seein' between you and Cole," Ike relayed to Renee.

"You do, Grandpa?"

"Sure, why wouldn't I? Cole's a good guy."

She saddened. "Yeah, but he's leavin' in four short days."

"Well, honey, enjoy it while he's here."

She mustered up a smile. "Okay, I will."

"Perhaps the two of you will continue on after all this is wrapped up."

"He hasn't said anythin' about that. I would like that, but I'm not goin' to push it. Do you think he cares for me?"

"I can see a glow in his eyes when he looks at you, that's for sure."

Renee exhaled a long sigh. "Perhaps he is in deep like I am, or maybe not. But I fear that he and I are searchin' for different out-comes regardin' us. I would like a lastin', lovin' relationship. He's only lookin' for somethin' casual."

"Is that what he said?"

"He was sorta clear about that."

Ike chortled.

"What, Grandpa?"

"People think they know what they want. That is, until they fall in love, and then by some sort of miracle, their goals change"—he snapped his fingers—"just like that."

"Well, I'm not gonna set myself up with any false hopes. I'll take what is offered and see if he comes to me completely."

"I think he will." Ike winked.

Inside the cabin, Cole finally got hold of Marla. "Marla, it's Cole. I'm sorry I didn't call earlier."

Marla placed her fork down on the restaurant's tabletop to concentrate on the call. "Give me an update. What's happening down there?"

"Nothing today. The Porters were not in town. I'm thinking tomorrow will produce some results."

"There you go again, Cole. I just want you reporting on Murky only. Perhaps I'm not making myself clear enough?"

Across the restaurant's table from Marla, Dule shook his head.

"Marla, I don't want to leave behind a situation where any of them can harm a hair on Renee's head."

"Oh no, Cole, the worse has taken root. This has become personal for you. You've fallen for the Stewart girl. That's it, this is over. You are to report back here to me in Philadelphia tomorrow by three in the afternoon for debriefing before you return to Cleveland."

Dule nodded in agreement.

"Marla, please listen to me. We can't jump ship now. Things have been put into motion that can't be undone. If I leave now, this entire town will be tormented."

"Three in Philly tomorrow, Cole. I don't think I need to remind you what takes place if you fail to show." Marla then abruptly ended the call.

"This isn't right," Cole grunted as he tossed his cell phone down onto the bed.

*****

MURKY, STERLING, AND Dalton made their way inside Joe's Tavern.

"A pitcher, Joe the schmo," Murky ordered before the trio sat down at the bar.

"Oh look, Mason is here." Dalton wickedly grinned. He shuffled down the bar and slid his left arm around Mason. "How's it goin', you fuckin' drunkard?"

"Please, Dalton, please leave me alone. My rheumatism is actin' up today."

"Mason, I don't really give a goddamn about you, so why would I care about your roomacrap?"

"Listen, if you let me be, I can give you boys some good inside information."

Dalton, unconvinced, chortled, "And exactly what the hell would that be?"

"That man up at Ike's place isn't who he really seems to be."

"You talkin' about Cole the mole, Mason Jar?" Murky probed. Mason nodded.

This snatched the brothers' undivided attention.

"What about him?" Sterling pressed.

"He's FBI," Mason reported.

Again, Dalton chuckled. "Yeah, right. You're a liar. This town with its worthless rumors is a damn joke."

"No...it's true. I saw his badge with my own eyes just a little while ago."

"In here?" Sterling interrogated.

"Yeah, he was here with the Stewart girl."

"What the heck do ya mean with her?" Murky sought.

"They were a-huggin' and kissin' while Joe got them their takeout." Murky scowled across the bar at Joe. "Is this so?"

Joe reluctantly nodded.

Murky became enraged and slapped the bar. "I'll kill that mole. Renee's my gal!"

"Is he FBI, Joe?" Sterling delved.

Joe again grudgingly nodded.

"Come on, we're goin' up to the Stewart farm. I have a score to settle with the mole," Murky growled.

Sterling grabbed hold of Murky's arm. "Wait, weren't you listenin'? This Cole guy is FBI."

"So?"

"So? He'll shoot you before you get within ten feet of him."

Murky raised his arms and shouted. "What the hell is the FBI doin' here?"

"I don't fuckin' know," Sterling replied. "What do you know about all this, Joe?"

Joe nervously responded, "Not much. The sheriff only knows that Cole is FBI, but he doesn't know why he's here."

"I don't give a shit who he is. I'm kickin' the hell out of that bastard." Murky asserted.

Dalton moved quickly and pinned Murky against the bar. "Damn it, Murky, listen to me. If we go stompin' up there, this FBI guy will shoot us on the spot."

"Dalton, I have to get that son of a bitch. He's stealin' my girl."

"Okay, bro, we'll get him. We just can't be foolish and rush on in. We'll set up an ambush."

*****

COLE PLOPPED DOWN on a chair on the porch.

"Why the long face?" Ike queried.

"I can't believe this, but Marla just pulled me off the case," Cole reported.

Renee's face flushed, and her eyes widened. "What?"

"Yeah, she said it's become too personal for me. She's never been comfortable with it from the start. I need to report to Philadelphia tomorrow afternoon."

"You just can't pick up and leave now. The Porters will raise havoc with me and the town," Renee fretted.

Cole raked his fingers through his hair. "I know that. I'm so sorry...I have no choice."

"No choice? So that's it? You come here and stir things up and just leave the mess for us to try to clean up?" she questioned with annoyance in her voice.

"It's not my decision. It's the way the structure of the Elite Four works."

"Well, the structure is just plain wrong!" Renee then stormed inside the farmhouse.

Ike shook his head in disgust and disappointment at Cole before he headed inside the residence as well.

*****

"I HOPE I made the right decision," Marla relayed to Dule.

He sipped on his after-dinner drink while she poked at her dessert.

"You did, baby. What else could you have done? This thing was about to blow up."

"Dule, you just don't get it. It will still ignite, but I had to pull Cole out of there and not risk exposing the existence of the Elite Four. So now, the crap will all roll downhill without a trained agent there to protect the innocent. People are going to get hurt or killed because of my decision. I probably shouldn't have gone after this case from the get-go. It had trouble written all over it."

"Marla, it serves no purpose to second-guess yourself now. You made what you felt was the right decision at the time, so leave it at that. What happens if Cole doesn't show up here tomorrow?"

"He'll show."

"Why? Just because you've spoken?" Dule scoffed.

"No…that's not all of it. It's more complicated than that."

"What then?"

She squinted. "There are some matters regarding the Elite Four that you don't need to know about, darling."

"Come on, baby, let the cat out of the bag."

"No, Dule. Speaking of cats, let's go. I want to get home and check on Tulie. She's been acting weary lately."

*****

RENEE ENTERED THE guesthouse without first knocking to find Cole lying on the bed with his packed duffel bag on the floor.

She lay down on the bed to snuggle up next to him. Cole placed his right arm around her shoulders as she rested her head upon his chest.

"I'm so sorry, gal. I apologize that I got you and your grandfather in this deep, and now I have to leave like some sort of coward."

She held him tighter. "You're no coward, Cole Walsh. You're the bravest man I ever known." After a few moments of silence, Renee reluctantly asked, "What time are you leavin' tomorrow?"

"Early. I need to get on the road to make it to Philadelphia by three in the afternoon. I wish I could stay here and finish this."

"What if you did stay?"

With a calm and direct voice, Cole replied, "I'd be a dead man walking."

Renee raised her head to look upon his face. "Are you serious?"

"I wouldn't joke about something like that. One of the codes in the Elite Four agreement deals with desertion and/or insubordination. The penalty is spelled out clearly. The other agents will hunt down the wayward agent to dispose of said agent, period."

"Why?"

"To protect the program. A rebel agent could become a talker. I agree with the protocol."

"Has it ever been put into action? The penalty phase that is."

"No...not that I know of, anyway. But make no mistake that they will carry it out."

She laid her head back down on his chest. "Then you are certainly goin' to Philadelphia tomorrow. I don't want you bein' hunted down."

"There's more."

"What is it?"

"When I pull out of here in the morning, you will never see me again. The rules forbid an agent ever contacting any persons involved with a case after that case is concluded."

"That's another stupid rule!" she snipped. "Can't you just quit the group?"

"No...nobody quits, not an option. That's considered desertion, and we already went over the results of that."

After another hush, Renee wondered, "Cole, are you goin' to miss me?"

"Of course I will. I'll never forget you, Renee."

Her eyes clouded. "And I'll never forget you."

He held her tighter.

"Can I sleep in here with you tonight?" she requested.

"I was hoping that you would."

Cole slept restlessly as Renee could find no slumber at all. She snuggled up firmer to his chest. She enjoyed the tingling sensation that surged through her body when she was in his company. She had never realized before how strongly someone could come to feel about another, how secure, peaceful, happy, and content one could arrive to be. But now, just as she was growing accustomed to feeling this enchantment, just as she was learning to love a man unconditionally, he was going away and to never return. How was she going to mend what was certain to be a broken heart? She knew deep in her soul that she would never forget Cole Walsh, and no matter what lay on the road ahead, she would never stop loving him. To her, he had become her everything. He was like a warm gentle melting of the snow come springtime, like the vapor of her breath on a cold night with the bright stars glowing in the sky above. This is what Cole Walsh had brought to her, what he had become in her life, and now that was all going away.

Renee recalled the adage that it was better to have loved and lost than to have never loved at all. But somehow that was doing little to ease her sorrow over his soon-to-be departure. Things would never be the same for her again, and for that, she was grateful. She hadn't realized how lonely she was before Cole Walsh stepped into her life and stole her heart away.

Renee listened to his heartbeat as the soothing sound eventually eased her into a peaceful sleep.

CHAPTER 49

"ANY LUCK WITH findin' out the FBI's mission here?" Jim asked Bob. The sheriff was at the diner's counter with a cup of steaming coffee before him.

"No, nothin' yet, Tiny. But I made a call to a buddy of mine with the state police. I can trust him to keep quiet while he pokes around to see what he can find out."

Macy Donalds was with her boyfriend, Paul Hartman, inside the diner.

"Why don't you take care of things here instead of goin' out on a wild-goose chase?" Macy snipped.

Bob glanced at her with confusion. "Huh? What are you talkin' about?"

"About two years ago, those three animals and their disgustin' father raped me up by Elder's Pond. I've never told anyone else, until now at this very moment, as I didn't feel I could come to you after it happened, sheriff. I knew you wouldn't do anything about it except spread the news around town like some sort of gossip machine. So again, those damn Porters get away with crime after crime. We have the felons of Harpersfield walkin' among us each day, and the best

you can do is sit in the diner drinkin' coffee. I'm scarred for life now with no hope of any sort of retribution."

"That's not so. I would have done somethin' if you would have come to me."

Paul, angered at the tragic news he had just learned, lashed out, "Oh, bullshit, Harvey."

"No…I would have done somethin'. I would have arrested them."

"Then go arrest them right now. She'll press charges, won't you?" Paul asked.

She nodded.

Bob's heart pounded as he quickly thought. "Um…I can't do that. The statute of limitations has passed. The crime happened too long ago," Bob lied.

Macy sobbed. "Well, I couldn't come to you. You're so intimidated by the Porters that you hide under a rock and let them run this town."

Bob quickly rose from his stool. "See ya tomorrow, Jim." The sheriff then shuffled rapidly out the diner's door.

"Yeah, run away from it like you always do, sheriff!" she shouted, and then she cried into the support of her boyfriend's arms.

Bob Harvey whisked the patrol car onto the road and headed for home.

*****

STERLING'S TRUCK IDLED up to the Stewarts' private drive. He then killed the engine, quietly rolling the truck to a halt near the end of the long driveway. From there, it was about two hundred yards to the farmhouse.

"Now, Murky, you follow my lead, and keep your friggin' head on straight. You got it?" Dalton instructed.

"That bastard is gonna pay for kissin' on my gal," Murky claimed.

"How do ya wanna go about this, Dalton?" Sterling inquired.

"Well, bein' that he's FBI, he's sure to be armed."

"He's stayin' in the guesthouse. I saw his boots outside the door last night," Murky disclosed, and then suddenly he blurted out,

"Damn. That's right. Renee wasn't in her bed last night, so she must have been in the guesthouse with mole. I swear, if he's fucked her, I'll cut his heart out!"

"Murky, maybe you should stay in the truck while me and Sterling kick his ass."

"No way, Dalton, I'm goin'."

"Okay then, we'll break into the guesthouse and ambush him. Ready?" Dalton asked.

"Let's do it," Sterling concurred.

The brothers quietly slid out of the truck and began trekking the remaining distance of the driveway on foot.

*****

YEN WILES WAS walking his dog before retiring for the night. Carter Porter, in a drunken state, pulled his pickup truck up to the curb next to Yen.

"Hey, Yen, come on over here," Carter called out through the truck's open window.

Yen made no movement toward Carter's truck. "Whatcha want, Carter?"

"Just come here a sec."

"Why?"

"Don't make me fetch you, Yen," Carter warned.

Reluctantly, Yen approached the vehicle with his dog leashed to his left wrist.

"How's Patti these days?"

Yen cleared his nervous throat. "Oh, she's fine. How's Bessy?"

Carter belched. "She's drunk, as usual. Got that money you owe me?"

Yen's expression became confused. "What money?"

"The five hundred dollars you owe me."

"I don't owe you any money, Carter."

"Sure you do, for services rendered. Now, cough up the money. I got bills to pay."

"Services? What services?"

"Oh, your daughter didn't tell you?"

"Aleescha? What about her? She's doesn't live in Harpersfield anymore. He and her husband Troy live up in—"

"Webster. I know exactly where she lives, Wiles."

Yen and Patti had shielded her well from the Porters as she grew up. They kept her in the house most of the time, and Patti homeschooled their daughter.

Yen swallowed. "What does Aleescha have to do with this?"

"Nothin'…yet. Show me the money, and I won't need to drive over to Webster and have my way with Aleescha. I bet she's got a fine bush between her legs." Carter wickedly grinned. "It'd be cool to screw an elementary school teacher."

"Carter, please don't harm my daughter."

Carter leaped down from his parked truck as Yen's German shepherd began to bark. "Shut the mutt up."

Yen tugged at the leash. "Quiet down now, Rocky." The dog continued to bark.

Carter placed his right hand on Yen's shoulder and gripped with force. Yen's knees bowed to the pressure. "The money. You're gonna pay me for services rendered, the services bein' that I'll let your daughter be. So do I get paid, or do I get laid?"

Yen grimaced. "Yeah…yeah, of course, you get paid. I'll have to go inside and write you a check."

"Just deposit it in my account at the bank in Waynesburg. If it's not there by tomorrow afternoon, I take a drive out to Webster."

"Please don't do that. The money will be there."

"It better be."

The dog growled and exposed its teeth to Carter. Carter released Yen from his grip, and then, using both of his oversized strong hands, he clamped the dog's muzzle shut. The German shepherd yelped in pain. Carter, with his large and heavy boot, kicked the dog in the chest area. Rocky collapsed on the sidewalk, and his body jerked as the canine grasped for air.

Carter hopped back inside his truck as Yen knelt to his pet's aid. Carter put the truck in gear and drove up on the sidewalk. Yen leaped out of the way at the last moment before Carter purposely ran the

over the dog with his truck, killing Rocky instantly. Carter laughed insanely as he sped away.

Yen yelled out in anguish, "Rocky!"

*****

MURKY SLITHERED OVER to a window of the guesthouse with Dalton and Sterling in tow. His eyes widened and his face reddened with anger as he spotted Renee on the bed in Cole's arms as the couple slept. Dalton was next to discover the situation, and he quickly covered Murky's mouth with his large left palm. He quietly pulled Murky back away from the window. Keeping Murky's mouth covered, Dalton whispered to Sterling, "Go to the barn and find a can of gas. We'll torch this place with them in it."

Murky yelled into Dalton's hand, muffling his voice. Sterling headed for the barn. Murky then broke free of the hold, and Dalton quickly motioned for him to keep his voice down.

"We're not fryin' Renee. That son of a bitch is probably forcin' her to be with him. She loves me, not him."

Dalton glanced around. "Okay, we'll set the main house on fire instead. We'll torch that. It should be one helluva bonfire."

After breaking an entry inside the barn, Sterling returned with a ten-gallon can of gasoline stored for the tractor.

With Renee's breathing rustling in his ear, Cole couldn't hear and respond to the criminal activity going on outside. The brothers quietly shuffled up to the farmhouse. Sterling saturated the porch area of the house with petrol. He then lit his Zippo lighter and tossed the entire ignition source onto the porch. "Burn, you old shiner," he chuckled as the flaming lighter plunged to the deck. The flash fire set off with a swooshing sound.

The Porters the engaged into a full sprint. The house was aged and the wooden structure very parched. The fire ignited quickly and rapidly spread. Soon, nearly the entire structure was licking with flames. The bright glow of the fire illuminated the property back into the cornfield.

The glow wakened Cole as he peered out the window near the bed. He jumped to his feet, spilling Renee to the floor.

"Holy shit!" Cole shouted as he rushed toward the front door of the guesthouse. Renee sprung to her feet. Cole caught a glimpse of the Porters on the run before they disappeared into the darkness on their jaunt down the driveway.

"Oh my god, no!" Renee cried out.

They moved quickly and came as close as they could to the fiery farmhouse, but the intense heat halted them in their tracks. Ike's bedroom filled with smoke as he slept, unaware that the house was in flames around him.

"Grandpa!" Renee screamed as loud as she could.

At the sound of her voice, Ike's eyes opened, and he immediately recognized the danger he was facing. He came to his feet in one jerked motion and opened his bedroom door. The hallway leading to the stairway was engulfed in flames.

Cole ripped Renee's shirt from her back with force, leaving only with her bra covering her breasts, and wrapped the torn garment around his nose and mouth. He attempted to inch nearer to the farmhouse, hoping the torn T-shirt would protect him from the heat and smoke. It was too intense, and Cole could not progress any farther.

Ike acknowledged that he was left with only one of two choices. Either perish in the fire, or leap out from the second-story window. He didn't hesitate to approach the open window, where he quickly jumped. His body descended and then slammed to the hard ground eighteen feet below, breaking three of his ribs. He struggled to his feet as the intense heat singed his gray hair. From out of the bellowing smoke, Ike staggered into Cole and Renee's line of sight.

"Grandpa," she whimpered before rushing to his aid. Cole joined her, and together they guided Ike away from the inferno. Cole eased Ike to the ground as Renee hurried to the guesthouse. She grabbed two hand towels and soaked them in cold water at the bathroom sink. She quickly made her way back to Cole and Ike.

Cole used one of the towels as Renee handled the other. They wiped down Ike's hands, neck, chest, and facial areas.

"I think my arm might be broken," Ike groaned. His eyes then teared over. "The house. The house is gone."

"Renee," Cole instructed, "my cell phone is on the stand in the guesthouse. Use it to call for an ambulance and the fire department."

"Okay, Cole, but they will have to come from Waynesburg, so we have to take care of him in the meantime. I'll get the first aid kit from the barn."

"Good thinking," Cole responded.

Renee darted away in a flash.

Cole glanced out toward the street and made out Sterling's pickup truck speeding away under the light of the fire. "It's going to be fine, Ike. Just lie still and try not to move around. Renee's getting help."

Ike coughed and then inhaled a deep breath. "I'm sorry I got sore with you earlier."

"It's okay, Ike, think nothing of it. Just try to save your breath for now, alright?"

Ike nodded in understanding.

Cole and Renee tended to Ike until the rescue squads arrived on the scene. Ike was then transported to a hospital in Knoxville.

*****

SHERIFF BOB HARVEY paced on his living room carpet, appalled at himself and mumbling, "You could help out that young lady, Macy Donalds, if you want to. The limitations haven't expired to still press charges on those savages. You could help her if you wanted to if you weren't so terrified. What is wrong with me? I'm the law in this town, not the Porters. But you know what happens if you rock their boat, Bob. They'll get ya for it. You'll pay dearly, very dearly. That poor girl, she must have only been fourteen when those brutes attacked her. What in the hell is the FBI doin' here? Do the feds know that I'm not doin' my job adequately? Naw, that can't be. Can it? Who am I kiddin'? I have no friend with the state police. I have no way of findin' out why this Cole Walsh is in town."

The flame from Bob's lighter trembled in his right hand as he lit a cigar.

"Yes, Mother, I know I'm a screwup, just like you always said I would be. 'Bobby boy, you're no good. You'll amount to a pile of crap just like your father did. But you'll be a bigger pile, Bobby, because you're so chubby. You came into the world whimpering, and you'll probably leave the same way. I swear if there were a home for worthless people, I'd send ya there. I hope ya prove me wrong one day, Bobby, but I doubt it very much.'"

Bob drew a lengthy drag from his cigar followed by a swig of whiskey from his glass. "Well, whatta 'bout you, Mother? I don't remember you doin' much of anything. You sat around and watched your game shows for hours on end. Then there was always that persistent rumor that you were runnin' 'round with Wridder Porter before he died. People say you started out with Wridder by givin' in to blackmail. You were protectin' your family. But Emily Gert said that you once told her that you had fallen in love with Wridder. How can anyone fall in love with a Porter? No, Mother, you weren't so righteous after all."

Suddenly the telephone sounded off. Bob snapped away from his thoughts and answered the call. "Hello?"

"Sheriff, it's Frank. I just heard on the police scanner that the Waynesburg fire and police departments are up at Ike Stewart's place."

"What?" Bob gasped. "What's goin' on? Why weren't we called?"

"Good question. I don't know why they didn't call us in. I had to hear it on the scanner. I think we'd better take a ride on up there."

"Pick me up in five minutes, deputy."

*****

THE ASHES SMOLDERED as the firefighters from Waynesburg finished off extinguishing the remains of the enormous blaze. The sole standing structure of the farmhouse was a brick chimney.

Cole and Renee sat on an old bench on the lawn while eyeing in disbelief at the ruins. Although it was a hot, muggy night, Renee trembled with chills as Cole wrapped a blanket around her.

"I can't believe it's gone. That house was in my family for five generations. Thank goodness Grandpa made it out. I wonder if perhaps he fell asleep with a lit cigar in his hand."

"This fire wasn't accidental, Renee," Cole disclosed.

"What do you mean? How do you know?"

"I spotted the Porters fleeing the scene."

Her eyes watered. "Oh my god, how long is that family goin' to torment this town and its people?"

"Are you two okay?" Webster police chief Brian Reynolds inquired. He was cruising the state route that led to Harpersfield when the emergency call came in. He drove over in the Webster patrol car to check on things.

"Yeah, just shaken a bit," Cole reported.

"What happened here?" Brian asked.

"The old man has a habit of falling asleep with a lit cigar in his hand," Cole replied.

Renee glanced awkwardly at Cole. He winked at her, signaling to go along with the incorrect explanation.

"That can be extremely dangerous. We see it from time to time. At least this time no lives were lost. You folks have a place to stay tonight?"

"Yeah, we have the guesthouse over there." She pointed out.

"Okay then, we're about ready to pull out. The fire chief will be along in the next day or two to have a look-see. You two take care."

"Thank you," Renee bid.

Brian moved back toward the flashing red-and-blue lights of his patrol car.

"Why didn't you tell him that the Porters set the fire?" she was quick to ask.

"Why? So they go arrest the Porters, and then I can't go after them?"

She brightened. "You're gonna get them?"

"You can bet your life I am."

"What about Philadelphia?"

"Renee, I was once at a crossroads to either help someone or myself, and I chose myself. I regret that decision, and I've learned from it. I'm not about to make the same mistake twice. Come tomorrow, the Porters are going to have to deal with their greatest enemy ever."

CHAPTER 50

"OH MAN, THAT place shot up in flames big time," Sterling celebrated.

The Porter trio were perched on the front porch of their house, drinking beer.

"I bet that pickled old man burned like a torch soaked in kerosene." Dalton snickered.

"Fuck that old shiner. One less obstacle between Renee and me," Murky added.

Carter's pickup truck then came bouncing up the driveway. He tossed an empty beer can out onto the lawn as he jumped from the rig.

"What the hell are ya boys up to?" Carter greeted, stepping up on the porch.

"We just torched Ike Stewart's place," Sterling disclosed.

"You did, huh? Why is that?" Carter calmly queried.

"Pop, the feds are here in Harpersfield. That shithead posin' as a farmhand up at Ike's place is an FBI agent," Dalton divulged.

"Why the hell is the FBI here?"

The three boys shrugged their shoulders in unison.

"He was layin' with my girl, Pop, so we torched the house."

Carter ribbed Murky, "You still got a hard-on for that Stewart girl, huh?"

"Oh yeah, Pop."

"Well, hell, we'll all have to do her sometime." Carter grinned.

"No, Pop…not this one, okay? I want her all to myself."

Carter glared at Murky. "Don't try to tell me, boy, who I can or can't fuck."

Murky submissively nodded.

"What should we do about the FBI?" Sterling changed the subject.

Carter lit a cigarette. "We'll take care of him. For now though, I'm goin' inside to get some pussy off your mama." Carter then headed inside the house.

After a few moments of silence, Dalton spoke up, "I got it! Why didn't I fuckin' think of it before?"

"What?" Murky quickly sought.

"Remember that time at Cletus Barrows's junkyard when he showed us how to wire a car in order to blow it up? He put on that fire suit, started that car, and it went into flames, and then he jumped out on fire and leaped into the pond. That was so cool. We could do that to this Cole's truck."

"Fry the mole! I like that idea. Good thinkin', Dalton," Murky complimented.

"Well, I am the smart one here," Dalton retorted.

Murky flipped up his middle finger, directing the gesture at his older brother.

Sterling jumped in. "First, we have to shut off the rest of the world from Harpersfield."

"What are ya talkin' about?" Dalton questioned.

"Well, if we are goin' to war with this FBI guy, we have to make sure the cavalry isn't called in."

"How the heck do we do that?" Murky quizzed.

"In the mornin', we cut the main telephone line feedin' into and out of town. Then we take a ride up to Memsey's Ridge and damage the cell phone tower there," Sterling schemed.

"Now, who's the smart one, Dalton? Looks like it's Sterling to me." Murky made a face.

This time around, Dalton was the one who saluted with his middle finger.

*****

BOB HARVEY RACED the Harpersfield patrol car up the Stewarts' driveway just minutes after the Waynesburg and Webster officials had departed. He sprung from the car nearly before it came to a complete halt. A dust cloud following the vehicle consumed him for a few moments before it dissipated.

Cole was checking the inventory of his ammo and had both his firearms out on the table inside the guesthouse when he spotted Bob and Frank stepping toward the guesthouse. Cole quickly folded a tablecloth over the weapons and ammunition.

Renee was in the next room using Cole's cell phone while speaking with the hospital in Knoxville. They informed her that Ike was doing okay, but they wanted to admit him for a few days for observation. She gathered information regarding visiting hours before she ended the call.

Bob rapped on the screen door of the guesthouse. Cole and Renee approached the door together.

"What do you want, sheriff?" Renee asked.

"What the hell happened here? Where's the house?" Bob inquired.

"It burned to the ground."

"How?"

"We think Ike fell asleep with a cigar," Cole reported.

"Why weren't we called instead of Waynesburg?" Frank sought after.

Renee retorted, "Because, deputy, we were in need of a fire truck and ambulance. Two things that Harpersfield is without."

"You still should have called us, Renee. We're here to serve and protect," Bob declared.

"That's a joke, sheriff. You two are nothing more than the Porters' puppets," Cole sounded off.

Bob softened and sighed dejectedly. "You're right. You won't get any argument from me there. Agent Walsh, I don't know why you

are here, and I realize you probably are not goin' to say what that is exactly, but I'd like to help in any way I can."

"Yeah, me too," Frank attested.

"If you guys want to help, just stay out of my way, okay?"

"Is it about the Porters?" Frank inquired.

Cole hesitated, and then looked to Renee.

She nodded her head.

"Yeah, deputy, it is. Now, I'll rid this town of the menace if you'll just leave it all to me. Okay?"

Frank and Bob eagerly agreed with a nod of their heads.

"And, sheriff, keep your damn mouth shut," Cole said firmly.

Bob raised his right palm. "Mum's the word this time. I solemnly promise, Agent Walsh."

CHAPTER 51

August 7

THE POWERFUL JAWS of a heavy-duty wire cutter (the brothers had stolen the device a few years earlier during a raid at a plumber's warehouse in Waynesburg while looking for copper piping to salvage) clamped down on the first of three telephone lines leading into Harpersfield. The cables ran along and then dropped from steel spider poles into a small block house that distributed communications into Harpersfield.

Dalton gave it great strength as the razor-sharp cutter sliced the line in half. Over a third of the landline telephones in town immediately went dead. Within minutes, the remaining two lines were severed as well, rendering all conventional telephones within Harpersfield out of working order.

"Jump back in the truck, Dalton! Let's get up to Memsey's Ridge!" Sterling shouted.

Dalton followed his brother's instructions, and soon the truck rolled along the road ahead.

"Ya got all three lines cut, right?" Murky looked at Dalton for reassurance.

"Yeah, I did. I can fuckin' count, ya know," Dalton growled.

"Then count how many times I punch that big fat head of yours," Murky bit out.

"You two assholes knock it off!" Sterling warned. "We have serious business to tend to."

The inside of the truck fell into a brief silence. After a few moments, Dalton and Murky shook hands in a mutual truce. Dalton then stared out the window of the truck and recalled a time when he was fourteen.

*****

"Pop, can I go to Elder's Pond and fish now?" Dalton inquired. He had just finished a long list of chores to do around the farm. Carter had been drinking most of the day with a woman he had brought home from one of his drunken episodes in Webster. The woman had been staying at their home over the past three days. Carter didn't explain to the boys, or to Bessy, who the woman was. It was as if she wasn't even there. She wore next to nothing with tight, short, cutoff Levi's shorts, a thin T-shirt, and was braless. She was obviously quite younger than Carter. She appeared to be about nineteen, perhaps twenty, but no older than that. She was a pretty young woman, but she looked to be spent. She seemed to have many miles on her at such a young age. She was sitting on Carter's lap on the porch sharing a beer with him. Bessy was in the house watching television. She couldn't care less about what Carter and the woman were up to.

"Mmmmmm, let me see, Dalton. Hell no," Carter growled.

The woman giggled.

"Please, Pop? The bass have been bitin' the past few days. I finished my chores."

"Ever feast your eyes on a fine pussy, Dalton?" Carter queried.

"Huh?"

"A pussy between a woman's legs," Carter explained.

The young girl playfully slapped Carter's left forearm.

Dalton's face flushed. "Sure, Pop. In the magazines you have around the house."

"So you've never seen one live and up close?" Carter persisted.

Dalton began to lick her tentatively at first, and then he attacked her area with his tongue. Her moans deepened, and she became moist between her legs. So damp, Dalton recalled, that she saturated his cheeks.

She grabbed hold of the back of the young boy's head and pushed his face deeper between her legs. Dalton was happy to oblige. She then eased herself and Dalton down onto the porch as she lay on her back and spread her legs to accommodate him. Dalton continued to stimulate her orally as she came to an orgasm. She then pulled Dalton up from between her legs, the young boy coming up on his knees. She then crawled across the porch like a cat on the prowl and helped Dalton to pull his jeans down around his ankles. She moaned and then flirtatiously grinned at the sight of his young and large erect penis. Slowly, she took his rigid erection into her mouth, and they both enjoyed the act of her oral technique upon him.

Soon, Dalton was hungry for intercourse, and he positioned her in a manner to execute the act as he recalled it from his father's adult magazines. Dalton mounted her as she guided his penis into her welcoming vagina. She bucked her hips, creating the necessary motion to make up for Dalton's inexperience. He remembered thinking that his virginity was now history. She felt so good, so warm, so wet as her walls caressed around his throbbing organ.

It didn't take Dalton long to realize he was about to ejaculate for the first time without the aid of his own hand. He began to discharge his semen inside her, and up to that day in his life, this was the greatest sensation he had ever experienced, but that would soon change.

With all the excitement and delight before him, Dalton had lost track of the whereabouts of his father.

Carter, while the act was in progress, had gone inside the house to retrieve what had become his son's worst nightmare. Just as Dalton completed ejaculating inside the woman, he heard the undeniable sound of his father's razor strap cutting through the air behind him. He had only seconds before contact to tighten his jaw and squint in preparation for the mighty strike. The strap met Dalton's bare buttocks with the sharp sound of a violent smack. Dalton's buttocks burned with pain as all the air rushed out from his body. He trembled, shook, and didn't have time to react before the second strike landed in the same area, which was now tender.

Dalton gasped for air as he rolled off the woman and onto the porch. The woman was shocked to see what was transpiring before her as she wanted to help Dalton but didn't know how. The next strike caught the boy between the shoulder blades as he struggled to his feet. Any bit of air that his lungs took in blasted out in a chilling cry. Dalton stumbled toward the steps of the porch just to have Carter kick him in the backside, sending him tumbling down the steps to the cement sidewalk below. With his pants still around his ankles, Dalton was unable to break his fall or make any effort to soften it. He crashed face-first into the cement, chipping his left front tooth. Blood oozed out from his gums and over his lips.

Carter wasn't through. "I said look at the beaver, Dalton, not screw it. You fucker, you greedy fucker, now you've soiled the bitch. You only screw when I say you screw, and always remember that I go first." Carter made a move to the stairs, ready for another attack on his son.

"No!" the woman shouted. "That's enough, you'll kill him!"

Carter then turned his attention to the woman. "Oh, what is this? You fuck 'em and now ya love 'em? What a joke. He's a fourteen-year-old boy, and you're a damn prostitute."

"I don't love him, Carter. But for Christ sakes, I have compassion for any human bein'. Can't you see he's in a lot of pain?"

Dalton took advantage of Carter's hesitation in order to pull up his pants and to step away from the porch.

Carter reared his arm back and sent the strap blistering the left side of the woman's face. The blow sent the woman back a few paces as she screamed out in pain. She then leaped from the porch as Carter was prepared to hit her again. She crashed to the ground, knocking the air out from her lungs. The blonde curly haired woman then struggled to her feet. She ran up the road, naked from the waist down, until she was out of sight. She never again returned to the Porters' residence.

*****

Sterling brought the pickup truck to an abrupt halt at the base of a cellular tower. He quickly unclipped his hunting rifle from the rear window bracket. "Grab your guns out from the back, boys, and let's do some target practicin'."

"We got our handguns with us," Dalton announced.

Over the next few minutes and dozens of rounds of ammo later, the Porters shot the tower's transformer, damaging it beyond repair. The cellular phones and radios in Harpersfield all fell silent.

The boys shouted out with a celebration over their accomplishment.

*****

"THAT SURE WAS strange," Emma relayed to Henry. They were inside their store when she sat her cell phone down on the counter.

"What's strange, Em?" he asked while keeping most of his attention on the young lady inside the store as she shopped down one of the aisles. Henry believed that every young person was a potential shoplifter, although he knew Macy Donalds well.

"The phones are what is goofy. I've been talkin' with my sister, Nancy, when the telephone on the wall went dead. So I called her back on the cell phone, and that just went all buggy. All I'm gettin' is static."

"Are you gonna buy that magazine, Macy? You know there's no readin' in the store. Either buy it or put it back," Henry pointed out.

"Yeah, okay, Mr. Gert. Sorry...I'll buy it."

"Alrighty then."

"Are you even listenin' to me, Henry?" Emma wondered.

"Yeah, Em, you said that the phone is actin' up."

"Both phones, Henry. Both phones aren't workin'. I wonder what is goin' on?"

"Well, call the phone company and see what's up," he teased.

"Very funny, Henry. You missed your callin' in life. You should've been a stand-up comedian." She made a face.

Macy then approached the counter. "How much for the magazine?"

Henry peered over the top of his eyeglasses at the cover of the magazine.

"It's six fifty. It's right there on the cover," Emma pointed out.

"I know, Mrs. Gert, but sometimes Mr. Gert gives a little discount."

Henry lowered his head into his shirt collar. He had broken a cardinal rule of his wife's, the miser.

"He does now, does he?" Emma placed her hands upon her hips. "Now, Henry, you know we have bills to pay. You just can't give the store away."

"For cryin' out loud, Em, the magazines are marked up 200 percent. We do fine. We have money that we'll never spend. We can't take it with us when we croak, ya know. We should be enjoyin' some of it anyway."

"I'm not discussin' this with you. Just sell things for what the price is marked, or I'll stop lettin' you mind the store," she warned. Emma then noticed Macy's cell phone inside her purse as the young girl fumbled for money to pay for the magazine. "Macy, will you do me a favor, honey? Can I use your phone for a minute to call my sister back to let her know I didn't hang up on her?"

"Oh, sure, Mrs. Gert. Here ya go."

Emma tried the cell phone, but it was on the brink as well. "Do any phones in this town work anymore?"

*****

"HOW ARE YA goin' about this, Cole?" Renee probed. He was seated at the small table in the guesthouse while loading his firearms. She was standing behind him, towel-drying her hair after showering.

"No more strategic plans, Renee. No more hoopla. I'm just going straight after them."

"Honey," she said while putting her arms around him, "I'm so worried. Those boys are sure to try to kill you."

"Well, that's what I'm trying to do to them."

"Won't you go to prison for murder since it won't be self-defense?"

"Nobody is going to prison." He glanced at his watch to see that it was nearly two in the afternoon. "In one hour from now, I will be a hunted man by three of the best FBI agents in the country. When I complete the destruction of the Porter brothers, I'm going to need to flee the country."

"Well then, I'm goin' with you when you flee," she was quick to respond.

He shook his head. "Oh no, you're not."

"Oh please, I want to follow you wherever you go. Cole...I...I love you."

He sat down the gun on the table and turned in his chair to face her. He could see it in her soft blue eyes, the love that she did indeed hold for him. The radiance of her skin, the mist in her stare, all told that she cared deeply for him. She was happy, yet sad that the man she just proclaimed to love would be leaving her soon.

He gave a wide smile. "Okay, we'll stay together."

They kissed with deep feeling. She glowed, and his heart raced for her.

*****

STERLING WHISKED THE truck to a halt in front of Gert's General Store.

"This fuckin' town is ours, brothers," Dalton declared. "Do whatever ya fancy. The ten Rs—rant, rave, ridicule, roar, rip, rifle, ruin, ransack, rape, and rob!"

Again, the three hooted and hollered as they spilled out from the vehicle.

Looking out the store's window, Emma gasped. "Oh my, we have some very bad company on their way inside."

Henry noticed that Macy was immediately frightened. "Quickly, sneak out the back, child."

Macy shuffled back through the store just as the bell above the front door sounded. Murky and Sterling strutted inside the store. Macy threw open the store's back door, only to come face-to-face with Dalton. Macy choked on a potential scream.

"Well, lookie here, it's the younger Donalds gal." Dalton smirked. "I haven't fucked you in a couple of years now. I could use another slice of that fine pie between your legs." He scratched his chin with the barrel of his handgun. "Yes ma'am, you have some luscious tits too, Macy."

Macy suddenly came up with a plan. She forced her voice to remain calm. "Dalton, you're the only one I want to remember from

that day in the woods. You're the only one I enjoyed bein' with. You felt so good inside me."

"Really?" he boasted.

"Oh yeah. You turned a little girl into a woman that very day. I'd love to have another go with you."

"Dalton? What the hell is holdin' you up?" Sterling called out.

"Just shut the fuck up. I'll be along in a bit."

"Well, hurry up. You're missin' all the fun in here. Murky has Henry in a headlock, and the old man's face is turnin' purple. It's so cool."

Dalton focused his attention back on Macy "So, you want my cock again, huh, bitch?"

She nodded with false enthusiasm. "Yes, badly."

He stepped to her and aggressively snatched her into his arms. He forced a kiss on her lips. She was receptive to his kiss only to get him to lower his guard a bit. Macy then reared back with her right leg, and with all the strength she could gather, she kneed him directly in the groin area.

Dalton buckled over in sudden pain and dropped his gun to the floor as she raced around him. Macy quickly rushed out the open door. He coughed and then shouted out at her, "You bitch! When I see you again, I'm gonna kill you!" It took Dalton a few moments to gather himself before he staggered into the store to join his brothers on their harangue.

*****

COLE WAS MAKING final preparations before heading into town. He secured the guns' holsters around his chest and packed extra ammunition into the pockets of his pants.

"What can I do to help while you're gone?" Renee asked.

He hesitated and then replied, "I need to talk to you about that, okay?"

She nodded.

"When you told about me the events leading up to Nate's murder, you said that it looked as though he was trying to make

it to an old fruit cellar deep in the woods to get away from the Porters, right? That he didn't make it to the cellar before the Porters assaulted him."

Again, she nodded.

"Let me ask you two things. Do you remember exactly where the fruit cellar is located?"

Renee gave a thumbs-up.

"Are you sure the Porters don't know where it's located?"

"I don't see how they would know. Why?"

He gently took hold of her right hand. "That's where we are hiding you out. We'll lock you inside the fruit cellar."

Renee's eyes widened. "What? No way, Cole, I'm not hidin' out in that old cellar. It's damp, and there are spiders down there. You're crazy if you think I'm goin' down there with all of them hairy wanderers."

"You told me that you weren't afraid of spiders," he teased with a grin.

"Well, I might have told a little white lie about that."

He chuckled. His voice remained calm and precise. "Listen to me, honey. When the bullets start to fly, those boys are going to want to retaliate. What better way to get back at me than to hunt you down and harm you? That's what they will surely do. I'm going to protect you, and there is no better way to do that other than the fruit cellar."

She was bittersweet. She was pleased to hear him refer to her as honey, but apprehensive over hiding in the fruit cellar. "Oh please, Cole, think of somethin' else, babe."

"I've thought it over several times, and the cellar is simply the best option. Anything less exposes you to extreme danger. We'll make sure that you have water, and we'll use lanterns from the barn so you'll have light. It'll only be for several hours at the most. When I've finished off the Porters, I'll come back and get you."

"What am I supposed to do if the unthinkable happens, and you can't get back to me? How will I get out of the cellar if I'm locked in?"

"You're going to have one of your grandfather's hunting rifles with you. For protection and an emergency way out, if needed. If I'm not back to you by dusk, then shoot your way out of the cellar."

*****

"PLEASE, FOR THE love of God, Murky, let go off Henry! He's not breathing!" Emma pleaded.

Murky ignored her.

"So, Emma, what do you know about the FBI agent in town?" Sterling prodded while swiping a strip of beef jerky from a large jar on the counter.

"Let go of Henry, and I'll tell you."

"No, that's not how it works, Gert. You tell us first, and then we'll think about lettin' go of Henry. By the look on Henry's face, you'd better make it quick. I don't think he'll fuckin' hang on much longer," Sterling said with a chuckle.

Emma spoke as swiftly as she could. "All I know is that he's an FBI agent posin' as a farmhand up at Ike Stewart's place."

Dalton was still taking deep breaths recovering from the shot in the groin delivered by Macy's knee.

"What's his assignment here, Emma? You seem to know everything goin' on in this goddamn town," Sterling mentioned.

"I swear to the almighty God, Sterling Porter, I do not know. Please let go of my Henry, you boys are killin' him!" she cried.

Sterling nodded at Murky, who then released Henry from the headlock.

Henry collapsed to the floor, gasping for air.

Murky then straightened his right arm and ran up and down the store's aisles, sweeping all the items from the shelves and onto the floor. Glass bottles of pickles, jelly, peanut butter, salad dressings, and cooking oils shattered upon the tiled floor.

Dalton shuffled over to Henry. "You fucker, you tried smugglin' the Donalds girl out the back." He then kicked Henry in the ribs. Henry grunted in pain.

Emma screamed.

"Shut her up, Sterling."

Sterling grabbed hold of the back of Emma's head, and then with force, he butted foreheads with her. A gash opened on Emma's forehead as she crumbled to the floor.

"Come on, we're gettin' nothin' worthwhile here. We gotta go pay the sheriff a visit," Sterling announced.

Henry was left behind and collapsed upon the floor of the store. After several minutes of gasping for much-needed air and oxygen, he was able to crawl to his injured and unconscious wife. Henry sobbed as he raked the fingers of his right hand through her gray hair. "Please wake up, Em. The Porters finally left. Please wake up and tell me everythin' is goin' to be okay."

He then laid his left ear flush to her chest to determine that she did indeed have a heartbeat. Suddenly, Henry felt Emma's left palm caressing the back of his head. He lifted his head to face her before they fell into a tight embrace and wept together.

*****

BACK IN PHILADELPHIA, Marla and Dule were seated in her kitchen as the clock on the wall designated the time with three chimes.

The room was silent for a few moments before Dule spoke up. "Cole's a no show. What now, Marla?"

Marla sighed. "Get each of the other three agents on a conference call for me, Dule."

"You got it, babe."

CHAPTER 52

STERLING, DALTON, AND Murky moved quickly across the street to inside the Harpersfield Police Station. Sheriff Bob Harvey was sitting behind his desk working a toothpick as Deputy Frank Collins was painting the brick walls of the only jail cell in town. Bob quickly rose to his feet when the Porters came crashing through the front door.

"Give us your gun now, Harvey!" Dalton demanded.

"Huh? What's this all about, boys?" Bob questioned.

Sterling marched over to Frank and pulled the deputy's handgun from its holster without resistance.

"Just stay inside the cell, Frank," Sterling instructed.

Murky pulled out his handgun. "Give up the ship, Bob the corncob, or I fill you with holes."

Bob quickly surrendered his handgun to Dalton.

"Good boy," Dalton commented. "Now, get over there in the cell with Frank."

Bob scurried into the cell.

"Give me your keys, both of ya."

They reluctantly handed over their keys.

Sterling then slammed the cell door shut, locking Harpersfield's only lawmen behind the iron bars.

After the Porter brothers hooted and howled, they stormed out of the police station to Frank and Bob's relief, but along with concern.

A shame-felt silence grew between the deputy and the sheriff.

Frank spoke up, "We are a pair of spineless cowards who do not deserve to be wearing these badges."

Bob's eyes clouded as he nodded in agreement. "I have never found the courage to stand up to the Porters, but the good Lord knows that I have tried. Once when I was a pudgy kid runnin' around Harpersfield, Carter stole my bicycle. I went home cryin', and my mother mortified me for not stickin' up for myself. My mother's opinions, though twisted at times, meant everythin' to me back then. So I set out the next day to get my bike back and to make my mother proud of me once again. I sat there in front of Gert's store for hours waitin' to see Carter and knowin' that he'd be with his brother Steadman. They were always together.

"My headstrong will to prove to my mother that I could be a man overrode my common sense that told me I was gettin' in way over my head. Well, along came Carter and Steadman ridin' double on my stolen bicycle. I stood up from the bench, cleared my throat, pumped up my courage, and then I marched right out onto Harper Street. My heart felt as though it would explode with fear as the Porter brothers approached me. I held up my right hand, signalin' for them to stop. But they didn't stop, they just kept comin', but I stood my ground like a fool. They hit me with my own bike, plowin' directly into me. I was knocked to the pavement, and the back of my head bounced off Harper Street. My world went into a spin, and I instantly had a severe headache that I wouldn't wish on my worst enemy.

"Carter and Steadman nearly lost control of the bike, but they held on somehow. I sat up and I cried, I cried hard. And they, well, they laughed. The harder I cried, the deeper they howled. A few of the townsfolk had gathered at the curbside to see what was happenin' on Harper Street. My humiliation was what was takin' place. I don't know what hurt more, my achin' head or my swallowed pride. But you know what, Frank? I wasn't afraid of them comin' back at me. I just didn't care

anymore. They could have beaten on me, and I would've just taken it. I was tired of the tortures stowed upon me by the Porters. I was tired of disappointin' my mother. I was sick and fed up with the whole damn thing. And they did come back at me. They did purposely run over my left hand with the bike, but I showed no emotion. My hand throbbed with pain, but I didn't make a move to console my discomfort.

"Then it happened. I don't know how to exactly explain it, but it was as though those ruthless punks could sense that I didn't give a hoot what they did to me anymore. I could take whatever they were goin' to dish out. I don't know if they got scared…I doubt they were scared…but they just backed off. I didn't get my bike back, but they rode off and let me be. I thought after that day that I would be immune to the Porters, that they would never tease or torment me ever again. Boy, was I ever wrong. The next day it was business as usual again as they stuffed my pants full of soil and pebbles and then lifted me into the air by my belt. I was back to bein' the pudgy kid that was defenseless, and all I could do was cry until they were through havin' their twisted fun with me.

"As I grew a bit older, I came to realize that there were two certainties in my life that were never goin' to change. I wasn't goin' to ever make my overbearin' mother proud no matter what I did, and that the Porters were never goin' to be civil. So here I am years later, the pudgy boy grown into a fat bald man still worryin' about what my mother thinks though she is now deceased, and now I'm locked up in my own jail cell by the next generation of Porters. I'm completely pathetic."

Bob shakily cleared his throat as Frank placed a supporting right hand upon his shoulder. Frank squeezed the back of Bob's neck, consoling his colleague and friend. Frank then decided that after years of silence, he would after all come clean. "Um…sheriff, you don't know the half of it…of the absolute terror that family is capable of bestowin' upon others."

Bob wiped a falling tear from his left eye. "What are you talkin' about, Frank?"

Now it was Frank's eyes that clouded up. "My grandmother told me somethin' years ago before she passed away that I have always held deep inside."

"May?" Bob inquired.

Frank nodded.

"I remember her, May Collins. She made the best chocolate cake for the bake sales that were held in front of Gert's Store."

"Yep, that was Grandma. Anyway, I never knew my grandfather, Gus. He passed when I was an infant. I was told that he had a massive heart attack while workin' the fields. I found out later that was a lie to protect my family and me. On her deathbed, May felt it was time that I knew of the secret. I was nineteen at the time, but no matter what age I would have been, no stage of maturity could have prepared me for what I was about to hear.

"It seems that my grandfather worked for Belmer Porter, but out of force and not voluntarily. He would pick up packages for Belmer when they would come in by rail. Grandpa would drive to the train station in Knoxville and deliver the box or boxes back here to Belmer. He went on two runs a month, sometimes three. Gus didn't know what was inside the boxes, and he never asked because he figured the less he knew, the better off he was. But he knew that whatever it was, it had to be illegal. Why else wouldn't Belmer pick it up himself?

"One day, as he was on his way back to deliver a box, Gus got into an accident with another car. It was a serious hit, but both drivers were okay. But the box had slid off the passenger's seat at the impact and slammed against the dashboard. Gus hadn't noticed the damage to the box and his car, and though it was gimpin' along, the car made it back here to Harpersfield. Upon delivering the box to Belmer at the Porter home, the box collapsed, spilling the contents onto the porch. Blue pills, white pills, green pills…pills of different shapes and sizes that where inside that box came rollin' on the porch from out of their broken bottles.

"They were prescription pain medication obtained illegally for sale on the streets. With that many deliveries and that many pills in each box, Belmer must have been one of the major distributors in southern Tennessee. As the pills spun, rolled, and finally came to rest on the porch, Belmer glared at Gus. Grandpa was frightened out of his wits as he bent to try to pick up the pills as quickly as he could. Belmer was fumin' and kicked Gus directly in the face.

"It would be over an hour before Gus came to. He was lyin' in the front yard of the Porter property. No one was around, so Gus struggled his way to his damaged car and got the hell out of there. He was goin' to assure Belmer that he would inform no one of the pills, but he never got the chance. That night, Belmer and his brother, Brutus, broke into my grandparent's house and took Gus with force out to the barn. Brutus knocked May unconscious with a single punch. Outside in the barn, Belmer and Brutus tied up Gus and then hung him from the rafters like a side of beef."

Frank became choked up as Bob gripped the iron bars and dumped his forehead onto the back of his hands.

Through spells of swallowing, Frank continued. "Those brutal bastards skinned my grandfather as if he were an animal. Using razor-sharp knives, they carved away his skin from the neck down." Tears rolled down Frank's cheeks. "God, I hope that he was dead before they sliced him up. May found his body several hours later, and from what I am told, she was never quite the same again after witnessing such a horrific sight. My uncle Don rushed over to console May and to cut the ropes that held my grandfather's body up in the rafters."

Bob cleared his throat. "Jesus Christ, Frank, what a thing to keep inside for so many years."

Frank sniffled. "It's been a Collins family secret for a long time. Of course, Sheriff Hughes listed the official cause of death as a farming accident. The family, the law, and the townspeople all knew to keep it all hush-hush, or they'd be the next victims of the Porters. So you see, Bob, you and I, we are pathetic cowards with handlin' the Porters, but we certainly aren't the first lawmen of Harpersfield to look the other way when it comes to the Porters."

*****

"DO WE HAVE everything?" Cole checked with Renee. The two were standing next to the barn, preparing to leave for the woods.

"Let's see, a lock and key, two large bottles of water, a roll of crackers, two lanterns, a rifle, and a small bag of bullets. Can you think of anything else, Cole?"

"I'd give you my cell phone, but it's not functioning at the moment. But here, take it in case it starts working later."

Renee inhaled a deep breath. "I guess I'm ready. Are you sure I can't take some spider spray with me?"

"You can't be spraying that stuff in the enclosed area of the cellar. You'll get sick," he replied.

"I'll just keep my eyes closed the entire time."

He kissed her gently on the left cheek as they began to head toward the timberline behind the cornfield.

*****

DULE POKED HIS head inside the kitchen. "Marla, I have them on the phone in the den."

"Thank you, honey."

Marla stepped inside the den as Dule pressed the conference call button on the desktop phone. "Barry, Janice, and Anthony, are you all still with us?" Dule inquired.

In harmony, they responded with a yes.

"Marla is here now."

Marla cleared her throat. "Hello, troops. I have some tough news. We have a wayward agent. A deserter. We all are completely studied on the action that is to be taken. You all are to drop whatever you are doing in your corner of the country and fly here to Philadelphia immediately. Understood?"

Each agent individually confirmed.

Dule then pressed the end call button. "Okay, Marla. I'm tired of being left in the dark. What is the group going to do?"

She whispered as she settled back into her large leather chair. "We are going to execute Cole Walsh."

Dule's eyes widened as he swallowed hard.

*****

COLE AND RENEE navigated the woods toward the fruit cellar. Cole realized that it was after three in the afternoon, which made him officially a hunted man.

After gathering the nerve, Renee queried, "Where do you suppose we land after this is over?"

"Well, it can't be a paradise. Those are the places where they will search first. I'm thinking Australia, at least we speak the language."

"Australia it is. Um…Cole, can we take Grandpa with us?"

He gently rubbed her upper back. "We sure can."

Renee brightened. As she strode along and stepped over a log, the small bag of ammunition tumbled out from her pocket and onto the forest floor. It went unnoticed by her and Cole.

"You're brave to be doing this, hon. To be taking on your fears and doing what needs to be accomplished. A lot of people wouldn't stare down life's troubles face-to-face like you're doing," he praised.

"No, I'm not brave, babe. I'm scared to death."

"Just because someone is frightened, doesn't mean that they're not courageous."

"I wanna share somethin' with you I've never told anyone before," she offered.

"Okay, shoot," he invited.

She cleared her throat and hesitated.

"You don't have to if you don't want to."

"No, it's not that. I'm just baskin' in the wonderful feelin' of becomin' so close to someone. To be able to talk about anythin' with someone without apprehension. To completely share everythin'."

"I agree…it does feel good."

"Okay, well, when I was nineteen, about two years ago, I witnessed somethin' I didn't respond to. It was horrible, and I was scared to death. I still feel a degree of guilt to this day that I didn't do anything to help."

"What was it?" he asked in a comforting tone.

"I was searchin' for Nate one day. He had escaped from the farm without completin' his chores. After checkin' the baseball field, I headed down to Elder's Pond. Nate would go there sometimes to fish and catch bass. I drove as far as I could into the woods and

then traveled on foot from that point. When I reached the ridge that overlooks the pond, it was there that I witnessed the horrific sight. Though the weeds were tall, and I could only see bits and pieces of her, it was obvious that the Porters were assaultin' and rapin' a girl. A bicycle lay crashed on the ground near a tree. The three Porter brothers, along with their father, had their pants pulled down. They were takin' turns on this poor girl. I could hear her weepin' from a hundred yards away. I froze. I didn't know what to do. I thought about rushin' in and tryin' to stop the madness."

"They would've raped you as well," Cole stated.

"Exactly, and I knew that. I thought the best thing to do was to let it run its tragic course, and hopefully, after they'd had their fill, they would leave the girl be and not kill her. But I couldn't slip away. I couldn't just leave that girl to those malicious animals. I was just about to run to her aid when Murky spotted me. My heart felt like it had been grabbed and squeezed by the very hand of fear. I think that was the only time in my life that I was thankful that Murky holds a torch for me. He gave me a single warnin' by pointin' to the woods behind me. He was tellin' me to flee, or they'd rape me or even worse. I could tell by the look in his cold eyes that there would be no further chances for me to get out of there with my life. I was so torn as to what to do. In complete confusion and sorrow for that girl, I turned back toward the truck and ran like the wind."

"You did the only thing you could do," Cole was quick to point out.

"Perhaps, but that doesn't make me feel any better about it."

He placed a comforting arm around her as they continued to navigate the woods.

"I cried all the way back into town. I immediately drove to the police station where I confronted Sheriff Harvey about the Porters doin' somethin' terrible out by Elder's Pond. But he simply stepped away from me like a scared rabbit. I took Grandpa and Nate with me back to the sight the followin' day. We looked around carefully to see if there was a body or perhaps a freshly dug grave. The leaves on the ground were rustled about, and there was a little bit of dried blood on the grass, but it looked as though the Porters let that poor

girl live. I'll wonder for the rest of my days who that girl between the strands of grass was." Renee's eyes watered. "I should've done somethin' more."

Cole reassured, "You did all that you could. You got out of that extremely dangerous situation, and you reported it to the police. It's not your fault that the sheriff didn't do his job. Stop being so hard on yourself. I'd be willing to bet that if that girl knew what you had done, she'd completely understand, and she would be grateful that you did what you could to help her."

Renee snuggled up tight against Cole, causing them to momentarily stumble with their walk.

A few hundred yards farther into the timber, they arrived at the well-hidden fruit cellar. All except the door to the fruit cellar lay underground.

"I guess Grandpa used to hide his moonshine down there," Renee revealed.

Cole grinned as he commented, "It was a booming business at one time. Okay, let's move these vines out of the way and open the door to this old crypt."

Within a few minutes, they gained clear access to the only door of the cellar. It took some strength, but Cole was able to pry open the large wooden door through the built-up soil in front of it. Once the soil was pushed out of the way, the door swung freely. He ignited one of the two lanterns and then entered the dark moist dwelling before Renee.

The room was cool and quiet. When the light crawled inside the room, Cole could determine that the cellar was about forty feet wide and thirty feet in depth. Shelves hung on the walls lined with old mason jars and rusted lids tied together by spiderwebs. Suddenly, three bats took to a noisy flight out the cellar.

Renee screamed out and clung to Cole.

"It's okay, hon, those were the only three."

"Are you sure?" she asked, out of breath, nervously.

He shined the light closer to the ceiling. "Yeah...there are no other flying rats." He sat down the lantern in the middle of the room and then increased the flame's intensity a bit. The room illuminated completely.

"I should have brought a sweater." She shivered.

"Here," he offered while removing his shirt, "I'll grab another shirt before I leave the farm."

She enjoyed gazing upon his muscular chest, arms, and stomach. "The insects are gonna eat you up on your way back to the farm," she concluded, accepting the shirt upon his insistence.

"I'll be fine. It's you that I'm worried about. Are you going to be okay down here?"

They placed her supplies on the dirt floor.

"I'm not crazy about it, but I'll manage. Just get back to me as soon as you can."

"I will, I promise."

They kissed before Cole moved out from inside the cellar, leaving her behind. He slowly closed the door and put the lock in place. He snapped the lock shut, trapping Renee away from the outside world.

"I love you, Agent Cole Walsh," she called out. "Be careful out there now."

CHAPTER 53

AFTER SECURING THE sheriff and deputy inside the jail cell, Murky, Dalton, and Sterling each fired bullets into the station's radio equipment, rendering it useless. Now all that Frank could think about was his wife and children at home and how he hoped to see them again. To his relief, the Porters boys shuffled out the station's door. Other than being locked up in their own jail cell, Bob and Frank were left unharmed.

Jim and Pam Tinelberg stepped outside of their diner after hearing the shots ring out from the police station across the street.

"What is it, Jim?" Pam anxiously inquired.

"I'm not sure, sweetheart. It sounded like Bob and Frank were firin' their guns. Maybe they are target shootin' out back."

"I've never heard them do that before. Perhaps I should call over there."

"Remember, Pam, the phones aren't workin'."

"Oh, that's right."

"I'll stroll on over and see what's up."

"Be careful, Jim."

Before Jim could take more than a few steps into the direction of the station, the Porter boys appeared on the street. Jim and Pam could observe that all three men were armed.

"Go back inside, Pam," Jim quickly directed.

"Oh no...God help us," she gasped as she dashed back inside the diner.

The Porters spotted Jim before he could make a move back inside the diner, and he froze with fear.

"Tiny, you son of a bitch!" Dalton shouted. The three brothers crossed the street to where Jim stood. "You fuckin' pointed a gun at us the other day. Nobody does that to the Porters!"

With all his strength, Sterling buried a punch deep into the pit of Jim's stomach. Jim doubled over with intense pain as Pam, peering out through the diner's window, screamed out. Jim was able to raise his left hand to signal Pam to remain inside the diner. However, she could no longer stand still when Dalton placed the barrel of his handgun against Jim's left temple.

Pam threw open the door of the diner. "Dalton! No! For the love of God, put the gun down! Please!"

All eyes turned to Dalton as the street fell eerily quiet.

Dalton glared at Pam for a few strange moments and then grunted, "Fuck you." He then pulled the trigger of his handgun, firing the gun and sending a bullet into Jim's head.

The shot pierced through Jim's skull and blew an exit hole a half inch in diameter out the other side of Jim's head. Blood and fragments of Jim's brain tissue painted the curb and sidewalk. Jim Tinelberg collapsed to the sidewalk where his body shook violently, his hands in a clawed formation.

Pam shrieked out a deep cry as she fell to her knees next to her husband.

"Don't mess with the Porters," Murky declared.

The brothers delivered celebratory high fives to one other. Sterling then kicked Pam in the ribs, causing her to buckle and collapse onto the sidewalk next to her Jim. Murky then grabbed a handful of her hair and smeared her face in her husband's blood that was pooled on the sidewalk.

Sterling quickly trotted to his pickup truck. He then steered the truck up on the sidewalk, nearly running over Jim and Pam. He purposely crashed the rig through the front of the diner, crushing and slinging tables and chairs along the way before plowing into the

counter, splitting the wood into large splinters. The truck came to a rest with the radiator steaming. Sterling jumped out of his truck, pumping his right fist in triumph. Dalton and Murky laughed at the destruction of the diner.

Stacy Hughes, who was in town staying with her mother after a spat with her husband, poked her head out of the laundromat to view the turmoil taking place over at the diner. She quickly ducked back inside to hide her pregnant self behind a line of clothes washers.

The brothers then made their way on foot up along Harper Street, shooting out business windows along the way. Emma and Henry Gert hunkered down behind the counter inside their general store. Fred and Merle Darton couldn't see far enough up Harper Street from their gas station to decipher exactly what was transpiring.

"Merle, go in the backroom and fetch my rifle," Fred directed.

Merle moved quicker than he had in a while to retrieve his father's firearm. He handed his father the rifle so Fred could load the clip of the weapon. They stood together near the front door of the gas station, craning their necks to gain a view as far as they could see up Harper Street.

Some ten minutes later, they distinctly heard a handgun's hammer cock behind them. Chills shot through their bodies as they feared turning around.

Sterling laughed insanely.

"Drop the gun, Fred the unmade bed," Murky demanded. "And don't even try to be brave, Merle the girl."

Without hesitation, Fred quickly tossed the rifle to the floor.

Dalton picked up the rifle and quickly unloaded the clip. He then glared at Fred Darton. "I'm only gonna ask ya one fuckin' time, Darton. Why is the FBI here?"

Fred trembled. "Please don't hurt us, Dalton. I heard that the FBI is here, but I swear to God, I don't know why."

Using Fred's own rifle, Dalton reared back and struck Fred in the mouth with the butt of the gun. The blow shattered Fred's upper dentures and fractured his jaw. Fred dropped straight back, stiff as a board, and collapsed inside the station, striking the back of his head on the cement floor that rendered him unconscious.

"Pop!" Merle shouted.

But before he could move to aid his fallen father, Sterling grabbed hold of his right arm.

"Drop your pants, Merle the girl," Murky ordered.

"What are ya doin', Murky, turnin' queer on us?" Dalton said with a smirk.

"Shut the hell up, Dalton." He then turned his attention back on Merle. "Now, drop your pants, you fat ass."

Reluctantly, Merle lowered his pants to his ankles.

"The underwear too."

Reluctantly, but knowing that he had no choice, Merle dropped his underwear.

Sterling chortled. "Look at that small little dick. What the hell are you ever gonna do with that, Merle? Any girl would laugh at ya."

Merle's eyes clouded. Merle's penis was of average size. The Porters were well above average and used those measurements as the standard.

"You damn crybaby," Dalton barked.

Murky then placed the cold steel end of his handgun's barrel flush against Merle's testicles. "Lazy fucks like you, Merle the girl, should never reproduce." With that, Murky squeezed the trigger, blasting Merle's testicles with a screaming bullet. Merle immediately passed out, falling to the floor. Blood spewed from between his legs.

"That was so cool, Murky," Dalton praised.

Murky took a bow.

"Now, that was a blow job," Sterling added.

The brothers hooted in harmony.

*****

COLE MADE ONE last inventory check of his weaponry before sliding inside his truck. He pushed the key inside the ignition and suddenly hesitated before turning over the engine. Intuition was telling him that something wasn't quite right. FBI agents called it a sixth sense that they carried around inside themselves. This feeling seemed to strengthen with experience.

He leaped from the rig to inspect beneath the truck. He observed nothing unusual but wasn't completely satisfied. He then popped open the hood of the vehicle, which proved that his hunch had paid off. A single red wire was visibly attached to the positive post on the battery by electrical tape. Cole's eyes then followed the trail of the wire, observing that it ran into the fuel filter's casing. He removed the casing to see the wire continued inside the fuel filter cartridge and into the fuel line itself. He pulled the wire out of the line to discover that it had ran all the way back to the fuel tank. He realized that if he had started the truck, it would have exploded into a ball of flame.

He ripped the wire off the battery's post and tossed it to the ground. He then quickly moved back inside the rig and started the vehicle without incident. He drove aggressively down the driveway, on a rush toward town.

*****

RENEE NERVOUSLY HELD the lantern as she looked around the fruit cellar. She spotted an old wooden milk crate against a wall and took a seat. She shivered, mostly of uneasiness rather than the coolness of the underground dwelling. It was whisper quiet within the cellar. She fidgeted a bit and then noticed an old scrapbook covered with dust inside another milk crate. She leaned forward to pick up the album. She brushed off the dust to see in her mother's handwriting the words "Jack and Beth" on the cover.

Renee opened the aged book to the first page to see more of her mother's handwriting. It went on to explain that she saved all their correspondences over the years as a reminder to her heart. The book contained love letters and photographs. Renee was fascinated as she read the letters. This was as close as she had ever felt with her deceased parents. The letters revealed that when they started seeing each other romantically, her mother was fifteen and her father nineteen. Beth's father, Renee's grandfather, Myles Cannon, who was now deceased, had forbidden Beth to see Jack. Myles felt that Jack Stewart came from a family that ran moonshine, and he didn't want Beth having any part of that.

One letter read,

My Dearest Jack,

I tried to explain to my father today that the moonshine business is now defunct, but he refused to listen. I can't bring up the subject of you without him grunting. I miss you so and hope that we can meet again soon.

In another letter, Beth wrote,

It hurts me so to talk about it, so I will write it down. Carter Porter has made me a sad young lady. He took away the very thing I wanted to give to you, Jack, my love. I wanted to save my virginity for our wedding night, but Carter stole that away. Steadman held me down while Carter had his way with me. I do not dare tell, as my father would take after them, and he would surely be harmed or even killed by the Porters. Please understand, my love, that this has changed nothing between you and me. The very day I turn eighteen, I still plan to elope with you.

Renee was furious at Carter Porter as she read portions of another letter, written by her father:

Beth, I feel your pain, and I wish I could make Carter Porter pay for what he has done to you. I love you so much, and I never want to see harm come to you. But you know that Carter and Steadman would torment me and my father, Ike. I just pray that one day God takes care of the Porters.

I love you and miss you tons,

Jack

Renee turned the page. Another letter was pasted there in her mother's penmanship:

> I'm so excited, Jack! Two more weeks until my eighteenth birthday, and then we can be together forever! I can't wait until our wedding night the day after my birthday, and I give myself to you completely. I hope I become pregnant that first night. I want to start our family right away!

Renee grinned. "You did get pregnant by Dad on your weddin' night, Mama. I'm livin' proof of that."

Renee's anger at Carter Porter for raping her mother when she was only fifteen continued to rise. This was the first time Renee had learned of it.

The book went on to reveal that eventually, Myles came around to accepting and liking Jack Stewart. There were photographs in the book of Nate and Renee when there were toddlers, and Renee giggled at the photographs of Ike when he was younger.

She closed the book and pressed it close to her heart. Renee planned to keep the album and the enclosed memories forever.

*****

"LET'S PUT TOGETHER a few bottle bombs," Sterling suggested. Dalton rushed inside the gas station and soon returned while dumping five individual liter bottles of soda. He walked the now-empty plastic bottles to the gas pumps and filled each one to about three quarters of its total capacity. Murky rounded up five shop rags and saturated them with gasoline. The dampened rags were then stuffed into the neck of the bottles.

"We have bombs!" Sterling celebrated.

Dalton then doused the fuel pumps with gasoline. As the trio moved away, Sterling ignited one of the bottle bomb's wick with his backup cigarette lighter. Murky heaved the improvised bomb toward the gas pumps. The brothers took on a full sprint away from the

station. The loaded bottle crashed into the fuel pumps. An explosion ensued, sending a fireball soaring into the air above. Most windows of the station shattered.

The sound of the explosion and the intense heat brought Fred to consciousness. He quickly rose to his feet and dragged his unconscious son away from the flames. All that he had worked for, the Darton family business of generations, was now engulfed in flames. With adrenaline pumping throughout his body, Fred was able to maneuver Merle's large frame to his pickup truck. A bit dazed but aware, Fred began the drive to the hospital in Webster.

Carter was inside the tavern talking with Joe when they heard the explosion of the station over the sounds of the jukebox.

"What the hell is that?" Joe wondered. He quickly stepped out from behind the bar as he and Carter made their way to one of the tavern's windows.

Fred Darton sped along Martin's Way, the only road leading into and out of Harpersfield. On the outskirts of town, Fred was late to discover a trap that the Porter brothers had set across the dip in the road. They devised a railroad tie pierced with sharp nails to lie across the width of the road. The tie was secured in place by cables attached to tent spikes driven into the ground next to the road. Fred had no time to apply the truck's brakes as the motor vehicle struck the railroad tie, blowing out all four tires. He struggled to maintain control of the rig until he could bring it to a halt. He sprung out from the rig to grasp that all the tires were flat.

Fred now had to travel by foot alone as he had no choice but to leave unconscious and injured Merle behind. He rushed to remove the railroad tie from the road, but then noticed that the booby trap was fixed with homemade pipe bombs. If the tie were to be moved in any uncertain manner, the pipe bombs would set off. Fred had to leave the tie in place across the road, crippling all vehicles coming in or out of Harpersfield.

He then began his quickened walk. He figured if he cut through the forest, he could make it to Highway 49 by dusk. He could then flag down a passing motorist for some help.

*****

"Wow," Joe gasped at the visible fireball. "Fred's station just exploded!"

"Yeah…it sure looks that way. That damn fat-ass boy of his probably farted." Carter laughed.

Joe shook his head. "This isn't funny, Carter. That station has been in the Darton family for many years. I hope Fred and Merle are alright." Joe then noticed that Carter was glaring at him. He had said too much and now realized it.

"Joe, you've lost your mind talkin' to me like that, you motherfucker."

"I'm so sorry, Carter. Let me fetch ya a beer." Joe attempted to step away, only to have Carter grab hold of the back of his shirt.

"Not so fast, Skidmore. Turn around."

Joe hesitated.

"Turn around!" Carter raised his voice.

Reluctantly, Joe turned to face Carter.

"Now, I'm gonna take a swing at you, Joe, to teach ya a lesson. You just stand there and take it like a man. If you duck and I need to swing again, I won't be happy about it."

Joe clinched his teeth and tightened his jaw, preparing for the strike.

Just as Carter was about to rear back his right arm, the door to the tavern crashed open. Dalton, Murky, and Sterling stormed inside the tavern, hooting and hollering.

"Hey, you're here, Pop," Dalton greeted.

Carter held up his right forefinger. "Hold on a second, boys. I have some unfinished business here." Carter then reared back and landed a solid punch to Joe's jaw.

Joe stumbled back against the bar. He shook his head, dazed.

"Now, know your place from now on, Skidmore, and get me and my strong, handsome, and rowdy sons a damn beer."

"Oooooh, that looked like it hurt, Joe the foe," Murky chuckled.

Joe stumbled behind the bar, rubbing his jaw, to deliver bottles of beer to the Porters.

"What ya boys up to?" Carter explored.

"Pop, did you hear that a fed is in town? That fucker up at the Stewarts' farm is FBI," Sterling reported.

"Yeah...you've already fuckin' told me that, nitwit. We'll have to do somethin' about that."

"We already are, Pop," Dalton disclosed. "We've booby-trapped the FBI guy's truck, cut off the phones, spiked the road, trashed the store, locked up the sheriff and his deputy, shot Tiny, beat Pam, put a lickin' on Fred, shot his boy, and blew up his station."

"I shot Merle the girl's balls off," Murky boasted.

The four Porters roared into a round of laughter.

"Sounds like my boys have been busy today. Sometimes this town needs remindin' that the Porters are in charge of things 'round here."

Sterling eagerly suggested, "Come back out with us, Pop. Have some fun rippin' this town apart."

Carter tittered. "Oh, I don't know, son. It's been many a year since I rampaged. I think my body is a little too old for that shit now."

"Come on, Pop. You can do it," Murky cheered.

After a brief hesitation, Carter blurted out, "Okay...why the hell not? Let's go for it, boys!"

The Porters then exchanged high fives.

CHAPTER 54

COLE ACCELERATED HIS truck to the dip in the road where he detected the spiked railroad tie blocking the way. He slammed on the breaks, but there wasn't sufficient distance to come to a complete stop. In near unison, the truck's tires exploded. The truck veered off the road and into a shallow ditch. The front bumper crashed into the wall of the ditch, bringing the truck to an abrupt halt.

Cole was uninjured as he climbed from the now-disabled vehicle and then up the incline to the roadside. He then spotted Fred Darton's pickup truck and quickly approached. Inside, Merle lay on the seat with a blood-soaked shop towel between his legs. Cole reached inside the open window of the truck to check and verify that Merle had an active pulse. Cole then saw thick black smoke rising from Harpersfield about six miles away. He quickly pieced the puzzle together. This was the doings of the Porters. They were rampaging through and tormenting the small town. Fred must have been rushing his son to the hospital when the vehicle's tires were damaged. Cole figured that the elder Darton probably set off on foot for help.

"Merle, if you can hear me, it's Cole Walsh. Hang in there, big guy. Your father went for help. I hate to leave you alone like this, but I need to get into town."

Merle then stirred, and his eyes opened.

Cole observed that Merle had regained consciousness. "Did you hear what I just said?" Cole asked.

Merle nodded.

"What happened to you?" Cole questioned.

In a gravelly, weak voice, Merle responded, "Murky Porter shot me."

Cole's eyes widened. "Why did he do that?"

"The Porters are destroyin' the whole town."

"I have to get into town," Cole declared.

"Are you really FBI, Cole?"

"Yeah…yes, I am, Merle."

"Good…Go get them bastards," Merle said weakly with a wink.

*****

A GREEN AND white Philadelphia taxicab pulled up to the curb in front of Marla's residence. Stepping out from the taxi was FBI and Elite Four agent Anthony Becth. After paying the driver, Anthony rang Marla's doorbell.

Soon Dule pulled the door open. "You must be Anthony?" Dule extended his right hand.

Anthony, forty-four years of age, was a bold-looking Caucasian man standing at six foot three and a fit 215 pounds. His thick hair was deep brown, as were his eyes. His complexion was scarred from severe acne during his teen years. He donned a suit and tie even when off duty and was a full-fledged agent.

His wife of twenty-four years, Margaret, was a law enforcer in her own right. She was a probate judge in the county where they resided. Margaret was completely unaware of the Elite Four. Anthony didn't feel that Margaret, being a judge, would understand or agree with the group's functions. Their children—Anthony Jr., Marissa, and Rebecca—were grown, though Marissa still lived with her parents in Gary, Indiana. Anthony Jr. and Rebecca resided in the Gary area as well.

"Who are you?" Anthony probed in his deep masculine voice.

"I'm Dule, Dule Brookside. I work with Marla at her agency."

Anthony appeared puzzled.

"I know about the group," Dule revealed. "I'm all for it, the things that the unit does, that is. You know, the missions and what they mean. Anyway, come on in."

Anthony stepped inside. "You're a tall son of a bitch, Dule."

"Yeah…I guess I am."

"Ever play any basketball?" Anthony gestured taking a basketball shot at a nearby waste basket.

"No, not really. You like sports, huh, Anthony?"

"Just baseball actually. I like my Chicago White Sox."

Dule pointed the way. "Marla is in the den."

Anthony followed Dule until they reached the destination. Anthony then strolled by Dule, and as he did, he warned, "Dule, if you ever speak of the Elite Four outside of the group, I promise, I'll kill you."

Dule had nothing to say; he only swallowed hard.

Anthony greeted Marla with a friendly hug.

She winked at Dule. "Do me a favor, honey. While you wait for the others, arrange to lease a van." She then closed the den's door in Dule's face.

*****

RENEE PACED THE cellar floor, humming several childhood songs that she could recall while attempting to keep the thoughts of bats and spiders from invading her mind. She then sat on one of the milk crates and quietly sobbed. She recalled all the stress and annoyance that Murky Porter had brought into her life.

For as long as she could remember, Murky had been there in some form or another to disrupt her existence. The earliest she could recollect was one afternoon in the autumn when her father was raking fallen leaves in the front yard of their home. She was about seven years of age and jumping into the pile of leaves as her father gathered them. The Porters' pickup truck came to a screeching halt in front of the Stewart house. A young Sterling, Dalton, and Murky leaped out from the bed

of the truck as their father plopped down from out of the cab of the pickup truck. Suddenly, the fun-filled afternoon turned to melancholy.

*****

"Why the heck do ya bother rakin' leaves, Jack?" Carter questioned. "The winds of early winter will just blow 'em all away anyway."

"Carter, I would rather you not use such foul language in front of my young daughter," Jack requested.

"Don't tell me how to talk, Stewart. I'll bust ya one in the chops." Carter then glared at Renee. "It won't be long 'til the youngin' there is ready for pluckin'. Yeah, another couple years, and she'll be growin' some hair on her pussy."

"If you ever lay a hand on my daughter, Carter, I swear I'll kill you," Jack warned.

Carter laughed wickedly. "You don't scare me, Jack." Carter then snatched the rake from Jack's hand and struck him in the chest with the handle. The forceful blow stung Jack to his heart.

"Stop hurtin' my daddy!" Renee barked.

"Shut up, little girl. Know your place," Carter growled.

"Give me a kiss," six-year-old Murky flirted with Renee.

"What? No way. You must be crazy," Renee claimed.

Jack took hold of Renee's arm and pulled her back away from Murky.

"See there, Jack? Looks like your daughter will carry a Porter baby one day. Hell, that would make us kinfolk," Carter grinned.

"I think it's safe to say that has about a snowball's chance in burnin' hell of happenin'," Jack disagreed.

Renee snuggled up to her father's lower left leg.

"Where's that pretty wife of yours today?" Carter sought.

"That's absolutely none of your business," Jack replied. Beth was up in Knoxville with Nathan. Nate's skin had been breaking out with eczema lately, so she took her son to see a dermatologist.

"I'm 'bout tired of your sassin', Jack," Carter cautioned.

"No one asked you to stop by. How about if you and your sons just move on, okay? You're upsettin' my little girl."

Carter cleared his throat. "Ah...yeah...sure, Jack."

Jack Stewart knew better than to believe that Carter had a soft spot.

"Hop back in the truck, boys," Carter directed.

Murky winked at Renee before turning back to the truck. Renee stuck her tongue out at Murky, making a statement that she was disgusted with him.

Carter revved the engine of the truck.

"Honey, I want you to run inside the house as fast as you can," Jack directed to his young daughter.

"Why, Daddy?"

"Just run, Renee. Run like the wind!"

Renee's legs tightened before she broke from her father's hold on her and leaped into a full run. She covered the distance to the house quickly, shouting back at her father, "Come on, Daddy. You run too!"

"Go inside, Renee!" Jack demanded.

She sprang through the screen door and stood inside looking through the mesh openings.

Carter backed the rear tires of his truck onto the pile of leaves that Jack had raked and punched the gas pedal to the floor. All the work that Jack had completed that afternoon was now gone as the spinning tires sprayed about the lawn with the gathered leaves. Renee watched in horror as Carter spun the truck around on the grass to face Jack. Her father took to a sprint as Carter accelerated the pickup truck. He steered the front bumper of the truck up to within inches of the running feet of Jack Stewart.

"Daddy!" Renee cried out through the screen door.

Soon, Carter had Jack pinned against a large oak tree next to the driveway. The front bumper of the now-stationary truck was pressed against Jack's thighs. The bark from the tree behind Jack pressed into the back of his legs.

It was then that Ike's pickup truck came bumping down the driveway. Ike was stopping by to see if Beth was back with Nate. Ike's eyes widened when he spotted his son pinned against the tree with Carter Porter's truck sitting idling, but ready to strike at any moment.

Ike leaped from his truck. "Carter. Please, for the love of God, don't do it," Ike pleaded.

The boys coaxed from the bed of the truck, "Go for it, Pop. Do it."

Carter grinned at Ike. "What do ya have to offer to save your son's legs?" Carter asked.

"I've got about sixty bucks on me," Ike quickly offered.

"Not good enough," Carter stated. He then advanced the truck a bit of distance, placing even more pressure on Jack's legs. Jack winced in pain.

"Okay, Carter. How about I keep ya supplied with moonshine?" Ike dealt.

"Now we are on to somethin'. You make the best shine, Ike. I want two gallons every week."

"Two? That's three hours of brewin' time. How about one? A gallon a week?"

Carter applied more pressure to the pedal. Jack called out in pain.

"Okay, Carter, okay. Two gallons it is!" Ike shouted.

Carter grinned wickedly as he finally backed his vehicle away from the tree.

Jack fell to the ground and immediately rubbed at his thighs. Renee rushed off the porch and knelt at her father's side. She hugged her father and wept. Jack's legs were deeply bruised, but not broken.

Carter, on his way out of the driveway, confirmed with Ike, "First delivery in two days, Ike." He then purposely slammed his vehicle into Ike's pickup truck, smashing out both headlights. Dalton and Sterling braced themselves for the collision, but Murky was busy gazing at Renee and didn't see it coming. He tumbled inside the bed of the truck, hitting his head on the rear of the cab, dazing him for a moment. Sterling and Dalton laughed at him.

"Shut up," Murky replied. "Or I'll hurt you, and I'll hurt you bad."

In what seemed like an eternity to the Stewarts, the Porters finally departed their property.

*****

"Damn you, Murky, and the rest of the Porters," Renee whispered to herself within the closed space of the cellar. She then shed

tears. "I've had no peace in my life because of that evil family. There must be justice somehow. If not by man-made laws, then by God's hand it shall be. I can't believe that demons like them can continue to torment and kill and get away with it. I refuse to believe that they will never pay for all that they have done to my family and to the kind people of this town. Go get them, Cole, and make things right, my love."

CHAPTER 55

THE PORTER BROTHERS were joined by their father as they stepped outside the tavern.

"Might as well burn down Joe's Place on our way," Carter suggested.

Dalton ignited one of the rag wicks before heaving the bottle bomb through a tavern window. The bottle crashed against the bar, splattering ignited gasoline some twenty feet in all directions. The bar and the walls immediately ignited in flames.

Joe desperately fought the blaze with a bar towel, but soon he lost the battle altogether. His shirt caught fire, and he bellowed out in pain as he rushed to the sink. After putting out the flaming material, Joe had little time to escape out the rear door of his tavern.

Within minutes, he watched in despair from the rear parking lot as the entire tavern was engulfed in a firestorm.

*****

Carter pulled his pickup truck up to a small door at the rear of the Porters' barn. On the cab's bench seat next to Carter was Sterling, and to the right of the eldest brother, Murky was seated. Dalton rode in the bed of the truck. The father and trio of brothers leaped from

the vehicle and quickly approached the door, which was secured with a heavy-duty padlock.

After fumbling with his key ring, Dalton zeroed in on the needed key and promptly unlocked the door. As Sterling swung open the door, he proclaimed, "The supply room is now open for business, Porter men. Select all you want and heave it onto the truck. It's lock and load time, my fellow soldiers. Leave nothin' behind now. We go back into town, fully equipped with weapons and a bad attitude." He grunted.

Lining the floor and walls of the secret storage facility was an array of weaponry the brothers had purchased and accumulated from the black market over the past three years and more. The arsenal included a cache of assault rifles, hand grenades, some four individually wrapped bundles of dynamite consisting of four powerful sticks each, and other assorted artillery. Most weapons, ammunition, and explosives were that of potent military grade. They were all extremely expensive on the illegal bazaar, but money was virtually no object for the Porters. And what wasn't purchased at a shocking elevated price was simply forcefully taken by the brothers using intimidation.

Within ten minutes, the bed of Carter's truck was nearly filled with weapons.

After gathering their arsenal, the Porters then continued their tirade along Harper Street. They blitz-bombed Gert's General Store, causing Henry and Emma to flee their beloved establishment, which was now engulfed in flames. Next was Tiny's Diner, where Pam had managed to drag her severely injured husband inside where she thought it would be safe. The flaming bottle bounced off Sterling's wrecked pickup truck and then slid beyond the counter. It tumbled across the floor inside the kitchen area and crashed into the stove. A vast grease fire ensued, and in less than a minute's time, the kitchen was now lost.

Pam attempted to clear herself and Jim out from the diner, but she was running out of time as the flames began to lick outside the kitchen and into the dining area. She realized deep down inside that Jim had been dead for nearly an hour now, but it had taken her this

long to finally accept the inevitable. With tears in her eyes, she kissed Jim on his forehead and then rushed out the rear door of the diner with the flames shooting at her. She could only tumble to the ground and cry in the tall grass and weeds behind the diner as her husband's body was incinerated inside the burning diner.

The Porters then unanimously decided that the police station was the place for their final bottle bomb. Bob and Frank were sure to perish while locked inside the cell. Sterling ignited the missile, and before Murky flung it through the large front window, Dalton, using his handgun, shot at the front window, shattering it and allowing the bomb's intended path of travel an unobstructed course.

Bob and Frank watched in horror as the flaming concoction crashed against a wall inside the station. Within moments, the room before them was in flames, and the large oak desk, the desk of four generations of sheriffs, was merely reduced to firewood. Bob panicked and began to tug and pull at the iron bars. The cell was aged, and the bars had developed some loose play in the lock mechanism over the years.

At first, Frank felt that the effort was hopeless, but then he slowly noticed that Bob was making some headway with the lock. Frank put his strength into the bars along with Bob, and together, they eventually were able to disengage the locked cell's door. They threw the door open and quickly navigated their way through the smoke and flares of fire. Bob led the way as they bolted out the front door of the station, only to be met by the Porters' gunfire.

Bob was struck several times while Frank ducked back inside the station. He fought his way to the rear of the station; his lungs filled with smoke as his hair and uniformed were singed. He staggered out the back door and stumbled to the ground a safe distance from the burning building.

Bob gasped for his last breaths. He mumbled, "You were wrong, Mother, I'm not worthless. I did lots of good for the people in this community. I just couldn't get over my fear of the Porters. God, please forgive me and take me into Your divine kingdom."

Sheriff Bob Harvey's life then expired in front of the police station as the burning building slowly collapsed behind his deceased body.

*****

"I'M HAPPY TO see the three of you all have made it." Marla welcomed the trio of agents. She paced before Barry, Janice, and Anthony in the living room of her abode. Dule stood ready near the front door. "We have a van out front waiting. Dule will drive us down to Harpersfield, Tennessee, as quickly as possible. I will go over the details with you during the trip, but for now, let's move it. So, everyone, let's jump into the van and get on the road."

*****

COLE MOVED AS quickly as he could on his march along Martin's Way. As he headed nearer to town, the clouds of smoke billowing out from Harpersfield thickened. He was full of adrenaline, but also fear ran through his veins. He recalled apprehending a serial killer in Cleveland a few years prior.

Agent Cole Walsh was required by the FBI to give a speech at a new recruits function in Baltimore, Maryland. Cole didn't want to deliver a dialogue, but there was no way out of it. The agency even supplied the topic: "The Capture of Randall Hern."

Cole cleared his throat behind the microphone before beginning his speech. "Randall Hern was a big man. He stood at six foot eight and weighed nearly 350 pounds. But if you looked at the child-like facial features of Randall Hern, you would think that he was nothing more than a large teddy bear. Randall Hern was no teddy bear. His eyes could turn shallow and cold as a shark's. Randall was appropriately named the Midwest City Killer. In a period spanning nearly seven years, he committed a series of gruesome homicides in the cities of Detroit, Pittsburgh, Cleveland, Buffalo, and New York. It was difficult to project in which of the five cities Randall would strike next.

"His pattern was erratic, only making sense to him. Randall would cut the heart out of his victims after killing them. He would then snap a photograph of the removed organ. A trophy, if you will." Cole sipped from his glass of water. The group of cadets looked to one another in shock over the beginning of the account regarding Randall Hern.

"Thanks to a lucky break in the case, Randall was spotted staying in a run-down motel on the outskirts of Cleveland, a mere nine miles from my apartment. It was me, along with two other agents, who were assigned to apprehend Randall Hern. To say that the other agents and I were frightened would be an understatement. This killer realized that he faced the electric chair if apprehended, so he wasn't going to surrender quietly. We entered Randall's motel room through an opened back window, and immediately, we were met with a stench that watered our eyes and made us want to vomit. A television was blasting away in the other room with an episode of the *I Love Lucy* show."

Again, Cole sipped from his glass of water.

"The other two agents flanked me as I slowly stepped along inside the motel room. I spotted the back of Randall's head as he sat in a chair in front of the television set. I held my handgun tight in my hands as I inched closer to his seated position. Agent Tom Narrows circled to my left as we slowly approached Randall." Again, Cole tasted his water. "Tom and I arrived at Randall's left side with our firearms at full draw. Unbeknown to us, Randall was at full draw as well. He had a handgun in each hand in his lap, one pointing at me and the other at Tom. When mine and Randall's eyes met, there was a feeling inside of me that I still find problematic to explain to this day. It was if my internal organs were being squeezed by a vise. Randall's eyes had a way of burning right through you. Before we could react, Randall's face grew with an evil grin, and he fired his weapons. Tom was struck in the chest, and a bullet tore through my upper left arm. I leaped back, and Tom crumbled to the floor. Now, sometimes you don't know how a young FBI agent will react until it's in the heat of the moment. Agent Donnie Slade, our backup behind the chair, panicked. He froze and could not get off a shot. I rolled

behind the chair just as Randall was about to stand up. I squeezed my trigger with all my strength, repeatedly filling the back of that chair with bullet holes. There was a hesitation that seemed to last forever before Randall finally spilled forward and onto the floor. Although I put four bullets into Randall Hern, he made it through surgery. Agent Tom Narrows died the following day, leaving behind a wife and two children. Agent Donnie Slade, in due course, resigned from the force. Randall Hern was sentenced to death row at the Ohio State Penitentiary, where he still awaits his date with the electric chair."

*****

MASON TURNER STUMBLED, frightened and intoxicated along Harper Street. The town around him was in disarray and on fire.

"Gotta bead on him?" Dalton checked with Sterling. The quartet of Porters were across the street from Mason. Sterling was leaning against a lamppost, peering through the scope of his hunting rifle at Mason.

"The crosshairs are on his head," Sterling reported.

"Fuckin' do it, bro," Murky urged.

Sterling then squeezed the trigger. The shot rang out as the bullet struck Mason in his temple. Blood splattered the sidewalk as well as Mason's shoe tops. Mason's body swayed momentarily, and he then staggered a few steps before buckling facedown to the sidewalk.

The brothers bellowed out in harmony.

"Wow, that was awesome!" Dalton howled.

"Mason probably shit himself before he folded up." Carter laughed. "Come on, boys. I wanna go get that Yen Wiles. We'll beat the hell out of him and then hump Patti."

"She's an old woman, Pop," Dalton pointed out. "I don't wanna screw her, yuck."

Carter threw his right arm around Dalton's shoulders. "Son, you don't know how good a screw an old woman can be. They want it bad. Patti's fat, but pretty for her age. Pussy is pussy, it all feels the same on the inside. Her eager beaver will swallow up your cock whole, like a vacuum cleaner." Carter sniggered.

"Hell, if it's gotta cunt, I'll do it," Sterling sneered.

The foursome then ducked back inside the pickup truck to head down through an alley on their way to the Wiles household.

*****

COLE ARRIVED IN town from behind the charred remains of Tiny's Diner. He spotted Pam Tinelberg sitting in the tall grass staring aimlessly into space. She was disheveled with ash and soot painted upon her skin and clothing.

"Pam?" Cole gently called out.

She did not immediately respond.

"Pam, are you okay?"

She then looked up at Cole with an emptiness to her expression. "Jim is dead. The Porters killed him, and then they burned down the diner."

"Pam, I need you to move away from the area. The Porters could come back, and they'll kill you next. Do you know of anywhere that you could hide out?"

She shook her head no.

"I'll help her," Stacy Hughes volunteered as she stealthily approached.

Cole knelt next to Pam. "Pam, Stacy here is going to help move you to a safer place, okay?"

Pam slowly nodded. Stacy took hold of Pam's hand and helped her to her feet. "I know where to take her, Cole. There is an old mine shaft behind the feedstore. There are others hiding out there as well."

"Good. If you come across anyone else along the way, take them to the mine as well."

Stacy then guided Pam in the direction of the feedstore.

Cole stepped out onto Harper Street to view a town in ruins. He quickly looked to every corner and rooftop of the few buildings that were left standing. He then spotted Sterling's smoldering truck inside the coals of the diner, figuring the brothers might be on foot. He pulled one of his handguns from its holster and began to slowly stride along Harper Street.

*****

IT WAS DUSK when Renee called out for Cole, only to receive no response. She decided to load the rifle to shoot her way out of the cellar's locked door. She reached for the small bag of ammunition in her pocket, only to discover it was missing. Renee figured that the bullets must be inside her bag of supplies. After a thorough search of her supplies, the small bag of shells was nowhere to be found.

Renee began to panic. Her breaths shortened as she swung the lantern around the confines of the cellar frantically looking for the bullets. In a last-ditch effort, she checked the chamber of the rifle, hoping that the weapon was loaded. It was not. She held back anxious tears as she forced her body against the door. The door was sturdy, motionless, and locked securely from the outside. She could not get the door to budge.

"Cole!" she shrieked.

*****

"PSSST....OVER HERE," Cole heard a frail old voice call out. He squinted through the fading sunlight of the evening to perceive Henry Gert waving him over to a storage shed behind where the general store once stood. Cole made his way over to Henry. "It's my Emma. She's injured with a good gash on her head. She's inside the shed." Henry pointed toward the small shack.

Cole entered the storage shed and saw Emma lying on the floor with a blanket spread on her. A makeshift compress was on her forehead spotted with blood.

Cole knelt next to Emma. "It's going to be okay, Mrs. Gert." Cole propped up her neck and placed a small cardboard box beneath her head. "You'll want to keep your head elevated."

In a weak voice, she asked, "Are you really FBI?"

"Yes...yes, I am."

"Please...please tell me why you are here."

"You'd better tell her, Cole, or she'll burst at the seams," Henry explained.

"I'm here to follow up on the murder of Nathan Stewart."

"I knew it," Henry blurted out.

"Why? What can be done about poor Nate at this point?" she pondered.

"I'm here to even the score with Murky Porter. I'm adding his brothers to the list now. Might as well throw in the old man while we're at it."

"That's not what the FBI normally does. I mean, I agree with it and all, but that's bein' like a vigilante."

"Hush now, Mrs. Gert. You need to conserve your energy," Cole advised. He then turned his attention to Henry. "She needs a doctor, but there is no way out of town or to get help here at this time. The gash is fairly deep, but thankfully, it appears as if it's through bleeding. Keep her warm, elevate her head, and maintain her talking, okay? I'll get back to you as soon as I can."

Henry nodded. "Thank you, Cole. And go get them bastards."

*****

STERLING CRASHED THROUGH Yen and Patti's front door. Unfortunately for the Wiles family, their daughter Aleescha and her husband, Troy Jacobs, were visiting from Webster. The foursome had been looking out the bay window at all the smoke billowing up from town when Sterling invaded the home. They startled at the intrusion. Sterling stood back to his feet while Murky, Dalton, and Carter entered through the now-damaged door.

"Oh my god, have mercy," Patti gasped before placing her hands over her mouth. Yen swallowed hard, and Aleescha began to tremble. Troy grew up near Knoxville, so he wasn't fully aware of who the Porters were or what they were capable of, though he had heard his share of the tales surrounding them.

"Your God isn't gonna help ya, Patti." Carter insanely grinned. "Take your clothes off."

"I get the daughter first, she's fuckin' pretty," Dalton bid. He then glared at Aleescha. "You get your clothes off too."

Yen and Patti's only child, Aleescha, was forty-four but looked no older than thirty, and she resided in Webster with her husband Troy Jacobs. Aleescha was an elementary school teacher and Troy an auto mechanic. Troy had recently found out that he was infertile; this explained why that after years of trying, they had not conceived a child. They were now considering adoption.

Aleescha was an attractive woman and full of zest. Her brunette hair she wore short at mid collar. Her green eyes rested below her rather thick eyebrows, but the look worked for her. She sported thin wired eyeglasses, and though she owned several pairs of contact lenses, she rarely utilized them. Her jawline was sleek and her teeth perfectly aligned thanks to a set of braces during her teens. Her build was slim and her breasts of average size. Aleescha had always appeared younger than her actual age.

Her husband, Troy, was an average-sized man of forty-six years old. A victim of male pattern baldness, only scant strands of hair remained on the crown of his scalp. The light brown hair that remained robust on the sides and rear of his head he allowed to grow rather long in length and unkept. Patti found this appearance to be unattractive and appalling. She felt that her son-in-law could improve his look by simply shaving his entire scalp area clean and smooth. His nose was large and his chin round. At times, Troy could be a bit outspoken and offensive.

Yen and Patti had shielded Aleescha well from the Porters as she grew up. They kept her in the house most of the time, and Patti homeschooled their daughter.

The women hesitated.

Sterling reared back and landed a hard punch to Yen's mouth, splitting Yen's upper lip. Yen shrieked out in pain.

"Okay, okay! Please don't assault my father any further," Aleescha pled. She then reached up and began to unbutton her blouse.

"What the hell are you doin', honey?" Troy questioned in confusion.

"I'm sorry, Troy, but I have to give myself to them, or they'll continue to assault my father."

She removed her blouse and then went to work loosening her skirt. Patti was stymied with fear and had not removed any articles of clothing. Carter then kicked Yen in the groin. Yen doubled over in agony. "Let's get with it, Patti," Carter warned.

With trembling hands, Patti commenced to disrobing. Yen was spitting up blood and stumbled back toward the bathroom.

As Aleescha stood clad in only her panties and bra, an unexpected stimulation began to override her nervousness. Her heart began to race with sexual awareness and excitement. The Porter men's complete attention was now on her every move. Their eyes eagerly waited in anticipation for the last of her attire to drop to the floor. They were nearly panting like wild dogs who had discovered a bitch in heat. She could see that Sterling had an erection by the growing bulge in his Levi's.

Other than Troy, Aleescha hadn't experienced sex with any other man. She eyed Dalton and smiled wide. She had always secretly found him to be handsome. With trembling but eager hands, she gained a grip on her bra. She unhooked the undergarment and then allowed it to fall over her breasts and fall to the floor. Aleescha's breasts were firm, milky white, and her erect nipples were of a soft pink. In a planned action, though she delivered a weak effort to make it appear innocent, she folded her arms to her chest as if to cover her exposed breasts, bringing her breasts tightly together. This caused her erect nipples to point directly at the Porter men.

They expressed their appreciation and excitement over the show Aleescha was presenting to them by egging her along.

Aleescha's upbringing was sheltered, which could be considered a foremost understatement. Yen and Patti were extremely overprotective of their daughter during her young years. The Wiles refused to allow their offspring and only child to attend public schools in the area. Her parents didn't want her in the vicinity of the Porter brothers or any other boys, for that matter. For this reason, The Wiles stretched their budget with Pattie attending classes to train as a private tutor for Aleescha's homeschooling. The young girl was never permitted to visit any friends at a friend's house, but really didn't matter at all seeing that the young girl was so isolated, the thought of making

a friend or two was all but impossible. The only "friend" Aleescha was able to claim was Anita Maxwell, who resided in Waynesburg. However, claiming Anita as simply a friend wasn't completely clear as Anita was the daughter of Dale and Helena Maxwell. Dale was the older brother of the former Patti Maxwell before she formally became a Wiles. This made Anita and Aleescha first cousins.

Aleescha spent countless days on end, and on occasion weeks at a time, without another child in her company. She would pass the time playing with her Barbie dolls, coloring books, playing checkers against herself, flipping through TV channels while using the remote until her thumb ached, walking the dog until the canine's tongue outlagged his tail, talking on her toy phone (she wasn't permitted to speak on a real phone unless under direct supervision of her parents), kicking a rusty soup can up and down the driveway, throwing a tea party for her stuffed animals, countless hours swaying her legs on her bed while staring blankly up at her bedroom ceiling, sleeping away sunny summer afternoons, and pacing the floor during cold winter nights. She had never attended a county fair, had no clue to what the inside of a movie theater looked like, no homecoming dance, and prom was out of the question. She often wondered how soda or coffee tasted, how did a boy and a girl become a couple, what it was like to stay up all night long at a pajama party, what it was like to have a friend call you on the telephone, if eating in a restaurant the same as dinner at home, how long were the aisles inside a grocery store, how many seats were in a school bus, did everyone talk to themselves at times, did all mail deliveries take place at the same exact time, what did delivered pizza look like. When she first had her period, she frantically wondered why she was bleeding from her vagina. Was she dying? Why was her chest expanding? Why was she told today that she would be going off to college in Knoxville soon? Could she take her Barbies along? Will she have a real phone? What about a driver's license? Will there be space in her dorm room for Darla (her imaginary friend since she turned nine)? The first thing she was going to do in college was to order delivered pizza.

Even though Aleescha felt robbed of her childhood, cheated as a teenager, and left clueless as an adult, she still loved her parents

dearly. She understood their misguided protection to safeguard their daughter from negative outside influences, but at the same time, they made their daughter a prisoner of sorts.

Aleescha was extremely intelligent to the books, but exceedingly dumbfounded to the world around her and was socially underdeveloped. As she entered her midforties, limitations and restrictions were a complete turnoff for her, and the driving desires to live footloose and fancy-free were like bait to a hungry fish—simply irresistible.

The majority of Harpersfield citizens were completely unaware that Yen and Patti had even conceived a child. On this day, however, Aleescha would make her mark upon the small town.

"Go for it, girl," Murky cheered and whistled.

"Yeah, have some fun with it. You've got me rock hard," Sterling admitted.

Aleescha began to sway her shoulders and her hips. She dropped her arms from her chest, allowing her breasts to bounce firmly and free of restriction. She ran her fingertips over her firm stomach and licked her lips, slowly running her tongue across her mauve lipstick. She gained a grip on the top of her maroon laced panties. Without speaking a word, the three Porter brothers anxiously nodded in harmony. Aleescha soothed at their impatience and excitement over her body. She then eased her panties over her hips. She turned until her back was facing the Porter men, and she bent at her waist, keeping her smooth, soft legs rigid. As she stooped, she lowered her panties down along her legs.

With the undergarment now down around her ankles, Aleescha remained in the vulnerable position for the Porters' pleasurable view. She was as excited as they were as they took in the sight that she was offering them. After nearly a full minute in that position, Aleescha then stood straight up and turned to face the men. Aleescha exposed her nude body completely before the Porters. They expressed a celebration with high fives for each other while gazing at Aleescha and the sight of her beautiful nakedness. Her vagina became increasingly lubricated with her readiness.

Her body was a most inviting sight for the Porters, unexpected as well. Aleescha's physique was more beautiful than they could have

ever imagined. Aleescha was forced to remain home for most of her upbringing, and her parents insisted that she wear oversized clothing. Aleescha had hidden away such a fine physique, and the Porters were now enjoying the enticing show.

Strangely enough, Aleescha was finding herself enjoying this situation as much as they were; the unusual excitement of the conditions had stimulated her desire to have sex with the Porter men, especially Dalton. Her level of eagerness soared to a height that caused her to nearly have an orgasm while merely standing in front of her captivated audience. Troy was angered that Aleescha was not resisting the Porters.

"Look at the gorgeous beaver on her," Murky admired. The three were appreciative of her pubic region.

"Wow, ya got a fantastic-lookin' pussy, Aleescha," Dalton complimented. Those words coming from Dalton caused her to swallow with excitement.

"Nice tits too," Sterling added.

The blunt talk about her most personal areas increased Aleescha's fire blazing from within. She had always been a free spirit sexually, but Troy was conservative between the sheets. She had kept her fantasies and desires hidden from him in fear that he wouldn't understand. She would have liked to have engaged into a spicy bedroom relationship with her husband, such as role-playing, viewing pornographic videos, and even possibly joining a nudist colony. Even partner swapping occasionally wouldn't be completely out of the question for her. However, this was all activity beyond Troy's realm of thought, leaving Aleescha frustrated and unsatisfied with her sex life. She often masturbated using a vibrator at times when she was home and alone. She had the sexual device hidden well to be certain that Troy never discovered it. He simply wouldn't comprehend the need for such a tool. She had never strayed on Troy, though there had been opportunities for her to engage in an affair.

Aleescha did, however, relax nude in a hot tub with her boss at one time while on a business trip. Aleescha and the principal of the school where she taught, Andrew Vermon, were attending a three-day seminar together in Indianapolis. The seminar dealt with the

topic of early childhood education. On the second night of their stay at a lavish hotel in downtown Indianapolis, Aleescha accepted the friendly invitation from her boss for a dinner date. They ate at a fine restaurant as Aleescha drank over the amount of her usual share of wine. Her head became light, and her mood, unexpectedly, grew with sexual excitement, wishing then that Troy were there with her. At the very least, he could satisfy her enough that she could drift off to sleep. But Troy was at home some five hundred miles away as well as her stashed vibrator.

Back at her hotel room, Andrew invited himself in. Aleescha thought nothing of it as Andrew was her supervisor and happily married to his wife, Ruby. Andrew was eighteen years older than Aleescha. Andrew talked Aleescha into another glass of wine from a bottle delivered by room service. As the alcohol consumed her even more, Andrew mentioned that the hot tub in his room was not functioning properly, but the hot tub in her room was working just fine. After another glass of wine, Andrew smooth-talked his way into convincing Aleescha that they should get into the hot tub in her room together, stating that it was for relaxation purposes only and it would be kept at a professional level.

When the two stepped out of their clothing, the appreciation of the sight of her nude body was evident on Andrew's eager facial expression. Although Aleescha did not find Andrew to be an attractive man, displaying her body before him excited her. The very warm water in the hot tub caressed her nudity, and her alcohol-induced enthusiasm nurtured. After another round of smooth talk, Andrew was soon kissing Aleescha.

When he broke from their kiss and began to stimulate her nipples with his mouth and tongue, Aleescha knew she had to stop it right then and there. If she wouldn't have brought it to a halt at that point, it would have eventually led to sexual intercourse. She fended against Andrew's advances and soon was out of the hot tub and throwing on her robe. She covered her body slowly, allowing Andrew one last gaze at her. She politely asked Andrew to leave her room. The next morning, she played as if she hadn't recalled the events of the night before. Andrew never mentioned it as well. Aleescha real-

ized before that night that she had exhibitionist tendencies, and that evening merely confirmed it.

When she was seventeen, Yen and Patti hired a duo of carpenters from Webster to remodel their kitchen. One morning, while Yen and Patti were busy running errands in Waynesburg, Aleescha put her plan into motion. She was surprised at herself that she gathered enough courage to carry out her strategy, but her excitement was the driving tool. With her heart pounding, she descended the stairs wearing only a Betty Boop T-shirt that barely extended below her buttocks.

Her minimal attire grabbed the attention of the two carpenters immediately. She figured one of the carpenters to be in his forties and the other in his fifties. Her exhibitionist fire within was burning hot that morning. She presented an innocent smile as a greeting for the men. She then removed a carton of orange juice from the refrigerator and sat on the counter. Then with a strategic maneuver, she reached up the cabinet to bring down a cup for the juice. In doing so, the T-shirt lifted along with her arms, exposing her naked buttocks to the carpenters. She then acted as though she was deciding on which cup to take, allowing the carpenters to gaze at her perfectly shaped buttocks for nearly a full minute. She then brought down a chosen goblet. To the men's disappointment, her shirt lowered while covering her backside once again.

However, Aleescha's show was not completed yet. In another calculated move, Aleescha purposely dropped the cup on the kitchen floor. She bent at the waist to retrieve the mug. Again, her T-shirt reacted and left her backside exposed. However, in this position, more than Aleescha's buttocks was on display for the two men to view. Her vaginal lips were in plain sight for the carpenters to gaze upon, less than three feet in front of them as they were on their knees on the floor placing tiles.

Aleescha was fully aware of what she was exposing to the remodelers. She fumbled with the cup twice before finally picking it up. She then poured the juice. Before heading back up the stairs, she quickly glanced at the men. She caught the two carpenters gazing at her before they snapped their heads away while attempting to get away with their gawking. Aleescha grinned inside as she could see both

men had an erection beneath their pants. She ascended the stairs and locked her bedroom door behind her.

She realized that the men enjoyed the view of her immensely, and they would surely remember it for years to come. They would certainly tell their buddies all about it. Aleescha powered up her stereo to drown out any potential sounds coming from her bedroom and then quickly removed her T-shirt. She plopped her naked body down on her bed. She spread her legs and cupped her vagina with her right hand and fingers. She masturbated for nearly twenty minutes, bringing herself to an orgasm on two separate occasions. It was that morning when she acknowledged that she was truly an exhibitionist. It went beyond only the show, however. She recognized at that very moment if the carpenters would have entered her bedroom, she would have had sexual contact with them. She was turned on that intensely. That was why she was sure to lock the door. It was her way of preventing the events of that morning from going too far. She simply didn't trust herself.

The carpenters finished up the remodeling project over the next few days. Aleescha avoided them after that morning, mostly to protect herself from herself.

"You're not touchin' my wife, you damn animals," Troy warned.

"Shut him up, Murky," Dalton directed.

"Wait!" Aleescha halted Murky in his tracks. "I'll take care of it. Shut up, Troy," she demanded.

The boys looked at each other and grinned.

"You want us to screw ya, huh, pretty girl? You want us to plunge inside that sweet pussy of yours, huh, don't ya?" Murky sought.

"Doesn't matter what I say. You're goin' to do what you're goin' to do no matter how I feel about it," she stated breathlessly.

"Answer the fuckin' question," Sterling pushed.

Aleescha glanced toward Carter trapping her mother to the floor. She quickly came up with a plan that would save her mother from rape and manufacture an excuse to do what she really wanted to do—have sex and lots of it.

On the other side of the living room, Carter was trying to force sexual intercourse with Patti.

"Well?" Murky growled. "Is the answer yes or no? Tell us, you beautiful naked bitch."

Aleescha attempted to sound nervous (which she was a bit, but it was with nerves of eagerness), to appear disgusted and filled with fear, but her weak effort was feeble at best. There was an undeniable tone of excitement in her voice. She playfully bit down on her lower lip. "I'll tell you what, all you Porter men. If you leave my mama alone, let her be, you all can then have your perverted, disgustin' way with me."

"Aleescha!" Troy scolded.

"It's for my mama," she fired back at her husband with her cover-up of an excuse.

Sterling called across the room to Carter, "Hey, Pop. The pretty and naked schoolteacher is dealin' us all a good fuck if we leave her mama alone. What do ya say?"

While he now nearly had Patti disrobed, Carter looked to the beautiful and nude Aleescha Wiles Jacobs. "Is that right, teach?"

She nodded her agreement.

"Do you even know what a good screw is?"

"If you let my mama go, I promise you, Mr. Porter, that I will give it my all."

He squinted. "We're goin' to have ya either way, bitch. You know that, don't you?"

She nodded. "I figured as much. But if you insist on assaultin' my mama, then when it's my turn, I'll just lay still, like I'm dead. However, if you set mama free, then I'll turn myself loose, if you know what I mean, Mr. Porter."

The three Porter brothers became very anxious and even more excited with Murky pleading, "Come on, Pop, take the deal."

Carter, becoming convinced of Aleescha's sincerity as his eyes inspected every inch of her alluring nude body, rolled from atop of Patti Wiles. Patti, as if she were a trapped wild animal finally being set free, sprang to her feet and then sprinted down the hallway to join her ailing husband.

Aleescha lay back on the floor and willingly spread her legs, allowing the men full access to her. Dalton pulled his erect penis from out of his pants and stepped toward Aleescha as she arched her

back and breathed heavily. She lifted her hips up from the carpet, offering her most personal area to Dalton. Just as he was about to mount her, he hesitated. "Pop has to go first, or he'll beat my ass."

"Well, get him on over here then," Aleescha invited, gasping.

"Pop, come over here! She wants to screw." Dalton chuckled perversely.

Carter wasted no time scooting across the carpet to settle upon his knees between Aleescha's elevated knees. He was quick to yank his pants down to his ankles and then plunged into her with Aleescha accepting Carter at his full length by swaying her hips to meet his thrusts. She moaned out in delight.

Troy stepped toward Carter in an apparent rage. Before he could reach his wife and Carter, Murky placed him in a strong headlock. Murky then pointed his handgun between Troy's eyes. "Go have a seat, Troy the wonder boy, or I'll blow your head clean off your shoulders," Murky warned. He then pushed Troy away.

Troy realized that if he did not comply, Murky would shoot him. Troy plopped down on the recliner.

Carter's penis was only the second one to have ever entered Aleescha's vagina, and she received it invitingly. She began to release all her inhibitions and desires that she had held inside herself for years. This excited aggression surfaced, causing the act of intercourse to become very satisfying for both her and Carter. She arrived at an orgasm, creating a stimulus where her vagina constricted and massaged Carter's penis. Aleescha moaned out in pleasure a bit louder as Carter ejaculated inside her. He then rolled off her, both of them breathing deeply.

"I tell you what, that gal has one fine snatch. Have at it, boys." Carter gave way.

Dalton was quick to maneuver himself atop Aleescha, and she was very willing for him. She was attracted to Dalton more so than the others. Their act of sexual intercourse was intense and very satisfying for both.

Within thirty minutes, all four of the Porters engaged in intercourse with Aleescha. She was then in no hurry to dress. She remained nude and softly squirming about on the light blue carpet.

"Stand up and put your clothes on, Aleescha. They're done," Troy demanded angrily.

"Uh-uh." Aleescha defied him. She then winked at the Porters. "If you boys leave my parents alone, I'll go along with you."

"Can we take her with us, Pop?" Dalton asked eagerly.

"I don't see why not. I think she's takin' a likin' to ya, Dalton." Carter grinned.

"Dalton is very handsome." Aleescha wrinkled her nose.

"Okay, babe. Put your clothes on and come with us," Dalton directed.

As Aleescha dressed, Dalton stepped over to the recliner. He placed the barrel of his handgun against Troy's right temple. Troy perspired and pleaded before Dalton fired the weapon, spraying blood upon the wall behind the chair. Troy's dead body folded up and fell to the floor.

Patti screamed as she raced up the hallway to see the horrific sight and then slapped at Dalton several times.

Dalton angered with a single warning. "Fuckin' stop it now, Patti!"

"Mama, please back off. He'll kill you!" Aleescha cried.

When Dalton saw Aleescha in despair, he softened a bit. "It's okay, babe. I won't hurt your mama." He then went into an embrace with Aleescha.

She maintained her hands at her sides. "Dalton, you didn't have to shoot Troy, for cryin' out loud!" she wailed.

"Well, babe, it's you and me now. I don't want you married and all."

"Come on, let's go back into town and fuck up more people," Carter directed.

They moved toward the door with Aleescha and Dalton hand in hand.

"Aleescha, for goodness sakes, don't go with them," Patti begged.

Aleescha turned to look at her mother and sniffled. "You don't even realize how terrible my life was as I was growin' up. I wasn't permitted to go anywhere. It was 'Aleescha, stay in the yard. Aleescha, don't go to the store. Aleescha, don't spend the night at your friend's house. Aleescha, don't go to the mall. Aleescha, don't look out the window. Aleescha, wear these ugly clothes. Aleescha, you won't go to school, you'll be tutored.' I grew sick and tired of it all, Mama. I felt like I was in prison."

"It was all to protect you, honey," Patti reminded her.

"Maybe I didn't want to be protected, Mama."

Dalton then squeezed Aleescha's backside.

"Please, honey, come to your senses. You don't want to run with those Porters," Patti pleaded.

The Porters chuckled.

"Bye, Mama."

"She'll send ya a postcard," Dalton snickered.

Sterling, Dalton, and Aleescha stepped outside before Yen appeared from the hallway and onto the front porch, yielding a loaded twelve-gauge shotgun.

Immediately, Murky drew his handgun.

Carter chortled as he reached over and took hold of Murky's wrists. "Put the gun down, son," Carter instructed. "Yen doesn't have the balls to shoot."

With confidence, Murky and Carter turned their backs on Yen and strode out toward Carter's pickup truck.

Yen simply could not bring himself to shooting another human being, even if they were malevolent.

*****

RENEE CRIED—HARD. The rays of sunlight coming through the cracks in the cellar door were all but gone now. The fuel in one of the two lanterns had run empty. She was now using the second and final lantern at her disposal.

Her crying settled as she came to realize that she must settle down and think things out if she were to deal with her dire situation. She also understood that there was not enough remaining fuel in the last remaining lantern to last throughout the night. She must afford the fuel sparingly, which meant enduring periods without light.

Renee twisted the knob on the lantern, choking off the fuel supply. The light faded until it completely extinguished. Renee blurted out a shriek as she adjusted to the total and complete darkness within the cellar's walls.

CHAPTER 56

STORM CLOUDS WERE on the horizon and rolling toward Harpersfield. The lightning in the distance had Cole looking out the window of the post office where he was surveying the town while searching the whereabouts of the Porter clan. "Hang in there, Renee," he whispered to himself.

He then moved some cartons of mail next to the window where he could sit and stalk as a predator. He then heard a shuffling noise coming from behind the counter. He pulled his handgun and slowly slithered around the counter.

Hunkered behind the counter was postmaster Claudia Williams, whom Cole had not yet met. Her eyes widened as she looked at Cole. "Please don't shoot me," she begged.

He extended his left hand out to her. "It's okay, I'm FBI Agent Cole Walsh." He quickly flashed his badge.

Claudia sighed in relief. "Oh, you're the FBI agent stayin' up at Ike Stewart's place."

Cole nodded. "News sure travels fast in this small town."

"You can bet the farm on it."

"I need for you to move to a safer place...um ..."

"Claudia. Claudia Williams." Claudia was thirty-eight and was the third generation of Williamses to serve as Harpersfield's postmaster. She bleached her hair, and her skin was overly tanned. She sported tiny eyeglasses and was a bit overweight, but it suited her well. She was divorced, and her sixteen-year-old son, Burl, was staying up in Knoxville for the summer with his father.

"Claudia, I need you to move over to the old mine where the others in town are hiding. Do you know where it is?"

"Yeah…but so do the Porters."

"I realize that, but if I can get most of you townspeople in one place, I can protect you better."

"Oh, I see now."

"So make your way there, and I'll cover you from here. Use the darkness to you advantage, and stay away from the streetlights."

"Okay. Can I ask you a question? Were you whisperin' about Renee Stewart?"

Cole cleared his throat as his face flushed. "Yeah…why?"

"You care for her, don't you? I can see it in your eyes when I mentioned her name. Well, she's a young and pretty lady, and you're a handsome man, so the two of you would make a great-lookin' couple." She smiled.

Cole fidgeted. "You'd better just head on over to the mine, Claudia."

*****

FRED DARTON DIDN'T make it to the highway by nightfall. He sat on a large rock to rest when he collapsed from heat exhaustion. He struck his head on the rock as he slid from his perch, and he lay there unconscious for nearly an hour.

*****

PATTI AND YEN were much upset and shaken to drive with any amount of steadiness. But Patti was able to gingerly guide their older model Chevrolet Malibu into town in search for their rebellious daughter. They were taken aback at the sight of the town in ruins.

"Lord have mercy, Yen. The town is in shambles," Patti gasped before her eyes clouded over.

"I just knew all this would happen one day. Those damn Porters are out of control. I tried to warn the sheriff, but he wouldn't do anythin' about it," Yen snarled.

It was then that Patti and Yen observed Bob Harvey's bullet-ridden and lifeless body lying on the sidewalk in front of smoldering ambers that was once the police station. They saddened at the sight and tightly held hands.

"It's all like a nightmare. But we're not gonna wake up, and everythin' will be simply fine." Patti sobbed.

"Wait, stop the car!" Yen blurted out.

Patti abruptly applied the brakes. The slow-moving vehicle halted immediately. "What is it, Yen?"

"I think I saw movement up ahead a bit. Someone is hidin' behind the big tree up there a bit."

Yen and Patti sat quietly while their hearts raced at a fever pitch.

Claudia Williams was dealing with a pounding heartbeat of her own as all she could see of Yen and Patti was the glow of their vehicle's headlights. She was using the large oak tree to keep from being spotted by any passing vehicle's occupants, though she already had been detected.

"Is it the Porters?" Patti nervously asked.

"I'm not sure. Maybe we oughtta turn around," Yen suggested.

"God, I hope that's not the Porters," Claudia whispered to herself.

The standstill lingered on over a few seconds longer. Suddenly, someone rapped on Patti's driver's side window. She startled and screamed out as Yen bit down on his tongue. Patti was soon relieved to discover that it was Cole Walsh standing next to her car. She quickly rolled down the window. "Oh, thank god it's you. I thought you might be the Porters. They kidnapped our Aleescha from us!"

"You two need to get off the streets. You're sitting ducks out here like this," Cole explained. "When I track down the Porters, I'll make sure that your daughter is safe. But for now, you must go into hiding with the others because there is no passage to drive out

of Harpersfield. The road leading out of town is a trap. Claudia Williams is just up ahead. She'll lead you to the others."

Claudia, after confirming it was indeed Cole next to the car, stepped out from behind the tree.

"I told ya I saw someone, Patti," Yen said. "These eyes might be old, but they're still sharp."

Claudia approached and caught Cole off guard with an embrace. She sobbed mildly into Cole's left shoulder as he placed a supporting arm around her back.

"I'm sorry, Agent Walsh, I just needed a hug. I'm so scared that it's makin' me weary."

"It's okay, Claudia. But I need you to find some strength and toughen up now. Help Yen and Patti to the mine shaft, okay?"

Claudia nodded as she broke away from her embrace with Cole.

"I'm not goin' into any mine shaft," Patti declared.

Cole crouched down to come face-to-face with Patti through the vehicle's open window. "If you don't go to that mine, I can't protect you."

"I'll take my chances out here. I'm claustrophobic. I would die a thousand deaths in an enclosed area," Patti claimed.

"If you stay out in the open, you may suffer the only death that counts. That will be at the hands of the Porters," Cole admonished.

After a few moments of silence, Patti changed her mind. "Okay, I'll go to the mine."

"That's a wise choice," Cole endorsed.

Cole helped Patti from the car. After she shut off the ignition, Patti began to cry deeply. She trembled and nearly stumbled to the ground. Cole grabbed hold of her left arm to support her from buckling at the knees. Yen raced around the front of the car to his wife. He took her into his arms.

"You still love me, Yen?"

He ran his hand through her short graying hair and then placed a gentle kiss upon her forehead. "You bet I do. I couldn't get along without ya, wifey."

"But sometimes I get mean toward ya."

"That's just your way, my love. I realized that years ago when I married ya. You've kept me in check over all these years. If it weren't for you, who knows where I would have ended up. In some no-good situation most likely. Yen Wiles's best move in his life is when he wed Patti Maxwell."

Cole and Claudia grinned over the love displayed by the Wiles couple.

"Now let's do what the FBI agent wants us to do. Let's move to safety."

Claudia nodded toward the Yen and Patti. "Come on, you two. Let's go into hidin'."

Yen and Patti followed Claudia's lead into the darkness toward the mine shaft.

Cole made his way back across the street to inside the post office. "I need to rid this friendly town of the evil that's been bestowed upon it," he mumbled to himself.

*****

THE VAN CARRYING the Elite Four agents ran over the spiked railroad tie on Martin's Way, bursting all four tires. Dule lost control of the van as it veered from the road, rotated completely, and then slammed into an oak tree before finally coming to rest upon its flattened tires. Anthony was knocked unconscious, Janice suffered a blow to her head, while Marla was buckled in tight and uninjured. Both Barry and Anthony each sprained their right ankles; Anthony's was a bit more of a significant injury. Dule suffered only a few minor scratches.

Dule kicked open the damaged driver's door and then hefted his body out of the van to the ground below. He came to his feet and pulled open the passenger's door and helped Marla out from the van. He then leaned inside and gave Janice support to exit the crashed vehicle. Barry leaped from the rig holding his left arm. "Anthony is out cold," Barry informed.

"Oh my god, is he alive?" Janice questioned.

"Yeah, he's breathing. Do we have a first aid kit?" Barry wondered.

"I always bring one with me. It's in the back, in my duffel bag," Marla said.

Barry limped to the rear of the van and retrieved a top-of-the-line first aid kit. He crawled back inside the van and split a capsule of smelling salts directly beneath Anthony's nostrils.

Anthony's body jerked as he came to while rubbing his head.

Marla and Dule were checking on Janice. "Are you okay? Do you know where we are, Janice?" Marla asked.

She nodded her aching head.

Dule held up three digits of his left hand in front of Janice. "How many fingers do I have up?"

"Three," Janice groaned.

Anthony aided the gimping Barry from the van, his limping more pronounced than Barry's was.

"Are you two alright?" Marla inquired.

"Yeah, my ankle is sore as hell, but we're going to be fine."

Dule then turned his raised three fingers to Anthony. "How many you see?"

"I'm fine, Dule," Anthony bit out.

A loud thunderclap boomed overhead, and then rain began to fall.

"Oh great, now this," Marla wheezed. "Okay, everyone back in the van. We'll wait out the storm before we walk the remaining distance into Harpersfield."

*****

LIGHTNING SHOT STROBES of flashing illumination through the cracks of the cellar door. Renee's body jerked with each thunderclap. She could hear the heavy rainfall outside the door as she pulled the blanket around her tighter while she sat upon the milk crate. She decided to consume some of the lantern's precious fuel reserve while waiting out the storm.

Renee twisted the knob on the lantern and struck the lighter. The lantern delivered welcomed light into her dark world. She rocked back and forth. "Cole, where are you?"

*****

COLE TRIED TO peer through the hard tumbling rain, but his visibility through the post office window was vague at best. The rain was coming down with a mighty force. If there was an upside to the timing of the downpour, it was that it was extinguishing the smoldering fires around town. Cole reached for his pack of cigarettes in his pants pocket and lit the tobacco. He inhaled a long drag before exhaling a cloud of smoke.

"Where the hell are you degenerates?" he growled. "If I don't spot them shortly after the storm passes, I'm heading up to the Porter homestead."

*****

RAINWATER INITIALLY BEGAN to trickle inside the mine shaft minutes ago, but now it had become a steady stream. The townsfolk quietly and nervously watched in a tight group as the water seeped farther into their refuge.

"How much do you feel it can travel before we have to move out of here?" Stacy Hughes inquired.

"These mines are old. Most of them are now completely collapsed," Deputy Frank Collins spoke up. "This is one of the few that at least the entrance is still intact, but what once was an entire mine is now caved in behind us. I don't know how much more water this unstable entrance can take."

"Shouldn't you be out there helpin' the FBI man, Frank?" Henry Gert snipped.

"I have my kids to think about, Henry."

"We all do," Patti Wiles sniveled. Yen attempted to soothe his wife.

"Want to hear some funny post office tales?" Claudia Williams made a sincere effort to lighten the gloomy mood.

Several in the group nodded.

"Well, the other day, Emily Montgomery came in with this small wooden box, and she said—"

"Help us get down there," a voice suddenly echoed down into the mine shaft.

"That's Fred Darton," Pam Tinelberg recognized.

Henry and Frank moved to the very entrance of the shaft and removed several of the plywood boards merely resting in place. Fred had his right arm around his wife Beverly, and Merle stood next to his parents while holding a makeshift compress to his groin area.

"Come on in, you Dartons. Get your butts in here and out of the rain," Frank invited.

The trio slid inside the mine shaft's entrance to join the other refugees. They were shivering, and their clothes were saturated with rainwater and mud. Fred had a torn strip of a sheet wrapped around his forehead and stained with blood.

"What happened, Fred?" Stacy inquired.

"Oh, I hit my head a rather good one on a big rock. I'm okay now. I was tryin' to make it to the highway for help, but I decided to come back to protect my Beverly. The Porters have Martin's Way rigged up so ya can't drive out of town."

"What happened to you, Merle?" Pam pondered.

Fred cleared his throat. "That bastard, Murky Porter, shot Merle's manhood."

Frank grimaced as if he felt Merle's pain.

"We have to get him to a doctor soon," Emma proclaimed.

"It's okay, Emma," Merle responded. "It's not bleedin' anymore."

"I think we all need to stay put until at least daylight, and hopefully the Porters will be through with their rampage by then," Frank indicated.

"Are ya goin' to arrest them, Frank? Or do they walk away yet again?" Beverly snipped.

Frank chose not to reply.

"The FBI man will get 'em," Henry claimed.

"That's one good man against four maniacs, Henry. I don't like those odds," Frank muttered.

"Where's the sheriff?" Claudia asked.

"He's dead. The Porters shot him as we fled the burnin' station," Frank sadly reported.

"Jim's dead as well," Pam sniveled.

"They forced my Aleescha to go with them," Patti whimpered.

"I saw Mason Turner bein' shot in the head," Stacy somberly added.

Joe Skidmore and his wife Judy, who were seated against a cold damp wall of the mine, had been quiet. Joe wrapped his pregnant wife in his arms and spoke up, "We've been a bunch of scared rabbits over the years. Lettin' those insane lowlifes rule our town."

"It's not just us, Joe," Henry retorted. "This has been goin' on for generations. The Porter family has always run this town. A person doesn't dare challenge them unless they wish to be six feet under."

After a few moments of silence, Pam asked, "Frank, can't you call in the state police with that radio clipped there on your belt?"

"No, I can't do that. The Porters shot up the radio base inside the station. My radio is now useless." Frank then tossed another piece of wood onto the dwindling campfire. He felt that he should do something more about the dire situation. With Bob Harvey now deceased, that made Frank the acting sheriff. He was torn between doing what a lawman should do and the cautions of being a family man.

*****

ANOTHER LOUD CLAP of thunder was followed by a bold streak of lightning.

"This storm looks like it has some nastiness to it," Dule remarked.

"I can see now why you're a detective, Dule. You're so observant," Anthony taunted.

Dule twisted within his seat to face Anthony. "What's your gig anyway, Becth? You've been on my ass since I met you earlier today. If you have something you want to say to me, just say it."

Anthony leaned forward in his seat. "Yeah, I do have something to say. It pisses me off that Marla let you in on the Elite Four. Why in the hell did you do that, Marla?"

Before Marla could respond, Janice chimed in. "Because they are screwing. It's obvious."

"No excuse," Anthony grunted.

"Unbelievable," Barry added. "He stokes your fire, Marla, and you spill the beans? What the hell is up with that?"

Dule retorted angrily, "Oh, and you are all so innocent? I hardly think so. I saw that you took Janice up to your hotel room that night in Philadelphia, Barry."

"Everyone, just knock it off," Marla demanded. "This is ridiculous! You're all behaving like a bunch of schoolkids. It's really none of your business as to why I let Dule in. I call the shots, remember? Do you believe that I would put the Elite Four in harm's way? Give me a damn break. Yeah, Dule and I are intimate, but I still would not have told him unless I trusted him as much as I do."

The van fell silent as the agents bowed their heads.

"And Dule, Barry, and Janice. What is this about a meeting in Philadelphia without my consent?" she growled.

A moment of awkward silence loomed.

"I called them in." Dule came clean.

"You did what? Why?" Marla called for an explanation.

"I was worried about you, honey. This case with Cole has you all twisted in knots. I was trying to get Barry and Janice to convince you to drop the case."

"Dule...if you ever make a move like that again, you'll be out on your ass. That goes for you, Barry and Janice, as well."

"Sorry, Marla," Barry mumbled.

"Yeah, me too," Janice seconded.

*****

THE BULK OF the storm finally passed, leaving behind only distant thunder. It was still raining, but not nearly as steady as it had been prior.

Cole decided to make his move. He stepped out in front of the post office and carefully looked each way along Harper Street. Taking a few moments to determine which direction to head, he settled on the intersection of Harper and Vine. The storm had knocked out the electric power in the buildings that were left standing and the few

residences upon the hillside. The streetlights continued to glow on stored solar power.

Cole treaded slowly with precision while examining every corner, each shadow, to try to avoid any possible ambush. Cole's right thumb nervously rubbed at the backside of his left fingers. He imagined about what it would be like to have a ring on his finger. A wedding band. Someone to go home to, someone to care for. Someone to care for him. However, he had gone his entire life without such a deep commitment. Would he be able to adjust?

As he grew older, he had felt that a certain something was missing in his life. An emptiness that needed filled. Was a wife the answer? Could any woman tolerate his demanding lifestyle? It was all so confusing for him. Would it be fair to bestow such a crazy way of life on an unsuspecting woman? Could Renee be the one for him? Would she be happy as the wife of an FBI man? Would she even accept if he were to propose marriage? Was their relationship merely a temporary thing for her? He was, after all, eleven years older than her. Does the age difference really matter to her? Does it matter to him?

Cole whispered to himself, "Get your mind back on the task at hand before you get your ass shot off."

*****

BEVERLY DARTON SHRIEKED as a large section of the mine's clay wall collapsed into the shaft. Rainwater from the strong passing storm was streaming inside the mine shaft at a rapid pace.

"Looks like we disturbed the mine's entranceway. Hopefully, the water stops right there," Henry observed.

"How about it, Henry? You used to work these mines years ago. What are the chances of this entire thing swallowin' us whole?" Frank questioned.

Like a war veteran with horrific memories of deadly battles, Henry Gert recalled his experiences as a coal miner, sometimes in the form of nightmares. The mines were unsafe, but that mattered none to the company raking in the profits. It was pushing the miners to their very limits, sometimes working as many as eighteen hours each day.

One night forever changed Henry Gert and shall always be etched in his mind. Henry, along with other crew members, were mining a hole up near Knoxville when the unthinkable occurred. It was shift change, and with lady luck on his side, Henry was one of the first nineteen miners to reach the surface, passing the reporting workers as Henry and others made their way out from the mine. Within moments after Henry had crawled out from the quarry, the earth in the immediate area suddenly shifted. The thick supporting lumber columns bracing the walls of the mine snapped like toothpicks. It all seemed to move in slow motion for those above the mine as the walls collapsed, turning the mine into a massive grave for 149 miners in all.

The miners safely on the surface panicked and sobbed as they feverishly dug with shovels and even with their hands at the tons of soil coal that had buried their coworkers. It was useless to try to save the lost; the excavators realized this but kept on burrowing late into the night. It would have taken weeks for bulldozers and large drill bits to reach and recover the dead, so it was decided to leave the mine as was and to place 149 makeshift tombstones at the site. The ironic thing about the incident was that mine was known as the 149th. As with many of the survivors that day, it was the last hole that Henry ever mined. He retired his hard hat after that tragic night.

Henry rubbed his jaw. "It's hard to say with any certainty, deputy. We've disturbed the structure. These shafts are incredibly old now, not many of them left. If she decides to go, we won't be able to hold her back."

"Well, I'm gettin' out of here then," Claudia stated.

Emma spoke up, "What then, Claudia? Face the ruthless Porters? No thank you, I'll take my chances down here."

"I hate those bastards!" Claudia shouted.

Frank observed Pam was withdrawing from the group. Her eyes were tearing up as she sat alone against the opposite wall of the collapsed clay. The group continued to discuss options as Frank took a seat next to Pam.

"I'm so sorry, Pam. If I'd done a better job as a lawman, Jim may have not been slaughtered by the Porters or any of the others for that

matter. Not even the murder of young Nathan Stewart was enough to make me brave."

She took hold of his right hand. "It's okay, Frank. You are no different around the Porters than the rest of us are. You have family at home that you must think about and protect. Jim wouldn't have wanted to live without his beloved diner anyhow. I just hope that someday those animals get theirs. That Harpersfield eventually gets even."

"Perhaps that FBI agent will deliver."

"I certainly hope so, deputy."

Pam broke into a sob as Frank consoled her.

*****

"I THINK WE can head out now, troops," Marla directed. "It looks like the brunt of the storm has finally passed."

"How are you going to do on that ankle, Anthony?" Barry asked. "Mine is feeling a bit better."

"I think I can manage."

"Perhaps you should stay back here in the van," Dule suggested in a sarcastic tone.

"Shut up, Dule," Anthony growled.

"Well, you're going to slow our progress," Dule pointed out.

"Drop it, Dule. Anthony is coming along," Marla snapped.

Dule sprung open the rickety driver's side door of the van before leaping out to the wet ground and into a puddle of standing water. Anthony immediately broke into laughter. Dule raised his right middle finger at Anthony outside the van's window.

Janice, Barry, and Marla glanced at one another before they all joined in a round laughter.

*****

COLE DETECTED MOVEMENT up ahead near the intersection, and he quickly ducked behind one of the light posts.

Aleescha, Dalton, Sterling, Murky, and Carter, on foot and unaware Cole was nearby, made their way across Harper Street and then up Vine Street, heading in the opposite of Cole's position.

*****

"OH MY GOD!" Claudia screamed as another section of the shaft's roof crumpled, nearly landing on Joe.

"I think we'd better get the hell out of this soon-to-be grave," Henry warned.

The group shuffled toward the entrance, but it was too late. The walls collapsed around them as the shaft instantly filled with mud up to their waists. The women began to shriek as Frank attempted to maneuver through the muck to help the others to safety.

Cole heard the ruckus, and fortunately, the Porters were now out of earshot. Cole had to pull back from his pursuit of the Porters to run to the aid of those inside the mine shaft.

Frank was able to push a pregnant Stacy Hughes to safety from out of the shaft. Next, he assisted Emma Gert through the tapering entrance as the walls and the roof above continued to give way. Cole was running toward the shaft, but he was over three hundred feet away. Frank encouraged Pam to move with all her might through the muck while he pushed her along. Pam came free of the clay's hold to join Stacy and Emma at ground level.

"Claudia, come on! Take my hand!" Frank shouted.

Joe and Judy Skidmore battled their way out from the shaft and prepared to help Frank from outside the shaft. Frank pulled Claudia through the muck, and at one point, she went under. When she surfaced, she was in a full-blown panic. She waved her arms frantically, striking Frank on the face several times.

"Claudia, settle down, calm down, or we'll both die down here."

Her arms fell limp while she wept.

"It'll be okay. Just trust me, and I'll guide you out of here."

Henry clawed his way out of the mine shaft and shouted back inside, "Come on, Claudia! You can do it."

Cole arrived at the entrance of the collapsing mine and quickly removed his holsters and guns, dropping them to the ground.

"Claudia and Frank are still down there!" Emma screeched.

Only a small opening remained in the mine shaft as Cole slid down through it.

"Wait, you're our only hope! You'll be killed," Pam squealed.

Cole ignored Pam and continued into the mine. Soon, Frank and Cole together were able to help Claudia out of the small opening. Just as Cole and Frank were about to make their own exit, the mine swallowed them whole.

"Oh no!" Stacy howled.

"Cole! Frank!" Joe shouted.

The group fell eerily silent as the muck pushed its way out of the now-filled mine's entrance. After long anxious moments, the group was about to concede that Frank and Cole were gone, dead.

Suddenly, the surface of the muck shifted before Cole's and Frank's heads sprung up from the muck's surface. Both men gasped desperately for air. Joe quickly moved to offer his hand. He pulled Frank from the muck and onto level ground. Frank and Joe then teamed up to pull Cole to safety. All were caked in mud, but the still-falling rain quickly rinsed the soupy muck away from their clothing and bodies.

*****

"HOLD UP A minute," Anthony requested of the group marching toward town. "I need to wrap my ankle before I can go any farther."

"Wrap it using what?" Janice queried.

"Um...your bra," Anthony responded. "Your bra or Marla's bra."

"My bra is staying right where it's at," Marla assured.

"Why a bra?" Janice mulled over.

Barry contributed, "Because a bra has hooks and/or velcro, and the elastic can be stretched to fit snug."

"Exactly," Anthony confirmed.

"I'll help you off with yours." Barry winked at Janice.

"I'm sure you would, Stone, but I can manage. Thank you just the same." Janice reached her right hand beneath her shirt and removed her bra without exposing her breasts. She then tossed the released bra over to Anthony.

"How much farther to town?" Dule asked Marla.

"I'm not sure, at least two or three miles."

"It's going to take us the rest of the night to get there," he retorted.

"Yeah…it looks that way, Dule. Probably better off hunting down Cole in the light of day anyhow."

*****

Reluctantly, Renee realized she needed to conserve fuel as she twisted the knob on the lantern. The cellar slowly fell pitch-dark. Her feet rested in a small puddle of water collected by the seeping rainwater. She laid her head down upon her knees and swayed.

*****

"DAMN, DALTON. WE just fucked her a few hours ago," Carter griped.

Dalton had Aleescha pinned against a lamppost on Vine Street with his hand beneath her skirt while pulling down her panties.

"I want some more of this, Pop," Dalton eagerly growled. She kicked her panties from around her ankles and accepted Dalton into her arms. She grinded her hips into him and moaned in ecstasy.

Sterling reached in from the rear of her skirt and stimulated her vagina with his long fingers. She bucked her hips into Sterling's grip. Aleescha then slid down along Dalton's chest and to her knees. She unzipped his pants and reached inside for his erect penis. His manhood sprung from his pants, and she grinned seductively. Aleescha took Dalton's throbbing penis into her mouth, massaging him with her tongue.

This was the initial period that Aleescha had ever performed oral sex on a man. She attempted the action upon Troy early in their relationship, but he placed his hand under her chin and guided her

head back up and away from his midsection before she could execute the sexual act. Troy was not interested in any foreplay, only strictly intercourse itself. Though Aleescha had never actually stimulated a man orally, she was certain that she could perform well if only given the opportunity.

She studied the way the women achieved it in the pornographic movies she had hidden away inside her house, on the top shelf of the hallway closet beneath a pair of throw pillows that were never used. Dalton tossed his head back and grunted out with excitement as Aleescha worked well with her lips and tongue upon his rigid penis.

Sterling positioned himself behind Aleescha and hiked her skirt upward. He pulled his erect penis from his pants and slid his manhood inside her welcoming and damp vagina. She moved her hips to match Sterling's rhythm without taking her mouth from Dalton. Everything about the Porter men was large, and Aleescha was enjoying the powerful stimulation that this delivered to her.

She pulled her mouth off Dalton's hardness for a moment to look up at him. She stroked him with her hand as she whispered, "I want you to explode inside my mouth, Dalton."

She returned her oral stimulation upon Dalton. Sterling ejaculated inside Aleescha's vagina. He grunted out, and she pleasurably moaned on Dalton's penis. As Sterling pulled up his pants, Murky dropped his Levi's. Within moments, Murky's penis replaced Sterling's member inside Aleescha's womanhood. Again, she purred as Murky entered her. Carter sat curbside smoking a cigar. He was aging and not able to perform as frequently as his young buck sons could. Murky's thrusts were fast and deep, causing the short hair upon Aleescha's head to bounce. He grinded his teeth, and his body trembled as he climaxed deep inside Aleescha. She continued to manipulate her hips even after Murky withdrew his penis from within her.

Dalton grabbed a handful of Aleescha's hair as his thighs tightened and stiffened. He released into Aleescha's mouth as his shooting semen oozed out from the corners of her lips. His breaths were short as he completed his ejaculation. Aleescha buzzed as she licked her lips clean.

"That was the best blow job I have ever had," Dalton celebrated.

Aleescha exhaled. "Well, keep me around, Dalton, and I'll give you one every day."

"Deal," he blurted out. "After tonight, my brothers, this piece is mine and mine only."

She rose to her feet and didn't bother to gather up her panties. "Want me to stay bare beneath my skirt?" she suggested to Dalton flirtatiously.

He eagerly nodded. Again, she purred.

The gang of five then continued their way along Vine Street.

*****

COLE ADJUSTED HIS holsters to his body. "I want you all to hide out in the feedstore."

"I want to go with you, Cole," Frank suggested with newly found bravery.

"I don't know if that's a good idea, deputy."

"Please. I want to make amends for all the times I've let the people down in this town. You could use a partner out there. There are four of them and only one of you. It's not like there are other FBI agents around here to choose from."

Little did Frank know that there were three FBI agents and a pair of private detectives on the outskirts of town.

"I'm also an Army Green Beret. I can handle four adversaries."

"Please, Cole, take me with you. Don't make me beg."

"Who will protect the women in the feedstore?" Cole questioned.

"I will." Joe stepped forward. "Chuck Arnold is outta town 'til Monday, but I know where he keeps the baseball bat and his handgun he has for protection."

"Cole," Frank pleaded.

Cole exhaled a long breath. "It's against my better judgment, but okay."

Frank's eyes widened with enthusiasm.

"Listen carefully to every direction that I provide. If in the heat of the battle I tell you to abort, you abort. Go it?" Cole ground out.

Frank nodded.

"Okay, the rest of you good citizens get inside the feedstore, and Joe, you get that gun."

"You bet."

The group headed to the feedstore as Cole and Frank made their way toward Harper Street while the rainfall finally ceased.

"How about a gun? I'm goin' to need a weapon. The Porters snatched my firearm from me," Frank explained.

"Where's the cruiser? I didn't see it anywhere around the charred station."

"It's over at Sampson's garage. Hank was goin' to change the oil, give it a tune-up in the mornin'. He lives over in Waynesburg and comes to the garage here in Harpersfield twice a week."

"Why not take the patrol car to Darton's for service?" Cole wondered.

"Oh, Hank's shop offers a discounted price for county vehicles, so..."

"Politics," Cole grunted.

"Exactly." Frank nodded.

"The Sampson garage is still standing, at this point anyway. We'll get the shotgun out of the patrol car," Cole directed.

"Good idea," Frank responded. "We won't need to break into the garage. The cruiser is parked out in the lot."

"Do you need to check on your family?" Cole asked.

"No, they're up at my wife's mother's place in Nashville for the week, thank god."

"Okay then, we get the shotgun, and then we'll go hunting for hoodlums."

CHAPTER 57

"THERE," ANTHONY STATED after securing Janice's bra around his sprained ankle. "That's much better."

"The only time I could get a man to wear my bra, and it has to be on his ankle," Janice joked.

"Hey, Anthony, does this mean we can call you a cross-dresser now?" Dule chortled.

"You know, Dule, each time you make a sly comment, it shortens your life span," Anthony commented as he gingerly stood to his feet. He gradually placed his weight upon the gimpy ankle. "I'll still have to walk with a limp, but at least some of the pain is in control now."

"He could probably use your bra as well, Marla," Barry playfully suggested.

"I already said no, Barry. Gravity is no longer kind to me. I wouldn't remain all perky like Janice over there."

Janice blushed and folded her arms across her shirt's chest area.

"Okay, are we ready to move again?" Dule inquired impatiently.

"Onward." Anthony pointed northward.

After slowly covering a few hundred yards, Janice questioned Marla, "Who is to shoot Cole Walsh?"

"The first to get a clear shot," Marla confirmed.

"No questions asked?" Barry sought.

"Nary a one," Marla confirmed.

Anthony sighed. "Boy, this isn't going to be easy. Cole is a good guy and one of our members."

Marla nodded but remained firm. "Yeah…but remember, Cole is fully aware of why we are coming after him. Be rest assured, if you don't get off a shot before him, Cole will certainly shoot you."

"I can't believe we are foolish enough to go up against a Green Beret," Dule uttered out.

"What do you mean we?" Anthony questioned. "You're not part of this, Dule. You're certainly not, nor will you ever be, a member of our team. If you mess me up anywhere along the way through this ordeal, I'll hack off your balls and then ram them down your throat."

Janice chuckled.

"You don't scare me," Dule bit out, though he was truly intimidated by Anthony.

"Enough!" Marla snapped.

*****

STERLING KICKED OPEN the wooden door of the old abandoned bowling alley, Memory Lanes. The entourage then followed Sterling inside the vacant structure. The building that once was loud with bowling balls crashing into pins had been deadly quiet for over a decade.

They made their way to the counter where a few pairs of bowling shoes, covered with cobwebs, were still stored within the slots of the shelving behind the counter. Sterling searched the office area and shouted out, "Fuck! Those bastards, Bob and Frank, found our stash of pot and coke again. It's all gone. The pricks probably torched it again."

"Well, they're dead now." Dalton snickered.

"Why don't you guys stop killin' people?" Aleescha suggested.

Dalton grabbed her left arm with strength. "Shut the hell up, bitch. You hang with us, you keep your back-talk at bay. Porter women know their place, and you'd better find where that is—and fast."

"I'm sorry, Dalton. I'm sorry. Please, forgive me."

Dalton shoved her hard and down onto the decaying wooden floor. "Stay down there for a while and keep your mouth shut. If you ever embarrass me in front of my family again, I'll kick your teeth in, you cunt."

Aleescha went into tears. Her skirt was hiked up above her waist, exposing her vaginal area. Carter looked to the delicate area and licked his lips. Suddenly, this situation was no longer fun and exciting for Aleescha. She pulled her skirt down over her hips before she stood to her feet. She now wished that she hadn't left her underwear back on Vine Street.

Carter inspected the guns, hand grenades, and dynamite they had carried with them after setting out on foot. Being as strong as the four men were, it was more gear than most could tote along. "Why did you boys figure you needed all this artillery?"

"Sometimes we have pounds of marijuana and cocaine in here, Pop," Murky reported.

"Yeah, and then that damn sheriff and deputy torched it," Sterling groaned.

"Okay, Sterling, you told me that already. The worthless sheriff and his flunky sidekick are goners now, so stop your whinin' about your stash," Carter relayed.

"Let's gather up our gear and head back into town to play some more," Dalton directed.

"Yeah, let's go and clean up the rest of the worthless shithole called Harpersfield," Carter declared.

✳✳✳✳✳

"STAND BACK, FRANK. I'm going to shoot the lock," Cole instructed.

"You'll hit the shotgun, and then it will be of no use to us," Frank pointed out.

"No, I'll only hit the lock."

"You have less than a half inch of gimme. The shot would need to be exact." Frank quickly realized his evaluation made no difference to Cole. Frank plugged his ears with his forefingers.

Cole fired inside the open driver's door of the patrol car at the locking mechanism securing the shotgun. The strike of the bullet hit clean, exploding the lock into two pieces. The intact shotgun tumbled back onto the passenger's seat and then slid down on the floorboard.

"Great shot, Cole!" Frank bellowed. The deputy rushed around the patrol car to whisk open the passenger door where he gained a solid grip on the shotgun before sliding it upon the roof of the vehicle. He then pulled out a metal box from beneath the passenger's seat and stuffed his pockets with shotgun shells. He then pumped five shells into the chamber of the firearm.

"I hear Porters are in season this time of the year." Cole winked.

Frank nodded. "They most certainly are."

"Well then, let's go and get our bag limit."

*****

IT HAD BEEN more than two hours since the lantern's light faded away, leaving the cellar in complete darkness. Renee decided she could squander a little more fuel to find some needed comfort in the light.

She fumbled to gain a grip on the lantern and then ran her fingertips along the oil lamp's frame until she located the knob. Within a few moments, a light began to glow. The illumination helped to ease her nerves a bit as her eyes adjusted to the weak light.

She picked up the scrapbook to leaf through it for a second time. She came across a photograph of Nate when he was around twelve. He was tossing a baseball with Ike near the barn. It was about this time in his life when he approached Renee with an awkward question.

*****

Renee was hanging freshly washed laundry on the line between the barn and the lamppost to dry in the breeze. Ike had been promising to fix the clothes dryer for over a month. Nate had been sitting on the porch for nearly twenty minutes, watching Renee as if he had something heavy on

his mind. She was fourteen, nearing her fifteenth birthday, and had yet to have a boyfriend in her life.

Finally, after gathering enough courage, her younger brother leaped from the porch and approached her. "Um...sis, can I ask you somethin'?"

"No, Nate, you're not borrowin' my stereo again. The last time you didn't put most of the CDs back, and the ones you did put away were in the wrong cases."

He fidgeted. "It's not that."

"Then what is it?" she sought.

After a hesitation, he asked, "What's it like to kiss a girl?"

She squinted at him. "I wouldn't know, little brother. I don't go around kissin' girls."

"Um...ah...you know what I mean. What's it like to kiss someone you're goin' out with?"

"Why?"

"Just wonderin' is all."

"You've been goin' over to Steven's Pass to see Myra Cooper, haven't you?" she teased.

"Well, sorta."

"What do you mean sorta? Either you are or you aren't."

"I only go up there to play baseball with her brother Doug."

"Doug is only about five. He's hardly big enough to play ball with you," she ribbed a bit further. "Do you talk to Myra while you're at the Coopers' place?"

"Sometimes."

"Do you tell her that you like her?"

"No!" he quickly said.

She pinned one of Ike's flannel shirts to the line. "Do you like her?"

He nodded.

"Then why don't you tell her so?"

"Because she'd probably laugh at me."

"Why would she laugh? You're a good-lookin' young fella."

"Well, she's older than I am. She probably thinks I'm too young for her."

"Myra is only a grade behind me. She can only be thirteen, and you're twelve. I would hardly call that a serious age gap," she chortled.

"If I tell her, and she says that she likes me too, how do I know when to kiss her?"

"Oh, Nate, why do you want to start so early in life? You got a bunch of bein' around in front of you for those kind of things to take place. But for now, you should just stick to your baseball and ridin' your bike."

"Yeah, well…I really like Myra a bunch. I think about her all the time. I just wanna know when to kiss her."

"I haven't had any experience with it myself," she revealed.

His eyes widened. "What? You're goin' on fifteen."

She rolled her eyes. "Oh yeah, Nate…I'm a regular old maid, I am."

"So you've never kissed a boy?"

"Nope."

"Do your friends know? They must make fun of you."

Renee took a deep breath. "All I can tell you is that if it's meant to be, you'll know when to kiss her. A voice inside will tell you when."

"You read too many mushy books," he teased.

"Perhaps, but I think that's how it happens in real life as well."

"So you think I should just come right out and tell her?"

"Yep."

"What if she turns me down?"

"Fall to the floor and cry like a baby," she said with a chuckle.

"Quit joking, I'm serious."

"Okay, okay…if she turns you down, just tell her that you still think that she's pretty. It'll give her somethin' to think about."

He nodded. "I like that idea."

*****

Renee smiled into the glow of the lantern. "You kissed Myra the next day, Nate. You came rushin' home to tell me as if your bike were a rocket. You never told any of the other kids at school that I was nearly fifteen and never been kissed. I love you, little brother. I miss you so much that it aches."

CHAPTER 58

"THIS IS GONNA be so cool," Sterling chirped. He watched as Dalton placed a bundle of dynamite between the fuel tank and the frame of the Wiles family minivan parked in the driveway.

"Please, Dalton, blow somethin' else up. My dad worked hard to afford that van. He ordered it special, and it took months for it to come in," Aleescha pleaded.

Murky quickly gripped her throat, cutting off all her oxygen. She jerked as she fought for air but couldn't break free. Murky was too powerful.

"Dalton, you have one with a mouth on her. You've warned her once, so I think we dispose of her now."

Dalton didn't show any signs of emotion as he continued to seat the dynamite. "Yeah, okay, Murky, shoot her."

Murky released his grip around her throat to aim his weapon at her.

Aleescha's heart raced. "What? No, please. Please don't kill me!"

Murky cocked the gun.

Aleescha desperately searched for anything to say to save her life. "Wait, I'll do anything. I'll have sex with you all again, all four of you. I'll give you sex anytime you want it."

"We get that from Tammy. We don't need your snatch any longer," Sterling growled.

"Or we'll just rape you when we want some," Murky bragged.

Aleescha realized she had only precious seconds remaining before Murky fired his weapon. She knew from secretly viewing pornographic material that many of men's fantasy was to watch two women engage in sex together. Aleescha had no lesbian tendencies whatsoever, but this was all about saving her life. "Wait, please wait! I've got it. How about this, boys? I'll have sex with another woman, and you all can watch."

Carter rubbed his jaw. "Now, we might be on to somethin' there, boys."

"Yeah, I'd do that for you guys to watch," she dealt.

"Who?" Sterling wondered.

"Me," she confirmed.

"No, you dumb bitch. What girl would ya do it with?"

"Oh, I dunno. How about Renee Stewart? Everyone knows that Murky is sweet on her."

"That would be cool to watch you and Renee lickin' each other's pussies." Sterling licked his lips.

"My Renee wouldn't do it with another girl," Murky asserted.

"You'd be surprised at the cooperation you can obtain while holdin' a gun to someone's head." Aleescha was quick to point out.

"No one is puttin' a gun to Renee's head!" Murky barked.

"Okay, okay...who would you all like to see me do it with?"

"Macy Donalds," Sterling was quick to suggest. "That girl has some great tits."

"Okay...Macy it is," Aleescha reluctantly agreed.

The boys became excited at the idea.

Sterling nearly stuttered, "Say that you want to kiss Macy's nipples."

"Huh?" Aleescha retorted.

"Say it. Say that you want to kiss Macy's nipples," he impatiently repeated.

"Yeah, come on, say it," Murky wheezed, nearly out of breath.

It took a lot for her to force herself to come out with it, but she knew that she must. "I want to kiss Macy Donalds's nipples."

Sterling's heart raced with excitement. "Now say that you want to lick between her legs."

"Ah, come on, you guys. Let's just wait until we get together with her." She attempted to stall.

"Say it!" Carter barked, causing Aleescha to jump.

"I...I want to lick between Macy's legs."

"Oh yeah," Sterling buzzed. He was listening to Aleescha with his left hand inside the front of his pants. "Say that you want Macy to play with your mound."

"I want Macy to play with my mound."

Over the next few minutes, Sterling continued to direct Aleescha to say what he wanted to hear until he ejaculated for the third time that night. The thought of what she was articulating secretly disgusted her, but it saved her life.

"Now, you can get the hell out of here. We'll find you and Macy sometime later tonight or tomorrow, and then the two of you can give us a show," Carter directed.

"Where will I go? I want to stay here with Dalton," Aleescha begged.

"You're too goddamn mouthy. Just get the fuck out of here," Dalton lashed out.

Aleescha realized that if she didn't depart at that very moment, she would be shot. She carefully placed the hand grenades she was holding on to on the ground before she quickly shuffled away from her parents' driveway and into the darkness of the night.

"There, the dynamite is ready," Dalton announced, sliding out from beneath the van.

"Light the fuse, Sterling, and get ready to run like the dickens," Carter instructed.

Sterling struck his lighter and touched the flame to the wick. The fuse came to life with sparks climbing toward the bundle of dynamite. The Porters nearly ran over each other as they quickly scurried away from the van. They jumped down into a deep ditch next to the road and plugged their ears with their fingers.

The smoldering wick reached the package of dynamite, and after a brief hesitation, the TNT exploded with a powerful force.

The detonation echoed throughout the valley. The van was lifted off its tires, and while airborne, the fuel tank created a subsequent blast followed by a sizeable ball of fire. The van twisted in the air before slamming down on the driveway in an upright position. The vehicle was engulfed in flames. The explosion shattered nearly every window of the Wiles home.

*****

"WHAT THE HELL was that?" Dule fretted as he stopped dead in his tracks.

"Dynamite," Barry replied. "One bundle, but set up to cause a second explosion. Perhaps gasoline or propane."

"That was a helluva echo. It had to be three, maybe four miles away, and it still trembled and brushed the air around us. That must be 6G4 grade," Janice pointed out.

"What's 6G4 grade?" Dule nervously inquired.

"The purest grade of all dynamite," Barry responded. "A bundle of three or four sticks wrapped together could level an entire house or building. A half dozen could bring down half a block or more. Powerful TNT, plain and simple."

"Holy shit." Dule swallowed.

*****

"THAT'S 6G4 DYNAMITE," Cole concluded as he and Frank watched the fireball climb up to the sky from about four miles away from their current position. They were in town while searching every dark corner for the Porter entourage.

"That's up there by the Wiles place," Frank reported.

"On foot, how long until we can get up there?" Cole questioned.

"Um…perhaps forty minutes or more."

"The Porters will be gone from there by then. I'm sure there is more dynamite from where that came from. We'll keep searching in town, and hopefully, we come across the hoodlums before the next explosion. They are not going to be able to resist coming into town

to blow things up, so we'll wait them out here instead of going on a wild-goose chase."

*****

"WOW, WHAT A fuckin' mess. That was so awesome," Murky bellowed.

The charred van's frame smoldered in the driveway as the Porters observed the ruins from the mighty explosion.

"That's some massive dynamite you boys have there," Carter approved.

"Let's go into town and blow some shit up," Dalton suggested excitedly.

"Yeah, we'll do that," Sterling agreed. "But first, let's go over to Mooney's Drive-In and blow up that old screen."

"Cool, let's do it," Murky agreed.

*****

COLE AND FRANK heard whimpering sounds coming from around the corner of Sampson's Automotive Garage. Cole drew his handgun while Frank held the shotgun steady as they slid against the outside of the building. Cole peered around the corner to see Aleescha Wiles seated against the building. She was sobbing with her head drooped to her chest.

He slowly lowered his gun as he stepped around the corner, Frank at his heels.

"It's Aleescha Wiles, Yen and Patti's daughter," Frank reported.

Cole stooped next to her. Frank and Cole both noticed that she was not wearing any underwear. Cole took hold of the hem of her skirt and lowered the garment farther on her legs to help conceal her private area. She appeared exhausted and spent.

"Aleescha, are you alright?" Cole asked.

She glanced up at him. "Who are you?"

"My name is Cole Walsh. I'm with the FBI."

Aleescha began to weep. "They shot and killed my husband. They raped me. All four of them. I only wanted to be with Dalton. Murky nearly shot me."

"When was the last time you saw them?" Frank questioned.

"About twenty minutes ago up at my parents' house before they blew up my dad's van. They made me leave, sayin' that I ran my mouth too much."

"You're very lucky to have gotten away with your life," Frank pointed out.

"Where is everyone? The town is a wreck. I can't find anyone. Is everyone dead?"

"Sadly, some are. The others are hiding away inside the feedstore. That's where I want you to head, Aleescha," Cole directed while helping her to her feet.

"Okay, I'll go there, but first I need to pick up...um...somethin' of mine on Vine Street."

"Your parents are safe in the feedstore with the others," Frank informed her.

"Thank god! I owe them a deep apology," Aleescha claimed before taking off on a jog toward Vine Street.

*****

"OH NO, PLEASE no," Renee gasped.

The last of the second lantern's light faded as the fuel reservoir ran dry. The cellar fell to darkness once again, and there it would remain until the morning's sunrise would seep through the cracks in the cellar's door, but dawn was still more than three hours away.

Renee stood from the milk crate and slowly felt her way to the door. She stepped back from the door a few paces and then rushed her body against it, ramming her shoulder against the solid wood, nearly knocking the wind out of her. The door didn't budge.

"Cole!" she shouted. "Cole, where are you?"

*****

"YOU'RE GONNA HAVE a rough time arrestin' those Porters. They won't go quietly," Frank remarked. He and Cole continued to search the immediate area around town.

"Who said anything about arresting them?"

"You're just gonna let them go?" Frank asked with a shocked expression.

"Nope."

Now Frank understood, but saw no need to come right out and say it. After a brief hush, Frank inquired, "Where's the Stewart girl? I saw the two of you together the other day. Seems you two are an item?"

"I safely hid her away, but she's out by now. She's probably here in town somewhere. She's armed, but I don't think Murky would harm her or allow the others to do so."

"Everyone in Harpersfield knows how Murky has relentlessly pursued her."

"Well, she doesn't care for him." Cole nicked a bit.

"Whoa, we all know that too. A little jealous, are ya there, FBI man?" Frank teased.

"That's ridiculous." Cole half chuckled. "Listen, deputy, you and I need to split up."

"Huh? Why? Just because I was razzin' ya a bit?"

"There are...ah...people looking for me. These people are planning to silence me. If you are with me when they show up, you might inadvertently share in the same fate."

"Jesus Christ, Cole. Are you wrapped up in the Mafia or somethin'?"

"Of course not."

"Well, I wish you luck, but I don't feel much like hangin' with ya any longer. Nothin' personal. I prefer my heart when it's beatin'."

"How about you going to the feedstore and holding base there? You can watch over the others."

"Will do."

"If you see Renee, tell her to stay put and not to venture out here looking for me."

Frank stepped quickly into the night.

Cole continued his search solo.

*****

"LET'S GO WITH two bundles of dynamite this time," Sterling recommended.

"Yeah," Murky concurred.

"Two bundles it is," Dalton confirmed. He positioned one of the wads of dynamite on the bottom left base of the old drive-in screen, and the second package he placed at the foot of the screen's right side. Dalton then motioned with a nod to Sterling.

Sterling moved over to the left side of the projection screen.

"We have to light the fuses at the same time," Dalton directed.

"Who the hell died and left you boss?" Sterling sneered.

"Just shut up and do as you're told, Sterling," Carter grunted.

Sterling positioned himself at the left bundle and Dalton at the right roll. They brought their flaming cigarette lighters near the fuses simultaneously.

"Ready?" Dalton prepared.

Sterling nodded.

They then ignited the fuses at the same time. The foursome then sprinted for cover inside the abandoned concession stand.

The pair of dynamite packages detonated in unison, blowing the wooden screen into splinters. Flying scraps of wood, some three feet in length, shot throughout the drive-in property like torpedoes. The windows of the concession stand shattered. A two-foot jagged-edged piece of debris sailed through the window of the concession stand. The flying spear protruded into the wall less than six inches above Murky's head. The Porters all dropped to the floor and placed their arms over their heads. Sections of splintered wood sprayed down from above for nearly a full minute after the explosion.

CHAPTER 59

"JESUS!" DULE YELLED. "They're blowing up Tennessee!"

"That was two bundles," Barry indicated.

"How far away, Janice?" Marla asked.

"Three miles, perhaps four. No more than four."

"I felt the aftershock," Anthony pointed out.

Dule grabbed Marla by the arm and pulled her aside from the others. "What the hell are we getting ourselves into, Marla?"

"Nobody said it was going to be easy, Dule. It's extremely dangerous. Chances are that not all of us will make it through this."

"Then why do it?"

"There is a member out there that is a risk at exposing the group. He has to be stopped at any cost."

"Why not just let the three of them go after Cole and not us?"

"I would, but I feel responsible for allowing this case to come to this point. I should have shut it down days ago."

"Those Porters, they're ruthless."

"We have some of the best guns in the country on our side. Just remain back in the shadows and watch them do their thing. It's really something to witness."

*****

"HOLY HELL TO shit," Carter gasped as he brushed away debris from his clothes before rising to his feet. "They probably heard that one clear to Webster." Actually, Waynesburg and Webster were a bit too far to have the explosions heard by the populations there.

"I got a hard-on over that one." Sterling snickered.

"The guy I bought this dynamite from said the stuff was good. He sure is right," Dalton pointed out. "We have one bundle left. Let's go blow somethin' up in town."

"Yeah, and let's load the clips in these assault rifles and shoot up everything on our way," Murky proclaimed.

*****

JOE NEARLY SWATTED Frank with the baseball bat as the deputy made his entrance inside the feedstore.

"Whoa! Joe, it's me, Frank."

Joe lowered the weapon. "Jesus, deputy. What the hell are you doin' back here?"

"I came to help protect everyone."

"What about Cole? Shouldn't you be helpin' him with the Porters?" Emma grilled.

"He sent me back here, Emma. I guess Cole has more problems than just the Porters."

"What do you mean?" Patti questioned while embracing her now-rescued daughter. Aleescha had arrived at the feedstore, with her panties back in place, about ten minutes prior and profusely apologized to her parents. They readily accepted her into their loving arms.

"He said that there were some individuals pursuin' him. People who want to kill him."

"What in the hell could that be all about?" Henry wondered.

"I don't know, but I wasn't stickin' around to find out."

"Aleescha informed us that the Porters have guns, grenades, and dynamite. How is Cole goin' to stand up against all that?" Joe questioned.

"Cole's not only an FBI agent. He's also a Green Beret from the US Army."

"Oh boy, those are some bad-ass dudes," Joe confirmed.

"What is a Green Beret?" Emma sought.

"You know, like Rambo? That guy that Sylvester Stallone played in the movies?" Frank pointed out.

"Oh yeah," Emma replied. "Then I agree with Joe about the bad butt thing."

"The Porters will probably be a little too much for Cole to overcome, but the Porters are certainly gonna have their hands full," Frank determined grimly.

*****

"WATCH THIS SHIT." Dalton grabbed his father's and brothers' attention after rendezvousing with Carter's pickup truck. He pulled the truck up to within ten feet from Tom Donalds's Chevy pickup truck parked in his driveway. Tom, his wife Missy, and their daughters Macy and Julie were in Knoxville where Macy was with the Waynesburg cheerleading squad competing in a state contest.

Carter handed his rifle to Dalton. Dalton slid the ammo clip inside the assault rifle and engaged the gun into the automatic position. He took aim, and with a slight touch of his right forefinger on the rifle's trigger, ten rounds quickly popped off. The barrel smoked as bullets sprayed quickly about the bed of the truck. Multiple holes were blown into the truck instantly.

"That is too fuckin' cool!" Murky roared. He then loaded his own assault rifle. He took aim at the house and, in less than three seconds, fired seventeen rounds. Windows shattered, and the aluminum siding buckled under the force of the shots.

Within a minute, Sterling had his rifle loaded, and the house developed into a withering target for the brothers.

*****

"MY GOD, IT sounds like a war off in the distance," Joe remarked.

"Those are assault rifles," Frank deduced.

The room inside the feedstore fell silent as each one of the towns-people battled insecure thoughts of their own. They were frightened, and as each anxious event unfolded, they became more apprehensive. They looked around the room to one another, wondering if they all would die on this night at the hands of the ruthless Porters.

Being that the Porter family had tormented Harpersfield since nearly the time of the town's existence, today's citizens of this small settlement in southern Tennessee, like their ancestors before them, could only imagine what a peaceful way of life must be feel like. Some of the people born in Harpersfield had chosen to move away over the years. However, there were those who had deep family roots in this town, and living there was all they had ever known.

The stressful life of sharing the community with evildoers could be seen on each of their faces. The Harpersfieldians showed early signs of aging. If an outsider were to guess the age of the citizens of Harpersfield, the estimates would probably be off target by an average of eight years or more on the high end.

"Where's Henry?" Emma sought in a near panic.

"He wandered off a few minutes ago," Claudia replied.

"Wandered off? Where to?" Emma squealed.

"Calm down, Emma, I'm right here," Henry said as he stepped back into the large room. He had several items in his hands.

"Whatcha got there, Henry?" Joe inquired.

"Well, everyone is feelin' so down, I thought we could use a diversion. Somethin' to cheer us up a bit. I went snoopin' around in Chuck's office and found a dart board and these darts. I also found an old newspaper."

Emma placed her hands on her hips. "Henry, have ya completely flipped your lid? What are we gonna do with darts and a newspaper?"

"Chuck has a pile of old newspapers in his office. The papers he saved when the stories were about Harpersfield. So I looked through them until I found the perfect one." Henry then held up the front page of the newspaper. In big bold print, the headline read, "Porters Arrested for Stewart Murder."

"See, the Porter brothers' photos are here in the paper," Henry pointed out.

"Mr. Gert, are ya sure you didn't get into any whiskey back there? You're not makin' much sense," Judy observed.

Henry paced over to a nearby wall, and using two of the six darts, he tacked the front page of the newspaper to the wall. He then stepped back about ten paces and threw the remaining four darts one at a time at the photo of the Porters. One of the darts struck and stuck between the eyes of Sterling's photograph.

"See?" Henry grinned mischievously.

A quiet moment passed followed by a mumbled laugh by all. Soon, the entire group was guffawing and waiting for turn at throwing darts at the Porters—well, their pictures at least.

*****

"HOLD UP, I need to rewrap my ankle," Anthony informed the group.

"Okay, everybody, take five while Anthony adjusts his bra," Dule chortled.

Anthony glared at Dule.

"Those were C115 assault rifles," Barry concluded after hearing the distant gunfire.

"With expanded clips," Janice added.

"Those are strictly military. How do civilians get their hands on them?" Marla questioned.

"Are you kidding, Marla?" Anthony spoke up while rewrapping his ankle. "There's a black market for nearly everything. No pun intended, Simmons."

"Oh great, now we're up against machine guns as well," Dule further worried.

"They are bigger, faster, and more powerful than any standard machine gun," Barry made clear.

"Oh thanks, Barry. That's a little more information than I needed to know," Dule uttered.

"Why didn't you leave the little girl back at the van, Marla?" Anthony kidded, referring to Dule.

Dule curled his lip at Anthony.

"Dule, you need to keep quiet," Marla warned.

Dule pointed to himself. "Me? What about him? He's the one so quick to be a smart-ass."

"I once witnessed a man being shot to death with a C115," Barry interluded. "It sliced him in half like a chainsaw. What makes them so dangerous is that the bullets are made to flatten when they first strike, and then spin down along the bone, tearing up everything in its path."

"Marla, I think I will go back to the van after all," Dule said.

"Suit yourself, but if the Porters find you before we find them, well…you get the picture."

After a brief silence, Dule recanted, "Okay, let's go get them, I suppose. You all better shoot them in their tracks."

Anthony snickered at Dule's apprehension.

*****

ACKNOWLEDGING THAT SOON it would be daybreak, Cole used the now-cooling charcoal embers from the diner's fire in a fashion that he was trained to do. He rubbed the dark coals onto the tips of both forefingers. He then painted several black stripes upon his facial area. This would tone down his light skin, making him a bit more difficult to spot in daylight. He still had a gut feeling that the Porters would head back into town to riot and destruct further. The temptation was just too great.

The Green Beret hunkered down in a ditch about a hundred feet off Harper Street. Here he would wait for his prey.

*****

"MERLE IS STARTIN' to bleed again," a nervous Fred Darton announced about his son. Beverly was tending to her boy, but there

was little she could do. She pleaded, "We need to get him to the hospital in Webster, or he'll bleed to death!"

"Fred and Beverly, there is no way out of Harpersfield, you know that. Fred, you ran over the trap up on Martin's Way yourself," Frank reminded.

"There has to be a way, deputy. I just can't sit here and watch my son die," Beverly sobbed.

Frank thought for a moment before snapping his fingers. "Perhaps a four-wheel drive can cross Sulfur River, but that's a big maybe. That river has more drops than a mailman's route. The undercurrent is strong, so if you go under, you might not resurface."

"I'll take my chances," Fred retorted.

"I can sneak across the street and get my Jeep," Joe volunteered.

"Fred, you have a big gash on your head. You can't drive," Claudia pointed out.

"Then I'll drive!" Beverly barked.

"That's ridiculous, Beverly. You're still recoverin' from your hospital stay," Henry reinforced.

"I'll do it. I'll drive Merle to the hospital." Joe stepped up to the plate.

"Thank you, Joe. May God bless you," Beverly bid before embracing him.

"Okay, get Merle ready. I'll get the Jeep."

Judy grabbed hold of Joe's left arm and whispered, "Joe, why do you want to risk this? I know that Merle needs a doctor, and I'm sympathetic to that, but let one of the others do it, please?"

"It'll be okay, honey. I'll be careful."

"What about the baby?" Judy queried while rubbing her stomach that would surely expand over the coming months.

"All the more reason I need to do this, Judy."

She shook her head. "I don't understand."

"One day I'll need to answer to our boy or girl. What am I gonna tell her or him? That Daddy had a chance to help someone, and he backed out? I don't wanna tell my child that. I want to tell them that I came through for a fellow man, that I helped another human bein' in distress."

She poked at his chest with her left forefinger. "You'd better come back alive, Joe Skidmore."

He embraced and then kissed his wife. "I will, darlin', promise." After another kiss from his wife, Joe announced, "I'll be back in a jiffy with the Jeep."

*****

THE FIRST HINT of daylight scattered across the horizon. The Porters were sitting along Martin's Way, indulging in beer they stole from the Donalds' home. They were unaware that four miles down the same road walked three FBI agents and two private detectives. The five in pursuit were also oblivious that the Porters were on the same stretch of road ahead of them.

"What do you guys wanna fuck with next?" Dalton belched.

"I'm wonderin' where the hell Cole the mole is at. I thought we'd run into him by now. Maybe he started his truck and blew up," Murky snickered.

"You boys go ahead and play some more if ya want. I'm headin' home. I'm tired. We've been up all night long, and I can't keep my eyes open," Carter remarked.

"Bye, Pop," the boys synchronized.

Carter took a shortcut through the woods.

Sterling gulped a long swig of his beer. "Let's go blow up somethin' in town."

"First I wanna go up to the Stewart place to see if Renee is there," Murky insisted.

"We can do that. I wanna see if Cole is charred inside his truck." Dalton chuckled.

"A fried mole. Man, that can't smell too good," Murky sneered.

The boys snorted. They stepped off Martin's Way from the opposite side of their father's departure. They cut through the timber on their way to the Stewart farm.

*****

THE MORNING LIGHT began seeping through the cracks of the cellar door, and it was a welcoming sight for Renee as her eyes slowly adjusted. She had been in complete darkness for nearly three hours.

*****

AS COLE LAY in wait, he recalled a time while in the army when the Special Forces were called upon for a secretive mission. Dr. Henning Mullins, a world-renowned nuclear physicist, had been kidnapped from his Florida home by rebels of a third world party. This group of rebels had ties to a country in the Middle East, which was attempting to develop a nuclear warhead. CIA officials were able to pinpoint Dr. Mullins's position in the jungles of Brazil, where he was being held captive. The 161st division of Green Berets were called upon to rescue Dr. Mullins. The doctor was to be brought home alive, if possible, but dead if a complete rescue was not conceivable.

*****

Soldier Mark Bridges swatted at a large bug that had landed on his right forearm. "Great, Cole, now I probably get malaria."

"Odds are against it, Bridges. Besides, I think that's the least of our worries right now. Satellite images show nearly two dozen rebels are protecting the camp, heavily armed."

The two were cutting their way through the thick forest using machetes.

"Dan and Kyle are coming in from the north, right?" Mark sought to confirm.

"Yeah, they parachuted in about an hour before us. We have to keep pace if we are to meet with precise timing."

"I wish they would have deployed more than four of us."

"That's the way it is. Remember that if this thing gets botched up, we're to kill the doctor. The government is not prepared to take responsibility for a nuclear holocaust."

"Yeah…I read the details."

Fifteen minutes later, the camp slowly came into their view. A tall barbed wire fence shaped the entire border of the rebel camp with four occupied guard towers at each point.

Cole whispered, "We have to get in there and out before dark. That only gives us about two hours. The helicopter is picking us up at first light in the morning."

"I have the tent on my back and anti-venom in my pack," Mark replied.

"Okay, our teammates should be on the north side of this fence. We can't use a radio, but my synchronized watch reads it's time to go. Lock and load, Green Beret Bridges, and let's get this mission accomplished."

It had been over three months since Dr. Mullins was kidnapped. In that time, with no apparent attempts at a rescue, the rebels' security had become a bit relaxed. Cole and Mark crawled up to the fence between the guard towers and cut away the links with a handheld bolt cutter. Soon, they slithered through the opening of the fence and continued crawling until they reached the first of four shacks. They stood to their feet and slid along the outside wall of the poorly built structure. It was then that they spotted their fellow Green Berets, Dan Pike and Kyle Sturtevant. Using hand signals, Dan informed Cole and Mark that Dr. Mullins was inside the third shack. The Green Berets teamed up and quietly entered the hut. One rebel stood guard outside of the doctor's room.

"Do your thing, Cole," Kyle whispered.

Cole snaked along the wall behind the guard. The others prepared to fire their guns at a moment's notice. Cole positioned himself behind the rebel, and in one quick motion, he wrapped his arms around the guard's head and snapped his neck. The rebel's body spilled to the floor as if he were made of flimsy rubber.

Dan moved forward and threw open the door of the room that held Dr. Mullins. Henning was seated on a cot gazing up at the ceiling when the door suddenly sprang open. He recognized the men as soldiers of the US Army.

"Oh my god, I am happy to see you men," Henning gasped. Then he realized that their mission could include killing him. He stood and put his palms up in front of himself. "I told them nothing, men. Not a thing, I swear. They beat me, but I said nothing."

"It's okay, Doctor. We're here to take you home," Mark reported.

Henning released a sigh of relief. Rather than trying to direct the actions for the doctor to follow, Dan threw Dr. Mullins over his left shoulder.

"Let's get him out of here," Kyle growled.

They moved with calculated precision, heading for one of the two gaps cut in the fence. They snuck back into the jungle without incident, but they knew once Dr. Mullins was discovered missing, the rebels would scan the forest in search of him.

They made camp on a small ridge overlooking their back trail. During the night, the Green Berets did not light a campfire in order to remain hidden in the darkness of forest. The glow from a fire would have given away their position. They alternated standing guard while the others slept. At first light, they moved again while heading for a meeting with the helicopter. In the distance, the forest echoed with the sounds of the rebels in search of Dr. Mullins and those that came to his rescue. The helicopter landed, and just as the rescue team was about to rush out of the brush to their transportation, several rebels appeared and sprayed the helicopter with gunfire. Before the helicopter could lift back off from the ground in an emergency exit, a bullet pierced the fuel tank, sending the helicopter into a ball of fire. The pilot was killed instantly.

The team ducked back into the forest to avoid the rebels. They were now without safe transport out of the thick jungle with rebels seeking them out.

"Dan, how far to the nearest village?" Cole asked.

"About thirty-five miles west," Dan reported after referring to his paper map.

"Okay, we head there," Kyle confirmed.

"That's a two-day hike," Henning wheezed.

"We don't have any other options, Doctor," Mark retorted.

They narrowly avoided the rebel soldiers that day, and after pitching camp that night, they continued toward the village the following morning. Two hours into the day, they realized that the enemy had surrounded them.

"How in the hell do they keep knowing where we are?" Mark wondered.

It was then that it came to Cole. He grabbed hold of Dr. Mullins's jaw, forcing his mouth open. After peering inside Henning's mouth, Cole

reared back and landed a hard punch to the doctor's jaw. Henning's head snapped back before he spit out one of his lower back teeth.

"What the hell are you doing?" Henning asked, grimacing in pain as his ears rang. Cole bent to pick up the tooth. He inspected what looked to be a cavity and pointed out a microscopic chip.

"This is a homing device. It works by radio frequency. This is how they know approximately where we are at all times. They must have embedded it after they drugged you, Doctor," Cole explained.

"Yes, they did drug me once," Henning confirmed.

Cole then tossed the tooth containing the chip into the brush.

"Sorry about the tooth, Doc," Cole apologized.

"That's quite alright, I understand."

"Cole, they're all around us and closing in. Let's form a guard-and-assault formation around Dr. Mullins," Kyle suggested.

"Good idea, Kyle." Cole grabbed Henning by the arm and led him to a tree. "Climb up the tree, Doctor."

"You've got to be joking. I haven't climbed a tree since I was child."

"It's that or be shot or recaptured by the rebels," Dan pointed out.

Henning leaped up to grab hold of the tree's lowest branch. Awkwardly, he shimmied up the tree. The Green Berets formed a circle around the perimeter with their weapons in the ready position. The noise in the brush and the voices of the rebels drew nearer. Soon, from the forest, two rebel soldiers appeared, walking directly into the trap.

Before they could react, Dan leaped onto the nearest one to him and sliced his neck open with a knife before the rebel could make a sound. Simultaneously, Kyle struck the other rebel in the chin with a forearm at such a force that it snapped the man's neck. The two rebels were killed instantly without being able to warn their cohorts.

Henning trembled as he held onto the tree. The brush around them was now moving with rebel soldiers. Cole nodded at Kyle, Dan, and Mark. They opened fire with their assault rifles into the brush. Bullets struck six rebels before the others could return fire. The Green Berets hit the ground for cover but continued to spray the brush with bullets. Three more rebels were hit before Dan took a bullet to the chest. He rolled while dropping his rifle. Kyle scrambled to his aid as Cole and Mark fired away, trying to hold back the rebels.

Within moments of reaching Dan, Kyle realized that his fellow soldier would probably not survive the gunshot wound. He then, as trained, turned his gun on Dan and whispered, "God bless." After shooting Dan, Kyle turned his gun and attention back to the oncoming rebels.

It soon became apparent that the rebels had gathered extra forces in the search for the doctor. Rather than about a dozen, the Green Berets were facing an enemy army of nearly sixty. Mark then caught a bullet in his throat. Blood gushed from his severed artery, and within a minute, Mark bled to death. Before Kyle and Cole could close the gap between them, Kyle was shot in the leg, then in the head. His body shook for a few moments after hitting the ground until he grew motionless. Cole dove into heavy brush as bullets struck all around him. After another two minutes of rapid fire from the rebels, the shooting mercifully ceased. The area fell deathly quiet until Cole heard one of the rebels bark out orders in their native tongue. Three of the rebels appeared from out of the brush.

They looked intently around for Dr. Mullins, who was perched in the tree above them.

Keep quiet, Dr. Mullins, Cole thought to himself as he watched the tree from about eighty feet away.

Henning's fear got the best of him, and his trembling caused enough noise for the rebels to look up and spot him. One of the rebel soldiers took to the tree quickly to gather Dr. Mullins. Cole realized that he was left with but only one option. The potential fate of millions of innocent lives rested in that tree. Dr. Mullins may have not helped the rebels to build a warhead yet, but it was only a matter of time until he'd break down from all the torture sure to come his way.

Cole peered through his rifle's scope and took careful aim. The crosshairs of the scope came to a rest between Henning's eyes as the rebel soldier was only two limbs away from reaching him. "Sorry, Doc," Cole muttered as he squeezed the trigger.

A single shot from the assault rifle struck Dr. Mullins directly between the eyes. His lifeless body spilled out of the tree and plummeted to the ground below. The rebels angered and sprayed the vicinity around Cole with bullets but failed to hit the Green Beret.

Another forty rebel soldiers busted out from cover, rushing toward Cole's direction, though they could not see him. Cole knew that his only chance at getting away with his life was clipped on his uniform's strap. He unclipped the shock grenade from the strap. The grenade was developed to set off with a piercing percussion that stifled anyone within a thousand yards of it. It was also packed with over eight thousand tiny but sharp pins that blasted out in every direction upon the explosion of the device.

Cole pulled the pin and heaved the grenade in the direction of the enemy soldiers. He then cupped his ears and applied pressure. The shock grenade hit the ground a second before it exploded. The extreme percussion dropped the rebels to their knees, and the flying pins struck nearly every soldier. The rebels screeched out in shock and pain. Cole took advantage of the situation to slip away into the forest unscathed.

Cole lived off the forest for nearly two weeks before he happened on to a friendly village. He was picked up by the US Army there. The possibility of a wayward nuclear holocaust was no longer a threat.

*****

"LET'S GO INTO town, Murky. There ain't nobody here," Sterling indicated.

"Yeah, and it looks like that Cole dude drove his goddamn truck away. I wonder why it didn't blow up. Are you sure you rigged it up the right way, Sterling?" Dalton questioned.

"I hooked it up right," Sterling retorted.

"Let's go, I want to try to find Renee in town," Murky said, standing in front of the charred remains of the Stewart farmhouse.

"We have to do a beer run. We're out of brew," Dalton announced.

"Hello? You numbskull," Sterling grunted. "We burned down the store, the tavern, and the gas station."

"Oh shit, that's right. Well, what are we gonna do for beer?"

Murky raised his right forefinger. "I got it. Man, I'm a genius. Remember a few years back when we were deer huntin' on the back of this property? We came across that cellar where the old man probably kept moonshine."

"Oh yeah, I remember that cellar. You are a fuckin' genius, Murky," Sterling praised.

Murky glowed with pride.

"Well, let's round up some shine before we go into town," Dalton growled.

Chapter 60

JOE GUIDED HIS Jeep to the very edge of the Sulfur River's bank with the bleeding Merle aboard. Joe knew the mysteries that surrounded this river, how the Indians from long ago avoided this running body of water. They believed that the river contained evil spirits that washed up from the river's origin, a natural sulfur mine many feet below the earth's surface. The water ran rusty and reeked of sulfur, as when a lit match is extinguished. The river was so acidic that fish and water plants could not survive its waters.

The river formed a natural border between Webster and Harpersfield. The sulfur content had eaten away at the river's bed, creating unpredictable ridges and sharp drops along its path. What made this extremely dangerous was that the water was cloudy, the bed of the river could not be witnessed from the surface. There were areas of the river that were merely three feet deep, while other parts could drop off to nearly sixty feet in depth. Because the bed of the river was exceedingly uneven, the currents were unpredictable and unstable.

Joe reached to the floorboard behind the front seat and brought two life jackets to the front. "Here, Merle, put this on," he directed while handing one of the two orange vest-type jackets to Merle. "I grabbed them from my canoe when I went after my Jeep."

Both men slid into their own jacket around their torso to a snug fit. "Are you ready?"

Merle delivered a nervous nod.

"Okay, here we go. I only hope that we've picked the right spot to cross."

*****

MARLA, DULE, BARRY, Janice, and Anthony made their way down Harper Street in the early morning light. There was an eerie quiet, and the air smelled of burnt wood. Buildings lay in smoldering ashes. Mason Turner's dead body was sprawled out upon the sidewalk. Cars and trucks parked along the street were vandalized. With no one to be found, it had the look of a ghost town. A chill bit the air despite the August heat.

"Jesus Christ, they have destroyed the town," Dule stated the obvious.

"Where is everyone?" Janice wondered.

"If it were you living in this town, where you would be, Janice? You'd either be dead or hiding out," Barry retorted.

"Those maniacs executed this well," Marla acknowledged. "They cut this small town off from the rest of the world. Besides the people here, no one knows what is going down here in Harpersfield."

From a roadside ditch behind them, the tall weeds came to life with the opening of Cole's eyes. He was a mere fifty feet from them, without the group's knowledge. Cole watched them intently as they moved very slowly along Harper Street.

"What I'm thinking is where is Walsh?" Dule asked in a shaky voice.

"Maybe he's dead. Perhaps they've killed him," Anthony replied.

"That's unlikely," Marla indicated. "Keep in mind, we are not leaving here without taking care of Cole or at least finding his body."

Cole thought to himself, *I have to find a way to deal with them one at a time.*

The group continued their way until they were out from Cole's sight.

*****

JOE EASED THE Jeep's front tires into the Sulfur River. "Fast or slow? What do you think, Merle?"

"Fast," Merle grumbled. "Let's get this over with."

Joe accelerated the Jeep and then popped the clutch. The vehicle rocked as it rolled across the uneven bottom of the river. The ride was rough enough that Joe was struggling to hold on to the steering wheel. Merle held on tight to the passenger's door.

"Come on, baby. Come on, get us across," Joe begged.

Merle closed his eyes and prayed, worried more about the river than his own bleeding now.

"A hundred more yards, Merle. Keep prayin', boy," Joe huffed.

The river's opposite bank drew nearer, as did the border of Webster.

"Fifty yards, Merle. I think we're gonna make it, young man. Looks like we picked the right spot to cross!" Joe blurted with excitement.

Suddenly, the Jeep leaped from an underwater ridge. With a plunge and a swirl, the Jeep disappeared from the river's surface. The rig quickly submerged and finally rested at the river's bottom, over twenty-five feet in depth. The rusty water poured inside the Jeep.

"Holy shit!" Merle shouted.

"Hold your breath, Merle, and when the Jeep fills, open you door," Joe instructed.

The two men held their heads above the rising water inside the vehicle as long as possible until the cab became completely filled with river water. Their eyes and nose instantly burned from the sulfur content of the river. Joe was able to force his door open and sprung himself out of the submerged Jeep. Merle was having difficulty with his door. He rammed his body weight against the door without success. Precious seconds were ticking away as Merle struggled. Joe was trying to swim to the passenger's door to help Merle, but his life jacket wanted to pull him upward toward the river's surface. Joe realized that if he surfaced, he would not have ample time to get back down to Merle before the Darton boy would likely drown. He thought about his unborn baby and the promise he made to his wife about returning to her alive. Valuable time passed as he desperately

attempted to save Merle. He released his life jacket, and the lone preserver rushed toward to the surface.

Joe quickly moved to the passenger door to grab hold of the handle. He used all his strength to pull the door open, nearly breaking a finger in the process. Merle was now in panic mode as Joe reached inside the Jeep to grab hold of Merle's shirt. He then pulled Merle out from the jeep. He held on to Merle's arm as they kicked their legs frantically, desperate to reach the surface in time. Merle's life jacket helped to propel them upward. The oxygen in their lungs was all but spent as they were forced to inhale the acidic water. Joe's head was the first to break out of the water, followed in less than a second by Merle's. They both gasped for air and coughed up water. Their throats felt as if they were on fire.

When Merle was able to fill his lungs with air, he cried. Fighting for enough air, Joe helped Merle swim toward the safety of the riverbank. "It's gonna be okay, Merle. We're gonna be fine. We're gonna make it to the bank. Just keep taking deep breaths."

Joe crawled out from the now-shallow water and pulled Merle up onto the bank. They both collapsed in exhaustion on the dry land of Webster's shore.

*****

"I REMEMBER IT bein' right around here," Murky disclosed. He, Sterling, and Dalton were searching the Stewarts' woods for the old fruit cellar.

"I think it was a little more that way." Sterling pointed to the right.

They stood looking at one another for a moment.

"Well, are you just gonna stand there like an idiot?" Murky snapped at Sterling.

"Ya know, Murky, if I weren't so happy right now, I'd kick the shit out of you," Sterling claimed.

"Yada, yada, yada, Sterling. I've kicked your ass before."

"What, Murky? A few lucky times out of about a hundred. I'd hardly call that an advantage."

"I'd hurt ya, and I'd hurt ya bad," Murky spurted out with his usual threat.

"Are we gonna get some shine or fight?" Dalton complained.

Sterling glared at Murky for a long moment before mumbling, "Shine."

They continued with their search and discovered that Sterling's hunch had paid off. They located the cellar.

As they approached, Renee could hear their shuffling about from outside the cellar. "Cole! Thank god, what took you so long, honey? Hurry up and get me out of here. I need to hold you and kiss you."

The Porters were stunned that Renee was inside the fruit cellar.

Murky instantly became angry at Renee's intimate references about Cole. "Why in the heck are ya callin' the mole honey?" Murky shouted through the locked door.

Renee's eyes widened and her heart pounded with fear at the sound of Murky's voice. "Murky?"

"Yeah, it's me! Are ya foolin' around on me with that mole?"

Now Renee angered a bit. "Stop callin' Cole that! I'm not messin' around on you, Murky. We have never, nor will we ever be, a couple."

Murky narrowed his eyes as his temper flared. Dalton and Sterling chuckled. Murky quickly raised his assault rifle to his shoulder and pointed the barrel at the cellar's door. He squeezed the trigger, spraying the door with piercing bullets.

Renee screamed as she crawled into a corner and curled up. Bullets hit and some ricocheted throughout the cellar. After about thirty rounds were spent, Dalton grabbed hold of Murky's gun, stopping the shooting. Renee sobbed as she quickly checked her body to see if she had been hit. She was relieved to find that she came through it without a wound.

"What the hell are ya doin', Dalton? If I can't have her, nobody will."

"Hey, I'm not against ya killin' the bitch. But let's at least screw her first," Dalton said with a grin.

"Yeah," Sterling agreed. "I don't know if I can cum again already. I have three times so far last night, but I'll sure try. That Renee has one fine beaver I bet."

"Nobody screws Renee except me!" Murky declared.

"Ah, come on, Murky. We'll let you go first, and then when me and Sterling are done with her, you can shoot her," Dalton dealt.

Murky mulled it over. "Okay, but I ride her first, and then I'm the one that gets to shoot her. But we're takin' her home to screw her. I wanna do her on my bed," Murky demanded.

"Fair enough," Dalton retorted.

Murky then jerked his gun out from Dalton's hold. He switched the rifle from automatic to manual. He placed careful aim at the lock and squeezed the trigger. The bullet buckled the lock, and it sprung open. Murky then stepped down the slight drop to the entrance of the cellar and removed the damaged lock. He threw open the door, and sunlight rushed inside, causing Renee to squint.

Murky's silhouette was standing in the doorway with the morning sun rising behind him. "Get up, bitch!" he barked at her.

Renee, at the tone of his demanding voice, realized that he no longer held a soft side for her. If she didn't comply with his every demand, he would most certainly kill her. She stood to her feet and trembled. She then made a desperate effort to help ease the tension. "Murky, you're scarin' me. I thought you loved me. Don't treat me badly. You're not supposed to hurt the one you love."

He grabbed hold of her right arm and slung her out from the cellar. The strong force of his aggression caused her to stumble out of the cellar and spill to the ground at Dalton and Sterling's feet.

Sterling crouched down. "We're gonna take you home in a little while, and I'm gonna get me some of that fine pussy of yours, Stewart." He mischievously winked.

"Not before me," Murky reminded as he exited the cellar.

Renee quickly came to her feet.

Murky aggressively grabbed a handful of Renee's hair, pulling her head back. "All that I've ever wanted was to be yours, but no, that wasn't good enough for you. I've tried and tried, only to have you turn your back on me. Well, not anymore because now you're only shit to me. I'm gonna screw ya, Renee, who is now my slave. You can count on that. I don't care if ya wanna screw me or not. We're gonna blow up some stuff in town, and then we're takin' you home with us."

"Damn, girl, your pussy is gonna be sore by the time we're done," Dalton chortled.

"You should've just come to me, Renee. Your brother would still be alive." Murky snorted.

Renee angered that Murky would blame Nate's death on her. She reared back with her right leg and kicked Murky in the left shin. He let go of her hair to grab his lower leg and limp around in a tight circle. Sterling and Dalton broke into laughter as Renee sprinted off on a run through the woods.

"Shut up, you derelicts, she's gettin away. Go after her!" Murky barked.

"Oh shit, our pussy is on the run," Dalton grunted before taking off on a sprint of his own after Renee. Sterling joined the chase while Murky still nursed his shin.

As she ran and navigated the woods, Renee shouted, "Help! Somebody help me!" She suddenly acknowledged that this must be the way Nate felt as he ran from the Porters on that fateful day. However, she couldn't run nearly as fast as Nate could, and the Porters had caught up with him. She soon realized that she was not going to remain in the lead much longer. She figured her only chance was to stop and fight.

She spotted a fallen branch with a jagged edge about twenty yards in front of her. She halted her pace to pick up the branch. With a speeding heart and trembling hands, Renee stood her ground, ready to defend herself.

Within moments, Sterling and Dalton came into view.

"There's our hot piece of ass, bro," Dalton sneered.

"She's got a stick." Sterling chuckled.

"What the hell are ya gonna do with that?" Dalton taunted. "You don't stand a chance, little girl. Put the branch down before we stick it up your ass."

"She'd probably like that." Sterling snickered.

The boys stepped slowly toward her.

"Put it down, bitch," Dalton warned.

"No!" Renee shouted, swiping the branch in their direction. "Don't come any closer."

Dalton kept her attention on him while Sterling slowly circled her. "Renee Stewart, you're no fighter. You're a wimp like your shit-head brother was," Dalton insulted.

"You shut up about Nate. You have no right to speak about him," she growled.

Sterling was just about to grab Renee from behind when she quickly turned and swung the branch at him, nearly striking his face. With her back now to Dalton, he rushed her from behind and swept her up into his strong arms. Sterling grabbed hold of the branch and ripped it from her hands. He then tossed the branch into the brush. She squirmed in Dalton's arms, but he had a powerful hold on her.

Sterling licked his lips. "I gotta get a good feel of those nice titties."

"No!" she screamed, again trying to break free of Dalton without success.

Sterling stepped over to her. He cupped his hands on each of her breasts and massaged her through her shirt. "Damn, girl, those are nice and firm. I'll have to tit fuck ya later when we get home," Sterling asserted. He continued to grope her up until he was suddenly attacked by Murky.

Sterling's head jerked to the left as a result of a blunt strike to the head from Murky using his own head as a weapon. A small cut opened on Sterling's forehead, and blood trickled down the bridge of his nose.

"What the hell are ya doin', Murky?" Sterling snarled as he wiped away some of the blood.

"I told you that I am first. I'm first and not out here, in my bed at home."

*****

"CAN YOU STAND up, Merle?" Joe inquired.

"Yeah…yeah, I think so."

With Joe's assistance, Merle slowly came to his feet on the riverbank.

"We have about a five-mile hike into town. Do you think you can make it?" Joe wondered.

"Do I have a choice?" Merle stated the obvious.

"No…I suppose not. If you need spells of rest, just let me know, and we'll take breaks, okay?"

Merle nodded.

*****

"HE LOOKS DEAD. He's got to be dead. Is he dead?" Dule asked Janice, who was checking for a pulse with her finger pressed to Mason Turner's neck.

"As a doornail," she replied.

"Well, what did you think, Dule? He was shot in the head with a high-powered rifle." Anthony rolled his eyes.

"Don't even start up again, you two," Marla warned.

"Where do we look for Cole?" Barry questioned.

"He already knows we are here, I'm sure of it," Marla claimed. "He's more than just an FBI agent, much more. He's a trained stealth soldier, compliments of the USA military. Be certain that we are going to need more than our weapons to bring down Cole Walsh. We're going to need our wits as well."

*****

"I SHOULD'VE GOT them Porters back for beatin' my mother," Merle said shamefully. He and Joe were making their way across an old abandoned field that was once a prosperous farm. The acidic content from the nearby Sulfur River had eventually invaded the soil, making crop growing impossible.

"What good would that have proved, Merle? Those boys would have killed you."

"Perhaps, but at least I would have had a little dignity, some pride. I curled up in the corner like a coward, as I always do when the heat is on."

"Ah, stop bein' so hard on yourself."

"It's probably a good thing that Murky shot my balls. What would any future son of mine be like? Just another wimp in Harpersfield."

"Listen to me. I've been a bartender and tavern owner for many years. In that time, I've seen many controversies. To me, the better man was always the one who walked away."

After a few moments of quiet, Merle delved, "Joe, do you think that Macy Donalds is pretty?"

"Um…yeah, she's a looker. Why?"

"Well, I've been thinkin' about askin' her out."

"Doesn't she see that Hartman boy?"

"Well, it isn't like she's married."

"No…I suppose not. So why haven't you asked her yet?"

Merle shrugged his shoulders. "I've only asked one girl out before, and she declined, sayin' that she was too busy with her work. I know that was a roundabout way of her tellin' me that I'm fat."

"You're much too critical of yourself, Merle. Lighten up a bit. Are you still bleedin'?"

"No, it stopped."

"Good, we should be in downtown Webster in about an hour and a half or so. There we can get you medical help and alarm the authorities to hurry their way to Harpersfield."

*****

"WE HAVEN'T HEARD anything for a spell now. I wonder if it's finally over?" Emma hoped.

"I don't think we should go anywhere until Cole comes back and tells us it's okay," Frank recommended. "Until then, we stay here in the feedstore."

"I pray that Joe and my Merle made the Sulfur River," Beverly said worriedly.

Fred placed a comforting arm around his wife's shoulders. "I'm sure they did, Beverly. Joe knows that river well, as good as one can, I suppose. They are probably at the hospital right now, and Joe has help on its way here."

"I'd love to see the look on the Porters' faces when the state police come whiskin' into Harpersfield," Henry scoffed.

"That should be anytime now," Frank cautiously estimated.

*****

"WE'RE TAKIN' THE old man's truck." Murky forced Renee in the direction where the vehicle was parked in the driveway.

"Her purse was in the guesthouse, just like ya said," Dalton revealed, stepping toward the truck.

Sterling grabbed the purse from Dalton's hands and fumbled through the bag's contents until he located the keys to the truck. "All aboard!" he declared.

"All of us are not goin' to fit inside the truck," Renee said.

"You're ridin' on my lap, so you might as well friggin' enjoy it. I'm sure my cock will get hard, and you will feel it throbbin' on your ass," Murky growled.

Rene winced at the very thought. Sterling dove into the driver's seat, and Dalton slid across bench seat to sit next to him. Murky leaped up to the passenger's seat and then flung his hand out to Renee. "Come on," Murky demanded.

With no choice, she reluctantly complied.

*****

THE GROUP GATHERED round Marla as Dule tossed his briefcase on the hood of a damaged vehicle near the charred remains of Tiny's Diner. He opened the case and handed some of the contents over to Marla.

"Thanks, honey. Of course, you all know what Cole Walsh looks like. These are newspaper photos of the three Porter brothers as they appeared in court nearly a year ago. Be aware of them as they are obviously armed, and they are extremely dangerous. If your life is threatened by one or all three of them, do not hesitate to take them out. Also, remember that you are to shoot Cole Walsh on sight. Now, it's best if we separate. Remaining in a group helps Cole and/or the Porters to monitor us. Each of you establish your own way around this town while Dule and I patrol together. If you come across Cole or the Porters, fire off your flare gun that Dule is now going to hand out. So let's check that our weapons are loaded, and let's do this."

CHAPTER 61

"I NEED A break, Joe. Not because of my wound, but because I'm out of breath," Merle requested.

"Okay, let's have a seat over there on that old fallen fence post."

After making their way to the makeshift bench, Merle confessed, "Ya know, I've been thinkin' I'm gonna change some of my ways. My dad is sure to rebuild the station, so I think I'll take up workin' on vehicles. It'll bring more money in for the family. Hopefully, the Porters will be in jail, so they can't rob us anymore."

"I think the Porters are certainly goin' to prison this time around. I can't possibly see how they'd get out of this one. They got lucky gettin' away with Nate Stewart's murder, but this time they won't be able squirm out of it."

"I hope you're right, Joe. Harpersfield will be a much better place without them."

"I couldn't agree more."

*****

"HOW ARE WE gonna get out of this when it's all over?" Dalton questioned.

"Easy," Sterling replied. "Who is gonna testify against us in court? If they do, they know that we or our relatives will kill their family members."

Renee was terrified to speak up, but her anger allowed her to do so. "I think you boys might be surprised. I believe this town is ready to revolt against you all. We are all sick and tired of the Porters' aggressions."

"Oh, whoa! Who has the bitch with the fuckin' mouth now, Murky?" Dalton taunted.

Murky nodded. "Yeah, you're right, Dalton. Can't be havin' a broad talkin' to the Porters like that." He then shoved Renee in the back of her head with force.

She folded at the waist, and her face crashed into the truck's dashboard. Her body snapped back upward, and blood from her nose sprayed on the dashboard. The momentum pulled her back into Murky's chest, and he quickly took a firm grip around her neck, wrapping his forearm around her throat. Renee fought for air.

Murky snarled into her right ear, "Don't you ever talk to me or my brothers like that again. If you do, I'll kill you."

"Cool," Dalton observed. "Her face is turnin' blue."

Murky released her just before she passed out. She inhaled a rasping breath of much-needed air. Murky then slid his left hand onto her crotch and cupped her between her legs. "My hand stays there. Now, for bein' mouthy, flash my brothers your tits."

Renee spoke with cloudy, pain-filled eyes. "Murky, I don't wanna do that, please."

"Do it, Renee, now my slave." He ground the words through his teeth.

"I thought only you wanted to view my body." She attempted to sway his demand of her exposing herself.

"Do it, goddamn it. For at least ten seconds." Murky delivered a final warning, grabbing a handful of her hair.

"Show us those knockers," Dalton cheered.

"Yeah! Nips, nips, we wanna see nipples," Sterling buzzed.

With complete reluctance, she pulled her T-shirt and bra over the top portion of her breasts, exposing them for the Porters to view.

"Now those are nice tits," Dalton admired.

Renee's face reddened with both anger and humiliation.

"That's a couple of mouthfuls worth there. Gawd, we certainly are gonna gangbang you later, girl," Sterling pledged.

Before she could lower her shirt down over her exposed breasts, Murky reached up with both hands quickly from behind her and pinched both her nipples in between his thumbs and forefingers. He gently rolled her nipples while peering over her shoulder. "I've been waitin' to see those hooters for a long time now. Finally, here they are in all their glory." Murky moaned with satisfaction.

She could feel his enormous penis become erect into the small of her back. She then forced her shirt over her breasts, disrupting Murky's connection with her nipples. Renee felt nauseated.

"That's okay, Renee. I'll get my flippin' hands back on ya again in a little while." Murky chuckled wickedly.

*****

"WHERE ARE YA goin', Frank?" Claudia prodded.

Frank was moving toward the door of the feedstore.

"I have a gut feelin' that Cole needs me back out there," he responded.

The group inside the feedstore were growing restless. Fred and Beverly sat quietly in an embrace, worrying over their son's well-being.

"If you leave, who is gonna protect us?" Claudia questioned. "Joe left, and that leaves Henry and Yen. No offense, gentlemen, but you're up there in age."

"You all stand a better chance if you stay together," Frank assured them.

"It sounds like it's over. Maybe we all should go home," Aleescha suggested.

"Yeah," Emma added.

"No!" Frank snapped. "You go back out there and then split up. The Porters will pick you off one at a time. This isn't over. I can feel it in my bones."

*****

"ARE YA GONNA sleep all day?" Bessy nagged at Carter. She was standing at the open bedroom door holding a steaming cup of coffee she had brought for her husband.

"What the hell is it to ya?" he lashed out before sitting up in bed.

Bessy strode to him and surrendered the cup of java over to her husband. "I'm worried about the boys. They haven't come home. They were out all night, and so far today, they haven't showed. And I heard explosions and gunfire."

Carter chuckled. "Oh, that. The boys are just havin' some fun is all. I was with 'em for a bit last night. They must still be goin' at it. That's my boys. I'm gonna swallow down some of this caffeine and head back out to join 'em."

Bessy placed her hands on her hips. "Who's gonna run for my whiskey today?"

"Who cares?" he snorted.

"Well, tell them to come home and get some sleep sometime today. And tell them to be careful and not get hurt."

*****

COLE, FROM HIS perch on the rooftop of the post office, surveyed as Janice crossed the street toward the building below him. She looked around carefully, everywhere except up. She stepped upon the sidewalk along the front of the post office.

Cole matched her pace from above, and then he leaped off the two-story roof. Like an eagle, he swooped down upon his prey. Before Janice could react, Cole plunged upon her, piling them down together onto the concrete. He had her wrists behind her back and restrained her with her own handcuffs within seconds.

"You scream, you die, Janice," he warned in a gravelly voice.

"Cole, you're not going to get away. Give it up."

"I have some unfinished business here first. Then you and the other agents can do with me whatever you decide that should be."

"There's no deciding about it, Cole. You know the rules. They are spelled out clearly. I'm sure you realize that we are here to kill you."

"Yeah, I'm fully aware of that. But I need to make sure this town is left to rebuild in peace and not in hell."

"You can't always be a savior, Walsh."

"Perhaps, Agent Stark. But this time I need to be. If I can't complete this mission, many innocent lives will be tormented and terminated."

Her voice softened. "Is it really that bad here?"

"Every bit."

"If you leave me here like this and those criminals happen by, I'm dead. I can't defend myself while I'm handcuffed," she pointed out.

"I'll hide you away inside the post office."

She glanced around at the charred buildings. "What if they torch the post office? Or blow it up with that high-grade dynamite they're carrying around?"

Cole hesitated before blurting out, "Damn it."

"You're just going to have to trust me, Cole. I'm on your side until this is over. Let me help you take care of these felons."

Long moments of silence passed before he bargained, "When I release the cuffs, you so much as make one wrong move, and I'll spill your brains on the sidewalk. You got that, Janice?"

"I got it, Cole. Come on, let's team up."

Cole removed the handcuffs. Janice rubbed her wrists. "You put them on a little tight." He reached out his hand to help her to her feet as she pledged her allegiance. "Let's go catch us some bad guys, Mr. Walsh."

*****

"AFTER MEETING COLE, I read up on Green Berets," Dule revealed. He and Marla were searching the tall grass that ran along behind the businesses on Harper Street.

"And what did you learn?"

"That they are not ones to mess with. They are trained to complete their missions regardless of who or what gets in their way. They

are precision killing machines. Do you think if it came down to it that Cole would kill us?"

"Yes, I have no doubts about that."

"Even you, Marla? He would kill you?"

"Most certainly. It takes a special breed to be an FBI agent. Even more so to be a Green Beret. Cole Walsh is one of the nicest people I know, but he's also one of the nastiest."

"Between you and me, do these agents stand a chance against him?"

"Barry, Janice, and Anthony are three of the finest in the country."

"That doesn't answer my question, Marla."

"You're talking too much, Dule. Just help me search for clues."

*****

"WE'RE ALMOST THERE, Merle. I can see the town now. How are ya feelin'?" Joe asked.

"A little weak, but I can make it."

"We'll have ya some medical help soon. While they tend to you, I'll get the police to respond to Harpersfield if they haven't already."

*****

"MURKY, TAKE YOUR hand out from between my legs please," Renee requested.

"No!" he barked. "If feels good there."

"Maybe to you it does, not to me."

"You screwed that FBI guy, didn't you?" Murky probed.

"That's none of your business," she bit out.

Dalton snickered. "That means she did the nasty with him."

"I can't flippin' believe that you messed around on me with that mole," Murky growled.

She angered, but her throbbing nose reminded her to keep things as calm as possible. "Murky, I didn't cheat on you. You and I are not a couple, so that doesn't make it cheatin' on you."

"Renee, your soft voice drives me wild. I can't wait to plunge my dick inside you," Sterling asserted.

"After me." Murky grinded his teeth.

"I know, Murky. You've said that thirty times now," Sterling said, rolling his eyes.

Renee's stomach churned at the thought of the three brothers having their way with her. Suddenly, she felt as if she would rather die.

*****

BARRY PASSED A small brushy area along Vine Street with his handgun at full draw. For a moment, he believed he heard a rustling in the brush. He concentrated on all that he could view in the brush. After deciding that it was nothing, he spun to continue onward. When he turned around, he came face-to-face with Cole, which startled Barry.

The barrel of Barry's gun landed in the pit of Cole's stomach. "Hold it right there!" Barry demanded.

Janice appeared from behind Cole, pointing her gun at Barry.

"Janice? What the hell are you doing?"

"Take your gun off, Cole, Barry."

"Huh? Why should I?"

"He has given me the skinny on what's going on around here. It's terrible, Barry, what these Porters are doing to this town and its innocent citizens. We can't just walk away from something like this. We need to set things right. Now put down your gun. You can either join us or walk away. It's up to you."

"You two feel this strongly about it?" Barry questioned.

"Absolutely, Barry," Cole assured. "After we take care of the Porters, you all can do what you want with me. But for now, there is no way I'm giving up. Janice decided to join forces with me. Now how about you?"

Barry looked to Janice. She nodded her commitment.

"Well, if it's good enough for Janice, it's good enough for me," Barry said while lowering his gun.

"That's great," Cole said with a sigh. "I figure that the Porters are not going to be able to resist coming to town, so we wait for them here rather than running around the countryside looking for them. You haven't seen a pretty young lady with dark hair and blue eyes, have you?"

"No, I certainly would remember that." Barry chirped.

Janice glared at him.

*****

JOE GUIDED MERLE to the desk of the Webster Memorial Hospital emergency room. A nurse was standing next to the receptionist where she observed bloodstains on the front of Merle's pants.

"Please, my friend here is in need of help," Joe pleaded.

The nurse, Jill Williamson, stepped quickly from behind the counter. "What happened?" she asked Merle.

"Some punk shot my, um…testicles," Merle replied.

"Oh my god," Jill gasped. "Let's get you on one of the examination tables right away." She then led Merle through a large door.

The receptionist, Marie Lovejoy, felt for Merle, but at the same time, she nearly chortled at his source of injury.

"I need to use the phone to call the police," Joe requested.

Marie sat the telephone on top of the counter.

Joe quickly punched in the numbers 911.

*****

EMMA CONSOLED PAM Tinelberg as she broke down over the killing of her husband, Jim. "Ssssh now, Pam, you know that Jim wouldn't take to you bein' upset like this."

"I hope those Porters rot in hell!" Pam cried out.

"I second that," Henry added.

"I can't believe our town is in shambles," Claudia wept.

Yen placed his left arm around the sobbing Claudia's shoulders. "It's okay, we will all rebuild."

"We can't bring back lives, Yen," Pam bit out.

"No, I suppose not." Yen softened his stance.

"Jim loved this town. He loved all of you. He once told me that if he had a chance to move anywhere in the world, he'd stay right here in Harpersfield."

The group looked at one another with somber expressions.

*****

"WHAT IS THIS?" Anthony asked as Barry, Janice, and Cole approached him behind the post office.

"You need to trust me and Janice on this one, Anthony. Join us along with Cole to take down these Porter criminals. We'll take care of Cole afterward," Barry explained.

"How does Marla feel about all this?" Anthony questioned.

"We haven't run into her yet," Janice replied.

Anthony shook his head. "She's not going to like it, not one bit."

"Are you with us or not?" Cole queried.

"If I'm not?"

"Then don't get in our way," Cole warned.

"Fine. I'll head back to the van," Anthony chose. "I'll have nothing to do with this. The three of you have shamed the Elite Four."

"Suit yourself, Anthony, but we haven't dishonored the Four. This is what it's all about, taking care of justice," Cole pointed out.

"Define it any way you want, but it's against the rules," Anthony reasoned out.

"Yeah, well, sometimes Marla is a little too conservative," Janice remarked.

"I'm not listening to any more of this. I'm aborting. Are you coming back to the van with me, Barry?"

Barry shook his head no.

"Janice?"

"No, I'm in this all the way."

Anthony glared with disgust before turning away to begin his long journey back to the van.

*****

"YOUR SCROTUM IS wounded, but your testicles are intact," Jill reported after her inspection of the wounded area.

This news brought much relief to Merle.

"Six to seven stitches, and you'll be fine."

Outside the room's large door, Webster police chief Brian Reynolds whisked through the emergency room entrance with Officer Gary Giles in tow.

"Are you Joe Skidmore?" Brian asked.

"Yep, that's me, Officer."

"What is goin' on in Harpersfield?"

"These brothers named Porter have taken over. They've blocked Martin's Way, cut off the phones, and set the town ablaze. They have killed at least three that I know of."

"When did all this start?" Gary questioned.

"Yesterday evenin'," Joe reported.

"I knew that soft Sheriff Harvey would let that town get out of hand," Brian criticized.

"He's one of the dead," Joe informed.

"Well, hell. He certainly didn't deserve that," Brian noted. "Are the Porters still on the rampage?"

"Yeah…they have guns and dynamite," Joe added.

"Jesus Christ," Gary grumbled.

"How about hostages?" Brian probed.

"I'm not sure."

"What about the deputy? Frank…?"

"Collins. He's still alive. Ah…I need to tell ya guys that there's a man in town, Cole Walsh. He's an FBI agent."

The officer's eyes widened. "What in God's name is the FBI doin' in Harpersfield?" Brian was baffled.

"That's what we all in town have been wonderin' ourselves."

Brian turned his attention to Gary. "I want a cruiser to rush over to Harpersfield, tell them to watch out for the trap in the road. Arrange for a helicopter, I wanna do a flyover. Call the state police and get them involved."

"Right away, chief," Gary responded, racing back to the patrol car to use the radio.

"Are you okay, Joe?" Brian asked.

"Yeah. I brought a young friend here to the hospital who has been shot. I lost my Jeep in the Sulfur River."

"That's one mean-ass river. I'll arrange for an officer to pick you up soon so that you can get a hotel room. With all due respect, Joe, you look like crap. You smell of sulfur, and you look tired."

"Thanks for your help, Chief Reynolds."

"You bet. Now, if you'll excuse me, I have a neighborin' town to get under control."

*****

"WHO THE HELL was that?" Sterling asked as they passed by Anthony Becth along an unmapped dirt road leading into town from the Stewart farm.

"I dunno, but he has a damn gun. I saw it holstered to his chest," Dalton described.

"Let's go back and take care of the mystery man," Murky suggested with an evil glint in his eye.

Renee guessed that the man limping along the side of the road was one of the agents hunting down Cole. She hoped with all her strength that Cole was safe. She acknowledged that she had certainly fallen in love with him.

Sterling slowed the pickup truck and turned the vehicle around on the dirt road. He accelerated the rig back toward Anthony. They arrived slowly at the section of the road where they had last seen Anthony, only now he was gone.

"Where the heck did he go?" Sterling wondered.

"How in the hell am I supposed to know?" Dalton snapped.

"There!" Murky pointed out the truck's window. "I saw movement in the woods."

Sterling brought Ike's truck to a halt. He and Dalton sprung out from the rig while Murky remained seated, forcing Renee to stay on his lap.

Sterling and Dalton quickly grabbed their assault rifles from the bed of the truck and marched into the woods.

Murky placed a kiss on the right side of Renee's neck. She leaned forward, trying to avoid his advances. He then did what she had been hoping he wouldn't do. He unbuttoned her Levi's and slid his left hand beneath her panties. His fingers raked through her pubic hair until he located her vaginal opening. His fingers played in the region as she winced. "Why are ya so dry down there?" he wondered.

"Because I don't want you touching me, Murky." Again, she could feel his penis become erect against her buttocks.

"Ah, come on, Renee who is now my slave. Relax and enjoy it."

"Please, Murky. Please take your hand out of there."

"Uh-uh. I like the feel of your pussy. I can't wait to lay my eyes on it. I bet it's pretty. I bet it tastes good too."

She then decided to do anything to get him to release his hand from the delicate area of her body. "You could ask Cole all about that. He seemed to enjoy his mouth bein' down there."

Murky instantly went into a rage as her plan worked. He ripped his hand from out of her pants. "Yeah…well, we'll see when we get back to my house. I bet my cock is bigger than the mole's is. Between my brothers and me, you're gonna get more cock than some girls get in a lifetime. Now, shut the hell up and squirm on my hard-on."

She remained still. He clutched a handful of her hair and pulled tight. "Right now, bitch." Reluctantly, Renee swayed her hips, grinding her backside onto Murky's Levi's, massaging his erect penis in the process. He moaned out.

Dalton and Sterling stood still in the woods while shifting their eyes, trying to detect any movement.

Anthony realized that he was being hunted as he hunkered down in a shallow ditch about fifty yards from the Porter duo. The FBI agent could not be agile on his ailing ankle, so he decided to defend himself in a stationary position. Anthony called out, "I want you two to drop your weapons now. I have a bead on you, and if you so much as flinch the wrong way, I'll fire. Now, drop the rifles!"

They heard Anthony, but they couldn't see him. "Um, I don't think so, motherfucker! Come on out and fight like a man!" Sterling shouted back.

Anthony then made the critical mistake of deciding to fire a warning shot. This only proved to give away his general location. He fired the shot about ten feet above Sterling's and Dalton's heads. Sterling and Dalton then opened rapid fire with the assault rifles toward the area from which Anthony's shot rang out. It immediately became apparent to Agent Becth that if he didn't shoot the brothers quickly, he would be struck. Bullets peppered the ground around Anthony as he waited for an opportunity to return fire. The assault rifles proved that they were too difficult to overcome as Anthony attempted to take aim at the Porters. He was struck four times without getting off a shot of his own. He dropped his firearm as his body slid down a slight embankment to the ditch below.

Dalton and Sterling then spotted the agent sliding down the embankment.

"He's hit!" Sterling celebrated.

CHAPTER 62

THE TOWNSPEOPLE INSIDE the feedstore assembled into a group embrace at the recurring sounds of the assault rifles on the outskirts of town. It marked the first echoes of attack in hours, dashing their hopes that the aggression was over.

"Why don't they stop?" Claudia cried out.

Patti comforted her.

"My god, haven't they put this town through enough already?"

"Yen, do somethin'," Patti pleaded.

"What do you want me to do?" He raised his arms. "Go out there and get myself killed?"

"No, of course not, honey. I'm simply scared." Patti broke down.

She and Claudia wept in each other's arms. Yen embraced both women.

"I've been thinkin' this over," Henry revealed. "We're just sittin' ducks here inside this here feedstore. I think we should hunt down the Porters ourselves. Maybe try to surprise them and take their weapons away from them."

"You're thinkin' crazy now, Henry," Emma pointed out. "Those boys are big, strong, and mean. They'd kill each one of us."

"Emma's right, Henry. We need to stay put and pray that Cole gets the Porters before they get to us. It's all we can do," Yen concluded.

*****

DALTON KICKED ANTHONY'S body to be certain that he was dead. Anthony did not respond.

"Who the hell is he?" Sterling asked.

"I dunno, never seen him before."

"Let's take his gun and his wallet," Sterling directed.

Dalton picked up the handgun from the ground nearby as Sterling pulled his wallet from his pants pocket.

"This is a nice piece," Dalton observed, admiring the firearm. Sterling flipped open the wallet to remove any cash when he viewed the badge. "Damn, this guy is FBI too."

"Why the hell is the FBI swarmin' around here?"

"I dunno." Sterling shrugged his shoulders.

"Anyway, we've bagged us a fed," Dalton proclaimed proudly.

"Hey, I have a great idea," Sterling disclosed. "Do you have one of the grenades on ya?"

"Yeah, I have one in my pocket."

"Help me move the FBI man over to that tree."

They dragged Anthony's body up against a large oak tree.

"What are ya plannin' on, Sterling?"

"Cut me a vine, Dalton."

His brother pulled a knife from his belt and sliced away at a vine hanging from a nearby tree. He then hauled the cut section to Sterling.

Using the vine, Sterling tied Anthony to the tree's trunk in a sitting position as he sang, "Tie the FBI man 'round the old oak tree." With Anthony secured to the tree, Sterling requested, "Give me the grenade, Dalton."

Dalton slapped the grenade into Sterling's right hand. It took some forcing, but Sterling was able to stuff the grenade inside Anthony's open mouth. Dalton laughed insanely. "I like the way ya think, bro."

"Ready?" Sterling asked.

Dalton nodded.

Sterling pulled the pin out from the grenade and then shouted to Dalton, "Let's run! Go...go...go...go!"

They sprinted as quickly as their long legs would carry them until they were about seventy-five yards away from the imminent explosion. They turned to witness just as the grenade detonated. The explosion was sudden and powerful, blowing up Anthony's head and ripping his neck clean off his shoulders. Fragments of Anthony's bloody skull and jaw toppled to the ground.

"Motherfucker!" Sterling chirped. "Now that was awesome."

The bark behind where Anthony's head had once been was torn away from the tree. The agent's headless body shifted a bit but remained in the seated position against the tree.

"I gotta hand it to ya, Sterling. You're an artist," Dalton bellowed. "That was beautiful."

"Yeah, that guy isn't gettin any head tonight." Sterling used dry humor.

Again, Dalton laughed insanely.

*****

"THAT WAS A grenade, T10 grade to be precise," Cole deduced from the sound of the explosion.

"How the hell are those idiots getting military-rated weapons?" Janice questioned.

"I was once offered all sorts of things like that when I was working undercover in Chicago. I tell you what, there's a market out there for nearly everything," Barry explained.

"There's Marla and Dule," Janice whispered, pointing toward the high grass.

Marla and Dule had yet to spot the trio.

Cole, Janice, and Barry quickly stepped behind the post office.

"She'll shoot us, I'm sure of it. The Elite Four is Marla's baby, and we are going against the rules," Barry reminded them.

"If we could only get her to listen to us for five minutes, she might see it our way," Janice assured.

"She won't give us that time," Barry added.

"Then I'll buy us the time," Cole planned.

"How?" Janice wondered.

"Just follow me."

Stealthily, the trio moved up behind Dule and Marla. Dule turned abruptly at the very moment Cole grabbed hold of his throat. Cole pinched down on the artery running along the side of Dule's neck, cutting off the blood supply. Marla immediately pulled her gun on Cole.

"Um…I wouldn't do that, Marla. Not if you want to keep Dule alive and breathing," Cole warned.

"What are you talking about, Cole? I'm going to shoot you and not Dule."

"If you shoot me, Marla, Dule will perish. You see, if I don't release my pinch on his vein exactly right, a surge of blood will rush to his heart and overload it. So if you shoot me, my hand relaxes too quickly, and Dule dies. It's that simple."

Dule's eyes widened, and with a weak voice, he gasped, "Marla, don't shoot!"

"What are you all doing together anyway? Why didn't you two kill Cole? Where's Anthony?"

"Marla, if you give us a chance, we can explain all of this," Janice bid.

Left with no choice, Marla dropped her weapon. "It had better be damn good."

*****

STERLING STEERED IKE'S truck along a section of Martin's Way between the roadblock and Harpersfield. Dalton was busy telling Murky the story of Anthony Becth's demise when the truck was suddenly bumped from behind.

"What the hell?" Sterling grunted. He glanced at the side-view mirror. "Hey, it's Pop!" He celebrated.

"Hey there, you pukes!" Carter yelled from his truck.

"Pull over, Sterling. I want to ride with Pop," Dalton instructed.

Sterling guided Ike's truck to the shoulder of the road as Carter pulled up beside them. Dalton jumped from the passenger's seat. Murky slid over to the spot vacated by Dalton while forcing Renee to remain on his lap, though there was now enough space for her to sit down.

"You boys still goin' at it, huh? I thought I'd hook back up with y'all." Carter grinned.

Dalton plopped down on the passenger seat of his father's truck.

"Sure, Pop. It'll be great to have you along," Sterling invited.

"Whatcha doin' now?" Carter probed.

"We're headin' into town to blow up shit. Then we're goin' home to get it on with Murky's girlfriend," Sterling explained.

"Oh, I see ya got that Stewart girl in there with ya. My my my, that's some piece of ass, I'm sure. I'll have me some of that too when we get back to the house," Carter stated.

"There went your turn to be first, Murky." Dalton chuckled.

Murky raised his left middle finger at Dalton.

Renee was getting sick more by the minute. She waited for an opportunity to escape. If they killed her if she attempted to run away, so be it. It was better than being forced into sex with those four animals.

"Let's get into town and blow up the joint." Carter winked wickedly.

Both trucks squealed their tires as they headed off.

*****

"WHAT'S THAT SOUND?" Emma asked while listening to what was transpiring in the sky above the feedstore.

"It's a helicopter!" Yen eagerly announced. "Joe and Merle made it! They got us some help!"

The group went into a round of celebration, none more so than Fred and Beverly Darton.

"Hurry and get outside to signal them, Henry," Emma gasped.

"I'll go with you," Claudia volunteered.

They stepped outside onto the deck of the feedstore, but it was too late. The police helicopter had already completed the pass. Nevertheless, they did not fret. Help was here, and the officials in the sky were certain to observe the town was in disarray and in desperate need of immediate assistance and rescue.

"Wow, the town is in shambles," Police Chief Brian Reynolds witnessed from the passenger's seat of the helicopter.

"I don't see anyone about," Pilot Jimmie Lang reported.

"Neither do I, Jimmie. They must be all hidin' out. There's a body lyin' next to the street."

"Should I land this bird?"

"No, we could set it right down into an ambush. We'll wait until a couple of our patrol cars get here along with the state police."

"Okay, chief. I'll set us down up on that hill over in Waynesburg, and we'll wait it out there," Jimmie planned.

As the echoes of the helicopter faded away, Marla, Dule, Cole, Barry, and Janice rose from the tall grass.

"I don't know if that's a good sign or a bad sign," Marla stated, referring to the police helicopter.

"If they get the Porters before us, the judicial system will probably fail us yet again," Cole indicated.

"I still can't believe that I let you all talk me into this." Marla sighed.

"You'll see, it's the right thing to do," Cole retorted.

"Okay, this is your baby, Walsh. Tell us what you want us to do," Marla said.

*****

"THEY HAVE THIS rigged up well, I'll hand that much to them," Webster Police Officer John Derns retorted to Officer Gary Giles. They were outside their patrol car at the roadblock set up by the Porters on Martin's Way.

"Why can't we just move it?" Gary questioned.

John pointed as he spoke. "See that fishin' line there? It's tied into caps inside those pipe bombs. If that line's tension changes, either by movement or cuttin' it, those caps snap, and the bombs

detonate. Now, I don't know if you've ever witnessed it, but pipe bombs are nasty stuff. Sharp fragments of metal fly everywhere in all directions. The line runs thirty feet to each side of the road, makin' it impossible to drive around it without settin' off the bombs."

"Any way of disarmin' them?" Gary inquired.

John rubbed his jaw. "The only way I see it is to detonate them from a safe distance."

"How do we do that?"

After thinking it over for nearly two minutes, John snapped his fingers. "Okay, we can do this, but we have to do it right with no room for error. We have about a hundred feet of thick coiled rope in the trunk of the patrol car we used last month over at the county fair to pull disabled cars from the demolition derby mess. With luck, I haven't gotten around to puttin' the rope back into storage. We tie one end to the railroad tie and the other end to the rear bumper of the patrol car. We then pull away from the trap to protect the car's radiator. You put the cruiser in gear while lyin' down in the front seat. I will be lyin' down in the back seat. We slowly roll away from the trap, and when the rope tightens, the railroad tie will move. The pipe bombs blow while we are protected inside the patrol car."

"Sounds like it could work," Gary stated.

"It's the only way I can see to pull it off," John said.

"Let's do it then," Gary committed just as Police Chief Brian Reynold's voice cracked over the car's radio. "106. Where are you, 106?"

Gary and John made their way to the car. Gary leaned inside and picked up the microphone as John gained access to the trunk.

"This is 106," Gary responded.

"Jimmie and I are perched on a hill in Waynesburg. Harpersfield has been assaulted horribly. Gary, we need to wait this thing out until state backup arrives."

"Confirmed, chief. We are just about to disarm the road trap out here on Martin's Way."

"Go ahead and proceed with that, but then wait until further word from me before doing anything further. Don't try to be a hero and rush into Harpersfield only to get yourselves killed."

"Confirmed again, chief." Gary then clipped the microphone back upon the base of the radio.

John unwound the rope to its complete length. "Okay, this is gonna be the most dangerous part—gettin' this rope tied on the trap without settin' it off," John warned. His heart raced as he carefully stepped up on the railroad tie and gingerly tied the rope to it. He next moved off the trap just as cautiously. He then knotted the other end of the rope to the rear bumper of the patrol car that Gary had turned around to face away from the trap. John then slid into the back seat and lay down. "Go for it, Gary."

Officer Giles placed the patrol car in the drive gear, and then he lay down on the front seat. The car rolled slowly away from the road-block. Within a few moments, the rope's slack tightened, causing the railroad to tie shift. Simultaneously, the six pipe bombs exploded, sending splinters of the railroad tie and fragments of metal flying through the air. The rear window of the patrol car shattered after being hit by debris. Several holes were pierced into the body of the car, and one of the tires exploded after being stabbed by pieces of the galvanized piping. A three-foot section of the road cracked beneath the power of the explosions.

When the fallout finally settled, the only sounds was that of what remained of the railroad tie dragging along the road behind the slowly rolling patrol car.

Gary reached up and jammed the car into the parking gear, bringing the vehicle to a sudden stop. John brushed shattered glass fragments from atop his body and checked for any abrasions. The men's eardrums rang from the mighty blast of the explosions. John detected no blood from potential cuts on his body. The glass shattered into round smooth edges, sparing John from certain injury.

Gary sat up on the front seat. "Son of a bitch, that was a helluva shake."

John rose from the back seat. "I told ya that those pipe bombs are nasty shit."

"Let's get the spare tire on the car to be prepared when the chief gives word to go," Gary directed.

*****

"HEY, THAT WAS the pipe bombs," Sterling rumbled.

"So what?" Murky retorted.

"Well, someone just got scrap metal blown up their ass." Sterling sniggered.

"Maybe we should go back and check it out," Murky suggested.

"Naw, let's get into town and win this war once and for all."

*****

"BOY, OH BOY, what is takin' the state police so long?" Brian asked Jimmie as they sat inside the idle helicopter. "I wanna get this bird back in the air."

"Just check your patience, chief. We'll hear from them soon enough."

"I'd like to just go in there and secure the town ourselves, but I'm not sure exactly what it is we are up against."

"I'll tell ya what we're facin', insane maniacs are what those Porters are. I had an aunt who used to live in Harpersfield, and I would visit her from time to time. I'm not fibbin', chief, when I say that the Porters are rotten to the very core. That family is possessed by a demon or somethin'. They have the entire town scared and eatin' right out of their hands."

"I remember about a year ago when the brothers got away with murder."

"Yeah, Harvey and the courts botched that up. Believe me, from what I hear, that isn't the only murder they've committed. The only difference was that time the body was found."

After a few moments of quiet, Brian blurted out, "What the hell is the FBI doin' in Harpersfield? It's eatin' away at me."

"Maybe it has somethin' to do with the Porters?" Jimmie guessed.

"Naw, I doubt it. The state police would probably handle that and not the FBI."

Jimmie shrugged his shoulders. "Well then, I dunno."

*****

"WE NEED TO split up with a planned gathering point," Cole explained to Marla, Dule, Barry, and Janice.

"How about the van right now, this minute, so we can get out of this demonic-ruled town and head on home?" Dule nervously suggested.

"Shape up, Dule," Janice snapped.

"Based on the explosions and rapid fire going on around here, it would seem we are up against something insurmountable. How do we fight that with only our handguns?" Barry put forward.

"Good will prevail over evil," Marla proclaimed.

"Oh, you can save the Bible school sermon, Simmons. I want some strategy from our Green Beret comrade here," Barry explained.

"The general rule is not complex. If you're seen, you're dead. If you miss with your shot, you're dead. The only way for us to have a chance at this thing is to work completely as a team. I'm not going to sugarcoat this. The odds are that one or two or perhaps all five of us will not make it through this. Mistakes happen no matter how hard you try to avoid them. But if you are taken down, try your best to take your pursuer down with you."

"I'm not doing this. I have too much to live for." Dule gulped.

Barry angrily retorted, "Then why did you come along?"

Cole looked at Marla. "Are you in?"

"You bet I am."

"Marla? What, are you crazy?" Dule questioned.

"No, I'm not crazy. Like these Elite members, I'm a fighter for justice."

"Even if it means risking your life?"

"You bet your ass."

Dule swallowed hard. "I guess I'll go with you, Marla."

"No, Dule, honey, I won't have time to babysit you. You're sitting this one out the rest of the way."

"What? Where will I go?"

Cole suggested, "There's a feedstore up the road a small distance, off to your left. That's where the others are hiding out. I'll take you over there myself because they are not going to know who you are."

"Marla, please come with me," Dule pleaded.

"I'll be there when this is over. Now, you go and sit with the townspeople and try to keep them calm."

"I was hoping they'd do that for me," he mumbled.

CHAPTER 63

"WHAT DO YOU think you're doin', Mr. Stewart?" the nurse inquired while stepping inside the hospital room. Ike was putting on his torn and slightly charred clothes in preparation to leave Webster Memorial Hospital where he was recovering.

"I need to get home to protect my granddaughter."

"Protect her from what exactly?" Nurse Laura Hinkley inquired.

"Oh, I know who torched my house, and they will now be after my Renee. I need to get on home."

"You live in Harpersfield, right?"

Ike nodded.

"Well, there hasn't been anything on the news about Harpersfield today. I'm sure everything is fine. Besides, Mr. Stewart, you're not ready to leave here just yet."

"Please call me Ike."

"Okay, Ike, but you're still not ready to depart. Now, you stop bein' so ornery and put your hospital gown back on. I'll be by a little later to check your vitals. You took in quite a bit of smoke from the fire, and I want to be sure that your lungs haven't suffered any prolonged damage. If I hear any news about Harpersfield, I'll be sure to let you know."

"I've tried callin' several people there, but the phones are down," he explained.

"That happens sometimes. Maybe somebody ran into a pole or somethin'. You just hop back up on that bed and stop thinkin' so much. I'm sure everything is simply fine over in Harpersfield."

*****

"WHAT DO WE blow up with our last bundle of dynamite?" Dalton turned to his father. They were now less than two miles from town.

"I'd say the post office. It's brick, so that should be awesome. I'd like to find Claudia Williams. I've always had a hankerin' to hump her while she's wearin' her post office uniform. Mmmmmm, that would be awesome. I think if I find her, I'll give her the Porter meat stick."

"Yeah…Claudia isn't bad for her age. She has a nice set of tits. Once, about ten years ago, we were roughin' up her son, Burl, in their backyard when we spotted Claudia dressin' in front of the mirror in her bedroom. We could see her through the open second-story window, and she had no idea we were watchin'. We couldn't believe it when she started playin' with her own nipples."

"No!" Carter gasped, becoming excited.

"Oh yeah, Pop. Then her hand slid down to her pussy. She reared her head back while she worked her pussy with her fingers. Man, I remember my cock was rock hard. Burl was so humiliated." Dalton chuckled.

"Goddamn it. Why couldn't I have seen that? See, she's divorced, and them divorcées are sure to be horny. So we're gonna blow up her post office, then we'll all take turns with Claudia."

"You go ahead, Pop. I'm gonna save mine for that Stewart girl." Dalton grinned.

"Oh yeah, that's right. We do have that fine piece of ass with us, huh? Well, Claudia can wait for another day. I want a slice of that Stewart gal too."

Suddenly charging up from the tall grass next to the road, Deputy Frank Collins fired the shotgun into the front-passenger tire

of Carter's truck. The tire exploded, causing Carter to lose control of the vehicle. Carter's truck veered sideways, and from behind, Sterling was not able to completely brake in time. The vehicles collided, causing Sterling, Murky, and Renee to jar hard inside the cab of the truck. The rigs came to a squealing rest in the center of the road. Ike's pickup truck, with Sterling at the wheel, steamed from the radiator. The hood was folded up, and both front tires were flattened. Besides a few bumps and bruises, the occupants of both vehicles were spared any serious injuries.

"Go get that son of a bitch Collins!" Carter roared.

The boys piled out of the crashed vehicles and grabbed their rifles. They hurried off on a run after the deputy.

Renee sat quietly in her grandfather's wrecked truck. Carter pulled a pistol from his belt. "You so much as even look like you're gonna run, I'll shoot you. You're not goin' anywhere until after you've screwed me and my boys," Carter warned Renee.

"There he is." Sterling pointed out Frank Collins, who was running across an open field.

Frank was no match for the speed that the Porters could generate. They closed the distance on Frank quickly, but were sure to stay out of shotgun range, yet within plenty of scope for their rifles. The trio dropped to their knees and took careful aim at the running lawman. Nearly simultaneously, they fired. In less than few passing seconds, Frank Collins's body was invaded by bullets. Frank collapsed to the one shot that shattered his femur bone, but what the Porters did not realize was that Frank was wearing a wraparound bulletproof vest beneath his uniform shirt, as he always had done.

"That idiot bit the dust." Murky snickered.

"Yeah, he sure did. These rifles rock!" Dalton buzzed.

"Let's walk up there and make sure the asshole is dead," Sterling suggested.

Frank lay in the tall bloodstained grass where the Porters could not see him. He was barely conscious and in terrible pain, but he had the shotgun ready to fire if they approached.

"Shit, he's dead, Sterling. We put a lot of bullets into his worthless ass. Frank the crank is no longer with us." Murky tittered.

"Let's get back to the trucks and fix 'em up," Dalton instructed.

*****

"I DON'T WANT to be trapped in here any more than any of you do," Dule admitted to the group inside the feedstore.

"Why didn't Cole explain to us what is goin' on out there?" Emma asked.

Dule shrugged his shoulders.

"Are you FBI as well?" Henry quizzed.

"No, I'm a private detective."

"What are ya doin' here in Harpersfield?" Claudia interrogated.

"That's a question that I've been asking myself repeatedly. It's a long, crazy story."

*****

"NO SPARE TIRE," Carter surmised as he kicked Ike's pickup truck's front bumper.

"Well, what the hell do we do now?" Sterling whined.

"We walk, you knucklehead," Carter snapped.

Murky yawned and grabbed hold of Renee's shirt, cupping her right breast. She despised the action, but she had long given up with fighting back Murky's relentless advances. She was becoming numb.

"I'm getting' tired. When I'm through cummin' inside you, Renee, now my slave, I'll be out like a light."

"By the time we've had our turns with you, little girl, you're gonna have a quart of cum in you and on you." Carter snickered.

The boys chuckled perversely. Murky slapped her lightly on her backside before he and his brothers geared up for the walk into town.

*****

JANICE STATIONED HERSELF behind the storage shed of the charred general store. From there, she could survey sections of both Vine and Harper Streets. Barry chose to climb a heavy-leafed

elm tree that grew next to Harper Street across from where the police station once stood. Marla resorted to the tall grass patch in the rear of the remains of Tiny's Diner. Cole returned to his perch upon the roof of the post office. All had their weapons loaded while ready to spring into action at a moment's notice.

It was nearly six in the evening when the town settled into an eerie quiet.

*****

"CHIEF BRIAN REYNOLDS?" A voice cracked over the radio. "Chief Reynolds?"

Brian quickly reached for the radio inside the helicopter. "This is Chief Reynolds, go ahead."

"This is Officer Larry Davis of the Tennessee State Police. I understand that you're in need of our assistance?"

"Yes, Officer Davis."

"Call me Larry."

"Okay, and Brian is fine here. We have a captured small town here in the southern section of the state. We believe that a family consistin' of a father and three sons have taken over the town. There are casualties, and the town is in ruins. We need to work together to apprehend these offenders."

"Let me guess, Brian. Harpersfield and the Porters. Right?"

"Exactly. How did you know that?"

"We've had any eye on those punks for some time now, just waitin' to pin somethin' on them."

"Well, you got that now. Where are you and the cavalry?"

"Mine and three other cruisers are clippin' along Interstate 281 north of Knoxville. We should be in Harpersfield in about an hour or a little more."

"Great, Larry, let me know when you're about ten minutes out. Jimmie and I will then get this bird back in the air and support you all from the sky. I have a cruiser with two officers waitin' your arrival on Martin's Way."

"Good enough, Brian. Talk with ya again in a bit."

*****

MARLA MILDLY TREMBLED, and her mouth was dry. Years had passed since her last stakeout. She tuned into the area around her and sharpened her concentration.

About three hundred yards to Simmons's left, Janice Stark leaned against the rear of the storage shed, completely alert as she recalled a stakeout several years prior that left her weak and weary.

It was a day in July near her home in Boston, Massachusetts. What was to be a routine mission turned out to cause her to think twice about her father's advice years ago that she should take up accounting rather than becoming an FBI agent. Daddy always worried about her so.

Matt Gerrod was a money man. There's nothing wrong with being rich, but it's not legal when you print your own money. Matt was one of the largest counterfeiters, not only in the States, but worldwide as well. If there existed a currency, Matt could reproduce the bills with a cunning likeness. The FBI had been trying to track down Mr. Gerrod for years, but at any given time, Matt could be anywhere in the world. The FBI caught a break when a member of Matt's network was arrested for an unrelated issue; he spilled his guts in exchange for avoiding prosecution. The FBI gathered two important bits of information from the felon. Matt Gerrod was currently in Boston, and so was a scheduled shipment of supplies to print some German marks. Matt always checked the supplies personally before accepting the shipment. The substrate and inks must be of the highest quality.

The shipment was to arrive in the Boston harbor, pier number 87, on this July night. Janice and two fellow FBI agents staked out the pier 87 landing dock and the adjoining small warehouse. The pier had been whispering quiet for several hours, and the agents were about to call off the stakeout, citing that the inside information was deceptive.

Suddenly, a boat appeared to be making its way toward pier 87. It was a yacht with a large man at the wheel while a beautiful woman, barely clad in a skimpy dress, sat on the railing of the boat's deck.

She was throwing her long hair back in the sea breeze and wearing sunglasses in the darkness of the night.

Janice quickly checked her photo of Matt Gerrod to the man driving the boat. It was not a match. The man on the boat was a bit larger than Gerrod. A seagull squalled near Janice, causing her heart to skip a beat. The tension on that pier was thickening, and it was apparent.

The yacht coasted into the pier. The man leaped onto the dock while the woman remained on board the vessel. From behind several large shipping crates on the dock, Janice could see and hear the duo.

"How long is this gonna take, John?" the woman whined.

"No more than an hour, Myra. Why don't you go below and make yourself a drink?"

"I have a glass nearly full already. Besides, Don and Heather are down there screwing again. That's all those two ever do."

"You and Heather are incredibly beautiful women, Myra. You're going to have men flocking over the two of you." John then tied the yacht to the dock. He stood at five feet eleven inches with a stocky African America frame. He donned a goatee, shaved his head bald, and sported a looped silver earring in his left lobe. He was wearing dress shirt and slacks along with shiny gray shoes. John Tykes was a runner. He would run anything—drugs, alcohol, tobacco (all for illegal minor sells), and counterfeit money. John made a good living as a runner.

Myra Germaine was a professional call girl with a hefty price tag. Her going rate for a night with a client was fifteen thousand dollars. At least three times a month, Myra was booked with a wealthy man. She and John met when John would bring customers to her at secret locations. Most of her clients were married and enjoyed the secrecy that Myra offered them. Myra would pay John two thousand dollars for each client he safely delivered and returned. Myra was twenty-seven years old and stunning. Her reddish-brown hair fell just short of her shoulders, and her soft green eyes shined in the dim lights of the pier. Her body was fit and yet curvy. She was tall at five feet nine inches and well groomed.

She was with fellow call girl Heather Lyles. Don Booth, Heather's client for the night, was enjoying his secretive evening on the boat. Don sold commodities on the internet and had produced a fortune in doing so. Don was every bit a legal man. As he indulged himself in Heather below the yacht's deck, he was unaware of the activities taking place topside.

John began unloading several wooden and cardboard boxes from the boat. As he stacked the cargo upon the dock, he was sure to keep looking around for both the expected company and any unexpected company.

After unloading the packages, John lit a cigarette and waited. Soon, Matt Gerrod, along with one of his thugs, appeared on the dock. Matt was an undersized man in his late forties. He was five foot eight at best and lanky. His face was clean shaven, revealing a pointy chin. He had large round eyes and an oblong nose. His skin was flush and pale even during the prime of summer, which proved that he was a man of nighttime hours and did not see much daylight.

From the shadows, after referencing her mug shot of Matt Gerrod as a match to the man now on the pier, Janice's heart raced.

Matt shook John's hand before inspecting the cargo. Once he was satisfied with the contents of the boxes, Matt signaled the thug to hand over to John a stack of legitimate bills. John made a quick check of the currency to be sure of its authenticity.

John was content and prepared to board the yacht when Janice sprang into action. She swept out from behind the empty shipping crates with her handgun at full draw. "FBI!" she barked. "Freeze right there!"

Without hesitation, Matt Gerrod leaped off the pier and into the harbor's water below. Myra stood up from her perch and screamed. John was wanted in three states and had no plans of cooperating with the FBI. He did, however, raise his hands at Janice's demand.

Feeling that she had John under control, the other two FBI agents rushed to take control of the boat. Then one of them jumped into the water to collect Matt, who was nearly drowning. Janice then made a critical mistake, a lesson that was trained not to do in the early stages of the academy. She assumed before securing him that

John was going in easy—no fight, no chase, and no struggle. She took hold of her handcuffs and eased her gun back into its holster. She even gave John a quick nod before stepping to him. Just as she was about to grab his left wrist to cuff him, fugitive John Tykes reached for his concealed handgun at the backside of his pants. Before Janice could react, John had the barrel of the gun buried into the pit of her stomach. The only word she was able to blurt out was "Wait!"

John fired his gun, sending the bullet ripping through Janice's torso. She tumbled to the dock at his feet. He jumped over her and fled on foot.

Janice was rushed to a local hospital and then journeyed by Life Flight helicopter to a facility near Washington, DC. She spent six hours in surgery, and at one point, the doctors feared that they would lose her. She pulled through the surgery and spent six days in the intensive care unit with her father at her side.

John Tykes was not apprehended that night, nor was he for over three years. He was finally arrested, thanks to an anonymous tip, at the Cleveland Harbor by none other than FBI Agent Cole Walsh. John Tykes was charged with assaulting a law enforcement officer and attempted murder, along with his other outstanding warrants. He was going to spend the rest of his life behind bars.

As for the caller with the tip, it was later discovered that it was the one and only Myra Germaine.

Janice looked down along Vine Street, knowing that whatever that road brings to her, she'd already experienced the worst.

*****

"WHY DON'T WE just throw her down in the ditch and do her right now?" Sterling recommended.

"Goddamn it, I said in my bed only," Murky insisted.

"Let him have his way with this one, he's in puppy love," Carter teased.

"I am, Pop. I've always loved Renee, but now the bitch has cheated on me." Murky then slapped Renee in the back of her head, causing her to stumble with a few wobbled steps.

Dalton then shoved her, nearly sending her to the ground. Murky grabbed her tightly around her upper left arm and forced her to walk side by side with him.

"There is no way I'm havin' sex with you or your brothers, Murky. The only way that is gonna happen is over my dead body," she claimed.

He clenched his teeth. "That can easily be arranged, Stewart."

*****

FROM HIS PERCH in the elm tree, Barry Stone could now see the group of Porters along with a young lady coming into view from a distance down Vine Street. He readied by taking a firmer grip on his handgun.

As the distance shrank away, Barry could make out the brothers with their assault rifles strapped to their backs. He looked at the sizeable weapons and then at his own handgun. "Oh boy, this isn't much of a match. But if I can take down one or two of them, that'll be a victory in my mind."

He leaned back against the trunk of the tree and rested his elbows on his knees to secure an aiming position.

CHAPTER 64

"THAT MAN, COLE, he seems as though that he's skilled enough to pull us through this," Henry mentioned.

"He's an idiot," Dule bit out.

"Now, why would ya say that?" Emma questioned Dule's bitterness.

"What, are you kidding? Cole is so full of himself, he probably whispers the words 'I love you' when he masturbates."

"Hey, buddy, you don't speak that way in front of my wife," Fred Darton pointed out sternly.

Dule realized his statement went a bit too far. He cleared his throat. "Sorry."

"Well, the Cole I met seems awfully nice to me," Emma commented. "I didn't see where he is conceited."

"Neither do I," Pam defended.

"You're just full of envy, Dule," Henry speculated.

"Okay. I'm sorry, alright? The guy is great, okay?" Dule surrendered.

Claudia looked at Dule in a flirtatious manner. "You're a tall man. You can sit over here next to me if you want," she invited.

"What don't you just toss your clothes over to him, Claudia?" Emma teased.

"Quiet, Emma," Claudia snapped.

"Thanks for the invite, but I'm a taken man, Claudia. I love Marla very much," Dule divulged.

"Who's Marla? Where's Marla?" Claudia questioned.

"She's the love of my life, and she's out there facing the enemy."

"What? The Porters?" Fred asked.

Dule nodded.

"That's crazy. They'll kill her," Henry stated.

"Marla can hold her own. She'll be okay...I hope," Dule claimed with nervous confidence.

"Let me get this straight," Aleescha began. "The woman you love is out there riskin' her life, and you're hidin' in here with us? That's cowardly and disgustin'."

"Keep your place, Aleescha," Patti reprimanded her daughter.

"She has the right to speak her mind," Yen retorted.

Dule fidgeted. "I know that it doesn't look good on the surface, but there's more to it than that. Marla just thought it would be best if I protected you people here in the feedstore."

"That's a lame excuse," Henry huffed.

Dule became frustrated. "What do you people expect me to do? March out there and get my head blown off? Well, I sort of like my head attached to my shoulders, thank you."

*****

BARRY TOOK CAREFUL aim and slid his right forefinger against the trigger of his handgun. The bead on the end of his weapon's barrel came to a rest on Sterling's chest. Barry inhaled a deep breath and then squeezed the trigger. The gun fired, but to Barry's horror, the bullet clipped a small branch of the tree, slightly knocking the projectile off course.

The bullet struck Sterling in his right upper arm. The Porters couldn't see Barry, but they were able to determine that the shot originated from up in the elm tree. Within a few short seconds, Barry was ready to fire again, but the Porters, along with Renee, were scrambling for protection behind obstructions.

The brothers opened fire with their assault rifles up into the tree. Leaves, bark, and branches snapped off the tree. Barry was hit repeatedly, taking in over two dozen bullets. His limp body plummeted from the tree, landing chest first on the sidewalk below. Blood oozed out of Barry's body from several locations.

Sterling, angry that he had been shot, rushed to Barry's body to shoot him three more times in the head. Barry's lifeless body jerked at the power of the bullets' impact.

"Who the hell is the nigger?" Carter queried as the rest of the group joined Sterling.

"How would I know, Pop, you idiot."

Carter clasped his right palm on Sterling's bullet-wounded shoulder, sending shooting pain down Sterling's arm. Sterling grimaced in agony. "Don't you ever speak to me like that again, son," Carter duly advised.

"I've been shot, Pop. That makes anyone cranky," Sterling countered.

"Stop whinin', Sterling," Dalton said. "It's only an arm wound. You'll pull through, you damn wimp."

Murky maintained a sure grip on Renee's left upper arm.

"What the hell is a black man doin' in Harpersfield anyway? Check his wallet," Carter directed Dalton.

After opening the wallet, Dalton shook his head. "Another goddamn FBI agent. What the heck is goin' on? They are sproutin' up around here like beans in a field."

Carter smirked. "We've downed two feds in one day."

*****

Marla peered through the tall grass, but from her vantage point, Harper Street was empty.

Janice peeked around the corner of the storage shed to observe the Porters hovering around the fallen agent Barry Stone. They were just out of her handgun's range. She would need to wait it out.

Cole raised his head over the lip of the post office roof to see the group standing at the intersection of Vine and Harper. He saw

that Barry was down, and the Porters were heavily armed. The way Sterling and Murky were positioned, Renee was blocked from Cole's line of sight.

*****

At the sounds of gunfire, the gathering inside the feedstore again went into a group embrace—all except Dule, who was overly concerned. He took his handgun into his grip and proclaimed, "I'm going out there. Those punks are not going to harm my Marla."

"'Bout time you grew a spine," Henry growled.

Dule rushed out from the feedstore's door. He then slowed his pace, moving from behind tree to tree. He remained parallel to Harper Street, about twenty yards from the pavement.

*****

"Let's walk over and blow up the post office," Carter directed.

"Okay, Pop," the boys replied in unison.

As they made their way along Harper Street, Janice gained a bead on them.

Dalton glanced over and spotted her at the last possible moment before she committed to firing her weapon. "Watch out!" he shouted.

Sterling dove to the pavement while Carter, Dalton, and Murky, with Renee in tow, positioned themselves behind a parked car.

Janice took a low-percentage shot, shattering the windshield of the parked car. She then pulled her head back behind the storage shed.

Sterling took steady aim directly at the shed and let his assault rifle roar. Bullets tore through the shed's wooden frame. Janice was able to maneuver around the first few bullets, but she was then overcome by the flying lead. Her body lurched wildly as bullets struck her body, one after another. Blood spewed from her mouth as she tumbled to the ground below. Another dozen bullets reached her, even after she was dead.

By the time Sterling eased up on the trigger, the barrel of the gun was heated and billowing with smoke.

"That's what we're talkin' 'bout. Way to go, Sterling," Dalton congratulated.

"Go check on your trophy," Carter prompted.

Sterling quickly moved to the shed with his now-cooling rifle pointed out in front of him. He peered around to the rear of the shed to see Janice Stark lying in her own pool of blood. Her eyes were open and her body motionless. He poked at her stomach with the barrel of his rifle to ensure that she was not responding. He crouched down next to Janice and frisked her for a wallet, stopping for a moment to caress her braless breasts.

"Small but firm, lady," he mumbled to himself. He located her wallet tucked inside the leg pocket of her pants. Before opening the wallet, he already knew she was FBI as well. The folded wallet looked identical to Anthony and Barry's holder. He opened it just the same to see the shiny badge and her ID card.

He walked back toward the road, waving the wallet in the air.

"Shit, they are like leaches around here," Murky expressed in disbelief.

"Yeah, well, we're winnin'. That's three feds that have bit the dust and zero Porters," Carter bragged.

*****

Dule strained to see the source of the gunfire without success. The Porters were only about one hundred yards from him, but around a slight turn in the road.

Cole could now see Renee had been captured by Murky, and he instantly angered. However, Cole knew that he must maintain a clear head and stay focused on the plan. Two agents were now shot dead (he was unaware of Anthony Becth's fate), so the force of the justice fighters was rapidly dwindling away.

Marla could had taken a shot from her vantage point; the Porters were within gun range. After mulling it over, she decided to wait for a better opportunity. As she settled back down into the tall grass, she was a little noisier than she attempted to be.

Dalton glared into the tall grass after detecting the sounds. Marla held her breath and committed to being completely still. Dalton was about to approach the tall grass when his attention was diverted away.

"Post office, boys. Let's go!" Carter commanded.

As they prepared their final bundle of dynamite by wedging it between the sidewalk and the foundation of the post office, Cole peered over the roof's edge from above. He took alert aim at the top back portion of Sterling's head.

Carter ignited the dynamite's fuse just as Cole fired his gun. The bullet entered through Sterling's skull and exited just below his left eye. Sections of Sterling's brain matter and his blood splattered on the rear of Dalton's shirt. Sterling's eyes remained wide open as he crumpled to the sidewalk as stiff as a falling tree. He was dead before he hit the pavement.

Murky looked up before Cole could get off another shot. "It's the fuckin' mole!" he shouted.

"Jesus criminy sake! He shot Sterling in the head!" Dalton screeched.

Murky peppered the roof's edge with rapid gunfire, forcing Cole to retreat.

"Holy shit, the dynamite's lit! We need to scurry now!" Carter yelled.

Dalton, Murky, Renee and Carter moved as fast as possible across the street and took cover behind a large metal garbage bin next to where the general store once stood.

Cole scampered as quickly as he could across the roof of the post office to the rear of the building. He leaped from off the roof just as the dynamite exploded, engulfing the post office into a powerful fireball. The force of the explosion flung Cole through the air and into a nearby telephone pole. He crashed into the pole with his chest, knocking the air from his lungs. He tumbled down fifteen feet before he slammed to the ground on his back.

Bricks and other debris rained down in the area, with one of the bricks striking Dule in his forehead. The blow knocked Dule unconscious as he buckled to the ground behind one of the trees.

Numerous bricks struck the large garbage bin shielding Renee, Carter, Dalton, and Murky from the projectiles. Several bricks sailed as far as to where Marla was positioned, but she was able to dodge out of the path of the descending debris.

The explosion ripped Sterling's deceased body in two pieces, slinging the sections of carcass out onto Harper Street.

When the bricks finally settled, a heavy cloud of dust billowed in the atmosphere.

"That bastard killed Sterling!" Dalton cried out.

"My son is dead!" Carter raged in anger. "Go kill the son of a bitch that shot my boy!"

Dalton and Murky rushed to the sight of the now-leveled post office in search of Cole. Carter soon followed, inadvertently leaving Renee behind.

She seized the opportunity to escape into a wooded patch behind Harper Street.

"Where is he? Where's the bastard who shot Sterling?" Carter demanded.

Cole, still recovering from the hit and fall, was a mere fifty yards from the Porters, but the thick cloud of unsettled dust was guarding him from their sight. He forced himself through pain to roll his body about ten feet in distance until he slid down a slight embankment.

"The explosion must have gotten him, Pop," Dalton assumed.

"Well, look around and make sure. If ya find that idiot, bring him to me. I want to shoot the moron between his eyes."

Dalton and Murky shuffled about the debris pile in their efforts to locate Cole. Carter began to weep as he stepped out onto Harper Street. He fell to his knees and took Sterling's upper body into his arms. "Oh, my boy, my sweet boy. They have killed you, my son. Your mother will be heartbroken. I promise to you, Sterling, that I will see your death avenged. I'll slice up the man that did this to you and feed him to the dogs. You didn't deserve this, Sterling. You're all good boys."

Dalton and Murky moved closer to the edge of the embankment just above where Cole was lying. Cole spent all his weakened strength to point his gun at the top of the ravine when he heard the

duo approaching. He realized that they possessed much more gunfire than he had at his disposal, but if he could shoot another one of the Porters before they shot him, he would give it all he had.

Dalton and Murky were nearly at the ravine's very edge when they heard their father whimpering out loudly.

"Come on, Murky, let's go take care of Pop. The explosion had to have gotten that asshole. Nobody could have made it through that big bang."

They stepped back away from the ravine, and Cole released a long quiet sigh of relief. He wanted to rid Harpersfield of the remaining three, as he now considered Carter a target as well, and he had to stay alive to complete that task.

Dalton and Murky joined their father at Sterling's divided body as the trio grieved together.

CHAPTER 65

"**JIMMIE, WE NEED** to get down there. We can't wait any longer. It sounds like a damn war goin' on over that hillside. Fire up this helicopter!" Brian commanded.

"Chief, I still feel we need to wait for the arrival of state police," Jimmie said hesitatingly.

"There are innocent people probably bein' slaughtered over there in Harpersfield. So what do you think, Jimmie? Do we wait, or do we get in there now and help those people?"

Within a few moments, Jimmie fired up the helicopter's engine, and the long blades began to rotate.

"You're makin' the right decision, James," Brian reassured. He then grabbed the radio's microphone. "John? Gary?"

John Derns picked up the radio. He and Gary Giles had been sitting in the patrol car awaiting word from Brian.

"Yeah, Brian, go ahead."

"Jimmie and I are takin' the bird over Harpersfield."

"But we haven't heard from the state boys again."

"Yeah, I know, John, but I'm sure you heard the explosions even louder than we did from up here. There are people bein' killed and tortured. I can't sit on this any longer. You boys with me on this?"

John looked to Gary. After a brief hesitation, Gary nodded. "Yes, chief. What do you need us to do?"

"Great, guys, now once we survey the situation from the sky, I'll radio you with your best way to approach town. If I can get off a shot at the assailants from the air, I'll take it. For now, keep sittin' tight until you hear from me again, over."

*****

RENEE QUICKLY CROSSED Harper Street, stepping along behind Carter, Dalton, and Murky while going unnoticed. She disappeared in the settling cloud of dust and headed for the ravine. If Cole survived the blast, he must be somewhere nearby. Her heart pounded over the fear that Cole, her newfound love, could now be deceased. She glanced around the immediate area for any clue that he may not have survived—his gun, a boot, perhaps a piece of clothing. To her relief, she discovered no such items.

She carefully stepped down the ravine and into a small wooded lot. Suddenly, without warning, she was grabbed from behind, and a large hand cupped her mouth. Her hopes of freedom drained from her body as she was certain that Murky had taken her hostage once again.

To her pleasant surprise, Cole whispered in her ear, "Babe, don't scream. It's me." He released his hand from over her mouth.

She quickly turned to face him, and she glowed. They came together in a heartfelt embrace and kiss.

"I was so scared, I thought you were dead," she sobbed.

"Hey, it's okay. I'm a little banged up a bit, but I'm fine. Did they harm you?"

"They knocked me 'round some, but they were plannin' things much worse than that. Thank god I got away when I did, and now, I'm finally with you again."

"We're not splitting apart ever again. You stay at my side, and I'll protect you until my last breath."

"It'll be my pleasure, Agent Walsh," she whispered.

Cole took a quick peek above the ravine and then coasted back down to Renee.

"You killed Sterling. The Porters are gonna be even more insane now," she pointed out.

"Good, when heads get lost in anger, that's when mistakes are made. Come on, we need to step back deeper into the woods to reassess the current situation."

"I'll go anywhere with you."

He gently took her by the left hand and led her away from the ravine.

*****

MARLA COULD SIT still no longer. She remained low as she moved through the tall grass, trying to gain a different angle while surveying Harper Street. She then spotted Dule unconscious on the ground across the street. "Oh my god, Dule!"

Marla threw caution to the wind as she sprinted across Harper Street to arrive at the aid of the man she loved. Just as she made it across the street, Dalton caught a glimpse of her. Carter and Murky then noticed the bewildered look on Dalton's face.

"What is it?" Carter grilled.

"I think I just saw another goddamn nigger in Harpersfield runnin' across the street."

"Let's kill the spook!" Carter roared.

Marla fell to her knees next to Dule and wiped the dried blood from the small cut on his forehead. "Dule, baby, it's me. Come on, honey, wake up." She slapped him gently on the cheek. Dule's eyes began to open slowly. She quickly kissed him. "Thank goodness you're alright. Can you stand up?"

Dule struggled to his feet, and in a spell of dizziness, his legs nearly gave in and buckled. He shook his head to gather his senses. He then nodded. She helped him to maintain his stand in time to see the Porters were in pursuit.

"Oh no, Dule, we need to move, now!"

"Hey, nigger bitch!" Murky shouted. "Hold it right there!"

"Let's go, Dule!" she wailed. They took to a run for the woods behind the feedstore. Dalton, Carter, and Murky were in chase. Marla

and Dule slid down a ridge top, nearly tumbling in the process. The pair then moved quickly to the edge of a creek that was a vein of the Sulfur River. "We have to jump in, Dule!"

"That creek is yellow," he observed.

"It doesn't matter! If we don't leap in, we are going to be shot!" They joined hands and leaped from the bank. They hit with a splash and inhaled in deep breaths of air before they submerged. The sulfur content burned their eyes and their nose as they remained still beneath the water's surface.

The Porters arrived at the top of the ridge and surveyed the creek's surface meticulously.

"Maybe they're in the creek," Dalton suggested.

"No way, that shit burns," Murky retorted.

"Well, let's shoot the water just in case," Carter instructed. They took rifle aim at the creek, and just as they were about to pull their triggers, the police helicopter flew directly above them.

"Son of a bitch!" Carter barked. "Shoot the flyin' pigs."

They raised their rifles upward at the passing helicopter.

"Oh shit, Jimmie, they got a bead on us!" Brian shouted. "Move move move!"

Jimmie dipped the helicopter into a hard right turn as the Porters fired. A bullet pierced the windshield of the helicopter. Jimmie was eventually able to guide the helicopter out of harm's way before they absorbed any further strikes.

"Come on, boys, they'll probably circle back. Let's find some cover," Carter directed.

The Porters made their way toward the feedstore.

Henry was looking through the feedstore's window. "Oh no, they are headed our way," Henry gasped.

The group came to attention.

"What'll we do?" Claudia asked frantically. "They'll kill us."

"We have to hide. Quick, everyone behind that large stack of bagged dog food over there," Yen directed.

They moved together to gather behind the stack of the large sacks just as the Porters stormed onto the porch of the feedstore.

*****

Marla and Dule surfaced after holding their breath until the last possible moment. They gasped for air and rubbed their sweltering eyes.

"What the hell is in this water?" Dule questioned.

"It smells like sulfur," Marla replied.

"How did it get in the water?"

"There must be a mine nearby. I don't see the Porters. Hopefully they moved on. Come on, Dule. We have to get out of this creek and track down the Porters."

*****

"Why are we runnin' for, Pop?" Dalton asked.

"That cop in the helicopter had a gun, you moron," Carter bit.

"Oh, I didn't see it," Dalton said. "You're gettin' older, Pop, I think you should take note that maybe I could kick your ass now."

Without warning or hesitation, Crater planted a hard right-hand punch to Dalton's forehead. The powerful blow snapped Dalton's head back and reminded him that his father was still boss.

They pushed open the door to the feedstore and stepped inside.

"Cops wouldn't fly around without guns, you knucklehead," Murky sneered.

"Shut your pie hole, Murky," Dalton warned, trying to clear the ringing in his ears.

"Knock it off, the both of you," Carter demanded.

The trio moved directly to the opposite side of the stacked dog food from where the townspeople were gathered. Pam and Emma covered their mouths in fear and to ensure complete silence coming from them. They all realized that death awaited them if they were detected.

Dalton was standing dangerously close to where he could possibly view the townspeople. The newspaper with the darts sticking in the Porters photos was on the wall behind Dalton. Carter or Murky could spot the makeshift dartboard at any moment.

Before they were discovered, Stacy Hughes put her brave plan in action to protect the hidden crowd. As she stepped forward, Pam

grabbed her arm and whispered, "Stacy, what are ya doin'? They'll kill you."

"Trust me," Stacy whispered back. She then strolled around the stack of dog food. The first of the Porters to see her was Dalton.

"Oh, looky at what we have here."

"Cool, somebody else to kill. Wait, two at that," Murky remarked, referring to Stacy's pregnancy. Dalton raised the barrel of his gun to rest upon Stacy's temple. She closed her eyes, praying quietly to herself that what she was hoping would happen would transpire. At the last possible moment, the opportunity presented itself.

"Wait! Stop!" Carter barked.

Dalton and Murky looked to their father with confusion.

"She's carryin' your little brother in that big belly of hers."

The townspeople stared at each other in disbelief from the other side of the stack. Stacy had purposely led Dalton away from the edge of the stack of dog food.

"Are ya serious, Pop?" Murky asked in disbelief.

"Yeah, I'm fuckin' serious," Carter snapped.

"Put the goddamn gun down, Dalton!" Murky bit out.

Dalton lowered his weapon. "We're takin' the boy to live with us after he's born," Dalton ordered. "Now, get the hell outta here."

Stacy moved quickly out the door of the feedstore, but not before Dalton fired a calculated shot at the door about a foot above her head. Stacy startled and nearly fell from the deck. She raced across the street in search of another haven.

"I think the helicopter is gone. What do we do now?" Murky wondered.

"Well, give me a damn minute to think, will ya?" Carter growled.

*****

"WE CAN'T GO back in there, chief. They have assault rifles. It would be suicide if we make another pass," Jimmie made clear over the noise of the spinning rotors.

"Just one more pass."

"I've never been insubordinate before, but this time the answer is no, chief. You can fire me if ya want, but I'm not flyin' this bird back over Harpersfield again until help arrives."

After a bout of self-reflection, Brain backed off. "Nobody is gettin' fired, Jimmie. I respect your decision. Go ahead and set us back down on the hill in Waynesburg, and we'll wait for the state police to arrive."

*****

MARLA AND DULE made their way up the ridge and emerged from the woods about one hundred feet from the feedstore. They peered through the windows of the feedstore to witness the Porters standing on one side of the tall stack of dog food and the frightened townspeople on the other.

"Oh no, Dule, they'll kill them if they discover them."

Patti spotted Marla and Dule and mouthed through the window, "Please help us."

"They need us. What are we going to do?" Dule worried.

"Um, let me think."

"There's no time for that. It's about time I did something with a bit of guts to it." He scampered away from Marla.

"Dule? What are you doing? Get back here. You'll get yourself killed!"

Dule positioned himself in the direct line of the window where the Porters were positioned. He whistled aloud to gain their attention. He then turned to pull his pants and underwear down to his thighs. He exposed his naked buttocks to them—he was mooning them! "Come get me, you pussy-ass Porters," he challenged. He then quickly pulled his pants up to his hips.

The Porters stormed out from the feedstore, leaving the townspeople in safety, and chased after a now-fleeing Dule Brookside.

"You son of a bitch, I'll blow your head off!" Murky shouted.

Soon, Dalton and Murky closed the distance between them and Dule, with Carter lagging behind.

Marla rushed along the edge of the wood line, keeping pace but remaining out of sight.

Dalton and Murky cornered Dule against a telephone pole.

"You're a dead man," Dalton promised.

"Nobody moons the Porters," Murky stated.

"It was probably like looking at one of your relatives, huh?" Dule goaded them and slyly grinned.

Dalton raised his rifle to Dule's chest as Carter joined them.

"Blow him away, son," Carter coached.

"Go ahead and kill me. I finally did something heroic, so I can meet my maker with a clear conscience," Dule proclaimed, although he was extremely frightened for his life.

From behind a tree, Marla placed careful aim with her handgun at Dalton. An instant before Dalton squeezed the trigger on his assault rifle, Marla fired her weapon. The bullet struck Dalton directly in his left temple. His body jerked and then stiffened before he fell to the ground below.

"Dalton!" Carter blubbered out.

Murky returned rapid fire into the woods from where Marla's shot rang out, though he couldn't see her.

Marla sprinted deeper into the woods as bullets sprayed all around her, striking nearby trees. With Carter's attention focused on the fallen Dalton and Murky's on Marla, Dule slipped around the telephone pole and ran off safely into the woods.

*****

"WHAT'S OUR NEXT move, Cole? They are shootin' up the town out there," Renee fretted.

"How much more dynamite do they have? Do you know?"

"The last explosion was their final bundle, but they have about seven or eight grenades. Listen, babe, I'm at the point where I am willin' to do whatever it takes to free this town of those hoodlums. If you think usin' me against Murky like a decoy or bait, I'll do it," she volunteered.

"That's awfully brave of you, hon, and it may have worked at one time, but I think you've worn out your welcome with Murky Porter. In other words, I think he's given up on ever having you completely. If that's the case, it renders you powerless with him. If he sees you again, he'll probably kill you."

"Well, what can we do then?"

"The first of those shots we just heard came from a Smith & Wesson Colt .45. That's the type of handgun Marla uses. Then it was followed by one of the assault rifles. I hope that she put down one of the Porters, but more so that they didn't get her with their return fire. We need to draw the Porters out without them wanting to shoot us, and I know exactly what that may entail. Come on, pretty gal, and follow me."

*****

MARLA AIMED HER handgun in the direction of the woods where the noise of someone rushing through the brush was heading toward her. She was relieved when Dule came into view. She lowered her weapon and ran into his open arms. They kissed several times.

"Are you alright, my love?" she asked worriedly.

"Yeah, baby, unscathed." He smiled.

"That was really brave what you did back there. Stupid, but courageous."

"Nice shot, baby. You nailed one of them," Dule said with a wink.

"Yeah, well, he was going to shoot the love of my life. That scared me to death to imagine life without you. Dule, when this is over, let's go back to Las Vegas, okay?"

"We were just there, Marla."

"This time I want to get married. I want to be Mrs. Brookside."

Dule's eyes widened in sweet surprise, and he glowed. "Are you serious? Marla Simmons wants to be my bride?"

She nodded and smiled.

"Well, my beautiful lady, I most certainly accept your proposal."

Again, they kissed.

CHAPTER 66

WEBSTER POLICE OFFICER Gary Giles watched in shock as Harpersfield Deputy Frank Collins, shot and bleeding, crawled up onto Martin's Way about forty yards in front of the patrol car.

"John, look." Gary pointed out the windshield.

"Holy crap. He's one of us. Quick, pull up there so we can help him!"

Gary started the patrol car and quickly covered the distance. He and John sprang from the cruiser.

"We're gonna help you into the car," Gary informed Frank.

The deputy was too weak to respond.

Together, Gary and John lifted Frank into the Webster patrol car. Gary turned the car in the opposite direction on Martin's Way as they sped away to transport Frank to the hospital in Webster.

*****

MURKY AND CARTER, dismayed and angry, walked slowly around town.

"If it moves, if it breaths, we shoot the damn thing, Murky!" Crater demanded.

"Ya got it, Pop. Everyone in this damn town is gonna pay for Dalton and Sterling."

*****

THE VICIOUS DOGS barked and snarled as Cole and Renee stepped onto the Porters' property. Undertaker, the large Rottweiler, made an aggressive charge at them. Renee screamed as the dog leaped at Cole. Cole caught Undertaker in midflight and wrapped his strong arms around the dog's thick neck, and with a forceful jerk, he snapped the dog's neck. The Rottweiler shrieked a quick yelp before his lifeless body fell away from Cole. The other dogs duly took note and backed off.

"You're my hero." Renee grinned and blew him a kiss.

They strode up on the porch of the old, ailing house. Cole reached for the door and slowly opened it. He and Renee entered the house to a damp, chilly atmosphere. As they made their way down the hallway, they began to hear singing coming from the living room. They moved into the room to witness Bessy Porter sitting upon the sofa with her back to them. On the coffee table in front of the sofa were several empty cans of beer and a cigarette in an ashtray with smoke billowing up from the lit tobacco. Bessy continued to sing.

> "Itsy-bitsy spider went up the waterspout.
> Down came the rain and washed it all about.
> Out came the sun and dried up all the rain.
> The itsy-bitsy spider crawled up the spout again."

Renee nervously looked to Cole as he signaled with a nod of his head for Renee to approach Bessy. Cole maintained aim on the back of Bessy's head with his handgun.

> "Itsy-bitsy spider went up the waterspout.
> Down came the rain and washed it all about.
> Out came the sun and dried up all the rain.
> The itsy-bitsy spider crawled up the spout again."

Taking each step carefully, Renee approached the sofa with her heart racing. When she nearly reached Bessy, Renee turned back to look at Cole.

"Itsy-bitsy spider went up the waterspout.
Down came the rain and washed it all about.
Out came the sun and dried up all the rain.
The itsy-bitsy spider crawled up the spout again."

Again, he nodded his head. Renee inhaled a deep breath before she gingerly moved in front of Bessy.

Bessy slowly glanced up at Renee.

"Itsy-bitsy spider went up the waterspout.
Down came the rain and..."

Bessy ceased singing and squinted at Renee.

"Hello, Mrs. Porter," Renee bid.

Bessy studied her face for a few moments. She then pointed her finger at Renee. "You're that Stewart girl, aren't you?"

Renee nodded. "Renee. I'm Renee Stewart," she confirmed with a shaky voice.

Cole took a step closer to the sofa at full aim.

Bessy reached for her smoldering cigarette and then took a swig from the can of beer gripped in her right hand. She belched before she spoke. "You must be here to see my boy, Murky. Well, he's not here right now, him or his brothers. I don't know where they are, and I'm worried sick."

Renee cleared her throat. "Believe me, Mrs. Porter, I am not here to see Murky."

Bessy snuffed out her cigarette in the ashtray. "Oh, I see. You must have a hankerin' for one of the other boys then. Is it Sterling or Dalton that has your shorts on fire?"

Renee curled her lip. "Um...neither. Mrs. Porter, this is not a friendly callin'."

Cole then took Bessy forcefully by her right arm and pulled her to her feet. "You're coming with us, Mrs. Porter."

"Who the hell are you?" Bessy snapped.

"That's not important. Now come on, let's go."

"What if I don't?" she snorted.

"Then you won't see your sons," Cole countered.

"Where are my sweet boys?" Her tone suddenly softened.

"That's why I'm here. I'm taking you to them."

"Well, let me grab a few beers to take along with me," she said.

"I'm not letting go of you," Cole replied.

"How 'bout it, child?" Bessy requested of Renee. "Will you fetch a few beers out from the refrigerator for me?"

Renee looked to Cole in confusion of what to do. Cole nodded his consent. "Yeah, I'll get the beer," Renee confirmed.

Renee stepped inside the kitchen to a disgusting sight. On the table was cooked pig hocks that appeared to be days old. Numerous houseflies were landing on and circling the spoiled pork. The stench was so foul that it nearly caused Renee to hurl. She turned away from the table to head for the refrigerator. The floor in the kitchen was soiled deeply with scum, mold, and mildew protruding out from between the cracks of the tiles.

She pulled open the refrigerator door to view more repulsive sights. Yellowing mayonnaise, lettuce that was nearly black, a tomato that was long since rotted, a pile of salami that had a buildup of fungus growing upon it, and cans of beer, plenty of beer. She removed two cans of the alcoholic beverages and then nudged the door of the refrigerator closed with her elbow to witness yet another horrific sight.

Standing upright and a mere ten feet in distance from her was Lucifer, one of the Porters' dogs. The pit bull was revealing his sharp teeth at Renee in a growl, and the hair on his back was standing up at attention.

Renee swallowed hard. "Nice doggy…Cole!"

Lucifer took to an attacking stance as Renee dropped the cans of beer to the floor. Just as the aggressive dog lunged toward her, the loud booming sound of a gun firing echoed through the kitchen area. Renee startled at the crack of the gun and covered her ears with

her palms. The suddenly limp dog slid across the tiled floor, leaving a trail of its own blood behind it.

Cole had placed his shot directly in the center of Lucifer's chest. The dog was dead before it ended its skid.

Renee's hands moved from her ears to cover her mouth as she inspected the fallen dog for any movement at all. Once she was convinced the dog was indeed dead, she turned to see Cole still holding on to Bessy's arm. He plunged his gun back inside his chest holster. Renee wept as she rushed toward him.

Cole placed his free arm around her. "It's okay, honey, it's over. You're fine," Cole reassured her.

Renee kissed his cheek. "Thank you. I'm sure glad you're a good shot."

Cole grinned. "I'm not so sure the dog would agree."

"Good to see that damn dog dead," Bessy said. "I hated that rotten mutt."

*****

"THAT WAS TOO close." Claudia gulped. "They almost had us. I think we should move somewhere else."

"Where would that be, Claudia?" Patti quizzed. "Nearly everything in town is burned to the ground or blown up."

"I think we should stay put," Yen advised.

"Yeah, me too," Emma agreed.

"I think we should move. If they came here once, they'll probably come back," Henry supposed.

"We stay put," Fred insisted.

"I hope that my Merle is okay," Beverly fretted.

*****

"WHERE THE HELL is everyone? I wanna shoot somethin'," Murky grumbled.

"They have to be hidin' somewhere. We'll find 'em," Carter pledged.

Cole eased out onto Harper Street about fifty yards in front of Carter and Murky. Renee remained back behind the laundromat. Cole led Bessy along with him. His left hand had a pinch grip on her throat, and his right hand held his gun to her head, point-blank.

Carter's eyes widened. "Bessy."

Carter and Murky moved quickly toward them.

Bessy raised the palm of her right hand. "Stay back, Carter. He'll kill me."

"Let go of my mama, mole!" Murky demanded.

"I don't think so, Murky," Cole said.

Marla and Dule joined Renee behind the laundromat. They watched as Cole conducted business.

Carter raised his rifle at Cole.

"Um, I wouldn't do that if I were you, Carter. If you shoot me, your wife will most certainly die. If my fingers release her throat too quickly, a surge of blood will overwork her heart. Add to that, at the first sounds of your rifle, I pull my trigger. Then you and your boy can scrape your wife's brains off the street," Cole cautioned.

"Put down your rifle, Pop!" Murky howled.

Reluctantly, Carter lowered his firearm.

Bessy began to weep. "Please help me guys. Please...I don't want to die. Not here, not like this anyway. I'm beggin' you, family, to please do as this man says."

"Okay, what do you want in order to let my mama go, mole?" Murky sought.

"It's simple enough, Murky. One word explains it all. Justice. That's why I'm in this small town, to see justice prevail. You and your brothers murdered Nate Stewart for reasons that were ignorant and meaningless. Since I've arrived here in Harpersfield, I've witnessed you Porters treating the people of this town in evil ways with no recourse to your actions. Look at me when I'm talking to you, Murky, you worthless puke. You are now looking justice straight in the eye."

"Please let my Bessy go," Carter pleaded.

Murky broke away from staring into Cole's eyes. He recognized that Cole was a very serious-minded and dangerous man. Nothing

near the dumb farmhand he had once portrayed. Of all the hatred, the wrongdoings, and the cold blood that ran through the Porters' veins, they did love their mother very much.

"So then what the hell is it gonna take, mole? Do you want me to turn myself into the FBI? Fine, take me, but leave my mother be."

"No, Murky the slurpy, it's not that simple. I'm gonna to hurt you, and I'm gonna hurt you bad." Cole mocked Murky's signature remarks. "I'm going to blow your brains out, if you have any."

From behind the laundromat, Renee pumped her right first into the air in commemoration of Cole's condescension of Murky.

"The FBI can't shoot a man that is surrenderin'," Murky asserted.

"Oh, that's true, but you see, I'm off duty. I guess you could say that I'm on vacation and that I'm freelancing."

Marla chuckled. "Oh, he's good...Very good indeed."

The group inside the feedstore stepped outside and onto the porch to witness the unfolding of the tense-filled standoff.

"You can't just simply shoot me. That'd be murder," Murky deduced.

"It seems to me that people have gotten away with that in this town before," Cole countered. Without looking directly at Carter, Cole warned, "You can take your hand off that grenade in your pocket, old man Porter. It'll take four seconds after you release it before it explodes. As fast as I shoot, those four seconds will equal six bullets into your wife's head."

Heeding the warning, Carter picked his hand clean from his pocket.

Cole could detect by the look in Murky's eyes that he was contemplating fleeing. "You so much as turn to run, Murky, and I'll put a bullet right through your ear. Now, drop the rifle."

After a hesitation, Carter quickly raised his rifle to his shoulder. Before he could take aim and fire, Cole turned his gun on Carter and fired two shots at the elder Porter's head.

Bessy screamed out a cry and kicked at Cole as Carter's body crumbled to the street. Murky took advantage of the moment to dart off the road to the other side of the laundromat from where Renee, Marla, and Dule were stationed.

"Hold on, I have to let you go easy," Cole instructed Bessy, but she continued to struggle. Cole's fingers released quicker than he planned. Bessy stepped away from Cole, and for a moment, her heart ceased beating. Her body trembled before her heart began to pump once again.

Murky shot at Cole, nearly striking the agent before Cole raced over behind the wall to join Renee, Marla, and Dule.

Bessy moved toward Murky. "Murky, come get your mama!" She sobbed.

"I have to get her before he does," Cole asserted. "She's our only trump card." He was just about to rush at Bessy when Murky intentionally opened fire on his mother. Bessy was hit numerous times about the chest and stomach areas. Her limp body plummeted to the street in a now-bloodstained sundress. The street fell eerily quiet after Murky finally eased up on his rifle's trigger. The bystanders paused in shock that Murky had just purposely slaughtered his mother for all to see.

Murky then shouted, "There you have it, mole! Your leverage is gone now, motherfucker. I'm too ruthless and headstrong for you to contend with me, you dickhead. I'm gonna kill you and then Renee, and then I'm gonna slay everyone in this stupid town." Murky then ducked behind the laundromat and sprinted off into the thick woodlands.

*****

"GARY OR JOHN?" Brian barked into the radio.

"Yeah, chief?" Gary responded.

"I've been callin' you for fifteen minutes. Where are you?"

"Back in Webster, at the hospital."

"What? I didn't authorize you to leave your post on Martin's Way. Whaddya doin'?"

"We discovered a fellow officer down. Deputy Collins of Harpersfield is in bad shape. He's been shot, so we rushed him back here to the hospital," Gary explained.

"You should have radioed me," Brian reasoned.

"Yeah, you're right, chief. Just caught up in the moment, I suppose."

"Well, you done the right thing, but you should've informed me. I pray that Frank pulls through. Anyway, hightail it back to Martin's Way and prepare to enter Harpersfield. The state officers are about twenty minutes out."

"On our way, chief."

*****

"ALL OF YOU, get back inside the feedstore!" Cole shouted from across the street. They quickly complied. He then looked the trio consisting of Renee, Marla, and Dule. "That means the three of you as well."

Dule shook Cole's hand as he passed by. "Good luck, Cole. Go get that bastard."

Marla patted him on the shoulder. "Put it to bed, Walsh."

Marla and Dule staggered in exhaustion across the street with Dule putting a supporting arm around her.

Renee's eyes clouded as she grabbed hold of Cole's shirt. "I don't suppose it would do much good for me to tell you to be careful. Would it?"

He shook his head no.

"I know you have to do this. I know it's your nature, it's who you are. However, Cole Walsh, I need to see you walk back out of those woods alive and in one piece. Ya hear me now? I love you with all my heart, and I don't want to spend tomorrow or the rest of my days without you. Murky has already taken the life of one man that I love. I pray to God he doesn't take another." Renee sobbed.

Cole gently pressed her head into his chest. "Hush now. I don't like to see you cry. You put on your brave face to help comfort the jittery townspeople. Watch over them until I get back. You have that certain way with people that make them feel at ease. Go and take care of them, sweetie, while I handle what is out in the woods."

They kissed, hopefully not for the last time.

Renee stepped across the street and waved back to Cole before entering the feedstore.

Cole moved out onto the street and obtained the assault rifle lying next to the fallen Carter Porter. He strapped the rifle over his left shoulder. He then removed two hand grenades from Carter's pockets.

After a short jog, the armed agent slowed his pace, and like a lion on the prowl, Cole flowed into the timberline.

*****

Renee leaned against the closed door of the feedstore and lowered her head.

"What's the matter, pretty young lady?" Marla asked as the group surrounded Renee. "I know Murky is the only one left and he's very dangerous, but Cole will know what to do."

"I'm scared. I know Cole can handle himself, but I'm still nervous."

Marla took her into her arms. "You've fallen in love with him, haven't you, child?"

Renee nodded into Marla's embrace.

"Ah…" Emma sighed. "He's quite a catch, Renee. Cole is a very handsome man."

"Thank you, Emma." Renee continued to sob. "But he hasn't told me that he loves me. I've told him that I do."

"Is that what else has you so upset?" Marla delved.

"Yes."

"I'll let you in on a little secret, Renee. Cole Walsh doesn't go around wearing his heart on his sleeve. No, he doesn't do that at all. He's had a tough life, yeah. He chose most of that for himself, but it's a tough way to go just the same. His sister drowned when he was young, and he once was in love with a gal who died in his arms. He's witnessed war and hardened criminals that most people believe only exist in books or movies. From experience, I can tell you that an FBI agent must develop a certain hardened shell that keeps them from going insane. Take my fiancé Dule for instance."

Dule wondered why he was been brought up in all this. But he sure enjoyed being referenced as Marla's groom-to-be.

"He believed Cole hated him," Marla continued. "Especially after their initial meeting. But you see, I knew it was just the opposite. If Cole gives you the time of day, you can bet that he likes you. I think that Dule has come to terms with that."

Dule nodded in agreement.

Marla stroked Renee's soft strands of hair. "Remember when I told you and your grandfather that you would never see me again?"

"Yes."

"Do you know why I came back here?"

"No."

"Because I called off the case. I called it off because I knew just by the sound of Cole's voice over the phone that he had fallen in love with you. He had become too emotionally attached to be capable of approaching the case in the assigned manner. You must be one special young lady in his heart for him to stray away from orders. That's completely out of his character. So you hang in there, honey, and don't fret. The words will eventually come from him. Until then, just let him say them with his loving and protective actions toward you. Those measures speak louder than any sentence ever could."

Renee tightened her embrace with Marla over her comforting words.

*****

COLE LOOKED OVER a gully above a ravine from behind a tree. He shifted his eyes slowly back and forth, attempting to detect any slightest movement coming from Murky. He readied himself and the rifle as he heard someone approaching from his left on the opposite side of a tree. The sound's distance closed to within a few feet when Cole sprung out from behind the tree and took aim at the intruder, nearly pulling his trigger in the process.

Dule quickly raised his hands. "Whoa, whoa, Cole, buddy. It's me."

"What the hell are you doing out here, Dule?" Cole whispered while lowering the rifle.

"Let's just say I'm feeling a little braver today than typical. I ducked out from the feedstore when Marla wasn't looking. I left word with Renee to explain that I left to join forces with you. I don't know if that's good or bad, but I thought I'd meet up with ya to get the last of the Mohicans."

Cole nodded. "Just so you know before fully making that commitment, Murky Porter is armed with an assault rifle, grenades, and an awful bad attitude. He's not in the best of moods."

"I'm in, Cole, if that works for you."

They shook hands.

"Okay, using your newfound courage, let's wrap this up and free Harpersfield of its malevolent activity once and for all."

*****

OFFICER GARY GILES committed a miscalculation that irked every chief of police across the country. The subordinate officer decided to speak with a reporter who appeared at the hospital after following the speeding patrol car carrying Deputy Frank Collins to the emergency room. Within fifteen minutes, the story of Harpersfield under siege broke into local programming on television sets across the tri-county area.

Two floors above Frank Collins, Ike Stewart watched the television from his hospital room while wondering all morning long why he hadn't heard from Renee. The live news story interrupted normal programming with reporter Judy Hilton standing in front of Webster Memorial Hospital. She described that a police source informed her that the town of Harpersfield was under siege by a family with the surname of Porter. That buildings and homes had been set ablaze and blown up with dynamite. There were casualties, and local police departments were waiting for the arrival of the state police to assist them in gaining control of the small town. The police advise all citizens to stay away from the dangerous situation in the small town of Harpersfield.

Ike sprung from his bed and dashed to the window where he viewed Judy Hilton on the front lawn of the hospital reporting live

as she spoke into a camera. He rushed to dress himself and moved quickly down the hall.

The nurse spotted him and shouted, "Mr. Stewart! I've told you to stay in bed."

"Sorry, I need to check out of this hotel," he blurted back before boarding the elevator.

Judy was wrapping up her live broadcast when Ike approached her. She lowered the microphone to her side. "Did it go off without a hitch?" she asked news cameraman Mark Burns.

"We got it, Judy, and as always, you looked beautiful," he said and winked.

"Always a-flirtin', Mark," she teased.

"It's what keeps my blood flowin'.

"Please, you gotta help me," Ike gasped as he neared the news reporter and cameraman.

Judy gave Ike a weary look. "And who are you exactly?"

"My name is Ike Stewart. I live over in Harpersfield, have all my life. I've been in this hospital because those damn Porters burned down my house while I was in it!"

Judy glowed at Mark as they swiftly came to learn that this Harpersfield story had real potential.

"What can we do to help?" Judy was suddenly captivated.

"My granddaughter and my friends are bein' held hostage in Harpersfield. I need to get there pronto. I know a back way into town very few are aware of."

Judy raised a finger. "Wait a minute…Stewart…Are you related to last year's murder victim Nathan Stewart?"

"Yeah, he was my grandson," Ike replied.

"My my, this keeps gettin' more and more interestin'." Judy widely grinned. She then stepped next to Mark and whispered, "What do ya think? Should we take the old fellow to Harpersfield?"

"Sounds kind of dangerous in that town right now. Maybe we should wait until the police have it under control."

"If we do that, Burns, the meat of the story slips right through our hands. This report could be the story of Tennessee over the past five years or more. We'd be the primary news crew on site. Think

about it, we'll be promoted in a heartbeat. Handed a reward or two. Perhaps even land a position with a major network in Memphis, Knoxville, or Nashville. The door is open and waiting for us to walk through it. So whaddya say?"

He hesitated a bit, but then beamed. "I like the way you think."

She then refocused her attention on Ike. "Okay, Mr. Stewart, we'll give you that ride into Harpersfield."

CHAPTER 67

"WE'RE TEN MINUTES out, Chief Reynolds. Meet us at the Waynesburg and Harpersfield border out on Martin's Way," State Police Lieutenant Darrin Styles informed Brian over the radio.

"We read ya, Lieutenant Styles. We'll meet ya there," Brian responded and then clipped the radio microphone back on the dashboard of the helicopter. "You heard the man, Jimmie. Get this bird back in the air."

*****

COLE AND DULE slowly descended an embankment, slipping from tree to tree. When they reached the bottom of the gully, Cole signaled for Dule to close the distance between them.

"There's been no movement or tracks that I can detect from Murky," Cole whispered.

"What does that mean?"

"That he is watching us. We must not be in range of his rifle just yet, or he would have fired. So we need to become difficult targets."

"How do we do that?"

"Move from obstruction to obstruction. Don't offer your complete broadness to any one direction or another. Make only your profile available."

"You're losing me here, Green Beret. I understand what you're conveying, but I don't know how to execute it."

"Just lag behind but not next to me and duplicate my movements. We need to remain at least fifty yards apart. If he gets one of us, then the other will have time to react for cover before Murky can take proper aim."

*****

IKE, JUDY, AND Mark were on the road on the outskirts of Webster inside a white news van. The vehicle was equipped with a small satellite dish upon the roof and blue lettering on the side of the van that read "WJYT CHANNEL 12 NEWS."

Judy turned her head toward the rear of the van from the passenger's seat. She addressed Ike, who was situated on the back seat. "So tell me, Mr. Stewart, what are these Porter brothers like?"

Ike was stymied over her attractiveness for a moment. "I'm sorry, I'm just so used to seein' you on TV all the time, and now you're right here in front of me."

"That's fine, Mr. Stewart. Now, what can you tell me about the Porters?"

"First, you can call me Ike. The Porters are as nasty as nasty comes. They have been mean and evil for generations of Porters. It's like it's in their bloodline or somethin'."

"You mean they are petty thieves that rough up the townspeople a bit?"

"Oh no, it's much deeper and crueler than that."

Looking at Ike's reflection in the rearview mirror, Mark queried, "Ike, what can we expect when we get to Harpersfield? Are the Porters gonna cut us some slack since we're the media?"

Ike chortled before answering, "Not quite. The Porters don't deal in slack, don't even know the meanin'. They'll harm you as well as anyone else."

Mark looked nervously over at Judy. "I dunno about this."

"It'll be fine, Burns. I'm a woman, which should buy us some respect."

"That'll make things even worse. With all due respect, Ms. Hilton, those Porters can have your skirt hiked up above your head before you knew what hit ya. They respect no one, not a soul, and that's the cold, hard truth," Ike described.

Judy, with less of a nervous appearance, asserted, "I'll take my chances. I need this story...exclusively."

"The first sign of trouble, I'm outta there," Mark affirmed.

Judy rolled her eyes at Ike.

*****

JIMMIE SAT THE helicopter down in a small field next to Martin's Way. He and Brian slid out from the helicopter to greet Lieutenant Darrin Styles and State Police Officers Dale Rhodes and Michelle Durham. Everyone shook hands.

"What are we facin' in there?" Darrin slanted his head in the direction of Harpersfield.

"We did a flyover a while ago. It's not lookin' good. Buildin's are down, a body on the road, and the Porters have assault rifles in their possession. They hit the chopper, so we got the hell outta there," Brian recounted.

"How many of them?" Michelle inquired. She was a petite woman, but a tough cop.

"Four. A father and three of his sons. They are all armed with guns and explosives," Brian disclosed.

"Explosives? What type of explosives?" Dale questioned. Dale was a rather tall man of solid build. He and Michelle saw one another on a personal basis, but have kept that quiet from the force.

"Dynamite, powerful grenades," Jimmie answered.

"Jesus Christ, where the hell did they get their hands on that stuff?" Darrin wondered.

"It's high-grade material too," Brian added.

"Well, I'm not leadin' my people into a slaughter," Darrin stated. "Let's get a SWAT team out here, and then we'll move on in. It'll take them about an hour or so to get here. Until then, we sit tight."

*****

COLE SIGNALED FOR Dule to halt in his tracks. Cole focused his eyesight and listened intently. He then heard the faint sounds of a rifle's safety being disengaged. At the last possible moment, he spotted Murky between a fork of a tree about eighty yards in front of him. Murky had the powerful firearm pointed directly at Cole.

With a sudden leap, Cole dove into a dense brush thicket to his right. Murky then opened fire, spraying bullets around and into the brush pile. Cole had already rolled out from the backside of the brush, avoiding the flying bullets.

Dule quickly took cover behind a large oak tree as Murky turned the rifle on him. Dule reached around the tree and fired off three shots with his handgun, though he didn't know precisely where Murky was located. The gunshots flew near Murky, but not close enough to pose a threat. Again, Murky made his rifle crack, peppering the tree that Dule was shielded behind. Bark from the tree split off in chunks, but the tree was large enough in diameter not to expose any of Dule's body. Murky shot until the barrel was smoking before he darted off deeper into the woodland.

"Are you okay, Dule?" Cole called out.

"Yeah, how about you?"

"I wasn't hit. Did you see where he went off to?" Cole sought as he cautiously approached Dule.

"No, he was gone before I peered around this tree. What do you want to do now?"

"We have to change tactics. Murky is a little more patient and smarter than I give him credit for. You stay put, find some decent cover, and watch as much of the woods as you can see. I'm going to make a large circle around and then work my way back here. Either I'll spot him and take him down, or I'll flush him back toward you. Be sure of your target, as it could be me heading back to you before

Murky does. I estimate it will take me about forty minutes to cover the diameter."

*****

"TURN HERE ONTO that dirt road just up ahead. It's a back way into Harpersfield," Ike directed.

"There?" Mark pointed out the window and stopped the van. "That's barely a trail. I'd call it a path and not a road. We'll get the van stuck."

"There's another way that's a little more of a beaten route, but it'll take an hour to loop around to where it is," Ike informed.

"Take this one, Burns," Judy directed. "I don't want to sacrifice another hour of time."

"Okay, but you'll be the one payin' for the tow and damage to the van, not me."

Mark swung the van from the pavement and onto the dirt side trail where the weeds and vines of the woods had nearly reclaimed it. This road was once popular with moonshine runners years ago, including Ike himself. The ride soon became jerky and bumpy. Judy held on to the dashboard to keep herself in the passenger's seat. Her large breasts bounced wildly in her revealing low-cut top. Her breasts nearly jumped out of her blouse as she was not wearing a bra.

This was the way that Judy preferred to appear on camera. Not only was she proud of her above average–sized breasts, but she felt that her revealing appearance would make people remember each of her live reports, especially the male population. Mark had seen her breasts exposed on several occasions. He was married and faithful to his wife, but still Judy had attempted to seduce him in the past and continued to do so from time to time.

Reporting the news, especially an exclusive breaking story, sexually stimulated Judy. Being that Mark was her personal cameraman, he was the male in her line of fire when her desires burned the hottest. She flashed her breasts to him, and he didn't attempt to stop her when she got that way. He was loyal to his wife but enjoyed Judy's exposure just the same. One night they were on assignment together

in Memphis covering a double homicide story. Judy and Mike where exclusively on the spot when the murderer was arrested by the police. Their news clip aired nationwide. This exclusive caused Judy's sexual appetite to soar. Back at the hotel, Judy and Mike where inside his room drinking from a bottle of champagne in celebration when Judy excused herself to go to the bathroom, and when she returned, she was completely nude. She seductively lay on the bed and spread her legs for Mike to view all her womanhood.

The combination of her inviting, alluring, and beautiful nudity, her playfulness, and the alcohol were drawing Mark to the bed like a magnet. He lay down on the bed next to her, and they worked their hands feverishly over each other's bodies. Their breathing was rapid and heavy as Judy reached her hand inside of Mark's pants. It was then that his faithfulness to his wife was being tested to the extremes. The love he held for his wife overcame his lust the last possible moment, and he quickly backed away from Judy.

He stood up from the bed. She realized why his sudden withdrawal took place. She reassured Mark that his wife never needed to know. That wasn't good enough for him. He politely asked Judy to leave his room and to return to her room across the hotel's hallway. Reluctantly, she dressed and stepped out from his room.

Several hours later, Judy was back inside her room with a man she met in the hotel's lounge. She was relentless in satisfying her sexual wants and needs that night. Even after his rejection with sleeping with her, Judy continued to try to seduce Mark when an exclusive news story surfaced. So he was fully aware at the end of today that Judy would be hot on his trail once again. He'd take in the view of her nude body, but he was certain he would it stop it there. He did love his wife. The station was about to slap a dress code on Judy, but that was before her ratings soared. Now, the station encouraged her revealing attire.

Ike noticed her bobbing breasts and enjoyed the view, but he realized that if she ran into the Porters looking like that, they would feast upon her.

"We're gonna bust the shocks on this van. You'll be the one to explain it to the station, not me," Mark said to Judy.

"Stop whinin' and just keep drivin'," she retorted. She then turned her attention back to Ike. Her voice was jumpy from the rough ride. "Ike, any chance I could interview one or more of the Porters? I wouldn't have them set down their weapons or anything. I just want the exclusive."

Ike squinted at her. "Is that all you care about? Gettin' the story?"

She looked outside the van's window for a long moment and honestly replied, "Yep."

"That's shallow, lady. There are innocent people under attack."

"You don't get far in my business, Ike, by havin' a heart. You need to put that all aside and get what viewers want to hear and see on the screen. I'm in this for the long haul. I want to anchor CNN someday."

"Remind me to stop watchin' your channel," Ike growled.

"No reason for haste, Ike. I'm just doin' my job."

"That still doesn't make it right."

"Right isn't always the right thing to do," she claimed.

"That's a bunch of hogwash," Ike responded.

"Be that as it may, do you think the Porters will grant me that interview?"

"News lady, if you go anywhere near those boys, they'll have their way with you, and then they'll part your hair with a bullet," Ike warned.

"That wouldn't be so bad, would it? Well, maybe the bullet part isn't so good." She grinned impishly.

*****

"YA KNOW, THERE was a time when Jim and I were havin' some serious problems. Things weren't good, not at all. I had found out that Jim was seein' a gal over in Waynesburg," Pam revealed as she confided in Renee. They were apart from the others a short distance inside the feedstore. Renee was leaning against a support pole, and Pam was sitting on a large bag of sunflower seeds.

"That must have been terrible," Renee assumed.

"Yes, it was, but now that he's dead"—her eyes clouded—"it doesn't seem so significant. We all respond to certain things in life a bit too harshly. He was seein' this gal, but I never doubted the love that he held for me. He promised to never see her again and

begged my forgiveness. I nearly ended the marriage, but I could see the deep remorse in his eyes. I struggled with forgivin' him until one day, someone cleared it all up for me."

"Who was that?"

Pam grinned. "Renee, it was Nate."

Renee looked puzzled.

"I was sittin' on the back step of the diner takin' a break between the breakfast and lunch crowds. After weeks of Jim and I barely communicatin', it was takin' its toll on me. I was spent, tired, and at the end of my rope. I started cryin', both from the hurt and the fallout from stress and tension. That was a few summers ago when Nate was washin' dishes for us to earn a little money. He had seen me from the kitchen window and could sense that I was in despair."

*****

"Is everything alright, Mrs. Tinelberg?" Nate asked as he sat down next to Pam on the step.

She wiped the tears away from her cheeks. "Um, thanks for askin', Nate, but it's nothin' you need to concern yourself with."

"Perhaps it would help to talk to someone about it, whatever it is."

"I think you might be a bit too young to understand," she stated.

"I'm fifteen now. I think I can handle it." He grinned.

*****

Pam smiled from her sitting position on the sack of seeds. "One thing about Nate, you could tell him anything. He had a way of makin' people feel comfortable around him. You knew as well that whatever you talked about, he kept it between just the two of you, and that's sayin' a lot in this rumor mill of a town."

*****

"So you think you can handle it, huh? I guess you are growin' into a young man now. Yeah, maybe it would help to talk about it," Pam consented.

"I'm all ears," Nate offered.

She sighed. "Nate, Mr. Tinelberg has been seein' another. She lives over in Waynesburg, and I guess it's been goin' on for nearly a year now."

Nate's eyes widened. "I'm sorry to hear that, Mrs. Tinelberg. How did ya find out?"

"I don't know what Jim was thinkin' 'cause I'm the one who takes care of our bills. There was a charge on of one of our credit cards for a restaurant and motel room in Waynesburg. It was on a night that Jim said he was goin' up at his brother's outside Knoxville to go night fishin'. I confronted him with it, and eventually, he confessed. He's promised that he will never see her again."

"Are you two gettin' a divorce?" Nate asked worriedly.

"I dearly love Jim…I'm not sure what all is gonna come out of this," she replied, her voice saddened. "What do you think I should do?"

Nate leaned back on his hands. "Let me ask you this, Mrs. Tinelberg. Do you believe that Mr. Tinelberg loves you?"

"Absolutely. I'm sure of it."

"And you just told me you love him. Isn't part of love bein' able to understand and forgive?"

"I know, Nate. I'm tryin', I'm tryin' hard, but I don't understand it all, and I'm not quite ready to forgive just yet. It's kind of left things in limbo for now."

"I'd say accept his apology this time. However, make it clear to him, there'll not be another round of forgiveness if he's ever unfaithful again."

"How do I…um, be intimate with him after all this? When I think of Jim touchin' that other woman, it makes my skin crawl."

"This is the way I think about things when I'm angry with someone. If they were to die that day without things bein' resolved, would the problem still be large enough for me to hold a grudge? Would I forgive the person before they put them six feet under? If I can answer yes to that, then I forgive them while they are still above ground, so that they know that I've forgiven them. When one decides to let bygones be bygones, then let it be just that. If you completely forgive Mr. Tinelberg in your heart, you'll forget about this other lady."

After a brief pause, Pam praised, "I believe you'll be a bit more than just a dishwasher in your lifetime, Nate Stewart." She hugged him in appreciation for his help and lending an ear.

*****

Pam eventually forgave Jim, and in a sense, their marriage became stronger than ever before.

*****

COLE READIED AS he detected noise approaching from his right. He quickly hunkered behind a tree. He peered around the trunk to see a deer leaping its way through the timber. The animal appeared a bit jittery. Cole had hunted deer for most of his life, so he acknowledged that a deer up and around in the hour before dusk was typical behavior; however, it was obvious by its body language that this deer had been spooked from its sanctuary. Cole was certain that Murky was nearby.

Then the unthinkable happened. From directly behind his left ear, Cole felt the cold barrel of Murky's handgun touch his head.

"You've run outta luck, mole. Drop your weapon," Murky demanded.

Cole hesitated.

"Now," Murky growled.

Cole then tossed his assault rifle to the ground.

"The handgun too."

The handgun landed on the ground next to the rifle.

"Before you kill me, answer me this. How the hell did you sneak up on me like that? That's never happened to me before." Cole believed again that he had underestimated Murky.

Murky glowed with pride. "Are ya kiddin', mole? I run drugs. You do that for ya livin', and ya learn to be a stealthy alley cat. And ya know, cats prey on moles for a livin'. It all comes to reason in the end, not my friend."

Cole couldn't help but not to believe that under the right circumstances, Murky Porter could have made a stellar Special Forces soldier. He had the untrainable natural talents. Be that as it may, he was an evil force that needed to be dealt with.

"So this is it, huh? You're just going to pull the trigger without ever really knowing?" Cole taunted.

Murky looked baffled. "What the hell ya goin' on about now?"

"Whether or not you could take me in a fistfight? You know, how real men settle things."

Murky firmed his lips with confidence. "Oh, I could take ya. I could kick your ass all over the county."

"Okay, if you're so sure about that, then there is no reason to prove it. Perhaps you could, perhaps not. So go ahead and just pull the trigger."

"You might be a big guy like me, mole, but I'd still knock your block off. No man has ever taken down a Porter in hand-to-hand combat. And that's a cold hard fact. Never has happened and never will. You can bet your sorry ass on that."

There was truth to Murky's claim. Over generations of time, no man had singlehandedly championed over a Porter in one-on-one fisticuffs. The Porters were simply too big, too strong, too powerful, too skilled, too stubborn, and too relentless. They would fight to their own death, period. No such thing as a mere bar fight or a simple case of road rage or anything else that would create a squabble found a Porter defeated. To triumph over a Porter, you would need to literally beat them to death and nothing short of that. To date, nary a Porter man had ever been on the short end of a physical confrontation.

"That sounds stupid," Cole taunted.

Murky pushed the barrel against Cole's head. "What sounds stupid?"

"When you mock people's names. We usually get out of that around the third grade, no?"

"That's it, you're a dead man." Murky engaged the firing mechanism.

Cole realized he had all but one last opportunity. "Well, I'm glad to see you're admitting that I could whip you in a stand-up, toe-

to-toe contest," Cole boasted. "When you pull that trigger, then you admit I could kick the shit out of you in a fistfight, period."

"Okay, asshole, have it your way. I'll kill ya with my hands instead of the rifle. It's just gonna be more painful for you." Murky chortled wickedly.

Murky kicked Cole's guns over a small ravine and then heaved his rifle down the same gully. He then clutched a fist with his large right hand and grinded it into the palm of his left hand. "Bring it on, mole. My daddy raised us well, and I grew up with two hard-knock bastards of brothers. You ain't got no chance. I'm gonna beat you into a bloody pulp and then head back to town to ram my big cock inside Renee's pussy."

"Usually at this point, I would tell you that it's best that you just turn yourself in, but you see, Murky, I'm not here to arrest you. I'm here to cut you out of life itself. So there will be no surrendering today. No, instead, I'm going to be judge and jury right here in these woods. I'm not going to show any mercy. In layman's terms, I'm going to kick your ass and then break your fucking neck."

"Well then, mole, you'll be the first to accomplish that. Let's get it on and see who is left standin', FBI man. I'm gonna knock around another fed for a bit, and then I'm gonna cave your face in. I'll give your best to Renee, the fine filet, while I'm ridin' her as if she were a buckin' wild bronco. You can bet my huge sausage will touch depths of her pussy your smaller dick couldn't reach." Murky then rushed at Cole to swing wide and hard.

Cole stepped aside, and Murky's momentum nearly carried him to the ground below. Cole rubbed his jaw in a mocking gesture. "Wow, now that really stung, Murky the slurpy."

Murky glared at Cole as he was instilled with every bit of confidence. "Just testin' the waters, mole." An eerie coldness then took over Murky's expression. His eyes nearly turned gray. "You screwed Renee. Didn't you?"

"You bet your ass I did, Porter."

Murky snarled in anger and rushed at Cole again.

This time, as Cole swept out of the way, Murky was able to hook his foot around Cole's shin, and with a jerk of his powerful leg,

he spilled Cole down to the fallen leaves upon the forest floor. He then moved quickly to Cole, and before the FBI agent could roll out from harm's way, Murky planted a kick with his heavy left boot into Cole's midback area. The breaking of a few of Cole's ribs could be heard, similar to that of the snapping of a small tree branch.

Cole grimaced in pain. Murky returned with another left boot in the same now-tender spot into Cole's back. Cole coughed up a few spots of blood. Murky then threw his large body into the air and plummeted down upon Cole with all his weight and strength. All the air inside Cole's body rushed out from his lungs.

"Big guys just fall harder!" Murky chortled. He then clutched a handful of Cole's hair and slammed his forehead hard against a protruding root of an oak tree. Cole's ears rang and his head throbbed. Again, Murky blasted Cole's head into the same root. And then again.

Cole realized that another collision with the root, and he would be knocked unconscious, then Murky would certainly kill him. With all the strength he could muster, Cole jolted his right elbow backward and caught Murky in the upper lip, knocking out Murky's right front tooth. The hard blow snapped Murky's head back, and he tumbled away from Cole. Murky grabbed at the intense pain pulsating inside his mouth as Cole stumbled to his feet.

"Is that all you got, Murky?" Cole continued to taunt Murky, though it agitated his broken ribs to speak.

Murky came to his feet. "Ya know, mole, Sterling was a tough son of a bitch. He kicked my ass most of the time, but I beat him every now and then. I'm the only one in the whole county that can claim that. So if I can beat Sterling's ass, I can surely kick yours."

Cole, after a quick check of his position, needed Murky to rush at him again. "Well, you don't need to brag about that anymore, Murky. I put a bullet into your worthless brother's head. Remember?"

Murky fumed and rushed at full force toward Cole. Just before they collided, Cole hopped upward to grab hold of a low-hanging tree branch. He elevated his body above Murky's attack, leaving Murky to slam chest first into the tree's trunk.

The collision stifled Murky, and he nearly plunged to the ground. He stumbled back some fifteen feet before finally regain-

ing his balance. Before he could arrive back to complete awareness, Cole landed a solid punch to Murky's left jaw, jarring loose a second tooth of Murky's. Cole prepared to throw his next blow when Murky surprised him with a jolt of his own. A powerful fist landed in the midsection of Cole's chest. Cole was thrown back a few paces as his heart skipped a beat. Murky then stepped forward and cast another powerful punch, striking Cole in the left eye. The massive strike shattered Cole's eye socket before he could shield his face with his arms.

Murky then kneed Cole in the groin area. Cole dropped to his knees. With a mighty right-handed punch, Murky belted Cole in the throat. Cole collapsed to the earth, gasping for a breath of air.

"I warned ya not to mess with me, mole. But I'm tired now and done with ya, you bastard. The time has come for you to die." Murky growled. He then slid down the ravine to retrieve the firearms, but in more pain than he expected. Murky would never admit to it, but he had taken a good beating at the hands of his foe. He gathered the weapons, sticking Cole's handgun in the waist of his pants. He strapped one of the two rifles onto his back and toted the other in his large hands.

He made his way back up the ravine, only to discover that Cole was now missing.

"Where'd ya go, mole? You gotta be nearby. You're a hurtin' little mouse. Okay, I'll find ya if that's how ya want to play this out." Murky wiped dried blood from his upper lip before he began to poke around the immediate area. "Come out, come out, wherever you are. I have some lead for the mole to eat."

Murky waited quietly for a few moments before he began to move slowly around the area. "You might as well just give it up, FBI man. I'll find ya. I bet your balls hurt, don't they?" Murky sneered. "I bet your throat feels like it's swollen to the size of a watermelon." Murky moved to the front of a small brushy section and peeked behind a large tree.

Suddenly, the brush area came to life with Cole's eyes staring from behind Murky. Cole leaped onto Murky's back and hauled him to the ground. Murky's rifle fired a round into the air.

From nearly a quarter mile away, Dule heard the gunshot. He thought to move toward the sound of the blast, but Cole had directed him to stay put. He used a tree to shield him from the direction of where the shot had rung out and waited to hear any further shooting.

Murky and Cole wrestled for control of the rifle. Neither men gained a solid hold on the gun before it tumbled away from their reach.

Maintaining a hold on Murky, Cole tried to pry the other rifle loose from Murky's back without success. Murky reached for his handgun. The rifle strapped onto Murky's back inadvertently fired into the air.

This was enough for Dule as he quickly marched across the floor of the forest toward the shot's origin.

Cole could no longer hang on to both Murky and the weapon as Murky's exceptional strength broke him free of Cole's take on him. Both men quickly stood to their feet, with Murky pointing the handgun directly at Cole.

"I'm gonna kill ya with your own gun," Murky snarled insanely. "I'm gonna shoot ya just like you shot Sterling."

Cole held up the palms of his hands. He realized that in a moment, he'd be dead. "Let me just say one thing before you pull the trigger."

"What would that be, mole?"

"You, your brothers, all the Porters will rot in hell. The way you treat people is evil, and there is going to be a place in Satin's fiery domain for you."

Murky chuckled. "Is that supposed to scare me, mole? I'm lookin' forward to it. People in hell probably play like the Porters do. We'll rule."

"Well, until then, you can forget about Renee. She'll never have anything to do with you."

Murky stepped up nearly face-to-face with Cole. He placed the barrel of the handgun against the underside of Cole's chin. "I'll let you in on somethin' before I blow your worthless head off, mole. I'm gonna fuck Renee. I'm gonna screw her good, better than you did. Then when my cum is still seepin' out of her, I'm gonna shoot her in the head."

A sudden and unexpected then noise grabbed Murky's attention.

Dule stumbled into sight, not knowing he was so near Murky and Cole.

With only a split second to work with, Cole took a leap of faith and wrapped Murky's head into his strong arms. He then peered into Murky's eyes and muttered, "Bye-bye, Murky, you stupid fucking turkey." With a powerful jerk, Cole twisted Murky's head.

Murky's neck broke with a definitive and strident snapping sound. Murky's body went lifeless as Cole released him to tumble to the forest floor.

"Jesus H. Christ." Dule swallowed. "You broke his neck. I've never seen anything of sorts before!"

Cole yanked his handgun from Murky's now lifeless grip. He groaned over the pain shooting from his rib cage as pointed the gun at Murky and delivered a bullet into Murky's forehead. Murky's dead body jerked. "That's for good measure, Porter," Cole snarled.

*****

SIRENS SCREAMED FROM a distance as townsfolk stepped out onto the porch of the feedstore. The WJYT news van pulled up onto Harper Street. With Judy equipped with a microphone and Mark sporting a news camera on his shoulder, they slid through the doors of the van.

Ike Stewart stepped down from the van.

"Grandpa!" Renee called out in glee. She scurried down from the porch and rushed to Ike's side. They quickly embraced.

Judy launched into interviewing the citizens of Harpersfield on the feedstore's porch while the Webster and Tennessee State police cars simultaneously rushed to a screeching halt on Harper Street. Two SWAT trucks blocked off each direction of the street leading out of town as the police helicopter hovered in the sky directly above.

*****

COLE AND DULE made their way from the woodlands. Cole looked as though he had been through a war, and in a sense, he had.

He was utterly exhausted but satisfied that Harpersfield was now free of the Porters' demented grip. His left eye was bloodred and swollen around the socket. His shirt was torn, and he had rake marks on his neck from Murky's fingernails. His ribs ached and his groin region was sore, but his heart was warm at the thought of reuniting with Renee soon.

Dule reached out to support Cole as they strode along Harper Street. Cole signaled to Dule that he could make it under his own from there. The duo shook hands before tumbling in a solid hug of mutual respect.

The late evening had reached its twilight as they stepped into the red and blue strobe lights of the patrol cars. The officers, SWAT team, reporters, and the townspeople watched quietly as their tattered hero made his way toward them.

"It's over!" Dule announced in victory, breaking the stale silence. "Cole took care of the last of them Porters!"

The group of Harpersfield citizens exploded into a loud round of applause.

Cole made his way to Renee.

Her eyes watered. "I love you, Cole Walsh."

"And I love you, Renee Stewart," Cole disclosed.

She collapsed into his open arms, and they kissed to a resurgence of ovation.

"Well, you did it, Cole. You rid this town of the menace. I suppose you'll be leavin' us now," Renee said softly.

"I believe you'd look great living up in Cleveland with me," he suggested.

She glowed. "Are you serious?"

"You bet I am."

"What about Grandpa?"

"There's room for him as well."

"Oh, babe." She melted before kissing him again.

CHAPTER 68

One Month Later

AFTER A THOROUGH investigation, FBI director Sydney Myles declared the Harpersfield incident an official case of the Federal Bureau of Investigation. This released any wrongdoings of the Elite Four organization. Sydney did mention to Marla that he knew everything wasn't on the up and up, and he advised her to stop doing whatever it was she had been up to.

She took his advice and officially dissolved the existence of the Elite Four. She decided to run for election to Congress. Marla figured that as a congresswoman, perhaps she could help produce legislation to be more favorable for the victims of crime.

She and Dule married two months after the Harpersfield incident and are now looking to buy a house together in the Philadelphia area.

*****

Three Months Later

STACY HUGHES GAVE birth to a healthy baby boy who was now a month old. Even after coming clean that day inside the feed-store that Carter Porter was the baby's father, Stacy named the boy Thomas Donald Turmac. Stacy gave her son's her soon-to-be ex-husband's surname as Donnie planned to father the child as it were his very own. She and the baby resided with her mother in Harpersfield after she and Donnie decided that their arrangement was no longer working out. She was already calling her newborn son Tommy.

*****

THE TOWN WAS rebuilding with the use of insurance monies and community charity drives that reached as far as Waynesburg and Webster. Joe Skidmore's tavern was taking on a more modern appearance, but Emma Gert and Fred Dalton were not so anxious to change things. The general store and gas station were being rebuilt to nearly the same specifications as their previous appearances. The innovative police station's construction was all brick. Pam had the innovative idea to erect the town's new eatery in the fashion of a 1950s diner, complete with an appearance of a train car encased in stainless steel. She appropriately named the new restaurant Tiny's Two.

The new top lawman of Harpersfield was Sheriff Frank Collins. Donnie Turmac had signed on as the new deputy. While the station was being constructed, Frank and Donnie were sharing the feedstore as a makeshift police headquarters along with the temporary post office. Postmaster Claudia Williams complained of the crowded conditions, but she was happy to have the daily company.

*****

Five Months Later

RENEE AND IKE were adjusting to their new life in Cleveland, Ohio. Ike fished nearly every day on the shores of Lake Erie. Cole

and Renee had become engaged and were planning a summer wedding the following year. Cole had asked Dule to be the best man at the ceremony, and his newfound friend had respectfully accepted. Marla would be a member of the party as well. Renee had asked her to be the maid of honor.

Renee was about to excitedly discover that she was pregnant with her and Cole's first child. Cole was hoping that the existence of the Elite Four would recruit new members and continue forward, but he understood Marla's decision to shut it down. He had thoughts of branching out on his own to continue the work of the Elite Four.

Cole had learned to love again, and he couldn't love any deeper than his deep feelings for Renee.

Ike was happy that Cole was about to become his "grandson-in-law" is how he put it.

*****

One Year Later

ALEESCHA WILES STEPPED up onto the porch of her new home. The tattered residence that once belonged to the Porter family now belonged to her as she had purchased it in a police auction at a low price with a promise from her father, Yen, that he would help her fix up the place. She opened the screen door, and with a set of twin baby boys bouncing upon her hips, she then scampered inside the house. The twins, results of the Porters' gang sex with her, she had chosen to name Vincent Marlin Wiles and Kenneth Joseph Wiles. She then closed the screen door to her newfound dwelling behind her.

Next to the house and perched upon the top branch of a tall oak tree, a vulture blinked its eyes while belching out a single screech from its sharp beak before taking flight to circle the skies above Harpersfield, Tennessee.